Also by R. A. Lafferty:

R.A.Lafferty
THREE GREAT NOVELS

Space Chantey

Fourth Mansions

Past Master

First published in Great Britain in 2018 by Gollancz
an imprint of the Orion Publishing Group Ltd
Carmelite House, 50 Victoria Embankment
London EC4Y 0DZ

An Hachette UK Company

7 9 10 8 6

A CIP catalogue record for this book is
available from the British Library.

ISBN 978 1 473 21341 8

Printed and bound in Great Britain by
Clays Ltd, Elcograf S.p.A.

www.gollancz.co.uk
www.orionbooks.co.uk
www.sfgateway.com

CONTENTS

Space Chantey

CHAPTER ONE

The Lay of Road-Storm from the ancient Chronicles
We give you here, Good Spheres and Cool-Boy Conicals,

And perils pinnacled and parts impossible
And every word of it the sworn-on Gospel.

Lend ear while things incredible we bring about
And Spacemen dead and deathless yet we sing about:—

And some were weak and wan, and some were strong
  enough,
And some got home, but damn it took them long enough!

NEW SPACE CHANTEYS,
Living Tapes, Sykestown, A.A. 301

WILL THERE BE a mythology in the future, they used to ask, after all has become science? Will high deeds be told in epic, or only in computer code?

And after the questing spirit had gone into overdrive during the early Space Decades, after the great Captains had appeared, there *did* grow up a mythos through which to view the deeds. This myth filter was necessary. The ship logs could not tell it rightly nor could any flatfooted prose. And the deeds were too bright to be viewed direct. They could only be sung by a bard gone blind from viewing suns that were suns.

3

Here trumpets blare. Here the high kerigma of heralds rises in silvery gibberish. Here it begins.

The war was finished. It had lasted ten equivalent years and taken ten million lives. Thus it was neither of long duration nor of serious attrition. It hadn't any great significance; it was not intended to have. It did not prove a point, since all points had long ago been proved. What it did, perhaps, was to emphasize an aspect, sharpen a concept, underline a trend.

On the whole it was a successful operation. Economically and ecologically it was of healthy effect, and who should grumble?

And, after wars, men go home. No, no, men start for home. It's not the same.

There were six of them there, Captains of hornets, those small craft that could go anywhere, six of them mustered out with their crews and with travel orders optional. And there wasn't an ordinary man among them. They were six full crews of the saltiest, most sulfurous men who could be combed out of the skies.

Roadstrum, one of the Captains, was as plain a man as ever lived, and now he spoke out plainly:

"I would say let us go directly home. We were boys when this began, and we are not boys now. We should go home, but I could be talked into something else.

"Dammit, I said I could be talked into something else!"

"A day or two on Lotophage might be worth it," said Captain Puckett. "We'll never be this close to it again and there must be something behind all those stories of the soft life there. They say it is Fiddler's Green and Theleme rolled together. They say that it may be Maybe Jones City itself. If we don't like it we can leave at any time."

"The Captains Roadstrum and Puckett are from World, are you not?" Captain Dempster asked. "In that case it is not at all in your direction home."

"We are from World," said Roadstrum, "and we know the direction home."

"Lotophage is supposed to be a bums' world," said Dempster, "and if you stay there long enough you turn into a bum."

"If you're afraid of it we'll mark you off," said Captain Silkey, "and perhaps you have less a way to go to be a bum than we others. But I see that you are afraid."

Silkey knew how to put the needle into Dempster. The only thing that Dempster was afraid of was being called afraid.

4

"Look at it this way," said Captain Kitterman. "We can't get flight clearance to World or to anything in that Arm for three days, but we can go to Lotophage immediately. We can spend an equivalent day there, we can spend two, and still be home without loss of time. I suggest that we do it."

"For myself," said the sixth Captain, "it is imperative that I get home. There may have been changes there. My wife is faithful within limits, but I do not know whether ten years transcends those limits. My children should have reached an interesting age. Besides, nobody ever stops on Lotophage for only a day or two."

"What think you, Crewmen?" Roadstrum asked loudly of the splendid array. These men were the salt of the skies, the one out of ten who had determinedly stayed alive through the whole war, very often hurt, absolutely refusing to be killed. Never had there been so many great fine men assembled. They were the tall ones.

"I'd give the very ears off my head to go to Lotophage and enjoy it," said Crewman Birdsong, "but the ears on my head and other shapeless things about me will be the obstruction. They have a regulation on Lotophage, you know; only beautiful persons are allowed the enjoyments."

"They bend the regulation," said Captain Silkey. "They use the wide idea of beauty. All the fine surging things they count beautiful, even though they be a little rough in texture. They don't bar one man in a thousand."

"I'm the man in a thousand in that," said Birdsong, "but I'll go; I'll try it. There's no world I'd visit so gladly."

They put it to the vote of their crews. Most of the men were for the side trip to Lotophage, the pleasure planet. Only enough men for one hornet crew wanted to go home directly. The sixth Captain (he shall be nameless, he shall be nameless forever) assembled the cravens and they went to their ready barracks to wait for flight clearance home.

The other five crews tumbled into their hornets to go to Lotophage.

"I have shucked a skin like a yearly snake," said Captain Roadstrum. "I'm an onion and an outer layer is sluffed off me, that of Young Soldier the First Time. But I be bigger and ranker for losing the layer. All who go home in the wrong direction, we fly!"

Where fiddlers scree'd and Rabelaisians loped, it was,
And Maybe Jones had walked the streets and hoped it was.

So glad a land, you'd never find a grouser there.

5

They said a man could really throw a rouser there!

Ah well, 'twas good enough for Lotophagians,
But how about the horny hopping shaggy uns?

How turned the bright-eyed crew to sleepy gooney guys?
How have a high old night with afternooney guys?

Lotophage was beautiful at planet-fall, subdued gold, afternoon color. Roadstrum, who captained the lead hornet, intended to take the planet from morning side as he always did, but somehow he failed. He came down in an afternoon world. Then remembered that it was always afternoon on Lotophage.

You could have shipped home whole boat-loads of sugar from the sweetness of their welcome. These people really made you feel wanted. They were even kind with Crewmen Birdsong and Fairfeather when they took them into custody.

"It is that only beautiful people are allowed at large here," the Lotophagians told these unfortunates. "We bend a point, we break a point, but you two are beyond the point entirely. It's into the dungeons below the light that the two of you go."

"But look at Captain Roadstrum with that broken nose on him," Crewman Birdsong protested angrily.

"We bend a point there," said a Lotophagian. "What's a broken nose? He's a beautiful man withall."

"Look at Captain Puckett with a muzzle on him like a coon," howled Crewman Fairfeather with much heat.

"We break a point there," said the Lotophagian. "Take him from the rear, or in no more than one-eighth profile. Is he not beautiful? But we cannot in heart say the same thing about you. It's the dungeon for you two."

"For how long?"

"Until you die. Or until we need the room for two more uglier than yourselves, which is not likely. You two just fill it up."

"Sorry, boys," said Captain Roadstrum. "Sorry, boys," said Captain Puckett and Dempster and Silkey and Kitterman. And the Captains and the crewmen went about the business of enjoying Lotophage.

As with all low-gravity planets there was a lassitude about everything. The indolence was reflected even in the subtropical flora. And no other life but the lazy one would have been possible there, due to the thin atmosphere. It was because of this that one could get high there so quickly. The air was almost entirely oxygen with no nitrogen filler, but it

6

was still very thin. But for those who love the lazy life, it was automatically induced.

Most flopped down where they were without even going to the nearest building. Why go further? Everything was available everywhere. They fell center-first into the slothful life. They slept hugely. It was hours later before any of them came to awareness again. Then they reclined Roman-fashion on the grass, and the sod rose and formed into contours to accomodate them.

"We used to lie on the roof at home when I was a boy and dream of this," said Cowper, one of Dempster's crewmen. "We'd dream how we would live on an island or planet, and the bananas would fall off the trees beside us. The coconuts would drop with a hole already in them for drinking; and after they were drained they would fall apart for eating. There would be a waterfall that turned a paddle-wheel that worked a music box, and you had only to whistle the key notes and it would take up any tune you wanted to hear. There would be cigarette vines dangling just above you, and you could snap one off and it would be already lit when you snapped it.

"It was big turtles, as I remember the daydream, who were taught to walk by with varieties of food on their backs. It was monkeys who were taught to prepare these foods."

"Ah well," said Captain Roadstrum, "when we travel we find how greatly our boyhood dreams are outstripped by reality."

Roadstrum had a four-foot-long pseudo-banyan fruit, actually a giant banana. He had been eating on it for many hours. He had a jug of rum-mix which he sucked with an attachment. The mix was under slight pressure so that he didn't have to suck very hard. At his side was a control panel of great selectivity. The invisible speaker, heard only by himself, would give him music or song, news or comment, drama and weird humor tales, gem-like repartee, or dirty stories.

He could squeeze a bulb in his hand and he would be flopped over into the warm water of the ocean pool where he could roll and float and dive. He could squeeze the bulb again and he would be transported back onto the grass by an ingenious lift. It was handy, and it was easy on the body.

In only one case did the panel fail him in information. That was when he asked it, "What day is this?"

"That answer we cannot give," the panel said. "It is ruled that, if you will not rise and see, it really does not matter to you. Besides, here there are not days. Here it is always afternoon."

The only clock available to Roadstrum without rising was the whisker clock. He felt by his beard that many days had gone by. He did not want too many days to have gone by. "Can you shave me?" he asked the panel. "Oh, sure," and the panel did it that quick. And this set the clock back to the beginning.

It was an easy life on Lotophage, and there was a whisper about the houris. The houris were among the things supposed to make the time pass so quickly on Lotophage. In particular Roadstrum had heard the whisper of an houri named Margaret, and now he rose to find her.

He stopped only to inquire of the health of crewman Sorrel. Sorrel, one of Puckett's crewmen, had thus far been their only casualty. He had put his jaw out of place while yawning. He seemed all right now but he would take it easy for a while.

Generally an houri would come on signal, even a thought signal, and swoop a man up in her arms and carry him off to pleasure. Roadstrum, however, being unaccountably energetic, was already on his feet when Margaret came to his unvoiced signal. He suggested that they go to the *Sleepy Sailor* a full hundred feet across the lawn.

Margaret offered to carry him on her twinkling shoulders, but Roadstrum was a bundle of energy even on this soft world and he walked on his own two feet.

In the barroom of the *Sleepy Sailor* there were many patrons sleeping or lounging on couches. But there were others of more hardy breed who sat bolt upright ("What's that mean, anyhow?" asked Margaret; "It means downright upright," said Roadstrum), and even some who stood with toe on rail. Some of the patrons were familiar to Roadstrum. There was Maybe Jones himself.

"Is this the place, Maybe?" Roadstrum asked him.

"No it is not," said Maybe, "though it fools me for a while every time I come. I'll stay here a while till I get a tip on a likelier place. This is very like the Place Itself as it is in the early afternoon, when things are beginning to rustle and make starting noises. But it never blossoms out as does the place; it never really gets into it. 'Things will start hopping along about sundown,' I always say, but here there isn't any sundown."

"I have heard about a place," said Roadstrum, "if you have ten thousand Chancels d'or for the tip."

"Always, always," said Maybe Jones, who always paid well for tips that might lead him to the Place Itself. "Here it is.

8

Now if you will mark down the rough coordinates here and whisper me a brief description of it I will be off to see." And Roadstrum gave it to him.

"I know a place that might be the place, Maybe," Margaret the houri said.

"Margaret, Margaret," said Maybe Jones, "you have given me ten thousand wrong leads, and yet I believe you could give me the right lead if you wished." And Maybe Jones was gone. He traveled forever looking for the lost pleasure place, and spacemen had begun to call it Maybe Jones City.

"Everybody loves it here," said Margaret the houri. "On Lotophage the law does not restrict. Elsewhere many things are illegal, as are we ourselves. We are forbidden to live anywhere else, and the penalty for disobeying that law is death. Where does that leave you if you happen to be immortal?"

"I have heard about you houris," said Roadstrum, "but the stories are confusing. It is said that you are older than people and that you will live forever."

"I sure hope so. I wouldn't want it any other way. But we change. I remember when I used to call myself Dolores and wore a rose in my hair and carried on like that. I remember when I was Debra and had a lot of style. I remember once when I was a Frenchie. Boy, it sure is fun being a Frenchie! But I don't remember very far back, only a couple of years. It seems like I always did have a lot of boyfriends."

"They say that you are timeless, which I do not understand," said Roadstrum.

" 'He moves a mighty turban on the timeless houri's knees,' as the poet says. I don't understand it either, Roadstrum, but you use a timeless device on your own ships when you make the big instant jumps. Who needs ships?"

Roadstrum sat on the timeless houri's knees and found it pleasant.

"The report is that you are completely immoral," he said.

"Shouldn't wonder if I am," Margaret answered.

"That you are not born, do not generate, and never die."

"No, I don't remember ever doing any of those things."

"In Earth legend, it is said that you are older than Eve."

"You don't understand women, Roadstrum. Never tell one that she is older than Eve. No, no, she was twenty-one years old when she was born; and I'm not one to whisper such things, but it wasn't a normal birth. I'm eternally nineteen. Sure, I remember her. She was the first of those fat house-cats."

"You have always had a bad name among good people," said Roadstrum.

"It's those fat house-cats who give us a bad name. I don't care for them either."

"It is even said that you do not live at all, that you are only a tall story that wandering men tell."

"There are worse places to live than in tall stories," said Margaret. "But you are in them yourself, Roadstrum, in all the jokes and stories of the shaggy-people cycles."

"Margaret, it is all wonderfully pleasant on Lotophage, but does it not seem as if they forgot to put the salt in?"

"You can add as much salt as you wish, mighty Roadstrum, but the water will not boil as quickly."

"What, Margaret?"

"To boil a lobster, one takes first a lobster—"

A Lotophagian citizen came in.

"The men who have died, mighty Roadstrum, how do you want them disposed of?"

"Died? How many of our men died here?"

"Only a dozen or so. You'd be proud of them, such happy lazy smiles on their faces when they went!"

"Well, do they bury here, or burn?"

"Oh no, neither. We use. One does not bury nor burn the essence of ecstasy. They provide the distillation of all pleasure. Those bar-snacks that you eat so avidly, are they not fine?"

"They are fine," said Roadstrum. "I wondered what they are."

"From men off the packet ship *The Yellow Dwarf*," said the Lotophagian. "Those men really ate and drank and roistered while they were here, day and night, I mean deep into the afternoon. They stuffed themselves and they spread themselves. They built themselves up while they were tearing themselves down. When they finally gave out there was nothing left of them but bellies and nerves. It's the jangled nerves, the fevered psychic leavings imbedded in the sweet fat that gives the particular flavor."

"The taste is powerful and tantalizing," said Roadstrum, "but the origin leaves a nameless doubt in me."

"—to boil a lobster, one takes first a lobster—" said Margaret.

"Your own men should have an even more unique flavor," said the Lotophagian. "We will call the product 'Lazy Man Ectasy Chips.' Give the word and we will have some of them for you quite shortly."

"All right," said Roadstrum, "go ahead. I don't know why

I gave it a second thought but there are a crowd of second thoughts hovering over my shoulder this afternoon."

"—and one puts it in a bucket of cold water," said Margaret. "Then one very very slowly brings it to a boil—"

A little shabby man was singing *Show Me The Way To Go Home*, an ancient folk melody.

"What are you called?" Roadstrum asked him.

"John Profundus Vagabundus," said the little man. "Deep John the Vagabon'. I'm the original old-time hobo. I've been wandering these thousands of years and I can't get home. I just can't make it."

"Why can you not?" Roadstrum asked him. "You are from World, according to your speech, and we go to World. We will take you when we go."

"But you will not go," said Deep John. "And if you do, I cannot go with you unless you compel me to. I have passed the last possible moment here and I am not able to leave."

"Why should you want to, Vagabond? Is this not the end of the road that every vagabond has looked for? It is the world of every complete pleasure without pain. And they are so glad to have us here. See, they have already made a plaque 'Great Roadstrum loused around here,' and they have set it into my favorite spot at the bar. What other place so welcomes visitors? This is Fiddler's Green, this is Theleme, it is the land of the Lotus Eaters, it is Maybe Jones City—(no, belay that last; Maybe says he isn't sure that it is)—it is Utopia, it is Hy-Brasail, it is the Hesperides. It is the end of every road."

"It's the end of the road, all right," the hobo said, "but I didn't want it to end. That's Fiddler screeing on his instrument in the next room, but he says he doesn't believe that this is the Green at all. And Frankie-Boy is in there too. He eats and drinks, and he carries on as even a red-nosed priest should not; he talks philosophy and he tells those whoppers; but he says that he begins to doubt that this is Theleme, after all."

"I'll just have a couple of words with those fellows and convince them again how wonderful it is," said Roadstrum.

Crewmen Crabgrass and Oldfellow and Bramble came into the *Sleepy Sailor*. Bramble blew a note on a pitch pipe and then he recited:

All lusty liquor with a crystal cask for it,
Whatever wished one only has to ask for it.

Tall pleasures piled in infinite variety,

11

Raw rolling gluttony without satiety:

And under sheen than all things else is awesomer
A golden worm that gnaws and gnaws and gnaws some more.

"Whence the doggerel, good Bramble?" Roadstrum asked.

"It's a popular epic composing itself these days," said Bramble. "It's called the Lay of Road-Storm, and it's about yourself."

"I understand now," said Roadstrum; "certain low fellows have been making cracks about the 'lay of Roadstrum' every time I set my hands seriously upon a woman here. But what is the 'golden worm' bit?"

"It's the way we feel," the crewmen shouted. "The golden worm is gnawing at our entrails. There is too much of it here, and it doesn't move along at a seemly pace. Captain Roadstrum, we are tired of lying around and going on little benders and jazzing these little girls here. We want to go on big benders. We want to find the big girls."

"What's to stop you, good men?" Roadstrum asked them. "It seems that everything is available here. It surely is here in the *Sleepy Sailor*. Can you think of any pleasure not to be found here?"

"No, we can't, Captain," said Crewman Crabgrass, "and it bugs us. How do we know this is everything, just because we can't think of anything else? We can't even get into places like *Shanghai Sue's of the After Dark Club of the Haystack* or the *Rowdy-Dow*. They all have signs on them, 'Open at twenty-one o'clock.'"

"There is surely plenty to do till then," said Roadstrum.

"Till then? Captain Roadstrum, there isn't any twenty-one o'clock here. It's always afternoon."

"Oh, those are only false fronts and signs that some of the boys from the tramp ship *Muley Cow* put up for fun," said Deep John the hobo. "They sure were good fellows from the *Cow*. I can taste them yet."

"False fronts or not," said Crewman Oldfellow, "they've sowed the seeds of doubt in us. If we sink back into it again now we'll be like the man who was drowning and didn't care."

"Good thing he didn't," said Roadstrum, "or he'd have worried himself to death."

"—passed the last possible moment," said Deep John the Vagabond.

"—heat the water very very slowly," said Margaret, "and the lobster will not stir till he is irrevocably boiled."

"Get your hot 'Lazy Man Ecstasy Chips,'" called the Lotophagian coming in with a great basket of them. They all began to eat great gobs of them, and they were the finest ecstasy chips anyone ever ate.

"These in particular," said Crewman Oldfellow. "I never in my life ate anything with so fine a flavor. I wish that Crewman Bigbender were here to taste them. Somehow they remind me of him."

"Let me see the tag on that bunch," said the Lotophagian. "Ah yes, they *are* Crewmen Bigbender."

They ate variously. It was all good. They drank. It was very good. They dozed. It was perfect.

"I don't care if I never wake up," Roadstrum murmured as he drifted under.

"—passed the last possible moment—" breathed Deep John the hobo.

"They are like all the others," said Margaret the houri. "Why did I think they might be different? I wanted to go back to World with them. I used to have a lot of fun on World. I'll wait me the centuries yet, and I'll yet find a man able to leave here after he comes. But he'll have to be a man in a million."

"I am a man in a million," said Roadstrum out of his shallow sleep.

"It is too late," said Deep John. "On the tomorrow we will eat 'Mighty Roadstrum Ecstasy Chips' and I'm sure they will have a mighty flavor. But I want to go home."

"I have the feeling that my life is in great danger," Roadstrum croaked nervously in his thin sleep.

"Never in your life will you be in such danger as you are at this moment," said Deep John. "You go under now and you can never come up again. And you have gone under."

"I never trusted a one-sided coin," Roadstrum mumbled in his sleep. "I never trusted a too-easy pleasure."

Roadstrum reared up suddenly like a great bear coming out of hibernation on Saint Casimir's Day.

"I have to go home at once," he said ponderously.

"They all say that but none of them do," Margaret told him.

"I am in great danger," said Roadstrum.

"Of course you are," said Deep John. "If you live through this, you will be in other dangers where your life is worth nothing; you will be in jams that will scare the very hair off your head. But you will never be in such danger as you are now here on Lotophage."

Bellowing like a bull, Roadstrum, the one man in a million, ran out of the *Sleepy Sailor* and began to kick the men awake. Most of them fought to get back to sleep or to death. Some of them really wished to leave Lotophage, and they said

13

so with great sorrow but with no hope. And some of them turned over on their faces and hung on, swearing that nothing could ever tear them away from this soft world. There were handles in the grass provided for hanging on. Lotophage was a jealous world and did not give up her victims willingly. Some of these men had befouled themselves, being unwilling to stir for anything at all, even to give their panels instructions to care for them.

Roadstrum rushed to the dungeon. "I'll get those two if I have to smash the place," he swore. "They, at least, will not be in love with it here. They will help me with the others."

He went to the dungeon and (thing beyond believing) Crewmen Birdsong and Fairfeather had just been released. Two men even uglier than they had arrived on Lotophage, and the hornet men were released to make room for them.

Two men uglier than Birdsong and Fairfeather? Are you sure? That is what the authorities on Lotophage decided. Two men from the *Smiling Skink* were put in the dungeon in place of Birdsong and Fairfeather, and they are still there.

In a frenzy now, Roadstrum fired up two of the hornet ships. He got Captain Puckett onto his feet and aware of the great danger of remaining. He promised to take Margaret back to World, where she had not been for several thousand years. He called to Deep John the Vagabond to come along if he was coming.

Roadstrum and Puckett and Birdsong and Fairfeather, Margaret and Deep John, jerked up those men who clung to the grass less tightly. They carried them, sniffling and sobbing, to the hornet crafts.

They enskied, they were in free space, and the most terrible of all dangers was behind them.

On Lotophage, as they left it, it was still afternoon of the same day and not perceptibly later than when they had arrived.

14

CHAPTER TWO

One needs for picture of the Laestrygonians
All hump-backed cuss-words and vile polyphonians.

"We'll cry a warning here though we be hung for it!"
The fact is, not a crewman had the tongue for it.

Those boys are rough, nor steel nor steinn can stay with them;
You'd better have viscéral blood to play with them.

That human meat and mind should ever rout the things!
It scares us silly just to think about the things.

We trim to decent measure these giganticals
And couch the tale in shaggy-people canticles.

Ibid

BOTH HORNETS were near inoperative. Somehow they had never shaken off the lassitude they had acquired on Lotophage, and they had been sluggish for the whole trip since. Puckett's hornet had to come down for an overhaul, and that of Roadstrum was nearly as bad.

"A planet, a planet," Puckett hollered over the communicator. "Find us a planet quickly, Roadstrum."

"The only one we can possibly make is Lamos," Roadstrum called to him.

"Lamos of the Laestrygons? But that's a primitive world. There will be no facilities for overhaul there. Pick another."

15

"I can't, Puckett. My craft won't hold, and you say yours is worse. Make ready for it. Do you still have your psych library and your tapes?"

"Oh hell no. We pitched them out long ago. Is there a people on this world? Is there a language?"

"Puckett, there's information here that I don't trust. A lot of these things were filled in by jokers for the fun of it, figuring nobody would ever get to such a world anyhow. The inhabitants are giant-like and primitive, it says, believed to be a species of Groll's Trolls."

"We've tangled with those big fellows before. They don't worry me."

"These are much bigger than ordinary, it says. They worry me a little. But their language, and this is the joker part of it, is given as something between Old Norse and Icelandic of Earth. How would primitive Troll people have Earth languages? And how such odd ones?"

"Try it, Roadstrum, try it, since you have psych tapes. We've at least fifteen minutes before our hard or easy crash. That's time enough for your men to learn any subject by psych. We shouldn't have pitched ours out, but we have a Norwegian on craft, Oldfellow. Did you know he was a square-head? We'll plug him into the brain-buster and then all plug in on him. Maybe modern Norwegian will bring us close enough. It's something to pass the last fifteen minutes and keep the men from getting nervous. It's all a joke anyhow. And we already know six basic dialects of the Groll's Trolls language. We'll probably encounter some variations of them here."

They came down on Lamos with their retrogrades shrieking. It was a heavy-gravity planet and their power was almost completely shot.

"We'd never make it if it wasn't all downhill," Roadstrum complained. "All right, men, into your pumpkin-picking cradles! We're going to hit hard!"

Ah, it was a hard crash for both the hornets. It knocked everybody out, cracked ribs and clavicles, ruptured lungs and diaphragms, and filled everybody with blood in mouth, nose, and ear. It was suffocating pain riding up through their unconsciousness, quite a long unconsciousness.

"I could open one eye if I could raise a hand to it to uncake the blood," Roadstrum groaned much later. "I could raise one hand if I could find the other hand to raise it with. I could stand on my feet if I weren't broken in the middle and hinder parts and if I hadn't suddenly doubled in weight. But all these things I will do yet. I am the mighty Roadstrum and I will perform the heroic feat of sitting up and prying

16

my eyes open, and even of raising my voice in exhortation."

He did so. He rose, not only to a sitting position, but onto his feet indeed. And he howled to his men to arise and encounter and defend. He got Crewmen Fairfeather and Birdsong up. He got the great Captain Puckett up and moving. He got the valiant Di Prima and Boniface, and Bramble and Crabgrass and Eseldon up and going, and the others had begin to stir. They had been hurt before often, and they knew how to rise above it.

They were out of their crafts. They were on a rock-strewn scarp with a little short sedge growing out of it. They were under a green-gray sky on a very heavy world, and they were surrounded by grinning giants or ogres, the largest sort of Groll's Trolls ever seen.

Listen, none of the men would head up to the navels of any of these creatures, and the men from the hornets were all fine tall men. These giants were splayfooted and thick as tree-trunks. They had shoulders two meters wide, humps on the back of their forward necks like bull humps, and heads that were howlingly huge. The ears on them were like nine-liter jugs, and their mouths were wider than their wide faces in defiance of all rules.

Margaret the houri was bubbling around, unabashed and unhurt, and was talking at a great rate to the grinning giants. And the language they were using was something between Old Norse and Icelandic of Earth. There wouldn't be much difficulty there then, but it was surely a peculiar business.

"I am Bjorn," said the leader of the Trolls in a voice that sounded as though he had great boulders grinding around in his gizzard. "The others of us have names which you may learn if you live long enough into this day. Come to breakfast now. Boys, you really better eat a big breakfast! You're going to need it."

"No, no," Roadstrum protested. "We must see to our crafts first. We must assess the damage and the possibility of repair. And then we have our own rations to serve us until we have made a study of the produce here."

"Little boy-men, you'd better forget about your crafts or boats or globes," Bjorn told them. "My little boy will fix your boats for you. He's mechanically inclined. And you had better forget your rations. If they produce such puny types as you they will not serve you for this day. We look at you. We look at us. We laugh. Come eat what we eat. You will have to eat the big breakfast of our sort because you are going to fight the big fight afterwards and we want you to be up for it."

"Wait, Bjorn," Roadstrum howled. "Don't let that big

17

fellow into the hornet craft with those seven big stone hammers. He'll smash things. He'll ruin us forever. I'll just stop him—"

But Roadstrum's feet were spinning in the air and Bjorn was holding him high and clear by the scruff of his neck.

"There is no big fellow going into your craft, good Roadstrum," Bjorn assured him. "That is my little boy Hondstarfer. I told you that he is mechanically inclined. He will fix whatever is wrong with your boats. In the meanwhile you will eat the big breakfast of your lives and then you will fight the big fight to your deaths."

"But he'll break up all the instrumentation with those big stone hammers," Roadstrum protested again, still flailing his feet in the air.

"Have you not trust in me?" the boy Hondstarfer called as he entered the first of the hornets. "Have you not noticed? One of my stone hammers has buckskin laced over it. I use that for the fine work. Do not worry, I will fix your boats, or else I will fail to fix them. This is the high logic. I am the best and only mechanic on Valhal, which is called Lamos by the ignorant."

A boy? He must have been a meter taller than big Roadstrum.

"Somebody stop that young fool!" Roadstrum called, still beating the air in the grasp of Bjorn. "If he meddles with the craft we're stuck here forever. Kill him or something, but stop him anyhow!"

"He who kills before breakfast will have bad luck all the forenoon," Bjorn gave them the proverb. "I would take it unfavorably if anyone killed him. He is my little boy and you will let him do what he wants. I am sure he will fix your boats. Nobody can chip stone or dress leather so finely as my boy; nobody can fit a balk or a beam so well. He is the best mechanic anywhere. And call him not a fool! You think we have no feelings just because we are slobs? Here comes the cars. Now we will go to eat the big breakfast. Try to play the men at the bord whether or not you will be able to play it in the field."

Here come the cars, Bjorn had said. Cars? What *were* those things sliding in through the low sky, skimming in not ten meters above the land, silently and flatly and raggedly? Wait a minute now. It is camouflage of some sort. They cannot be big flat slabs of stone sliding about in the air with giant Trolls standing on them! But they sure did look like big slabs of stone, some of them twenty meters in diameter, some of them only a tenth as wide. There were ten-man and five-man and one-man slabs sliding along flatly above the ground.

And when they came down they still looked like stone slabs, and they were.

Well, how do stone slabs as heavy as these (and the smallest of them were so heavy that twelve men could not budge them at all on the ground) cruise about above the land with no mechanism whatsoever.

"Crewman Bramble, how is that possible?" Captain Roadstrum asked.

"It isn't. Our wits are scrambled, our eyes fail us; it is not possible at all."

"I see that you have never encountered a science as advanced as ours," the boy Hondstarfer said as he came out of one of the hornets to enlighten them. "This is so far beyond you that I am not sure I can explain it to you. You yourselves are caught in the electromagnetic dead-end, so you are hardly able to imagine a thing like this and you doubt your eyes. We are fortunate. We have no surface metal on our world, or perhaps we would have been caught in the same dead-end. Is this not much neater? Our cars operate naturally on the static-repulsion principle."

"How can that be?" asked Crewman Bramble, who knew the theory of everything. "The static-repulsion principle can move nothing heavier than feathers."

"What do you use for feathers on World?" the boy Hondstarfer asked in amazement. "Here it will move stone slabs of a pretty good size, and it would move mountains if they weren't rooted so deeply into the land. This is a dry world and one without metals in its surface. It is mostly of pure flint. So we take slabs of chert or impure flint from the mountains, and there is sufficient static-repulsion between the slabs and the surface flint to enable the slabs to glide and fly."

"It is impossible," said Crewman Bramble.

"Shall I tell you the supreme scientific law of the universes?" Hondstarfer asked. "Hold onto your ears or they may fall off at the magnitude of the disclosure. It is all scientific laws crushed into one. Like charges repel. Think about it."

"Where do the slabs get their charges, Hondstarfer?"

"I don't know."

"Why don't all the slabs fly about all the time?"

"I don't know."

"Why do they fly so lightly in the air and then sink so heavily to the ground?"

"I don't know."

"Will it work for anything besides flint and chert?"

"I don't know. There isn't anything else on our world."

"Well, how do you steer the things?"

"It's all in the way you rub your feet on them. But you will have to put felt boots over those metaled things you're wearing. Here, the women come with small children's boots for you to slip on. Anything else would burden you so that you couldn't move."

Women? Dame elephants rather. They were very large, though not so large as their men-folks, and broad and almost shapeless. They were smiling and mysterious and ineffably wild, unbeautiful, ogresses, giantesses. But Crewmen Fairfeather and Birdsong and others went for them. Being somewhat grosser in their choices than the other crewmen, they were completely taken by these great creatures.

"I have never been so humiliated in my life" said Margaret the houri. "The giants all say, 'Go away, little girl, go away to your mother. Eat the big breakfast and someday you will grow up to be a real woman.' Real woman! Fellows, if there was ever tenth-rate competition, this is it. And I can't compete."

"You go now with my father and the others," the boy Hondstarfer said, "to eat the big breakfast and then to die the big death. And I go to get a bigger stone hammer and still a bigger one. It is fun to work on your flying boats. There are so many things in them that I will have to change or throw out completely. It is no wonder that they break down, they are so primitive."

"Come, come, little boy-men," big Bjorn called. "Mount on the two stone slabs set aside for you there and come to the breakfast hall. Follow us. Oh, you must all put on the little felt boots over your metaled ones. Were you not told? We go now. You follow."

"How do you get these blimy things off the ground?" stone-slab Captains Roadstrum and Puckett called out to the giants after they had assembled their men on the slabs.

"Rub your feet, little boy-men, rub your feet!" laughed Bjorn and Hross and Hjortun and Fjall and Kubbur and all those shaggy giants. "Were there ever such dolts? How do you get your own flying boats off the ground? Rub your feet, little things, rub your feet."

The Captains and crewmen rubbed their feet on the big chert slabs, drew hot sparks; and then the slabs jolted and rose from the ground and glided crazily along. They learned the tricks of steering and gaining height quickly. These were really easy vehicles to operate.

And now they had the impression of great height when they were no more than five hundred meters in the air, an impression that they never had in the hornets. It was all sheer down-drop in the windy air, and these things had no side-rails of any sort on them, and they tipped and swerved.

"The magic carpet!" said Crewman Bramble. "We have evidence now that the medieval Arabs of Earth really used such. They worked only over the very dry rock deserts, flint and chert deserts; and they were not carpets only, but thin slabs of stone covered with carpeting. Antiquarians have assured us that the evidence is overwhelming that such things were really used. I didn't believe it. I don't know how they could have worked. I don't know how these can work."

They came to the face of a sheer mountain. They hovered in the air in front of a black hole in the face of that rock.

"Come in to the breakfast," Bjorn called. The ogres drifted into the black interior on their stone slabs, and the men followed them in. And came down hard. The static-repulsion principle seemed to fail when they were in the heart of the stone here.

"Clumsy!" taunted Bjorn. "Clumsy!" taunted Blath and Hrekkur and the other ogres.

"You are the new guests here," said Bjorn in the cave darkness. "Tell the sun to come in, little Roadstrum."

"I'd as well tell the wind to lie down and the waves to be quiet," said Roadstrum. "I don't know what you mean."

"You are a boy-brained blockhead," said Bjorn. "What words do you use to order the sun when you are on World? Here it is simple to recite the words. You say, 'The sun, come you in,' and the sun comes in.

"The sun, come you in," Roadstrum said valiantly, wondering at himself. And the sun came in.

It was not, of course, the big sun of Lamos, but the little sun, the little boy of the big sun. It came in through the doorway of the cave, a hot yellow ball three meters in diameter, and it rose up to the roof of the cave and shone there. It was bright and hot, and the cave had been very cold. Water began to run down the walls, and globs of ice to fall.

"What is it?" asked Roadstrum of Crewman Bramble.

"It is the little sun, the little boy of the big sun," Bjorn interrupted. "Does not the sun of World have little boys also?

"What is it really?" Roadstrum asked Bramble.

"Some type of ball lightning," said the crewman. "But no, I see that it is a glowing stone. It must be a very small asteroid captured in the queer ambient of this nonmetallic world. It will glide around as the other rocks, and it should burn up if it is the proper texture. I don't know by what means it obeys voice commands. It burns but it does not burn up. I haven't worked out a theory on it yet. I suppose that Bjorn's hypothesis is the best one; it is the little boy of the big sun."

"We have roast bull first," said Bjorn, as a big bull was driven to them from some inner space of the cave. "Roadstrum, you are the high guest; skin the bull."

"I would need first a long steel knife to kill it," great Roadstrum said. "And then skinning knives and tongs and an A-frame and a block and tackle to handle it. Give us the equipment, Bjorn, and myself and five or six of my men will have it killed and skinned within the hour."

"You are really the great Road-storm?" Bjorn asked in wonder. "Little boy-men, you don't know how to skin a bull. Fjall, skin the bull."

Fjall broke the horns off the bull and threw them away. Then he put his fingers in the horn holes and broke a girdle out of the skull. He peeled all the skin off the skull. He broke the front hooves off the animal and peeled the skin up the legs; then he did the same thing with the back quarters. With his great thumbnail he then slit the skin up the belly. He rolled the hide back over the hump and shoulders. Then, going around behind the unhappy animal, he caught the bull by the tail and jerked the entire skin off in one piece, leaving the bull bawling and bare.

"See how easy it is when you know how," Bjorn said. "Now, Roadstrum, spear the bull on that pike and raise it up to the sun in the roof and roast it. At least you can do that."

"I cannot raise the bull on that pike," said Roadstrum. "I cannot even raise that pike."

"Oh helvede! Spear the bull and raise it up, Hrekkur," Bjorn said, and Hrekkur did it. That little boy of the sun roasted it thoroughly and quickly with a great dripping of burning wonderful grease and a powerful aroma. They ran other bulls through then, skinned them like gloves, and roasted them whole on spits held high in the small sun.

"Let us not get ahead of the count," said Bjorn. "I doubt me a little whether the boy-men can eat a bull each. We will see. Why do you hesitate, Roadstrum? That first bull is yours. Take it, take it in both hands if need be, and eat it up valiantly."

But Bjorn was right. The boy-men from the hornet crafts could not eat a whole bull each. It took three, and sometimes four of them, to devour a whole bull. And they ate pretty heavily too.

Hey, they brought oat-cakes bigger in diameter than a man is high. They brought onions as big as the head of

Burpy, and he had the biggest head of all the crewmen. They brought in honey-mead in casks large enough to make houses out of. And the breakfast beer! They knocked a bung out of the cave wall itself and the beer flowed, black and strong as Irish porter, in a great stream. It was a mountainful of beer they had there.

You think that was all? They had pork pies with a full-grown boar in each of them.

"Roadstrum, Roadstrum," Bjorn chided. "Do not throw away the tusks. One eats them too. They will make a man of you. It is the same with the teeth and the hooves of the stallions that we come to in the next course."

"And the antlers of the stag too, big Bjorn?" Roadstrum asked, for he would not let the huge fellow out-talk him in any case.

"Oh certainly, little Roadstrum. The accepted way is to swallow them without crumpling them or abridging them, but I see that you have neither the mouth nor the gullet for that."

Well, the boy-men from the hornet crafts acquitted themselves pretty well after they had gotten into it. They were slow starters is all. The mightier of them ordered another round of bulls and ate them with only two men to a bull. They ate those little baked whole foxes as though they were peanuts, and the baked rams as though they were cashews. They devoured the beavers, as was the custom, pelts and all. They developed a taste for whole roast wolf and nearly ran the Laestrygonians out of that commodity. And they found eagle stuffed with meadow mice to be a really different tidbit.

They found also that there is this about honey-mead: the second gallon that one drinks is better than the first, and the third is better and more intoxicating than the second. They got as high as orn-eagles, and as stuffed as pigs on acorns.

"Tell me in truth, little Roadstrum, was it not a great breakfast?" Bjorn asked.

"It was a great breakfast, Bjorn," Roadstrum said in all honesty. "In all my life I have never eaten a more filling one."

"And now, Roadstrum and all your small things, we fight," Bjorn announced. "We fight the great fight to the great death. You'll like this part of it, for I begin to see that you are really good fellows and men after all."

"With what do we fight, and for how long?" Captain Puckett asked.

"We fight with the stone-tipped spears and pikes and

23

with stone battle-axes," Bjorn said. "We have little boy-sized ones that you will be able to lift if you wish to use them. Or, if you have weapons of your own, you may use those; and we fight till everybody is dead. How else is a fight?"

"Can we use our hand blasters?" Captain Roadstrum asked.

"We do not know what are hand blasters," said Bjorn, "but if they are weapons, you may use them, of course. Now, Roadstrum, dismiss the sun and we will go out. Say only, 'The sun, go you out.'"

"The sun, go you out," said Roadstrum, and the little sun unhooked itself from the ceiling of the cave and glanced brilliantly out of the gaping door.

They all mounted their stone slabs, rubbed their feet, and zoomed out of the cave entrance into the sunlight, that of the father sun, not of the little-boy sun who had been in the cave. They landed in a great meadow. Captain Puckett sent Crewman Birdsong back to the hornet crafts to get a hand blaster for each man.

"Do you want one, Deep John?" Captain Roadstrum asked the vagabond.

"No, I always use a piece of coal-car coal swung in a bandanna," said the hobo.

"We do not know what is coal-car coal or bandanna," said Bjorn, "but use them if they are weapons."

"A good solid rock will do for the piece of coal," said Deep John, "and a little sling I have here to swing it in. And I believe a little stone slab I have my eye on could be used both for vehicle and weapon."

"You are sure you want to use those little things, boys?" Bjorn asked when the hand blasters were brought to the crewmen and passed around. "They are so short and light, how will you kill one of us with one of them? Better take the stone-tipped spears and then we will have real sport. You boy-men are small but you seem to be fast. With the stone spears you will kill some of us, at least, and we will have sport."

"No, we will use our blasters," Roadstrum said. "And I will tell you, Bjorn, that it will be strictly no fight. I do not understand your custom in this, but we do not intend to fight till all of us are dead. We desire very much that none of us be dead. And we will fight till all of you are dead only if it is absolutely necessary."

"Spoilsports!" called Hross and Kubbur, the big giants. "Dog-warriors," Fjall jibed. "Little-girl men," Hrekkur derided, "you are not men for a fight. You are not men at all."

"We are men," said Roadstrum, "and we are masters of

men. Bjorn, bring a pig or a sheep and I will show you how easily and at what a distance one of these blasters can kill."

"Do you not insult us!" Bjorn cried angrily. "Pig-soldiers! Sheep-soldiers! Let us see you kill one of our men with one of your blasters. Then we will know whether they are weapons for men."

"No, no, I could not kill a living man or—ah—ogre for demonstration," Roadstrum said.

"I could," said Crewman Fairfeather. Fairfeather had always been something of a blow-top, but there was something different about him now. He had a grin on him that was almost like the grins of the Laestrygonians. He seemed to grow larger. He looked like—well, he had always been the ugliest of the crewmen, now he was nearly as ugly as the Laestrygonians themselves—he looked like one of the giants, that same happy insane look in the eyes.

Fairfeather shot big Hrekkur with his blaster. He tore a big hole in the giant and killed him.

"Now you've torn it!" said Roadstrum angrily. "We'll probably have to kill them all. Watch for their moves."

But all the giant Laestrygonians were whooping with laughter.

"Killed him! Killed him!" they whooped and roared. "Man, he did look funny when you killed him so easily."

"Look at his face, the side of it that's left. He still doesn't believe it."

"Hey, the boy-men got a real weapon going."

"Show us again."

"Kill me."

"Kill me. Hey, little fellows, kill me with one."

"Easy fellows," big Bjorn said. "We can't use all our fun up in one moment. You'll all get killed this day. We don't want to have our sport over too early; and remember, we have to kill the boy-men also. Are we ready? Onto your stone slabs all and into the air for battle!"

"Must we fight on those things in the air?" Roadstrum asked.

"There are no rules. We do whatever seems the most fun," Bjorn said. "Fight where you will. We like to come zooming at each other on the stone slabs and transfix each other with our spears as we crash together. Fight on the ground if you wish, but we will zoom down and spear you on the ground."

"We will try it both ways," said Roadstrum.

Both men and ogres got on their stone slabs and, rubbing their feet on them, lurched up into the air. They fought with two or three men or ogres on a slab, or with only one on a slab. The men could not steer or maneuver as well as the ogres could, but they learned rapidly since their lives depended on it. And it is very hard to kill with a blaster when riding one of those stone broncos in the sky and shooting at a fluttering evasive target.

Crewmen Fairfeather and Birdsong and Crabgrass were speared with stone-headed spears and killed, but each of them took an ogre with him. These crewmen died with curious whoops of laughter, quite unmanlike, quite ogre-like.

Crewmen Di Prima and Kolonymous were knocked off their slabs and killed in their fall to the ground. Crewman Oldfellow was cloven from crown to crotch with a stone battle-ax, and he died in the both parts of him. And every blaster shot by every man had missed. Only Fairfeather and Birdsong and Crabgrass had killed ogres, and only these had taken stone spears after the unsuccess of their blasters.

"To ground, to ground," Roadstrum ordered. And all the hornet craft men grounded their slabs. "The low air is the element of the ogres and we can't get them there," Roadstrum explained. "We'll stay on the ground where we can take steady aim, for we cannot do it on those wobbly slabs in flight. And they'll have to come down to our level to try to spear us. Here, here, let's form in rings of about five men each, and one can blast them front-on from which-ever direction they come."

They formed so. The Laestrygonian ogres swooped around on their slabs in the low air and devised tactics. And then a large stone slab hung in the air directly over every five-man group.

"Blast up," Roadstrum ordered.

All blasted up, and they tore some holes in the stone slabs. But they could not tell whether they killed any ogres. And not one blast in five went all the way through its slab. Those were good stones.

"We wait them out," said Roadstrum. "They cannot spear us unless they expose themselves, and we have them out-ranged. We wait while the poor giants make up their slow minds. I wonder what signal they use for surrender?"

"Whup! Whup! Whruuupp!!!" It was like an earth-blast shaking the very ground under all of them. One of the stone slabs had dropped suddenly in dead-fall and had smashed and killed all five men stationed under it. Blood running in little rivulets from under the edges of the stone slab, and wild hooting laughter from the low skies!

26

"Scatter," roared Captain Roadstrum. "Scatter," roared Captain Puckett. And the men all scattered pretty nimbly.

"Crewman Bramble, go up on a small slab and scout," Roadstrum ordered. "Find us an open-face cave or a haven of some kind under an overhang where they must come in to us and cannot drop on us."

Crewman Bramble scraped his feet on a small stone slab and was airborne, followed by whooping giants with stone-tipped spears.

"Up and fly at random," Roadstrum ordered them all. "Stall and evade and blast. We will learn the low-air tricks. We have them outranged, and there is no excuse for letting them kill us so easily."

So they were all up in the air.

But the only one who was doing any good was Deep John the Vagabond, called by Captain Roadstrum their native light-horse auxiliary. The old hobo had a very thin, very small stone slab, with a sharp cutting edge which he made to be the forward edge. He was able to attain very rapid flight on this and come in behind the flying giants. At first he used his handy rock in its swinging sling, crashing it into what should have been the brain-base of the giants, but he could attain nothing against their bull-humps. Then he used his slab itself for a weapon, swooping in beyond them at a very high speed and calculated height, and just plain slicing their heads off with the forward cutting edge of his slab. Their heads hit the ground with thunderous thumps, and the crewmen could keep track of the kills of their ally.

But say, those giants did have a happy time of it, no matter that a few of them were beheaded. They swooped in on the men on their flying stones, fluttering and banking and using their slabs like shields, and then suddenly struck with their long spears and spitted the men. There was laughter that made the low skies ring like bells whenever they did this. There was even louder laughter on the part of the giants when one of their own folk was killed and blown apart by a blaster. It seemed to be the funniest thing they had ever seen.

And in truth it was funny to see one of them blown apart and come down in huge bleeding hunks, the great head usually broken free and landing with a brain-spewing crash. There was never a folk who took such delight in bloody slaughter as did the Laestrygonians.

After a long while, Crewman Bramble came sailing back to the men, a spear quite through his shoulder giving him a rakish and almost heroic appearance.

27

"Follow, follow," Bramble called. "It isn't much, but I have found something."

They followed him to a huge stone platform under an overhanging ledge, and all the remaining men landed on this. It was at the end of a pocket, the smaller bit of a wedge, and it could be defended. It had a natural parapet, breast-high, and all were behind it with their blasters. There weren't many of them left though, six or seven, and more than twenty had been killed by the giants. How many giants were left they did not know. The men had never counted them, and they did not know them all. The giants all looked very much alike to the men. Here the giants could come at them only one at a time, and they would be fair shot for every blaster.

One of them swooped in on his slab and was blasted to bits very close. His slab staggered away and crashed into the cliff-side very near the haven. The men were covered with a rubble of broken stone and were drenched with the giant's blood.

Another came in, and another. One came in all the way, leaped from his slab, and killed both Crewmen Burpy and Fracas with a single spear-thrust, and was then blasted to death by Captain Puckett. But the shattered bulk of the giant near crowded them out of their haven and left them knee-deep in blood behind their parapet.

Still could be heard the idiot ear-rupturing laughter and hooting of Vetur and Fjall and many nameless giants in the low sky. Still could be heard the happy strong voice of Bjorn.

"Little boy-men, did you ever have so much fun a fight as this? Hey, it's a rousing thing, is it not? We always like to show our guests a good time."

Quite a few hours had gone by in all this. It wasn't swift. It had been all the tedious maneuvering of battle that is not done in an instant. But the men were all soldiers and they began to enjoy it. And still they were incomparably weary.

"One hour the break," came the big voice of Bjorn from the swooping low sky. "It is the noon. Come out and loosen up, and the women bring the water."

"Is it a trick?" asked Captain Puckett.

"No, they are not capable of tricks," said Captain Roadstrum. "Let's get out of here for a while."

They got onto their stone slabs, rubbed their feet, and lurched out into the sunny soft air. The big women of the Laestrygonians were rising on stone slabs with huge jars of

28

water for the giants, and Margaret the houri came with a pretty fair sized jug for the men.

"I will *not* let those cows bring water to you," she announced. "I bring the water to you myself. Hey, I've been killing some of those cow-women, one at a time, and unbeknownst to the others. Bjorn is right. This killing can be a lot of fun."

"So far this is the oddest day I've ever half spent," growled mighty Roadstrum, as he took his noontime ease on a stone floating in the low sky. "I don't understand the setup here at all. There is neither rime nor reason to it."

"I bring rime," Bjorn called in his loud voice. "Who needs reason?"

The grinning Bjorn slid his slab near to that of Roadstrum. Then he blew a solid note on a jug flute that he had between his legs. And then he declaimed:

> *The little bug has got the glitter eyes of him,*
> *You can't go by the pepper-picking size of him.*
>
> *We look and hoot, 'That must be only half of him.'*
> *We laugh at him and laugh at him and laugh at him.*
>
> *He be tall eater and a taller topian,*
> *No mind the little fellow's microscopian.*
>
> *We pitch a party, sling the dangest dangeroo.*
> *Whoop, whoop and holler! He's a hero-hangeroo!"*

"What in hound-dog heaven is come over you, Bjorn?" Roadstrum asked in wonder. "Is that Laestrygonian verse?"

"Sure is not, little Roadstrum. That is Road-Storm verse, your own high epic. We make verses of it here also, as do folks everywhere. It is so long a time since we have had a certified hero in our place. You think we be so nice to you if we do not know who you are?"

The grinning giant dripped rivers of sweat onto the earth below, and his voice was full of thunder. Roadstrum remembered an old mythology where the first rain was the sweat of such a deity-hero, and the first thunder was such a voice. But now Bjorn changed and became all business.

"The noon is over!" he cried in a voice that made big cracks in a high cloud. "All back and make ready for the fight. Scoot, little men, back to your haven. Last one there gets killed!"

The last one back to the haven was Crewman Ursley, and he was killed at the very entrance of it.

29

Now came the rocks thrown by the slab-hands of the giants, rocks near as big as the men themselves. This was the mortar attack from cover. Crewman Mundmark was struck by such a rock. His limbs were unstrung, he burst asunder, and he died. Crewman Snow was similarly slain, but in louder fashion. The rock didn't strike him full but it sheared near half of him away. He howled and roared and screamed. Crewman Snow was very reluctant about the dying business, but he died nevertheless.

And yet the men were killing possibly two for one. They blasted arms off the giants that were reared back to throw. They blasted every one dead who ventured into the open. And there hadn't been many giants, or men.

"How many of us left?" Captain Roadstrum asked as though he were counting patrols and batteries and battalions.

"I see myself. I see you," said Captain Puckett. "I do not see any others."

"How many of you dog-hearted giants are left?" Roadstrum called loudly.

"Only myself," came the strong voice of Bjorn. "Come out the two of you and we will see who is dog-hearted."

"I go," said big Captain Puckett. "I always did want to die a hero's death."

Puckett went out with his blaster blasting. He smashed rocks open as though they were eggs. He knocked an arm and shoulder off of Bjorn when he had only half a shot at him, and the happy laughter of Bjorn over it was one of the great things.

"I will show you a hero, a hero," Captain Puckett swore.

"Dead hero, dead hero, come to me," Bjorn jibed. They were out of Roadstrum's sight now. The sun was in his eyes as he peered, and it would soon be dusk.

There were a dozen more blasts, a dozen more hooting laughs almost too big even for a giant, and then a last blood-clabbering scream.

"The little boy-man was a hero after all," Bjorn called. "Shall I toss your dead hero to you, Roadstrum?"

"Toss him," Roadstrum called. And the body of Puckett, impaled on the great spear, came sailing in. Roadstrum caught him somewhat, stretched him out, and gave him the hero's salute.

"Hurry!" Bjorn called with some urgency. "The sun sets, and we two are left."

"What is the hurry?" Roadstrum called. "I fight well in the dark."

"No, no!" the giant cried. "Be you not difficult! All must

30

be dead before the sun goes down. Hurry out and be the hero too."

"A hero I am not, Bjorn," Roadstrum blared. "Alive I will bide a while, and it is now my brain against yours."

But Roadstrum lied, hardly realizing it. Some time before, in the time of the ten-year war, Roadstrum had caught the heroes' disease during one of the campaigns. It is infectious, and it stays with one to some degree forever. It usually took him every third day along about sundown, coming with a sudden chill and a quick steep fever. Always he had taken precautions so that he would do nothing rash while the heroic fever was upon him. But this was the third day at sundown and the fever came suddenly; and this time Roadstrum had not taken precautions.

He jerked Bjorn's great spear out of the body of Captain Puckett. He selected a stone slab, rubbed his feet on it, and veered out of the haven.

"Up and at it, Bjorn of the dog-liver!" he called boldly. "We fight your way to the death."

"Have we time?" the giant cried. "Thunder! Have we time? The sun goes down."

"In the high air it shines yet," Roadstrum called. "Up and at it, Bjorn."

There were two giants laughing in the sky! Roadstrum had turned himself into a giant with as boisterous and happy a laugh as the best ogre of them all. Now they came at each other on wild pitching stone slabs, the most rampaging stallions ever. Bjorn had his second spear, shorter but heavier than the first, and Roadstrum had found the strength to heft and haft the great spear itself. A pass, and both were slashed and gouged, and each left a hunk of meat on the other's spear.

"Higher," Bjorn called, "the sun fails. Faster, the final sortie. Up, up, Roadstrum, the sun must catch both our spears."

They went up very high. The sun was on the bloody points of both their spears, and all the world below was dark. Then they charged, each on his snorting stone slab that neighed and surged and had come alive. Roadstrum caught big Bjorn in the middle of the belly, where it is mortal to an ogre. To swerve then, in the millionth of a second! But there was not time to swerve. Bjorn's eyes laughed at Roadstrum as he died, and his heavy spear had the man through the center breast. Roadstrum's slab was the higher, and it sliced Bjorn through at the groin. The two heroes came together in death, transfixed on each

31

other's spears, and fell a very very great way to the ground that was now in night darkness.

"Ah, well, I died a hero and a giant," Roadstrum said, for every man is allowed one sentence after death.

So now all were dead on both sides. It had been close, though. For a while it seemed that they were not going to make it. The giants had told the men that the fun is all spilled out and lost if all are not dead by the fall of night.

Dead and splattered. Gathered up and carried. By what? By whom?

But even in dreams *they* are not. They are on the other side of dreams. It was incredible enough that one of them could carry Roadstrum, a giant among men. But how could one carry Bjorn, who was a giant among giants?

Death is for a long time. Those of shallow thought say that it is forever. There is, at least, a long night of it. There is the forgetfulness and the loss of identity. The spirit, even as the body, is unstrung and burst and scattered. One goes down to the death, and it leaves a mark on one forever.

"Come to the breakfast!" boomed a voice so vast that it shook the world and all the void between the worlds. "Come to the breakfast!"

And there was another voice rilling on in saucy silver, that of Margaret the houri.

"I see that I am going to have to make some changes here," Margaret was shrilling angrily. "You eat, you fight, you die, you sleep, you wake up, and you eat again. But where does that leave the women? You are going to have to find an hour every day for them."

"Yes, yes," said Skel and Mus and Fleyta and Belja and Toa and Glethi and Vinna and Ull and Raetha, and all those other Laestrygonian dames with the more difficult names, "you are going to have to find one hour in the day for us."

"I think for a long time there is something missing," big Bjorn was saying, "but there is no time for anything else. We breakfast, and then we fight till all are killed, and then it is night. We are dead all the night, and then we sleep for a very little while at first sun. Then is it time for breakfast again. Look yourself at the sundial, little witch-child. Can you see any time for anything else on the sundial?"

Margaret the houri lifted a boulder larger than herself and smashed the sundial.

"I will make a new dial," she said. "I will make it different and with an extra hour. There has to be time for the women. And now I will instruct the women on what they will do in that hour."

"How did I get back here, Maggy?" Roadstrum asked the houri. "Was I not dead?"

"Of course you were. And I was Valkyrie last night (the others showed me how to be one) and I carried you back from the battlefield. Sprained a shoulder doing it."

"But how was I dead and now I am alive?" Roadstrum persisted.

"Do you not understand yet, little Roadstrum?" Crewman Birdsong asked him. "Hey, it was a rollick, wasn't it?"

Little Roadstrum? From Crewman Birdsong? Roadstrum was *not* little, he was a giant of a man, he topped Crewman Birdsong by a head.

No he didn't. He didn't come up to the nether ribs of Birdsong. Crewman Birdsong had become a giant, as had Crewman Fairfeather.

"Why has it happened to you two, and not to great Roadstrum and to great Myself?" Captain Puckett asked, for now he was alive and awake again.

"Some have it and some do not," said Crewman Birdsong. "You two, and the most of you, must have had mental reservations when you went into the thing. I thought all along that you fellows weren't as joyous and wholehearted in the battle as you might have been. If you let yourselves go completely today and enter into it with a happy howling heart, then I believe you can make it."

"But what is it? How does it happen? Where are we really?" Roadstrum asked.

"No? You really don't know? Valhalla, of course. Here the heroes fight to the death every day in glorious and cloud-capping battle. And every morning they are reborn to fight and die again. I can see where it's going to be a lot of fun."

"Doesn't it become kind of tiresome after a while, Bjorn?" Roadstrum asked the giant of giants.

"Why no, not really, Roadstrum. You know how it is with everything. They all pall a little after the centuries begin to mount. But this is better than most things. Stay with us; you will be a mighty fighter yet."

"We have a choice to make, Captain Puckett," said Roadstrum.

"Let us first go see if we *do* have a choice, Captain Roadstrum," said Puckett.

They gathered their men, except Crewmen Birdsong and

33

Fairfeather, who had already become giants and who would remain in any case. They went down to their hornet crafts to see if anything at all could be done to repair them on this world, to see if the mad boy Hondstarfer had left anything of them.

Well, at least the shells of the hornets were still there, but there was a great amount of the works scattered around on the rocky ground.

"I couldn't see any use for a lot of that stuff so I left it out," said the boy Hondstarfer. "They will both fly now, but one of them will break down again after a little while. This one here is perfect and will fly forever. On the other one I made a lot of mistakes. You'll have more room in them now if you ever use them. Those long things I took out were what was taking up all the room."

"Those are the main drives," said Crewman Boniface.

"Ah well, the ships are fixed," the boy said, "but one of them will break down again."

"They will fly?" asked Crewman Humphrey. "Men, men, let's go then! I've had enough of this place where they stuff you full of bull and then hunt you down and kill you every day."

"No, of course they won't fly," said Roadstrum. "How could they fly without their main drives?"

"Oh, they'll fly," the boy Hondstarfer said. "I fixed the clumsy things. Did my father Bjorn not tell you that I was mechanically inclined?"

"However could you fix such intricate machinery with nothing but those seven stone hammers there?" Captain Puckett asked.

"I didn't, I couldn't, I only thought that I could. I had to go get that."

They hadn't noticed it before. They'd thought it was a tree. Hondstarfer hadn't fixed their hornets with those seven little stone hammers. He'd used a *big* stone hammer. Was it ever big!

"Hey, I want to be a hobo," Hondstarfer cried as Deep John the Vagabond fluttered down on his favorite slab. "How do I go about it, Deep John?"

"It isn't like it used to be," said Deep John. "It all seems much smaller and narrower since we took to the skies. The spacious days of it were on World in the old railroad time. But you'd need a time machine to get back there, Hondstarfer."

"Oh, I've got a time machine," the boy said, "also a space-racer. I think I'll go to World and turn myself back and be an old-time railroad hobo."

34

"Well, what is the choice?" Puckett asked. "Do we try to fly in something that can't possibly fly? Or do we stay to be killed again and again and again?"

"Wait, wait," called Margaret the houri. "I'm going with you. Those giants aren't as much fun as I thought they'd be. You get tired of them after a while."

"That's true, that's true," said Roadstrum. "We have our choice. Let's make it. I was a giant for my moment. I can be one again if I'm called on to be. Shall we say that Hondstarfer could not fix these things to fly? Shall we say that the stone slabs of this world could not fly? Load in whoever wants to go! We fly! We fly! We've flown on less."

And to their own amazement they began to load in.

"Wait, wait," big Bjorn called coming down to them. "Will you not stay to the breakfast?"

"We will not stay to the breakfast," Roadstrum said.

"You will do better today," Bjorn stated. "You begin to be giants. Today you will be able to eat a whole bull, Roadstrum."

"I am able to, yes, Bjorn, but I do not want to eat a whole bull. I can be the giant whenever I wish, and I am afflicted with the heroes' disease that smites me every third day about sundown. But we will fly! There are skies we have not seen yet! There are whole realms still unvisited by us. We will not be penned in even a giants' pen. We fly!"

"In that case, Roadstrum—ah—it is an embarrassing thing to say—in that case there is one thing we must do before you leave."

"Do it then," said Roadstrum.

"We do not want to be overrun with amateurs," the giant Bjorn explained. "If everybody knew how much fun it was here, then everybody would come. We want only such fine farers as yourselves who come by high chance. You must promise never to tell anybody how much fun it is here."

"We promise," said Roadstrum. "We will never tell anybody how much fun it is here."

"And there is one small thing that we must do to make sure that you keep your promises," Bjorn added.

"And what is that?"

"CUT YOUR BLOODY TONGUES OUT!"

Two of the Laestrygonian giants grabbed each man and threw him down; and a third, stepping on his man's throat to force his tongue out, grabbed it and pulled it out still further to its absolute extent, and then cut it out with a stone knife, roots and all.

Here was the creamingest pain ever. Here was utter frustration. Who may battle and defy and get revenge when deprived of tongue and voice? And besides, they were near dead from the loss of blood, near a more final death than that of the night before.

But they crawled and dragged themselves in, gagging and green, and loaded dying into their crafts, with Roadstrum going last.

"Here is one final thing beyond the final," said Bjorn. "—Ah, I am truly sorry to see you looking so green and puny—one very last surety you must give before you tumble dying into your boat. You must write on this paper that my little boy has here, for my boy Hondstarfer, as you may not know, can read. You will use your finger and the blood from the roots of your tongue. You will write 'I will never tell anyone how much fun it is in this place.'"

And mighty Roadstrum wrote with his finger and his tongue's-roots blood "I will never tell anyone how much fun it is in this place."

They took to air all bloodily and retchingly,
They made new tongues, but didn't make them fetchingly,

And flew through chartless skies where none had fled before;
Whatever came, at least they'd all been dead before.

But one thing worked, whatever else might nix the things,
That hammer-handling kid had really fixed the things.

All bloody luck they ever got away like that,
They sure did never want another day like that!

And Roadstrum shucked another layer fretfully:
One gives up giantizing most regretfully.

Ibid

36

CHAPTER THREE

All lost in space, the hide-bound inner side of it,
With roaring rocks that gave them quite a ride of it—

Ah better Dobie's Hole than such vortexicon
That stoned them all and spooked the cowboy lexicon!

They guessed wrong guess and reveled in unheedingly
(Where clashing rocks turned strange and roared stamped-
ingly),

And ate High Cow, and fell beneath the curse of it,
And bantered suns, and ended up the worse for it.

They had the horns and hump and very prime of it,
And rather lost themselves about that time of it.

Ibid

THEY CAME AMONG the clashing rocks, "the rocks wandering."
It was a thick asteroid belt moving at a respectable speed,
and it was necessary that the hornets match its direction
and speed for safety. Besides, since they were lost, they
might as well go where the rocks were going.

The wandering rocks were mostly about the size of the
hornets themselves, rounded and not too rough. They were
thickly clustered, one every thousand meters or so. "And
we called that thick!" the men said later. They were gray
bumbling things in the gray twilight, and some of the men
got out and rode on them.

"They've got eyes on them," said Crewman Oldfellow.

"Probably the mica glint," said Captain Roadstrum.

"No, no, not like that at all. Eyes like a calf, like a buffalo calf that I saw at a World zoo once. I look sideways at one of them, he looks sideways at me, and we see each others' eyes. But when I look at one of them directly, his eyes disappear."

"Ah well, maybe your eyes disappear also," said Roadstrum. "You'd be the last to know."

The clashing rocks kept their distances and positions pretty well; and yet it seemed as though they became somehow more numerous, as though they spawned when the men were not looking.

Roadstrum sent his men out to mark and number the one hundred nearest rocks. And then they rode along and studied the traveling rocks for an equivalent day.

"There are two forty-nines," Crewman Lawrence reported then, "and we numbered only one of each number."

"Then I have bumblers for men and they are not able to count to one hundred," said Roadstrum angrily.

"That is not so," Crewman Bramble protested. "I made the dies myself and I made them true. But now there are three number nines each bearing my genuine and original die of that number."

"There are five number sevens at least," said Crewman Crabgrass. "It sure does get crowded now."

"Do you hear snorting, Roadstrum?" Captain Puckett called from his hornet. ("False tongue, false tongue," warned the communicator.)

"Space noises, Puckett," Roadstrum called back. ("False tongue," warned the machine.) "And they become even noisier," said Roadstrum. "But would you call it snorting? Well yes, I guess you would. Puckett, where in glare-eyed space are all these rocks coming from? And what is the excitement and fear that seems to be running loose among them?" ("False tongue," the communicator warned again.)

The communicator always gave this warning now, whenever a man spoke from one hornet to another. The "False Tongue" sensor had been built into the communicator from the beginning as guard against space things that may counterfeit the human voice and so interfere and subvert. But now all the crewmen had false manufactured tongues in their heads, and their communicators warned them against themselves.

All except Deep John the hobo. Deep John had in some manner escaped the attention of the Laestrygonian giants at that time. "I was the only one able to keep a civil tongue in my head," Deep John liked to say.

Margaret the houri had also kept her own tongue, but the communicator called "False tongue" at her nevertheless. The machine read her as something not quite human, and her tongue also.

"It is snorting, Roadstrum," Captain Puckett called again. "It is snorting and bawling and trampling. Hear the heavy hooves of it!" (False tongue," said the thing.)

"We spooked them, Captain Roadstrum," Crewman Threefountains said mysteriously. "Some of these breeds spook easy. Man, are we ever going to have a rumble!"

"They are perverse roaring rocks," said Crewman Bramble, "and I do not believe that the spherical is their real form. And the closest one, rubbing on our very windows there and threatening to break in, bears the number three and five-eighths, and we made no fractional-number dies; and yet it is a die made by my own hand; no one could counterfeit me there."

They went another equivalent day, and the churning rocks were like to crush them all. "Each of the pawing rocks has a brand as well as a die number," Crewman Trochanter said then. "It's a sun-brand, but I don't know what sun."

"There's dust," said Roadstrum, "prairie dust, but how could there be dust out here? And our scan-can reads that there is a break in the thing, half an equivalent day ahead. We'll break out of this then, no matter what we break into."

"The way out of one known fusillade of rocks is Dobie's Hole," said Crewman Crabgrass, "and the hole is not bad. But the way out of the other known congress of clashing rocks is the Vortex. It apparently leads to sure death; nobody has ever come out of it again."

"It's death here," said Roadstrum. "We will take the side break when we come to it. We are lost, and we will not know whether it is Dobie's Hole or the Vortex. Hey, what curious things are you men doing with the ropes there?"

"We don't know," the men said. "We just found ourselves doing it. We have a compulsion to form the ropes into such running loops as these. There is something we must do with them when the time comes."

"Roadstrum," Captain Puckett called from his hornet, "the jostling rocks have gone insane! What's the name of this madness?" ("False tongue," warned the communicator.)

Deep John the hobo took the communicator and called from Roadstrum's hornet to Puckett's:

"The name of it is stampede."

39

"I think so too," Puckett answered. "Roadstrum, my men are making running loops in ropes, and they don't know why." ("False tongue.")

"So are mine, Puckett," cried mighty Roadstrum. "It will offend someone when it is done; but what is another measure of trouble added to what we already have?" ("False tongue," cried the machine.)

It was as though they were coming to a great river, and the stampeding stones were filling it up and running over it on the backs of their bogged comrades. But at this river in the sky (for half an equivalent day had passed), there was a second ford breaking off hard to the left. The hornets took the branching, coming into a region where the rocks pressed them less hardly. But now the men broke out of the hornets and began to do things clear outside of reason.

Crewmen Crabgrass and Clamdigger went for the horns of a little calf-rock they had selected, a rock even smaller than a hornet, not above five times the size of a bull elephant. And they had the thing by the horns, but how will a small asteroid have horns?

Then all the mad crewmen from both hornets were outside, shouting and making ritual motions with their ropes. They flew flying loops around that calf-rock, more than a dozen of them. They jerked it along their own new way, both the hornets dogging it. The men all gave voice to varieties of barking and hooting, and the calf-rock was bawling. The dust was deep and stifling and smelled of flint sparks.

"It's a thing too tall for my reason." Roadstrum slung out, "but I get the high excitement myself. We are pulled along at a great rate on our new course, but we will not let the doggie go! Onto it! Kill it! Skin it! Break it down! Devour it!"

They were out of the concourse of rocks now, except for the calf-rock whose neck they had broken and which died. They had escaped from one of the known fusillades of rocks, and their way of escape was not Dobie's Hole. It was the Vortex.

Nevertheless, the men, working dangerously, had begun to dismember the calf-rock, and some of them had lit space-primus fires to roast it.

"The horns and the hooves to Captain Roadstrum," Crewman Threefountains roared, "and the fat of the hump to Captain Puckett."

"What is it all, Roadstrum, what is it?" Puckett called.

"False tongue," warned the communicator.

"Oh shut up!" Roadstrum told the communicator. "Crew-

40

man Bramble, disassemble the bogus-intrusion safeguard. It drives me crazy."

"All right," said Bramble, and he quickly disassembled it.

"I don't know what it is, Puckett," Roadstrum called then, "but there's something about the aroma as they begin to roast the meat. A space-primus fire really has no odor, so how should it smell to me like sage-brush and buffalo-chips? Why should the meat smell to me like buffalo meat roasting, when I never smelled buffalo meat? The closest I ever came to it was my grandfather telling of eating it when he was a boy, at a rodeo on the Fourth of July at the old Hundred and One Ranch. And how is it that the men have got such magnificent horns and hooves off a round rough rock?"

"It's one of the sacred cattle of the sun we have killed," came the voice of Puckett. "We knew before we were born that this was forbidden. Now we must die the fiery death for the offense. You have the lead hornet, Roadstrum. Turn into the near sun with it, and I will follow. Let us be consumed by fire. There is no more hope for us."

"You're out of your wits, Puckett. What cattle of what sun?"

"The sun so great that it is known as *the* sun, Roadstrum. It is the nearest sun to us. Let us turn into it at once and be consumed for our sacrilege!"

"Puckett, if I had one of Hondstarfer's stone hammers here I'd fix your head for you. You're gone daft!"

"What, Roadstrum? I was outside for a moment trying to figure this thing out. Holy cow, it's an odd one! I heard you talking as I came back in."

"Puckett, you were giving me a balleyowl about the cattle of the sun and telling me we must turn into this nearest sun and be consumed."

"I was not, Roadstrum! Curse that sleazy little sun! Someone is trying to call us to our deaths. We'll not go into that little sun, and we can't go back through the stampeding rocks. It was the other sort of false tongue talking to you, not me. We're into the Vortex for good, so let's provision for it. Come out and feast, Roadstrum! Ten men couldn't eat the bull-hump of this calf, a hundred men couldn't eat the loins. Bring out a few kilos of pepper and a firkin of Ganymede hot-sauce."

"Curse that sniveling little sun, Puckett. For time out of mind and belly I've never seen such a thing as this!"

Did they ever carve up that big young bull! They were into the Vortex itself, going at unlawful and unnatural speed, caught by a force that none had ever broken, but they weren't going hungry into it.

41

They feasted on that big carcass that had seemed to be a rock. They questioned nothing. They were going at a speed where all the onrushing stars appeared violet color ("Lavender," said Crewman Crabgrass. "Lavender world laughs with you," said Crewman Trochanter), where all sequence was destroyed, where any answers would have to come before the questions.

The space-primus fire had become a pungent campfire. Crewman Threefountains played on his harmonica as the crewmen still gorged on the offworldly beef. Then they had branding-iron coffee from somewhere, and horse whisky. They had left the sniveling little sun and were going into a vaster black sun that had gobbled up its own light. It was night now, but it wasn't an ordinary night.

And then they all fell to singing old campfire songs, whether this should be the end of them or not. They sang such old songs as "Eight-Eyed Lucy Jane" (it's plain she isn't plain), "I Lost My Heart on Wallenda World" (to a woolly Woomagoo), "The Green Veronica," and "The Grollanthropus and His Girl."

And they were rushing into the Vortex at two hundred million kilometers a second, and there was no possible way to break out of it.

> *They felled a flipping doggie, made a bobble-up,*
> *And dropped to mokey sun that worked the gobble-up.*
>
> *It swallowed time and flow in loins and liver yet,*
> *And voided all that ever gave the Giver yet.*
>
> *One countered not with care or even laughter it,*
> *It drew in whole and pulled the hole in after it.*
>
> *Use but a thumb to gull the gulping glutton there!*
> *That hammer-handling kid had put a button there!*

Ibid

"I always wanted to study an involuted, massive, black-giant sun," Crewman Bramble said. "I dreamed as a young man how interesting it would be to have plenty of time to study one and at close range. We will have the time of our life for it now and a very close range. I say it all again, but I have a false tongue in my head in two different senses. Roadstrum, I never wanted so little to do a thing in my life!"

"The equivalent-day recorder has gone crazy," said Roadstrum. "Look at the days flip over. Why, Bramble, there's nine days passed while we talk here."

"That idiot kid Hondstarfer must have meddled with it as he did with everything else on the crafts," Bramble guessed. "Still, it's peculiar that it should begin to misfunction after all this time."

"Captain Puckett," Roadstrum called over the communicator, "has the equivalent-day recorder gone crazy on your craft?"

"Yep, gone crazy," Pucket answered. "We've been amusing ourselves with it. We've got to amuse ourselves with something as we drop to our deaths. Do you know, Roadstrum, according to this thing, I've aged a year in the last baseline hour? Hey, this would make a man old fast if he went by it, wouldn't it?"

"It's a damned dumb thing that the equivalent-day recorders should go wrong on both hornets at the same time," Roadstrum growled.

"It was a damned dumb kid we had meddling with our equipment," Bramble complained. "But so far we've figured out a purpose for everything he did, except the equivalent-day recorder now, and the *Dong* button."

The *Dong* button was just that, a big green button with the word *Dong* engraved on it. You pushed it, and it went *dong*. Well, that was almost too simple. Should there not be a deeper reason for it? And the small instruction plate over it didn't add much. It read: "Wrong prong, bong gong."

"There's no more to the button than is apparent?" Roadstrum asked Crewman Bramble.

"Yes, there is more. Everything on our hornets works by the static-repulsion principle now, you know. And the *Dong* button contains one half of a static-repulsion couple. But wherever in wall-eyed space the other half of that couple is, I don't know. It isn't on the hornets."

Well, they were well-fed by the space-calf that had masqueraded as a rock until they had slaughtered it. They were well provisioned by its leavings. They were rested and well, and they were falling to their sure deaths.

So the men busied themselves, or they did not, according to their natures. They had fun variously. And now and again one of them returned to one of the crazy equivalent-day recorders.

"Look, look," Crewman Crabgrass chortled. "I'm a month older just while I was in the john. You guys always did

43

say I took too long there. And I'm two years older than I was when I finished my third breakfast a while ago."

"A man could live a lifetime every two days by that thing," Crewman Snow laughed.

But the crewmen laughed less loudly when they discovered (about the time that the equivalent-day recorder had racked up five years since the beginning of its malfunction) that they had all aged about five years in appearance during those short hours.

Thereafter they whistled softly and spookily and began to look at the recorder with something like frightened awe. And they looked at each other furtively and did not meet each others' eyes.

A little later, Crewman Mundmark died of heart stoppage. He hadn't been too old a man, and he had kept in pretty good shape. But he had lived the violent years of a spaceman, and with twenty years suddenly piled on top of that (for it was about twenty years now) it was no great wonder that he should die.

There were balding pates and graying heads popping out all over the place. Crewman Ursley lost three fingers suddenly. There was nothing happened to them. Suddenly they were gone. A bandage bloomed briefly where the three fingers had been, and then there was only old scar tissue. And Ursley gazed at his changed hand in understandable amazement.

"Whence have I this sudden, great, old scar-gash on my cheek?" Roadstrum croaked out baffled. "When have I lost me my fine right eye, and how is it that I find myself carrying that eye (in pickled form) in my pocket?"

"These are all incidents of the lives we would have lived out were we not falling into the blind black sun," Crewman Clamdigger gave the opinion. "These are the losses and mutilations that we would suffer in our normal lives, and they show on us here as we come to these equivalent years in our fall into the Vortex."

"There was an old World movie named 'Death Train' of which I forget the plot but remember the impression," said Crewman Crabgrass. "And at the end of it they were in a runaway train going into a long tunnel to their deaths. So are we."

"It reminds me of a freight train I caught out of Waterloo, Iowa one night about three hundred years ago," said Deep John the Vagabond. "Man, that train did have an eerie mournful sound to it, and the clicking of the rails—why I can hear the same clicking of the rails now."

"So can we all," said Roadstrum, "but how would there

be rails clicking when we are going at a thousand times the speed of light?"

"Roadstrum," Puckett called from his hornet in a much-aged voice, "I've turned into a bald-headed, pot-bellied, crabby old man with no teeth and not very much vision. I don't like it."

"I don't like my own aging, Puckett. Have any of your men died?"

"Yes, about half. A good thing too. They're not much good for anything when they get to that age. Roadstrum, this will have to be goodbye. I'm too old and stove in to get outside the sphere these last two years—ah—that is, the last thirty minutes. It's happening faster now, you know."

"Myself, I will try it once more," said Captain Roadstrum.

Roadstrum went outside the hornet sphere. He had always liked to go outside, but now it was unpleasant and very difficult. He could not comprehend that positive black light nor the distortions of space. With the reversal of the curvature, the turning inside-out of mass and moment, it seemed that they were already inside the bulk of the black sun, but they rushed forever faster into the deep Vortex.

Roadstrum barely made it back inside. Still, he was proud of himself.

"I always said I'd live to be a hundred," he boasted. "Holy Cow, am I not a ramrod straight and imposing man at ninety-four! A Gray Eminence! Maggy, has it any effect on you? What does that mirror you are so busy with tell you?"

"Really, Captain Roadstrum, twenty or even twenty-one is not a bad age. I study myself as I come to that. No, I do not age as quickly as you do, but I age. I like me when I'm young. I like me when I'm old. I bet I even like me when I get to be twenty-two or even twenty-three."

"What, all the men dead except Hobo John?"

"Yes, all the others, Roadstrum, and now it catches up to me also. I had won a delay some centuries ago, actually I won the delay in a gambling game with a certain Power, but now both my basic and my extended life come to an end," said Deep John.

"It hasn't been a bad life, but it was rather disappointing that the last two-thirds of it should pass away in less than an equivalent day. Seems unfair, but we did kill that calf, and perhaps we shouldn't have. We should have known that such odd cattle would have belonged to someone. What, dying, Hobo John?"

"Might as well, Roadstrum," said Deep John the Vagabond, and he died.

"Be there any living on the other hornet?" Roadstrum called.

"None but me," came the crackling old voice of Crewman Oldfellow. "And I'm about to turn in and die myself. It's funny, Captain Roadstrum, they called me Oldfellow because I was the youngest man in the crews, and the name stuck. And somehow it never seemed to me that I'd really get old. I got to die now, and I doubt if we'll ever meet again. But if they *do* ever let you visit up our way, look me up."

"I will, Oldfellow. Pleasant death to you."

Margaret the houri had just made a little cake.

"Happy birthday, Captain Roadstrum," she called out cheerfully now.

"What, what Mag, what's this?"

"You just turned a hundred, Captain. Eat it."

"I will, Mag. Say, did you ever notice that a man gives off a pretty strong odor for about a second when he dies. Well, they're all gone but me, and now I go. It was nice, but shorter than I expected."

And he went into death snooze. Why not? He was a hundred and eight at least by the time he had finished the cake. It was going faster now.

"You are like all the others," said Margaret. "Why did I think you might be different?"

"Snuff, snuff, snooze," Roadstrum breathed in his death slumber.

"To boil a lobster, one takes first a lobster— Will not that rouse you again, Roadstrum? 'Passed the last possible moment,' Deep John would say, and now he is dead. Are you dead also, Roadstrum?"

"Mighty near." Roadstrum spoke out of his death sleep. "Leave me in peace."

"What was that word, Roadstrum? Peace? It's a fine word for the mob, but it will gag the one man in a million. Shall I say it again, Captain? Peace."

"I *am* one man in a million," Roadstrum protested out of his deep, old-man sleep. "Maggy, it does gag me. Why, I'll erupt out of the grave and stage my own ressurrection."

And he did manage to sit up, looking very much like Lazarus.

"How old am I now, Mag?" he asked in his reedy voice.

"A hundred and twenty, Captain, and it goes faster."

"That's not a bad age for a real man. What went wrong? There is a way out of everything, but somewhere we took the wrong turning, the wrong prong."

46

Then he looked at the *Dong* by his side, the button that the boy Hondstarfer had put there. "Wrong prong, bong gong," said its instruction plate. Roadstrum pushed this button as he had many times before, and it went *dong* as it always did.

Then Roadstrum fell back once more into what seemed to be his death slumber. But now there was somehow a change in the low purr, in the cosmic sound.

"I had better just hop over to the other hornet and push the button there too," Margaret said, and she did.

Yes, a fellow smells a little high for the short second just before he comes back to life, just as he did for a short second after he died. Margaret snuffled her nose at Crewman Oldfellow, and left. She went back to Roadstrum's hornet. It was her regular place. Everything was much as it had been before, except that the equivalent-day recorder had begun to run backwards as soon as the *Dong* button had matched the other half of its coupler with something in the black sun. And pretty soon Roadstrum came out of his death slumber on the same side he had gone into it.

"Mighty rum thing, Maggy, mighty rum. You remember what the high poet said:

The eating, aging; empty ogre got 'em there;
They fell into the well that had no bottom there.

Let us expunge that couplet, Maggy, for it was writ of ourselves, and we are entitled to edit our own epic. Perhaps the black sun did get us, but in the time reversal thing he did not. This is a most handy button. Now we can back out of anything we get into, as long as we are with the hornets."

It was fun watching the men return. There was something comic in their difficulty in accepting the thing. "You're kidding. It couldn't really happen like that," they all said. They were a bunch of cranky old men, and then they began to get younger as hope welled up in them. They came back, every last one of them. Roadstrum had his rogue eye back in his head, unpickled and serene. The scar-gash left his cheek. And Crewman Ursley had his three fingers back on his hand.

But there is a weirdness in almost all actions done backwards. It wasn't as much fun regurgitating the space-calf as it had been eating it. And they did have a blue hell of a time putting that thing back together. Roadstrum hated to give up the magnificent horns and hooves, but there was no way out of it. You go on that backwards jag and you'd better expect the improbable.

Certain bodily functions are unusual and almost unpleas-

47

ant when done in reverse; but to get out of a hole like they were in, you will put up with a lot.

They were back among the clashing rocks, "the rocks wandering." They were out of those rocks again on the other side of them. They were lost in space again; but the equivalent-day recorder was running normally now, in the right direction and apparently at the right speed.

"Whyever did we choose that path into the clashing rocks over all other possible paths?" Roadstrum asked in amazement.

"Give a look at the other possible paths, Captain Roadstrum, as you looked before," said Crewman Crabgrass.

"I look. I shudder," groaned Roadstrum. "I'm not sure but what the terrible course we just backed out of is not the best one. Horror, horrors everywhere we look."

"One thing, Roadstrum," Captain Puckett called from his hornet. "We didn't lose any time on that side trip. We came out at exactly the same moment that we went in."

("False voice," warned the communicator, "false voice.")

CHAPTER FOUR

He won a thousand worlds, and made the bums of them,
And mocked the Gentry for the broken thumbs of them.

He propped the Universe, but propped it jerkily,
For mighty Atlas after Georgie Berkeley.

He climbed the Siren-zo and made a clown of it,
And plucked the high note from the very crown of it.

Hold hard with heels and hands and crotch and cuticle
For episodes becoming epizootical.

Ibid

"I believe that I have found a sure way to beat the games,"
Roadstrum said. And all the men groaned.

"Give it up, Captain Roadstrum," Crewman Clamdigger
begged. "The smartest gambling men in all the worlds are
here; and a mental man you are not."

"This is a sure thing," Roadstrum insisted.

"Give it up, Captain," Crewman Trochanter pleaded.
"There are men here with luck growing out of their fingers
and toes, luck in their eyes and voices, in their minds and
in their nether-minds, in their beards and in their bowels.
And there is no man of us, even with false tongue, who can
say 'Lucky Captain Roadstrum' without laughing. A lucky
man you are not."

They were down on Roulettenwelt, the gamblers' world.

49

This was the showiest of all worlds, and it was said that the streets there were paved with gold. Actually, only the Concourse, the Main Mall, the Royal Row, Broadway West, Vega, and Pitchman's Alley were paved with gold, and these only in their central blocks, not over five thousands of meters of roadway in all.

And crewmen went into the big houses and watched the big gamblers; and they listened to the tall stories about them. There was Johnny Greeneyes, who could see every invisible marking on cards with his odd optics. There was Pyotr Igrokovitch with the hole in his head. Pyotr was the most persistent suicide of them all. Following heavy losses in his youth he had shot himself through the head. It had not killed him, but the shot had carried away great portions of the caution and discretion lobes of his brain. The passage through his head had remained open, with pinkish flaps of flesh covering the holes fore and aft.

Now, whenever Pyotr suffered heavy losses, he jerked out his pistol and shot himself through the head. It was all for a joke; he always shot himself through the same passage; and the "brains" which he appeared to spew out the back opening with the shot were in reality only phlegm that had gathered in his head. But it was rather a weird thing when seen by one for the first time, and Pyotr very often killed spectators standing behind him.

There was the Asteroid Midas, a big-beaked bird of a gambler who could do things with card and dice and markers in his long talons that seemed unlawful. There was Sammy the Snake, who held his "hands" in his mouth, or in his little forked tongue darting around. The last man who accused Sammy of cheating and who made a grab for the hidden card lost his arm clear up to the shoulder. But the man still insisted that Sammy *did* have a hidden card, that he, the man, had succeeded in grabbing it and even then held it in his hand, and that he would prove the thing if Sammy would only give him back his hand and his arm.

There was Willy Wuerfelsohn, Jr. Willy, as his father had been, was a devoted gambler. The father had died of starvation, being nineteen days and nights in a gambling session without eating or drinking. Willy senior was a well-liked man, and there were many people at his funeral mass.

"Requiem aeternam dona ei, Domine," the priest said rather near the end of it, "and now we pay special memorial to him by the one thing he loved most."

The priest and the pallbearers dealt out hands of hasty poker on the coffin and bet and played. They showed, and the winner was about to pull when a hand came up out of the coffin. It held, of course, a royal flush; and the hand raked the money into the coffin with him.

"—per misericordiam Dei requiescant in Pace," the priest concluded. Then they took him out and buried him. A remarkable man, as was his son.

"I know these are all the finest gamblers from all the worlds here," Roadstrum said. "So much the greater opportunity. This thing can't miss, can it, Crewman Bramble?"

"Of course it can miss," Bramble protested. "We haven't even tried it."

"No need to try it till the big money is down," Roadstrum said plainly. He went to the table with the biggest gamblers of them all and tried to get into the game.

"How much have you to bet, Captain?" Johnny Greeneyes asked him. "You may be a big space captain and still only a little man for money. This game is not for boys."

"I have two space hornets and one million Chancels d'or that is my mustering out pay, and ten thousand of same I had in tip from Maybe Jones," Roadstrum said with all the pride of a well-heeled space captain.

"Captain," said Johnny Greeneyes, "the lowest chip here costs one billion Chancels d'or. It was Maybe Jones himself who set this lower limit when he last played with us. It has to be that way, you understand, to keep the kids out. But there are lower tables for lower folk. There are even some where one may buy a marker for as little as a hundred thousand Chancels."

Roadstrum went grumbling and found a lower game. He bet his million and ten thousand Chancels and lost. Then he laughed, reversed it, bet them, and won.

He had in his pocket the *Dong* button from his hornet, and with this he could reverse any happening and run it through again with corrected hindsight. Crewman Bramble had completed the *Dong* with the other half of a floating couple, supposed to reverse things in any really dire emergency. And Captain Roadstrum, with his impassioned participation, turned every gamble into a dire emergency.

It worked again and again. Sometimes Roadstrum even won a hand without needing the button for replay. When he had several billion Chancels, he went to other tables and other sorts of games, testing it and making sure before he went to try the big boys.

The device worked again and again. At dicing, Roadstrum sometimes had to turn it back for as many as a dozen different throws to make his point, for he wasn't a lucky man. It worked perfect at roulette. That was simple one-repeat stuff. It worked well at roustabout poker. Roadstrum had more trouble at other poker games, the feedback of his own gaming affecting the betting and drawing of the other players. Sometimes he had to run it through twenty times before he won a hand; he wasn't a very good poker player.

It would seem that all this replaying took a lot of time, but it didn't. One goes into time, one backs out of it again, and time is as when one started. Nor did others even notice the *dong* of Roadstrum's button; all things in the sequence were forgotten by the others and remembered only by Roadstrum the principle.

Then Roadstrum went back to the table with the big gamblers. He convinced them that he was now a man of substance, and they played with him. Golganger was now in the game. Golganger was a creature of a species with a difficult name. He was peculiar in the extreme, and he had thirty thumbs on each hand. How that fellow could shuffle and deal.

But Roadstrum noticed with satisfaction that all thirty pair of Golganger's thumbs had been broken somewhere along the way. And that Asteroid bird had had his talons broken more than once, that was clear. Sammy the Snake had a crook in his forked tongue that he had not been born with, and all the men of them, Pyotr, Johnny Greeneyes, Willy Wuerfelsohn, had had their thumbs broken several times in their lives. On Roulettenwelt, as on most of the worlds, a shifty dealer will finally be spotted; he will be dragged out by honest men, and they will break his thumbs painfully; and he cannot be a shifty dealer for another month or so.

"Ah, you gentry of the broken thumbs," Roadstrum mocked, "you have been taken before, all of you, and I will take you now. I work you like putty in the palm!"

They played, and Roadstrum won. The big gambling men smiled at him and played some more, and Roadstrum won some more. Then the big men began to play seriously. Roadstrum had to run one set through more than fifty times to beat Johnny Greeneyes on it. Roadstrum's own thumb was quite sore from pushing the *Dong* button so many times. And still Roadstrum won.

"You have won all the money we have with us," Pyotr Igrokovitch finally said, and he shot himself through the head. "It isn't really much money, but to keep the game going we will let it stand for a medium-sized world. All right, does everybody bet one medium-sized world?"

"You fellows really own worlds?" Roadstrum asked.

"Of course we do," said Sammy the Snake. "Money is

only for the warm-up. The game doesn't start till the title-tokens to worlds come onto the table. Are you nervous, Little Captain of the Early Luck?"

"No, no, I'm not nervous. It's just that I never played for worlds before."

They played and Roadstrum won. He won and won. He won big. He owned more than a hundred worlds now. He had become a mogul in the universe. Many High-Space-Emperors have fewer worlds. Many Confederation Chiefs rule fewer.

"I be King Roadstrum now," he said proudly.

"King Roadstrum, I want to have a word with you," said Crewman Bramble.

"Yes, what is it, Bramble?" Roadstrum asked when they had gone apart to talk.

"I've been following the *Dong* button on the scope, Captain, that is, King," Bramble said. "The pulse becomes a little erratic. That Hondstarfer was an inventive kid, but he wasn't really a careful worker. The button should be worked over. There could be a failure."

"Keep watching it, Bramble. I want to make a couple of big grabs before I quit. If the pulse becomes too erratic, let me know."

Roadstrum went back to the table and continued to win. Johnny Greeneyes got green all over. The great crest-feathers of the Asteroid Midas wilted down as his spirits fell. Sammy the Snake was suffering the miseries, and there is nothing sicker than a sick snake. Pyotr shot himself through the head six times in quick succession, banged his empty pistol down on the table, and cursed.

"I quit," said Willy Wuerfelsohn, Jr. sullenly. "I've only three of four worlds left, and I'll need them to get back in a game in the morning."

"One thousand worlds," Roadstrum said. "I be High Emperor Roadstrum now."

"High Emperor Roadstrum, I want a word with you," said Crewman Bramble.

"This is it, boys," Roadstrum told the gamblers. "It has been a pleasure, and I don't know any man who wins so graciously as I do. —Well, Bramble, it was getting even more erratic, was it? Well, it was a good little button."

"No, no, Roadstrum, the pulse has cleared. It's working perfectly now. Go on with the game. Let the sky be the limit."

"I have won skies enough this day, and my eyes are so tired that I can hardly tell the green suits from the blue. Here, take little *Dong* and put him back in the hornet.

And round up the men. We are off to visit other worlds, perhaps even some of the one thousand."

Crewman Bramble took the *Dong* button back to the hornet and began to round up the man. And great Roadstrum went down to the men's room as he had been meaning to do for some time.

"Here, here," he told the attendant. "I'm no commoner. I own a thousand worlds. Put tissue with the Emperor's Crest on it into the stall for me. I can use no less."

"Put a Chancel d'or into my hand and I will," said the attendant.

"Double or nothing," Roadstrum snapped

The attendant looped a coin and won. They doubled and doubled, and the attendant won. Roadstrum flipped a coin and still the attendant won. Roadstrum no longer had a *Dong* button in his pocket to reverse his calls with.

They cut cards for it, and the attendant continued to win.

"It's a hundred thousand Chancels now and a bit more," the attendant said. "Do you want to go ahead?"

"Sure, double you again. This time I win," said Roadstrum. But the attendant won.

"It's three hundred billion Chancels now," the attendant said; "do you want to keep on?"

"I'm about to the end of my cash," Roadstrum said. "How about title to a medium-sized world?"

"All right. I always wanted to own a world," the attendant said. The attendant won the world, then two, then four, then eight, then sixteen, then thirty-two, then sixty-four—

"But I don't have anything to worry about," Roadstrum said. "I only have to win once to come out of it." But it was the attendant who won and won and won.

"How many worlds did you say you had?" the attendant asked after a while.

"One thousand exactly."

"You owe me a thousand and twenty-four. Give me the titles to the one thousand, and sign this I.O.U. for twenty-four worlds. I can trust you to supply them in a reasonable time?"

"Yes, I'll win them, or buy them somehow, or conquer them. I am a man of my word; I will get you your worlds. Now please, put the Emperor's Crest tissue into the stall for me. I've certainly paid enough for it."

"Can't," said the attendant. "You're not an Emperor anymore. You've lost all your worlds. You're a commoner again. Use plain paper."

The attendant still owns those worlds today. He is High

Emperor and he administers his worlds competently. He is
a man of talent.

> *A thing unseen is on its face unseeable;*
> *a being, savored not nor heard, unbe-able;*
>
> *and be assured there's naught at all outside of us*
> *unless perceived by one or by a pride of us,*
>
> *nor someone see it move it will not move at all,*
> *and damn! he had a husky guy to prove it all!*

Ibid

They were down on Kentron-Kosmon, an insignificant
world. And yet, in the middle of Space-Port there (a cow
pasture rather; it wasn't much of a spaceport) there was a
nice plaque of electrum and on it was lettered: *This is the
Exact Center of the Universe.*

Whether or not the plaque spoke the truth, this was the
only world that had such a plaque. And the people of
Kentron (there weren't very many of them; it wasn't a very
big world) had a sort of cockey pride over their centrality,
or over something.

But all the hornet men were flush (even Roadstrum had
partly recouped his fortunes on Pieuvre World), and they
wanted to have some fun. And Kentron had one fame besides its central location. *It is always Saturday night there,*
was a proverb about the place.

"The fact is, we're so knob-headed dumb that we can't
count the days," said a crinkly-haired young female, "so we
call them all Saturday."

Well, *you* try to count them. A full day lasted about
one equivalent minute. Imagine thirty seconds of daylight
and thirty seconds of darkness! *If you want to do something in the dark, you'd better do it fast,* is another proverb of Kentron, and it has a certain challenge to it. On
Kentron they had pace.

The men explored Kentron quickly. It was only about five
kilometers around it. It had twenty-five high class hotels
on it, and each man and one houri established himself in
one of them as king or queen for the time of the visit.
It had about five hundred blind-crows, pubs, winegardens,
or beer-cellars, and several of them seemed to be lively.
There was a lot of laughter and music going on; the people
were fair of face and figure and quite friendly; the weather
was almost perfect with its constant variety (one gets neither

very hot nor very cold in thirty seconds); the whole little world seemed to be a series of continuing floor shows; and moreover there was challenge.

Almost central to the planet and to the universe, was a little carnival. There was the Corn-Crib (you had heard all the jokes before, you had met all the girls before somewhere, and you still liked them both); there was the Big Casino with its warning sign *Dong buttons disallowed* (the word had got around); there was a Wrestle-the-Alligator Tank, a tattoo parlor, and the Booth. The big, good-natured-looking man in the booth was the Challenge, and they all felt it.

He winked them a great wink and the twenty-four men and one houri winked it back at him. He was a man of their own measure.

There were signs posted variously about the big fellow's booth. *I'm the guy who keeps it all going. If I weren't here, you wouldn't be here either. I know it all, I'm a smart-aleck. Loan-sharking and fencing. Any time I can't see you, you've had it. Country-style wrestling and scuffling done.*

There were, moreover, dozens of telescopes stuck around the booth, one big one pointing straight down into a hole clear through the planet; and the big man moved his eye rapidly from eyepiece to eyepiece, using them all. He had three sets of earphones on his ears, and he was surrounded by whole banks of instruments and scopes that he scanned constantly.

"Just what is the pitch here, friend?" Roadstrum asked the big fellow. "What is it that you do?"

"Anything and everything," said the big man. "I see them all. I do them all. I know them all. I throw them all."

"You don't look very deep to me," Roadstrum grumbled.

"Oh, I'm not. It isn't my profundity that makes me a mental marvel, it's the amazing detail of my perception. There is nobody else who can keep so many things on his mind at once. Ask me anything, anything at all, Roadstrum."

"Big fellow, if you know it all, then you can answer one small question that bothers me. We are on a very small world here; it should not have an atmosphere; it should not have a gravity of any consequence. By rights, we ought to be in our spacesuits now and wearing our static-grip boots. But we move about free and easy, breathing and functioning, and with our usual weight and balance. We have noticed that this is so on many small worlds. We appreciate it, but we do not understand it. How can it be?"

"You men are from World," said the big fellow. "Therefore you know of Phelan, who was also from World, and therefore you must understand Phelan's Corollary."

"Certainly we know it, or at least Crewman Bramble does," said Roadstrum. "He does much of our knowing for us."

"But I doubt that even he knows the Corollary to Phelan's Corallary," the big fellow said. "It states that 'As regards very small celestial bodies of a light-minded nature, the law of levity is allowed to supercede the law of gravity.' I call it the compassionate corollary. If I had to sit here all these ages in a spacesuit, I don't believe I'd make it."

"Get out of the way, Captain Roadstrum," Crewman Trochanter blared. "This fellow advertises country-style scuffling. Let him try great Trochanter at the wrestle. Answer me, fat-face; who is the saltiest sky-dog of them all?"

"I am," said the big man. So he and Crewman Trochanter joined in the big wrestle. Trochanter put everything on the big guy, and the big guy twisted around in it like he was made of Rega-rubber. He was always craning his head and neck out of a hold to glance through one of his telescopes or scan a bank of instruments. Trochanter threw him flat on his face, and the man twisted his head for a gawk into the telescope that looked straight down through the planet. "Just in time," he said. "I almost let a couple of them get away from me that time." Then he raised Trochanter up and slammed him shatteringly on his back, forming a spread-eagle indentation in the hard ground, seven feet long.

All the men looked kind of funny then. Trochanter was as good a country scuffler as you'll find anywhere. But spacemen can't let a tough carney keep the hop on them. One of them would have to toss him, if they had to go through the whole list.

"Who is the saltiest sky-dog of them all?" Crewman Clamdigger demanded.

"I am," said the big man. "Just a second till I scan all the scopes again and make sure everything is spinning right. All right, man, have at it."

That big fellow pinned Crewman Clamdigger so fast that it was spooky. He was good. He knew every trick, and he out-stronged them all. But still it was required that they all try him. "Who is the saltiest sky-dog of them all?" a crewman would demand. "I am," the big fellow would answer, and then the battle.

He threw them one after the other. Di Prima, Kolonymous, Boniface, Mundmark, and after each brief set-to the big fellow rushed back to peer through the spyglasses and give a quick listen through the earphones. Burpy, Fracas, Snow, Bramble, he tossed those four mighty quick. Deep John

57

the hobo; that was an odd match. Deep John has a special hold, "the double caboose," and if the big fellow hadn't countered it with the "little-Frisco switch" he'd have gone down to defeat there. Crabgrass, Oldfellow, Lawrence, Humphrey, each one asked who was the saltiest dog of them all, and each got his thumping answer.

The match with Margaret the houri was even odder, with preternatural elements sprung in. She turned herself into a brindled wildcat and went for his throat. Got a good piece of it too. But he got her soundly with the "cat-cracker." And yet, after she was back in her houri form, she was still licking good salty blood off her chops, his not hers, and looking more than half pleased with herself.

Eseldon, Septimus, Swinnery, Ursley, one, two, three, four, he took them. He took Crewman Threefountains. Then he tangled with Captain Puckett. This was a groaning, bulging, eye-popping contest. It lasted all through a thirty-second night, and all noticed that, when the two grappled strenuously and almost to the death, the stars in the the sky dimmed and nearly went out.

"That was too close," the big fellow breathed heavily after he had left Captain Puckett unconscious on the ground. "Mind if I strap on my fourteen-direction tele-goggles for our encounter, Roadstrum, and my three pair of earphones? I just can't allow myself to be held away from it so long." He put the things on.

"Use anything you want to," Roadstrum shouted. "It will avail you nothing. Who is the saltiest sky-dog of them all?"

"I am," said the big man. And they went at it.

Roadstrum was fast as well as mighty. He was stronger than great Trochanter or great Puckett, and faster than Crabgrass or Clamdigger. He knew the "funny-man back-off," the "gandy grapple," the "mule-skinners' mangle" and the "surgical hammer."

The big guy countered with the "three-jaw cruncher," the "bandygo back-breaker" and the "badger-trap." The short days and nights flickered by, and Roadstrum was looking better and better. He was aware to every possible trick, and a particular awareness came into his mind now.

"This guy is carrying me," Roadstrum said to himself. "What does he want?" And he tumbled the big fellow with the "coon-cat crotch-hold."

"I want a favor of you, Roadstrum," the big fellow answered inside Roadstrum's head. "Promise to grant me one small favor, and I'll let you throw me." And he smashed Roadstrum one with the "Samoyed sledge."

"Anything to soothe my pride and save my reputation,"

58

Roadstrum thought back into the big fellow's head. "Let me throw you then, and make me look real good." And he sent the big fellow crashing with the "down-under dingo-trip."

"It is a bargain," the big fellow thought back into Road-strum's head. And he did make it look good. He turned green when Roadstrum clamped him with the "Ruttigan rib-racker," he went down in pain when the great Captain applied the "double bull-whack," and he allowed himself to be pinned in the "big spider."

Roadstrum was the victor. Roadstrum was the saltiest sky-dog of them all.

"You men go enjoy yourselves for the nonce," said great Roadstrum, "and take the pleasures of the planet. I have certain soothing things to say to this glorious vanquished man. Be you away. It becomes a private thing."

The men, their plaudits sunk now to a mild roar, trekked off whooping and hollering and praising their Captain.

"And what is the small favor I am to do for you, big fellow?" Roadstrum asked graciously.

"Mind the booth for me, Roadstrum, while I go to the john. I have no relief man here."

"Why of course I will. That's a small enough favor."

"It is more important and more intricate than it appears," the big man said. "Let me explain it to you." And he explained to Roadstrum the use and importance of the tele-scopes and earphones and instruments and instrumental scopes.

"It is fantastic," Roadstrum said. "And it really is of such importance? I'll do it, of course. I'm a man of my word. But I had no idea that so much depended on it. The responsi-bility worries me a little. You will be right back, you say?"

"I will go to the john, Roadstrum, and I will come right back," the big fellow said. The big fellow left. And Roadstrum devoted himself to the business of watching the booth. It was intricate almost beyond belief; it required a degree of concentration that took a lot out of a man.

The down-telescope through the planet had a sixteen-way prismatic mirror on the other end of it (where it emerged downside planet), and integrating those sixteen sectors into a meaningful hemisphere was a mind-straining task.

The three sets of headphones that he was wearing now brought neither audio nor radio to the ears of Roadstrum, but rather three families of cosmic tones. The instruments and scopes led him to sense the various waves and fields of the universes. But none of these was the main thing. The main thing was the centrality of his mind that was tangential to every body in the all-everything-extent. What did not touch him in one of his senses or apperceptions was not.

"I am holding it," said Roadstrum. "It may be that I am the *only* one holding it at the moment. And if I let it go, if I fail, then everything fails. A few dozen or a few million bodies cannot survive alone. Each one that drops into the void of inattention will weaken the whole and topple the balance.

"It pulses, it all pulses with my own effort. The balance holds, and the lost ones are plucked out of the void each time. But it was near that time there! I must be stronger. And it becomes still nearer every time that the lost ones should careen the sound ones and draw all into the void with them.

"Why doesn't the big fellow come back!"

You see, the big fellow didn't come back right away. Quite a few of those hasty days and nights flipped past, and Roadstrum realized that a great part of an equivalent day had already gone.

Roadstrum could not leave the booth until the big man returned. Captain Puckett had offered to watch the booth for Roadstrum. Various crewmen had offered to watch it, but Roadstrum had to refuse. They were all good men, but they just weren't good enough. The responsibility was too great. Roadstrum must maintain the booth till the big man came back. If he did not, the skies would stagger and fall down, and it would all be gone.

Now rankling anxiety and envy rose up in him. He swore that he'd let the worlds fall down after all if the big fellow didn't return soon; but he knew he'd never do that. He would keep the thing going as long as he possibly could. If everything ended, it would be the end of himself also.

But he'd like to be having fun, as Puckett and the crewmen were. It was all a frolic on Kentron. This was one place where laughter was literally heard around the world. Roadstrum was amazed and amused to hear the booming laughter of Crewman Trochanter coming to him from every horizon. He'd have been more amused if he could have added his own laughter to it. There seemed also to be quite an amount of female glee mixed in with the large lilting voices of the crewmen. They were all on an antic, a revel. And Roadstrum, whose present business was to sense everything everywhere, could not help but feel it all.

"Bless the bony-headed, splayfooted bunch of them," Roadstrum said. "Bless the fine native folk who are entertaining them so gaily. And curse the big man if he do not come back quickly. I'm crushed under the weight of this job. I'm avid to be at the pleasures of this world."

But the big man did not come back right away, not for an equivalent day, not for three of them, not for an equivalent week. Roadstrum, of course, could not allow himself to sleep, hardly to blink. The responsibility was far too great. His eyes had become red-rimmed, and his ears were turned into sounding brass. His mind was in such a tangle that the far worlds reeled drunkenly, and only with the greatest effort could Roadstrum steady them again.

"The strength, the grandeur, the majesty of that big man," Roadstrum said in awe. "He has held it all going for years and centuries, so he said, and I am weary after two weeks of it? Imagine his concentration, his width and depth of mind, his spaciousness, the power and the tide of him who could master it all so easily, and I stumble awkwardly through it. Imagine the serenity of that man, the peace-in-power, the scope, the dynamism, the balance! Imagine him with a spit run through him end to end and he roasting on it! *Why don't he come back?*"

For it was a fact that the big fellow didn't come back right away. There was a lot going on there on Kentron, and Roadstrum was missing it. He was not missing it completely, of course, for whatever he missed completely simply was not. He monitored Kentron as he monitored every world everywhere. It was the personal participation in it that he missed.

For one thing, it was now carnival season on Kentron. There had seemed a sort of carnival atmosphere about the place from the beginning, but now it was real carnival. There was high roistering going on such as you do not find everywhere every day.

"Ah, I have relief," Roadstrum said suddenly. "And from World, of all places! He's a curious round-headed young boy, a Living Buddha is what he is, and he holds it all in his concentration and observation without instruments. I'm freed for the moment. I'll go find the big fellow and see what's been taking him so long. I will—

"No, I will not! The young boy slipped beyond it. He is tricky. He really wished to exterminate it all then, after he had such a good hold on it. Had he lulled me and perhaps two or three others, he'd have done it too. We barely saved it in time. Aren't there any others now? Ah, there's a solitary creature on Goffgorina who holds it all and lets it go and holds it again; but he isn't a steady creature. Now there's a mountain-strider on Peluria who holds it all

61

for a while. Those fellows are all quite capable, to do it without instruments, but none of them understands the importance of it. At any moment there may be a dozen sustaining persons scattered through the universes, but they cannot be trusted allwhere and allwhen. And what if there comes the moment when there are none? The responsibility is more than I can bear.

"I have to see it all in total depth all the time!" he bawled out. "I have to see every apple tree on World, every apple on every tree, every worm in every apple, every entrail-parasite of every worm, every cell of every parasite, every molecule of every cell. I have to see and understand every nucleate particle of every heat-happy sun, I must know every follicle of every trinominal plant on Ghar, every awn and glume of the eimer-wheat fields of New Dakota, every eagle of the Nine-Sky worlds, every mite in the underfeathers of every eagle, every microbe on every mite.

"I must know in which hand Crewman Clamdigger holds the coin in the game he plays with the girl at this moment. I must know the date and the head on that coin, and the flaw-stamping in the obverse lower scroll. I must know the man who made the slightly-flawed die that stamped that coin. I must know his niece. I must know the fellow she went out with three years ago once only. I must know the little kernel growing on his adrenal and beginning to give him trouble. And I must know the million rogue cells in that kernel that will be ten million tomorrow. I must know every object everywhere in many powers deeper depth.

"The spyglasses, the scopes, the instruments are but mnemonics and guides. At every moment I must see and feel the totality of it and all the ultimate detail in this great mind of mine. I stagger under the load of it.

"WHY DON'T THAT GUY COME BACK?"

The big fellow, you remember, had not come back right away, and now several equivalent months had gone by. Carnival season was over now, though there was still a lot of whooping and hollering on Kentron. Now it was the cloud-catcher season. The fleet went out, and the crewmen took the two hornets along with it (they told Roadstrum they'd be back for him bye and bye). The fleet spread its webs of spidery silver and silver nitrate, and caught and formed clouds in the nets. They dragged their catch back to Kentron with them and forced it to rain and lighten on the little world. So it was another festival-time, the Lightning-Lupercal that out-carnivaled the carnival.

Then it was hunting season on Kentron, then field-sports

season, then social-sports season. All the men were having howlers, except Roadstrum.

"If I have to see every atom in the universes, why can't I see the big fellow and know what's delaying him?" Roadstrum asked himself. "Why? Because he's a Subjective, that's why. He's a Subjective, just as I unhappily also am at the moment. I wish the big fellow would come back."

The big fellow came back.

"Thanks, Roadstrum," he said, "I'll take the booth over again."

Roadstrum tore the equipment off himself and collapsed to the ground from the steep weariness of it all.

"Where were you?" he moaned. "You were gone six equivalent months."

"Roadstrum, I'd been tied to that booth for a couple hundred years. Now I'm ready to go for another long spell. But a man does need a break sometimes."

"I had no idea it was so difficult or that so much was involved in it."

"I tried to tell you, but words will not convey it. One has to be inside it to comprehend the magnitude."

"How did such a thing begin?"

"Don't you understand? It *was* the beginning. It's the only thing there is. But it was haphazard for so many aeons that it spooks me to think about it. There were always three or four maintaining it, but there was no one person shouldering the responsibility. 'Somewhere there must be one person strong enough to take it all over,' I said to myself in a direful moment, but the strongest person I could think of was myself. I've been doing it ever since. A few centuries ago Berkeley gave it a philosophical basis, but could I get him to shoulder the thing itself? Yes, for a year or so. And then the flannel-mouthed Irishman talked his way out of it and I had it again. Well, it's a job."

"Is it really so important in every detail?"

"Yes. You are a detail, Roadstrum. If I put you out of my mind for a moment, then you are not. By my attention I hold it all in being. Nothing exists unless it is perceived. If perception fails for a moment, then that thing fails forever."

"Suppose you neglected but one aspect of a faraway thing for but one moment?"

"Sometimes I do. On several of the worlds there are beautiful roses that have no odor. It is because I forgot to smell them for one brief instant. There are several curious bobtailed little animals in various systems. It is because, for an instant, I forgot to think of the ends of their tails.

Here you will find a blind or deaf or halt creature; it is because I did not give them my full attention in one moment."

"Well, you are certainly a sturdy man to stand up under it."

"Yes, but I hate to be misjudged. They say that I bear it all on my shoulders, as though I were a stud or a balk. It is not my great shoulders, it is the amazing head on my great shoulders that maintains it all."

The crewmen were ready to go. They heard of a world that made all others seem trivial. Now that Roadstrum was freed from watching the booth, they said to come along, Captain, and let's be with it.

So they readied the hornets.

"I never did know your name, big fellow," Roadstrum said in parting.

"Atlas."

What thing they were and what an architecture yet,
What song they sang is not beyond conjecture yet.

Where heroes' bones for ages strewed the shore about!
A murdering song that men can say no more about!

They came in cresting waves and boldly tried for it,
And broke and blanched and balked and burned and died
*   for it.*

A tune that must ensorcel them and rot them all!
The missing note was really what had got them all.

Ibid

They came to Sireneca. "There is something the matter with the spelling of that," Roadstrum said. "It doesn't look right." This was the world of the Siren-Zo, the Siren-Animal, which is either a creature or a musical mountain or a manifestation or a group of very peculiar folks.

"I really wasn't ready for another truculent world," Roadstrum said. "We've had it so pleasant at all our stops since leaving Kentron Planet."

They had been to Nine Worlds; they had taken over Nine Worlds. They had been involved in the work and recreation for which they were best fitted, and it had really been quite a pleasant interlude.

There had been leagues and anti-leagues on Nine Worlds, there had been conspiracy and war and revolution, there had been crude butchery, and there had been really fine weaponry. The twenty-plus men from the hornets made themselves at home in the situation. They were wonderful fighting men, the least competent of them able to command armies. They took command of troops on opposite sides of the broil (at one time there were five different sides to the battles), and they connived and gained.

Roadstrum himself was probably the finest fighting man in the universe, and now he discovered that he was also a master diplomat. At the time when they had had to make new tongues for themselves (after that little embarrassment on Lamos of the Giants), Roadstrum had made a forked tongue for himself. He was now as polished and pleasant a liar as you would ever want to meet, and he took all those folks in every conference.

The trouble on Nine Worlds was that things had been a little too loose. Now the hornet men came out on top, and they tightened things up a little. They brought in nine world-managers from Guild, and they laid down rules to be followed. For now Roadstrum was absolute owner of Nine Worlds.

"I know that none of you men wish to be burdened with property," he said, "or I'd give you a world each, as long as they lasted. But since none of you have any such desire—"

"I have," said Crewman Snow. "I want a world."

They hadn't known before that Snow was a grasping greedy man. It was hard to understand how a hornet crewman (they were a free and easy lot) could want to be burdened with ownership of a world and the income of billions of billions of Chancels every quarter, but there is someone like that in every crowd.

Roadstrum gave Crewman Snow title to one of the worlds with very bad grace. He sent the titles to the other eight worlds by dispatch to the men's room attendant on Roulettenwelt, reducing his debt somewhat.

So the Nine Worlds affair had been pleasant easy business, and now they had come to another tough world. They were already hooked on Sireneca, and they hadn't intended to be. They had joked about it coming in, but they had known that it had its hook in them already, that they would have to kill it or be killed by it.

"Will you pour hot wax in our ears as was done the first time, Captain Roadstrum?" Crewman Clamdigger jibed. "And tie yourself to the mast? But we don't have a mast."

"I will pour hot lead into your throats to still your chatter," Roadstrum said. "We are fools to be into this thing but we cannot back off. It isn't as good a tune as that. When we find the lost note and fit it in we will probably discover that it is a very ordinary tune."

"We haven't heard it yet," Crewman Threefountains said.

"In our modern times we always hear a thing before we have heard it," Roadstrum maintained. "Our instruments have already recorded it and broken it down. Crewman Bramble reads the score and is entranced by it, up to a point. He is the most intelligent of us and he enjoys music in the most intelligent way, reading the score without the noise to distract. The others of us, for our insufficiency, are doomed to listen vulgarly.

"But we all know that there is something wrong with that tune, even before we come to it. Our instruments are experiencing frustration, and so are we. 'Something missing, something missing,' they transmit. 'Imperative that the missing element be found. Not very good tune anyhow.' Yes, there's the final high note missing in the tune, and we must find it or we will never sleep again. Many brave men have given their lives for this and failed. I say that we will not fail! We will force the missing note from the thing. And then we will kill it so it will no more be a hazard to farers."

Sireneca was mostly ocean, mean ocean with steely choppy waves following a strange harmonic. They did not have free flow, nor real crest, nor tide. Something was missing from the ocean waves. Their tune was the tune of the planet, and it was an incomplete tune.

There was but one small continent or island on Sireneca, and in the middle of it was the animal, or the mountain, or the folk. The hornets had set down on the flanks of this thing, and the crewmen made ready to solve it.

"Let us tackle this as a strategic problem," said great Captain Puckett. "You had better let me handle this, Roadstrum. A strategic man you are not. Formulate the problem, Crewman Bramble."

"The problem is to force the missing note from the creature or creatures so that our apprehensions and frustrations may be quieted and our sanity restored. The ancillary of the problem is that we do this without ourselves perishing, as all other farers here have perished."

"And what is the nature of the opponent, Crewman Bramble?"

"That we do not know, Captain Puckett, nor whether it is a single or plural thing. In earliest mythology it was referred to as the Siren-Zo or the Siren-Animal, as being one. But in appearance it is many, as we now see it, in the form of various well-bodied, golden-haired, singing women on the numerous outcroppings of the musical mountain. In what manner they kill all who try to come up to reach them is not known. Our only procedure seems to be that true one—trial and error. I suggest that the most useless man of us begin the climb now, and we will see how he dies."

"Crewman Nonvalevole, start climbing," Captain Puckett ordered. "Make for the nearest of the goldie-blondes there."

"All right," said Crewman Nonvalevole, and he began to climb the musical mountain up to the nearest siren. There was an odd thing about his climbing. Often the rocks of the mountain shivered under his feet as if to throw him down.

"The mountain itself is the creature," said Captain Roadstrum. "The scree and the boulders are part of its hide, and it shivers its hide like a World horse. The whole thing is alive. The blonde maidens are but tentacles of the thing."

"May I tangle with such a tentacle!" said Crewman Crabgrass.

"We must find the mortal center of the creature and attack it there," Roadstrum continued. "We will not kill it by scratching its hide. But when we do find its mortal center and kill it there, then, I believe, in its moment of death agony, we will hear the missing note. That is my conjecture."

"Oh be quiet, great Captain Roadstrum," all the men said. "A conjecture man you are not."

Crewman Nonvalevole had now climbed nearly to the nearest blondie siren. She rolled limpid blue eyes at him and sang in wonderful brass. It was a green-country foot-shuffling tune with a touch of boogie and a touch of ballad, none of your fancy things. It was the sort of tune that faring men themselves sing, but incomparably better, and with a rich beat and swing. The hornet instruments had been wrong to call it "Not very good tune anyhow," for it was good. It rose to the high stunning happy pitch—and then nothing. The climax note was missing and it drove them all crazy.

And then it began once more. Again and again it rose, and left the gaping silence at its apex. Men would perish of hunger and thirst yearning for that missing note. It had to be found.

Crewman Nonvalevole was up to the shimmering blondie now. Singingly she smiled at him and patted her golden knees. The crewman sat on her blonde lap and enfolded her in passionate arms.

There was lightning without thunder. The blondie brushed ashes and cinders out of her lap, ashes and cinders that were all the mortal remains of Crewman Nonvalevole.

"That was sudden and consuming," said Captain Puckett. "Did you get a reading on it, Crewman Bramble?"

"Twelve thousand amps, nine million volts, a little over one million cycles. A pretty good jolt. She never missed a note either, except the missing note itself. And I am sure that I heard a hint of that too, right at the frying moment. It didn't sound, but it was near to becoming a sound."

"The almost-sound was from Crewman Nonvalevole, not from Siren-sis," said Captain Roadstrum. "In his moment he did come near to voicing the note. I believe that I am on the right course. I have this intuition that we must go for the interior vitals. The outer hide of the thing is dangerous."

"Be quiet, Captain Roadstrum," said Captain Puckett. "An intuitive man you are not. It's a pretty good electric chair they have though."

"It isn't new; it's been done before," Crewman Crabgrass cut in. "They have them on Womboggle World, electric chairs in the form of beautiful women so the condemned can die happy."

"Who is the next most worthless man?" Captain Puckett asked. "That would be Crewman Stumble, I believe."

"I'll not go up!" swore Crewman Stumble. "I am not worthless to me. Send a dummy man up."

"That's what you are," said the relentless Captain Puckett. "You will go up, and you will trail a ground wire behind you like a tail. We will see if this one crisps you as thoroughly as that one fried Crewman Nonvalevole. We will get several of these fryings and we may be able to establish a pattern as to the way they work."

"Well, all right, but I don't like it," Crewman Stumble grumbled. Crewman Bramble attached a ground wire to Stumble like a tail, and Stumble began to climb the mountain toward the swishing blondie on a low left ledge. She ground out the ballad, fluting brass and a touch of fiddle music, in her buxom voice. Crewman Stumble became livelier the nearer he came to her, and she sang him up to her with an ever heftier voice, all the foot-stomping ascending notes, except the final one. The top of the tune was still missing.

Crewman Stumble finished his up-jaunt with a wild surge to the blondie's outstretched arms, leaped aboard her spacious frame, and locked around her with arms and legs. She intruded a laughing note into the ballad, but not the note itself. Then she gave him a smooch that was one of the great things.

Once more there was lightning without thunder. Then the blondie was brushing the ashes and embers of Crewman Stumble off her breast. And the damnable song rose and fell again and again, and the top of it was always missing.

"Did you get a reading that time, Crewman Bramble?" Captain Puckett asked.

"Yes. I believe it is the beginning of success," Crewman Bramble stated. "The ground wire made a difference. It vaporized, of course, and the reaction killed three other crewman near this end of it, but we do show progress. We begin to establish a pattern. It was only eleven thousand and fifty amps that time, eight and a quarter million volts, and the frequency remained the same. This time we'll use a heavier ground wire . . . hell, we'll use two of them!"

"Who is the next most useless man?" Captain Puckett asked, looking around.

"Enough!" Captain Roadstrum announced ponderously. "I am taking command once more."

"But, Roadstrum, we are proceeding according to scientific testing methods," Puckett protested. "Please don't interfere. A scientific man you are not."

"An excess of science will leave none of us alive, Puckett. Scouting patrol, see how we may find entrance to the thing itself! We itch in its hide, and it scratches us to kill. But it cannot scratch us if we are inside it. I have old folk memory of ascending the thing inside. We will find the passage."

The scouters scouted. They went on hornet instruments when bankrupt of other ideas. The instruments told them that the mountain-animal was indeed hollow, or at least had an open anal-oral passage, and that the entrance could be found, very deep and under water. The instruments indicated just where that passage was, but shuddered when asked whether there were dangers involved.

"As the finest diver and the finest all-man, I will go first," Captain Roadstrum announced. "Do you all follow me like close tails. If we drown and die, remember that one death is as good as another."

"No it is not," said Crewman Mundmark. "I'd rather die crisped by one of those blondies than drown in black water."

Captain Roadstrum dived a great dive down into the black water, in under the shelf of the continent that was also the mountain and the creature; and all the men followed him. He dove till it seemed that his lungs would burst. They did burst a little, bye and bye, and this gave him some relief. It also left a dark red trail that the men could follow. Then they all broke surface in a black cavity very deep under the thing. The only light was a garish dark red one far above them.

"It goes five hundred meters up and is a tricky climb," said Captain Puckett.

"We are tricky men; we can climb it," said Captain Roadstrum. "Do you see it now, men, do you see the form of the creature? It is a big rambling spider-form inside here, and the mountain is a living shell it has built for itself, for it's a mixed creature. The tune has a deeper tone inside here, and one can make out the words, but what do they mean. 'Da luan, da mort,' over and over again. 'Da luan, da mort,' what does that mean, over and over again, Crewman Bramble?"

"It's the treadmill song out of an Irish cycle," said Bramble. " 'Monday and Tuesday and Monday and Tuesday and Monday and Tuesday,' so the poor slaves had to sing at their labor for the puca. And finally a great savior came and broke the charm. 'And Wednesday too,' he said, and then it was all over with."

"Roadstrum is the great savior who breaks the charm," Roadstrum announced. "I will set a Wednesday-term to the monster. But there are other elements in this. Is not the climbing up of the giant spider and the slaying of it an Arabian-cycle thing? And did not Hans Schultz, in the green-island cycle, have a dream of the same thing? Upward, men; we are onto a great kill!"

Hawsers, cables a meter thick they climbed—and these were but the fine silks of the giant spider. The hairs on its toes were even thicker, and the men blasted them, beginning the attack. A note of alarm crept into the mountainous singing now. The creature knew that it was invaded but did not know how or by what. The creature sent tremors through its webs that threatened to dash the men down to their deaths.

"We must go inside the creature and kill it interiorly," Roadstrum announced when they had ascended a hundred meters. So they all entered the vulgar cavity of the thing and continued to climb upward.

There was still light, more so than before. It was more garish, redder, more threatening than it had been. That first light had been but the reflection of this. The mountainous interior spider had nine outside eyes and one great glowing interior eye by which he liked to contemplate himself. This was the spookiest light ever seen; and was the spookiest place, but one, in all the universes.

"The big red interior eye like a beacon is the mortal center of the creature," Roadstrum announced. "We will kill it there and it will die. And we will get our missing note then, or we will die too, from deprivation. It goes into a frenzy now as we close in on it. Who is the scareder, we or it?"

"We are, we are," the men cried. "We're the scaredest men ever."

The singing mountain had become hysterical with fright of the small things climbing up its maw. The song was really a racy one now, a lot of good fever in it, a black-blood beat that was solid. It rose and moaned, and only the top of it was missing. But it had outlined itself now, and the final note, when it came, would be worth it all.

It was now seen that the entire mountain-creature was one single instrument, and the whole planet was its sounding box. The blondie-orifices were but small reeds of this amazing organ, the giant web-threads were quivering strings.

Now the music-mountain was frantic, and so were the men. "Somebody dies pretty quick now," gasped Crewman Cutshark, "either we or he, and I don't much care which so long as it is swift."

"Mind those quivering stalks there, Cutshark," Roadstrum warned. "I believe that they emit a very strong digestive juice."

"Touch one, Crewman Cutshark," Captain Puckett ordered. "Observe the data, Crewman Bramble."

Crewman Cutshark touched one of the stalks, and he dissolved. The flesh was whisked away from him like vapor. He was only rather dirty white bones, and then the bones also dissolved.

"What did you get, Crewman Bramble?" Captain Puckett asked.

"Eleven million dissolution units at a base of—"

"Leave off the science stuff or I'll clamp you all in irons," Roadstrum warned. "Upward, men, to the big kill. It's but fifty meters above us, and death licking at us every spot of the way. Hey, listen to the way it's beginning to scream now! That really jazzes up the tune."

"That's me screaming, Captain Roadstrum, and I don't figure on stopping for quite a while," Crewman Threefountains screamed.

Ah, the baleful red-glowing inner eye of the monster, which was also its soul and its mortal center. It blazed with red and black fire, and crackled and stunk. The tune began a new ascension, many times more powerful than it had been before, hysterical with horror, giddy and gibbering, hate-hopping, and yet quite the best thing of its sort ever done. All it needed was the top of the tune, and that

71

moment drew very near. The whole mountain was lashing out frantically, flinging thousand-ton boulders out of its quivering hide, moaning and bursting asunder.

"Now, men, now!" great Roadstrum cried, and he dove upward into the giant living eye. And all dove into it, rending it, killing the thing.

The note. The missing note sounded. It was worth it. It was fulfillment. It was water after deserts. It was the top of the tune. They all heard it. And nobody would ever hear it again.

It sounded the note in its last agony. Then the whole mountain died.

Roadstrum kicked the mountain open and they all went outside. The mountain was smaller than it had been, and it shrunk down still smaller as though the air were being let out of it.

The tune was gone and forever. Its missing note would no more be a hazard to that sector of space. All the crewmen felt deep satisfaction. They had heard the dying note of the Siren-Zo and their thirst was quenched. The blondie appendages had become broken dolls.

All loaded into the hornets for further adventures. It was early Wednesday morning.

72

CHAPTER FIVE

On Polyphem, a sneaking, snaking mood they found,
And something odd about the tasty food they found.

They gazed to see the passive sheep and lambs about,
Nor guessed themselves to be the woolly rams about.

The leader, he a sullen stormy blokey there,
Defiled the bord and put them in the pokey there.

And one became so gross they couldn't carry him,
And one so queer and cold they had to bury him.

But some got out alive from it, and well they did,
And lived for worse, but none knows how the hell they did.

Ibid

THE KID HONDSTARFER, back on Lamos that was Valhalla, had told them that one of the hornets would break down after a little while. He said that he had made a lot of mistakes on one of them. But they had worked perfectly since that time, and the Captains and crewmen had forgotten that advice.

Now the hornet of Puckett broke down. Or it broke, and it had to come down somewhere or perish into pieces. Puckett told Roadstrum to go on and leave him. Puckett had a way of putting it on pretty thick, sort of a wheedling way, sort

73

of a "but of course one space captain would never leave another in distress" way of presenting such things. Roadstrum felt a strange body twinge which he mistook for the call of duty. He said he would never leave a mate in distress.

"I believe a little creative mutiny is called for here," Crewmen Trochanter and Crabgrass and Clamdigger told Captain Roadstrum. "We are a little tired of caring for the boys in Boat B, and we're not too happy about yourself."

Roadstrum had a way of putting it on pretty thick himself.

"Be there man among you who doubts my demesne or destiny, then I have fared in vain," he said. "I bare my throat to the treacherous steel—"

"All right, all right," the three tough crewmen capitulated. "We're with you, all the way and in everything. Only spare us the 'act.'"

"It's Polyphemia or nothing," Roadstrum called to Puckett over the communicator. "There's not another world we could possibly reach."

"You said the same thing about Lamos of the Giants," Puckett protested. "Roadstrum, there's *got* to be another world."

"Oh, that wasn't really so bad, Puckett. Thinking back on it, it was sort of fun with the giants. There really isn't another world we can reach if you're coming apart. Polyphemia is better than nothing."

("False tongue," voiced the communicator.)

"Oh all right, Roadstrum, we'll go down then."

But the communicator was right. Roadstrum did speak with false tongue unwittingly. Polyphemia was incomparably worse than nothing.

But it looked wonderful enough coming into it. Great green grass! but it did look wonderful! It was a pastoral world, said the manual. The Polyphemians were simple shepherds. They raised sheep and goats, made a little cheese and whey, drank sweet milk, ate fine lamb and kid, perhaps wove a little wool, the manual said, lived in fleece or hair tents, and supposedly played pastoral airs on wooden flutes.

"It cloys, it cloys," said Crewman Clamdigger. "Let's think a little more about that mutiny, men."

"Ah well, maybe there'll be shepherdesses," Roadstrum told them.

"Combing wool and churning butter, not for us," said Crewman Trochanter.

They landed badly. The facilities on Polyphemia were the worst in the universe. They felt eyes watching them, wolfish eyes, not sheep eyes. But the only one who shuffled up to meet them was a lank, dour shepherd. They supposed he was a shepherd, but he wasn't combing wool.

"A happy day to you," Captain Roadstrum boomed. "I suppose it isn't every day that fine, cheerful, interesting strangers come to visit you."

"We hate strangers," said the Polyphemian. "And we hate spacecraft. We hate just about everything."

He shriveled them with a look, and he spat green.

"But we are in dire distress. One of our crafts is crippled. We will need time to repair it, and perhaps we will need your help," said Roadstrum.

"We are tone-deaf to the call of help," said the sour shepherd. "We are deaf to almost everything. There is only one sound we hear a little. We call it the green whisper."

Roadstrum gave it to him: the soft sound of an educated thumb ruffled over the edges of high-denomination bills. The shepherd heard it. It is a dangerous double-bladed sound. It has got a lot of people in trouble. But the hornet-men were confident of their ability to handle anything.

The shepherd gave a grunt that was perhaps assent. He gaped his face in what might have been a grin. And he was suddenly joined by quite a number of his fellows.

"Just what is it you want, strangers?" asked one of the new shepherds, who seemed to rank a little higher than the first one.

"Why, if not hospitality, at least a hospice," said Roadstrum. "We are space-weary. We would rest. We would eat and drink. And then we would examine the facilities here."

"There is only Drovers' Cottage," said the leading shepherd. "You can rest there now. You can eat with us in the hall this evening. And there are no facilities on Polyphemia."

"How is the food here?" asked Crewman Trochanter.

"Monotonous, mostly," said the shepherd. "There is one particular food that sets us up, and we have not had it in months. We get pretty tired of plain mutton."

Well, the shepherds guided the crewmen to Drovers' Cottage through rich meadows and pastures populated with herds of sheep.

Sheep? Are you sure they are sheep?

The lodgings were bad. Drovers' Cottage was not a palace. But heat was not needed, and there were tallow candles provided for when they should be needed. They were fed a little, though the sun was still high in the sky. It may have been mutton, but most curious tasting mutton. Then porridge, perhaps, that may have been weevily. They even were served perry from the runted fruit of the land, and became one-tenth happy on it.

But the sheep worried Roadstrum, and he looked out at them and puzzled about them.

"I'm not a farm boy, but there's something the matter with those sheep," he maintained.

"It is my considered opinion that they're woolly enough and dirty enough to be sheep," said Captain Puckett. "Is some third thing required? Why, Roadstrum, you must admit that they're sheepish enough to be sheep. Therefore they are sheep."

"Crewman Bramble, are they sheep?" Captain Roadstrum asked.

"The only thing about sheep I ever studied was sheep's liver flukes parasites, or it may have been sheep's flukes liver parasites. Let me see their parasites and I'll tell you quickly enough whether they're sheep. But I never studied sheep as such, and I doubt if anyone else did. There was no such course at Cram College."

"They walk on two legs when they're not down eating," Roadstrum said. "Is that right? Do you think it right they should walk about on two legs, Crewman Clamdigger?"

"I never studied sheep either, Captain. I say, according to the principle of subsidiarity, and no local law countervening, let them walk on two legs if they want to. Is it our business how the sheep of Polyphemia walk?"

"Well, there is something peculiar about them as sheep," Roadstrum held out stubbornly, "and sooner or later I'll think what it is. I believe I'll just go out and have a talk with those fellows."

Many of the sheep were still eating in the meadow, and they ate awkwardly, as though it were a learned thing for them to eat that way. And others of the sheep were gathered in a low tavern. Roadstrum went into this with some misgivings. He had not heard of sheep as congregating in taverns. "And yet I suppose that they should be classified as social animals," he said; "why should they not meet in taverns?"

It was a shabby sort of tavern they had there. The bar was of rough unfinished wood that had never known polish, the stools and benches were badly made and wobbly, very poor things. "They look as though they had been made by sheep," said Roadstrum, "and I suppose they were."

Roadstrum hardly knew how to begin. He had never talked with sheep before, nor associated with them at all.

"Are you a sheep?" he asked one of them finally.

"Why, yes, I'm a sheep. What else would I be?"

"You look almost as if you were a very shaggy man."

"Ah well, I wouldn't say that. I suppose I'm a sheep. I have always been a sheep."

"Well then, what would you say is the difference between a sheep and a man?"

"A man will eat a sheep. But did you ever hear of a sheep eating a man?"

"Don't believe I ever did," said Captain Roadstrum.

There was something sorrowful about the sheep. They ate and drank dully from a vat that contained foul vegetables, leeks and ramps and strong gross turnips, and rank things that were very earthy but not of old Earth. They were fat, whether men or sheep, and they smelled like sheep.

But there was no real merriment, as there should be in a tavern. They drank a potion that seemed to be potato beer. Roadstrum took a bowl of it out of curiosity. It was mildly alcoholic, and it should have enlivened the tavern.

"Do you ever have music?" Roadstrum asked. "Anything to liven up the place?"

"We sing a little sometimes," said the sheep he had been talking to. "We do not sing well."

"Let's try it," cried Roadstrum. "Come on, fellows; let me hear one of your rousing songs! I am a stranger with a great curiosity about you. Some of you start with a few bars, and I will lend my own wonderful voice to the melody. Sing, sing!"

"Well, all right," some of the bolder sheep said.

They sang flatly, but they sang:

> "The docker-man a-drawing near,
> "he don't appear at all appall us.
> "He whets a knife and sheds a tear.
> "We haven't any tails at all us."

"We haven't any tails at all us," Roadstrum gave them the last line back in hearty chorus. It wasn't a bad little tune, but the words gave Roadstrum a turn.

"Why, you fellows haven't tails at all, have you? Not even docked stubs. I thought sheep always had tails unless they were chopped off."

"Not on Polyphemia," said the sheep Roadstrum had been talking to. "That must be some other kind of sheep somewhere else."

"Come on, lads; give us another verse," Roadstrum cried encouragingly.

"All right," said the sheep, "if we must." They sang flatly once more.

> "For greeny grass to graze and grout
> "we couldn't eat the stuff or store it.

> *"They took our gimpy gullet out*
> *"and gave us seven stomachs for it."*

"*And gave us seven stomachs for it,*" Roadstrum bawled
out in melodic response. "Ah, I believe there is a bit of
folklore or ovine-lore hidden in that stanza," he said shrewdly.
"You were not naturally ruminants? And you have been
made into such? This becomes one of the most curious things
I ever ran into. I suspect that you are not sheep at all."

"We have to be sheep," the sheep said. "Who else would
have us?"

"Well, no need to be sheepish sheep," Roadstrum encouraged. "Let us have one more stanza and be glad of
our respective states. You think it is all possum and red-
eyed gravy being a man? Sing, hearties, sing."

And flatly they sang once more:

> *"Ah Jennie was a gambol lamb,*
> *"a lamb no more is gambol Jennie.*
> *"Subducted by a Sweedish ram!*
> *"We all got yen for yeaning Yennie."*

"*We all got yen for yeaning Yennie,*" Roadstrum roared out
in raucous chorus. "Why, fellows, you have wonderful songs
and you are wonderful singers! No? You don't think so?
I guess you're right. In no other company in the universe
would I be the finest singer present."

A man came in. A man and not a sheep. A villainous
looking man. He passed out little slips of parchment to some
of the sheep, and then he left again.

And the sheep seemed even more depressed than they
had been.

"Your call?" the sheep-bartender asked Roadstrum's friend.

"Yes. For tomorrow," the sheep said sadly.

"We all have to go. That's what we're here for."

"I know. But I hate to leave Agnes and the children."

The sheep was very fat and very sorrowful. Roadstrum
was very interested in the sheep as being his friend, and
was especially curious about the parchments.

"What is it?" he asked the sheep. "What does your slip
say?"

"It says my name," said the sheep, "and it says tomorrow."

Respecting the sheep's reserve, Roadstrum did not pursue
the matter, but he felt that something was very wrong.

Oh well, the sheep got a little happier as the afternoon
progressed. They sang some more, and they did a little
better when they weren't urged to it too strongly.

They passed the cup that impels, and their fat faces
began to glow. They even told stories. There is a whimsy
to sheep stories that is like nothing else; humble and bashful,

and yet with a real cud of humor. And shaggy sheep stories are a special form. But do sheep, in fact, have stories and humor and song?

Roadstrum had always believed that he had troubles enough of his own. He seldom borrowed trouble, and never at usurious terms. He knew it as a solid thing that sheep do not gather in taverns and drink beer, not even potato beer; that they do not sing, not even badly; that they do not tell stories. But a stranger can easily make trouble for himself on a strange world by challenging local customs.

"But I am the great Roadstrum," he said, suddenly and loudly. "I am a great one for winning justice for the lowly, and I do not scare easily. I threw the great Atlas at the wrestle, and who else can say as much? I suffer from the heroic sickness every third day about nightfall, and I am not sure whether this is the third day or not. I say you are men and not sheep. I say: Arise, and be men indeed!"

"It has been tried before," said Roadstrum's friend the sheep, "and it didn't work."

"You have tried a revolt, and it failed?"

"No, no, another man tried to incite us to revolt, and failed."

"Tell me about it, sheep."

"Another man, another traveler talked to us as you have done. 'Early in the morning you must revolt,' he said. 'You must refuse to go where they herd you; you must refuse to be butchered. You must take up stones and clubs in your hands, and beat down the men who would take you to slaughter.' That's what the man told us."

"And that is what I tell you," said Roadstrum.

"Ah well, it was the shortest revolt on record," the sheep said. "In the morning, some of us did take up sticks and stones in our hands. And then the whistle blew as it does every morning. Those who had received their notices for that day threw away their sticks and stones and broke rank and went, jostling each other, to their slaughter. You don't think we'd want them to have to blow that whistle at us the second time, do you? And who ever heard of sheep picking up sticks and stones and going to battle. It just isn't in our nature to revolt."

There was the gonging of a great bell that signaled it was time for the animals to go to their cotes. It was just sundown, and the sheep should be snug in the fold by dark. They all said good night, and shuffled out very sheep-like.

And so it was sundown, and it was time for Roadstrum and the other hornet men to go dine with the high Polyphemians in their hall.

"Did you find out anything about those fellows, Roadstrum?" Captain Puckett asked him as he joined the others.

"Puckett, they do not look like sheep, and they do not act enough like men. There is something the matter with the whole business."

"I would not worry about it," said Puckett. "Remember the hornet-men's code: Never incite a local populace unless there is something in it for you."

Well, they were set down at quite a big table with all the big Polyphemians, and the Cacique of Polyphemia was at the head of the table.

"Are you not afraid to come unarmed into our hall, little men?" the big Cacique asked. "Do you trust our hospitality?"

"We trust all hospitality everywhere," said steady Roadstrum. "We have been on a hundred worlds, and nowhere has the bord been defiled We trust the hospitality of all men when we break bread with them. We have eaten giants' bread on Lamos and cotton candy on Kentron World, and we have not met treachery Treachery, where it comes, does not touch the silent oath of the bord. This is respected on all worlds."

"Eat hearty, eat hearty!" said the Cacique. "How do you like our food?"

"The double oath of the bord does not require that we lie," growled Crewman Trochanter. "It is insipid You must know that yourselves."

"It is not our best food, but it is the best we have to offer at present. For ourselves more than for you we regret this; nobody loves fine food so much as do we. We expect a finer food shortly, but for topological reasons you will not be able to partake of it. But we will bless you in that hour when again we eat our fine food."

"I have a complaint, a very serious complaint," said just Roadstrum.

"Strangers may not lodge complaints till they have been in residence here for ninety days," the Cacique said, "and no stranger has ever remained with us that long."

"My complaint won't hold for ninety days. I accuse you people of eating men."

"You could not have heard of—but no, their arrival was not logged, any more than yours was If you are given another life, good Roadstrum, you should learn to post your arrivals more carefully, let people know where you are But that is another matter. What is it you are speaking of? Get to the point."

80

"I will. You are slaughtering some of them in that building now."

"Oh, you mean the sheep? For a moment I thought that you meant—"

"They are men, and you know it."

"I know it, and you know it. But the sheep don't know it, and the documentation does not know it. We are logged as a pastoral planet, given over almost entirely to the raising of sheep. Will you argue with the Gazeteer itself? I can show you the pedigrees of all these creatures, and they are sheep pedigrees. They are good eating, but there is better. Do you know what it is?"

"I do not. But this I will not eat," said mighty Roadstrum, and he overturned the great bowl of spicy goulash. "Sheep this is not."

"You could have waited till we had finished," grumbled Crewman Clamdigger. "The stuff is good. And you said yourself that the sheep did not act quite like men."

"We are insulted," said the Cacique. "You have defiled the bord. On all worlds one eats what one is given, and one praises it."

"All praise to this flesh!" howled Roadstrum. "Flesh of our own flesh! We eat not our own kindred! On your feet, men! It's a rumble! Awk!"

And not a single brave man came to his feet. They were manacled in their chairs where they sat. Trapped chairs! They had fallen into the most childish trap of them all. They shook the hall with their fury, but their bonds were strong and so was the hall. And all the great Polyphemians were laughing.

"We told you that there was a finer food," the Cacique of Polyphemia chortled, "and that there were reasons why you could not partake of it. But we will partake, and we will begin to do so tomorrow. We have it so seldom. Tame servile sheep is tame food indeed. You were right to call it insipid, but it is the best we have for our daily fare. But there is a better, Roadstrum, a better."

"What, you toothy androphage, what could be more vile, or better in your view?" the furious enchained Roadstrum demanded.

"Yourselves, woolly Roadstrum, rampant ram! It is everything that tame sheep is not. It is the finest of fine foods for our own fine selves. We will have to arrange to have it oftener. Ah, rage, Roadstrum, and all your fine men! Rage and grow fat in your rage. In our own way we love you, and we'll waste not a gout of you."

So Roadstrum and Puckett and all their furious men from

the hornet crews were dragged, amid sky-splitting noise by all concerned, into a dungeon to be fatted for the kill.

Margaret, of course, was not with them. She had made her own arrangements with the high Polyphemians. There were the two great Captains, Deep John the Vagabond, and either seventeen or eighteen crewmen. There is a point of issue here.

Twenty of them had been dragged in, counted, and certified. But a little while later there were twenty-one of them. The big Polyphemians told the counter that he had made a mistake, and that he would go in the pot for it. The counter maintained that he had not made a mistake, that he had counted correctly, and there had been only twenty. The counter was correct in this, but he went into the pot nevertheless.

How the twenty-first man happened to be there, why he was not there at first and where he came from, and how he differed from the rest of them are things of great moment.

A Polyphemian pokey is much like a pokey anywhere. Deep John asserted that this was so, and he had been in more pokies than all of them together. And yet there was something special about this one, and it had to do with their special purpose of being there. They were fed lavishly. And they were mocked. "Rage, and grow fat in your rage," the Cacique had told them. Well, they did rage, and they ate, and they raged again. There was little else to do.

It was rank fare, but there was an abundance of it. Crewman Starkhead would not eat at all. Crewman Burpy ate to excess. The rest of them attempted to practice moderation, but they were hooked into eating more and more. With the rank leeks and ramps were also habit-forming mushrooms of an intoxicating sort, compelling them to eat more and yet more, and to rage and rave. Their moderation became more and more immoderate, and they came somewhat to like the low food. Worried and restricted men will eat to ease their worry, and they grew fat in spite of themselves. Except Crewman Starkhead.

Margaret the houri visited them, but not often. She had been consorting with the high Polyphemians, and Roadstrum accused her of being faithless.

"But of course I am faithless, great Roadstrum," she said. "It is our nature to be."

"Haven't you any loyalty at all," he asked in his sorrowful voice, putting on the act a little.

"I don't think so. We weren't constituted with any," she said.

"But I am sure you would work for us against the Polyphemians."

"Work against those fellows and get put in the pot? Not me. And they're not bad at all. They're so blamed mean that it's fun. There come times when we like our fellows real mean," she said.

"We will remember that when we are out again and you with us," threatened Crewman Trochanter. "Mean, Margaret, real mean. And you won't like it."

"Oh, but you're not going to get out. You're in it for good, and they're going to eat you up every one."

But Roadstrum used his special wheedle on her then, talking to her privately in a low voice through the grille. What words he used we do not know; but remembering that he now had a forked tongue, and that he had become something of a diplomat on Nine-worlds, we know that he found apt words.

Margaret did agree to work for them and spy for them. She still wanted to go to Earth with them. She had heard that the men there were willing.

It was on the following morning, their second day on Polyphemia, that Di Prima was taken. He had always been the fattest of them. He went with a joke on his lips about his name and he being the first of them taken, but in spirt he was uneasy. And the other men all raged at the idea of one of their companions being taken and being roasted and stewed and then eaten. They roared and ranted, and the Polyphemians mocked them to still greater fury. And they ate in their wrath and put on a sheath of hasty angry fat.

Late that night one of the Polyphemians came to them and told them that Di Prima hadn't been very good.

"Fat enough, but not rampant enough," he said. "But we expect much more of all of you. Rampant rams! Rage and grow! Oh you will be prime stuff!"

And they were all driven almost insane by the angry mushrooms in their broth. But Margaret came to them a little later and told them that the mocking Polyphemian had lied.

"Yes he was good! I always liked Crewman Di Prima, but I never liked him so much as at the banquet. He was the best man ever. Really!"

"You ate? You ate part of him?" Captain Roadstrum asked, and he was aghast.

"What else would I eat? He *was* the banquet. And he was good good good!"

Thereafter they all thought of her a little differently, now that she had feasted with the high Polyphemians and had eaten one of them. And she also thought of them in a different way and looked at them with odd anticipation.

Crewmen Fracas, Snow, Bramble, and Crabgrass went to be eaten, one each day. Bangtree went. Oldfellow and Lawrence went. Each went a little less gallantly than had his predecessor, and now the jokes on their lips were of a strained quality. They were still the brave crewmen, but it does rag you this being taken out and eaten one at a time.

"We can't go on like this," Roadstrum moaned. "We have to play our ace to survive. Why, oh why, won't they take our ace? Another day and we'll go clear mad and eat him ourselves. How can they resist him?"

Their ace was the twenty-first man who had appeared among them after the correct count had been twenty. The secret about him was that he was not a man at all but a kit. He was a kit, and the men had each one of them carried a part of that kit strapped to his belly to be assembled when a real emergency arrived. Their situation in the Polyphemian dungeon was such an emergency, and they had assembled the kit.

His name was Esolog-9-Ex and he was a build-it-yourself pseudanthropus kit. You never know when you are going to need such an automaton, and many hornet-men had formed the habit of carrying such portions of one.

The men had had fun with Esolog-9 in the past, particularly in the happy days of the war. You remember the time they had constructed him into a cardshark? Into a hillbilly? Into a peddler? One of the best had been when they constructed him into a crackpot general. This pseudo-general issued a series of the weirdest and most asinine orders ever heard. They resulted in more than ten thousand men going to their deaths needlessly. It was excessive, but it was funny.

On Bandicoot the natives had found parts of such a kit on dead soldiers of the back-drift of the war, had assembled him into a ruler, and he still rules Bandicoot today. For these kits could be built to be anything in man form.

And in the Polyphemian dungeon the crewmen had built Esolog-9 into a fat man. He was not an ordinary fat man. He was made to rant and rave more than any of them. And another element was set into him, a sialagogue that tantalized the men, that set up such a flow of juice in them all that they almost drowned in their own slaver. They'd have stuck a fork in him if they had one. The wonder is that they did not eat him themselves. And the high wonder of it all is that the Polyphemians had left him so long.

Day after day the Polyphemians selected other men, fat, but not so fat as Esolog; succulent, but not so succulent as he; ravening, but not with his own special rage.

"Why do they not take him?" Roadstrum moaned again. "We go to our deaths, and it seems as if they will leave the finest one of us till last."

And the point is that the Ace-in-the-Hole, Esolog-9-Ex, was booby-trapped. To eat him was to suffer the swelling death, the exploding death. One would swell and swell and swell, to three times one's size, to nine times one's size, to a thousand times one's size. One would explode and completely destroy oneself and everything around.

"Why don't they take him, and we be released from our misery?" all the men groaned.

Then, one afternoon, Margaret told them that the Polyphemians would take Esolog-9 that very night. They knew, of course, that Esolog was the best of them all, and they had been saving him for a very special occasion. That special occasion had arrived. Some cousins of the Polyphemians from another place had come to visit them. That night would be the finest of all banquets, and Esolog-9-Ex would be the crown of the feast.

"He will destroy them all," said Roadstrum. "Then you will bring us the keys to the dungeon, Margaret, and we will escape. But see that you are at a safe distance from it, and most especially see that you do not eat any of him."

"I say I will not, and I say I will not," said Margaret, "but can I be sure that I will not? Oh oh oh, he will be good! How can I say I will not eat a little bit?"

"Margaret, Margaret, it would be your destruction," Roadstrum warned. "You must be very shrewd in this. Do not eat any of him. And be far distant when the Polyphemians have eaten fully."

"I say I will not, and I say I will not, but can I be sure I will not?"

The Polyphemians came for Esolog-9 in the early evening. He went to his death as dapper a dog as ever went, and his joking was genuine. He was cool; he hadn't a nerve in him. You had to admire him, even if he was no man at all, but an assembled kit. And he raved and ranted as was expected of him when in the hands of the Polyphemians. He was perfect.

The men waited the news, and Margaret brought them hourly bulletins. She reported that the Polyphemians had begun on him. She reported a second time that the Polyphemians had devoured him all except for a few pieces hardly to be seen. And finally she reported to them that the Polyphemians had begun to swell and swell and swell.

"You know where the keys are, Margaret? You will be able to find them in the wreckage?"

"I know where they are. I will bring them to you as soon as the show is over."

"And don't get too near, Margaret."

"No, no, I'll stay well clear of it."

And Margaret did not have to report to them when the big thing came. It was a rumble like walls going down; it was a sound like a distant dam bursting. Then it was an explosion that shook all Polyphemia to its deepest roots.

By the time their ears were functioning again, Margaret brought them the keys and let them out. Starkhead did not come out. He had eaten nothing since they entered. He was peculiarly inert and cold to the touch and offensive to the nose. One never admits that a hornet-man is dead, it is against the code, but they buried him there in the floor of the dungeon.

And they could not budge Crewman Burpy. He had grown grosser and fatter than any of them, fatter even then Esolog-9, but the Polyphemians had passed him up. He was too placid; they had such sheep of their own; there was nothing rampant about him. He had grown so heavy that he could no longer stand on his own legs, and they left him without a lot of regret.

Freedom from the dungeon, and now the freedom of the skies. No need now to repair the crippled hornet. There were men left to man one craft only, and it would be a little crowded, so large had they grown.

Deep John looked at himself. "Men, men, it was hobo heaven," he said, "and out of it alive. Whoever saw a genuine hobo with such a pot on him."

So they enskied. They were in high space. And in time they would regain their fine lines and their wonderful tempers. Freedom freedom!

"Boys, I don't feel well," said Margaret the houri.

"You shouldn't, you female cannibal," Roadstrum growled. "You saved us in the end, but you didn't treat us at all well in the middle."

"Boy, I feel terrible," she said.

"It is a wonder you do not die of remorse," said Captain Puckett.

"Remorse this is not. I'm going to burst."

"Look out, look out," Crewman Clamdigger warned. "Maggy was fat, but not that fat. She's three times the size she was when we loaded in the hornet."

"You ate, you ate part of him!" Roadstrum howled furiously.

"Only a little sliver. I don't care. It was worth it. Boys, I'm going to burst."

And she had already taken up three-quarters of the hornet and crowded all the men, gasping and straited, into a tight corner. She had begun to rumble, and she would go any minute, and all with her.

"She'll blow! She'll blow!" howled the frightened men. "She'll blow, and she'll blow up the ship and all of us with her." And there came the still deeper rumble that one hears just before the sundering explosion.

Perils! And there would be more of them. And they were still years from home.

The Chantey pleads a lapse and leaves a doubt of it.
We don't know how the hearty crew got out of it!

What tales you hear with reason may you doubt them all.
They could not be! And yet the men got out them all.

Remember not the jokes they made to bluff it off,
What ghastly thing they suffered, and to sluff it off.

Withhold the question where such brave men cry a lot.
Remember also hornet-crewmen lie a lot.

Ibid

87

CHAPTER SIX

A feckless fate had foiled their path and ditched them there.
A lady with a lilty way had witched them there.

She thought to light a scorchy flame at least in them,
And had to settle for the risen beast in them.

Fell dangers from the charmer and the hair of her,
Beware of her! Beware of her! Beware of her!—

As deft and devious as Ancient Niccolo—
Now sing her song, strum harp, and pip the piccolo.

Ibid

IT WAS scramble on all their data. Their direction and course were gone. They found themselves in the mysterious realm of middle space, which has no real bearings. But there are shoals and obstacles there.

"What is here, you confabulating canister?" Roadstrum demanded of the data log. "What things are these drifting in the space about us?"

"Here there are warlocks and mandragoras and witches," the navigation data log issued.

"When your machines start to go droll on you you're in trouble," Roadstrum growled. "I can get wise answers from my men. I don't need a machine for that."

"He thinks he is men," Crewman Bramble explained. "He has been with men always and does not know other machines."

"Fix the idiot thing, Bramble. Fix it," Roadstrum ordered.

So Crewman Bramble fiddled with the data log a while and then announced that it was fixed. "Bad connection," he said. "That's what I always say, isn't it?"

"All right, Log, now give a straight answer," Roadstrum ordered. "Where are we, and what are these drifting things about us?"

"Here there are warlocks and mandragoras and witches," the log issued once more. "Kill me, torture me, I can say nothing else."

"Who has been feeding nonsense to this machine?" Roadstrum demanded.

They had narrow misses of collisions with things that apparently weren't there at all. The things seemed solid till very near approach, and then they faded to mist. It was illusion space they were in.

"Ram them, ram them," Roadstrum roared every time an object loomed up. "If we pass through them without harm we will know that they aren't really there."

"All right," issued the data log, and they rammed through several objects that had seemed quite solid, jagged, rocky, quite large bodies.

"What if we don't pass through them without harm, Roadstrum?" Captain Puckett asked.

"Don't know. I suppose that will mean they are real, if we have a real collision."

"And it may mean that we aren't real any longer," said Crewman Clamdigger. "We could get unreal awful easy smashing into one of those things that was really there."

There was another one of them looming up, a round little world of gold and green. It was overdone. It was too arty to be real. Whoever had thought it up may have had a certain feeling for art, but none at all for planetary dynamics.

"That's the phoniest one yet," Roadstrum laughed. "Ram it, Log, ram it. I can see into the mind that made it up."

"So can I!" cried Margaret furiously. "It is Aeaea, the Aeaea mind. I hate her! Ram it, canny can, ram it!"

And the navigation log soared the hornet into ram it, and then somehow slackened off a little. They came in at too low a speed for a real ramming job, and the world took on further reality from their hesitation.

"You fumbling idiot," Roadstrum fumed. "You half accepted it on its own terms, so now it is half there. Too close to it to veer now, and it's getting too solid to take a chance going right through. Slow it and land. What happened to you anyhow?

"Lost my nerve," the navigation data log issued.

"Oh, that damned Aeaea!" Margaret exploded again. "I've run into it and her a hundred different times in different parts of the universe. She and that silly planet of hers! She doesn't have a regular place. She hangs it anywhere. And now we've got to land on it. I hate her!"

They landed on Aeaea. They made a bad landing. They first buried themselves in the soft surface that was like smoke. Then they had to back out and let it solidify. They got out and walked, and it was tricky. Aeaea hadn't made her world very thoroughly. For the place was not charted and not generally believed in. The surface was full of nothing-holes. But it firmed, it firmed, it became a workable theory, it became a fact.

"Aeaea!" Roadstrum hooted. "We all know that it shouldn't be here. Whoever heard of coming onto a myth in actuality. I'd say annihilate all myths and be done with it."

"Easy, easy, fine Roadstrum," Margaret cautioned. "What do you think I am?"

"Oh, but this breaks it, Maggie! It would hardly startle me to hear the lady sing."

"No, no, Roadstrum. Give her an ear and she'll take it all. She's worse than the Siren-Zo, and she has a more hideous song. Let's zoom away from this place; it becomes too solid."

But it did startle Roadstrum when he heard the lady sing. It startled them all when they heard it. It was high and clear, and not far away. There was an artiness about that singing that is beyond art. It would have been better if it were not quite as good, but it was remarkable singing.

They were in the center of the singing, and they were all trapped. Then they were in the center of a new silence, in a world inside the song. And there was a nice enough lady there, but could she be Aeaea herself?

"We are strangers, lost and bemused," Roadstrum said to the lady. "We landed here by accident. We are looking for the lady who was singing, the lady who (according to silly myth) is identical with the planet and who sang the planet into being."

"And now we have found you," Margaret interrupted rudely. "Scat, you wood pussy, down on your four legs and skat!"

"The Margaret be mute!" the lady ordered, and the Margaret was frozen into an angry crouching statue. Fire in her eyes and slaver on her mouth, but she could not move or speak.

"I am the lady," the lady said then, "and there is no

lady here except myself. I am Aeaea. To my notion there is no other lady anywhere. And I resent your calling this a silly myth. I made the myth and it is not silly; charming rather. Well, come along, come along! You are my things now, and you will come when I call you."

They all followed her like children—they did not know where.

They came to fine quarters, or perhaps it was that the fine quarters came to them. These things seemed to form about them, and there was no real distance traversed.

"A dish, a doll, a droll, a dream," Crewman Clamdigger breathed.

"A girl, a grig, a gleam, a glom," Crewman Trochanter gobbled.

And Margaret hissed. She would never remain entirely mute, that one. She was still unable to move, yet she was still with them in their quarters. There was something the matter with these quarters. They seemed not to be designed for people at all. For something, but not for people.

"Be you all at ease," said the lady Aeaea in her musical voice. "When you have rested and eaten there will be time to admire me. The Margaret may eat from the bowl on the floor, and the rest of you in your fine stalls—ah cubicles. The mighty Road-Storm will come and talk with me."

"A larkin, a limpet, a lass!" admired Captain Puckett. They liked the lady.

"All right, girl," Roadstrum said when they were alone. "I have a few questions. They will be to the point, and I want answers."

"I doubt that you could understand the answers, " Aeaea warned. "I see now that you are a common simpleminded man, and we maintain a very high intellectual average here. It will be difficult to communicate."

"Who is the 'we' that maintains so high an average, girl?"

"Only myself now. My father has been dead these last several centuries."

"It should be easy to maintain a high average with only one entity."

"It is. I am mistress of all the sciences. I go so far beyond all else that my work is called magic. I manipulate noumena, regarding monads as points of entry tangential to hylomorphism. As to the paradox of Primary Essence being contained in Quiddity, the larger in the smaller, I have my own solution. The difficulty is always in not confusing Contingency with Accidence. Do you understand me?"

"Sure. You're a witch."

"Exactly, but I frown on the name. Very unscientific. But I am no ordinary witch. I studied in Salamanca the hidden."

"Salamanca, the underground witchcraft school? But that was on World, in the Indias, in the New Latin Lands."

"There are entrances to it on World, Road-Storm, but do you not know that the underground lands are shared by many worlds? It is all one underground, a vast place, and it is but a trick on which globe one will surface on coming out. This is the reason that the inside of every world is so much vaster than the outside. You are fooled by the shape of these little balls on which things live and crawl; you see the universe inside-out; you see the orbs as containing and not contained. I will teach you to see it right if you please me."

"On with it, witch, on with it."

"I am the consumate scientist, Road-Storm. Science has suffered in having her name applied to mechanics, an ugly stepchild of hers. Matter itself is a humiliation to the serious. We cannot make it vanish forever, but can make it seem to. For my purpose that is even better. All matter can be modified as long as it is kept subjective. Let us keep it so."

"Yes. Let's do that, Aeaea."

"Those who fail to understand my science may call it magic or hypnotism or deception. But it is only my projection of total subjectivity. I will bring one of my creatures and you will see what I mean."

"Bring it on, gay girl! Hey, I feel as lively as a monkey here," Roadstrum laughed.

Aeaea left him then, and her singing filled the halls when she was gone. They were fine halls of marble, polished travertine. No crack or grain at all in their walls. But if one took a total subjective view and wished them to be less perfect? Yes, they were not really travertine, but an inferior marble; not marble really, but ordinary limestone; not that either, but adobe, mud really. Roadstrum kicked holes in the walls, and a great part of them fell down.

"Why hokey!" he said. "I can make marble halls myself. I wonder how many others know how? A thing like that could come in handy."

Then he formed them to travertine marble again, being very subjective about it. He heard Aeaea coming again, her wonderful singing drawing nearer, and he was a little leery of her. She would know many tricks, and he had only partly learned one of them.

She came singing, and she brought a pet raccoon with her. Roadstrum guffawed to see the thing. This was real art! You would practice a long time before you made a thing as comic and clownish as that, and yet at the same time calling out all compassion and sympathy. A coon would no more be only a coon to Roadstrum; this one was really a person. A burlesque, of course, a caricature and a perfect one, a simulacrum with a soul. It was a solid cartoon of a little animal made by a real master.

"It's good, Aeaea," Roadstrum said heartily. "I never saw anything better even in the Natural Arts Museum on Camiroi. Has he seen it? You really take him off with that?"

"Has who seen it, Road-Storm? Of whom does it remind you?"

Roadstrum chuckled with real amusement. "It looks just like Puckett. I might almost say that it is Puckett. What other animal but a coon would he look like? Was it live to begin with, Aeaea? Did it really look like that, or have you only made it look like that?"

"I have explained to you, Road-Storm, that there is no difference between appearing and being, so long as we keep matter subjective. You have not paid attention."

Ah, the angry and at the same time pathetic eyes on that coon!

"Just like Puckett himself, Aeaea," Roadstrum mused. "Even the tail is the sort of tail he'd have if he had one. This is a new art that surpasses anything. You are a genius, Aeaea."

"I have always thought so, Road-Storm. He is so sweet, the little raccoon, but if he bites me one more time I'll break out every cute tooth he has."

"Let's get Puckett here to look at this. Will he recognize himself in caricature?"

"Mighty Road-Storm, do you not understand yet?"

"Understand what? Would Puckett be offended?"

"Of course he is offended. That is why he bites me."

"What? What? I don't believe it. This is not Puckett."

"It is. There is no Puckett anywhere except here. This is High-Captain Puckett, commander of hornets. This is your friend and companion in his new form. You see him like this, I see him like this, he sees himself like this, and therefore—"

"Oh shut up, witch! I don't believe you. I'll find him."

Roadstrum went roaring through the halls to find High-Captain Puckett. Aeaea sang behind him and all around and laughed as she sang. Roadstrum found Crewman Humphrey.

"When did you last see Puckett, Humph?" he demanded of him.

"I don't know," Humphrey fluttered oddly from his upper lip. "He went with the lady, I think. He looked kind of funny."

"Puckett looked funny! Look at yourself, you straddling kaymo! What's happened to you?

"I don't know," Humphrey fluttered with that rubbery lip. Humphrey *did* look funny. Humphrey had always looked funny, but this was different. Roadstrum would think of the difference in a minute.

"There goes Puckett now," Crewman Eseldon brayed suddenly. "See him there climbing up that plant."

"You ass, that's a coon!" Roadstrum roared. "Was there ever such an ass?"

There never was. The horrible truth swept over Roadstrum in waves while the weird singing of Aeaea rose and fell. It had happened to all those men. The likeness had been so good, and he himself so upset, that Roadstrum had not noticed it happening.

Humphrey had looked funnier than usual. Humphrey had turned into a camel. That's enough to make anyone look funny. "But what right has she to turn my men into camels and coons?" Roadstrum asked angrily. "They are persons inviolate and should not be subverted to animals. Aeaea, Aeaea, come here and give an accounting!"

Crewman Eseldon was now an ass. He had always been one, but now he was one physically. The change seemed to have got all the men. "Hollering won't do it," Roadstrum hollered. "It's time I did some rapid and dynamic thinking about this thing. Come you together here, men, creatures, animals, pseudomorphs, companions of my bosom. Come together here and we will hold congress on this affair."

They came, they came. Was this only group hypnosis? Or had they actually changed? Aeaea said that seeming and being were the same thing. Roadstrum attempted to fight her on her own ground. He became very subjective about it all. He had been able to turn travertine marble to clay-mud and back to marble, but he could not turn these things back to man-form.

Crewman Septimus was now a rabbit. With that cleft upper lip and those pink eyes he could not say anything else. Crewman Swinnert was a hog, a good solid hog, the kind you'd like to be if you had to be one. Ursley was a bear. Margaret the houri was an alley cat (that was the first mistake that Aeaea made; it was not a metamorphosis for Margaret to become an alley cat, that was her true form).

Crewmen Clamdigger and Threefountains and Trochanter, three tall stags, great horny wild stags. Those boys had always had a lot of spring to them, and now they were ranging and leaping wildly. Deep John was a polecat. "I always did like folks to treat me with a certain decent reserve," he said. Crewman Bramble was a fox. He had always been the smartest of them, but if he was so smart how come he was taken in this?

"If any of you have any ideas, tell them to me," Roadstrum begged. "Fortunately for you all, the lady Aeaea has an imperfect idea of animals. I believe that she has led a secluded life, that she has never seen real animals. She leaves you with the powers of human speech, for an instance, and that is rare in animals. But I at least have remained a man, and out of my great mind I will fabricate some device to free you from all this."

And they laughed at him. They who had been captain and crewmen and hobo and houri laughed at the Captain Roadstrum, laughed foolish giggly gobbly animal laughs. And he was furious.

"Ah, she left you your men's voices, but she took away your men's brains. Foolish gibbering things hardly worth saving. But for the great love I bear you in your real forms I will find a way to save you yet. I am a man yet, and I will find the way to lead you back to the man context."

They laughed and giggled yet. You have heard stags laughing? You have heard donkeys and polecats laughing? Yes, but have you ever heard a kinkajou laughing? It runs down your spine like an idiot, that laughing. That was Crewman Lawrence in his new form.

"There has to be a converse to all this," Roadstrum maintained, but he was full of doubt now. "I'll break the spell or the science of her singing yet. As the only man left it devolves to me to do it."

There was high laughter in the singing now, and Aeaea came to them assembled there. They all gathered around her, except Margaret, and were completely charmed by her. Animals! Animals!

But Roadstrum was more than surprised when Aeaea swung him up under her arm and set him astride her shoulders. It was pleasant but puzzling. Either she had become very large or he had become very small.

The reflection in the polished wall gave him the answer.

Mighty Roadstrum had become a very small ape. Angrily he leaped down. He didn't like it.

"Many men have become the pet apes of beautiful women," he gibbered in monkey voice, "but I will not have it happen to me literally. And I was small ape all the time that I trumpeted I was the only man left? No wonder that the animals laughed."

But it had happened; it had happened to all of them. How does one accustom himself to being an animal? Roadstrum refused, and held apart. But Aeaea became the center of the lives of the rest of them, and in a day or two she had them hooked.

They were her animals. She maintained their jealousies, fondling one and then the other, keeping them subservient to her. They were her creatures, and she gloried in them.

It would seem that she must be injured or crashed or slashed to death or ground to death, and Aeaea did not seem the durable type. Half a ton of camel in her lap was no great thing, perhaps, but when she went into her frolicking wrestle with Ursley the bear it was a fearful thing. When she went for canters with Eseldon the ass she bore him on her back as often as he bore her on his, and he was quite a big donkey, yet they seemed to have a gay, galloping time of it. The coon and the kinkajou slashed her with teeth, the three great horny stags leaped all over her. Stag-man Trochanter learned to balance with all four feet on her shoulders, and he was big as a horse.

"It is all in being subjective, Apie Road-Storm," she explained. "But of course I am slashed and I bleed, and I am crushed and ground down and broken. I want to be. I have a passion for these things. It is the animal in myself. And yet all these things are in my mind only. They are private fantasies of mine, as are you, most wonderful of apes. You all love me, you know. If you did not, I would make new fantasies."

All loved her except Margaret the alley cat. And Margaret was a violation of Aeaea's thesis. It was axiomatic that all her creatures should love her, said Aeaea; therefore the alley cat loved her also. But Margaret had hateful ways of showing her love.

But Roadstrum still plotted for freedom. He plotted with Margaret the alley cat, with Deep John the polecat, with Puckett the raccoon, and with Bramble the fox.

But had not Bramble died and been eaten by the Polyphemians? No, he had not, it only seemed that he had. He was always too much of a fox to be taken and eaten, but the trick by which he evaded it will not be given here.

Something was working in Roadstrum's little ape head. When he had been a man he had always known when it was time for action; particularly he had always known the last moment when action was still possible. He knew now that that moment was come very near. He was sinking deeper in his animalness every hour.

Puckett the coon resisted, but with entirely too much deference. "We should let the lady know that we do not always wish to remain animals," he said. "We must present this protest firmly to the lady. We must take the bull by the tail, as the ancient adage has it, and tell the lady that we are not entirely pleased with our state."

Then a blinding light burst on Roadstrum, and he saw the truth of the situation. Many things Roadstrum was not, and it was sometimes wondered why he was the natural leader of all the men. He was their leader because he was a man on whom the blinding light sometimes descended.

"I've got it, I've got it," he shouted. He gibbered it like an ape? No, he shouted it like a man. He had his man's voice back again. "I've got it, guys, I've got it! We have been taking the bull by the wrong organ. The witch has played a semantic trick on us. We were already pretty salty animals when we came here! It is toy animals she has turned us into. We have been working against ourselves, trying to be men again, but to be her idea of men, since we live in her context. But she does not know real animals, or men.

"Listen, listen; what we must do now is become more animal, and not less animal. Assemble, assemble all.

"Toy creatures, puppets, tame things!" he thundered. "Be real animals! Raise it up in you! Show the witch what real animals are. Resurrect the old beast!"

"No, no," they twittered. "Aeaea has already turned us into animals with her singing. Someday, but not today or tomorrow, we will become men again for a little while, if she will permit it. But we are animals now, Ape. Your words are mixed."

"Hear my man words, hear my animal words!" Roadstrum bellowed. "Be you not toys any longer! Stir up the wild business in you. You have to be real animals before you can be men. How could Roadstrum be the tame ape of any woman? Puckett, be you a real boar coon while you are a coon! Humphrey, be you a cob camel at least! Ye three great stags, be rampant and musky stags! Ursley, let out the great growl, be a bear and not a toy bear! Septimus! Swinnert! Eseldon! All! Raise it up in you!"

97

The arty singing of Aeaea turned into a scream, but a sincere one. Reality, raw murderous reality broke into her contrived world. Terror had come to the planet Aeaea, and it would never be the same again. The lady Aeaea had become a sniffling screaming old lady now, and only Eseldon the ass remained with her. An ass is all she deserved.

No, no, it cannot be given here! The blood would be all over you, on your hands and in your heart, and you would never be able to get rid of it. It was horrifying, animal, human slaughter, the brutish murder of a concept and a person. It would sear your eyes to watch it.

Of what did the great revolt consist? Some say that it was a cosmic gang-shag that left the lady near dead and in terror for the rest of her life, never again to dabble in toy animals. But most agree that she was left dead indeed, though perhaps not from her own viewpoint. And some say that it was an elemental surge, so much more horrifying than a mere attack that it cannot safely be put into words.

Margaret, of course, was in the middle of it. Nobody had ever doubted her animality.

"I'll shred that lark; I'll shred her yet," she had sworn. And Margaret grew to be a larger and larger cat. "I see myself as a very large cat, you all see me as a very large cat, she will see me as one, and therefore I will be one." Margaret had become bobcat sized, leopard sized. Her tail twitched and her whiskers vibrated. She'd have that song-bird; for Aeaea, in her terror, had begun to look very like a bird. Ape and cat and coon and fox had been practicing at seeing her as a bird, and it worked.

Margaret went for Aeaea, and they all went for her. She was torn open in throat and breast, she was rent apart, she was ground down, she was trampled and stomped, she was bitten and clawed, she was defaced (that Margaret took the face clear off of her with a final sweep of her tigress claws), she was annihilated. She was dead.

Dead, dead, nothing left, except the song that had turned into a scream that still hung in the air. And the bloody pulp that had almost no resemblance to a body. She was stubborn, though, that Aeaea, and she had her own philosophy.

"I am as I have always been," said Aeaea. "You can all see that there is no blood on me." Well, there was quite a bit of blood around, much of it on the cat Margaret. She reveled in the feathers and blood on her paws and face, quite a bit of blood.

"I see myself as unhurt," Aeaea continued (there was the broken remnant of a body on the ground, and there was the voice in the air). "Surely you all see me as unhurt. Therefore

I *am* unhurt even though (as it happens) I have just died horribly. Now you had better all be gone. I hate sticky farewells, and what is left of me has become very sticky."

"Aeaea, whichever is you, the voice in the air, or the bloody thing on the ground, there is a flaw in your philosophy. You really are dead, you know. You begin to fade away, and so does your world. Hey, we'd better get off this thing while there's still something left to get off!" Roadstrum trumpeted.

"Would you sing for us once more," asked Humphrey the apprehensive camel, who was becoming uncameled.

"Yes, do," said Margaret. She was back in her human or houri form now. "How about 'Mouth Full of Feathers'? That's a good boogie song. Or the 'Dying Canary.' I always did like the 'Dying Canary.' " Margaret was a little cruel.

"I can sing no more," said Aeaea. "I fade, I fade. But do I not carry it all off well?"

She did, she did. But now the murder howl had gone over the space-ways, and they were all outlaws to be hunted. And decent people would no more give them haven.

She sought with song to make the towsle toys of them,
She hadn't recked the ruddy reckless boys of them.

She sold her reputation for a song she did,
And paid a reparation for the wrong she did.

The "Songstress Murder" made the space-ways gape to hear,
The stunning scandal, murder, wreck, and rape to hear.

A killer clan! The avid law is chilled for it,
And deems that they be hunted down and killed for it.

And Roadstrum cast a youngish pelt aside of him,
And came down near the tough essential hide of him.

Ibid

99

CHAPTER SEVEN

The cream of Horneteers, the high elite of them!
And sky-wolves snapping at the bloody feet of them!

In Guimbarde town, it rude! it raw! ramshackle it!
They sought the crushing, crashing way to tackle it.

For noble lies and every royal whopper there
They'd kill the kerl who couldn't tell a topper there.

Inside the Club itself, the most exclusive yet,
Came snuffling death:—and they be more elusive yet!

From flying hoosegow, sudden-swift, the ratter ran
Who cut all trails and read the Gypsy patteran.

He blew the blast! And they be hustled well and gone.
And after that they went a while to Hell and gone.

Ibid

IT WAS the most exclusive club in the world, in all the worlds, and this is a mighty pale statement to make about it. Let us emphasize that it was hard to get into.

It was a hundred and thirteen stories up by one count, a hundred and nineteen by another, and nobody was sure how close either might be. Naturally the Club did not have a room or suite number, no more than did any other thing in those buildings.

It was in one of those weird, wooden buildings of Guimbarde Town, and the buildings of Guimbarde Town have neither elevators nor zoom-rooms. How could they have? There is no corridor nor shaft in any of them straight enough for such contrived transportation.

It was in one of those thousand-odd steep wooden buildings that crown Blind-Raven hill, tall shanties, most of them over a hundred stories (there is no exact count in any of these buildings) that the Club is found. These buildings lean together and prop each other up; and when one of them topples and falls (and it happens quite often) several others will usually fall with it.

The building no longer had a name, or at least no name that applied to all of it: there were local names that applied to various parts of it. Long ago it had been the Ramshackle Hotel, but the lower nine stories of it had sunk into the mud (they used no foundations in Guimbarde Town) and various tribes and peoples still lived subterraneously there. At a little later time, a dozen upper stories had fallen from the building onto the Greenglanders Building and had been incorporated into that; and very many of the middle stories had burned. But to make up for what it had lost, in simple justice it had received thirteen stories fallen from the old Potters' Steeple, dropping from the sky, as it were. These were conjoined crookedly to the old basic (these segments never do fall straight), and all the higher stories later added to the building were crooked.

Well, how *do* you get up even a hundred and thirteen or a hundred and nineteen stories to arrive at the Club? You go up those old outside stairways, and they sure are dangerous! There will sometimes be five or nine stories missing from the stairway, and there you must scramble. There are places where you must pay toll or fight your way through. There are cliff-dweller Indians in the mid-sixties who drink out of the skulls of those who thought it a safe thing to go up that stairway.

All this, you must know, is the finest section of Guimbarde Town, not the meanest; and Guimbarde Town is the finest city on Yellow Dog. Yellow Dog itself has lost its world license, is now a proscribed world, and is inhabited mostly by shiftless and shifty persons.

So it is seen that the Club is not an easy place to get into. Why not come down to it from above, you say, in gracious copter or in sky car? They don't use them there. The skies over Guimbarde Town, and indeed over the whole of Yellow Dog, are infested by Megagaster birds that can take all but the largest craft in a single gobble. And yet Roadstrum and his brave outlaws *did* come down into the Club from above.

"How can we land? How can we land?" Roadstrum had fretted at the top of his voice.

"Leave it to Bramble," said Captain Puckett. "He'll think of something."

"Leave it to me," said Bramble. "I'll think of something. Hey, you know those nineteen cases of Mumuckey mustard that we have carried for so long a time? Often we've had little room for food or water, and have been forced to sleep three deep. Some of you have howled that we should throw the mustard out so there would be room for ourselves. 'Let us keep them,' I said every time; 'we will find something they are good for.' Now we have found it. We will foil the Megagaster birds with our mustard, and we will land on this planet."

Willing crewmen got out and, working dangerously, coated the entire hornet craft half a meter thick with Mumuckey mustard. Then they came into the dangerous sky of Yellow Dog.

What happened to them? What happens to every craft that enters that dangerous sky? They were gobbled up in one bite by a Megagaster bird.

One account is that they went right through that bird like yellow flame. Another is that it bounced them around nine times in its maw and then spat them out with a cry of disgust and horror. They crashed down through the top dozen flimsy floors of a building and came to rest in the Club. They got out of the hornet craft and looked around.

It was dark there. The more exclusive a club is, the darker it always is. There was no light there at all except the luminescent eyes of some of the creatures present. This, however, was light enough, once they got accustomed to it.

"This is the Improbable Club," said the President-Emeritus in a heavy muffled voice, "and you things have made an improbable entry. Many unqualified persons have attempted to crash this Club, but you have done it literally. Whether you will be able to qualify for our high membership is another thing. It will not matter. We accept, for a brief moment at least, all who come here as members. We will quickly measure you one way or another. We have no living ex-members. Sit you down, all, and unwind your ears. Remember, each topper must be topped."

"If not?" Roadstrum asked boldly, not understanding this jabber at all.

"The stopper," said the President-Emeritus. This worthy

seemed hardly human, but he was a genial person, in a hard-eyed sort of way.

"What's the fellow talking about?" Roadstrum asked Crewman Bramble. "What is this Improbable Club that we have fallen into?"

"I'm not sure, Captain Roadstrum," said Bramble. "The name is, perhaps, an euphemism. There is a crest on the old weapons-rack in the corner, and it reads 'Club Menitros.' Is this the Club Itself whose very location is unknown, the club for membership in which Emperors might give their right galactic segment, the club so exclusive that for a full century it had no members at all? Is this the High Liars Club itself?"

Roadstrum and all the crewmen bowed their heads. "If it be so, we will all try to be worthy of it," they murmured.

The half-dozen members were drinking loopers, the green-lightning drink, and now a liveried waiter brought them to the crewmen also.

Margaret the houri, who had been larking around in other parts of the building, came in to them now.

"I met a fast-talking fellow and I'm going to World with him," she said. "I'd go with you, but the word is that you're not going there."

"But yes, we will go in our hornet as soon as we are sure we have given the slip to the sky-police," Roadstrum said.

"Three families have already moved into your hornet," Margaret said. "You couldn't get them evicted in a month. Besides, the word is out that you're not going anywhere in that hornet, ever. I guess I'll just go to World with this fast-talking fellow."

"Our fellowship begins to break up," said Roadstrum sadly. "Goodbye, Margaret, you'll miss us."

Deep John the Vagabond, who had likewise been making connections, came back.

"I'm going to hook a night freight to World, fellows," he said. "I'd go with you, but the word is out that you're not going to World. And where you are going, I don't want to go."

"The word is not out until we put it out," Roadstrum said. "I myself intend to go to World very soon."

But Deep John had left them.

"One of the members there reminds me of someone," Roadstrum whispered to Puckett. "The fellow with the green scarf."

"He looks familiar to me also, Roadstrum," said Puckett. "I'm on the verge of thinking whom he reminds me of."

And there was another fellow there who seemed to be, like the hornet-men, on trial membership. He was a curious creature with a knot in the middle of his forehead, with one red eye, and with the other eye covered by a patch.

"You may begin, Probationary," the President-Emeritus said. "Be not nervous. In a very little while you will either be a member, or you will not be."

But the red-eye began nervously for all that.

"I come from a very poor planet. We have no exports except our own citizens, going to better ourselves in other places. We have no talent, can perform few tasks, and have no trade on alien worlds except one. We work as traffic lights."

"As traffic lights?" Roadstrum asked, though he was not sure that a probationary member should be asking questions. "How as traffic lights?"

"All on our world are born with one red eye and one green eye," the creature said. "Our eyes shine brightly, as you see that my red eye shines brightly here now. We offer our services, we stand on corners in fair weather and foul, and we blink first one eye and then the other. The pay is everywhere miserable, the conditions are hard, but it is a livelihood."

The President-Emeritus motioned to three ushers, and they approached grimly.

"Why is the one eye bandaged, and what is the knot in the middle of your forehead?"

"If one wished to work on a good corner anywhere, and have a little better conditions, he had to have an amber eye also," the creature said, very nervously. "The amber eye is not natural to us, so I have had an implant but it is not yet completely formed. It will grow, and it will break open, I believe, by springtime. In the meanwhile my green eye is inflamed. It's the messages I have to flash on it that have done it in. The 'walks' and the 'don't walks' I can manage easily enough. It's the special things, the 'No left turns except on Sunday or before eight A.M.,' things like that have inflamed it. It isn't easy to flash a variety of messages."

"Enough of that," said the President-Emeritus. "I believe you hardly qualify, and if you continue with your jabber it will get worse. Why can folks not understand that this Club is not for amateurs?"

The ushers slit the fellow's throat, opened a trapdoor in the floor, and dropped him through. He fell three hundred and fifty meters, the building having a lean there and this part of the story being out over empty air.

"I understand what he meant," Roadstrum whispered

to Puckett, "when he said, 'In a very little while you will either be a member, or you will not be.' I am not sure that all our men will be able to qualify. They are good ordinary liars, but the extraordinary is expected here."

"That fellow with the green scarf bothers me more and more," Puckettt whispered. "He reminds me very much of someone we have met in our travels, something about the brow, something about his grin."

And it was to the fellow with the green scarf that the President-Emeritus turned now. "Give us one of yours, Horace," the P-E said, "anything to get the taste of the late ineptitude out of our ears."

"Sammy the Snake!" Roadstrum said suddenly and loudly. "Pardon me, sir, but are you any kindred of Sammy the Snake, the gambler on Roulettenwelt?"

"My cousin," said the fellow with the green scarf. "I am Horace the Snake. Fellows, these travelers know Sammy."

All the crewmen could see the resemblance now. It was something about the brow, of course, and something about the grin. It was also the flickering forked tongue and the thirty-meter long torso. Cousins! they could almost have been brothers!

"Ah, I'll tell you about the time I used to be a baseball player," Horace began. "I had natural disabilities for this sport, for it had been originally a human game not designed for snakes. And, after humans, it was the giant frogs who played it best, especially at my chosen position, shortstop. Those fellows could really get the hop on a ball. And I, a poor earth-crawler, had to make my way by diligence and persistency.

"In my apprentice years I had a mighty sore mouth from catching that ball, and I never could throw it at all. But I could reach it. With my tail anchored around second base, I could flop my head all the way to third, or first, instantly. In my ninety years on the diamond (we snakes are long-lived) I had fifty thousand double plays and ten thousand triple plays, all unassisted. This, I believe, is a record."

"How would you bat, Horace?" Roadstrum asked, entranced, for he had never heard Horace's stories before.

"Couldn't very well, Roadstrum. Had to take the bat crossways in my mouth and bunt. I'm telling you I really had a sore snout in my apprentice years. But I stayed with it and I learned. You've heard pitchers say they'll jam a ball down a fellow's throat. They did to me. I've swallowed more baseballs than any ball player who ever lived. The worst thing is, they passed a special ruling that I was out whenever I swallowed a pitched ball. I never did believe they should have charged me more than a strike for it."

"Still, if you *could* lay down a bunt, any sort of bunt—" Roadstrum saw the possibilities.

"I could and I did, Roadstrum. I got where I could lay them down, and they didn't have to be very good. I could stretch my length and have my head on first base before anyone could blink. And once I was on first, I was as good as around. I hold every base-stealing record in baseball. When the bases are ninety feet apart, and a fellow is a hundred and five feet long, how are you going to tag him out?"

"I believe I know a way to stop that stealing." Crewman Trochanter grinned evily.

"I think I know what you mean, Trochanter." Horace the Snake smiled. "Horse-Hoof Harry tried it once when he was playing first base for the All-Star All Stars. Weighed nine tons, that fellow, and what hooves he did have on him! I still wake up screaming when I remember how he tromped on my tail just as I went into my stretch."

Crewman Trochanter chortled.

"But it was the last tail he ever tromped on, Trochanter," said Horace the Snake. "It was just about the last thing of any sort he ever did. I felt kind of sorry when his widow came around to see me that evening; but, as she said, it's all in the game."

Another person, perhaps human, had come into the Club. He was talking in a low voice with the President-Emeritus and with others. There was cursing, and the phrase "bird-killers" was heard.

"We had a bat-boy named Bennie," Horace the Snake continued. "He was a bat-boy literally, too small to handle the bats, but he flitted around merrily in the air."

"And how he could catch flies!" said Crewman Bramble.

"I hate a guy who's heard them all," said Horace the Snake.

One of the Club members, a florid colonel type, who dressed in the human style, was telling a steep tale of witty warfare and cunning conquest. The high hero of this was a great leader named Alley-Sally. It was a racy tale, and it excited Roadstrum.

"Puckett, Puckett," he whispered avidly, "just listen to this great stuff. Listen how it goes. What I would not give to be in on a campaign like that one! What I would not give to meet such a leader."

"Roadstrum, Roadstrum," Puckett chided. "It is yourself and ourselves he talks about; our own epic. Alley-Sally is yourself, Road-Storm. You remember that bit he's telling now, the six-day war in Wamtangle? Sure, that was a passing smart trick you devised there, Roadstrum. It's part of our own story he tells."

"Oh, I know that, Puckett. But he tells it so much better than it happened! Listen how they did it, Puckett! Listen to how smart their leader was! Oh, if I could only have been there!"

There was a lot of boy still left in Captain Roadstrum.

"One of the hornet-men will now tell a tale," said the President-Emeritus. "A slander against the hornet-men has been brought into this Club within the last several minutes. I do not believe this slander, but I say it is time the horne-teers were tested. If they fail the test, then they be not members of the Club, and it will not matter if the slander is true. We will make it quick. Let one horneteer tell a colossal lie, and all be judged by it."

"Let me," said Captain Puckett. "A raconting man you are not, Roadstrum."

And this is the high tale that Captain Puckett told:

"When I was quite a young man and filled with the spirit of adventure and space-faring, I went out to the Daedalian Chersonese and visited a world known as Demetrio Four. Being an undisciplined youth (I speak of that time now in sorrow, having become a moral man in my maturity) I fell into a liaison with a local girl, one Miseremos. She was the light of my life and I was completely impassioned by her. Our affair went along charmingly, until one day her four brothers came and seized me. They examined me very carefully, and in a way that I could not understand. They said that, things being the way they were, Miseremos and myself must marry. I was not adverse to this, loving the girl mightily, though I resented somewhat the manner and compulsion of it.

"And marry we did, though I was quite puzzled by some of the accompanying rites. Then followed the weeks of deep enjoyment, though I was more and more puzzled. I felt strange and uncertain, and my wife, apparently, did not. 'Your brothers spoke of *Things being the way they are*, Miseremos,' I told her one day. 'And I look at you and wonder. How are things, Miseremos?'

"'Do you not understand, dear Puckett?' she asked me. 'Oh, surely you understand! With us on Demetrio Four it is not the same as with folk elsewhere. We maintain our own most peculiar custom in this.'

"I hadn't known of that custom at all, but I was caught by it. On Demetrio Four it was not as it is elsewhere. I had heard the vaunt, 'The men of Demetrio accomplish what

107

no man else has ever done,' but I had not understood it. With my dear Miseremos on Demetrio Four, it was I who had become pregnant."

"It reminds me of the young wife," said Horace the Snake, "who complained to her mother, 'My Robert is the most wonderful man in the world, but he simply can't bear children.' "

"My period was an easy one," said Captain Puckett, "and at length I gave birth by the natural method. It was a beautiful baby boy. Our joy was almost complete, and I had no suspicion that my time of shameful failure was at hand. Ah, better I had died in childbirth than have endured such shame!"

"What was it, good Captain Puckett?" asked the President-Emeritus. "In what did you fail shamefully?"

"Couldn't lactate," said Puckett. "My wife's brother had to nurse the child."

The Club members conferred among themselves. Puckett and Roadstrum and all the crewmen were being weighed in the balance. Was it good enough? Would the hasty tale of Puckett get them into the Club before the crisis (which they all felt but none of them understood) broke?

"Puckett, I didn't know you were ever on Demetrio Four or in the Daedalian Chersonese at all. It isn't in your record," Roadstrum whispered. "And the custom isn't mentioned in Fisher's Customs of the Nineteenth Sector. And, come to think of it, there are Demetrios One, Two, and Three, but there isn't any Demetrio Four."

"Be a little less of a boy for the moment, Roadstrum," whispered Puckett. "If we fail the Club, we have our throats slit. If we get into it, there is still a threat mounted here against our lives and liberties, but I believe we can claim asylum as members of the rarest club of them all."

"For one crime there is no asylum even in the Club," whispered Horace the Snake, who had sharp ears for whispering. "For all other crimes we give asylum, but for the most heinous crime in the universe we give no asylum."

"What is the most heinous crime in the universe?" Roadstrum asked.

"Killing a songbird."

The President himself came in dressed in the robes of his office. He conferred with the President-Emeritus and with the others. They were being very grim about the matter.

"I believe I understand it now," Crewman Bramble whispered to the Captains. "The arrival of a little while ago, he who looks at us so balefully, is not a man but a sherlocker. We are tracked down."

Yes, they could all see it now. The thing was a sherlocker, a sky-dick, a snuffling hound. It was a ratter, and they were the rats tracked down. The pipe and the deer-stalker hat were not adjuncts, but parts of its contrived head. It was a burlesque of an old architypical human head, the Baker Street prototype, but the thing was a hound and it went on four legs (which they had not noticed before).

The President of the Club spoke now.

"In great sorrow I speak. All you the crewmen are accepted as members and are duly inscribed. But that members of the highest Club of all should be guilty of the most heinous crime in the universe! We will meet no more for one year, and we will deck our halls in mourning for a nine year period. Your accuser will speak now, and we share your contempt for him. But as for yourselves—how the shining ones have fallen!"

The thing, the dog, the sherlocker, the sky-dick, the ratter cleared his throat and began.

"I am the latest model of sherlocker, the finest tracker in the universe. Here I had no real starting place since the site of the crime was a contingent one, having no regular location in real space. I had only the smell of a toy that the Roadstrum had played with when he was three years old, some knowledge of the thought patterns of the Bramble, and the information that Margaret the houri had no heartbeat and no heart.

"With great good fortune I first cut the trail after cruising nine megaparsecs at random. A little later I spied a bent clump of grass in empty space, and still later three twigs that pointed. Here and there I noticed that the hydrogen atoms were all bent in a certain direction. Shrewdly I noticed variations in the cosmic flux; something had passed to alter it. Then I cut the trail for the second time and had my direction.

"I am the snufflingest tracker ever, and I can read any patteran ever laid; one of my ancestors was a Gypsy dog. As I closed in on them I deducted a multitude of details. I was able to deduce the middle name of Crewman Trochanter's maternal grandfather (from the asphyxan in the wake of the hornet), the secret fantasies of Crewman Ursley (from a muted resonance in the Hondstarfer stone-drive), the scalp-itch of Captain Puckett (he is allergic to the Stoimenof salt in the galley of the hornet). It is all down in my notes. I tracked them here. There they sit confounded! Arrest the criminals!"

"Slit his throat!" Roadstrum howled, coming to his feet in the grip of what seemed to be a good idea. "He has told

109

the truth at a meeting of the High Liars. Kill him! Kill him!"

"Of course we'll kill him," said the sad President. "We'll slit his throat, and we'll drop him through the trap like the dog he is. But not before he's blown the whistle on you."

The sherlocker blew an old-style police whistle. Three hundred coppers boiled into the room, manacled the brave hornet-men, and dragged them away to the terrible place from which, it is said, there is no returning.

The place itself, and ne'er a good word spoke of it,
You shiver when you even make a joke of it.

Though some go cocky, gaily in hand-basket there,
The most fare sadly in a clammy casket there,

Where Dante doled "l'orrible soperchio
Del puzzo—e gran pietre in cerchio."

Undying pain and gaping loss, no doubt of it.
A wide way leading in and no way out of it!

But none have told the blackest horror shrouded there—
Tall teeming terror—but it sure is crowded there!

Ibid

They were taken as prisoners to Hellpepper Planet. They were up in court there before Tiresias, the blind Theban prophet, who had considerable to say about the workings of this place. Tiresias was not really blind; but he had weak eyes and he wore blue glasses. His underlings called him Blinky.

"You are up for the rape and murder of the person and planet of Aeaea," said Blinky. "I assure you all that a shudder ran through Hell itself here at the news of your crime. Have any of you regrets?"

"Regrets?" Roadstrum asked in a hollow voice. "My only regret is that I didn't get to hear that fellow tell more of his story at the Club. There were these space warriors, you see, Blinky, and there was their noble and heroic leader, and they—"

"Roadstrum, Roadstrum," Puckett protested. "It was our old story that he told. 'Twas of ourselves."

"I know that, but he told it so much better than it happened. How can I be happy in Hell with my ears itching for more of it?"

"A little order here," Tiresias requested severely. "Something is wrong. This babbling fool cannot be Roadstrum himself?"

"Something is indeed wrong, Blinky," Roadstrum said evenly. "This silly place cannot be Hell itself?"

"I own a certain disappointment in both," said one of Tiresias' lieutenants, "but it is, and apparently you are. If you have come with high expectations of anything, you have come to the wrong place."

"Have you any defense for your damnable crime?" Tiresias asked sharply.

"Do you want a lawyer?" the lieutenant asked. "There are plenty of them to be had here."

"We'll be wanting no lawyers," said big Roadstrum. "We've made our pan, so we'll fry in it. Is that the way the saying goes? Let's just take a look at the accomodations here, fellows."

"You are not free men to be making examinations," said Tiresias. "You show signs of levity, and that is the one thing not permitted here. This place is for serious persons only. If you are not serious now, by hell you'll get serious pretty quick! Hear it! You are sentenced to durance forever. Process them, minions."

"Hold it!" Roadstrum roared. "Hell, this isn't Hell! Crewman Bramble, you're the nearest thing to an intelligent man we have in our party. Can this hayseed place with that pathetic ineptitude on the bench be Hell itself?"

" 'They order things so damnably in Hell,' as the philosopher said. I don't know, Captain; I just don't know. It might be."

"Puckett, go that way," Roadstrum ordered. "Trochanter, go the other. Blinky, shut up. Report back to me within the hour on the size of this place and the torture facilities here. Now then, Blinky, while they're about it, I'll just have a look at that register of yours there and see who is signed into this place. Kstganglfoofng!! It's hot!" (Roadstrum sometimes used high-Shelta swear words, as did many skymen.)

"Of course it's hot, Roadstrum. Everything is hot here," said Blinky Tiresias, "and you won't get used to it."

"That's all right; that makes it a little more like the real thing. A man'd have to have asbestos hands to handle that register, but why are the names in it writ so small?"

"Everything is writ small here, Roadstrum. There's such a lot to be crowded in."

"But you do torture, you do rend and tear, and break and burn?"

"Certainly, certainly, Roadstrum."

"You have all the monsters and stenches, all the white-hot rocks, all the pits of flame, all the soul-burning regret, all the horror and shrieking without end?"

"We have it all, Roadstrum. You will have your surfeit of it."

"But it bedevils me, Blinky, where you have room for it. This is a small place."

"We haven't room for it. It's awfully crowded. Millions and millions, you know."

Looking generally bedraggled and with their feet smoking, Puckett and Trochanter were back from their explorations.

"I believe it's a fake, Roadstrum," said Puckett with deep disappointment. "This isn't the Hell I believed in. It's as though we looked at it all through the wrong end of the glass. Oh, there's torture enough, crude and raw, and there are the millions of sufferers. But it's all too small, too small."

"It isn't a hundred meters across," declared Trochanter. "And the tortures are repetitious. No real imagination in them. Not what you'd like. I think we'd better shop around for a better Hell before we commit ourselves here."

"You can't," said Tiresias. "You're already committed here. This is all the Hell there is."

"Be reasonable, Blinky," said Roadstrum. "What reason have we to believe you? It seems inadequate to my men and it seems inadequate to me. This petty place cannot be—"

"This petty place cannot be Hell, Roadstrum? Ah, but it is, my friend. That, you see, is the hell of it. Minions, minions, we waste time. Prepare them."

"Blinky, where are the towering flames?" Roadstrum demanded.

"It's all high-frequency cookers, Roadstrum. No smoke, no flame, no mess."

"But it's too small. There is not even room for all the old-time horse-thieves."

"It is crowded, yes, but we make room. Get with it, minions. First you will miniaturize them."

"Miniaturize!!!" howled Roadstrum. "Miniaturize!!!" howled they all.

"Nobody will ever miniaturize me!" Roadstrum roared. And then he broke loose with an inexcusable display of shouting and bad manners:

"It stifles, it shrinks! Where are great fires and the bottomless pits? Where is the howling of the triply-damned, and the clanking of monsters? I'd go to Hell in black glory if it fell to my lot, but I will not abide in this place! It's a rumble, men; rise in your wrath! Break out of it!"

"It's a rumble," they roared like cresting waves, great

112

Puckett and Trochanter and Clamdigger and Threefountains and all.

Man-a-bleeding, but they broke out of that place! You say it can't be done, but they did it. Their expectations had been too high, and no second-rate Hell could hold them.

In a way, this was their greatest feat. No one else had ever broken out of there before. But they were still in sad straits, without craft, lost and in great pain, mired in the boiling swamps a little to the south of Hell. How, how would they ever get off of Hellpepper Planet? Was it possible that any of them should live through this thing?

CHAPTER EIGHT

More gory episodes omit we ken of them;
The Chantey sings ten years filled up with ten of them.

Of crewmen dead we weep, and what a row they had!
And some had gotten home but none knows how they had.

All high adventures, twined as vermicellio,
Through carpers carp "the thing's distinctly paleo."

Great Road-Storm wished he'd never seen the first of it,
He didn't guess the last would be the worst of it.

Penultimate we give with wry apology
This mithermenic of a new mythology.

Aliunde

ROADSTRUM always said that he walked home from Mars,
the last lap of his journey. This may not have been true.
He had fallen into habits of untruth somewhere along the
way. But he came home, home to Big Tulsa the marvelous,
the Capital of World.

He arrived alone, in evil case, to find troubles in his
house. He was broke and bewhiskered and tired to the
marrow of his bones. And yet he was a man of means,
so he made a short visit to replenish those means.

The bank had been modernized. It was a transparent
young lady who waited on him. It wouldn't have startled

him on one of the other worlds, but it did at home.

"I am unsure," he said. "Are you people?"

"I also am unsure," said the young lady, "since our position is presently under litigation. Actually we are the newest thing in people. Soon there will be none produced in the old manner. You will have to admit that it was a very grotesque arrangement. Here is your account, Mr. Roadstrum, supplementary name Great Road-Storm."

"Ah, it shocks me to see how it has shrunken." Roadstrum studied it. "It may yet be enough for a modest life, but something has gone amiss with it."

"There have been some fabulous withdrawals, sir. Not many fortunes would have survived such. Is this all you wish to withdraw now, sir?"

"That is enough for now. And block the account."

"Block the account? Penny will be furious."

"I hope so. Thank you, young, er—lady."

Roadstrum went to his house. Little Tele-Max was playing out front. Tele-Max was still little. Roadstrum had been gone for twenty years, what with one thing and another. The kid was a runt or he'd have grown bigger than that.

"Hello, Papa," Tele-Max said.

"Hello, Tele-Max. How did you know me?"

"From your pictures. You have become a legend; but that was several years ago; you're pretty much on the shelf now. There is nothing older than yesterday's legends."

"I know it. But what is that hellish racket, Tele-Max? You'd think even the trees would drop dead from that terrible noise."

"Oh, that's Mama and the suitors, and the song they always play. The trees did die from the noise. These are artificial trees."

"Suitors? What are they doing, having a party?"

"Papa, they've been having a party for twenty years."

"What do the neighbors say?"

"I don't remember any neighbors. I guess they all left a long time ago."

"That song is like salt in an open wound, Tele-Max. Did not your mother used to play it to excess many years ago? Did I not once destroy the tape of it?"

"So family tradition has it, Father. But they have worn out more than five hundred tapes of it since. That is the latest version they are playing now, by the Chowder Heads. You could hardly have heard it before."

"All thanks for small favors. I've been made a monkey out of by singing that *was* singing, and should I fall to this? I tell you what, Tele-Max, your mother has not seen me for

115

twenty years. Another couple of hours will not matter. I will have to find the strength to face this. I wonder what I did about the suitors the first time. Wasn't there a first time?"

"The first time, Papa? The story is that you impressed them by shooting an arrow through twelve holes in a row. Later you killed them."

"What is an arrow, Tele-Max?"

"I don't know either, Papa."

There is one place where all the important persons of World come at least once a day, the Plugged Nickel Bar; and Roadstrum's old mates were all, in their own way, important persons. Roadstrum entered the portal (it had only a single narrow door) and the only one of his old friends he saw was Margaret the houri.

"Are you ship, shape?" he asked her.

"I am always ship," said Margaret. "I remember you a little. Were you not a pet monkey that I once had."

"I was a pet monkey, but you didn't have me," he said. "Want to tie one on, Maggy?"

"Maggy? I, sir, am Charisse, or perhaps I am Chiara. I have been trying on roles. This time I shall assume a very arty role. Everything has become very arty on World."

"Ah well, Charisse or whoever, want to swing a gantry?"

"What an antiquated expression! No, I do not. No offense, but not with you. You are a space-ace. Don't you know that they're dead?"

"Most of them are."

"Oh, they're finished. The swish boys are all the thing again. I will get me a very delicate one, a limp limpet. It is all the thing to be very delicate and a little weary."

"I'm a little weary, but not that way. Sorry to have seen you Charisse, or should I say Chiara?"

"Melisand. I just believe that I will be Melisand."

"Hey, Cap'n," a huge slack-faced man called to Roadstrum. "Come bust a bottle with me. I think I used to know you before I got muddled in the head."

"And after the holocaust, God made green grass again!" Roadstrum roared happily. "Trochanter! Spleen of my spleen and aorta of my aorta! Trochanter!"

"Easy on the sloppy stuff, Cap'n. I like you too. Let me poke you one to see if you're real. A lot of them aren't. Hey, you are real."

"Of course I'm real!" Roadstrum swore, picking himself up from the floor (Trochanter poked hard). "Did any of the other men survive? Have you seen any of the others?"

"I talk to Cutshark and Crabgrass quite a bit."

"Trochanter, Crewman Cutshark died in the maw of the Siren-Zo, and Crewman Crabgrass was eaten by the Polyphemians. They're dead."

"I didn't say they weren't dead, Cap'n. I just said I talked to them quite a bit. I'm addled in my wits now, I've told you."

Trochanter, the crewman without peer! He was as rough a fellow as Crewmen Birdsong and Fairfeather, who had remained on Lamos to become giants. He was a hornier stag than even Crewmen Clamdigger and Threefountains. An incandescent, heavy, tall man. But some of the light had gone out of him now. He was still heavy, but not so—

"You aren't as tall as you used to be, are you, Trochanter?" Roadstrum asked him.

"Nope, burned the bottom half-meter of my feet and legs off on Hellpepper Planet. You remember that ruckus, Cap'n. Hottest ground I ever saw there! Say, I talk to Crewman Clamdigger sometimes too. I think he's alive. He seems solider than Cutshark and Crabgrass."

"Ah, several of us have survived, then."

"Cap'n, anytime you want to go again, I'll be here. You can't tell. You just might want to go again sometime."

"I will remember," said Roadstrum. "It is very unlikely, but if I ever go again I will certainly take you along, Trochanter."

"Captain," called the nameless houri, "if you *really* want to go again, I'll forget the Charisse and Chiara and Melisand bit and go along. And Crewman Clamdigger *is* alive. He bought the shell of a junk hornet with his last Chancel. It hasn't any drive in it, it won't go at all, it's not worth a thing, but he lives in it and broods. If you do go again, we have the beginnings of a crew."

"It is very unlikely, but I will remember it, Margaret the shape, and great Trochanter the crewman without peer!"

Roadstrum left the Plugged Nickel Bar with mixed feelings. He had regained part of the strength he needed to face things at home. He strode along with resolute step, and suddenly he discovered that his resolute steps were not reaching the pavement.

He had been grabbed by the hair of his head, lifted up by a great hand, and was pulled into a second-story window. There was booming laughter that reminded him of that of Bjorn on Lamos. But it was Bjorn's little boy, Hondstarfer.

"What on the wall-eyed world are you doing on World!" Roadstrum howled. "Hondstarfer, you are ungent for my sore sclerotics! Hey, did you ever get back far enough to be an old-time railroad hobo?"

"I got back there, Roadstrum. That's why I came to World in the first place. But the other hoboes wouldn't accept me. They were afraid of me. They said I was a railroad bull. What's a railroad bull, Roadstrum?"

"Don't know exactly, Hondstarfer. I didn't even know the old vehicles were sexed. What are you doing now, you old hammer-handler?"

"I'm a design engineer for the IRSQEVWRKILOPNIX-TUR—"

"Yes, I know the bunch. They're a good outfit."

"—MURFWQENERTUSSOKOLUV—"

"I know the bunch, Hondstarfer. This is their building here, is it not?"

"—SHOKKULPOYYOCSHTOLUNYYOK—"

"Dammit, Hondstarfer, I said I knew the bunch. No use giving me the entire initials of the agency. How are you doing with them?"

"—TWUKKYOLUVRIKONNIC—that isn't the entire initials of the agency, Roadstrum; that's the short form. Oh, I'm doing pretty good. I'm a seminal genius, they say, and I have the most sophisticated tools ever devised to work with. And I do build some good things for them. I'm quite successful. I'll tell you something, though. In the daytime, with all those sophisticated tools, and particularly if someone's watching me, I just stall around. But at night—"

"Ah, at night! What do you do then, Hondstarfer?"

"Put away those damned sophisticated tools and get out my stone hammers. That's when I build the good stuff. Don't give me away, though, Roadstrum."

"No, I won't give you away. Hondstarfer, poor addled Crewman Clamdigger has purchased the shell of an old junk hornet, and—"

"I've seen it, Roadstrum."

"Of course it wouldn't be possible to put it in flying condition."

"I could do it in about an hour, Roadstrum. I'm good on those hornets. You going to fly again? I want to go along."

"No. I don't think there's a chance in a thousand that I'll ever fly again, Hondstarfer. It is just that my mind dwells on the old days."

Roadstrum left Hondstarfer and the MURFWQENERETC Building then. He had regained the strength he needed to face things at home.

That song was still going on, and it was still the

Chowder Heads singing it. Roadstrum groaned within himself.

Then he went in and killed the suitors. It seemed to be what was expected of him. It was fun while it lasted. You know how those things are.

So he had everything now. He had dear Penny again. He had come back home in his deep maturity, home to green World, the world of his youth. He was still a man of means (there were many accounts that Penny didn't even know about) and he had the ability to multiply those means. He still owed titles to several worlds to the men's-room attendant on Roulettenwelt, but he saw that by shrewd management he would be able to pay the remainder of this debt.

He had honor, he had respect, he was a high hero. He still had his health, despite the deep inroads made by events. He had sloughed off all the outer layers of him and became the essential onion, pungent and powerful and of an immediacy that sometimes brought him close to tears.

He had, you may have forgotten this part, one eye in his head and the other eye in his pocket. He took the other eye in his hand when they wished to discuss matters, and now he talked to it straight.

"Eye, my eye, everything is wonderful with us. We are home in peace. We have wonderful Penny again. We have the world of our youth. We are honored and respected and one other word which I forget. We have come to the peaceful end of our journey. Why does that sound less exciting every time I say it.?"

The eye in his hand winked at him dourly. Eye was a tough old gump, not much given to easy enthusiasms. Roadstrum put it back in his pocket and once more contemplated his good fortune.

He would stick it out at least a week, he had promised himself. He had already stuck it out for three days, and that's nearly half a week. He didn't hang around the house much anymore. The Intimate people were doing a series on Penny, and there were always half a dozen of their fellows there getting down her poignant memories of her dead suitors, the more than a hundred of them.

"There was Thwocky," she had said. "Shall the first installment be my memories of Thwocky? He was the one you killed first; you remember, Roadsty? Drove the spindle of the player right through his head. Now, of the permissive-motivation of Thwocky, in the impulse patterns and lassitude-conjointment, there are nine salient aspects which I shall discuss as I build up the foundation of our intimacy.

This can best be understood in the nimbus of the empholeuon motif, which—"

Penny had always talked like that, but sometimes he hadn't listened. Now he found it harder and harder to seal off his ear. But it was still wonderful, all wonderful. He had honor and respect and another word which he had forgotten. He was home from his life journey, he had peace and benignity and benevolence and all good things and happy.

But there was one word in this setup that didn't sound right to his ear. Ear, not ears, he now had but one. Which word? What was wrong with a word? What was there of trickery about a word?

He thought of it while the afternoon deepened into evening. He thought of it while the artificial locusts began to chatter and hammer in the artificial trees. He went home and locked himself in his soundproof room, while Penny was telling revealing things about her suitors.

All things possessed in perfect peace for the rest of his life! And one word was wrong there? What word was wrong?

"Eye, my eye," he said as he took it into his hand. "All things are wonderful, and can you say that anything is wrong?"

But the eye closed on him in disgust.

Honor, respect, enjoyment, peace, conjugal love, ease, peace, benignity, peace, perfection, honor, peace. What was wrong with one of the words?

Peace. How does that sound again? Peace.

It exploded inside of Roadstrum. He erupted out of the building in a place where there had never been a door, strewing sheets and beams of the building after him.

"Peace?? For me?? Roadstrum, man, it is yourself you are talking about. Let you not hang it around your own neck! I am great Road-Storm! Peace is for those of the other sort!

He found his foxy forked tongue, and the roots of a deeper tongue that had been torn out, and gave great voice.

"I will be double-damned to a better Hell than Hell-pepper Planet if I will have my ending here in peace! Peace be not the end of my epic! An epic has already failed if it have an ending. I don't care how it ended the first time—it will not end the same now!

"I break out of it! Nobody will sing the last lines of me! A crew! A craft!"

His great voice reached all the way to the Plugged

Nickel Bar and to the MURFWQENERETC Building. The great voice set up echos in old addle-brained crewmen, in a heartless houri, in an overgrown kid from Stone World.

Roadstrum ran away from the bloodless buildings and stood in the open. He took again from his pocket his off eye, his last companion.

"Eye, my eye," he trumpeted. "Look at me! There are places we have never been! There is blood we have not spilled yet! Shall we let them restrict us to a handful of worlds. Eye, my eye, are you with me?"

And the eye came alive and gave a really joyous wink. A hammer-handling kid was already at work on the junk hornet. The lights turned on in dim-witted crewmen who became incandescent again. And others of their kind gathered to them.

"Men! Animals! Rise you up!" Roadstrum roared. "To come to the end of a journey is to die. We go again!"

Roadstrum got a craft and a crew. He went away once more.

Alas, we have the terminal report of him!
The coded chatter gives the sighted mort of him,

How out beyond the orb of Di Carissimus
His sundered ship became a novanissimus.

His soaring vaunt escapes the blooming ears of us,
He's gone, he's dead, he's dirt, he disappears from us!

Be this the death of highest thrust of human all?
The flaming end of bright and shining crewmen all?

Destroyed? His road is run? It's but a bend of it;
Make no mistake, this only seems

the end of it.

Fourth Mansions

CONTENTS

I: I THINK I WILL DISMEMBER THE WORLD WITH MY HANDS

"For there are all these obstacles for us to meet and there is also the danger of serpents."
Interior Castle: Teresa of Avila

THERE IS entwined seven-tentacled lightning. It is fire-masses, it is sheets, it is arms. It is seven-colored writhing in the darkness, electric and alive. It pulsates, it sends, it sparkles, it blinds!

It explodes!

It is seven murderous thunder-snakes striking in seven directions along the ground! *Blindingly fast! Under your feet! Now! At you!*

And You! You who glanced in here for but a moment, you are already snake-bit!

It is too late for you to withdraw. The damage is done to you. That faintly odd taste in your mouth, that smallest of tingles which you feel, they signal the snake-death.

Die a little. There is reason for it.

There was a young man who had very good eyes but simple brains. Nobody can have everything. His name was Freddy Foley and he was arguing with a man named Tankersley who was his superior.

"Just how often do you have to make a total fool of yourself, Foley?" Tankersley asked him sharply. Tankersley was a kind man, but he had a voice like a whip.

"An enterprising reporter should do it at least once a week, sir, or he isn't covering the ground," Fred Foley said seriously.

"You do it oftener," said Tankersley. "Why is your nose bleeding, Foley?"

"I do it oftener because I'm more enterprising than your other reporters. Oh, my nose bleeds every time I get caught a good one there."

As all cats (and especially tigers) are loose in their skins, this Freddy Foley was loose in his face. There was room there for far more things than his winking innocence and his easy grin. There was room for multiplex character that Freddy hadn't developed yet, for expressions he had never used. It was a face unplowed, though momentarily bloodied.

"This should count for several times," Tankersley went on. "This goes beyond being a total fool. Do you know what position Carmody Overlark holds?"

"Special Assistant to Secretary of State."

"Right, Foley. And you come here with this cock and bull story—"

"Capon and steer story rather. Surely you know that much about the Mamelukes."

"And because his given name is Carmody, and because there lived more than five hundred years ago a man named Khar-ibn-Mod— Say, your head is gashed badly too! Did someone do it to you on purpose?"

"Yeah, they tried to kill me, I think. And this Khar-ibn-Mod had the exact appearance of Carmody Overlark. It's a face that could happen only once."

"Some similarity. An old woodcut is hard to compare with a face that neither of us has seen except on paper or screen. Who tried to kill you, Foley?"

"I don't know exactly. I could figure it out, but this Carmody Overlark story is much more important, and I request permission to follow it out."

"Well, you are most certainly denied that permission,

Foley. How would a man who died five or six hundred years ago—?"

"But we don't know that he died. History is strangely silent on that point."

"History is strangely silent on millions of small details. History would more likely note it if he didn't die. And that is all you have?"

"Oh no, Mr. Tankersley. I've come on quite a few more details and they all confirm my theory. The difficulty is that they sound a little improbable. If you won't accept the possibility that Carmody Overlark and Khar-ibn-Mod are the same man, then you sure won't accept the less conventional details. They make the main statement sound like the time of day."

"And I'm about to bid you the time of day, Foley. I believe I'll put you on the seismic disturbance case."

"No sir. I already know all about that. It isn't interesting when you know it."

"You know what's causing the low-grade seismic disturbances coming from the hills northwest of the city these last several evenings? Then you know more than quite a few smart people know. Tell me, Foley."

"No sir. You'd believe me even less than you believe the Carmody stuff. They aren't low-grade disturbances, though. There's a lot of twisted stuff in that bunch but it isn't low-grade. It isn't even physical. The little earthquake jolts are mental, but they fool the people who feel them."

"I don't believe you know what low-grade means in this sense, Foley. But they certainly are physical. Mental jolts will not fool or affect instruments."

"Yes, Mr. Tankersley, I believe they will. But I want to stay on the Carmody story. Mr. Tankersley, did you ever feel that someone is sucking out your blood or ichor, draining you of the fluid that might let you become a little more than a man? Or did you ever feel that there

was a net cast over us and we were all held in this
net by a hegemony of spiders as yet unidentified?"

"Those spiders are my reporters, Foley, and they do
spin some pretty thin stuff. Now I will tell you one
thing: there are *stories* that reappear with the same
faces when they should have been dead for more than
five hundred years. And there's a special aspect to reappearing stories about reappearing men: follow one
out and you will be killed for it every time. I don't
know why this is so but I tell you that it is. They may
have attempted you already and you too dumb to
know it."

"No sir, I'm not too dumb to know it. I know they're
trying to kill me or scare me to death."

"Ah, why don't you take off the rest of the day and
get drunk, Foley?"

"I did that Monday on your advice. I'd still rather have
followed up *that* case."

"Well, it was better than having you go off quarter-
cocked on the Knoll story. That would really have gotten us laughed out of town. And this thing now, *drop it!*
No more Carmody stuff. No more stuff of men who
live for centuries or who live more than once. Try one
more bender for my sake now, and I hope to see you
tomorrow morning, red-eyed and trembling, with your,
ah, sanity restored, and ready for work. Get out of here
now."

"Yes sir," Freddy Foley said, and he got out.

Good eyes but simple brains, that was Foley. He really
could see at levels where many folks cannot, where Tankersley could not; where even Jim Bauer sometimes
could not.

The Harvesters had begun to meet in the evenings at

the home of James Bauer. It was a nice place on
side above a lake and Bauer had named it ?
the mansion.

("*Morada,*" an ashen voice conveyed, "besides meaning a dwelling place, means a sojourn; but *morada* also
means mulberry-colored, or violet, or purple: the color
of the sky at dusk in mid-winter, the color of snakes in
shade.")

There were seven of the Harvesters. It takes at least
seven to make up a set at brain-weaving, and this was
their favorite game. They met in the evenings especially,
and often in the daytimes, for they all had a sort of
entanglement going about each other. Apart from each
other they were powerful in their persons. Together
they became critical mass.

Morada was the home of Jim Bauer and his wife Letitia. The Manions and the Silverios lived quite close
by, and this made six—just short of the critical mass.
Bedelia Bencher was free to be anywhere at any
time. Now she came to Morada every evening. She completed the weave. Thereupon there were low-grade
seismic disturbances, earthquake jolts which were mental but which fooled instruments and men.

The weave was a most peculiar perfect circle—it had
two discrete ends. One was the airy Bedelia Bencher.
The other was the massive Jim Bauer.

This Jim Bauer was in oils, in the splotchy sort of
oil-painting that Eakins did do well, that should have
been sketchy in result, and wasn't.

(*Wait—a bird just fell to earth not eighty feet from
this Bauer; fell to earth with every bone in its body
broken. It was a large dusk-flying bird of the kind that is
called Night-Hawk, and it fell with resounding concus-
sion. Only a bird that is already dead will fall heavily
like that. Nothing to be done about a dead bird. Continue.*)

Even when in motion, James Bauer seemed always to

be posed for such a portrait. He was a big, young-looking man, and it was all choice beef that hung on him. He had a rich voice and he had been a rich boy. This still made a difference to the two other men present (or coming into presence), though they all were passing rich now. These three had been to grade school together at St. Michaels, and they still adhered together for all the differences and years. It made a difference that Jim Bauer had been the rich kid, that he had been to Europe and to Rio while he was still a boy, that he had been off to rich-kid boarding schools some of the years. It made a difference that he had known the names of operas and things like that, that he had had French cigarettes in French packs when the other ten-year-old kids could hardly come by one cigarette a week.

And this rich-kid air still clung to Jim. A large part of his aura, of his psychic power, was built out of the group remembrance of such things. Well, what is any person's influence built out of if not of trivial but clinging things?

Bauer means farmer or peasant, which Jim certainly was not. It means a knave too. It also means a pawn at chess, but Jim Bauer believed that he was no one's pawn. He was a biologist at Bio-Lab of America. He was a New-Left Actionist; so had his father been, so had his grandfather been. He called himself a Centrist, but he belonged to the eccentric. He was intelligent, or at least of very tough brains, startling mental stamina and well-bottomed memory. He was a pan-math, a catchword artist. He was the Bishop's left-hand man. Jim said that he himself was a privileged mutation, that the whole world was mutating, that it could only be saved by such privileged mutations as were the Harvesters.

Bauer had invented the seven-handed game of brain-weaving. Do not try it! It is a seven-bladed sword; it is no joke. It really can be done, and that is the fearful part of it. Bauer said that it was a patio game; he also said that the health and balance of the world depended on the seven of them playing it well. Bauer spoke with a colorful and intricate rumble. He had copied that rumble from someone; he had practiced it and developed it. It was a part of his psychic power now. It was a personage rumble.

Bedelia Bencher came onto the patio at Morada, and certain flowers in a bowl lifted their heads and followed her.

"I thought those were artificial flowers," Bedelia piqued.

"They are," said Letitia Bauer, "but they've learned to raise their heads when you come just as natural flowers do."

"Has your little Freddy busted on this one yet, Bedelia?" Bauer gave out with his clattering rumble, he also lifting his head at Bedelia's coming. "Have you heard any echos that he's busted on Carmody Overlark? Oh, Freddy is our patsy and our proof! Let us no longer doubt that we can influence minds distantly when we put minds together here. We can sift Freddy Foley like wheat. Soon we'll be able to sift the whole world. It comes the harvest, Harvesters! We can brain-weave, we can influence. 'Bust grandly over the man Carmody Overlark,' we wove to Freddy, and he caught it across town. 'Goof gloriously, Freddy!' we wove, and I felt him take it up. How could anyone touch a man like Carmody Overlark? But your little Freddy has busted on him, I know it, I feel it! It was about mid-afternoon today. Have you heard echoes of it, Bedelia?"

"Echoes? Earth-rumbles!" Biddy Bencher crinkled. "Tankersley called my father; my father called me. 'You'll have to find another boyfriend to play with,' my father said. 'You find me one who's so much fun,' I told my father. Tankersley called me. 'If your father didn't own such a piece of this paper this kid would have to go,' Tankersley told me. 'Why do you fool with the fool anyhow, Biddy?' he asked me. 'He's out of his mind, that Foley kid. He's clear crazy, and he hardly seems to realize that he is. You can't hang a story like that on a dog.' 'But what was it, Mr. Tankersley, what was it?' I asked in my innocent way. 'Wild fillies couldn't tear that story out of me, Biddy,' he said. 'You couldn't hang a story like that on a dog; how could you hang it on a man as untouchable as Carmody Overlark?' But I don't know what it is yet."

This Bedelia (Biddy) Bencher was a drawing in red chalk by Matisse. She was red-haired and lightly freckled and beautifully bony (the last her own description). She had a lustful mouth and innocent eyes, and was full of green passion. She was nineteen years old and had been nineteen for quite a while.

"How can anyone as stupid as you are have a near-genius rating?" her father once ranted. "Those mind-raters must be out of their minds."

"But I've always been near genius, dear Father," Biddy had answered. "We have always been close."

Biddy had no mother. She had been born, she said, near-grown and nubile from her father's forehead. "You can see the scar yet," she'd say, and the father Richard Bencher did have a livid scar across his forehead, but he had a different explanation for it. Biddy *did* have a brain, however, and the seven-minded game of brain-weaving would have been impossible without her.

"Find out, Biddy, what little Freddy has pulled!" Salzy (Ensalzamienta) Silverio cried as she materialized there on the patio. This Salzy was a bit by Degas, yet he would never have guessed the twisted passion of this dark, gay, unsmiling young woman. "Not twisted," Salzy once said of her own passion, "it is helical. That sounds better."

(*A mouse in mimosa roots nine feet from Salzy was blinded with blood and died quietly with its brains exploded. Odd, though: that mouse died with a smile.*

Salzy, in the aura of her, was a gentle and unknowing murderess of many small bits of the ambient.)

"We will not do another thing that involves Carmody Overlark directly," Arouet Manion said dimly. It did not seem that these persons arrived at Morada or entered the patio there. It seemed that they were already there in potential and now became realized, one by one. "We went for Carmody by name and face; we wanted him to play a hilarious joke on himself at a diplomatic function. And he exploded back at us, almost blew our brains out. Yet there is a vacuum there also. He isn't real, you know. We aren't the only ones who have stumbled onto brain-weaving. I can hear that Carmody laughing in my mind yet, and him more than a thousand miles away all the time. And when we linked him with the Foley caper I felt him flow through our minds again. 'Goof gloriously, Freddy,' we wove, but Overlark himself added something to that weaving. I'm almost afraid to find what idiocy Freddy has busted this time."

This Arouet Manion was a Reynolds piece. Having a Reynolds face, he appeared more profound than he was. But that maker touched many of his characters with his irony. (*One hundred yards away a good man fell from grace in an instant, sinning silently to himself, and then reaching for the telephone to actualize that sin; it was the sin of calumny. It was not an ordinary sin to this man. It came to him in a wave of sticky evil, as an outside influence.*) Manion had a size and strength of both mind and body. It might be of poor quality, but there was a lot of it, enlivened by boundless energy. Manion was a doctor, a psychiatrist. He was a semi-pro psychologist and an amateur philosopher. He was also a Teilhardian and a concordist. Being so, he was a man completely without humor, but also there was nothing serious in him. Turgid, yes, but not serious. But he was one of those who were beginning to move the world, literally.

"We need a new target," sparked Wing Manion, who crackled in the air every time she moved. (Was Wing Manion as sparky a woman as that?) "I say, let our new target be Michael Fountain. He's the most informed man we know. He is also, I believe, the best man we know. It's simply that he's a man of no energy at all. A low-pressure fountain is our Michael. Let's weave power for him, then, so he can move the world. He's the one we need to be Lord of the Harvest."

Wing Manion reminded one of a fish done by Paul Klee: not in her actual appearance, of course, but in her style. Yet she was good-looking, and Klee never painted a good-looking fish in his life. Those Klee fishes, though, they have passion.

(*Instruments at a seismograph lab in the city picked up low-grade seismic disturbance as Wing Manion solidified into the group, bringing it nearer to critical mass. These curious little jolting earthquakes had been recorded for several evenings and there were distracting elements to them. Really, they were not real. "Impulsion without content," was the interpreted reading of the seismometers. Without content? Wing Manion? Those machines are feebleminded.*)

Wing Manion was devoted, she was kind. She loved kids, she even loved rocks. Biddy Bencher said that Wing Manion was a sexpot who happened to be a saint and so was complicated back on herself. Being married to an incompetent psychologist didn't help.

"Don't you think we're being a little too godly in all this?" Hondo Silverio asked the bunch of them. Hondo startled them all anew every time he came into presence, struck them with shivers of fear or at least strangeness. Yet there was no better man anywhere. "Has God called us to be Harvesters? Jim Bauer says that God has called him. Arouet Manion says that God-in-process has called him. Well, nobody has called me except my own depths, and those caverns aren't to be trusted.

We've stumbled onto a trick that frightens me. We really *can* move men and mountains. We really can determine, to an extent, what the world will be. Shouldn't we be giving rather than taking?"

"No, we should take always," Jim Bauer said. "We are Harvesters and we harvest."

"We have come onto the trick of amplifying and projecting psychic energy," Hondo continued. "Look out! By a trick or coincidence, we are all of us people of powerful passion carelessly channeled. By another trick we could turn into rutting animals. We are a bunch of psychic athletes, but we are neither very good nor very wise people. What right have we to pour fire into Michael Fountain or into anybody? We came onto an easy and harmless vehicle in Freddy Foley. He doesn't know what hit him, but I think he enjoys being the half-cocked fool. But we ran into stark and laughing mystery when we tackled Carmody Overlark himself. It's almost as if he were mind without real body. I have the feeling he could have annihilated us if he wished. Let's be careful."

This Hondo Silverio could have been by Ingres. (*Out at St. John's a five-year-old boy had been dying, but he didn't die. His temperature fell six degrees in six seconds. He was well. "It was the big snake, my friend the big snake," the boy said, "he made me well right away. Why don't they let the big snake be a doctor, and make the little doctor be a snake?"*) Hondo was a petroleum geologist and a driller. But he was also historical geologist and archeologist. He said that he had found his wife Salzy in Mexico City. But she said that he had blasted her out of a Mexican shale-formation where she had been in an old and evil stratum with serpents and saurians. There was sometimes a frightening gaiety about this couple, something of serpentine mottled green humor, wholly uncontrollable under-strata of recklessness bursting up in artesian fountains of water that was frosty with forbidden minerals. Oh, Hondo meant it when he said that they should be careful. He meant especially that *he* had to be careful.

"We *hope* that there will be danger in releasing these things," Letitia Bauer said with great seriousness. "We call ourselves the Harvesters and we talk of harvesting a better world. What I want is a livelier life and a deeper one, a life worth living and a death worth dying. I'd see the whole white froth of accommodation and present ease swept away in a moment if it would give us anything deeper." (*Over a hill, and not at all far away, a middle-aged couple jumped to their feet in trembling and horror. It was that damnable harp again! The sudden sounding of it was not pretty harp music. It was unworldly, atonal, now muted, now thunderous, horrifying and charming harp music. For three evenings it had played like that, enough to affright the dead. The harp, a newly acquired antique, was in a room by itself. It harped, but there was no harper, and it had no strings.*) "Ah well, be it that widow and orphan and the weak and deficient are delivered from their poverty, then," Letitia Bauer continued (herself sounding very much like a harp without strings), "but let the strong never be delivered from their struggle! If we have not this hope of danger, then all is lost in a swamp. Each one of us has a dangerous power in his own person. We have it very much more than seven times over when we set up a weave. Dangerous powers are not really dangerous unless they are used. Let us use them! Tonight we will pour what fire and what danger we can into Michael Fountain. There is no man needs them more."

Letitia Bauer was the pale or moon-colored, slim woman whom Burne-Jones had painted several times: as Beggar Main, as Norse Goddess, variously.

The world jerked. Seismometers recorded high-grade seismic disturbance as the brain-weave now came rakishly and dangerously into action while the seven burgeoning persons of it seemed sometimes at ease, sometimes in passion, sometimes doing other things or nothing at all. But they reached critical psychic mass now, and every act of theirs would give a wobble to the world.

The brain-weaving was something that the Harvesters themselves did not understand, though they had developed it deliberately. Now they gathered the power and the goal to themselves, and they projected it. They did not, any of them, understand it completely in their own persons, but they understood it more completely when the seven of them were linked together. Surely they would understand it in near totality when they had linked more and more strong persons to themselves. These seven were all projecting persons and they could feel their own effect welling through.

Jim Bauer, mixing drinks at the little patio wheeled bar, had broken into rumbling and powerful song. Bauer had to have a big belly to support his big chest to support his big rough song. And he had to have a powerful neck to support the powerful and massive head in which so much of his activity was carried out. There was reason for everything in the spreading construction of him.

Bauer projected with big hands, almost with holy hands; he mixed drinks with hands that were like the hands of God-over-the-world. He was the Harvester in his hands, and it meant something. He came at the mind of Michael Fountain then, came with massive head and barrel chest and great hands and rumbling spirit, and slipped off. Came again, slipped again badly, swore with a joyous rumble, came again as he mixed Michael's name with his powerful song, encountered strangeness that he had not known to be in that Michael Fountain, welled in and wrestled with that strangeness.

Bauer was doing things with lime and sugar and tinkling glass rods, and at the same time he was burglarizing a mind eight hundred miles away. But was not Michael Fountain right here in the city?

Somewhere and not right here in the city, a bewildered young man sat upon a battered bed, clasped his hands to his head, groaned deeply, and at the same time grinned a prodigious grin. The young man liked the encounter that stunned him, he liked the new violent pain in his head; he liked all new violent things whatsoever. "I have a new horned-bull in my head," the young man said. He swayed with the pain of it and grinned more goblinishly.

Wing Manion had peeled off a robe and gone down the crumbling steep concrete and iron stairway from the patio to the lake. She was into the chilly December water, and then down deep under the water and crouching in the secret mud. She encanted the name of the quizzical man who was her friend, as much as he knew how to be a friend to anyone. She would give a fiery sword to this Michael and he could turn it which way he would. She would teach this Fountain how to flow! She came to the man in his rumpled house and room.

Michael Fountain knew her mind instantly. He liked Wing Manion, perhaps, more than the others of the group. But he slipped off from her instantly and almost untouched. He had always been an avoiding man. But Wing was puzzled in her surge. James Bauer was not there at work, and James had given the strong feeling that he had entered the mind. Wing broke water and reviewed and memorized the entire world in one intaking flash. Then she descended shimmering under a shelf of striated rock into a catfish castle. She came again at the mind of Michael Fountain with fire and metal and water, and again she slipped badly from him. She came again, slipped, and then struck the mind-trail of James Bauer and followed it seeking entrance. And the entrance she found was the most unexpected sort.

Here was a new area, weird even to Wing Manion, and she added her own weirdness and excitement to it. Who would have imagined that there were such enchanted and crooked groves in dry Michael Fountain? Jim Bauer was there also, and the network had made its first linkage.

"I had no idea there was such a man as this inside Michael Fountain," Wing thought, like a catfish bubbling. "Why, that makes him everything we need. I will give this man inside the sword, I'll teach him to flow. Oh, how I could teach him, how he could teach me! What flow! What a flesh-fountain he is!"

"Now I have a new *bruja* in my head," a young man said. "I like the fire-witch. Which of us shall be burned up first? A bull and a witch, and I rise and go somewhere. There is something that this lout is called to do."

Michael Fountain, the dry man, paced the floor of his cluttered living room with the beginning of worry. Two of the young people had come at him, venturing, and he had sloughed them off. But they had fastened onto something, either inside him or outside him, they were fastening onto something that might already be wild enough without their mind-meddling. And they had accidentally brushed a third something: this was not the powerful, awakening, grotesquely grinning young man with a new bull and a new witch in his head (Michael knew this young man somehow, either inside or outside of himself): this was another and weaker man, a man who had somehow been caught in the cross-blast of it and had died of it. "They've killed a man, unwittingly," Michael Fountain said. "Somehow I will find out who it is tomorrow. In any case I will have to force the wild ones to give up directing their gadget."

Salzy Silverio had gone around the shoulder of the little lake to an overhung natural rock-garden under the cliff. She coiled herself there in the mossy rocks of serpentine shale and water trickled down on her. She was full of her own helical and otherwise twisted passion. Her husband Hondo went around to her, carrving drinks. There were green mottled sparks when the auras of the two of them came into contact. Oh, these were both gracious and benign and urbane persons, full of all graces and grace! Theirs was intelligence and vitality and kindness. and amid. their strong coiling passions was a great center of compassion. They were the great and intelligent and superior and noble snakes such as rule one of the distant worlds of which one reads. Salzy had once stated. when in one of her double-helical moods, that her husband Hondo had two pizzles, as have certain snakes. "Oh. is that true?" Letitia Bauer had demanded at the time. "I'll have to find out whether you're joking or whether it's true. It could be true, you know." "It could be true," Salzy had said snakishly.

Hondo and Salzy had entered the brain-weave, and now there were five additional linkages added to the one that had been before. "That there be fire in the Fountain and new snakes for old!" they wove. They brushed the conventional Michael Fountain but lightly, slipping off and shivering him, and entered at once into the weird young man who was possibly interior to that Michael, who was possibly far distant from him and yet known to him. And that young man was now on his feet, he was running, loping in that ungainly but rapid and tireless way that big men of his race have. He was loping down dusky but warm December streets toward the river. Inside his gloriously bursting head was a she-snake of his own high people, one who had been blasted out of old sleeping shale-strata; and with her was a noble creature as male as himself, deep with artesian welling-up.

Arouet Manion entered the brain-weave with cool pantheistic elegance. He would bring ancient ice and not fire to the Fountain. His spiritual fathers had taught him that the highest goal was to put out the lights of heaven, but the next highest was to exalt the earth. He really had this mystic attachment to the earth and he could communicate it. He had a real place in the brain-weave; it could not have worked fully without him; it may be that his place was to pervert it, but place it was. He touched the surface Michael not at all, he was immediately into the young man.

Arouet did not inhibit the fire-force and violent surge of the mind and network he entered. He sent a rale and tremor through it all, and then a giant reaction. He was like explosion and shattering of ice followed by a steeliness and outre precipitation. The wrongness of the man set up roaring tensions and angry despondencies but it strengthened the intrusion. Its false mystique would influence and move this new dynamic mass for the stark life of its surge. It added its diabolical gaping nothingness, and the reaction to that was white fury. The mind of Arouet Manion had great natural energy wrapped around a void, and it contributed a new angular velocity and a mad rain of strange particles. The brain-weave would not work fully without Arouet; it' would not work fully if any one of the seven were missing. "Pray that it may not work, pray that it may not work at all," Michael Fountain gasped, white and trembling from near brushes with it.

The linkages multiplied, and then multiplied again as Letitia Bauer came with her own ashen and angular passion and swift hope of danger. The brain-weave was fabricating a new and uncontrollable personage in the name of Michael Fountain, but did he know it? He knew it in fright and agony, and he slipped away from it again and again. He had felt the death of one man caught in it accidentally; he felt the total penetration of another. But were not both of these himself in some way?

The brain-weave had entered, deeply and forever, into a mind under that of Michael Fountain, and yet it was a mind associated with his. Had the brain-weave made a new mind and a new man and named it Michael Fountain?

A ghost in red chalk completed the brain-weave, a red wraith of disarming simplicity and shattering profundity: so young an anima that she still had not shook off the poltergeistic manifestations of her own adolescence; a numinous pink spook, lazy with summer lightning and instantaneous with blood-gaiety, shyly murderous, with a laugh like breaking crystal, eldritch and ethereal: Biddy Bencher the young red witch.

They had completed the heptameles, the seven-person weave. It was full to overflowing, and it overflowed with a lightning-line of power.

A loping lumpkin of a young man had fallen in half faint and full pain against the guard-rail of the bridge, bleeding and glassy-eyed. He was struck by the line of power so that the thin soles of his shoes smoked. Such strikes had killed others, but this one would transfix and animate him.

Now he burst into a real *carcajada,* a guffaw, an elephant laugh. He came onto his feet again. He still reeled, but now he reeled with a swagger. He was Miguel Fuentes and he had just become a main person in the world.

"Now I have a *canelón,* a cinnamon cookie in my head," the young man joked with a thick tongue: for *canelón* means gargoyle as well as cinnamon cookie, and Biddy Bencher was both.

"Get out with you all now!" the germinating man ordered. "You have done me! You have changed me the man, and I will remember what I must do. I think I will dismember the world with my hands as though it were a *cabrito*, a kid to be barbecued. I will remember the big thing and I will do it."

This timeless man (who had lately been a young man) lurched across International Bridge and set about effecting certain things in the world.

II: EITHER AWFUL DEAD OR AWFUL OLD

Simplicity into the world all bare,
Unweaponed, careless, witless, artless clown,
Lays hands on curly anacondas there
And drags the very dragons through their town.
Simplicitas: Orthcutt

BIDDY BENCHER came into the Scatterbrain Lounge later
that night. She was fevered and spent, but quite alert
and full of monkeyness.

In the floor of the Scatterbrain there was a bronze
disc countersunk, and on it was the inscription THIS IS
THE EXACT CENTER OF THE UNIVERSE. Whether it *was*
the exact center is an unsettled question. Hugh Hamtree, who owned and operated the Scatterbrain, said
that the disc was already there when he took over the
place. The previous owner, Birdie Mounteagle, was remembered as a whimsical man.

"Freddy, little left eye of an owl," Biddy cried when
she saw young Foley there, "did you not have a startling
idea today? I had heard, no, I had felt, that you had
something going. Had you not a one-in-a-million idea?"
Lustful mouth and innocent eyes, this Biddy was a cinnamon cookie full of arsenic.

"Biddy, I still have the idea, but how do you know?
How are you people monkeying with me?"

"We don't monkey. We infuse with real live pop-skull
and green lightning. I have to know. What was the rare
idea, little frog-foot, and how did it go?"

146

"The same as all my one-in-a-million ideas. I'm not allowed to follow it out. I'm not even allowed to think about it." That unplowed face of Foley was getting faint plow-marks now.

"Did old Tankersley order you to get drunk and forget about it?"

"He did. And it isn't as much fun when you take it for medicine."

"How can men retain positions of authority and remain unreceptive to such striking ideas as yours? Ah, what was the idea?"

"I don't want to talk about it, Biddy," Freddy said stubbornly.

"That's a black lie. You *do* want to talk about it. At least *I* want to talk about it. And are we not one, my own mouse-ear?"

"We are one if you say we are, Biddy. Well, I had the notion that perhaps Carmody Overlark (everyone has heard of him these last several years) was the same man as Khar-ibn-Mod, a Mameluke diplomat who served an Egyptian Caliph some years back."

"How many years back, Freddy?" (*Those* are innocent eyes?)

"About five hundred years, Biddy. It seems sillier when I say it out loud."

"Why, it doesn't sound silly at all, little blueberry bush."

"Why are you about to bust then, Biddy?" (How can he be a man yet, when this she-kid treats him like a kid?)

"It's my new diet, Freddy; I eat nothing but bubbles now. But I can see how Mr. Tankersley might not dive right into a story like that without being pushed. Why do you think they're the same man, bendy pretzel?"

"Ah, they look a lot alike and their names are kind of alike," Freddy said sadly.

"Theories have been built on slighter bases. They

didn't stand up very well, though. How would Carmody still be around after five hundred years, little honey-locust? Wouldn't he be either awful dead or awful old?"

"There's an alternative, Biddy, but I shiver-at mentioning it. Laughter of a loved one can be very cruel. Not that you would laugh at me till I'm gone."

"And not that you love me when I'm not here. Will you tell it to me all at once or a little at a time?"

"A little at a time, Biddy. I love you but I don't trust you. I can hear Bauer and Manion hooting now when they find out what you've made me do. But there's something to it, Biddy! I know now that there is. You've put me onto something real with your meddling. Biddy, find out all that you can about Carmody Overlark. I'm going to find out what he does and how he does it."

"The guy might have gotten froze in a block of ice in that Egyptian river," the proprietor Hugh Hamtree interrupted. "Then they might have just found him and thawed him out a couple of years ago. They deep-freeze a lot of things now. I can't see where they lose any flavor at all. If he was froze solid quick enough—"

"Leave us, Hamtree," said Biddy. "Our private conversation is not meant for outside or outsized ears. There's a man at the front bar who wants a drink and is too shy to ask for it. Your new cashier is being talked into cashing the hottest check in town, and your check-in boy is robbing you blind at this very minute. Be off, or I'll push you into your own ice-maker machine and freeze you solid quick.

"Freddy, little corn-ball, I'm with you to the end, which may not be very long. It's possible that you're using someone's old kidney for a brain, but you're still my boy. I remember several times you've been right when you hadn't any business to be. I was always for the underdog, and, doggy, you're way way under. How can I help you?"

"Find out everything you can about Carmody Overlark,

Biddy. Your father and your friends know people who know details about government people. Find out any odd stories that attach to Carmody Overlark, particularly any new ones that have attached to him in the last year or two."

"All right, Freddy, little oyster, I'll find out what I can. Now I have to leave you and go to find another man in his chambers. Don't be jealous. He's only one of those fascinating older men."

"I have to go see a man too, Biddy. He may already be in bed. He may be provoked with me for waking him up. He gets provoked with me quite a bit. Can I call you a taxi?"

"No, my man is within close walking distance. Will you walk out with me? My man gets provoked with me a lot too. Which one of us are those fellows whistling at, my own woolly-worm? Oh, do you turn this way too? We'll walk together a while, then. I'm very worried about this man. It's been several hours and I haven't heard any news or sirens about him."

"Why would there be? What is it? Should there be news? Shall I call my paper?"

"No, I'll call by his place first. By the amount of powder we poured into him, there should be an explosion by now, Freddy. I turn in here. Oh, is your man in this apartment building too? I tell you, little green cantaloupe, we should have made a tiger out of that man by now. He should have started to pull the world down around our ears already. You take a man as smart and great-minded as he is and build a fire inside him. Oh, how did you know to punch seven? That's my floor. Hey, that's got to be yours too, that's the top floor in the building. Here. Thank you, Freddy; you go on to your own man now."

"You go on to your own, Biddy. Oh, were you coming to see Michael Fountain too? He doesn't know I'm coming. Does he know you're coming?"

"No, I don't think he does. He'll be doubly surprised. Knock and step back, Freddy. He may really have turned into a tiger. He might blast us."

"He's left the door ajar, Biddy. I think he's expecting us, or someone."

"Probably world personages already flocking to—" They went in.

Michael Fountain had only a night-light on. He was wrapped in an old bathrobe and sitting deep in an easy chair. He was sixty years old, lean and lined, only a fringe of pinkish hair around his pate, craggy featured, with a hook to his nose like that of a Plains Indian or an Armenian, but he was perhaps too pale to be either.

"I want to talk to Bedelia, and Freddy wants to talk to me," Fountain said kindly. "Where shall we begin?"

"Oh, begin with Freddy, old earmuff. It will be bloody enough when you start on me," Biddy said, "and you may soften a little in the meantime."

"You think you may have a great silent laugh at Freddy and his caper, Bedelia, and that I will be laughing too. I believe, though, that the several capers of your group have gone past the laughing stage. Just what is it that you want to know about Overlark, Freddy?"

"First I want to know how you knew I wanted to know about Overlark, Mr. Fountain."

"I monitor a few of the antics when I suspect that they are becoming dangerous. The scavengers, who call themselves the Harvesters, instructed you to goof gloriously about Carmody Overlark. What is it, Freddy?"

"I think there's something odd about him. I want to know if you have anything odd. In particular I want to know if there's been any significant change in him in the last year or so, since the beginning of his meteoric rise."

"If he's risen like a meteor then it's quite a dim one,

for he isn't generally known at all. Oh, reporters and dilettantes will have heard of him, of course, but he isn't a big name. There *has* been one change in him in the last several years, though. He changed his name."

"Oh. From what and to what? And when?"

"From Charles to Carmody, and just about two years ago."

"So the Carmody from the beginning has been Carmody only about two years. Why did he change it?"

"He gave numerology as the reason. And you're about to say that an intelligent man does not believe in numerology? But a man doesn't have to give a reason to change his name legally."

"Did he have anything to hide, Mr. Fountain?"

"As Charles Overlark? No, I don't think so, Freddy. He was obscure, but not much more so than he still is. He was and is wealthy. He's always been a heavy contributor to the party. He's a man of natural status. Beyond that he's known simply as a brilliant amateur."

"At what?"

"Ah, an intellectual, a legend, an amateur of all the arts, and a patron."

"Was he actually an artist in any field?"

"I don't think so. I believe he only collected."

"And as an intellectual, has he actually produced anything?"

"Not that I know of. I believe that here he also collected: intellectuals. It was always assumed, however, that he was incredibly brilliant."

"Always, Mr. Fountain? Or only as an afterthought? Would it be possible that his reputation was inserted back in time a little, and that actually he had no reputation at all before his rise?"

"Yes, that would be possible, Freddy. This sort of thing has happened before. The facts that one has always known were sometimes not really known as late as yesterday. Actually, if I should examine my conscience, I'd have to admit that I had scarcely heard of him at all till he was suddenly prominent in his small niche. But there is a retrospect given to him in some manner so that it seems he was always known.

"He isn't a new appearance, though. There have been several well-documented pieces done on him. We can take him back, always in the best circles, to his birth; and we can take his family back as far as we want to go."

"But until his modified meteoric rise he really had nothing but his money to recommend him? He could have been a dolt for all we know?"

"He could have been, Freddy, but he isn't a dolt now. My experience is that dolts are always or ever. . . . I believe that's all you can think of to ask me at this time. But you also wish to ask me questions about another man?"

"No. About the same man, Mr. Fountain. What do you know about Khar-ibn-Mod?"

"Hardly anything, Freddy, but I know all that is known about him. I'm surprised that you should even know the name. I didn't know you were a student of the Mohammedan Middle Ages."

"Do you know how he died?"

"No. I don't recall any mention of his death anyplace. How did he die, Freddy?"

"I don't think he did. Have you ever seen the old woodcut of his face that's in the Cambridge *History of the Middle Ages?*"

"Yes. Let me flash it into my mind a moment. I see what you mean, Freddy. He *does* look a little like Carmody Overlark, doesn't he? It's always handy to have good recall as I have. Does the glorious goof consist of this similarity, Freddy?"

"Partly. Recall it again. Does Khar-ibn-Mod have what you would call an Arabian or Egyptian face?"

"Not what *you* would call one, Freddy. But particular

faces don't really follow racial rules. Besides, the Mamelukes were mostly of Christian European slave origin, taken very young and raised with great selection for their particular duties. I'd say that that face is probably Moravian. So is Overlark's. And the names do chime a common tone, don't they, Freddy? No. I don't laugh at you; I've met such coincidental ghosts before. Anything else about your man or men?"

"Do you know whether Khar-ibn-Mod suffered from asthma?"

"Not that I know of. He didn't live in an asthma climate. But he could well have suffered, and we would still be ignorant of it."

"Carmody Overlark suffers from asthma—these last two years. I found out that much about him myself. Thank you, Mr. Fountain. It's your turn, Biddy."

"Oh. Yes, Freddy, leave us now. Mr. Fountain has some harsh things to say to me and they are not for callow ears. Out, little crackerjack-prize, out."

"I will not. You've witnessed my own bleeding of words, my own great goofing. I'll hear what comes to you. Besides, I'm still a reporter, and you two become momentous people in a very peculiar business that's going on."

"Your little group has killed my favorite nephew and namesake, Bedelia," Michael Fountain said.

"Mikey? Has he died? But he wasn't expected to live. We didn't kill him, he was dying anyhow. Not that I'm callous. Did they call you that he was dead?"

"No. I called them first, to be sure. I had the feeling. He had just died, and I'm not quite sure that he would have otherwise. You and your group are playing a dangerous game, Bedelia, a dangerous and ignorant game."

"Of course we're ignorant. We're pioneers as well as Harvesters and we go into unknown regions. But we're going to set fires in very select persons; we're going to mutate them with a great psychic wave sweeping over them in the evening time when certain rays are most likely for it. And we've done it to you, Michael, we've done it to you. We've made change in you, and now you'll use your great talents in ways you refused to use them before."

"No, you have not done it to me, Bedelia."

"But we have! I was in your mind, we all were. You slipped us, and then we took you from under. We got you, we exploded in you."

"No, you did not. I slipped you, and then I slipped you again, clumsy kids that you are. But you killed Mikey, invoking the same name, and you may have entered another somehow."

"No. You. We were in your under-mind. We reveled there. You don't know it now, but you *will* know it. We've planted you and it grows in you."

"No, Biddy, I slipped you almost completely. I'll have to find out who you did revel in. I will have to see about undoing the harm you've done to somebody. It was not myself, it was not Mikey except glancingly, but it was somebody somehow attached to me, for I felt it strongly. I cannot at the moment imagine who it was. I have no other namesakes that I recall. But it was somebody whose mind has touched mine, who was in a certain accord with me, a young man's mind, and I do not know whose. You're sure you don't know who you bit into, Bedelia?"

"Yes, it was you, you!"

"Not at all. You assault strangers, and at a distance, and perhaps to their deaths. It has to stop."

"It will *not* stop, Michael, old moss-rock. We break new roads. We induce the new human evolution. And you can't even guess what we will do next."

"Of course I have guessed it. You will attempt mutation on yourselves, or perhaps it will be mutilation. It will not work."

"It will work! We've seen the castle on top of the hill.

We'll climb that hill, we'll be the first people ever to climb it. We'll be the first super-people, the first people able to grasp the vision. And we'll lead the rest of humanity up to it. We wanted you to be our first leader, but you've failed us."

"Don't do it, Bedelia. It is likely to kill one or all of you."

"What of it? Surely the chance is worth taking. Despise us, loathe us! We'll show you. We'll redeem you all. We'll make the breakthrough to intellectualized, celestialized, chthonized, socialized, paranaturalized, cosmosized, one-other-word-that-I-forgot."

"Oh shut up, Biddy!" Fountain snapped angrily. "Freddy, drag her and her drivel out of here."

And Freddy Foley dragged Bedelia Bencher out of Michael Fountain's apartment.

" 'Twas thus they stoned the prophets!" Biddy sang defiantly as the door slammed intolerantly behind them.

"You're all of you stoned, Biddy," Freddy told her, "and not on honest hooch either. Get off it, Biddy; that's a crazy bunch you're running with."

"You will notice, Freddy, that my feet do not touch the sidewalk," Biddy said a little later. "I am walking on air two inches above the sidewalk. I would walk higher but then I'd be too high to walk with you."

"You're too high to be walking with anyone anyhow. But why'd you just stumble if you're walking on air?"

"Air-pocket. Oh, I am etherealized, Freddy, I'm a new person entirely. I'll go to my own place now and become cosmic. I don't blink anymore, I haven't blinked for hours; I believe that blinking is a trait of mankind in the transitional stage. I will never blink again. I will not close my eyes again ever, not in life nor in death. I am mistress of all worlds and visions. I will go and paint weird pictures on my eyeballs now. Why not? I don't need them for seeing. I can see with every part of me.

Why are you turning into the alley, Freddy? That's the back door of City Museum down there."

"I know it. The night watchman is a friend of mine. I go talk to him sometimes when I can't sleep at night; and, Biddy, I sure can't sleep at night lately. Not since you snakes spit snake juice in my eye. And now my own girl has turned into one of the snakes. I wish I hadn't seen it happen, Biddy."

"But I am glorious now, Freddy, glorious and glorified. I've already learned a lot of the patter that we Harvesters use. Now if I can figure out what it means I'll be two steps up. I haven't really turned into a snake, Freddy. Good night."

"And find out what you can about Carmody Overlark, Biddy."

"All right, little back-end of a glowworm, I will."

Freddy rapped on an old bronze panel of the back door of City Museum. "One hundred and nineteen long knocks and one short" was the code between the friends, but Freddy never had to knock that many times. The door whispered open. The friend was a young man named Selim Elia, a young Syrian man who loved the museum and faithfully watched over it by night.

"Freddy cannot sleep at night." Selim smiled as he closed the outer door again and led Fred Foley through the dim entry-room. "He sleeps well in the daytime but he sure can't sleep at night. Are the flaming ducks after you again, Freddy?"

"Something like that. Dead ducks keep flopping up in live people, yes, dead snakes and toads. Did you ever look at your girl and suddenly discover that she had toad's eyes, Selim?"

"Mine has basilisk's eyes, Freddy, much more sophisticated. Is it the live things or the dead things that are bothering you tonight, Freddy?"

"It's those that won't make up their mind which they

are. See, there are these brain folks that Biddy runs around with, three Shes out of Haggard and three Borgia types out of Baron Corvo. They mix up this brain stuff and put it out in psychic jolts. It knocked me to my knees the first time they used it on me. Tonight they tried it on Mike Fountain. He slipped them, but it killed his nephew and bit into someone else. Now they're raising up something that would be better dead, and they've put me onto a man who ought to be dead. I want to wander around the museum a while. I *know* the things here are dead."

"No, Freddy, they are not. There is not one dead thing here. You don't understand, Freddy. It is not natural for things to stay dead; it sure is not natural for people to stay dead. You can hear them still, all over this place at night, rocks, bones, skulls, whole people. They get tired waiting for time to get up."

"Selim, your mother was a wanton dromedary. Let's go through the dead rooms. Which is the Aztec room, this? Yes. But it's never too peaceful here. Even the stone faces don't seem dead enough."

"Oh, they are not, Freddy. Look at the mean eyes on that one, and his head no bigger than an apple. Don't put a finger near him, you might lose it. That one got crossways with a rock witch over a girl. The rock witch shrunk him first and then turned him into stone but he sure didn't kill him. Do his eyes look dead?"

"No. But they're only mica or rock-crystal set in obsidian stone. There's nothing alive in here except the imagination."

"All right, then *put* your finger near it, Freddy, try it."

"I will not. Let's find something deader than these rocks."

Freddy Foley looked at dolls, at stuffed wolverines and kit-foxes, at Indian artifacts, at suits of Spanish armor curiously boys'-sized. But he had a new lead growing in his mind. He avoided a room on three sides of it, going around and looking at other things. Then he went into the Egyptian room and Selim Elia followed him.

"Now, this is dead," Freddy said. "These are things you can have confidence in. The same dead things here forever. Pta bless Egypt!"

"Ah, but we have one new piece, Freddy. It is a life-mask and that is unusual. We have many Egyptian death-masks, but this is specifically called a life-mask. It is a molded portrait made on a man then living, and it is the finest thing we have."

"Whose is it? I don't want to see it. Where is it?"

"Behind you, Freddy. We've had it for only two days. It has been verified and authenticated before we got it. The life-mask is that of a civil servant who served under Akhnaton, the heretic king of Egypt. We don't know the man's exact station."

"Special Assistant to Secretary of State," Fred Foley said.

"Really? You have toad's eyes yourself when you try to be mysterious. It's behind you, Freddy. You can't see it the way you are standing."

"Oh, I can see a little without eyeballs myself. How old is the life-mask?"

"Oh, King Akhnaton lived around 1350 B.C., or around 900 B.C., if you follow the timetable of Velikovsky."

"Well, what's the name of the mask?"

"Kir-Ha-Mod is the translation, but we are not sure of the vowels. I myself believe that it should be translit-terated as Kar-Ha-Mod."

"I think so too," Fred Foley said, and he turned sullenly to look at the mask. "Ah, it's yourself!" he jibed at the thing. "And it's my belief that you are only the mask of a mask, sir. Tell me, Car-whatever, do you know who is wearing the mask itself today? Selim, did you just slip a piece of paper into my pocket?"

"No, Freddy. I'm standing ten feet from you. Tell me what this is, Freddy. Mystery doesn't become you."

"It's the same face three times, it's the same name three times. Selim, how would you say Overlark in old Egyptian?"

"Ka-Ra, which means both the food of Ra and the soul of Ra, is also the word for a lark. I don't know what Overlark means, though, other than a name."

"Neither do I. This piece of paper, Selim, which you *didn't* slip into my pocket, gives a certain address, and it tells me to go there right now."

"You are a reporter. Go there. It may have been in your pocket for hours, though, and you just noticed it now. You may have put it there yourself and forgotten it. You know how you are. But go there, tonight or in the morning. Remember, you're the boy who never passes up a tip on anything. You told me so yourself."

"I'll go right now. It says right now. It says to come alone. I'm scared of it but I'll go. Say, those guys are talking Mexican-Spanish and they're cooking up something big. They might really jolt the world, that guy and those he's gathered."

"What guys, Freddy? Those of the address where you're going?"

"Oh no, other guys entirely. Selim, I bet I know something that they don't know about their own brain-weave, and they invented it."

"Who, the Mexican-Spanish plotters?"

"No, the Shes and the Borgias, Biddy's group. You get plugged into their brain-weave and you stay plugged in. They plug into someone else, and you're connected too. And sometimes now I'm connected with him and they're not. Well, one snake-pit at a time; I'll go to the address. It's a spooky part of town, especially this late at night, but I knew it when I was a kid and I still know it. Good night, Selim."

"Good night, Freddy. And, Freddy, you aren't the

only one who's noticed the resemblance of the life-mask to Carmody Overlark. It's been a joke around the museum for these two days."

III: IF THEY CAN KILL YOU, I CAN KILL YOU WORSE

> We have gone higher and deeper than anyone
> has gone before. We have solved problems that
> were always regarded as impossible of solution.
> We have reached a certain firm height in mate-
> rial and physical and spiritual being. We have
> come up in powerful, loose, integrated move-
> ment, and with profound freshness and creativ-
> ity in our group soul; and we have seen the high
> pastures beyond. We come to the verge, to the
> mansions of the fourth height, in a moving mo-
> ment of dizzy expectation and extreme danger,
> up under a new Heaven with a new Earth in our
> hands. *Don't drop it!*
>   *Second Trefoil Lectures*: Michael Fountain

FRED FOLEY swung along with a jauntiness of expectation. This was a section of town that he had always
been a little frightened of, but the frightening elements
were from his childhood.

There had been a brick factory here once. The
offices of the company were still here, but the hive-
shaped baking kilns were now at another location. It
had been from the intense fires of those kilns that
Freddy Foley, walking in the evenings with his father
and not yet four years old, had got his idea of Hell.
Should he be probed even today it would be found that

he had a concrete idea of Hell, that it is hive-shaped like a brick baking kiln and of an eye-burning fire inside.

And with this idea was an early story told him by Sylvester Larker, that they had put a little boy into one of the kilns and burned him up. No reason was given for this. In small boys' stories no reason is ever given for any act, nor is it asked. They burned the little boy all up except his eyes, which turned into agates. These were the same two agates that Sylvester Larker used for taws. They would seek out the marbles for themselves, they never missed; Sylvester Larker had been marble champion. And he had given these two agates to Freddy.

All his life, people would be giving valuable things to Fred Foley unasked: gifts, powers, lives, worlds, secrets.

Also, in this part of town, there had been the brick pit itself, likely the deepest hole on earth. It had a narrow-gauge railway track down in it, and the little cars that shuttled back and forth were wound up from it by cables. There had always been water in the bottom of the pit, however much they pumped it out. And once a little boy had drowned there. He was of Freddy's age, four then, and he was the first dead person that Freddy was ever permitted to see.

There were other elements in that old section which had abiding effect on Freddy Foley. The people of that neighborhood had kept both cows and hogs long after it was forbidden by ordinance to keep them in town. And pigeons—all the families had kept pigeons. There is no accounting for the manner in which pigeons had become sinister to Freddy; it was surely in connection with some story which he no longer remembered. In the early days of that neighborhood, many of the houses still had barns; the barns had lofts, and lofts always have pigeons.

Hound dogs too. The Stamfords had hounds, the Dugans had hounds, the Collyers had both bird-dogs and hang-dog hounds; and kids who have strings of hounds are just naturally tough. This is fact, whatever the explanation of it.

There were the railroads, very strong in the complex of memories. The district was in the V of two lines which joined forces there before they went downtown, and it was there that they always hit their whistles. There had been sidings to the cottonseed-oil plant, to the brickyard, to a fire-belching foundry, to a boiler-maker's. There was the waste land that is always about rail junctions, bogs, weed patches, small pastures, large vacant lots, genuine woods with streams, clay cliffs honeycombed with boys' and hobos' caves, and the Old Show Grounds. The Show Grounds held the carnivals, all the circuses except Ringling's, which was too big for it; and in times between it was always occupied by families of Indians, Gypsies or Mexicans.

Among these was the Larker family. The Larkers could have been any of the three, or could have been something else. Toney, who was Freddy's age, said that they were Indians, that they really owned the whole town-site, that they were going to take it back and make the people pull down all the buildings, and then they would kill them all by putting green rawhide around their necks and setting them out in the sun. This shrank the rawhide and strangled the people to death.

Sylvester, who was two years older than Freddy, said that they were Mexicans, and for proof of this he had a Mexican knife that had killed sixteen men. But Leo Joe Larker, who was the oldest of the Larkers and four years older than Freddy, said that they were Gypsies. He said that they could tell who was going to be murdered and who was going to die that year. He said, moreover, that they could work magic, and that he himself had raised a man from the dead.

But Freddy's father had said that the Larkers were a black-necked bunch of Irish tinkers, the last of them, and that the world would be better when they were gone. The Larkers had a shack that was clapboards on the bottom and canvas on top.

This was the first time in a dozen years that Freddy had been back to that district where he had been raised. He knew about where the address would be. He was going to a meeting with a person whose name he did not know, answering a summons which he had received in an unknown way. "Walk there, and talk to no one, and do it at once," the note said. "You will barely have time."

The face of this district had changed somewhat, but the feeling of it had not. Freddy knew that it was still occupied by the toughest boys in town and that they were no longer small boys. As reporter he knew that the bars here were dingier and rougher than bars elsewhere, that most of the burglars in town lived here, that crimes of violence in the district had a shamefully high index, that there were stories going around more macabre than those Freddy had heard in childhood.

The quarter had always been built up in tight knots of buildings separated by empty spreads. There was something oriental about the crowdedness of the buildings, something medieval about the high-gabled look of them. There were still the vacant lots, still the woods that threatened to take over the whole place with a sudden rush, still the street lights broken out as often as they were replaced.

The house of the address (it had to be the address, though it could not be read in the dark) was a tipsy four-storied frame building with no light at all except a cigarette in the open door. It was a squat earth-giant winking with a small red eye. But what gave Fred Foley the creeps was that he knew what man was standing there, and he couldn't have. Ah well, a fellow who raised a man from the dead when he was no more than nine years old will always have a certain presence about him.

"Hello, Leo Joe," Freddy said boldly. "Is it yourself I am to meet?" It was Leo Joe Larker standing there still unseen, either as blood-curdling boy or as man.

"You know my name? I underestimated you. I'll have to find out how you know my name, since it wasn't told to you," said the black gap behind the cigarette.

"You haven't changed, Leo Joe, except in your voice. I used to know you when we were boys. I can't see you in that dark doorway, though." Nothing was changed in Leo Joe except his voice. But the voice was all that could be encountered of him. If the boy's voice could not be recognized in the man, and if the man himself was invisible in the dark, then what was it that identified him?

"You haven't changed from before?" Freddy added.

"Not changed from what before? But yes, you were the fearful little boy. You had a dog named Popcorn," the voice said.

"And now I am Fearless Freddy," Fred Foley said. "I ask you again. Is it with you that I have this informal appointment?"

"No, Foley, I'm an interloper."

"I'd rather deal direct, Leo Joe."

"I'm putting in first claim on you."

"What for?"

"If you're threatened in any way tonight, and you will be, just consider that I have an override on all threats to you."

"But if my meeting isn't with you, how do you have any part of it?"

"Never mind my part. Upstairs you're going to be threatened by a couple of rough-talking gentlemen. They overdo their threats. But then they also overdo their execution of them. They can kill you, and there's a fair likelihood that they will. It's one thing to be threatened in a very heavy and outmoded style; it's another thing to be killed in that same outmoded style."

"What will they want me to do?"

"They'll want you to lay off the line of inquiry you're on."

"Well, what do you want me to do?"

"I want you to stay on it, Foley. Be dumb, blind, blundering, and silly, but stay on it. You may be dumb enough to get to the core of it."

"Well, will you help me with it, Leo Joe? I'm totally in the dark."

"No, I won't help you. And you seem able to see in the dark tonight. No, you have to go on your own all the way with it. I'm just telling you *not* to lay off. If they can kill you, Foley, I can kill you worse. If they can scare you, I can outdo them at that too. Now go up to your appointment. You better not be late."

"What will I do?"

"Whatever they tell you to do, don't. Whatever they tell you not to do, do it. But say what you have to, to get out of there alive. And don't keep any more appointments in dark rooms with people you don't know."

"If the appointments are in the line of my inquiries, I *will* keep them. Ah, do you ever see any of the old kids, Leo Joe?"

"I don't know anything about old kids. I'm probably not who you think I am." The man came out of the doorway still wrapped in dark, passed by Freddy Foley silently and disappeared. He didn't look much like Leo Joe Larker should have grown up to look like; he hadn't sounded like him at all. The dark glimpse had shown a man who might be a Negro. The voice, remembered now, had something of that tone. Nevertheless, Fred Foley believed that this interloper man had been Leo Joe Larker when he was a boy.

Foley entered the dark doorway of the building. He

felt his way up the stairway. It wasn't too difficult. All these old wooden apartments were built alike. This one, Freddy now suspected, was empty and condemned; and he knew that the only light he would see would be one coming from under the door of a room on the top floor. He knew his appointment would be in such a room, though the note hadn't told him of that.

Freddy saw the slit of light as he shuffled to the top step. He opened the door and went in. He pulled up a chair and sat down at the table with the three men. "It's your move," Fred Foley said.

"You've been asking questions about a man who has been replaced," the first man said heavily. It was pretty dim in there. The light that Foley had seen slitted under the door was from some sort of carbide lantern such as hunters use. The lantern was sitting on the floor and did not illuminate the faces of the men well. Apparently the utilities were off in this building. "Don't you know that you can be replaced as easily?" that first man asked.

"No. If I thought I could be replaced, I wouldn't worry so much about myself. How can I be replaced?"

"By another man named Fred Foley who would be identical to you in appearance. But he won't be going around asking questions," that first man said.

"Actually I wasn't asking questions about a man who has been replaced," Freddy said. "I think I've been asking questions about a man who replaced another. That's where my interest lies."

"Then you're asking questions about the wrong man, Foley. Your own situation is like that of the man who was replaced. You should wonder what happened to him."

"I hadn't given him a thought. All right, I wonder what did happen to him?"

"He ended, Foley, and without a trace. It can happen to you, tomorrow, even tonight. You would not be at all. You would be worse than dead. And not only would there be no trace of you, but there would be no one wondering where you went. Another Fred Foley would be walking around in your clothes, wearing your face and your body, living in your rooms, holding your job. But he wouldn't be you. And you wouldn't be anything, anywhere."

"So I should stop asking questions?"

"You should stop even thinking questions," the second man at the table said.

"The replaced man may not be in complete oblivion," Freddy hazarded. "I may follow that line of inquiry by being a replaced man and seeing where it leads."

"We won't be mysterious about it," said the third man at the table. "It leads to physical death. Some of the victims die in pretty heavy agony. Some of the dispatchers get a lot of fun out of it. It's my own kind of fun. You can follow that line of inquiry if you want to, Foley, but it will be hard to get your story back from the other side."

Foley passed his hand before his eyes. There wasn't anything there. It had been as though a strand of gossamer or spider-silk had touched him. Those things aren't very thick. It would take a lot of them to entangle a man. It was an old spider-silk, though, and it dangled out of a web of old memories.

This room, this old rooming house, was on the edge of the Old Show Grounds where the carnivals used to set up. Foley remembered one show where a man sawed a lady in half. What happened, someone had told him, was that the man didn't saw her in two at all; it was a trick. But what really happened, Leo Joe Larker had told him (Leo Joe the boy who seemed to have grown into an altogether different man), was that the man sawed her in two all right and she died. Then they got a different lady to show the people out in front. They used up about five ladies a day with the act. Freddy had always believed Leo Joe's explanation of how it was done, rather than the weak silly stories that others had given him. "But what do they do with all the dead ladies?" he had asked Leo Joe at the time. That had brought on another story, for there *was* an unusual dispostion of the bodies of the sawed-in-half women. It wasn't very practical, though, and he doubted if these three men here would use the same method. What he had asked then and what he almost asked now was "Why would anybody want to kill all the ladies?"

But what he really asked out loud now was "Why would anyone want to kill Fred Foley?"

"Why *we* might want to kill you is that you have asked too many questions," that third man said. "You asked them of quite a few people. You even asked them of one person who belongs to our group."

"You should wear badges."

"Bravado doesn't become you very well, Foley," said the second man at the table. He was leaner and sharper and more silent than the other two men. "You have little nervous tricks that indicate that you aren't brave at all."

"I know that, men. But I also have sudden impulses that make me so brave that I scare myself. Don't count on me being either way. I don't."

"I doubt that we'll have any more trouble with you, Foley," said the first man. "One way or another, *we will see to it* that we don't."

"Remember, it could happen to you tomorrow," the third man said. "It could happen to you yet tonight."

That was dismissal. Fred Foley left them. The slash of light was under the foor for a moment after he closed it on them. Then it was extinguished. They had put out even the lantern. Fred Foley felt his way down the stairs, bumped into a wall at one of the lower landings (those old apartments were not built absolutely alike, and besides Freddy had now lost the illusion that he could see in the dark), came finally out of the shanty doorway and into the dark street.

The effect that the men had had on him was submerged somewhat in the effect that the district had always had on him. He discounted the encounter much as he used to discount the stories of the Larker boys. But he was not quite sure that those three men might not kill him that very night, just as he had never been quite sure that Leo Joe Larker had not raised a man from the dead.

He walked rapidly the mile toward downtown and his own rooms. He talked to himself, and then to another.

"Take it easy, Miguel," he said. "You can't get it all rolling in one night. Hey, you're gathering a pretty salty bunch already, though. How could I find you if I wanted to join you?"

He was getting a sort of contact with someone who had also been assaulted by the brain-weave. He called him Miguel and not Michael, but he knew there had been a link between the two.

He wasn't through for the night. He needed to ask more questions of someone. He wouldn't go back to Michael Fountain tonight. That man would surely be short with him on a second visit. Fred Foley needed to talk with someone who knew more things than did Michael Fountain.

But there was no such person, not in his acquaintance.

Well then, he needed to talk to someone who knew sorts of things that even Michael Fountain didn't know. And there was only one such person, a blockish ungainly fraud, but he did know things outside the lines.

And here was his very broken and unkempt street here on the edges of shanty-town. Fred Foley turned down it toward the diggings of Bertigrew Bagley.

The authors of the brain-weave believe that they have

transmitted somehow through polarized one-way glass; but it is two-way. The return way is open even when the senders are unaware, and all those who have been touched by the weave are themselves somehow in touch, even when the weavers or Harvesters are asleep.

Thus Freddy Foley now sometimes impinged on the entity for whom he had found the name of Miguel. (He still believed it to be a separated fragment of Michael Fountain. But Miguel, raising an army to take over the world, had already enlisted eight men, three of whom knew where they could get rifles, and this all in one night. Fred Foley knew of this part but he didn't know how to appraise it.) Freddy also impinged on the devious mind of Carmody Overlark, but this always lost him in a laughing swamp.

However, one portion of the brain-weave itself was not now completely asleep. She was wandering in a fitful delirium, not frightful (for it was one of the Shes out of Haggard and nothing could frighten them), but puzzling (even to her of the initiation and the strong psychic powers), frustrating, a rambling-in-waste-places delirium. "I have borne a child out of my body," she said, "I expected him to be beautiful and full of light. Instead of that, he is a deformed monkey." (She had not actually borne any child out of her body except Iracema, a girl who was now eleven years old; but this was another sort of image.) "I wonder if anyone else will notice that he is a deformed monkey," she said. "Many babies look like deformed monkeys, and people are polite about it. I could be loud and confident and carry it off, I know; but perhaps it would be better to destroy the child and bear another one tomorrow. A great thing will happen to me before that, and the child I bear tomorrow night may really be beautiful and full of light."

(This She was the ashen-haired, pale or moon-colored slim woman who had been painted by Burne-Jones several times. She was Letitia Bauer, the danger-loving one of the Harvesters; but even she was not sure in her surety.)

Then the slob came into Freddy's mind. This may have been because he now neared the slob's diggings; or the slob himself may have been a target of the brain-weave. The slob was the sort of man that the Harvesters might try to have fun with, just as they had had fun with Freddy himself.

Two crammed and ponderous minds in two such different containers. Michael Fountain was the very image of distinction, urbane, mannered, of regal appearance and voice, respected in the several communities: an elegant decanter. Bertigrew Bagley was fat and ungainly, grown old ungracefully, balded and shaggy at the same time, rheumy of eyes and with his mouth full of rotten teeth, discredited, violent and vulgar: an earthen pot, and a cracked one at that. But he knew some things that even Michael Fountain didn't know.

Fred Foley had been there once before, as a reporter, trying to pin some ugly rumors on the flush-faced old mountebank. He hadn't been able to pin them on him, and he had been treated better than he deserved.

Freddy went down the three steps to the heavy door and pounded on it. He knew (he shivered at the memory of it) that there was another flight of steps leading down inside. He pounded harder and had the feeling that his pounding could not be heard. He remembered that all doors into Bagley's den were iron-sheeted and muffled, and could be barred with series of long steel bars. He remembered something else. He struck a match to see, and it was so. There was still the plaque there: DAMNED DOOR NOT LOCKED. COME IN.

Freddy went in fearfully. Fearless Freddy was afraid of certain small things that had bitten him before. He stepped carefully, knowing it would be no good. He avoided one rolling thing and slipped on another. Fred Foley fell down the flight of stairs.

He cursed, but not unhappily. It was always adventure to visit Bagley. The place was dark and empty. Then it leaped to half light, and the big man came in and filled it, laughing with a hooting like hippopotami, slipping into a big chair made of a barrel cut down, ensconcing himself behind a big table built out of freight skids.

"You do it best of anyone who comes to visit me, Foley!" Bagley boomed. "Anyone who falls down stairs like that can't be all bad."

"That was a trap!" Freddy snapped, somewhat elated however and knowing that nothing was broken. "Stairs should be kept clear."

"No, they should not," Bagley told him. "Steps are made to put things on. A man is entitled to store what he wants to on his own steps; there's no better place for sorting things out. A man has to use his eyes, Foley, even in the dark. What's the idea of coming here without an appointment?" Bagley was a crackpot, but it was not an ordinary pot that had cracked. It was a giant grotesque Gothic garboon.

And always at Bagley's just around the corner of eyesight, was the dog-ape, the plappergeist that served Bagley. Freddy could not see the thing directly, but he could see its friendly wink. The thing liked Fred Foley. This spook-animal-person went through walls easily and could be inside or outside.

"You ought to have a light so a man could see where he's going, Bagley," Fred said.

"I have one light in the place; that's enough. I said what's the idea of coming here without an appointment?"

"Would you have given me an appointment if I'd asked?"

"Of course not. Damnation, man! I didn't know you

had a bottle! You should have hollered that you had it before you started down. You could have broke it when you fell."

This Bagley had a fantastic erudition (though much of what he knew happened not to be so), a fertile mind, a gift for invective that had left scar tissue on the great and near great for a generation and a half, a wanton contempt for all mankind except a few always temporary favorites, and a deep love for a red-necked brawl. You will remember him writing under the by-line of B.B.B. (he was known as Beetle-Browed Bagley) before he was totally discredited.

"Well, what are you after, Foley?" Bagley asked him after Foley had opened the bottle, pulled up a sort of cobbler's bench, and joined Bagley at the big table built of freight skids. "You came as a slippery reporter before and tried to hang me with a raffish rope. And now I believe that you are involved with a group that has tried to burglarize my mind. They cannot do it. I've a series of long steel bars that I can set into the doors of my mind also. What are you after? I ask you. You don't love me enough to visit without a motive."

"I have a motive, Bagley," Freddy said. "You rode an old horse that got you laughed off the public scene: the old Hidden-Hand running through History and Affairs. It's quite a nag. Now I find myself riding the same horse."

"You're sure you know which end of the horse to get on, Foley?"

"No."

"Because I didn't either. It's a double-rumped cayuse. I never did find the head."

"Did you ever really have anything, Bagley?"

"I thought I did. Now I'm not sure. I believe I was close to something, but I may have been mistaken as to its shape, size, color, and motive."

"Did you ever have anything on Carmody Overlark?"

"Him? No. He rose after I had set. He has all the earmarks of one of them, though. I do not use the phrase as cliché. You have heard of the archaic smile and such. Let me assure you that there is such a thing as the archaic ear. He has it, and most of them have it. The ear is the only appendage of man that has evolved at all during the recorded or pictorial history period. This would be clearer, of course, if the ear left skeletal or bone remains. But the archaic ear has a touch of Pan, and all these repeaters have it.

"When I say this, Foley, I see a look in your eye that is familiar to me; it has been turned on me often enough. When I threw it all over and retired, Foley, I went to a doctor, the least quackish I could find. I asked him to go over me from stem to stern (I told him I didn't know which end my brains were in) and tell me frankly whether I was crazy. He did a thorough job on me, probing both mind and body. When he was finished I asked him for his decision. 'Am I crazy?' I asked him. 'One of us is, Bagley, one of us is,' he told me. That's about as fair a verdict as any man has ever given me."

"I was wondering if there's also an archaic look in the eye."

"Yes. There is, and you have just used it. The ancient skepticism. Which part of the horse are you working to, Foley?"

"The nether ribs, I think. You hinted once that there were certain types of contrary men who occurred so persistently in history that you were double-damned if you didn't suspect that there were certain *individuals* recurring in history."

"Yes, I did hint that, and for that I was crucified upside-down like St. Peter. It's a good thing I didn't say it right out loud. What is your question, Foley?"

"Did you have any theory or idea at all to go with your harebrained hint?"

"There are several theories. Reincarnation seemed to me to be the most likely. I have about a thousand pages of tables worked out, but they don't really jibe unless I cheat on them. I have even applied what I call my epicyclic adjustment to them. In Ptolemaic astronomy, when it was found that the planets did not act as if the Earth were the center, then it was necessary to plot their courses as smaller circles about points on larger circles. The theory had to be propped up.

"When I found that chronological reincarnation was not the answer to the reappearance of perverse men, then I had to add a grotesque appendage to my theory. An evil man dies; and he is followed by another evil man of startling similarity. But the death dates and the birth dates do not coincide. In my thousand pages of tables, I have only six cases that may possibly fit, and even with these I have to juggle a handful of days, or assume minor errors. So I have posed the possibility to myself that the dead man does not necessarily come to inhabit the boy at his birth, or at his conception (for I also tried to make that fit), but may appear in him in early childhood, or with the coming of the years of reason, or even later."

"At the merging of latest youth with middle age?"

"You mean Carmody Overlark? I don't know. That seems a late entry, but there are others even later. My theory remains a very rickety one, however much I prop it up. Can't you afford better whisky than this, Foley?"

"No. But you're convinced there is something in your theory?"

"I am convinced that certain evil men reappear in history in their own personalities. I am still looking for the explanation of it. I believe you have begun to nibble at the same bait."

"You're convinced that they're evil? All of them evil?"

"Certainly. What need has a good man to return?

They are crawling evil. This Overlark whom you are tracking down, you surely see that he is of evil effect."

"Not at all. I was hoping that the returning genii were a benign influence. I've been looking for something to hope in for a long while."

"Foley, man, he's of the old crippling persuasion."

"You know, Bagley, that your views were never popular, even at your peak. And now you've been reduced to a party of one."

"Oh no, there's many of us around, and each of us is worth a thousand of the others."

"Overlark is a brilliant man in the Humanist Tradition."

"At the name of which even buzzards gag."

"I can understand the reason for your unpopularity, Bagley. But now I'm only interested in the reappearances themselves. I haven't attempted to analyze the effect of them."

"My old dog is restless outside, Foley. Someone is laying for either you or myself. I have been beaten up once already this week, and that's par; so I suppose someone is after you. Don't get yourself killed too easily. Foley, you are a slack-eared pup and a disgrace to the Irish. I'd throw you down the stairs if we weren't already at the lowest level. Now sit quietly and finish the bottle, and then you'll have to go. You may not be completely hopeless, however. Once you get your hands onto the thing you will learn a little of its nature. You'll feel the rot of it, the leprosy that will not be stamped out. And you'll see that its face is always respectability. But if you follow it up to the end you will not be respectable yourself. You'll be branded as I have been; you'll find what a tight setup they really have. And you'll see how it is almost impossible that their leaders could have become so astute in a single life. And as you look back you'll come on a man, and you'll come on him again and again, and you'll know that he is the same man just as well as you know anything at all.

"Then you'll wonder (Lord how you'll wonder!) how many of them there really are. How wide is that preternatural brotherhood? There've been a hundred points where mankind was frustrated from real clarification and grace. At each of those points you will find one of those evil men. Who directs them? And why do they obstruct while they mouth progress and enlightenment?"

"You believe in preternatural brotherhoods, do you, Bagley?"

"Belonging to one myself, certainly I do."

"Well, I don't agree that they're evil, or that they're plural. I know one man who has lived too long or too often. But you, Bagley, see everything in black and white."

"Say, that's a pretty good phrase, Foley. Wait a minute till I write it down. Oh, I have some men in my collection who've lived a dozen times. I do not see everything in black or white. I see most things in the four or five central colors or forces. In the middle, of course, is that malodorous worm whom we call common man. He is mud-colored. And around him are the four sorts of creatures who assail him while they claim to love him, but mine is the only sort that actually loves him. Foley, did someone tell you tonight to stop asking questions?"

"They did, and I won't. I'll ask questions till my larynx falls out."

"Boy, you're in danger. Myself, I've always been able to counter them or evade them, but you're not that smart."

"I'm as smart as I need to be, Bagley. What are the four sorts of creatures?"

"Oh, it is all allegory and beyond the comprehension of flatlanders. Foley, a supreme word of contempt is

178

'flatlander.' Somehow there is the belief that people in the Dark Ages believed that the world was flat. They didn't. But it is the contemptuous ones of today who have made a really flat world that is the sad answer to everything. What is wrong with the world and why is it not worth living in? It's flat, that's what. Foley, I have a little room under this rough floor. It's black and full of water but it has a cot. Go down there, they are after you tonight. I know these things. If they come here they will only work me over and I've been worked over often. But they'll kill you if they find you here. It'd mean that you were still asking questions."

"Dammit, fat man, I *will* ask questions and I won't hide. Now tell me what the four sorts of creatures are. I'm not stupid. That's only the permanent impression I leave."

"Oh, the four sorts of creatures that surround the Castle are the Pythons, the Toads, the Badgers and the Unfledged Falcons."

"Oh what botching! Unbotch it, Bagley. Where do you get your drivel?"

"I have it anciently from my own ancient person and position. And beyond that, there are hints of it in the unguarded passages of Anacharsis Clootz, *who was one of us*. Some of it's from the beautiful things of a lady named Teresa Cepeda, born a little after Columbus died. He only discovered continents; she discovered the Castle itself. Hers also was a Spanish venture and it will be weighed in the final balance. Did you know that nations as well as persons will be judged at the final judgment? She will be judged for Spain."

"If I didn't know that you sometimes have a kernel inside the rotten shell I'd give up on you, Bagley. Get specific. What sort of creature am I? Which are you?"

"You are one of the malodorous worms, Foley, the commonality of mankind, the simplicity. Me, I'm a badger."

"Damn if you're not, you snap-jawed fool. Well, what are the others?"

"Your meddling friends, the mind burglars, what do you call them? the brain-weavers, the Harvesters, they belong to the pythons, Foley. But always remember that pythons are prophetic. I don't know why this should be. It seems unfair; prophecy should be given to worthier creatures. These pythons sometimes call themselves the intelligentsia, sometimes the gnostics. They are not knowing, though, they are fools. But they are the proverbial fools who rush in; and, rushing in, they take by storm. Remember first that they are snakes; and second that they are prophetic snakes."

"You may be both parts right about them, Bagley. But I'm still interested in a man or men who live more than once, or seem to. Do they classify among your creatures?"

"Cetainly. The revenants are the toads. They sleep or they die under stones for years or centuries, and then they come out from under the stones. But there is either a legend or fairy tale of the toad with a jewel set in his head. These returners really have the jewel, and it may be the jewel of knowledge. They have this bright thing, just as the pythons have their prophecy; and I wish we had it ourselves."

"All right. What are the badgers? Tell me about them. You are one."

"Foley, it would take many hours to tell about us. We entrench in the earth and we retain an old empire. I don't joke. Ours is the real; but even if I should tell you all about it you would regard us as a network of lodges or curious societies or comical conventions. Can you not see that it is your apparent government and world that is these things? Foley, there are alternate worlds going on all the time, depending only on the vision. There is a double reflection. I do not accept yours, and you sure would not accept mine. But I say that mine is alive and that its more favorable time-track may still be selected. X-ray eyes, Foley, ghost eyes, fish eyes, shadow flesh, and white golden air. Halo. Aura. Corona."

"As your doctor said, Bagley, one of us is crazy."

"You cannot see my world at all, Foley. You see and hear about current states, but have you heard about Greater Armenia and Greater Ireland as political entities? Have you heard of Christendom still living? Do you know who still governs by entrenched right?"

"Tell me, Bagley, tell me. I'll be able to do the piece on you that I was going to do a year ago, and Tankersley won't fire me for the Carmody caper after all. Who rules, Bagley?"

"I do locally. I'm the Patrick of Tulsa. The Congregation of Patricks is a complex network, with Exarchs, Crolls, Autocrats, Larkers, Aloysii, Patriarchs, and so on up to the Emperor himself."

"This is rich stuff, Bagley. Well, who is the Emperor?"

"I regret that the office has been vacant for more than a thousand years. But the authority still remains, though it is held in abeyance."

"Oh brother! All right, I'll eat the whole animal down to the gamey rump! What are the unfledged falcons?"

"Foley, you should know these things without asking. You are a rare combination, with the simple mind and the complex eyes that see on the primary five levels. The unfledged falcon appears more reptilian than the reptiles. But sometimes it grows, it is fledged, it flies. At its best, to me, it is only mediocre: it was the Crusades; it was the Ottonian Empire (an interloper); it is firm but doltish authority. At its worst it is the fascist thing. But it is fledged only as a reaction: I see a present example of it. Oddly, I am getting this from your mind. A young man has been torched with this fever only this past evening. Already he has raised twenty-five men. He may even get the falcon off the ground. His name comes to me as Miguel. Is that right?"

"I think so. I was about to walk out on you. Now I'll wait a minute. You lifted that out of my mind neatly, though I don't know who dropped it in there. Yes, I believe he's trying to raise an army, from the very bottom, but I don't know who he is or where. Do you?"

"No. But I know that the time is due for the reaction, the fledging. There are probably a hundred such movements starting right now in the world. One of them will take hold and shake the world, in months, even in days. It is no help to us, though. Foley, the whisky's gone. You'll have to go too. I only tolerated you for it."

"I'm going. Tell me, though, fat man, what does Patrick mean, as a title, not a name?"

"It means patrician, both as a title and a name."

"Bagley, you're not normal."

"Not always, but more than most. I try to live by certain norms, squarely as a square. One meaning of *norma*, a norm, in Latin is a carpenter's square."

"I tell you, Bagley, that you vary from that square. Isn't the word for that abnormal?"

"Not the only word. Me, I'm enormous."

"Yes you are. Bagley— Oh, nothing."

Foley went up the cluttered stairs and out the heavy door, leaving the impossible or enormous Bertigrew Bagley who was Patrick of Tulsa in an alternate. He caught again a corner-of-the-eye glimpse of the dog-ape-plappergeist that served Bagley. The thing thumbed its nose at Freddy happily, then made the Levantine gesture, then the African. Plappergeists are vulgar spirits. Only a trick of the light or a trick of the imagination, of course, yet a thing was there and it was in accord with Fred Foley. Less simple fellows would be unable to see the thing, even out of the corner of the eye.

The quick fox leaped through dark streets, superb in his sensing now. Foley was lately a member of a brain-weave and he had eyes all over him. He had better have! An unlighted car roared out of the street and up on the sidewalk after him, and men boiled out of it when it missed him and half crashed. Through a gap then, down a half-alley, over a fence, up an old outside stairway, across onto a lower roof, on and on. Freddy might be a simpleton but he was an agile simpleton. They did not have him that night.

He lost them, and continued to lurk and sprint for the fun of it. Easy into a trap (they were waiting for him outside his own door), coming so close they could taste him; then into a darkness that he knew, down a quick back block and into the night door of his own newspaper building. Into the night company of his peers, too many of the sleepy loungers and early boys for him to be followed there.

But somebody was after Fred Foley and they weren't kidding.

IV: LIAR ON THE MOUNTAIN

The python is a gentleman,
No common snake uncouth.
He prophesies from a lush divan
In a fortune-teller booth.

The little naked falcon biff
Bound with intengent tethers!
Beware the dreamy falcon if
He ever grows some feathers.

Till new day come, the toad plays dead,
Down in deep earth unlawful.
He has a jewel in his head
That sets it aching awful.

The badger faces down the dogs
And with the powers wrastles,
A steadfast rock in squishy bogs,
A patrick in his castles.
    New Bestiary: Audifax O'Hanlon

TANKERSLEY DISCOVERED Freddy Foley about noon, tilted
back in a chair in open-mouthed sleep. The Tank woke
him by kicking the chair out from under him.

"Are you still on the Overlark jag, Foley?" he rumbled with kindly thunder.

"Yes. Yes. Still on it." Freddy was a little startled. It

was a sudden but not unpleasant awakening. "I request permission to continue—"

"Let it go for a day, Foley. It'll keep. Get on the plane to San Antonio right now. You should be able to catch some sort of hedgehopper or nonsked to Del Rio from there. Then get to Vinegaroon any quick way you can. Something is happening there that's so simple-minded that I have hopes you may be able to understand it. I sure can't."

"Oh, that's only Miguel trying things out a little," Freddy said. "I think he just wants to take a United States town for an hour or two to proclaim himself, to get his name in the papers. He has only twenty-seven men. He can't do much with them yet."

"Foley, who in peyote-pickers' heaven is Miguel?"

"I don't know exactly; not to tell, anyhow."

"You've been sitting in that chair for eight hours, they say. How could you know what's been going on down in Vinegaroon, Texas in the last hour? *Do* you know?"

"Yes. I told you: Miguel has taken the town with twenty-seven men from Mexico. It isn't serious. He did it just to get people hearing about him, and because it will do him good in Mexico that he was able to capture a United States town. He'll be back in Mexico by the time I get there, though, and I did want to see him."

"Foley, how could you learn such howling nonsense when you were asleep? It just happened, whatever it is, or it's still happening. How do you know about it?"

"I work all the time, Mr. Tankersley, even when I'm asleep. I'll bet I'm the most under-appreciated reporter on this paper."

"Get down there and find out what happened, Foley, right now! I sure can't believe the funny stuff that came over the wire. And while you're down in that bend of the river, see if you can find out anything about that recluse, O'Claire. I'm not sure how close he is to Vinegaroon. Nobody is quite sure where he lives. Find him, though, if he isn't too far out. He's some kind of wilderness baron—"

"No, he's a patrick, Mr. Tankersley, not a baron. I'm not sure they have barons in their system. Anything else, Mr. Tankersley?"

"That's it, Foley. Ah, you'd better get up off the floor first thing. Somehow I don't have complete confidence in a man who's lying on the floor."

"Yes sir," Fred Foley said. He got off the floor and caught the plane to San Antonio. From San Antonio he flew in a private plane with a young man named Donald R. Clark to Pumpville. Donald R. sold computers and there was a rich rancher near Pumpville who might buy one. In Pumpville, Foley got on an army copter and flew the fifteen miles to Vinegaroon. All of this, from the time of the floor takeoff, was about two hours.

Vinegaroon was full of soldiers. "Hey, boys, why do you not come till they have already leaved?" the Mexicans in Vinegaroon gibed at the soldiers. The Mexicans had liked the invasion of their town. It set them up a little. The Texans of Vinegaroon were merely puzzled. "We can't figure what they wanted at all. They came in, a double handful of them, with old rifles. They said they were going to occupy city hall. We don't have any city hall. They said they were going to occupy the radio station. We don't have a radio station either. 'Hell, this is as bad as Mexico,' they said. They said they were going to occupy the telephone exchange and the post office both. 'I myself am the telephone exchange and the post office both,' Miss Villareal told them. 'They are my front two rooms. Come in and occupy.' She talked Mexican with them then and they went in. When they came out again they shot a few shots into the air and sang some songs. 'What happened in there?' we asked Miss Villareal. 'The leader, Miguel, bought a six cent stamp,' she said, 'and he made me Alcalde. Now

I am Alcalde, Mayor of Vinegaroon.' She can be mayor if she wants to. I'm the elected mayor and I'm supposed to get a hundred dollars a year for it, but there's never any money in the treasury. We don't have any treasury."

The Texan who told this to Freddy Foley didn't seem very much concerned. "It may be some sort of Mexican holiday we don't know about," he said. "It may have been a sort of pageant or reenactment of something, but our own Mexicans don't know anything about it being a special day. Hey, write it up real big, will you? Make it an invasion! Don't make it sound like a joke. We'll get a couple of tourists if you make it sound like a real invasion."

An army colonel was trying to find out what this leader had looked like. Various of the inhabitants had drawn pictures of him. "I can draw better than any of those," Freddy Foley said. He drew a picture of what Miguel really looked like. "Yes, that's him," the people said. Freddy went in with Miss Villareal to her two front rooms. She was the telegraph office too. He filed his story with her.

"Come on out to my place for a while," a big tawny man told Freddy. "I bet you never saw a place like mine."

"You don't know where I could find a recluse named O'Claire, do you?" Foley asked him.

"I'm O'Claire," the man said, and Freddy got in his pickup truck with him. Things were falling right for Freddy today. They always did when he was out for stories. Freddy Foley was a simpleton, but he was a simpleton that things fell right for.

They were riding through buffalo-grass and sagebrush and mesquite country. This O'Claire was a jolly man who talked away as endlessly as the country without seeming to say any more than it did. He was big, and sandy-colored in both hair and skin. He was either of late middle age or else ageless. The pickup truck moved like a little boat, covering wide, rolling distances easily; then there came a change in the motion, a roughness, as though the little boat were in a nipping cross-tide. Freddy noticed that they were no longer on a road, but it was not really rough. The unevenness was cushioned by the tussocks of buffalo-grass. The mesquite grew closer and bigger, the grass grew ranker, it became a thicket country; and the boat was going uphill, weaving and picking its way. The jolly O'Claire suddenly became musky and weird, without ceasing to be jolly.

"I am completely self-sufficient," said the O'Claire. "I don't need the world at all, and the world doesn't believe it needs me. I am everything. I am all I need. I can get along without the world better than the world can get along without me."

"Nobody can get along without the world," Freddy said. This was getting to be heady country. That was probably the first generalized statement Freddy had ever made in his life.

"For my time of waiting, for my time of exile, I am completely self-sufficient," O'Claire said. "I really have to be, to set a model for the rest of the world."

"Just how long is your time of exile, Mr. O'Claire?"

"Oh, all my life so far, and probably all my life for as long as it extends. There is the world huddled there. And here am I camped before its front gate. The world is afraid to look out its front gate. It knows that *I* am here."

"It's possible that you don't understand the world," Freddy said. That was the second such statement he had ever made in his life.

"No I don't, don't understand it at all. All I know is that I am appointed to camp at its front gate and be self-sufficient. I believe that I am to guard it that nobody enters that front gate. Nobody ever does, though. The world is a closed thing, Foley. See the little peccary pigs, Foley. They're running in bigger flocks here than they do inside the world. We will take one. *You* will take one. I insist that you have that pleasure." The little pigs were running in bigger bunches, the country had become more thicketed and forbidden, and they were rising much higher.

"How do I do it? I never took a peccary, O'Claire. I'll do it, though, if it's done."

"Here's a little leather lashing. Hold it in your teeth, Foley. Now I'll race up alongside one. Dog it, Freddy. Throw it and tie it. That's all."

"You're kidding."

"No, I am not kidding. I want you to have this pleasure."

O'Claire raced the pickup alongside a little skittering peccary. Freddy dove out and dogged it, just as the darting little boar had given up and broken speed. Freddy landed on it, and boar and boy rolled over and over a dozen times: the pickup had been going at a great rate of speed. The slippery little squawker doubled back on itself and doubled again, like a greased snake, and tusked Freddy horribly. But Fred got it on its back with its four feet together and lashed them tight.

O'Claire backed the pickup alongside. Was it possible that that sandy man was a little white about the edges? Had he expected Foley to do it? Freddy threw the little trussed boar into the back of the pickup. It was about fifty pounds and it sure was mean.

"Do you eat them?" Freddy asked. He was bleeding pretty badly about hand and forearm and cheek. That little pig had known how to use its tusks.

"Oh sure, that's my main meat. I eat it fresh, and I also preserve it. I have over a thousand pounds of it set back in one of my caves. I hole up a while in the winter months."

"It gets winterish down here?"

"It does when you're high enough, and I live high. Who wants to live below the frost?"

"You really dog the peccaries from your pickup, O'Claire?"

"Sure. It's easy. You did it well the first time, outside of getting tusked."

"Who handles your pickup when you dive out on one of the things?"

"Oh, I have it under voice control. It backs and stands like a real dogging pony. I'm serious. A self-sufficient man has to be good on gadgets. I just flip that green toggle on the dash and I have it under voice control. Say, you don't see a house around here anywhere, do you?"

They had come to pretty high country by now. They hadn't ridden twenty-five miles, and Foley hadn't noticed any country this high when he flew into Pumpville with Clark. There was a big stream of water booming down the thicketed hills, and it had been a smaller stream lower down. That could not be. The place was unnatural. The earth sounded hollow below them. They were near the crest. How could there be so much water flowing down?

"No, I sure don't see any house around here," Foley said. "And I didn't expect to see such high mountains around here."

"Ah, those—I make them myself. I told you I was self-sufficient. I was hoping you'd say you couldn't see any house. Nobody's ever been able to find my house: that's why they call me a recluse and a legend. Well, here we are."

"It's like everything was doubled here, O'Claire," Freddy said.

"Everything that has substance will cast shadow, Foley. My things have substance. Don't get the things mixed up. Most people's things are shadow only."

O'Claire parked the pickup where it stalled, with its

nose pointing up at forty-five. Foley got out with him but he sure could not see any house there.

"We'll string the little pig first and let him bleed," O'Claire said. He pulled three oak poles out; they were already chained together. He hooked on a little snatch block and set it up. He set a little clamp around the hocks of the animal and swung it into the air. He hooked it on. He stabbed it into the throat and it gushed a fountain there. Where had O'Claire pulled this sudden equipment from? It was a little shed there where the mesquite grew close to the mountain. You wouldn't have noticed that it was a shed if there hadn't been a little equipment in it. It was just a little cove of mountain-colored rocks. O'Claire led the way up staired rocks either through the shed or behind it. They were up on a rock ledge that was either ceiling or deck or portico. They went through rooms of a sort that held furniture of a sort, but you would hadly have guessed that they were either rooms or furniture if O'Claire hadn't been with you. There was water running and falling, and the sound of bigger water above.

"What's up there?" Freddy asked. He was losing direction in the several quasi-rooms and could hardly decide which was inside and outside.

"Oh, the fountain," O'Claire said, "one of the primary fountains of the world."

"There can't be a fountain on a mountaintop," Freddy protested.

"A while ago you were thinking there couldn't be a mountaintop," O'Claire told him. "You didn't see it when you flew in. Hardly anyone comes onto one of these fountains unless it's shown to him, but every river in the world begins with one. The cartographers don't know about them and the geologists don't know, but they are so."

"It can't be artesian," Freddy insisted. "Artesian water

must come from higher ground somewhere and there isn't any. There can't be a fountain here."

"Behold it, though," O'Claire said, and there was quite a fountain there. "This is right at the front gate of the world and the world doesn't know it's here. None of it's as large as it looks. The lake—it's nearly circular—is only ninety feet across, and the fountain in the center gushes up only thirty feet. Even the roaring isn't as loud as it seems. A decible recorder gives a low level of noise. There is quite a bit of illusion on my mountain."

Musical thunder of the fountain. Climbing churning water that was golden or white or green or blue or thunder-color. Height above height of it, fountains bursting out of fountains, castles of water piled on top of castles. Whole nations of spirits living in the towering columns of foam. The living airy shocking sudden smell of fountain water, salt and sulphur and iron, and fresh. And the vast bottomless lake of which the incredible fountain was center.

"O'Claire, how deep is that thing?"

"Don't know, Foley, I've always been afraid to sound it. There's things here I'm not supposed to understand. I'm a patrick and my job is to guard this door of the world. But there are caves below the lake, dry caves. This whole height is like a sponge, full of caves and passages. I know that if I sounded the lake it would sound far deeper than the caves below it and it'd scare me. It's full of fish, though; full of shellies, full of grandpappy frogs and big turtles. I could live on its produce forever."

"It's full of big blacksnakes too," Freddy growled, "big ones, five or six there."

"Sometimes they are seven, sometimes eight, sometimes nine," O'Claire said, "but they aren't snakes. They are all the tentacles of one amorphous creature. I believe that every primary fountain has one. This one tries to escape, and if he ever escaped into the world there would be disaster beyond telling. He leaves the center sometimes and tries to climb out onto the shores. Then I beat him back. That's the main reason I am here."

"Oh snake hokey, O'Claire! Who beats him back when you're off in town?"

"There is an oyster that whistles. I hear, and I come back at preternatural speed from wherever I happen to be. Foley, do not look blank at me! You should light up to the magic of the oyster that whistles! And the tentacled fountain-devil has never slipped me once. I believe that a few of them (from other fountains, not from mine) do slip into the world from time to time, though. They are what does the damage to the world. You would not know of any such new seven- or eight- or nine-armed creature wreaking havoc recently, do you?"

"Maybe I do. O'Claire, you're a liar as high as your mountain."

"That I am, little Fred Foley, that I am."

"Miss Villareal warned me of you, I think. She gave me a sort of blessing: 'That you be safe from *cascabels* and their brothers, and toads, and unborn things, and the mountaintop liar.' You are the mountaintop liar, O'Claire."

"Certainly. How about pancakes for supper? Feed a few sticks into the *horno* there and get it hotted up."

Then O'Claire whistled sharply, a whistle cutting through the roaring of the fountain.

"Hey, Peggy, bring the milk!" he called loudly.

"I didn't see that little clay furnace when I came up here first," Foley said. "It looks like it'd heat up quick, though. O'Claire, what are *cascabels?*"

"Rattlesnakes, Foley, but don't pay any attention to Miss Villareal's blessing other than to be protected by it. She is an intuitive person but weak on her zoology. The black creature is not the *cascabel*, but the *pólipo maldito*, the misnamed serpent from the beginning. The toads are toads indeed, but they have servitors who will kill to protect their reputations. And by unborn things she really means unfinished or unfledged things. She hasn't quite the words for the four creatures. And neither she nor you need fear the mountaintop liars nor any patricks. We patricks stand ready to serve and to save. I believe that God must be out of his wits that he does not call on us yet. We await that call forever. Yeah, just mix the buckwheat flour and the honey and crush in a little of the rocksalt; it's from the fountain too. A little butter then, and afterward the milk."

"*I knew a liar on a mountain,*" Freddy sang softly to the tune of High Noon.

"*He had a pancake for a house.* Where's the milk, O'Claire? Everything else is here.

"*He keeps a polyp in a fountain.* What will I use instead of milk, fountain water?

"*He gets'um milk without no cowse.* Hey, is that Peggy?"

That was Peggy, a little she-goat who came up to the lake. O'Claire milked her into a wooden bucket, enough for the pancakes, and gave it to Foley. Freddy mixed and poured into a pan and set that into the *horno*. He mixed some more in another pan and O'Claire gave him a very cold sausage to cook with it.

"Is that from the pig we just killed?" Freddy asked. "How so quick?"

"No, no, it takes four days to get the high taste out of one of those animals even if you know what you're doing. This is last week's pig. Use a lot of it, Foley, I love sausage. Now then, I have white wine and red wine, beer, sagebrush tea, corn whisky, peach brandy, tequila, mead (which is honey-whisky), milk and buttermilk, but no coffee. Can't grow it here and I grow everything that I use. What will it be, Foley?"

"Honey-mead," Foley said. "I've read about it, but

I've never seen it or tasted it. Were those stone benches there when we first came up? Was the stone-slab table? We're all ready, then. O'Claire, I am the best mountaintop pancake and sausage cooker in the world. What's that fruit and where did you get it when I wasn't looking?"

"It is brother to the chokecherry and half-brother to the sandplum. I grow them, Foley; I grow everything I need. I am the self-sufficient man."

"The whole supper is a mountaintop lie, O'Claire, but it's good. My own touch, you know."

It was really too early to be a supper. It was, as a matter of fact, the first meal that Freddy had had that day: It was very bright sunlight yet, none of the twilight stuff. Whatever Freddy saw on the mountaintop was there. "But where did you get the cheese, O'Claire?" he demanded. "You didn't go down."

"Oh, I get the cheese from goats' milk and cows' milk. I keep three of each. I have a thousand pounds of cheese ripe, and more ripening. I have much more honey than that, whole caves full of it. I run about a hundred hives. I have granaries full of buckwheat and barley and corn and Mexican beans. I have amphoras full of blackberries; they go so good with turtle. I have a mushroom cellar that is directly under the fountain. I have peanuts—you wouldn't believe the quantity of peanuts I have. I have whole vats of cactus syrup. See this shirt? I spun and wove it myself out of yucca fiber. I grow my own flax, I shear my own sheep, I make my own shoes and jackets from my own leather. I grow my own tobacco and make my own pipes. The basin below the fountain lake is my power pool. I close the dam for an hour when I want power, then I let my donkey generator churn and run my power tools. I cut my own timber, I make my own charcoal, I fire my own clay pots, I stave my own barrels. I have a house of twenty rooms, but they are scattered, no two together, the furthest a mile apart.

This is my fountain room. I have a fortress, I have an arsenal, I have a library and observatory. I know the caves under me better than does any other living person, but there are many others who know parts of them, and there were almost always a few people living in them. These caves are very deep, and they go lower than the bottom of the great river itself. I can duck into a cave entrance five feet from me (you do not see it) and go through eighteen miles of passage dry-shod and come up in Mexico. I could hide armies in my caves."

"I think about a little army now, of one Miguel. Could it hide in your caves?"

"Miguel knows me. Mine is one of the several great minds that had influenced him before he was recently struck by that gaggle-brained lightning. He has visited me before. I expect him to come again. He may be able to line up a dozen such havens. How are you in accord with him, Foley? I don't catch that part."

"I don't know how I am but I read him somehow. I don't even know his last name."

"Fuentes. That is 'Fountains.' You are about to ask whether there is some connection between him and the savant Michael Fountain in your own town? I believe the boy wrote to the man several times, relying on the name coincidence for introduction. I believe the man answered, giving some good advice which is now being ignored. And I believe the boy is presently right in ignoring this good advice."

"He can't get anywhere with his games, of course. Like taking over Vinegaroon."

"No, he can't get anywhere, Foley, not for more than the long hour. He *will* take over the world, of course, but that will be for hardly more than a decade. Even so, he may decide to throw his power to another. For a little while the world has become a vacuum crying to be filled. Miguel is a compassionate boy and cannot stand to hear it cry. That's the way they all start, but they all become a little coarsened as they move along that way. It's possible that he will simply back the world into a corner and then give it over to . . . to I don't know whom . . . before either he or the world is too much damaged by it."

"I hadn't noticed the world being a vacuum, O'Claire."

"Yes, it is bankrupt, just when it believes itself doing famously."

"Exactly what are you, O'Claire? You talk so much and you don't say anything."

"You were with another one of us last night, Foley. I believe, though, that you had figured that out. His dog was restless, but nobody has ever seen his dog. You had a story there, a poltergeist or plappergeist story, and you muffed it."

"Bagley? Are you and he really of the same species, O'Claire? Yes, I know the jokes about Bagley's invisible dog, but it was written up years ago. Besides, it isn't exactly a dog and it isn't exactly invisible. I saw it myself. Well, no, I didn't really see it, but I saw it wink and flash happy obscenities, and I know what it looks like if I ever do see it. You are a patrick like old fat man Bagley?"

"I am Patrick of Pecos, Foley, and you guessed it before you started down here. My realm goes from the Glass Mountains and the Santiagos on eastward as far as the Sutton Plains and Eagle Pass, and it includes all the Serranias del Burro south of the great arc of the river. Foley, there are three hunting men below, and they are masquerading as conventional hunters. They will pretend to see a buck deer and they will shoot, but they will be shooting at us. We withdraw now."

And they did withdraw, away from the fountain on the hilltop and into the maze of rock castles, and then into a furnished room. "But they'll find the remnants of our supper, O'Claire," said Freddy. "They'll find everything we left scattered around."

197

"No, they won't find a thing. I also have an invisible creature, a plappergeist who serves me, and he'll clean it all up. They won't even find the fountain or the lake. They'll be led astray. They won't even discover that it's a mountaintop. They'll find that it's quite a low hill, as you saw that it was from your plane."

"Well, which one of us do they want to kill, O'Claire?"

"You in particular today, Foley. And myself every day. They have fixed your interest on the reappearing men again, though, since they're warning you away from them. And the reappearing men aren't really very interesting, Foley; not nearly as interesting as I am."

"Do all patricks read minds, O'Claire?"

"Naw. None of us do. We're just smart. You've got a story on Miguel, Foley, if you know what to do with it. And you've got a story on me if you know how to handle it. These are both better stories than anything on Overlark. Myself, I doubt that men reappear. It is only a shape of mind that reappears. Theirs is a Fountain Inside-Out, the Vortex. It sucks you down. Forget it. You'll be a long time getting the story on Overlark. It won't be very good when you get it. Nobody will believe it. And you will be either confined or killed in getting it. I resent him and his. I consider us patricks to be much more important."

"Well, the Overlark story is the one I will have to get, O'Claire. You talk like a friendly oracle, so be one to me. *Is* there a conspiracy against the world by certain men who seem to live again and again?"

"Oh, a few of those things must have got together a long time ago, Foley. I guess they try to run the world. So do we patricks."

"Do they try to run it for good or for evil?"

"If there are such things as good and evil, then their effect is evil."

"In that case, what can I do about it?"

"In that case, there is nothing you can do about it. I

insist that they aren't that important; but they think that they are, and they kill partly from vanity. I believe that they do not like to be annoyed by the callow."

"How exactly do they effect their evil, O'Claire?"

"In no one way exactly. They do it in such manner that it can hardly be traced to them. There are a few narrow passes where a group can ambush the world, and some of them are always there. They themselves believe that they are the gyroscope to prevent the world from jumping its tracks, from progressing to the next Mansion, as the Lady called it. There was one period, only a few centuries ago, when the civilized core of the world had reached a certain peak—not the highest peak that it was meant to reach, but it had reached a reasonably sound balance at a good level. There was even hope then that the world could make the transition to a still loftier level without disaster. There was present, however, a group of these men or these things which we are talking about. They decided the direction of the world was not to their liking; they believed the world was a bone misset. They broke it, to set it again in their own way. Millions died, and the new setting was in a slightly different direction."

"Was it a great war, O'Claire?"

"No. Not a war at all. It is sometimes called the Plague or the Black Death."

"And they actually loosed that on the world?"

"Indignation does not belong to the historical perspective, Foley. The plague did surprise them by its violence, but be careful that you do not slander the nature of a thing, even a disease. It had a gentle nature. It killed within three days and with no great pain. Its characteristic was a rather happy sort of delirium. There was, besides, a compassionate element to it which I have seldom mentioned. It struck down adults only, seldom children."

"You will not make me love it, O'Claire. What were

some of the other narrow passages where the Overlark sort interfered?"

"Oh, once there was a country and generation of unusual oppression. The people were ground down by the monarchy, the nobility, and the newly-monied. It seemed that there was no way out of it except a cleansing revolution. And indeed the revolution was begun, and with high hope. Then the members of the group interfered, evilly, as you would say."

"And it failed?"

"No, it succeeded. That's the point, Foley, you will never be able to trace anything to that group. But the revolution succeeded in such a way that it might have been better if it had failed. It was not clear gain at any rate, not a clean turning. And it could have been.

"And there was a later time when sincere men tried to build an organization as wide as the world to secure the peace of the world. It had been tried before and it had failed before. Perhaps if it failed this time it would not be tried again for a very long while. The idea of the thing was attacked by good and bad men, in good faith and bad. The final realization of it was so close that it could be touched with the fingertips. A gambler wouldn't have given odds on it either way. It teetered, and it almost seemed as though it would succeed. Then members of that group interfered."

"And it failed, O'Claire?"

"No. It succeeded, Foley, as in the other case. It succeeded in so twisted a fashion that the Devil himself was puzzled as to whether he had gained or lost ground by it. And he isn't easily puzzled.

"There have been any number of like cases. There was one in particular that is the most interesting of them all. You will be especially interested in it, Foley, for it concerns your prey Overlark in one of his earlier manifestations, one that you haven't stumbled onto yet. Thunder, Foley, thunder, it's late! I must hurry. I'll fly you to San Antonio instantly so you can catch the Tulsa plane and be home tonight. Come."

"No, wait, O'Claire. I don't need to be home tonight. Tell me this instance."

"No, Foley. I've got to get you out of here right now. Get in the plane."

How was there a plane there? How had O'Claire fired it up already? How were they airborne so swiftly? How was the mountaintop no more than a low hill when they looked back at it? Why couldn't Foley see the fountain and the lake now? What had happened to the fountain? If we are out of fountains then all is lost.

"O'Claire," Freddy said, "I feel that all the fountains in the world are dried up."

"Naw, they don't dry up, Foley," O'Claire said, "but sometimes their waters must run underground for a while. That's been the case for a few centuries. This does impoverish the surface world. Wit becomes witless and the daily bread goes stale. Both wealth and poverty lose something of their special enjoyment. And I'm told by people of the flesh that even the generative act isn't as much fun as it used to be."

How were they in San Antonio already?

"Wait, O'Claire," Foley begged. "It's thirty minutes till my plane time. You can tell me about Carmody Overlark in that earlier manifestation."

"Foley, the oyster just whistled," O'Claire said, looking a little mad. "The monster is trying to get out of the fountain: I've got to get back there with unnatural speed."

And O'Claire was gone from there with unnatural speed, back into the air too quickly for any clearance or regulation. Gone. Gone.

"*I knew a liar on a mountain,*" Freddy sang softly and grinned. But he wished that he had gotten that last lie out of O'Claire.

V: HELICAL PASSION AND SAINTLY SEXPOT

> So they get it into their heads that it is *arrobami-*
> *ento*, or rapture. But I call it *abobamiento*, fool-
> ishness.
>
> *Interior Castle*: Teresa of Avila

THE HARVESTERS were met again that evening in Morada, the home of the Bauers.

Bedelia Bencher brought a red rose to Letitia Bauer
—"for your death"—but neither of them understood it.

"We come to the problem again and again," Big Jim
Bauer rumbled, beginning on the big thing rapidly, and
there was an overpowering medical smell in the room,
compounded with the usual odor of mysticity that the
Harvesters exuded. "As to the world and the people
of it, we have come to a too early perfection more
quickly than we imagined, for all that it's taken these
thousands of years to bring us here. If there is not to be
another cycle of rise and bust we must make a breakthrough right now. The limit isn't set so high as we
imagined. The ancients were correct that the limit, the
sky, could almost be reached by thrown rocks and shot
arrows and catapults. We're pressing against that sky
now. Soon we'll be crushed flat between the unyielding
sky and the upraised earth. In all our amplitude we
now come to the new narrowness. I believe that humans
have been at this crisis-plateau many times before and
have always failed. This time we will not fail. We will

break through. We will shatter the sky. We will be free to complete our growth."

"I've always hated that sky and all it stands for," Arouet Manion whined sharply, like a saw cutting through elm-wood. "One of my spiritual fathers swore always that we must first put out the lights of heaven. I agree that we must shatter this heaven-sky completely and forever. It's no more than a filthy membrane that prevents us from being born. Let's use words correctly for a while. The love business is gone and over with. We can now speak of the higher love or the cosmic love, but we all know that it must be a great surge of hatred that will break through the sky. We've climbed up through our puling infancy; we've come into our awkward and disgusting adolescence; and we all know that we've been two utterly different creatures in those two states. Tadpole does not differ nearly as much from the frog as we do from our earlier and later state, except in appearance. But now we'll break through to the third state, to full adulthood. There hasn't been even one fully adult human being from the beginning of the world until now. We'll correct that tonight. We'll finally, the seven of us, become creatures of the third state, adults."

"I feel there's something hellish about it," Wing Manion protested. "Who are we to shatter the sky, even by metaphor? There's a framework and a timetable somewhere for us to follow, I'm sure of that. Isn't it arrogance and dishonesty for us to break that up?"

"Certainly, certainly, arrogance and dishonesty," Big Jim Bauer agreed heartily. "Arrogance and dishonesty are exactly what we need. We'll find likelier words for these virtues in due time, but they're the exact names in the present context. We can clean it up, we can clean it all up when we have the time for it. Oh, it's the easiest thing in the world to move and bend the limits on the local level. I've already done so. I'm not called the bishop's left-hand man for nothing. I knead him like a lump of sour dough. I had but to use a few phrases which Arouet lifted from Teilhard, and he made them his own. We become now the Overpeople of the Third Testament, I explained it to the bishop. The father was the type-figure of the First or Old Testament, the ancestral, chthonic, black-earth beast figure, our origin and our animality. The son was the type-figure of the Second or New Testament: that momentary puling thing that was called Love, that momentary puling thing that was called God, the awkward adolescence of ourselves. Now we come to the holy spirit who is the type-figure of the Third Testament. This is ourselves when we shatter the sky and become full and free people." Jim Bauer rubbed his big hands in complete pleasure with himself.

"I explained it to him and I explain it to you," he went on, "that God was the missing link, a weak categorical imperative for a weak interval, but necessary. May that dismal interlude quickly be excised from our unconsciousness when we've become adult. God stood between the beasts and man in the evolutionary sequence: lower than full man, of course. And now we'll be done with that figure forever. God could never be spoken of as holy without laughing, but man may be spoken of as holy after tonight."

"How did the bishop take it?" Bedelia Bencher asked Bauer. "Doesn't he ever get chock-full of you? I do sometimes."

"He took it completely and trustingly as a backward child would, Bedelia. He's even going on television with a presentation of it when I've cleaned it up a little for him. The camera-eye, for him, is the pearl beyond price. For this he's given up and traded all that he owns. 'But what will a man receive in exchange for his soul, or his intellect?' I taunted him a little; but he only grinned vacantly. Both of us know that he never had any soul, or intellect. But we are untouchable from that quarter, and also from the legal sector. We've played with our power over others, having good game with it. Now we'll turn back our powers on ourselves, and we won't be playing. Tonight the seven of us will make the big jump. We'll become the first of the privileged mutation. We'll shatter the sky like the dirty glass it is, the unauthorized membrane that has shut us off from life. We'll become the first of the new people, the Third Testament of the world."

"Well, will we be the end of it then?" Letitia Bauer asked. "What if we receive everything ever and I still want to say 'No, no, that is not near enough'? I *will* say it. I hate to be the end of anything. If we break into the last land, I'll hate it, even if it is infinitude. There *has to be* something beyond even infinity for me. Is there no hope of danger beyond?"

"Of course there is!" Jim Bauer boomed. "We'll be the beginning and not the end. Even the little murky half-brained theologians, grubbing into a thing long dead, have speculated that Three as the number of persons in the Godhead was never more than a contingent number. They speculate that there may be as many as five, or seven, or even nine persons in what used to be called the Trinity. Even such little pigs'-eyes as they may look a little ways forward. I tell you that there may be many thousands of stages or person-types in the humanity thing, and we now break intrepidly to only the third. There is hope of danger for millions of years, Letitia, forever."

"We're clear on the medical aspect," Arouet Manion said. "I'm an M.D. I was a general practitioner and surgeon before I became a psychiatrist. And James Bauer was a medical doctor on his way to becoming an eminent biologist. We'll set the stage for the induced mutations now, and each of the seven must give every aspect of himself."

"Will it hurt?" Bedelia Bencher asked cheerfully.

"Certainly, certainly," Jim Bauer said. "It doesn't have to, as far as the surgery goes, but we want it to. We want to bring out the agonizing awareness of every one of us in every possible way. Begin the inward-turned brain-weave, all of you, while we get ready for the rest of it. Weave it to the ultimate! It is ourselves we are mutating now."

The helical passion of Salzy Silverio stung them all with the strength of it, for all that she was gobbling little cheese snacks and chattering inanities with Bedelia Bencher. The weave needed the passion of Salzy more than any other thing. It was possibly the strongest element in the whole weave.

A strong smell of ammonia had been released into the air. There were two large brass-colored spheres there and they sent lavender lightning dancing between them across the room. They raised a lot of acrid ozone with their eerie sparking, and also raised all their spirits unaccountably. The pink hair of Bedelia rose up from her head into quivering extremities from the charge in the air and there was a garish corona about her.

"It's all hokus, of course," said Hondo Silverio in an easy voice that seemed to come out of a nest in the rocks. "It's my own arranging. It sets up something of the primitive conditions of the world when life sparked for the first time; or at least something of the laboratory myth of those probable conditions. It was a hoax that first time too, but a primitive glob *did* allow itself to be hoaxed by it and was conned into coming to life. The hoax has been a condition ever since then, and will be forever. And the first glob, you know, was itself a mutation, and against stiff statistical odds. The normal didn't slip in till later, sideways and ashamed of itself, and the normal has never been of any use to anything: not then, not now, not ever. We're tampering with the double-helix centrality of our own body cells, and the helical passion of my own serpentine wife has already set it to going. Come with it, all of you! We need show-boats tonight, we need outlandish showoffs! Outdo your-selves! Scatter the ectoplasmic confetti. This is carnival!"

"Throw serpentine, you old serpent," Wing Manion called out, like a laughing fish. "Throw streams of it. It's a water carnival, but we're the seven-headed dog at the bottom of the water. What's the dog doing down there anyhow? Does anyone remember the name of the seven-headed dog?"

James Bauer and Arouet Manion were arranging for the surgery, but they had everything draped in plush purple instead of antiseptic white.

"We disregard all infecting!" Bauer boomed. "We welcome it. How can infection hurt us? We are ourselves setting about the infecting of the world. How can we fear what we'll get from each other? We wish to get everything possible from each other. What can environ-mental germs do to us? We ourselves are evolutionizing all environments tonight."

"Mighty sloppy medical practice," said Bedelia Bench-er, but who can take seriously a girl with her pink hair standing on end? The contribution of Bedelia to the weave had always been a sort of cosmic hilarity.

And she was into the weave now, pink and pungent, the numinous spook, the cinnamon cookie, the mad ani-ma who had never left off being a kid. Plappergeistic and poltergeistic, the lavender lightning was about her especially, the witch who was no more than a sketch in red chalk. She had really never had a body, that Bede-lia, only a chalk sketch of one. This gave her a certain lightness, and there was enough heaviness in some of the others. Summer lightning, lavender lightning inside the walls, and hazel-colored sparks out of her eyes. She had been, perhaps, the primordial mutation—light enough to come to life—and the heavier normal things had not arrived till later.

Hondo Silverio was now into the weave with his mot-

tled-green humor and his ancient nobility. "You forget
sometimes," he had said once, "that the first motley,
the first mottled-green clown suit, was a snake suit. We
were the original humorists. Our sudden scaring of people, that's the best practical joke of all, and it never
wears out."

And what he said now was "We need even the very
first types for this induced mutation and don't forget
that the original person-type was a double one, and that
the nobler and more humorous half of that original father
image was the snake."

A noble snake was Hondo, but he seemed to crawl
less than the others.

Once more Jim Bauer was projecting his person with
big hands as he arranged instruments and vials and
needles. He was a joyous rumble, the arrogance and
dishonesty that was needed to break the stifling sky-
limit on them. He was power, do not doubt that. He
was rumbling spirits. He was smashed fountains. He was
lightning.

He struck like lightning.

Bauer, with blinding speed and incredible force,
smashed his wife Letitia in the face with a stunning
chopping knife-blow, felling her. She screamed but once
as she fell. He had gashed her suddenly and deeply
with the ghastly Harvester mark. She bled deep red as
she went chalk-white. Perhaps she was killed by that
one blow; her head lolled as though her neck was broken.

Danger!

But was it such a dirty danger she had wanted?

She came strongly into the weave at the instant of her
fall, in with the whimper of death but still with that
same crying for danger. All the ashen and angular passion that this moon-colored slim woman could give she
gave them. But she had broken and died at that moment of first bloodshed, and they all acquired pieces of
her. The gouging of the sector out of her head, the long

needle into her side under her arm where the lymph is closest, the deep rasping and inoculation of the round, were all bloody and botched with her. They were meant to be.

Arouet Manion slid into the brain-weave with his own cool elegance, his chilly passion for these hot things. Arouet loved the blade; he loved the needle; he was a sadist in these things. He slashed and gouged. He had the cold passion for blood. "The old barber-surgeons were right," he whined dreamily. "Bleed the patients, bleed them all, bleed them for everything! It weakened and killed the patients, of course, but it brought such soul-filling satisfaction to the barber-surgeons. I love it, I love it!" There was something almost inelegant in the Arouet elegance carried so far.

Wing Manion, the speckled Klee-fish, the saintly sex-pot, swam into the weave with a billow of underwater excitement. She belonged to the waters that are under the world, and she bled pale but ancient fish-serum instead of blood when she was gashed in head and side and round. Oh, she bled a small bucket of it, though. There was a lot of it in her.

"The mechanism of this is quite simple," Jim Bauer rumbled as he struck Salzy Silverio such a bloody, deep, blinding gash on the head that she fell to the floor stunned. The power was in the rumbling sound of Bauer's words, not in their meaning. "We extracted serum and specimen from each of you some time back," Bauer growled out like a throaty lion, "and little glots of flesh, nerve stringers, samples of every sort of cell. We made living broths of these, and we mixed in the tissues of mutating worms and newts. We shot the broths through with high voltages and frequencies, we bathed them in every sort of ray, we bombarded them with strange particles, we encanted them: 'Mutate, damn you, mutate,' we encanted. We took one half of each broth and distributed it among the other six. Now each one of us will receive back most of his own, but a little of all the others. There are a dozen triggers inside the broths, the serums. They reenter us. They should produce cellular explosions inside of us. We'll mutate in our smallest cells and in our total symbiosis. Each of us has now received three violent wounds and has received the serums into them. Ah, isn't the pain exquisite? Fainting again, Arouet, and you love it so much? There is an additive to the serums, the most painful known. It harms nothing, but it tortures. We want us all to feel it to the utmost.

"What, two others of you are still conscious? Are there two others here as strong as myself? The men are gone under, and two Shes remain unbroken. Bedelia, you surprise me! I didn't know that you were one of the strong ones."

Bedelia Bencher was not particularly strong now. She was retching violently, and her pinkishness had turned to purple. She had probably lost a quart of blood, and she was blinded by the ammonia fumes and the lavender lightning from the brass spheres. But she was still conscious.

And Salzy Silverio was most certainly conscious. Her mouth was in motion without words; her lips were moving with the illusion of a double-helix motion, a snake-mouth motion; her frame was shaking, her eyes sparked with hate and green laughter at the same time.

This Salzy had not collapsed for long when she was struck down with the gaping head wound. She would be the last to give up, always. She was conscious and snapping with color. She even flicked her tongue out from broken moving lips. She was the twisted passion itself.

Jim Bauer, swaying and falling all over himself, already far over the threshold of pain, opened wall jets to let measured amounts of noxious gas into the room. This would bring unconsciousness to all of them for a half hour.

But Bauer stayed on his feet by blind last effort, until the blackness or the purpleness should overwhelm him. He wanted to savor the pain and arrogance and hate as long as possible. He deliberately walked on the bodies of all six of his companions as they lay on the floor, heeling lavishly into vital sectors. He trod last on the sinewy, lithe, snake-strong body of Salzy Silverio, on stomach, on breast, on throat, while she watched him with defiant snake's eyes bright with hatred. Then Bauer collapsed in a final spasm, falling heavily atop the firm fish-body of Wing Manion.

Salzy Silverio closed her inner eyelids, her snakes' eyelids, but she could still see as though through mist and she would not give up her consciousness. And the brain-weave itself remained fully conscious.

They all came around about the same time. Hondo Silverio opened windows to clear the room. It had just come on deep twilight while they had been out. They were all new people now, of course; they had mutated. There was truly a stronger linkage among them, a stronger mastery of the world. They had shattered the sky, and now there was no limit at all upon them.

They would have looked disheveled and disreputable to other eyes, but to their own new seven-faceted eye they did not.

"Are we all all right?" Salzy Silverio asked with a certain huskiness in her voice. After all, big Jim Bauer had stood on her throat and ground a heel into it; but it could have been a very elephant and it wouldn't really have hurt her. And, of course, nothing could ever hurt her again, now that she had mutated.

"Yes, all are all right," said James Bauer. "Except Letitia, that is. Ah—she's dead. I somehow expected that, though."

"Isn't that a little bit awful?" Bedelia asked sharply.

"We are all of us consummately awful now," Bauer

rumbled, "in the real meaning of the word. We are filled with awe of ourselves, and we are completely awe-inspiring."

"Oh shut up that stuff!" Bedelia flared angrily. "Your wife is dead. This should bring you out of your silly daze. For one thing, there's the legal thing. I think you murdered her. You must have broken her skull, you struck her so terribly."

"Oh, possibly, possibly; yes, I'm sure I did. But it's no great matter."

"No great matter?"

"Of course not, Bedelia. You have some carryover, I'm afraid. It's almost as if you hadn't mutated completely. Oh, I can get a new wife easily enough, and I will, within the present hour. As for my legal aspects, don't you realize that we're now the masters of the law and of everything?"

"No, I sure don't realize that," Bedelia protested. "I think it's horrifying."

"A little horror makes the soup taste better, Biddy," Salzy Silverio consoled her. "Don't you just love to come onto threshing monsters in a bowl of soup? I think the new way will be fun. I've taken a liking to the arrogance and hatred bit already."

"I'd marry you, Biddy, on the spot," Bauer said, "but that wouldn't expand the brain-weave, and I believe it should be expanded by one more now."

"You sure as hell would *not* marry me, you final pig!" Biddy swore.

"Of course I would, Bedelia. We're not ourselves now, we all belong to each other. But I believe we should expand the weave by one. Letitia is still in the weave, you know. We can still feel her. We can still talk to her."

That was true. Letitia Bauer was still in the brain-weave. They could hear her ashen weeping in waste places somewhere, they could still feel the moon-color and slimness of her.

"I believe it might be well to have several dead people in the weave," Bauer mused, but even his musing had the sound of muted thunder. "It will give us better perspective to have several dead people in our communication. Which one would be best? Oh well, I'd better get to the marrying part first and then return to the murder. There's a girl going by on the sidewalk."

Jim Bauer went out and took the girl by the hand. He pulled her into the house, and she came along in dazed fashion. "We're married now," he said. "Your name is Letitia Bauer now. See her dead body there. Look like her. Look like her! I tell you. You cannot set up a will against any of us. We are the will of the world now. Look like her. *More.* That's close, but *more.* I can compel you, you know. Yes, that's about right."

It wasn't about right. It was perfect. The new girl *was* Letitia Bauer now. She had had to age about twelve years. She had to become moon-colored of skin and ashen of hair. She had to slough twenty pounds and become slim. But when one of the new mutated masters compels a thing, it must be done.

"Strip the old one, Wing," Bauer ordered. "Strip them both. Then clothe the new one after she's been properly bloodied and inoculated and introduced into the weave. She'll mutate easily enough now, I believe, and the old Letitia will help her. Hondo, get rid of the body. Go bury it almost anywhere. Nobody will see you. If they do, it won't occur to them to prevent you. We are new people now and no one will interfere with us. Arouet!"

"What of me, Bauer? You can't order me. I'm as mutated and masterful as you are. No one can stand first here."

"Of course not, Arouet. We've all become the same person. But that person is speaking through my mouth now. Arouet, don't you believe it would give our brainweave more balance if one more of us would be rid of the body? In some ways, death brings even closer communion; notice how close the dead Letitia is now, closer than the living. One more, do you think?"

"Yes. Here, give me the .45, James, I'll do it. You mean Hondo when he comes back from disposing of the body?"

"No, I mean you, now, Arouet. And I'll use the .45. No man can shoot himself without being a little clumsy about it. I'll do it."

"No, Jim, no, no!" Arouet Manion ran out of the room, he leaped a hedge, he disappeared.

"He'll come around in a little while," said James Bauer, "or I'll go find him and kill him. We have to expect these spotty starts. We've been mutated only a few minutes, after all. I suggest that we all take our rest this night as did the first chthonic father-image on the seventh day. Our accomplishment, after all, is much higher. Now I have a new wife, or an old wife in new appearance, to bloody and then to bed. Begone, fellow Harvesters. We're in constant contact anyhow. We're all one person now."

"I'll give you a ride into town, Biddy," Wing Manion said. "I'll let Arouet run a while before I look for him. Of course, he'll be easy enough for any of us to find any time, now that we're all the same person. He always was yellow. Now that he's mutated, he becomes ocher. Didn't he turn positively ocher when Jim Bauer was about to kill him, Biddy? Oh, it will be exciting, being mutated and all, don't you think so, Biddy?"

"It may be exciting. It won't be as much fun as I thought it would."

"Oh it is goofy, Biddy," Wing Manion said, "being new and powerful and all that. I'll bet that's what the first primitive glob said when he was hoaxed into coming to life with all that ammonia in the atmosphere and all those high-powered rays barking around. 'Oh it is goofy,' I bet he said."

214

Freddy Foley was with his boss Tankersley. He had been getting kind words for a change.

"Those were two very good stories you got today," Tankersley said. "I wonder sometimes why I keep you on, but I guess it's because you often get good stories. You show real empathy with this Miguel. You get right inside him. And you really believe that his movement may pick up momentum, that it will be dangerous, that he'll be unable or unwilling to stop it, and that he'll still be a nice kid when he topples the world? I don't believe he'll really endanger the world, but some of the movements may. Every crooked-neck plum tree in the world may be bearing bloody fruit by next season. And the other story, you did a fine job on that, even if you violated the first item of the reporter's canon."

"How, Mr. Tankersley? I got all my information from O'Claire directly, and I discounted it just as I thought it should be done. What canon did I violate?"

"Spelled his name wrong."

"I couldn't have. There isn't any wrong way to spell it."

"It is A-u-c-l-a-i-r-e. French, not Irish. Sorry, Foley, in a more perfect world everybody would be Irish, but in our own imperfect world they are not. Auclaire."

"Really muffed that one. Mr. Tankersley, do you know anything about the patricks?"

"Hardly anything. Some sort of lodge or society. Pretend to take themselves seriously, like the Baker Street Irregulars. I believe they also use a little esoterism such as may be picked up from the Los Angeles quackeries. They have titles and things. Pretend to divide the world into realms ruled by themselves. Do a piece on them if you want to, anything to keep you off the Overlark lark."

"I'm not off the Overlark bit for good."

"Get off it for good then, Freddy, or your head will roll."

Freddy went and borrowed some pictures from the morgue. He had collected others here and there. Some he had been forced to steal. He went with them to the lodgings of Michael Fountain. And Michael was distraught.

"I thought there was ritual murder a while ago, Foley. I was sure of it. It came from our mutual acquaintances who have become vile. I read them back, as they tried to read me. They murdered Letitia Bauer. I know that they did. But then a little later the happening was expunged."

"I got a little of that too, Mr. Fountain. And then a little later I got it that she was all right after all. I put it out of my mind then. I have some things on Carmody Overlark I want to show to you and talk to you about."

"I just talked to Letitia Bauer on the telephone," Michael Fountain said. "No, she certainly was not all right, she said. She had a blinding headache. Yes, she said, there had been insane experiments going on at their place and she had had about enough of them. So nice of me to imagine that she had been murdered, she said, but she hadn't been really. Everything is all right now, Mr. Fountain, she said, and you come to visit us again when we are once more sane which I hope will be soon. Well, there's something there that I don't understand, Foley. Probably it was a very strong mental projection of ritual murder. They do play black games, your friends. Yes, I'll gladly look at anything you have on Carmody Overlark. Anything to get the Harvesters out of my mind."

"Pictures, pictures," said Freddy, and he laid them out on the table. "I have two piles of pictures here, all of them of Carmody Overlark. This stack here has pictures of Carmody that are more than two years old. This second stack has pictures of him that were taken within the last two years. Look at them closely and tell me if they're all of the same man."

Michael Fountain studied the pictures closely for some time.

"Yes. I'm familiar with all of them except two," Fountain said, "and they're among the less clear. Yes, Freddy, all those are pictures of Carmody Overlark."

"I know they are. But are they all of the same man?"

"Is there a difference? I'd say immediately that they were all of the same man, except that you're the second person who's asked me such a question. How can they all be of Carmody Overlark and not all be of the same man?"

"I can't explain."

"Neither could my other questioner. I can be cryptic myself but usually I avoid it. You stretch it a little far, Foley."

At the side of Foley's face, just out of vision, drifted a strand finer than silk. He resisted the temptation to brush it off, but he felt that a spider had cast on him a second time.

"Who was the other man who asked about Carmody, Mr. Fountain?"

"I won't tell you. You don't know him, I'm sure."

"But I want to know him."

"I won't tell you who he is. He questioned me in confidence."

"So do I. I ask his name in confidence."

"No. You don't have enough of my confidence for that."

"Is it true, Mr. Fountain, that the patricks have invisible servitors, plappergeists, who protect them?"

"Oh, I suppose so. Bagley's invisible dog can be seen, though. I've seen it. It only takes sharp looking. But it's more like an ape than a dog."

"And do the returning men also have servitors who protect them, and are they furtive but not invisible?"

"Yes, that's true. You'll be confined or killed if you

keep asking questions about Carmody Overlark. I don't know why. He doesn't seem that important to me."

"Mr. Fountain, who would be most likely to know whether the earlier and the later Carmody Overlark are the same man?"

"You might ask his wife."

"I hadn't thought of that. Thank you. I will."

Freddy Foley went to the Scatterbrain Lounge to see if Biddy would show up that evening. The problem remained. There is a truism that things equal to the same thing are equal to each other, but this truism may not be true. The pictures of the later Overlark were also the pictures of Khar-ibn-Mod and of Kir-ha-Mod. And the pictures of the later Overlark were also pictures of the earlier Overlark. Why then were not the pictures of the earlier Overlark also the pictures of Khar-ibn-Mod and of Kir-ha-Mod? They should have been, but they weren't.

When logic breaks down something else should take over. But it wouldn't come to Freddy, it just wouldn't come. Whatever it is that makes a man what he is and not another man, it seemed to break down here.

Then there exploded into the Scatterbrain Lounge the man that Freddy least expected to see of all the men in the world. It was O'Claire, no, no, Auclaire.

"Foley!" the tawny man cried and gripped Freddy and was frantic. "It escaped! It escaped from the fountain! Now it is loose in the world! It is loose in this very city! Where is it? Do you know? It has some affinity to you. Answer me, Foley! Come alive! It's important! The thing is a world-eater!"

"Man, I don't know what you're talking about," Foley sputtered in amazement. "What are you doing here, Auclaire? A mountaintop lie doesn't come to roost here. You're off your head. What are you looking for?"

"The creature from my fountain, the seven-armed

creature that has snakes for tentacles. *It's loose in the world, I tell you!* It's loose in your own city!"

"You're insane, man. You were only pleasantly crazy this afternoon. Now you're clear gone."

"Foley! Listen to me. *There it is! It's coming to us now!* There is a walking tentacle of the damnable world-eater itself, and nobody rises to kill it or confine it! She's one creature of it, one snake of it! Get back in your place, creature, or I'll beat you back!"

"I will *not* get back in my place!" Biddy Bencher sparked, for she was the walking tentacle of the world-eater. "The whole world is my place now. Why yes, I am one snake of it. What of that? I'm a mutated person now. I'm part of the being that grows and inherits the world."

"Aaagh, then I'm too late," Auclaire moaned, and all the fire went out of him.

"I'm wounded, Freddy," Bedelia grimaced, "and the turban on my head isn't the style; but in a day or so I'll unveil the Harvester mark on my forehead in all its brilliance. And your friend here, Freddy? You do have the most interesting friends."

"So do you, Biddy. Biddy, this is Mr. Auclaire, the Patrick of Peços."

"Oh, I've met patricks before. I love them all, don't I, Freddy? Why don't you go see Mr. Bagley? He's Patrick of Tulsa."

"You refuse to go back to your prison, creature?" Auclaire asked, trembling.

"I refuse to go back to my prison," Biddy said. "I don't even have a prison to go back to. And don't call me creature, little snake-hunter. I am now the essence of uncreated ecstasy."

"I was hoping I'd be able to drive you back to your place," Auclaire moaned, "but I see that I'm too late and you've already fragmented. Yes, I'll go see the local patrick and we will attempt tactics. Oh, God help us all! Why didn't you stay in your fountain as God intended you to do, creature?"

"No, no, I didn't leave the fountain," Bedelia protested. "The fountain left me. Oh, I'd forgotten all about when I lived in a fountain. It's like in another life. But now we build new fountains, new upwellings."

Auclaire left them there. He was defeated. All the fire had gone out of him.

"Did you kill Letitia at your gangeroo tonight, Biddy?" Fred Foley asked.

"Yes. How did you know, Freddy? But it was only for a little while. We fixed it up later. I forget just how, but she's all right now. And now I can communicate both with Letitia dead and Letitia alive, so we've added one to our number. But I shouldn't be talking of such things to a sample of non-mutated humanity. Change the subject, Freddy."

"All right. Have you picked up any stories on Carmody Overlark, Biddy?"

"Oh, I'd forgotten about him. Why is he important? I myself am much more important than he is, now that I'm mutated and super. But it seems that I did hear a couple comical things on him. What do you really want?"

"Is there any new oddity that has attached to him in the last year or two?"

"Oh yes. He keeps rats. And he soaks his head in a bucket. He didn't used to do either."

"*Soaks his head in a bucket?* Biddy, this is me, Freddy. We're friends. Now what was it that you meant to say when you said that he soaks his head in a bucket?"

"I meant to say that he soaks his head in a bucket. He keeps one in his office always, and there's one for him wherever he goes. I don't know why."

"Anything else?"

"On Carmody, no. On you, yes. I have this information of myself, being now transcendent and super and traveling through so many minds at will. You have decided to leave town this evening. Well, there's a man waiting to kill you at the airport, and another at the bus station. There's a third one waiting to kill you if you stay in town."

"Oh well, dead if you do and dead if you don't. Where did they wound you tonight, Biddy, other than the forehead gash?"

"The side, under the arm, close to the lymph."

"And where else?"

"The left round."

"Yes, I thought you sat a little gingerly."

VI: REVENGE OF STRENGTH UNUSED

There is what seems like a regular pattern of excavated cities. From the bottom, three cities, each more advanced in artifact and building, one atop another; then a city of total destruction: following above will be three more cities showing advance and again a fourth showing total destruction.

It is possible, however, that this most common cycle is actually the failed or broken cycle. Much more rarely do we come on the cycle of the full seven cities: at Leros, at Lough Dorg, at Angkor Kong, at Chichen-Ticul. In these cases we find the first three cities of ascending worth, then the fourth or "confusion" plateau which reveals contradictory and exciting values, fragmentary but contained destruction, and grandiose foundations: above this in each case are the fifth and sixth cities, which can only be called marvelous both in their attainments and in their balance and their prophecy: above these are the truncated bases of the seventh cities, which are absolutely unique even in their low remnants.

In each case, the local legend is that the final cities (having become perfect) were taken up to heaven in every stone and person.

The Back Door of History: Arpad Arutinov

"THERE AIN'T no way, Charley, there ain't no way we can blow it," one drinking young man was saying to another. This seemed to be a catch-phrase born that very day. "There ain't no way, Charley," one woman was saying to another there.

"Boy, I sure can blow it," Freddy Foley said. "There's lots of ways I can blow it yet. Sit here like I'm coming right back, Biddy. I'll see you some other day, some other where."

"Be careful, Freddy, little acorn; you're going to take the airport limousine, and there's a man going to kill you if you show up at the airport. —But why should I warn you? You both belong to unmutated humanity and I'm above such things now."

"You're walleyed and beautiful, Biddy, and you have a fever and you will die in a few weeks. Hey, I can prophesy too."

Fred Foley went around the corner and caught the airport limousine just as it was pulling out. The driver was a friend of Freddy's and Freddy sat in back in the baggage place. But if anyone had wondered, Fred Foley had been on the airport limousine.

There is one dark crossway down under old viaducts, and Fred Foley rolled out of the limousine there. There was a small station of a prehistoric carter service there, and Fred Foley was in and out of it quickly.

Who remembers when they still had passenger trains in this part of the country? Who was the last person ever to ride on one? Now there is a deep secret about this. This prehistoric monster is not dead. Though passenger trains no longer run, yet there is one coach-car hooked onto a Kansas City run at night. Foley got on it. No one, not a fossil, would look for him there. It was one in the morning. There were only five other persons in the coach and four of them were fossils. The fifth one was of that fearsome breed who might want to talk.

Freddy took a book from his bag. It was a rather serious book with which he intended to put himself to sleep, *Painting and Reality* by Gilson, but it had one of those false jackets slipped over it. You know the kind, *Safe-cracking for Pleasure and Profit*, *Arson Can Be Fun*, *Care and Feeding of the Polecat*, *Seduction for the Anxious Amateur*. The jacket of this book was *Brain-Surgery Self-Taught*. Freddy read it and dozed till there was a tug on his arm. It was the fifth man.

"I beg your pardon, Doctor," that fifth man said, "but that's a title with which I am not familiar. I am Doctor Jurgens, a general practitioner, not at all a brain specialist. I am interested, however, in anything at all that pertains to our profession."

"O'Claire, Doctor O'Claire, with an O, not an A-u," said Freddy. "It is a real pleasure, sir."

"I sometimes believe, Doctor O'Claire, that we general practitioners get a larger picture of the world than do you more talented specialists."

"Yes, I'm sure that you do, Doctor Jurgens."

"Yet I must make a confession before I proceed further. I am lately disbarred. I am appealing the action. I have done nothing wrong. But there is a penalty for doing things differently. You need not continue to talk to me if you do not wish to."

"I'm quite willing to talk to you," said Foley-O'Claire.

"Thank you. It was for an unorthodox paper of mine that I have been disbarred. 'The Precursors.' You may have read it."

"I'm a little behind in that department, Doctor Jurgens. There's so much literature in our profession that, as they say, it's very difficult for a man to remain a-breast. I'm sure there's a copy of it at my home office; I'll make a point to read it. What is the main thesis of it?"

"That there is a Precursor, a forerunner to every great disaster, to every great epidemic, to every high happening of every sort. You will recall that there was a failure of the apple crop the year before the great

Gothic assault on Rome, a partial but quite serious failure of the grape the year before the battle of Tours, and the pomegranate harvest was far below average the season before the great Persian attack on Attica. We might even couple the crop failures with the great militancy happenings: cabbages and Crecy, millet and Malplaquet, turnips and Tourcoing."

"Watermelons and Waterloo?"

"O'Claire, I'm thunderstruck! That was right under my nose all the time and I never guessed it. Yet it's a fact that 1814 was a poor watermelon year in the United States, in Africa, and in Russia. I had always equated the quince crop with Waterloo, but you have opened my eyes."

"But isn't this a rather odd field of interest for a doctor?"

"Oh, this isn't my field. I only cite these historical commonplaces by way of analogy. You can find Precursors in the field of minerology, in literature, in politics, in weather. My field, of course, is Precursors in the field of medicine."

"Ah, now you fascinate me, Doctor Jurgens."

"To every great epidemic, O'Claire, there is a Precursor, apparently unrelated, impossible of connection, yet infallible as to prediction. When the Precursor appears, then the more serious epidemic will follow as surely as season follows season. I maintain that if these were correctly analyzed, then the great epidemics might be prevented. These run in advance, sometimes a year or more in advance, and this gives time for worldwide precaution.

"For an instance, a full year before an outbreak of meningitis in an area, there will be a minor, barely reported, outbreak of cotton-mouth accompanied by quite small irruptions on the inner gums. I cannot prove the connection. Medically there would seem to be none.

But the coincidence is so uniform as to be more than coincidence."

"Yes, I had noted it myself," said Foley-O'Claire, "but perhaps I hadn't assigned to it the significance it deserved."

There are people who do not like to talk to crackpots, who are bored with boors, who shy off from fools. Foley had none of their reluctance. His profession was gathering information. He knew that fools talk on while wise men hold their tongues, that he could get more information from one fool than from seven sages, that if any man talks long enough he will say something. Besides, he had nothing else to do.

"There is another striking example or coincidence," Doctor Jurgens continued. "Two years before every outbreak of influenza (which always varies as to type) there is a heavy outbreak of erythema, or rash, which also varies as to type. Again there can be no medical connection, but there is some connection."

"It would seem that the Precursors, the predictors, could be crossed up," Foley-O'Claire said. "An epidemic depends on contagion and contagion depends on many tenuous threads easily broken. The Precursor could be made a liar."

"I hope so, O'Claire, for that is my mission. I cannot, however, find where it has ever been a liar. I'm trying to make a liar out of it now in one of its most horrible predictions. I'm going to the capital with my appeal. If I cannot make a liar out of it, then there is something unnatural about the Precursors. It will mean that they are of another realm, that they are real predictors of the future, that the future cannot be altered. I have made a personal adversary out of this Precursor. And such very small blisters they are!

"Between the fingers, O'Claire, right at the base. They itch a little, and then they are gone. There's not one —

person in a hundred who really notices them or seeks medication for them."

"I had such just last week," said Foley-O'Claire. It was true. He had.

"Half the nation had such just last week, O'Claire, and now they've forgotten them. They've forgotten them so completely that I wonder how it happened to be noted the other times. Yet it *was* noted, and clearly, but in so random and offhand a manner that it seems a miracle. Boccaccio mentions it, Defoe mentions it, the Welshire Chronicles mention it twice. Everywhere do we find the clear account of this peculiar between-the-finger itching coming about a year before the Thing itself."

"The Thing? What is it, Doctor Jurgens?"

"Oh, the Plague. It'll be here in the present year, you know, unless of course I can persuade the Federal to take steps, just what steps I don't know, to stop it. Well, good night, Doctor. My time is upon me. The natural cycle, you know."

"Oh? What is that, Doctor Jurgens?"

"The thirty-four hour cycle, the natural cycle. I fall into it whenever I'm taking long journeys. You have never noticed why we do not want to go to bed at night? Or why we do not want to get up in the mornings? How can we be expected to adjust to the cycle in just a few thousand years? Wherever mankind originated, we know it was not on this world. It was on some planet body with an equivalent thirty-four hour day. This may narrow the hunt for our original home on that day after tomorrow when we really go looking for such things. Good night."

"Tut, Doctor Jurgens, tut," said Foley-O'Claire. "That's scientific heresy you talk."

"Doctor O'Claire, it has been said that a heresy is the revenge of a forgotten truth. I say that every monstrous appearance or movement is the revenge of a strength or variety unused, of a vitality untapped in us. And it looks like a good year for monsters."

Doctor Jurgens flung himself into a deep seat and went to snoozing. Then Foley also napped a few of those quick naps that may be taken only on trains. There was a special element in them for him now, though. One who has been touched by a brain-weave will no longer snooze or dream alone. He will do it out of the vortex.

What the mind of the brain-weave was doing tonight (and it was the mutated Jim Bauer mind that was dominant in it; the rest of them were tired) was killing people, or causing them to kill themselves. Jim Bauer, and the brain-weave through him, seemed to have selective hatreds. He killed a dozen of them. He was killing the thirteenth. "I wouldn't have killed some of those," Fred Foley said to himself, and also said back through the entire brain-weave, "Some of them are pretty good people, some of them are a lot better than Jim Bauer. It's going to be a lopsided world if they keep killing that sort of people."

The thirteenth man didn't much want to go. He sat at a table and scrawled on paper, *I do not kill myself. I have no reason. This is dream-stupid. Even if I wished, I have no gun. And now I have a gun before me, and where did it come from? But I don't know how to shoot it. I never shot a gun in my life. But yes, now I know how to shoot it.* There was a lot of pressure in that brain-weave, icy elegance, green-mottled humor, helical passion, cinnamon-colored dying, ashen weeping of dead Letitia, danger-incitement of live Letitia who wondered in her broken sleep what sort of living nightmare she had been gobbled up by, Klee-fish and the comical death-bubbles, O'Claire's octopus escaped from the fountain and loose in the world, patricks alerted, and the third stage of the world perhaps beginning.

Something else through the brain-weave that the weave itself didn't know how to monitor, two young men who had become kindred by being touched by the tentacles. Real blood flowing on the border now in savage night fighting. Thirteen of Miguel's men killed in a busted raid, and thirty joining him to replace them. How is a man going to sleep with that stuff going through his head?

Foley had to change trains in Kansas City. He went to the telegraph office. No, he didn't want that stuff to go by wire, though. He phoned Tankersley and got that man up. He gave the names and stations of thirteen prominent men who had just died or suicided.

"You'll vouch for it?" Tankersley asked him.

"I'll vouch for it, Tank."

Then Freddy gave him an eyewitness account of bloody doings on the border.

"You're sure this happened, Freddy?"

"Most of it did. The rest of it will happen momentarily. No use waiting for it to happen to print it, not if it's sure. Rely on me, Mr. Tankersley."

"Where are you, Freddy?"

"Kansas City."

"How come you sound so funny?"

"I'm half asleep. Print it, Tankersley, just as soon as you can."

And Tankersley would print it just as soon as he could. It had to come right or he was dead. And it did come right. It all happened.

A mother put an eleven-year-old daughter on the train at Kansas City. "Don't blow it, kid," the mother said. "Ain't no way, Charley," the daughter answered. So it had become a byword of the times. Everything was coming right up to the point of perfection, rich harvests abounding, pearls beyond price to be dug from every field, all well with the country and the world, no hurry, we were just about there. Any danger of busting it or blowing it finally? Not on the popular level there wasn't. "Ain't no way to blow it, Charley," the people said.

Freddy read two pages, then dozed till there was a tug on his arm, a blue-eyed tug (Freddy, touched by the weave, could now see in all parts of him).

"I beg your pardon, but I was wondering if you were *One of Us?*" asked the man with the snapping blue eyes.

"Possibly, just possibly," Foley said.

"I am a rooted man, sir," said Blue-eyes. "There are those who chop off their own roots in the name of the old 'new' fashion. They wither from that moment. But radix-form mock roots burgeon out of the ground and surround them grotesquely, and these nourish nothing. I say that a man should not allow himself to be surrounded by such weightless weirdness. His own weirdness (that most necessary thing) he should keep inside himself where it is a strength. Beware that you not chop it down or cut it out of yourself. It grows again, externally and poisonously, unsustaining roots. I noticed the jacket of the book you were reading. It is a facetious title, but you do not seem to be a facetious man. Then I asked myself, Why should a man put such a jacket on a book other than for a joke? Why, for concealment, I told myself. What you are actually reading is not for prying eyes. The book (and it may not be a book) does not correspond to the title on the jacket. That is my guess."

"There is a fascination about guesses which must remain unverified," Freddy Foley said.

"I believe that it is a precis, a resume of your own project," the blue-eyed man said. "You may not care to discuss it. I do not care to discuss my own project, but I can always spot a fellow inventor. Every time I go up to Washington with one of my new great inventions, and it is several times a year, I see others who are quite unmistakably of my kind. We inventors are a curious breed."

"Ah, we are that. We are not as other men," Freddy said.

"Though I would not reveal the slightest detail of what I am carrying, yet there is no harm in telling you that it is basically an Enervator."

"I surmised as much."

"But perhaps you have surmised that I have only invented one more relaxer? No. If that were the case my trip would not be of so great moment. If that were the case I would not be followed and shadowed. There is one man in this coach who sleeps with his ears and eyes open and misses nothing. He is a shadow. His job is to watch and follow someone, and that someone cannot be other than myself."

"Or myself," said Freddy.

"Most inventors have the tendency to overestimate the value of their own inventions," said the blue-eyed man, "and perhaps you overestimate yours. The shadow-man looks at *you* with veiled eyes, it is true, but that is only so he will not seem to be looking at me. No, I'm sure that it is me he is following. What I have is a device that will change humanity completely, that will erase the decades and centuries, that will enable one to span—but I cannot tell you more. My life is in danger as it is."

"Why should your life be in danger for inventing a relaxing machine?"

"I tell you, it is much more. It will enable man to remove death to the incredibly distant future."

"It would seem a boon. Who would prevent it?"

"Those who have already achieved my aims without my machine. There *are* such men. I have reason to believe that there is a small jealous group who will kill to prevent their special benefits from going to all humanity."

"I've more fear that humanity will be killed by special benefits going to it unasked," Foley said. "It's a cat that's going to be killed with too much kindness. I wish you'd put a relaxer on all over-kind and over-zealous groups."

"But I will, sir. So many things appear out of due season. I'd freeze them a while. Ah—we both understand that I have been talking nonsense. My machine is not like this at all, but it may be of some aid in integrating the personal and world ego. We both understand that 'Enervator' is no more than a code description."

"Yes, we both understand that," said Fred Foley. That Fred Foley drew some strange ones, but there *was* a shadow-man on the coach and he was as likely shadowing Fred Foley as the blue-eyed inventor.

The rails were making rhymes to the tune of *Kansas City Star*:

> *Piles of money, piles of barley,*
> *Piles of peace, each man a king.*
> *Ain't no way to blow it, Charley,*
> *Ain't no way to blow the thing.*

Really, everything was better than it had ever been before, if you didn't look too closely behind the screen. "Bad news, bad news!" Tankersley stormed sometimes. "What do they make reporters out of nowadays? Can't anybody find just a little bad news to lead off one more edition?" There wasn't much bad news any more. In two more weeks a popular president would be reelected. People were sharper and kinder and happier than they had ever been. All molehills had been leveled. The world was flat and tidy, a perfect takeoff platform for . . . something. Ah well, what are a few bat-wings in the night, a few pet hydras escaping from fountain prisons, a few men living too many times? More power to them. And by dusk of the day that was dawning Fred Foley would come to the fine place itself, Washington the Capitol City, where all difficulties are resolved.

"Your creature had *not* escaped, Auclaire," Bertigrew Bagley growled. "What's the matter with you? Have you only one set of eyes? It's back in your fountain now, at any rate. I can see it. I don't believe it ever escaped into the world at all."

"No, Bagley, no. That's a simulacrum in my fountain now. It left it there to fool me. The thing itself is loose in this city and in this world. It has fragmented into seven or eight people but it still has its unity. The arms of it are persons. They always have been. We were wrong to believe that the arms of the polypus were movements. We saw them as Communism and as Secular-Liberalism and as such deadly things, but it is only when they inhabit persons that they are dangerous. That Foley knows the names of all of them, but he has slipped me. The sorrel-snake woman is the only one I know."

"Go easy on the sorrel-snake girl. I've a great affection for her. She doesn't laugh at me as viciously as most of them do. Oh, *I* know all the members, Auclaire. I can have my dog kill them easily enough, but I'm not sure that I should. We lived with dragons in the earlier days; why are we fastidious now? Every fine castle used to have its own dragon in the cellar. Every fine world has always had."

"This one is deadly, Bagley. It is one of those which has not raised itself, has not broken loose for centuries. It begins to eat up the children now. It killed thirteen good and high men this morning and it has hardly come awake yet."

"Three of those men needed killing, Auclaire. You've

got to admit that, whichever side of the aisle you're on."

"And the worst part of it, Bagley, is that it won't do any good to have your dog kill the members. They have already set up a real weave. They have already mutated. And one of them is already dead and it makes no difference at all. She comes on even stronger and weirder after she's dead. And the leader, what is his name?"

"Jim Bauer. He's the biologist, but he knew all along that the biology of the thing was only part of the hoax, only part of the trigger."

"He is torn between two ideas for strengthening the weave now. He will either kill himself and go to hell—he believes that he might do better work from there—or he will enlist an actual demon of hell and expend the weave to nine members. He is already playing Demon Lover with both his dead and his living wife—what is their name?"

"Letitia."

"Letitia—Happiness. I wonder if she really wanted it? She got on that danger kick instead. Maybe it is her sort of happiness, but she comes through mighty pale and drawn. Should we contact the Patriarchs of Greater Armenia and Greater Ireland?"

"Oh, I've already done that, Auclaire. They say that they have escaping creatures of their own, much more momentous ones than we have here. And the Patriarch of Greater Armenia reminds me of another thing. God still regards all four sets of us things as exterior creatures, not to be allowed into the castle or the world, not good for the castle or the world. To Him, at the moment, we are not much better than the python-nest things, than the resurrection toads, than the gnashing falcons. Even our sometimes alliance with the falcons, as better than the other two, is not completely pleasing to Him."

"What must we do then, Bagley? Oh yes, I remember

what the Manual says we must do. 'Serve faithfully for aeon after aeon, that He may be convinced of our good will. Guard the hydra-pythons that they may not escape into the world. Unravel the mystery of the resurrection toads even if it takes us a million days. Mitigate the menace of the falcons, but use it against any greater menace that might arise. And after long and faithful service, He may admit us into the castle.' Bagley, I keep hoping that every thousand years we serve may be the last."

"It would be pretty ironic, Auclaire, wouldn't it, if the other three sets also believed that they were serving faithfully? That they might also some day be admitted to the castle? You know, there's a story that we *were* in the castle once, that we set up our own primordial weave, and that we mutated; and that we got thrown out then and became exterior creatures; and that we have to labor like trolls to redeem ourselves. Say, my dog is one-quarter troll by blood. I'll ask him sometime how hard they really work. We may be overdoing it."

Odd talk, that, is it not? Not very. Not from patricks. They often talk like that when a couple of them get together. They are some sort of lodge or society. They pretend to take themselves seriously, like the Baker Street Irregulars. And they pick up a little esoterism such as you get from the Los Angeles quackeries. They have titles and such, and they pretend to divide the world into realms such as Greater Ireland and Greater Armenia.

Jim Bauer, as a matter of fact, did not kill himself that day. Neither did he kill Arouet Manion. The sickly fear of death that was on Arouet added a curious and glittering element to the weave. Imagine a man being afraid of a little thing like dying, a mutated man at that. But cowardice might be as necessary an element as arrogance and dishonesty and hatred to make a weave really work.

Bauer postponed his own death for a while, regretfully, as he believed there was still much work to be done in generating the weave and he believed he could do it better in the body. Later, later he would do it.

But he did enlist an actual demon named Baubo to join the weave. This expanded the membership to nine. We will see how it works, we will see how it works.

VII: OF ELEGANT DOGS AND RETURNED MEN

> ... For I have written at great length of these
> Mansions (the fourth), as these are they where
> the greatest number of souls enter. As the nat-
> ural is first united with the supernatural in
> these, it is here that the devil can do most harm.
> *Interior Castle*: Teresa of Avila

IT IS A southern river town with some pretensions of
being a city. It is intended to be beautiful, and often it
is. It has more greenery than most, and it uses its water
areas (both natural and contrived) well. There is grace
in the general placement of its public buildings, and it
has one quality which only the distinctive cities have:
it is never seen for the first time. It is always recognized
as something once known and forgotten for a while.

And like every southern river town it has its canker.
Every one of them has it somehow, like a beautiful belle
with a loathsome disease. There is no point in stirring
needless enmity (though it *is* fun) by naming the names
and recounting the venoms. But it's a fact that they are
a mean bunch of towns: many of them are likable, but
all of them are mean.

Every plain mean town in the land, Kansas City,
Natchez, Wilmington N.C., Cape Giradeau, Cincinnati
(certainly it's a southern town; it doesn't matter which
side of that river it's on), Morgan City, Memphis, Lare-
do, Baton Rouge, St. Louis, Louisville, Richmond, New

Orleans, every really mean town in the country is a southern river town.

The capital has its own orneriness, as pervading as the others, but it isn't the same sort. It never was a fun town. It is not a robust sin town. Its fleshpots have no real juice in them. Its vices are effete and heterodox, and its moral rot is a dry one. Though its people have come there from all parts, yet they are not all sorts of people. They are very much of one sort. The ethic climate here nurtures an ancient, evil, shriveled thing. It is of the inhabitants of this city that the prophet spoke:

> Of those who do not have the faith
> And will not have the fun.

There's an odor about all these southern river towns that isn't entirely due to their dank rivers. Here there is a sense of being in a tightly closed room even when outdoors. Still, it's a pretty and pleasant town to come to in the evening.

Oriel Overlark shouldn't be a hard person to locate. Fred Foley would find her, ask her one question, and then go back home if, of course, he got the answer. There are several thousand persons in Washington whose whereabouts will always be known to everyone. Anyone in the trade will know.

Freddy looked up Mary Ann Evans. She'd know where Oriel Overlark was at the moment. Mary Ann was a casual acquaintance of Foley, but now he must originate the fiction that they were very old friends, and Mary Ann must go along with it. She was a lady reporter, and her stories were entirely of the ladies.

But she looked at Fred Foley with amazement, almost with awe. Nobody had ever done that before.

"Foley! How did you do it? How did you know? You had some of them almost before they happened, all of them before or right at the moment when they were discovered. I think there are pickup orders out for you. Your paper denies knowing where you are. You're going to have to answer some real inquiries. *How did you know about them?*"

"About what, Mary Ann? That's the strangest greeting I ever got from anyone. I just blew into town."

"About the thirteen suicides, if that's what they were. Were they? You must be the one who knows all about them."

"Was my name on that story? That was way back early this morning."

"Your name wasn't on it—you'd be torn limb from limb for it by now if it had been. Your boss-image Tankersley *is* being. But we were able to track it back to you easily enough. What are you following up on now? Six of those suicides were here in Washington, but of course you know that."

"Oh, I'm not doing anything of a followup, Mary Ann. My part of that one is finished with. All I came to Washington for is to see Oriel Overlark and ask her one question."

"What a cover, but who'd believe that? When did you start doing ladies' features? Fred, you're so much older and more mature! I can't believe it. I never saw a kid get over being a kid like that. It's only a year since I saw you."

"It's only a week since Tankersley told me he wished I didn't look so much like a kid. He didn't think I'd ever get over it."

"In one week you've matured and deepened like that? What's happened to you?"

"Nothing at all, Mary Ann. And I sure haven't matured. Now, can you tell me where I can find Oriel Overlark, now, at this moment? I want to ask her one question, and then I want to go back home."

"There are very many people who want to ask you

very many questions, Fred. Why the Oriel fake? Is she connected with the suicides?"

"Oh no. This has nothing to do with that. I want to ask her one question, that's all."

"For what she's worth, Fred, let me tell you that she isn't worth anything to you. I've done three pieces on Oriel myself, trying to see her in three dimensions. It didn't work, though. She looks brilliant, but she's a flat person. Not even low relief. She doesn't have three dimensions.

"Carmody was an art collector, you know, before he became adviser to the advisers. Oriel is a piece of art. Not profound art, but striking new art for all that. She's a novelty piece. She's been imitated and parodied, but only in a small circle. She'll never be a widespread fad. Why do you want to talk to Oriel? What kind of question do you want to ask her?"

"I want to ask her a question about Carmody."

"Why don't you ask Carmody the question about Carmody?"

"I will, if Oriel doesn't give me the answer. I guess I really want answers from both of them. I may have to add them together. Oriel might not know all about Carmody. I'm sure that Carmody hasn't researched Carmody to any depth, doesn't really know much about Carmody, but—"

"—added to what *you* know about Carmody, you should have it complete. Is that it, Fred? There she is now. And if you have to ask me which she is, then you don't deserve any answers at all."

"No. I don't have to ask which she is, Mary Ann."

Freddy and Mary Ann were dining at Proviant's, and the Oriel party had just entered. Certainly nobody would have to ask which was Oriel, even though several of those in her party were prominent. She didn't take the center. She took a position where it was even a little hard for them to see her. But she *was* the center.

Proviant's was a Germanish sort of restaurant. Mary Ann hadn't known that Oriel would come here. It is more likely that Freddy had made her come here through some power he had from being brushed by the weave. They could watch but not hear the Oriel party from here, and Freddy's first impression was that Oriel was not so flat as all that: that she might have dimensions that Mary Ann didn't suspect.

"She's isn't really pretty," said Mary Ann, "yet men look at her as if she were. Her eyes are too close together; her hair grows too far down on her forehead; her ears aren't a bit good, but she seldom shows them. She hasn't enough jaw, and her neck lacks only a little of being scrawny. Her shoulders are her best asset above-board, but they're not in it with those of her two friends, and you don't even notice them. She doesn't know how to sit. She doesn't know how to walk."

"But you'd recognize her in a crowd, or at a great distance, Mary Ann."

"Yes. She's too light in the body and too heavy in the legs. Her ankles are good, though, and her feet, particularly the insteps. But honestly I can't give her much else."

"Her hair?"

"Oh, her hair's by Schwob. I thought you'd know that."

"Not the color."

"The color is about ten percent Schwob. He has a way of putting the highlights in. It wasn't exactly that color before, but it was close."

"It's blue-blonde. There can't be a color like that, can there? Or it's like ashen-blonde seen under a blue light, and the light here isn't. Gahh, I've had one too many, no, two too many, ashen-blondes lately."

"Really, Fred? Is that what's matured you? If only she hadn't those washed-out blue eyes."

"At least they aren't green, Mary Ann." (But possibly Oriel's eyes were a bit green.)

"Fooled you, Fred. I felt that one coming. I didn't listen. She isn't at all intelligent. And she isn't a good talker or a good listener. It's just that she's always had it. She's even richer than Carmody. Oh, there's Carmody joining them now! I didn't suspect he'd join them."

"I did. That stuff is hard work, though," Freddy said.

"Shall we barge over and I make the introductions, Fred? There's really no painless way to do it. They'll make us feel like commoners in any case. It's their only talent that I really envy. Whatever it is that sets them apart and makes them that sort of people and not our sort I don't know."

"Oh, I've been puzzling lately what makes a person what he is, and not another. My puzzle's really the same as yours. I remember now where I met Carmody before. I had a slight notion that I'd known him. He wasn't at all the sort of man one would remember or notice, for all that he was rich and open. But this Carmody has carried over some details from the old."

"Not notice that man? Fred, how can you say that? Everyone would always have noticed him and remembered him. Why, the smoothness is just dripping off him."

"I know it. But he isn't the same man. I've got that part of the answer now, I'm sure. I really had my trip for nothing. But I don't believe that either of them will tell me how he does the trick."

"Is this something that I'm not supposed to understand, Fred?"

"I don't think they want anyone to understand it. They're nervous and unsure."

"Nervous and unsure? Them? Never, Fred."

"Why do they have people everywhere to kill people who ask questions, then? I wouldn't do that unless I was a little bit nervous about something."

So Freddy went over to where the august party was

settling down again after the arrival of Carmody Overlark.

"Mr. Overlark, I doubt if you remember me," he said. "Fred Foley. I knew you a little at Hot Springs three years ago. You were a cheerful loser at the races and you sometimes stayed up after dark."

"Yes, Foley, I got out among them a little more then," Carmody Overlark said. He had a twinkle on him, but not what you would call a merry twinkle. Something other, of a different humor. And, yes, he did have archaic ears. "I've less time for diversions now, but I still enjoy them. I remember you. A newspaper man, aren't you? And there may be something you want to talk to me about in my and your official capacity?"

"What would be the easiest way to go about it, Mr. Overlark?"

"It's a vicious circle with only one possible solution. I'll have to make an appointment for you with my secretary, and he'll make an appointment for you with me. Here, I'll write a brief note. He'll be able to decipher it, but you may not be. It's the only way you can get to see him, and seeing him is the only way you can get to see me. It may be a day or two; I'm quite busy. Good evening. And good evening, Miss Evans."

They were dismissed, but Freddy had the scribbled note. Freddy and Mary Ann went back to their table.

"Don't be resentful, Fred," she said. "Besides, he really *is* important. He wasn't being rude, just direct. And you do have an appointment for an appointment."

"That's not my resentful look, Mary Ann. Pray that you never see that. But he doesn't remember me. He never saw me before."

"Naturally not. Why did you make up that silly story about knowing him at Hot Springs? Anybody could have found out where such a prominent man as he was three years ago and made it fit in."

"Oh, I did know Carmody Overlark there, Mary Ann.

I spent part of a large night with him, but I'd forgotten it. He was such an easy man to forget."

"Fred, you're off your noggin. Nobody could ever forget that man."

"He *was* easy to forget, and I had forgotten him, till it came back to me a moment ago. But that man there never saw me before and I never saw him."

"Why did he say that he had, then? How did he know that you were a newspaper man?"

"He said he knew me because he knows as much about Carmody Overlark as one man will bother to learn about another for a special reason, and he realized that I probably *had* met Carmody. And he knew I was a newspaper man because I look and act like one, and because I'm with a newspaper woman, you."

"Tell me about it, Fred. If I were onto anything queer I'd tell you about it."

"My mother used to tell me that lying would make my tongue black. What really made my tongue black was chewing walnut hulls for tobacco, but she always thought it was my lying. You'd no more tell me if you had something live—"

"Oh I know it. My tongue's black."

They ate. It was good. They talked. And once Freddy left the table briefly. It was not coincidence that another person left another table at nearly the same time. It was planned that way, but the way the planning was implemented is harder to explain. Foley had his own way of getting an idea across, especially with his new-found maturity, and he was more capable than most gave him credit for.

And now he had made another appointment, which did not involve a secretary. He had hopes, for the first time, that perhaps the trick would be explained to him after all.

Anyhow, he had a date with Oriel Overlark now.

Freddy and Mary Ann left Proviant's. They ditched each other. Mary Ann went to make inquiries on whether there was really anything new on Carmody Overlark, on the fifteen suicides, on tip-man Freddy Foley who had now won inner-circle fame for a story he'd already put out of his mind.

Freddy walked not quite at random. He walked rapidly in the bright streets and slowly in the dark ones. "That damned spider," he said and brushed his hand across his eyes, but there wasn't any spider, only a silk streamer out of some web attached to him. He doubled and redoubled. He knew the tricks. He came up behind the man who had been following him and collared him firmly.

It was the inventor from the train.

"Not that you worry me," Foley said, letting him go again when he saw what fish he was, "and not that I care about being followed, but I *am* curious. Why have you been following me?"

"I wasn't," said the man. "It only seemed like it. Actually I was following the man who was following you—ah, this is a little hard to put into words—the man who was following you so he wouldn't seem to be following me. You were just a little pawn we maneuvered around. Then you maneuvered to get behind both of us. You didn't notice him at all, but he's waiting quite near. He's a better shadow than I am. Why was it that you noticed me and didn't notice him, since he was between us most of the time?"

"I don't know. Well then, why were you following the man who was following me?"

"To keep him in sight. And because I didn't quite understand the situation. I still don't. It's almost as if there was something important about *you*. I told you back on the train that there was a man in our car who slept with his eyes and ears open and missed nothing. He was following me to destroy the secret of the remarkable invention I carry, and perhaps to destroy the inventor too. That is the same man who is still waiting a little ways off. You had the idea that it might be you he was following, as though your own invention (whatever it is) could be of such import. Now I'm a little in doubt myself. It's a blow to my pride, but it just *may* be you he is following. Are you in danger?"

"Not in immediate danger, I don't believe. I've passed several darker corners than this where it could have happened if it was meant to happen tonight."

"Say, I'm Crabtree, Carlyle S.," the man said. "You *should* know my name, but most inventors are uninformed and unacquainted outside of their own narrow field. I except myself. Most don't know their own next door neighbor in the speculative neighborhood. Yet I'm an important man, and possibly you are, since you also seem to be a focus of interest. You may regard me, sir, as a little sawed-off joker with a lot of talk who'd be no good in a showdown. But I boxed at Tech, school middleweight champion. I'm still handy. Shall we go jump him and see what he's made of? We could cut him off both ways from here."

"It might be fun, Carlyle S., but we wouldn't find out anything, and I'd lose a possible lead. A man following you can sometimes lead you to a place you wouldn't otherwise be able to find. Now, Carlyle, I'm going to phone a man from the corner drug store there. He's given me things in the past. Do me a favor and watch my shadow for a little while. I'll be right back. We'll talk some more, then, and you may want to go with me and talk to this man also."

"His name, sir, in case something happens to you, and I may be stubborn enough to follow it out myself?"

"Harry Hardcrow," said Fred Foley. "I don't know his number till I look it up. I don't know his address any more either. He's known in the newspaper business, if you would want to find him."

"And your name, sir? I don't even know that."

"Fred Foley. I'm also in the newspaper business, but not as well known. Watch my shadow for a while. But nothing will happen."

"I believe that something *will* happen, Foley. I have an instinct for these things and I've never been wrong yet. Something very direct will happen suddenly, but I will try to be ready for it."

Foley went into the corner drug store, looked up the number and phoned Harry Hardcrow. He got him at once. Hardcrow seemed half glad to hear from him. At least he placed him. And suddenly Hardcrow seemed much more interested. Fred Foley had new fame as a tipster going for him.

"Foley, honest, I want to see you and talk to you. I want to ask you about— But honestly, I have something big I have to cover right now. I do want to see you later. You may be able to do something for me, and I'll do almost anything for you. Could you come by my place about midnight?"

"Oh sure, Hardcrow. You still live at the same place? Yes, I can find it."

Foley left the drug store and walked back to meet Carlyle S. Crabtree, the inventor. He thought he might go to the hotel and talk till time for the meeting with Hardcrow. An inventor might have a mind that would hit on overlooked corners of a problem. Besides, Crabtree seemed like a man who would stay with a friend, once he had become a friend. In a way, they had pact between them.

But Crabtree wasn't standing where he should have been. Foley approached the dark spot very slowly. If Crabtree weren't there— But he was there, as Foley saw with the absolute opposite of relief. Foley was always cool. He should have been doubly cool with his new maturity. Cool! What he saw froze him solid for a minute.

Carlyle Crabtree wasn't standing there, but he was lying there. And the way he was lying, Freddy knew that he was dead. He was lying on his face, dragged back into the doorway of an unlighted shop. He had been knifed deeply and his life still ran out in black blood, but the main bleeding was over with. He had no pulse. He had already begun to go rigid.

Freddy was surprised that he remained calm. But he had been calm in tricky situations for several days now. After all, according to Mary Ann Evans and to his own new feeling, he had achieved maturity. But what now?

The shadow was nowhere to be seen, but he might still be near. He had killed once, he might intend to do it again. But Freddy began to get mad.

"I'll have you for this!" he called loudly. Then he was silent. He had no wish to be associated with the death itself so he worked rapidly. He turned Crabtree over. The man hadn't even been gone through. He still bulged in the same places. Whatever interest they had in Crabtree, it hadn't been in what he was carrying.

Foley took out a very large, very full manila envelope that Crabtree carried inside his shirt. He had known that Crabtree carried his most precious possession there. The chubby little man wasn't that chubby. Freddy also took the money-belt and the wallet, as such things can be handy.

He finished with it. But he had his new instincts and insights, and also his old reporter instincts. They shrilled at him "Plant! Plant!" Freddy had been wrong at first. Crabtree *had* been gone through. Someone had a very great interest in what he had been carrying, to frisk so quickly and completely, and to substitute authentically.

Freddy had begun to like the little inventor, but he left him there and walked rapidly toward his hotel. Two people were signaling his mind. This business of distant people talking to him was something new these last two or three days and he didn't attempt to account for it. They had to be people who had also been brushed by the brain-weave, for that acted somehow as communication satellite to bounce the messages. But this was Bencher, Bedelia's father. Had the weave attacked him too? Or had he had some earlier encounter? After all, he did have a great scar on his forehead from some youthful encounter, and it was very like the mark the Harvesters had inflicted on themselves lately.

"Stay there and wait, Freddy," Bencher was saying. "I'll get you out of there."

"Stay here and wait nothing!" Freddy snorted. He had picked up his shadow again after two blocks and he didn't intend to make a mistake. Freddy was very alert now and very angry. Turning a corner, he paused and listened. There was nothing to be heard, though he fancied he could hear another man listening. Foley reversed. He was fast. He thought he could collar that shadow quickly and have him, knife or no knife.

The shadow was faster. Foley couldn't run him down. He followed him around another corner, and the shadow had disappeared completely. But there wasn't any place he could have disappeared.

"Stay there, Freddy, you have to stay there," Bencher was saying again. "I'll get you out, I'll get you over the wall somehow."

"Over what wall?" Freddy asked. Finally when Freddy had neared his hotel, the shadow was there again, but further back.

"Ah well, this is your game," Freddy said. "I'll find a game that I can play better than you. There's no use getting cute now at this end of the trail. If you followed me before, you know where I'm staying." Freddy went into his hotel.

"It's simply diabolism," Bencher was saying. "I don't know why my daughter became involved with it. It isn't that she's brainless, it's just that she's still a kid.

I'll figure it out. I'll sort out the different powers involved. This simple diabolism I can whip. Stay there and don't worry. I'll get you over the wall."

"Leave it, Bencher," Freddy said. "I'm not behind walls, and I can whip simple diabolism myself. This is more complex."

Freddy went to his room, bolted every bolt, checked windows and such, went into the bathroom to be safe from possible gunfire from outside, and dumped all the Crabtree loot onto the floor. He even sounded the wall between his and the bathroom of the next room. It sounded firm and untampered-with.

But the second voice came now. It had waited politely for the first one, Bencher's, to finish.

"You know who I am," came the slightly-slurred, slightly-accented voice of Miguel Fuentes to Freddy's inner ears. "We have not met but we know each other. We are both brushed by the devil-weave, and we can fox back and talk by it. I want to make proclamation. You will proclaim this for me from the capital of your country. Let me talk now. You will not need to write it down till later, or you can phone it in to someone and not write it down at all. I know you are like me, you have a memory for words, and you will remember all of mine exactly.

"I make proclamation of who I am and what I will do for the world. I was roused to my activity by devils for a devils' game, but I will not do devils' work. This is a mistake that the devils make, that they believe they have the ordering of things. They cannot remember that very often these things turn against them: that they can start a wind but they cannot order which way the wind will blow. This is what I am: a poor man, but a good man at several trades; a man of brains who has never used his brains until now; a bad man very often, but one who was never so dishonest as to pretend that his bad was good; a slob, *un chapucero*, there is no word in English to say what sort of slob I was; a strong man, particularly in the arms and back and loins and legs; a humorous man even when the great gash of false justice and misery cuts across the whole world picture.

"Why has this thing come to me? Why, because it did not come to another man, I suppose. The world is in need of ordering, and there is no other man who steps forward and says 'I will order it.'

"I will be called fascist. I and mine will *be* fascist in the old Roman sense, not in the sense of the modern sniveling things that are of the left and not of the right. We will be fascist in the real sense and sign of the fasces. This is the battle-ax bound in with sticks and rods, and the meaning of it is authority by steps. Ax cuts sticks as threat, sticks beat dogs, and dogs (when comes an unusual revolution) eat up ax. This is like the hand and fist game that children play when they put out their hands to challenge each other: rock breaks scissors, scissors cuts paper and paper covers rock.

"As to the last part of my instance, the revolution where dogs eat up ax, I will proclaim it in a moment what elegant and bristling and false dogs those are, and how they are not of the people at all but are vicious prey on the people.

"This is the fault of the world, this is the reason that it needs ordering now: it is bankrupt in the middle of its wealth, and it offers a life that is not worth living. It has stolen their old poverty from the people and given them meaner things under new names. It has brought back a slavery that is more abject than any in history, though its chains are not of iron but of peculiar compulsion. The world has befouled itself and it needs to be cleaned. Think of me as the cleaner of the world. If I use a little blood instead of useless detergent, it is to cleanse it the better.

"I speak good words of Indians, the earth people of earth. I have traveled to countries and continents as sea-man and irregular soldier and I have seen that it is the same everywhere. There are always the earth-people (I will call them Indians, though they have other names in other places; there are even blond and red-headed Indians, and fair and black and the color *morado*); and there are the ravening dog- or wolf-people who prey on them. It is the dog- and wolf-people who use revolution and the liberalism-slavery trick and the devil catchwords to disorder the world. In every land of Latin America and in most lands of the world, there have been at least three revolutions by these dog-people (some of blood, some of idea only), and all have been in the name of the earth-people. Now there are the great families and groups who rule and enslave everywhere. They pass the dog-lie that it is the old stubborn rich families, that it is the old stubborn church, that it is the old stubborn ways that are obstacles. This is all lying. It is always the new rich dog-families and groups, the novel church of the itching ears, the ways of new hell that enslave. And it is these dogs who rule always who ask falsely for more revolution; it is they who bleed false blood for the new poor who are their own creation; it is they who preach love instead of law. For the law obliges them and restricts them. But it costs them nothing to use the word 'love.'

"I call them the elegant dogs, and I begin to kill them now. They rule the world but they do not believe that there is another world above and after.

"I speak good words of church who is mother here and also hereafter. But it is for real love of church that I will kill certain judas priests and judas bishops and almost all of judas editors and journalists.

"But for our great compassion, we will not kill so many people as many might wish. Of most of the elegant dogs we will only pull the teeth. 'This is no good,' says an adviser who joined me only today. 'Those dogs will grow new teeth. Kill them all.' We will see. If they persist in growing new teeth, then it is time to kill them.

"We will kill only such persistent false voices as can not otherwise be silenced. In all the world we may have to kill no more than one million liberals, communists and doctrinaires. The rest will shrivel, for a time at least.

"I understand, with my new insight, the four powers that are on the fringe of the world. I have now become actionist and captain of one of those powers. I understand the abiding men and the returning men. I understand which support us and which support the dog-faced octopus.

"Am I so sure that I am right? No. I am not. A man who is sure he is right is always wrong. But I am sure that the elegant dogs are wrong. A patrick whose mind I encounter tells me that God still regards all four sets of us things as exterior creatures, not to be allowed into the castle or the world, not good for the castle or the world. I believe that God is mistaken in classing us with the other powers, and I will convince Him of His mistake. But I will do what I have to do, even though I was roused by devils and have not yet the full approval of God. That will come if I do my work well.

"To all the governments and governors of the world: Wait and do not panic. I am coming to relieve you of your governing as soon as possible. Do not abuse anything while you wait. You are on time and sufferance. I come quickly, but there is a whole world to occupy. I will kill only the anti-life people who speak of unwanted people, as if there could ever be too many people, as if there could ever be too much of this highest created excellence. I will kill only unreformable liberals, and elegant dogs who oppress, and the evil returning men who are fine and yellow in toadflax.

"To the world in disorder: Wait. Persevere. I come to order it now.

"Proclaim that, Foley, proclaim it. It will really come about."

"All right, Miguel, all right. I'll proclaim it," Freddy said. "Yes, I will remember it all. Leave me now. I have my affair with elegant dogs and returned men fine in toadflax."

VIII: THE LINE OF YOUR THROAT, THE MER-
CURIAL MOVEMENT

> What adders came to shed their coats?
>   What coiled obscene
> Small serpents with soft stretching throats
>   Caressed Faustine?
>   Swinburne

In his hotel room Fred Foley examined the money-belt and billfold he had taken from Crabtree. Finding nothing of interest in them except money and identification, he made a bundle of them to parcel post to the police. He examined casually the contents of the large manila envelope. This, he decided, he would keep for further study.

It was the detailing of Crabtree's latest invention, the design of a cubicle. The cubicle would be the size to hold a man lying down. It would be airtight and nearly indestructible when sealed. The purpose of it was obscure, though the papers said it was an Enervator. "Who wants to be enervated anyhow?" Foley asked himself.

There was considerable electromagnetic apparatus, minute controls to maintain conditions and large controls apparently to set up conditions. There were many pages of mathematics and schematics which could not be digested casually; by many persons they could not have been digested at all. But Foley, who had been a science feature writer, had a talent of going to the heart of a thing and he soon had the basic idea of it.

"But it's all wrong," he said.

"Of course it is," said Hondo Silverio. "It's a substitution, but an ingenious one."

"It isn't an Enervator, of course," said Richard Bencher. "It's an Hypnotic Dredge. Even in its wrongness I can see that the original is meant to bring up the strengths and varieties unused, the vitality untapped, to awaken the interior nourishing weirdness and so demolish the exterior mock-root poisons. Stay there, Foley; I'll get you over the wall."

"No machine will do it—not this, not the original," said Hondo Silverio. "But they're afraid of it and have intercepted it. They're terrified of our interior strengths."

"I didn't know you two were tuned in," Freddy said. There was a note by Crabtree to the effect that the thing had never actually been tried out. There was writing that Freddy called the "A" or Crabtree hand; there were some that he called the "B" substitution or other hand, but this was so near to the Crabtree hand that Foley did not know how he distinguished them.

There was a feeling about all this that Foley had from the first, a feeling which he knew would persist no matter how deeply he delved into it: that was the feeling that the whole thing was a hoax.

At the same time there was the even stronger feeling that Carlyle S. Crabtree had been in no respect a hoaxer. But can a straight man perpetuate a hoax unwittingly? No, not that man. He might perpetuate some nonsense, or a failure or an ineptitude, but never a hoax.

But this smelled of hoax all through it. "Well, I'll leave it here a while," Freddy told himself. He would go out. He knew that his room and his things would be gone through while he was out. No matter. Whoever they were, they already knew what it all was, and he didn't.

Freddy went out for his meeting with Harry Hardcrow. He stopped in the street in front of his hotel and whistled loudly. "Coming?" he called then. "Coming after me?" But his shadow was not to be seen. Then a taxi rolled around the corner and stopped to his hail. Freddy got in. He had the feeling that he would be taken to his destination whether he gave it or not, but he was skittish of testing it. He gave the driver Harry Hardcrow's address.

"Not that you aren't, and not that I'm not," said Harry Hardcrow, who often talked that sort of shorthand, "but I'm wondering if your visit is casual or urgent." He shook hands with Foley. "You had a slight tone of excitement when you talked to me on the phone earlier, Foley. And you appear now still more excited. Has anything happened in the meanwhile?"

"Not that I recall, not anything important," Fred Foley said. "Oh yes, there was the murder of a man whom I knew only a little bit. But he had been waiting for me when it happened. It shook me a little more than has come to the surface yet. But it wasn't involved with my main line of inquiry, so we'll let it go for the moment."

"It *may* be involved with your main line of inquiry, Foley. What *is* your main line of inquiry?" Hardcrow asked.

"I'm looking for the answers to a couple of questions that will sound asinine to you, Harry, though not so asinine as if I'd put them in their first forms. The first one I ask seriously, though it sounds almighty trite. What's your opinion of the state of the nation and the world now, Harry?"

"Worse than perfect, Foley—jittery, almost hysterical in certain circles. And nobody knows why. Two years ago it was the best it had been in decades, maybe the best ever. *And everything has improved since then.* Two years ago there was real feeling of hope and trust all around the world. Differences had almost disappeared. Health, national, physical, moral, and financial, was good. Crime was down. And there had come that sort of creative gaiety that marks only the very great eras. We had come into one of the really golden ages. It wasn't just the arts, Foley (though they were burgeoning as not since that short springtime in Florence half a millennium ago); it wasn't just material prosperity (we've had that before, though not so solid nor so unmixed); it was just a general breaking into the light after many years of work on all fronts dedicated to the advance. It was a good harvest in sight after a long labor."

"I know how it was two years ago, Hardcrow. And I know a little how it is now, though the worst is kept from us peasants. But how has it become worse while getting better? What has happened in between?"

"It was a series of unprecedented advances that somehow left us far in arrears, Foley; a program of wise and probably perfect moves that left us in a stupid situation; a whole array of undoubted improvements that has nearly reduced us to a shambles. Nobody knows just what has happened. And all are trying, on the advice of the best minds available, to restore some sanity to our position."

"On the advice of the same best minds available which engineered the unprecedented advances, Hardcrow? The wise and probably perfect moves, and the array of undoubted improvements? We slide back two steps while we advance one."

"It's easy to criticize, Foley, but one doesn't do it in time of crisis. It may be that our position really is improved, so much so that we're allowed to see some dangers now that had been hidden from us. Or things might have been worse had it not been for the careful plannings and actions. It may be that these have taken the edge off a terrible debacle that was due for us."

"And it might not be. Who's chopping us down, Harry?

Hardcrow, you were stitting here right in the lap of the nation's pulse, to turn a metaphor. Have you noticed the appearance of a series of brilliant 'new' men who may have something to do with our backward improvements?"

"I have noticed the new men, Foley, and they're what gives me hope. We may be in a transition canyon when we thought we were on top of the crest, but these new men will lead us out of it. I've been fascinated by them; I've asked myself 'How is it possible that we should be so rich in talent?' "

"You seem hypnotized by this, Hardcrow."

"Yes, I am a little. I believe now that our setbacks are only temporary, or only in appearance. I believe that these new-appearing great minds will advance us along that great road."

"As far along as we were before they appeared?"

"Much further along, Foley, all the way. Our premature flowering may now become the real thing. Oh, I know the snide hints that have been going around the country. I'm sorry to see that you appear to have fallen prey to some of them. I'm not yet ready to believe that our advance has been thwarted deliberately, surely not that it's been thwarted by those who seem to be advancing it most."

"When will you be ready to believe it, Hardcrow?"

"Never, I hope. Tonight I saw a new prospect. I'm on fire with it. Foley, there's expectation in the air, and nothing the stodgy people can do will sour it. Tonight I was present at the unveiling, so to speak, at the introduction to Washington of perhaps the most flexible and curious mind in the country. We can't fail in anything when we have such men as he. I believe that he, as well as other such brilliant men, will get us off dead center, will fill our sails with billows once more—"

"A sail-seaman you're not, Hardcrow. What sort of apple is this new man?"

"I'd say a crabapple for a joke. For coincidentally his name is Crabtree."

"Not Carlyle S.?"

"It certainly is. How could you have known, Foley? You aren't big enough to have entree to— You aren't high enough in the trade even to know of such a man. Still, you *did* scoop the country on the suicides, and on some of the happenings of the Fuentes fascist fellow. And you do seem to have come along remarkably, Foley. Is it only a year since I saw you? You seem older now, and much more—"

"Mature, Hardcrow. It's my new maturity. Yes, I'm big enough now to hear stories of big men when they appear."

"Well, you've been a science feature writer, and I understand that Crabtree had some standing as scientist and inventor in the hinterlands. You knew he was in town?"

"Yes."

"That's odd. *Nobody* was supposed to know. Still, how perspicacious of you to guess that *he* would be selected for high position, since it hasn't yet been announced. He's a wonderful inventor. Marvelous ideas!"

"Most marvelous. How long, exactly, Hardcrow, is it since this great unveiling of this flexible and curious mind? How long ago was it that you saw Crabtree?"

"Why, I've just come from the meeting. None but us selected correspondents was there. And the officials and dignitaries. It isn't twenty minutes since I saw him last."

"And it isn't much more than two hours since I saw him dead, Hardcrow."

"What are you saying, Foley? Are you trying to fish a story out of me? I'm onto your cracked talk. Don't try it with me. What are you trying to say?"

"That I'm fortunate to be near the actual birth of one of these new men, Hardcrow. It makes me feel a little

like a midwife. Can you tell me what Carlyle S. Crabtree was wearing?"

"Foley, do you doubt that I was there, just because
you weren't selected? I can do even better than tell
you what he was wearing; I can show you. Naturally
cameras were forbidden. And just as naturally every
correspondent had his own pinhole camera. We'll just
roll them out. Here. Here's a good one of him on the
very first picture."

"Yes, that's Crabtree all right, Hardcrow. Or it's so
near to Crabtree as to deceive all except the elect. I'd
give a lot to know how it's done. And it's his same
clothes, baggy pants, jacket and all. I wonder what they
did about the knife-cuts in the jacket and shirt? Hey,
I wonder how they got the blood back in him? And if
they had a body left over? He was a nice fellow."

"Seems to be, Foley: a plain man as all very great
men are. He came dressed just as he arrived in town.
But he's absolutely incandescent with ideas. What was
that other stuff you were talking, Foley? You seemed
to be talking nonsense, perhaps dangerous nonsense."

"Yeah, I know. Crabtree was wrong at the last, though.
The shadow wasn't following me after all; he was following Crabtree. Or there may have been one on each
of us and they may have been in concert. I still have a
little pride in my own importance. Did Crabtree provide anything startling?"

"With the simplicity of the truly great he had carried
things of the highest importance in a large manila
envelope inside his shirt. Imagine, Foley, these were
things that may change the whole destiny and nature
of man."

"Crabtree took the manila envelope out of his shirt?
You saw him do it?"

"Yes. A pandora's box in a manila envelope. That is
what he took out."

"Then I wonder what I took out."

"It will take years to analyze it, Foley. But it will be wonderful."

"It may be. But Crabtree rather wanted to put it into effect without waiting years. He was even a little in a hurry that it be done at once. He was afraid that certain groups would prevent it. I see that they have. And so a new man is born."

"Foley, there's something about your attitude that I don't like," Harry Hardcrow said harshly. "There are some things you don't have any business guessing if you don't know other things. A newspaper man has got to know when to keep his mouth and his mind shut. You might end up dead."

"Isn't that the usual fate of men, Harry?"

"There have been other times, Foley, when you seemed ready to disassociate yourself from the mainstream. And you've been throwing out insane hints for ten minutes. Unless you explain them you'd better leave at once. You may be too hot to handle as it is. I don't intend to get my hands burned for any unlicked cub."

"There's another question I'll have to find the answer to, Hardcrow. How do they subvert minds like yours? You aren't stupid. You've been here in the middle of it. You do know part of something that's going on. You weren't always servile. You weren't always scared. Is there more than one way of intruding a new man into an old? Are you entirely the Harry Hardcrow who used to be? He could look at both sides of a coin."

"So can I yet. And I know which side is heads."

"You know more than you say. Those are prisoner's eyes looking out of your head. But you've thrown in with it."

"I said that I was one of the selected correspondents, Foley. I'm selected on most things. One must give up a little bit to be selected. But most aren't even given the chance. Foley, before you call anyone a sellout, you just think if you were ever good enough to be given the chance. Who ever wanted to buy you? Few are selected, and none of them turn it down. And those who howl at the distant scent of it are those so far below consideration as to make it comical."

"It is comical, Hardcrow, and I'm laughing," said Fred Foley. "But in my way I go on." Foley tried to brush something from his sleeve but there was nothing there.

"Is there any way you could step out of the room for a minute, Harry," Fred Foley asked, "and let me talk to the other Harry for only a bit?"

"I am the only Harry Hardcrow," said Harry, "and I'm about full of you, Foley. Get out of here right now."

"Goodnight, Harry," Fred Foley said to the harsh mouth and flushed face. And then, more softly. "Goodnight, Harry," to the prisoner's eyes inside the man.

Freddy phoned the Miguel Fuentes proclamation to Tankersley. That man had become somewhat meek about accepting anything Freddy gave him now.

"Are you sure, Freddy?" was all he asked. "If you are, then I'll print it."

"Oh yes. I've got it right. That's just the way he wants it to be run."

Fred Foley went back to his room. The room had been gone through, but they hadn't been messy about it. "They'll have to open my head to find out whatever I'm carrying," he said to himself.

Freddy looked at himself in the mirror. It was true: he had become a little older, and much more mature. He had a new respect for himself. Then a short night in bed and a rugged one.

Fred Foley had never adjusted to the twenty-four hour cycle of this world, and often in his trade he had avoided it. Usually he did not go to bed till he wanted to and he did not get up till he wanted to. He was strongly on the thirty-four hour cycle of the world from which people originally came. But sometimes he had to adjust a little, and he did have an early next-morning date with a woman who was riddled with riddles.

Pungent dreams then, and irritating wakefulness. And a spooky wasteland between. Fred Foley was a message center sometimes with all sorts of froth swirling about him.

James Bauer was being opposed by a strong and intelligent man, Richard Bencher, the father of Bedelia. This Bencher was tough of mind and he had real depth. He was direct. He was smart. He could go to the actual (that which acts upon the ambient) center of an apparatus, so he went directly at the mind of Jim Bauer. Bencher had had youthful encounter with some such thing before. He had come out of it, defiant and victorious, and had lived a concentrated and successful life, but he had been inattentive to many of the small details of his life. One of them had been his daughter Bedelia. Now he would make amends.

Bencher had begun to smash and break the weave; and Jim Bauer, bellowing in his resonant soul, had called the brain-weave to fight back. But was Bauer really the master of the weave? There were some strong persons in it.

Hondo Silverio was arranging his own encounters. He was suggesting to Bencher that they should kill James Bauer and destroy his residue-brain by a method which Hondo believed would work. And he suggested that he, Bencher, should then join them in the weave in place of Bauer. This startled Richard Bencher. "How do you know when a snake's kidding?" he asked himself. "I know so little of their psychology, but I must learn. No, I will not do it," he said. "That's mad."

When Bencher fought a thing he fought it all the way, but this would be harder than he thought. He could tackle Bauer front-on. He was as tough a man in mind and body and spirit as was Jim Bauer. They could battle like bulls. But what was he to make of the mottled-green humor of Hondo Silverio which he did not find entirely evil? Inhuman, yes, but not entirely evil.

How of those other psychic athletes in the weave? How of Wing Manion the saintly sexpot and Klee fish? For a moment he thought that he encountered in her the mind of his dead wife. How of Salzy Silverio of the helical passion? She shook him till he was dizzy and half mad. How of Arouet Manion the elegant devil who was so much a concordist that he brought in the slime of a thousand worlds and reveled in it? There was the ashen-ghost Letitia Bauer and the ashen-flesh Letitia Bauer, one dead, one in hypnosis, both in masochistic agony and longing. There was real mystery and cyclonic energy about that strange duality which Bencher did not begin to understand. And there was Bedelia herself, and the real demon who had joined the weave, and these two had become unnaturally close.

"Gad, she's had some odd boy friends," Bencher battled, "but not a real demon before. She's loose in her mind. This one even makes Freddy look good. That such a she should come out of my loins!"

Richard Bencher, for all his scope and determination, was confused in the multiplex thing he encountered. Even his own daughter refused to come out of the weave, but she would not herself attack him. She even invited him to join the weave, as had Hondo Silverio; her own suggestion was that he kill Arouet Manion and take his place in the weave. In her conscious state, Biddy did not know anything about this battle or this offer, however.

Salzy Silverio of the spiral passion was drawn insanely to Bencher, as she was to all strong men. And Wing Manion was trying to explain to him what it meant to be a Harvester; and how, perhaps, the Harvesters were more important than the harvest.

One who battles a dragon must watch that he be not

ensorceled by the beauty of any part of it. Dragons are sometimes iridescent in some of their limbs and append- ages. They are curious and arty and there is a sort of rousing music in their bellowing and fire-snorting. Rich- ard Bencher had him a battle; so many parts of the opponent were also parts of his own curious self.

Other messages, other persons and scraps of persons, other flitting souls around other scorchy flames.

Michael Fountain was wringing his hands over a bro- ken world. He knew so much, but he did not know how to fix a world. His latino namesake at least knew that much.

Miguel Fuentes was executing nine men after a night- court sentence in the middle of wild chaparral. It was an unpleasant thing to have to kill these unreformable elegant dogs, so he did it himself. Then he was sobbing disconsolately with his head on the rump of a burro.

"He's even younger than I am," said Fred Foley. "There must be *someone* else who could order the world."

There was the invisible dog of the patrick Bertigrew Bagley, who was more ape than dog, and who could sometimes be seen if one knew how to look. Foley saw him now, and the plappergeist winked solemnly at him. Freddy knew who he was then. He was the island- ape who used to be in the Katzenjammer Kids in the funny paper. But all grotesque funny paper characters have independent and exterior existence, unknown usu- ally to their drawers. It was good to have the dog, the ape, the polter-plappergeist on your side. He was smarter and more mischievous than other dogs or apes, and he could kill effectively.

There was Carmody Overlark, the urbane toad with the jewel in his head. Was it for pain of that that he had to soak his head in a bucket? But this Carmody had a talent in full which Fred Foley had only a little and that only these last several days: he knew when he was in anyone's dream anywhere. He became himself in the dream, and not an image of him. He came in astringent and powerful. One dreamed or thought of Carmody Overlark at his peril.

A short night and a rugged one. It was not the pungent dreams or the irritating wakefulness that was the worst. It was the spooky wasteland between. Did people, when they were still on the world whence they came, when they were naturally adjusted to their longer day-night cycle, suffer from dreams at night, from wakefulness, from wastelands? Or are these only of the present period of adjustment? Take them away and you take away something. Amputate them and we bleed; they are part of us now.

Patricks and falcons, dog-faced hydras with more and ranker arms than one could count, people who popped up in unlikely centuries, castles and mansions, and a house named Morada that had a broken stairs going down from its patio to . . . what?

Finally dawn-morning came.

"Damn, it took you long enough," Freddy told the shining wench.

Freddy Foley rented a rent-a-car in the morning and drove out to the morning-Maryland hideout. He found it more by instinct than by the Oriel description, which had been brainless and hurried. He caught a whiff of it as he came near, the something distorted in the morning light, the unreality and impermanence of the surroundings, a too-shrill music to hear with proper ears, the sick poetry, the paleness of grass and bush as if a great stone had just been rolled away exposing it all. But Foley had been through that choppy and building-pocked countryside before and it hadn't been like that. Lately, however, he had been learning to see with other sorts of eyes, with Harvester eyes, with patrick eyes, with falcon eyes, with toad eyes. A man misses so much if he uses only one set of eyes.

The house was nearly hidden by the pale boscage. It was elegant and low—"squat like a toad, close at the ear of Eve"—it was the place, it could not be the hideout of any other creature. Freddy had not known she was like that the evening before. Now he caught it all before he saw her.

Oriel Overlark met him at the door, throat and gills aquiver. She jibbered in silver, she shined like green bronze, she was the most striking and puzzling thing that Freddy Foley had ever seen.

"Did you bring them? Didn't you bring any part of them? Did you bring part of them in yourself? Be open, boy, or I'll crack your brains like walnuts and eat them right now. I want them, I want the two of them right now. How did you attach to it? I want to merge with it! Help me to merge with it right now!"

"The people of the brain-weave, Mrs. Overlark? How did you know about them? Do I have their smell on me? They barely brushed me. We'll forget about them. I want to ask you several questions, that's all."

"Oh questions! I want the spiral passion and the mottled snake humor. I want his body now. More, I want hers! Has anything from them entered into you? I want you then, right now."

Oriel had clasped Freddy and he was shocked by the heat of her. A body heat of a hundred and twelve at least is unusual in an old-recension human. Freddy would have sworn also that she had two hearts beating furiously. And her eyes, they were made to look at, not to see out of. "Throw hither all your quaint enameled eyes" ran through his head. A nameless emotion burst up through Freddy Foley and almost exploded in him.

"Tell me about him," the jewel-eyed creater pleaded. "Has he really two of them? How is she? The writhing, the convolutions—tell me, show me."

"I barely know the couple on sight, Mrs. Overlark. They are weave people and I *have* been brushed by the weave, but that's all. Hey, cut that out!"

An overpowering emotion still more upwelling in Freddy Foley! It would burst him! And into his quaking breast came certain spoof lines of Chesterton:

> Or didst thou love the God of Flies
> Who plagued the Hebrews and was splashed
> With wine unto the waist, or Pasht
> Who had green beryls for her eyes?

The emotion overpowered Freddy completely. It burst him asunder.

"You're laughing at me!" Oriel Overlark gasped in white amazement. "Oh, I am wounded! I am dead! How could anyone be so ungrateful? Don't you know that's the only way we can be wounded?"

Well, it had been that or rupture himself. Freddy'd had to do it. By the time he had gotten rid of the bigger globs of laughter, the torrid Oriel Overlark had turned to ice.

"I'm sorry, really I am," Freddy explained. "Your eyes are like nothing else. Your form is like nothing else. Your passion, perhaps, belongs in the weave itself, and I'm sure you've been in weaves like it. It's only that I'm a boor, one without the true lower feeling, and I don't understand these intense things. Now pout for a moment (you do it wonderfully), and then answer some questions."

But Freddy nearly burst again. "The gold and flowing serpent" ran through his mind, and Oh those lines!:

> Scorpion and asp, and amphisbaene dire,
> Cerastes horned, hydrus, and ellops drear.

Oriel Overlark was all those things, and pretty besides, and who was the oaf who would not appreciate this, wrapped as it was in kata-chthonic passion and overly sweet poetry?

"I don't believe at all in asking questions," said Oriel in a sulky and lifeless manner. "Still less in answering them. Both use up time, and time is the one thing we have so little of."

Oriel had been badly wounded by the laughter and was still gasping. She had been mortally affronted and her jeweled eyes had gone dull.

"Mrs. Overlark, kid, green-eyed doll, I've lately been searching for a group of people who seem to have plenty of time," Fred Foley said. "Centuries of it."

"No, nobody has plenty of time," the wan Oriel said. "Almost all have about the same amount of it. Every day we live we get a day older. It's frightening. We look for a way out of it but we don't find one."

"How long have you been in a hurry, Oriel?"

"I've always been in a hurry. I must make every minute count. Every second must be of the highest interest. You somehow gave me to believe that you would be of highest interest. The line of your throat! The mercurial movement of your body! Please don't disappoint me."

"I'll have to; I'm not geared to that at all. Nobody can stay at high point all the time."

"Yes, at high point all the time, every living minute," Oriel insisted. "There has to be variety, excitement, even a new kind of calm, a sharper agony as is mine at the moment, an additional facet. It must be really new, and it must not last long. After a while, real variety is hard to find. Then we must lie fallow to whet the appetite and to save the precious days."

"Well, this won't take too long. What I want to find out, Oriel, is this: was there any significant change in your husband Carmody Overlark about two years ago?"

"What I want you to do is not ask me any questions

270

at all. Of course there was! There's always significant change in him—two years ago, two days ago, two minutes ago I'm sure. That's why he's so wonderful."

"I have a curious theory, Oriel, that the Carmody Overlark of more than two years ago was not the same man as the Carmody Overlark of today."

"But of course not. He's never the same. He's protean. He's a chameleon. All of us are."

"Who is us?"

"Please don't ask questions. It's annoying. If you won't be passionate, go away. When you looked at me last night I thought you had more in mind than asking questions. If you want answers to questions go to the encyclopedia."

"You may be one, Oriel. Are you quite sure that the Carmody Overlark you were married to two years ago is the same man as the Carmody Overlark you're married to now?"

"I have been married to only one man."

"For how long?"

"Oh, who knows? It's so hard to figure. You have to subtract so much, and add a little, and who keeps track? That's the frightening part, keeping track. Even figuring it out takes time and I don't have the time."

"I met Carmody Overlark several years back. He was not the same man I met last night, but he sure looked the same."

"No, that was just a little goof we— I never knew him at all; I only saw him once. I don't go in for the details. They're handled. Haven't you been told that it's dangerous for you to inquire along this line? I wouldn't want anything to happen to you. The line of your throat! The mercurial movement—"

"I know, Oriel. Oh, my life's been threatened. Three men told me they'd kill me if I didn't lay off, and one man told me he'd kill me if I did. I figured they canceled out. I believe that the Carmody Overlark of today is the same man as a Khar-ibn-Mod who lived something over five hundred years ago. Would you know anything about that?"

"A rather humorous piece has already been done on certain coincidences between my husband and that man."

"My piece, if I do it, may not be humorous."

"Your piece, and you will not do it, would not be believed in any case."

"I'm puzzled about one thing, Oriel. I had understood that the Mamelukes were abridged men. Are you sure he's so wonderful? Or does this reanimation that I'm tracking down consist of more than I supposed?"

"Oh, you don't understand it at all. Line of your throat and all, you just don't understand it. The methods weren't at all those which you call by the same name. Actually, there was a thousandfold increase in passion. Perhaps it's a good thing that the uninitiate aren't acquainted with it. It wouldn't do at all for a weak race. And yet some of the contemporaries do have something. Oh, the people in the weave! Oh, yourself if you wished!"

"The man who was Carmody Overlark until two years ago, what happened to him, Oriel?"

"I imagine they killed him. I hadn't really thought about it."

"Don't you care? After all, he *was* your husband."

"He was *what*? How far off can you get? How can you only guess a little bit and miss the rest so far?"

Oriel was fiddling with her hair. She was becoming bored. Even the exquisite agony of rejection had lasted too long. She fluffed her hair out as though to cool herself. Then Freddy saw it and understood a little more about her.

"You don't understand anything about me, do you, sleeping *Adone?*"

"Yes, now I understand almost all about you, Oriel."

"What made you understand?"

"Your ears. Miss Evans said last night that your ears

weren't at all good and that you seldom showed them."

"She'll suffer for that remark. My ears are excellent."

"Yes they are. But they're archaic ears."

"Of course. Should I get new ears each time?"

"You also are one of the reappearing persons?"

"Certainly. And now that you've guessed a little of it, what can you possibly do with your knowledge? There's a group in one of our finest institutions; they're there just because they guessed just about so much. I can arrange it quite easily that you join them. Insanity is only the refusal to accept facts as they are. That we are unassailable is one of the facts that are."

"Why are all of you so nervous and jittery and guarded? Why do you have to kill or confine to protect your secret?"

"Oh, because we're in such a hurry and passion, and because time runs out so fast."

"What happened to the Oriel Overlark of before two years ago?"

"I really don't know and I really don't care. She may be in one of the institutions for claiming to be me, or she may be dead."

"Don't you use the old bodies?"

"Sometimes, in a way. Again sometimes, in a lesser way. You don't have to know."

"Do you know anything of your group substituting for an inventor named Crabtree last night?"

"The man who became Crabtree last night is an old friend of mine. I welcome him back. He's one of those of the thousandfold passion. I don't know anything about the man who was substituted for."

"How are you able to substitute so well without being detected?"

"Oh, we're mimics. It's an ancient art. And we also force them to mimic us, back in time—you wouldn't understand it. We keep our own appearances, but we also assume the appearances of the persons we replace. You'd have to know more than you ever will know about the old mimicry to understand how it's done."

"I know a little about it by comparing pictures and images. What's the object of all this? Why do you slow down and obstruct the world?"

"I don't make policy. Partly it's just that we intend always to run the thing and we can't let it have loose rein. We do it because we want to do it and for other reasons that are not for you to know. We do it because the world and its people are our footstool and we don't want our footstool to become too grand. Ask my husband when you have your interview with him. He'll elude you much more adroitly than I can. And I imagine that after you've talked to him you'll be put away in one way or another."

"I may have something to say about that."

"Not very much, mercury movement, not very much. The others will not regard you as an ornament, as I do."

"Are there others of your talent who are not of your group?"

"Oh, there are randoms. Have you known some?"

"Maybe. I'm not sure. How far back do you go, Oriel?"

"You shouldn't ask the age of even a reappearing woman. Quite a ways back."

"As far back as Carmody?"

"Oh no. Not nearly so far back. I was picked up much later. We recruit, you know. We must, since we don't generate. And some of us are lost accidentally. We've tried for centuries to outlaw embalming. We've succeeded only locally and for short periods. We leave elaborate instructions and commands for our own disposal, and yet the abominations still have their way with some of us."

"But all of you will die some day. And then what?"

"But all of *you* will die some day. And then what shorter what? All of you alive today will die long before we do. And no one of you has come back to bring an authentic report."

"Haven't you any consciences at all?"

"I haven't. No, I don't believe that any of us have. There are signs that you uninitiates are also losing yours. We're both behind and ahead of you in the evolutionary scale, spanning quite a space. No, we've sloughed our consciences completely if we ever had any. And now you've overstayed your welcome. I thought you'd have the passion, would at least be a man, or an animal, or even a reptile. Really I like them best. It's a long time since I've had such a letdown. I could have given you an experience you won't otherwise get in life, and I did expect a little variety from you. We are all of us consummate sensualists."

"I'm sure you are, Oriel. Two more questions even though I am overstayed. Why does your husband keep rats?"

"A hobby. You don't need to know any more."

"And why does he soak his head in a bucket?"

"You ask him."

"I will."

Fred Foley left the morning-Maryland hideaway.

"The line of the throat, the mercurial movement," Oriel said.

" 'Or keep it as a cistern for foul toads
To knot and gender in,' " Freddy Foley said.

IX: BUT I EAT THEM UP, FEDERICO, I EAT THEM UP

The ascension, when it comes, will be in the regular sequence, but rising a stage above the old pattern and continuing to rise. We will have had our spring, our summer, our autumn. We will have our winter then, and it is the breaking season: we will break upward into patterned rise, or we will break down.

This must not be the Fimbul-winter, the destruction winter, the wraith winter of the fulminous monstrous unwarming fire laid by the Frost Giants; not the withering sub-tropical winter, the torpidness that brings the four exterior creatures through the gates; not the inanity winter, the loss-of-nerve winter. After such spiritual and psychic frosts we can have only repetitious sick springs.

It must be, in some manner, an evergreen winter, a singing winter "a summer bird which even in the haunch of winter sings" a time of swift sanity, of right ordering and careful law, of interior handicraft and joiner-work. "Who are these spectral forms coming with pale sickles? The year's harvest is already in. Begone, pale harvesters, it is another season now."

It is only after our winter of swift sanity and steely nerve that we will have our second spring. It will not be repetition, it will not be beginning again in the old way. It will be a tumultous springtime higher on the helical, the ascending spiral; with birds more

> songful, colts more clattering, earth more burgeon-
> ing, spirits more exalted, sky more eternal. It is
> only after we have broken the wraith winter that
> we may have our helical springtime, that we may
> finally enter our Fifth Mansions. And then the rest
> is all sheer and joyous ascent.
>
> *Prose Poems*: Maurice Craftmaster

FREDDY FOLEY was putting his affairs in order, inas-
much as that can be done in a short time. He had a
happy head on him while he did it even though the
fuliginous Harvesters were romping and wrecking
through its inner channels. He discovered, as had Richard Bencher, the iridescent limbs and rousing music
of parts of their dragon.

The manila packet of Crabtree was now consigned
by Freddy to a responsible man, Michael Fountain, even
though Fred was now convinced that it was a hoax and
the original packet had been put to other use. Michael
Fountain would be able to guess much of the original
thing from the false shadow of it.

And he met Salzy Silverio in the middle of his mind.
"The snakes are shedding their skins early this year,"
Freddy said. "It means an early and auspicious spring."

Freddy phoned the lawyer back home and instructed
that man to consider his Will Number Three as his only
last will and testament, and to destroy wills one, two,
four, and five. Freddy hadn't many tangible things to
will anyone, and yet there were some things in that
which were worthy and almost tangible.

And Bedelia Bencher was on the edge of his mind,
impudent and exasperating. Pink sulphur, scented rosy
fire and all, he would not give his girl over to any sec-
ondclass devil. This part was not over with.

Freddy had made up several packages and large
envelopes. He went out to mail them, sending the big
heavy envelope to Michael Fountain by registered mail.

Then he went to get a shave and haircut so he would be his best under scrutiny.

"I have born other children out of my body," said an ashen ghost in Fred Foley's cerebellum while he was in the barber chair. "They are all of them deformed monkeys, or snake children, or elongated toads, or queer fish, or specter children. Fortunate that they have already perished! I am lost, I am confused. But I will still go another way. I will not go the way they have set for me. Tonight, if it is night, today, if it is day. I will bear another child who is beautiful and full of light. They cannot dominate one who is indomitable."

Fred Foley gave himself a pep talk and then went directly to the doctor's office. He did not go to just any doctor. He went to the one doctor of really solid reputation. There was one thing he wanted to be sure of and to have the proof of.

"Be careful, Freddy," said an intelligent and superior and noble snake out of its coiling passion and great center of compassion. This was as Freddy came into the anteroom at the doctor's. "Think, Freddy, who directs your steps there. Should you not turn and leave as rapidly as possible? This kind of doctor you do not need."

"This kind of doctor I may well need," Freddy told the projection of Hondo Silverio. "With you things romping in my head, I have to have a guarantee of my sanity before I go on."

"Go right in, Mr. Foley," the appointments girl said to Freddy's outer ears, and Fred Foley went in.

"I'll state my reason for coming as quickly as possible," Fred said to the doctor of solid reputation. He couldn't see the doctor's eyes, only the glint of light on his glasses. But there had to be eyes of solid reputation behind them. "I want to be certified as sane. Is that ever done, Doctor? I want you to go over me very carefully and then give me a written opinion that will stand up legally."

"Well, no, it really isn't ever done, Mr. Foley, not quite like that. A man doesn't ask for such a legal certificate without a legal threat. Has your sanity ever been questioned?"

"Oh, a little bit, here and there, you know how it is, Doctor. It's usually in a kidding mood that people tell me that I'm crazy. Ah . . . some of them are serious, though. But I have reason to believe that my sanity *will* be questioned, and that quite soon. I believe I may be railroaded, and without recourse. I'd like to have the opinion of a competent doctor on record before that event."

"Most committed persons believe they're railroaded, Mr. Foley, but most don't suspect it before it happens. Are you given any alternative to being put on the rails?"

"I was once given the alternative: to shut up. I didn't do it. It's probably too late for that now. Well, go over me and tell me how sane I am."

"You must be prepared for the possiblity that you *are* a little off, Mr. Foley, and that if you are sent up it will be for a reason. You seem to have delusions of persecution."

"They aren't delusions, Doctor. Two sets of threats have been given to me, one on my life, one on my freedom. I was awake and not suffering from hallucination both times. My hearing is better than normal, it's acute. My knowledge of people is sound. I've been threatened to make me lay off a peculiar line of questioning."

"Then lay off. That's what a sane man would do. A sane man solves his problems in the most direct manner. Laying off would seem the most direct manner for you."

"But I don't want to lay off."

"Then you probably *are* insane, to an extent, on this one subject. Why don't you want to lay off the thing that threatens your life?"

"I have a certain amount of stubbornness. And I have my principles."

"Neither is a sign of sanity, Mr. Foley. More often they're the opposite. An insane man will always have a considerable amount of stubbornness, intractability. And he'll have *very* strong principles, though usually for very weak reasons. A sane man bends to reality, and his principles die a little as he gets older. Yours should at least have begun to weaken. You aren't a child. Children, you may not realize it, are never sane. But sanity should have begun to develop by your age."

"We may not mean the same thing by sanity. I was sane when I was a boy, Doctor. This is one thing I do know. And other boys were mostly sane. Some of them have lost it, a little, when they come to be men. I don't believe I've lost very much of mine."

"No, we certainly don't mean the same thing by sanity, Mr. Foley. You have a backward idea, an insane idea of it. Sanity is adaptability to the world as it is, even though that world may be a little insane by ideal standards. You seem to be in fine health, and I'm sure that your senses are acute. Your attitude isn't truculent, so far. If committed, you probably wouldn't make a difficult patient; that's one thing to be thankful for. The difficulty of adaptation is always harder on the patient than on the overseers. Now then, Mr. Foley, let's examine your attitude toward reality, taking into consideration that your profession is based largely on fiction. When you fictionize in your reporting—do you realize it?"

"Certainly I realize it."

"And you're never carried away by it, never to the point where you can't see the difference?"

"Certainly I'm carried away by it, or I wouldn't be any good at it. But I believe it's the same way an actor is carried away. And I do see the difference between the fiction and reality, where it's necessary to draw a difference; most of the time it isn't necessary, it doesn't matter."

"You think it doesn't matter what you reject and what you accept, and how you handle it all? Mr. Foley, suppose you interviewed a very magnetic man who said that he had ridden to other planets in alien space-craft? Would you be immune to his evidence?"

"I sure hope I wouldn't be immune to anyone's evidence about anything, Doctor. I wouldn't reject any evidence for anything without examining it, not as reporter. And your question isn't merely a supposition. I *have* interviewed *three* such men who said that they had ridden to other planets in odd craft. And all three of those were magnetic. They projected the stuff, they talked the stuff, and they said that the crafts were driven by the same magnetic stuff. Two of the men certainly didn't convince me, though they did make good copy. But that third man had my mind wide open for quite a while."

"Oh. What closed your mind to his insane ideas then, Foley?"

"He told me he'd arrange for me to take one of those quick trips to another planet. But he never showed up for the appointment."

"I see. And if you *had* taken such a trip, would you have believed it?"

"Certainly I'd believe it. If I had actually done it, then of *course* I'd believe I had."

"Even knowing that it was impossible? That's bad, Mr. Foley, bad."

"If I had done it, Doctor, then I'd know that it *was* possible. He shouldn't have stood me up. That shook my trust in him. He did send me a postcard, though, from Ganymede. He explained, not too implausibly, that their takeoff was hurried and that they'd been forced to leave without me."

"A postcard from Ganymede, Mr. Foley? Do you

realize what you're saying? Ganymede is one of the moons of Jupiter, or at least one of the large planets. How could you believe—"

"Actually the card was postmarked from Pueblo, Colorado, Doctor. It was one of the disappointments of my life."

"You wanted such things to be true?"

"Oh yes."

"Bad, Mr. Foley, very bad."

"Bad that I should want the marvelous to be true? I would think that normal."

"Only for children, Mr. Foley. You have a decidedly immature attitude toward the world. That isn't completely damning in itself, but let's go on a little further. If you were told that a new race of giant snails was going to take over the earth and abolish mankind, how would you react?"

"I'd react by considering my informant and questioning where he got his information. If he had even the slightest snail-horn of information, I'd follow it out. I'd try my mightiest to find out whether there really was a new race of giant snails trying to take over. I'd examine all the evidence my informant could give me, and all that I could invent myself, always with an eye as to how I could turn it to account. I'd consider the treatment—quizzical, facetious, sensational, or who-knows-after-all?—even before I had anything to treat. If there were real evidence, Doctor, I'd really follow it out. I can see the banner on my feature piece, *On the Track of the Giant Snail*, in my mind's-eye now. Believe me, I'd try to be the first to interview the snail leader."

"You would actually spend time on such a report, Mr. Foley?"

"Yes. I may *spend time* on that very thing whenever I'm through with what I'm on now. There's bound to be an interesting story in it: if not of the giant snails themselves, then perhaps a story of a man who believed in giant snails."

"Worse and worse, Mr. Foley. Now then, what would you do if you had the report that there was a race of superhumans secretly ruling the world to the detriment of normal mankind? Would you credit the report, Mr. Foley? Would you examine it? In a way, this is the test. There *is* a pattern of such belief in a certain form of insanity."

"Oh, is there now, Doctor?"

How many strands would it take to bind a man, and each of them so much thinner than a hair? Would you believe a report about secret spiders? Or would you refuse to believe it even after they had tangled you in their webs?

There was an abnormality about this doctor. It bothered Foley while they talked. What it was slipped away from him, but he hovered over it. He would have it in a minute.

"You don't answer me, Mr. Foley. *Do* you believe in a race of superhumans? Now then, what if it was reported, or it came into your mind somehow, that this race of superhumans had one slight peculiarity which distinguished them? Would you see this peculiarity wherever you looked and would you imagine a conspiracy? Would you imagine you saw this peculiarity on people in the streets? That you saw it on someone following you? That you saw it on someone you came to for advice? That you saw it on a doctor whom you came to visit?"

"Such as archaic ears, Doctor?"

"Such as anything, Mr. Foley. Is archaic ears one of the forms that your delusion takes? Do you imagine that a race of men with funny ears is out to dominate the world?"

"Either I'm imagining it or it's happening. Yes, I believe that certain old people with funny ears are out to dominate the world. It does make me sound as if I were a little off, especially since nobody else seems to see such things."

Foley was tempted now to doubt his own sanity, the doctor had put it all so smoothly. He was tempted, but he didn't really doubt. He had evidence before his eyes now, if his eyes were still good. The doctor had the funny ears, no doubt about that.

"Bad, Mr. Foley, very bad," the doctor was saying again.

"Doctor, how did I come to seek you out?" Freddy Foley asked suddenly.

"How would I know, Mr. Foley? I suppose you came to me because I'm a doctor of solid reputation."

"Well, who *told* me that you were a doctor of solid reputation?"

"It could have been almost anybody, Mr. Foley, for I am."

"How did I even learn your name and address?"

"I don't know, Mr. Foley. It was probably given to you by someone who thought you really needed a doctor. Or you could have had it from the phone book."

"I could have, but I didn't. Doctor, I don't *know* your name and address. What brought me here?"

"Your feet, perhaps. A vehicle? I don't know."

"I never heard of you. I never heard of your solid reputation. But I never even thought of going to any other doctor. I didn't ask any of my acquaintances the name of a good doctor. I came directly to you without asking directions or anything else. I came directly to a man I had never heard of, already convinced that he was a man of solid reputation. How was this put into my mind?"

"Ah, now you believe that the super-people can control your mind? Bad, Mr. Foley, very bad."

"How did you know my name was Foley? How did

your appointments girl know it? How did you know I was a reporter?"

"Have you suffered these gaps of memory and information before, Mr. Foley? Is it that you become a little excited now? If you will allow me, I'll give you a sedative, and then we'll delve a little deeper into this."

"You come out of that chair and I'll knock you back into it, Doctor! You're not giving me any sedative!"

"My, aren't we violent! The symptoms continue to unfold."

"You can stow that, Doctor. I know when I'm being taken. You're one of them."

"I am one of them? Soon, Mr. Foley, as your mind weakens, everybody will be one of them. You'll see them everywhere you look. It will be the whole world in conspiracy against you."

"I considered that once before, Doctor, but it didn't hold up. It isn't the whole world in conspiracy against me, it's a small bunch of you in conspiracy against the whole world. How was it done to me, Doctor? By subliminal or subvocal suggestion? How?"

"Your suggestions follow a pattern of a familiar dementia, Mr. Foley. You can believe any or all of them. I'm not sure that it will be well for you to be walking the streets. You *have* shown signs of violence."

"I'll show more signs if you try to stop me."

"I can have a pickup order out for you within seconds, Mr. Foley."

"Why bother? I still have an appointment in the parlor of a bigger spider. He's at least a little curious about me or he wouldn't be willing to see me. He's at least a little nervous about me or he wouldn't have detoured me here. And I have the feeling that I'll be watched by archaic and many-faceted eyes when I go to his parlor."

"In the parlor of a spider, you say. Sheer infantilism.

Yes, Mr. Foley, I would be willing to give a certificate concerning your sanity, but it would be the opposite of the one you came for. But you're right, you will be closely watched wherever you go. There's really nothing you can do in the little time you have left."

Foley left that doctor of solid reputation. He came angrily and alertly out into the street again, careful of ambush, careful of everything. But there is a danger in being too careful, and he knew it; it makes you too tight.

And now Foley was tempted again to doubt his own sanity. He *did* see the distinguishing mark, those damned odd ears, on people in the street: newsboys, shoppers, loitering messengers, hurrying tourists. Either he was going crazy, or another galloping suggestion had been implanted into his mind. Those ears were on the shop-girls, on the policemen, on little colored kids no bigger than toys, on kind old ladies. He thought about post-hypnotic suggestion and such rubbish; he thought how an ordinary thing will sometimes appear extraordinary as though seen for the first time; he thought *This is it, Freddy, this is it.* But for all that, he decided that if he had gotten into the state he could get out of it.

He squinted his eyes. He could make the strange ears appear. He could make them go away. He could see the snakes. He could cast out the snakes. He had once learned this from an old snake-watcher.

The snake-watcher had told him how to stop seeing snakes. This was when Freddy had been on the jail beat. One *can* stop seeing snakes: it takes great strength of mind, intense concentration, deep resources of courage, and a blind denial of the obvious. But the giant effort to make the snakes go away can be made. The difficulty, the snake-watcher had said, is that it takes so much out of a man that he is left weak and shaken and has to be restored. And the handiest restorative is just what made him see snakes in the first place. "Learn to live with them, learn to live with them," the old snake-watcher had advised.

But if hallucinatory snakes can be made to disappear by giant effort, so should archaic ears be capable of being modernized. Foley made the giant effort, and then the people in the streets no longer had peculiar ears. Or rather, they no longer had the archaic ears of the reappearing folks. They still had peculiar ears; Fred hadn't noticed ears much before; he saw now the thing that many people never see, that ears themselves are forever peculiar.

Having seen this much, Freddy went further with sudden insight: he saw that people themselves are peculiar by nature, that there is no norm. But this didn't help much.

"What I need now is one rich and powerful friend who'll be faithful to me to the end," Freddy told himself. "I need a foul-weather friend. There has to be somewhere at least one person who cares what happens to me, one who has a gracious way with money and no fear at all of embarrassment or danger. There has to be one person who'll stand by me whether I'm crazy or not, one who'd enjoy a battle. If I had such a friend I'd communicate at once and give a hint of what just might happen to me. But do I have such a friend?

"Yeah. I do. Besides, it might shake her loose from that demon she's stuck on. She likes to be needed and I need her now."

Biddy Bencher, whatever else was wrong with her, was such a friend. She had a gracious way with money (her father's), she certainly had no fear of embarrassment or danger. She was more likely to stand by a crazy person than a sane one. And she did love a battle. She was a foul-weather friend all the way. So innocent and yet so foul. She was the one. Nobody was more loyal, to more things. She changed loyalties like coats. Well, it was time for her to put on her Freddy-coat again.

Freddy called her up, not by phone. Other forms of communication had come onto him lately almost without his noticing them. He got her but could not get her attention. She was lounging on subterranean beaches and wild dogs were tearing her apart. "You're missing pieces, you're missing the best pieces," she kept calling at the tearing dogs. "All you're tearing off is the legs. Don't any of you like the white meat?"

Freddy couldn't get her attention that way. Finally he called her on the telephone and she answered on the fourth ring. "Hello, Freddy," she answered at once. "I was playing the record-player and I couldn't answer until that movement was finished. Sure, I'll come there if you need me. Where will I come? Where is there? Is this Freddy or have I answered a dead phone?"

"I'm in Washington, Biddy. I'm fine, as fine as one can be in Washington, temporarily fine, but possibly I won't be free by the end of this day. If I am confined, in all likelihood it will be at the Asilo Santa Eliza, and they'll deny that I'm there. Come get me out if you don't hear from me again."

"Freddy, little short end of the stick, phone me at home late tonight if it hasn't happened. If I don't hear from you, I'll fly there and be there in the morning. I understand, dear, I know what kind of people they put in Santa Eliza. I always knew you were a little, but I don't want other people thinking it, and I sure don't want it made official. Are you on the same jag, Freddy?"

"Yes, the same jag, Biddy."

"There must be something to it, then. If it was just a crackpot idea they wouldn't lock you up. They don't lock up crackpots. I know they don't. Shall I bring Papa?"

"Yes. He said once to wait and he'd get me out. I wasn't in yet then, but I think he had a futuristic insight."

"I'll come either on bat-wings or by commercial flight, Freddy."

It is good to have one rich and powerful friend.

An hour and a bit to the west another young man found himself circumscribed and threatened with confinement. Hasty army units of two nations had him nearly in a pocket. United States forces, with plane and copter overhead, with radios sputtering back and forth and up and down, mobile with jeep and track, toothed with rifle and automatic rifle and bazooka and machine gun, covered both sides of Canyon Creek to its nearly dry mouth and spread out both ways along the Rio Grande itself. Mexican forces had worked out of the wild and rocky mountains of Serranias del Burro and covered most of the near south shore of the same big river. Little armed river boats stood ready with roaring power barely muted, and ripped here and there in the chocolate colored water.

Miguel Fuentes and his one hundred men; no, his sixty men; no, his twenty-five men, were nearly in the bag. But their numbers and grouping dwindled as streams sometimes dwindle into the sand in that region. Half of them had merged into the roving Mexican patrols; many of them actually belonged to those patrols, but now they had a new loyalty.

Fifteen men and a leader. Where had the rest escaped the closing net? Then three men down with gunfire. Twelve men and a leader into a canyon between rough bald-headed hills, and the covered mouth of the canyon was right on the river. Got them from both ends, got them from sides, covered them from above, harried into the last turn; shouts, warnings, expectations, rattle of hard weapon fire. Final caution, and the converging troops came together.

The bag was closed, but there was nothing in the

bag. Every way out still closed. Most minute search. Counsel and cursing. Air to ground to air communication in two languages. Flame throwers firing every thicket. Where were the twelve men and their leader? They had gone into the short bare canyon, they had not come out of it, and they were not in it.

"Federico, Federico, hey Freddy," a voice communicated from cave via weave to distant city. "Do you watch the trick? Hey, is that ever a trick!"

"Go away, Miguel, I have no time for you," Freddy Foley communicated. "I've got a noose around my own neck and I'll have to learn to like the feel of hemp."

"Noose I'm talking about," Miguel exulted. "*Hombre*, was there ever a noose around me! You have watched, I know you have watched."

"I watched you but I had other things on my eyes," Freddy communicated. "Anybody could do it with a setup like that. But how will I do it?"

"You know where I am? In the very middle of the earth I am."

"You're down in the complex of caves that Auclaire the patrick told me about, Miguel. You'll get lost in them and never get out. They're thirty miles each way and nobody but the patrick knows their windings."

"And can I not compel the mind of the patrick Auclaire? Now I give you statements which you will proclaim."

"I haven't the time for you, Miguel. You're taking things by the wrong end of the stick. You're as vile a thing as the other creatures."

"I may be so, Federico. If it is so, then I am called to be vile; it is my mission which I may not question. If I am as vile as the other creatures, yet I am *not* the other creatures. I beset them, I cut them down. I am the snake-eater. What, is the snake-eater not as vile as the snakes? But I eat them up, Federico, I eat them up.

I come soon to my hour. Now you will proclaim the statements I give. I compel your mind to this.

"I have loosened more than eighty men, more than eighty seeds. They are scattered even now. They find quick places to root. They are completely instructed by me, even if only for short hours. They will root, they will grow, they will form other groups immediately. Tell the world that I am down in the middle of the world now, that I am under the ground in a grave. And tell them that I will emerge on the third day as a sign and a wonder. Is that not a blasphemous way to put it! Hey, it is fun to cut these holy corners sometimes and shake the elementals. Proclaim it for me, Federico. I compel you to."

"I know you do, Miguel. Rot your brown bones anyhow! I'll proclaim your stuff and then I'll be shed of you. Emerge on the third day as a sign and wonder! Oh brother!"

"A tip, Federico, a tip. You also will go underground, be hunted into a hole, be trapped underground inside a confinement and inside yourself within that. You will be invaded, you will be dead, you will be buried underground in a peculiar grave. And on the third day you also will emerge. Don't knock it, Freddy, it's a good trick."

"Get out of my head, Miguel. I've had enough of you."

"But you will proclaim my statement, Freddy. I compel you to."

"I know it. I'll do it. And then we're quits. Gah, they're worse than reptiles before they're full-feathered!"

Fred Foley phoned Tankersley and gave him the statement of Miguel Fuentes.

"He really has the Messiah fever, has he, Freddy? Say, there's a group in Norway came out for Miguel today, and one in Indonesia. And about all they know about him they have from our own dispatches. Sure, I'll run it, Freddy. You've kept us ahead of the world on it so far."

Then Freddy started out toward the office of Carmody Overlark. He didn't know where Overlark's office was any more than he had known where was the office of the doctor of solid reputation; but his feet would bring him to it.

Something clicked in Freddy's head. The appointment he had been wanting had come through. Overlark had given the word that Foley was to be admitted at once, and Foley was coming at once.

X: ARE YOU NOT OF FLIMSY FLESH TO BE SO AFRAID?

Ere Mor the Peacock flutters, ere the Monkey People
   cry,
Ere Chil the Kite swoops down a furlong sheer,
Through the Jungle very softly flits a shadow and a
   sigh—
He is fear, O Little Hunter, he is fear!
                          Kipling

OVERLARK'S secretary had a rough, white, unfinished face that seemed to Foley to express cruelty and cowardice. "You are his dog and you mirror him," Foley said softly to himself.

This may have been Foley's imagination. The secretary might have been a nice enough fellow but he wasn't the jolly type. He had smoky eyes that almost made it appear that he was blind.

"I have no idea why Mr. Overlark is willing to see you," he said, "but I must write down your reason for visiting him. What is it?"

"I want to give him some advice," said Fred Foley.

"He is hardly in need of that, from you at any rate," the secretary said.

"Since that's the commodity he deals most in he might want a new line of it," Foley said stoutly. "Mine is a little out of the ordinary and it's given freely."

"He has sent out instructions that you be admitted,

Mr. Foley. I had just made attempts to reach you but I failed."

"No, you succeeded, smoky-eyes, you succeeded. You reached me nicely."

"Go in then. But I beg you not to take any more of his time than is necessary. His time is very limited."

"So is mine, but I haven't learned to budget it so finely."

Oh it was a plush place inside, but a different plush than Freddy had imagined. It looked like an office where a great amount of work was done, and this surprised him. It was large but still crowded, containing files (files which were themselves works of art in their haunting ornamentation), two very large tables that could have been conference tables if only the piles of bulletins were ever cleared off them, several desks that were almost cockpits with the amount of instrumentation about them, and a variety of taping and viewing and communication equipment. And there was Carmody Overlark himself, an ornamental man.

"You were intending to ask me questions, Foley," said Carmody Overlark (he didn't ask Foley to sit, but Foley did, and it seemed to irritate the man), "but I imagine I'll do most of the talking. First off, and naturally, we are not alone, in case you have any wild ideas."

"Why are you afraid of little Fred Foley?" Freddy mocked him.

"I'm afraid of nobody, Foley. I'm physically capable but I seldom task myself with the duties that belong to subordinates. I hear you've been acting oddly today. Why?"

Carmody's eyes weren't those of a prisoner looking out; they were those of one who had taken refuge within. He didn't want out. He wouldn't come out.

"I went to a doctor this morning, Mr. Kar-everlasting-Mod, to get an opinion on myself. I don't know whether that's odd behavior or not, but the doctor was odd. He tried to get me to doubt my own sanity."

"He tried to get you to recognize your own insanity, Foley. That's the first step toward a cure, and we have cures for everyone."

"There's a proverb about the cure being worse than the disease, Mr. Overlark. I want to ask you some questions about a strange movement. I believe you're near the center of it," Freddy said, and Carmody looked at him with eyes like shattered glass. They were disconcerting, those eyes. One couldn't look into them; one bounced off their facets.

"What you want is to startle me with how much you've guessed, Foley, and to force a full revelation from me. That's pretty childish. Don't you realize what a nonentity you are?"

"No. I've never admitted to myself that I'm a nonentity. I have always believed that every man—"

"—is entitled to his mete of human dignity. That's really a very late idea and there's nothing to it. You're here without any advantage at all. What possible circumstance would impel me to tell you everything or anything?"

"The circumstance that I'll soon be put out of the way and won't be able to use the information. And the sort of pride that holders of tight secrets take in revealing such secrets to their captives."

"I have no such pride, Foley. Oh, maybe a little. No, that's not at all the circumstance that would impel me to tell everything or even nearly everything to you. But there is such a circumstance."

"Is it present?"

"Oh yes. But barely. It seems to me, from what I've heard of your activities, that you've already discovered the essentials about us. This is: that we live when we want to live, that we go into a non-aging state that is very near death when we want to do so, and that we live again, and then again: that we try always to live at most heightened experience and to spread ourselves out for as long as we possibly can; and that we do not permit interference. What else do you want to know about us?"

Fred Foley understood in a sudden glimpse that Carmody Overlark was mad. What, "The Sanity of the Centuries" (that had been one of his titles when he was Khar-ibn-Mod) was mad? Absolutely. He lived in a different world entirely. He didn't see the world before him, not even with his multiplex eyes. *That* was madness.

"Why don't you live and die and live again without bothering the world with your doings, Overlark? Why do you impose a deleterious effect on the world?"

(*I've been wrong about him,* Foley thought. *What I guessed, what he himself believes to be the way of it, isn't the truth of the matter at all. There's much less here than meets the eye.*)

"Let me go back to the beginning, Foley, or a little before," Carmody said. (There was always laughter just behind his voice, but it had no real merriment in it.) "You'll see that one man's deleteriousness is another man's delectation. The world is for ourselves and not we for the world. Anything we do to the world is right, so long as it gives us pleasure. You believe you have some sort of standards, and you haven't. Most of the things that you believe are eternal are really very recent. We of the older recension aren't bound by them. We've been in combat with you for a long time. You believe, in one of your theories, that we're in control of the world. We aren't. But we have been, and we will be whenever we wish. It's a day you will fear to see, that we come fully awake again. And we do come awake now. We will regain the world. Certain later interlopers have for some time ruled heaven and earth. Now we come back—ruthlessly."

"Don't you believe the others also have rights?"

"The others have had the run of their rights long enough. They are the interlopers, and it's time that the ancient line is restored. —Oh, Foley, I misunderstand you completely; that's always the difficulty of conversing with infants. You mean *people*. You mean do people have any rights? Oh no, I don't believe that people have any rights."

"Are you and yours not people, Carmody?"

"No. Not in every sense. Our apotheosis was effected very long ago." Clear mad; this man with the edgy eyes, with the complexion that was sometimes ghost-lighted and sometimes dead-fish color, with the laughing tainted cruelty and the sick fear. If he was on top of it all, why was he so scared?

"A man doesn't become a god, Carmody, except for purposes of rhetoric," Freddy said. "I assume that your apotheosis was like that of the Caesars."

"Foley, the next time you skim through the *Lives of the Twelve Caesars* (for you will be allowed books in your confinement) see if you can guess which three of those emperors were of us—for three were. They were already gods. Their confirmation in public godhead was only that the public be appeased."

"You're giving an ironic twist to the words, Carmody. What real effect could your auto-apotheosis have?"

"It was an act, an utterance, a statement that became true as it was uttered. Let me say simply that this is always a possible development of man. Oh, not of every man, but of many. Many more than you'd suppose. There's the one man in a thousand, perhaps the one man in a hundred, who is capable of turning into a god. This is as true as that many bees could turn into queen-bees, should the proper historic surge be present. You find it extravagant that I should speak of historic surge as applying to so small a thing as a swarm of insects? But it's also extravagant that we should apply it to so small a thing as a swarm of men. The point is that a small hive of bees has more claim on you to importance than you have on us. We're much further above you than you are above the bees. You'd feel no compunction in the destruction of the bees of a region if for some reason it worked to your profit or ease —let's say that the bees of a region bore what seemed to you to be a disease. And we would feel no compunction at destroying most or all of you, if it should be necessary or convenient to us, and it may well be."

"Yes, I do find your ideas a little extravagant, Carmody. When you speak of being gods you actually mean an elite group of demagogues, a bunch of supermen (in your own opinion)."

"You don't know what I speak of, Foley. I was once a tribal deity, literally and actually. All of us were."

"How many is all of you?"

"The first clutch of us, the first dozen; and it was many times that many millennia ago. I was a true tribal deity, Foley. I exceeded even the rest. I was deified, and as a deified one I had access to the several veins of secret knowledge. We were all of us remarkably intelligent in what was a very intelligent age, one that didn't yet hobble on the crutches of literacy and compilation. What we knew we knew directly. We formed a confederacy and established Olympus. We destroyed the Titans, and we ruled. I beg your pardon, Foley, but I caught a country expression going through your mind: something 'as a peach-orchard boar.' It seems I've brushed this expression in minds of men talking to me before. What is it? Even in our earliest mythologies there's nothing about a peach-orchard boar."

"You've forgotten your mythology then, Carmody," Fred Foley told him. "I assure you that the peach-orchard boar is there strongly, early and late. But when you speak of destroying the Titans and ruling, you don't speak literally."

"Oh, but I do! Olympus is actually a phonetic equivalent of the name of our old high mountain lodge. We were gods and we lived there as gods."

"And you interfered in the affairs of men like the Homeric gods?"

"We did, and we still do. We *are* the Homeric gods, though much older and more crafty than Homer supposed. We're also the gods of wilder epics. Like all epic gods, we had our twilights and resurrections, and we— Foley, I warn you! *Don't do it! You're dead on the spot if you do it.*"

And Carmody Overlark had risen to his feet in pale fury.

"Don't do what?" Fred Foley protested. "I'm honestly puzzled. I'm unarmed and completely without a plan. I really don't know what you're talking about."

"Don't laugh at me, Foley! You're dead on the spot if you do! I will not tolerate it. You laughed at my poor wife, but I will not tolerate being so wounded. You're brainless if you try it. I'll have you killed at once. I mean it."

"Continue, Mr. Overlark. You were telling me a good story and I wouldn't break it up, even though I nearly break up myself. I'm properly quelled by your threat; I don't want to be killed on the spot. That's no laughing matter for me. Continue."

"I will. Perhaps you don't know that laughing at us was the offense of the Titans themselves. For that we slaughtered them, and no such battle has been seen since. We're not only tribal deities, Foley, but also national heroes. There's one element common to all national heroes: that they disappear, and that they will come back. We're the thing behind that archetype. It's part of every national lore that the national hero will awaken again and lead like a Messias. There's even a variant Jewish belief that the Messias has lived before, that his appearance will be a returning rather than an advent.

"Now then, behind every legend is fact, and behind these legends is solid fact. The national heroes, under their own or other names, lived and seemed to die. But they only slept. And they will return. Most of them, most of us, have done it several times. I was such a legend myself long ago, and the last written traces of my own legend have now nearly disappeared."

"Your ears twitch, Carmody," Foley said. "Is that a property of archaic ears?"

"Foley, ours are the itching ears mentioned in scripture. They itch for novelty; we're not ashamed of that. And they do twitch physically. Oh how seldom are new things heard! So often they itch in vain! I was saying, Foley, that the last written traces of my own legend have nearly disappeared, so now I set about renewing my own legend."

"I'll have to take all this with a kilo of salt, Carmody," Fred Foley said, "being under death threat not to laugh and all. But I simply don't accept it."

"Why not? You had already convinced yourself that I was a returnee."

"I had, Carmody, and you've just now unconvinced me. You're a wraith that settles on a man and alters him. You're an insane spirit with no real substance, an influence flowing through. But you aren't a man, and you never were."

"I am a returned man as you first believed. I and my group are powerful enough to rule the world. Being so powerful, would we not be in legend?"

"Possibly, Carmody, but not so neatly; not with all the known names."

"The neatness is a modern accretion, Foley. Often the legend-cloak is draped over an unworthy dummy."

"Not as national heroes, not as peoples' heroes. You're against the people."

300

"No. It's they, in their ingratitude, who sometimes turn against us. We began as people of a sort, as men. After we were men we were tribal gods. We each have our tribe that we sometimes inspire and that we follow with interest. My own is a diaspora tribe that's older than the Jews and has forgotten its name; sometimes it's called the Intelligentsia. This is a people and a race, though it's forgotten that it is."

"It's no wonder that the Intelligentsia is inhibited from becoming intelligent."

"And when our tribes follow false gods, then we visit our wrath on them—as did a certain neologist among the tribal deities."

"This is like something out of Freud or Jung, Carmody. It isn't real."

"What is, Foley? We ourselves have always been puzzled as to what constitutes reality. We even have a sort of bet among ourselves as to who'll find the valid answer."

"But if you aren't real, what sort of visiting wraiths are you? Are you like winds blowing on a man and making him look a little bit like another man? Are you thin spooks influencing by fear and yourselves fearful?"

"We do influence by fear, but we deny that we are fearful. But how could you be if you had no— Oh, there are some things that can't be explained! It's so much easier to obliterate than to explain."

"And you really have no morality at all, Carmody, and you regard all our ethic as man-made?"

"Certainly. And *you* have no morality, Foley. You have only the memory of a morality. There are so many of these memories and nothing that is origin to them. Where were these original things? I was there. Where were they? It's always been in the past tense. Man has never been moral, but he's always remembered that he had been moral. It's a sort of backward aspiration. But you wouldn't understand it, Foley."

"I begin to understand some things too well. But when all is said and done, you're men only, or less than men, not more."

"But all isn't said and done yet, Foley. We are still men, in a way, but we are not *only* men. It wasn't a mere empty gesture, the rite of our assuming the godhead. It meant something."

Carmody Overlark was no more than poltergeist or plappergeist like the dog-ape of Bertigrew Bagley. He was even inferior to that sometimes invisible creature. He worked the fear trick; it was the only trick he knew. He came out of nowhere, a wraith frozen with fear, and he communicated that fear. By means of it, he seemed to have his way, a little bit, over the fearful. And there are always plenty of fearful.

"But you're not eternal or all-powerful or all-knowing or all-kind," said Freddy. "You're certainly not all-kind. What does your godhead consist of?"

"But we are the nearest things to the eternal. We are, at least, very powerful and very knowing. Oh, there have been marches stolen on us, we don't deny that. Here and there we weren't as astute as several others. But we'll see how it finally comes out. And to ourselves we are all-kind, Foley. We give ourselves all precedence, as is right."

"Who stole the marches on you, Carmody? You have me curious there."

"Oh, once there was a traveling man from Ur, and one made a promise to him at an oasis. The promise wasn't strictly kept but the memory of the promise abides. There was the Galilean thing. There was, what partly combined with it, the Grecian thing. We'd seen many come and go, and we were too complacent. But we're not content to run behind for long. We've bled it near to death in half a dozen drawn battles; it can't get even a draw any longer. Our old enemies are all dead, and it's only the parasites growing out of their bodies that we must subdue now."

"And you really regard us as no more than bees, or perhaps ants, Carmody?"

"Oh, as a little more. But if our planned ecology demands that you must go, then most of you will go."

"And you believe you can't be prevented?"

"Of course you can't prevent us. You could no more prevent us in anything than bees could prevent the removal of one small hive where men wished to build a building. Oh, it's possible that some of us may be stung a little, but that won't prevent your removal."

"Why are you so scared, Carmody, if you're so powerful?"

"Why do you keep referring to me as being scared? Anyway, haven't you known men who were scared of bees? But our planned ecology does demand that most of you be removed, so you will be removed."

"How you going to do it?"

"It isn't hard. Not after you've done it a few times."

"Why do you keep rats, Carmody?"

"How do you know I do, Foley? I keep rats like I keep people, to play with."

"Do your rats have any connection with your plans to remove most of mankind?"

"I don't know what you mean."

"Do you intend, by means of rats, to reintroduce the plague for the destruction of mankind?"

"Oh yes, we'll use the rats, among other things, for that introduction. And we'll use the plague, among other things, for the destruction, but only as a sort of secondary tool. The plague is a dull weapon and not to be depended on; it needs a very dry tinder and ideal conditions for a sweeping spread. We don't have those conditions now. You're a damnably antiseptic generation, a seven-times-washed abomination. I don't know where you get it—certainly not from us. The plague will be

303

only one of the secondary aids. We have a primary tool that's never failed."

"What's that, Carmody?"

"Hysteria. Fear."

"My father used to say that if I repeated 'This is only a bad dream' three times the dream would go away. My father was wrong there. When I said it three times it always caused it to solidify into a very bad dream indeed. I have most of your pieces now, Carmody. I only need time to put them together."

"You'll have plenty of time during your incarceration, Foley."

"I *do* have one more question, though, about a thing both abrupt and silly."

"Ask it then. But I warn you, if you laugh, you're dead."

"Why do you soak your head in a bucket, Carmody?"

"Ah, Foley, I'm glad you asked that, I really am. Because, before I tell you about it, I must do it. It's past my time for it, and I'm gasping like a fish out of water, which is what I am in a way. I was afraid I'd have to have you taken away before I was finished playing with you, Foley. But now that you've mentioned it, I'll do it. If you're looking for something grotesque about me, this is surely it. There's nothing so grotesque as a fish out of water, and you may as well watch."

Foley followed Carmody Overlark into the next room. The "bucket" was a large crystal ewer or bowl, transparent, and the water in it was still astir as though it was freshly poured. Foley recalled the sound of gushing water in the background as he had talked to Overlark. Well, let the toads have their fountains too! Even the patricks have fountains.

When Carmody Overlark took off his shirt, Foley was surprised at his remarkable musculature, for he had seemed a slight man. He was tanned, but there was something else. There was a very fine graining to his skin that reminded a little of fish skin—though that thought would not have come if fish had not just been mentioned.

Overlark breathed out deeply, emptying chest and collapsing his whole upper body in the expelling. Then he plunged his head and neck and shoulders into the large bowl and began to breathe the water deeply. If this was fakery it was good fakery, and it hadn't been rigged just to impress Freddy Foley.

The man, if he was a man, was breathing very deeply under water—if it was water. His eyes were open and they had a new snap to them. He grinned, a not altogether man grin, a not altogether fish grin. It was the grin of a tribal deity full of rogue power and eternal youth, one at home in all the elements. Something false about both the power and the youth, though.

Fred Foley scooped water and tasted. It was half salt—brackish, like tide-turning estuary water, or water from the sea very near the mouth of a great river. Or it was like water from an ancient ocean, one with less salt in it than have the oceans now. But why did Fred Foley think of that?

There were minute plants in the water, and small fish. It was not tap water. It was either drawn from a particular source, or carefully mixed. Foley had a sudden belief that there might be an upwelling of that water in that room, even though it was an upper-floor room, just as there was an upwelling of water on Auclaire's mountain, though there were dry caves below.

Well then, this was something that did not explain itself at all. Carmody Overlark had had his head under water for more than five minutes, and the water itself was in constant change or parade. There were schools of small fish that passed through it laterally. They did not follow around the curve of the bowl, they disappeared. And other sorts of fish appeared, all traveling a parade in the same direction, coming out of the glass itself (for all that could be discerned of them), traveling across the bowl in a straight line and disappearing into the glass wall again. There was optical illusion or there was strong current flowing through that bowl.

Was the underwater breathing of Overlark somehow the key to suspended animation? It was a funny key; it didn't seem to fit any of the locks. It was plain that an ordinary man would be dead, as it was now ten, now fifteen minutes that Overlark had his head and breathing below the surface. It was plain that he was not an ordinary man.

Then the water went out of the bowl. It could not be said that it drained out, for there was no drain. Air followed water in the current-parade across the inside of the bowl, and then the inside was dry. Overlark pulled his head out. He was beaming and greatly refreshed.

"Wonderful, Foley, wonderful. You should try it. There's nothing like it to set a man up."

"You almost convince me that there's something to you, Carmody," Fred Foley told him. "It makes you seem a little more than a man."

"Oh, not on account of that am I more than a man. It really makes me a little less, since I'm not a complete master of the air element. At one time I was somewhat ashamed of my need to return to water, but I've since talked myself out of that shame."

"After all, a tribal deity has no need for shame."

"Exactly, Foley. But you still don't understand, do you? It isn't really a mystery. It's just that I go back a very long time."

"Why doesn't your wife soak her head in a bucket, Carmody? If she does it, I haven't heard of it."

"She doesn't go back nearly as far as I do, Foley. She's a recent acquisition, a recruit of only a few hundred decades back. But we very old ones came from the sea and we're not completely free from it."

"I don't understand it at all, Carmody. I had some

theories worked out about this suspended animation business, but this head soaking doesn't tie in with them at all."

"I was born in the deep sea, Foley, before there were either monkeys or men upon the earth. I have the need to return from time to time, as those born on the land do not. I was one of the first to come out onto land, into the middle of that sky-beach, one of the first to learn to live above the water. And our first Olympus was in such sky, but still the ocean tide rose over its floor. You won't find traces of it on mountaintops, Fred Foley. Its palaces were sea-level caves (the top of the sea was then our sky) and they're now below the water. Ah, it was a long time ago, hundreds of thousands of years."

Fred Foley had a sound grasp on time. He knew the difference between hundreds of thousands of years and hundreds of millions of years, as many laymen do not; and he knew that the time before there were either monkeys or men upon the earth was impossibly distant. What then? Carmody Overlark apparently believed all that he said about himself. But was he not an impossible poltergeist, visible only for his borrowed body? And are not poltergeister really simpleminded creatures, for all their oddments of knowledge and false knowledge? Do they entertain superstitious beliefs, about the world, about themselves? Have they their own ghostly mythology? "You think people are silly to believe in ghosts?" an old man had asked Fred Foley a long time ago. "Boy, you should hear some of the things that ghosts believe in!"

"Oh, I led them up onto the land, or up into the sky," said Overlark. "It's all a question of viewpoint. We're sky-fish, all of us, and I was first."

"You're insane, Overlark," said Fred Foley, "but we'll let that go for a while. You said when we started that there was one condition (which I hadn't guessed) under which you might be impelled to tell me everything. And now you've told me almost everything. What is the condition?"

"That we might want to recruit you. We do recruit, now and then, to keep up our numbers."

"You have no idea how quickly I'd refuse, Overlark."

"You have no idea how quickly you'd accept, Foley, if it were finally offered to you. It hasn't been yet, but it may be. In any case, you'd first have to serve your period of incarceration. Then we'll have a look at your state of mind. But no one ever refuses. We're sensitive and we don't risk refusals. We ask only those sure of accepting. I believe you'll be sure of accepting in several days. Now I'll have them take you away."

"But why, Carmody? Why are you afraid to let me go? And you not of flimsy flesh to be so afraid?"

"I'm of flimsy flesh, yes, and now I need a quick snack, and I'll be rid of you first."

"And in this case you're still a little ashamed of being seen? Do you eat them live, Carmody? The rats, do you eat them live?"

"I do, yes, like kids eat popcorn." (This gave Fred Foley an uneasy turn, and the belief that Carmody was reading him a little too deeply. Whatever had happened to Popcorn, his little dog? Had the Larker kids really eaten him as they said they had?) "The second reason for having them take you away, Foley," Carmody Overlark continued, "is that you're crazy."

"On what evidence?"

"On the evidence of a man in your own profession, Foley, a man named Harry Hardcrow. He'll testify that you talked insanely last night. On the evidence of my own wife, who's stated that you were like a man with no mind at all. On the evidence of a certain doctor of solid reputation; he's a true expert in the field. Or on the evidence of myself.

"Or, if you don't really want to be taken away as a

lunatic, you can be taken away as a murderer. A man was murdered last night. He was last seen in your company. This unfortunate man was traveling under the name of Carlyle S. Crabtree, but that wasn't his true name. Carlyle S. Crabtree is an eminent man well known to us. The derelict who was cruelly murdered was a poor deluded fellow who had somehow picked up this name. The light was poor last night, in the doorway of that shop, and perhaps it can't be proved directly that you killed the man. But it can be proved that you handled him dead, and that you didn't report it. A fairly tight case of murder could be made against you. It was an especially cold-blooded murder."

It may not take too many of those spider-silk strands to bind a man after all. And the spider never leaves off working. Ah well, maybe Fred Foley was crazy. He was talking on the upper floor of a building on a sky-beach with a plappergeist, a mere troubling wind or wraith, who was visible only because of occupying a body not his own. The spook, with all his other disabilities, was insane, and lived in terror. And yet by transmitting part of that terror in which he lived, the spook might just have enough leverage to affect the world.

"Yes, that murder *was* a little cold-blooded, Carmody. It made me mad then and it still makes me mad when I think about it. Well, whistle up your buckoos—but I'll chop a few of them down before they drag me off."

"Curiously, my feelings are with you in this," Overlark said. "I don't love my buckoos; I enjoy seeing them chopped down, so long as I have plenty of them left to carry out the task. I tell you, Foley, when *I* am in such a spot (and I have been), I take the first one high, the second one low, and the third one dirty. After that, it usually turns into a melee."

Freddy's thoughts were along the same line. He didn't

hear any whistle, but Overlark had somehow given the signal, and buckoos boiled into the room. Freddy took the first one high and clean and sent him staggering. He took the second one low. But there it ended. The third, the fourth, the fifth, the sixth, came over him in dead heat and near killed him. The melee had been brief, and Fred Foley was trussed.

He raged and raved a little but they took him away. They took him, and they buried him in old buildings. This was the first day of that burial.

XI: "I DID NOT CALL YOU," SAID THE LORD

> —and one fears heights, and he shall be afraid
> in the road ... before the silver cord is snapped
> and the golden bowl is broken, and the pitcher
> is shattered at the fountain ...
> *Ecclesiastes* 12, 5-6

THEY WERE a very intelligent bunch at the Bug, but
Foley realized after a while that some of them had a
faulty orientation. It was in the emphasis they placed
on various things, in their center of interest which
seemed sometimes a little off-center, in their serious
treatment of the comic, in a distorted sense of proportion. Yes, there was something a little wrong with many
of the inmates of the Bug.

The Bug was sometimes called Old Central, or The
School, or Little Eli, or The Chambers. It was called
Happy Hollow, and the Paddock. It was called the
Bat-Roost, the Bughouse, the Boobyhatch. One of the
inmates called it the Nutcracker Suite, and one of them
called it The Long House ("long and lazy" is "crazy" in
Australian rhyming slang, and you go to any nuttery
in the world and you will find one of those gentlemen
from the south). But those of Fred Foley's new circle
referred to Old Wanwit on the Potomac simply as the
Bug.

The Bug was the institution of old buildings to which
the buckoos of Carmody Overlark had taken Fred

Foley for his incarceration and burial. Here were kindred souls, likewise buried: Bophry, Moyer, Framble, Bryant, Sloan, others, very nice fellows, and each one with a great jagged crack the whole length of him.

The first afternoon of burial is always a time of loose ends. Foley walked the lush lawns of the Bug and talked to himself. There was nothing wrong with talking to oneself in the Bug, even with talking out loud to oneself.

"Now here is the problem," said Freddy. "Nobody has examined me, and yet a complete report is filed on me showing that I was minutely examined. The report was already prepared before I was brought here. This is known as efficiency. To how many of my companions has the same thing been done?

"Many of my companions are disoriented. They have a fine jargon but they've lost touch with reality. They can seize on an isolated point and treat it interestingly from many angles, but they can't relate that point to the world. They can take a joke as the point of departure of a thesis, but they can't understand that joke as a joke. But I'm here as one of these, and the world can't tell the difference between us.

"There are people here for the same reason I'm here: because they believe there's a group possessed of either very long life or returning life, and because they believe that this group conspires against the world. How do I differ from them?

"Is the only difference that I can recognize a joke and they can't? But what if it's all a joke about the returnees and I can't recognize it? Then am I also insane?"

And Fred Foley walked straight into a tree.

"I'm at least getting careless with my wits," Freddy said. "Normal men don't get so preoccupied with their thoughts that they walk into trees. But there's one consoling thought: it may be that those of my type weren't insane when they were committed here, that they've become a little odd from the atmosphere of the place, or from those constant shots they give us. But that thought isn't as consoling as it might be. How am I to avoid the atmosphere of the place? How am I to avoid the constant shots? And how am I to avoid being here a long time?"

And one other detail made Fred Foley doubt his sanity a little. Leo Joe Larker might be there in the Bug. And he repeated an earlier warning:

"Whatever they tell you to do, Foley, don't do it. Whatever they tell you not to do, do it. Be dumb, blind, blundering, and silly, but stay on it. You may be dumb enough to get to the core of it. You're on your own with it all the way. I'm just telling you *not* to lay off. If they can kill you, Foley, I can kill you worse. If they can scare you, I can scare you double. Now, go to your appointments. Oh, I forgot! You've already been to your appointments. You're in here with us now. A lot of good it did you to be dumb and blind and silly. You didn't come any closer to whipping the thing than us smart ones did."

"Are you all right, Leo Joe?" Foley asked him. There was a puzzle about this Leo Joe Larker. He was a Negro now. There was no doubt about that. But he hadn't been one as a boy. Mexican, Gypsy, Indian maybe, or dirty-necked Irishman, but Negro, no. He didn't grow up to look anything like himself as a boy, his voice was not anything like that. He was, however, the same man who had spoken to Freddy from the darkened doorway one night. Yes, and he *was* Leo Joe Larker who had raised a man from the dead when he was a little boy. You're sure of some things, even after you're crazy.

"Why do you call me by that name?" Leo Joe asked. "That isn't the name I'm committed under."

"Foley isn't the name I'm committed under," said Fred, "but you called me by it immediately."

"I know it. But that Leo Joe stuff wasn't the name I had been going by either. I'm not even sure that I remember it. Are you sure that's my name? I'm probably not who you think I am. Say, why's that fellow so afraid of heights all of a sudden? He didn't used to be like that, did he?"

"What fellow, Leo Joe? Oh!" The fellow was James Bauer. He wasn't there, of course. He was back at home sitting on his own sometimes chilly patio. But a weaver, a Harvester wouldn't mind a little thing like it being chilly. In the lake down below, Wing Manion had been swimming every evening, and very often Hondo and Salzy Silverio swam with her. It doesn't get too chill for Harvesters, not even in mid-winter.

Rather odd that Leo Joe Larker should follow Fred Foley into the weave, though. Well, who can say what was odd about Leo Joe Larker?

James Bauer, thirteen hundred miles away, was trembling. He was the master of the weave and he was trembling. He went to the edge of the patio, to the concrete and iron stairway that led down to the lake. He put his hand on the iron rail and he shook.

"It isn't as high as all that, Foley," Leo Joe said. "It's only twelve easy steps down to the water, and the water there isn't four foot deep. I never did see a fellow so scared of heights as he is, though. You know it, he just got that way. He wasn't scared of them before."

This wasn't a projection like a viewing screen. It was being there with a piece of each of the senses. Every person brushed by the weave could read back into it, and sharp persons who brushed those brushed-ones could also read back into the whole apparatus.

"Arouet, Arouet Manion!" James Bauer was thundering from his far-away patio, and Arouet entered there from the house, frightened also, but not of heights:

"You compelled me so I'm here," he said. "You're in a passion. What are you going to do?"

("The heavy one is going to kill the other one, Foley," Leo Joe Larker said in the Bug enclosure. "You know that, don't you? Is there any way to stop it? Is it real?" "It won't happen for hours, or days," Fred Foley told him. "No, I don't know any way to stop it. No, it isn't completely real, Leo Joe, but it almost is. Pieces of it are real.")

"It's intolerable, Arouet," said big Jim Bauer. "The heights! How can anyone abide such heights? The highest mountains of earth aren't even anthills before these heights. One who falls here will fall through black space for eons. Is there no protection?"

"Your fear is of depths, not of heights, James; and like my fear of death it strengthens the weave," Arouet said. "You mock me for mine, I mock you for yours. And our anger feeds the weave."

"There's one thing I must do while on this pinnacle," Bauer rumbled. "I kill you this time. Crawl on your belly, Arouet. You'll grovel for many hours, and then you'll die. Grovel, man! I compel you!"

And Arouet Manion was on the stone floor of the patio. He was black with fear.

Foley caught something of a plappergeist just around the corner of his several senses. So, there was a patrick in the Bug! The creature-familiar was there.

"Can you change it to some other scene, Foley-Smith?" Bryant asked as he joined them. (But Bryant was not the patrick.) "That sure is a funny set you have. It doesn't have any chassis, and you can see it with your eyes closed. Why don't you let the fellow that's putting the speech together come in? I like to put speeches together myself."

"All right, Bryant," said Fred Foley, "if you're interested." These inmates of the Bug were some of them very psychic people. One has to be very psychic to hook in so easily on a brain-weave twice or thrice removed.

This was Michael Fountain, a sixty-year-old lean and lined man, craggy featured, with only a fringe of pinkish hair around his pate, with a hook in his nose like a Plains Indian or an Armenian, and too pale to be either

Michael Fountain was lecturing into the dictaphone. Such first-draft lectures were then transcribed for him, and from them he prepared his fine final renditions. He was dictating sequences for a superb lecture which he would name *The Golden Glass Bowl.*

"I will posit a student questioner of the intelligent but naïve sort," Michael was dictating, "and I will answer his questions. It is no matter that the questioner is at the moment imaginary." (That was in error, but Michael did not understand it. A real questioner would send a question into Michael's mind now by means that Michael still did not accept. The first questioner was a man named Greyhorse, who was intelligent but not in in all ways naïve.) "Any lecturer worth his salt and salary," Michael Fountain was continuing, "can call up whatever questions he wishes from the students sitting before him. He can pick out the most unlikely student for it, and he can elicit from that one just the question he wishes. This is done by gesture, by expression of expectation, and by the dropping of key phrases. It has always been known that an intelligent lecturer or teacher could do this. I explain the tactic to you since you here present are all destined to enter the intellectual elite. One sign of that is simply that you are attending my lectures. Were you not of the potential elite, you would not be here. But the students, even the students of the elite, who speak and think entirely in the prescribed catchwords (especially those who believe themselves the most independent), will sometimes grow angry at themselves for this, will sometimes feel themselves frustrated and insufficient. And yet they cannot deny that the trends and the questions come out of their own mouths and minds; out of the shallowness of their minds, however, while leaving the depths troubled but uncontributing.

"Ah, the questioner asks why there are still pockets of poverty and misery in the Golden Glass Bowl that is the world. There are these remaining pockets, my young friend, because there are still pockets of stubbornness and pride. 'Is not a poor man still entitled to his own measure of stubbornness?' I hear my young friend ask. No, he is not, I answer. Nobody is entitled to even a small measure of stubbornness any longer. Beasts may be stubborn; men may not be. 'And are not the poor entitled to even the crumbs of pride?' my phrase-mouthed questioner asks again. No, my friend, they are not! Not even the crumbs of pride can be allowed, not to the lowest of men, not to the highest. This would be apparent to you if you considered words in their real meaning. Birds and baboons have pride, perhaps; men may not have. It has never been a part of true men. The rich have had to give up all vestiges of pride long ago. They stuttered and protested, but they gave it up. It was a good bargain for them. Wealth and ease are better than the old vestige. And the stubborn poor can also enter into wealth and ease if they give up that old cumbersome burden. It were easier for a camel (*camelus camelops*) to pass through the eye of a needle than for a man burdened with pride to enter into the golden heritage, as an old prophet said. Ah, do we have another questioner?"

("Let me have at him once, Foley," said Loras who claimed to be an alien. "Have at him, Loras," said Fred Foley.)

"Ah, this questioner asks why we have given up the stars and the outer space," said Michael Fountain easily. "I always smile when I receive this question.

We have given them up, and all plans of further studying them, of ever visiting them, because we must set a limit to ourselves. It is very curious the persons who ask this question. So often it is those who might be called moral. Is it not ironic that those who believe that one wife is enough do not believe that one world is enough? How is it possible to reverse things so? We become free by a restriction. We restrict ourselves to one world so that we may enjoy one world fully. Our total freedom here is our compensation. Blot out the skies! There is nothing beyond our one sun. There is no world beyond our one world. The Golden Glass Bowl which we hold in our hands is singular and unique. Do not go whoring after strange worlds!"

("Let me have him, Foley," said the man who was possibly Leo Joe Larker, or who was possibly not the person they thought he was.)

"Ah, the questioner asks why we made it so small and why we are throwing it away," Michael Fountain lectured into the dictaphone back there in the south midlands of the country. "And I understand what he means. And the answer to the second part is that we are *not* throwing it away; at least I believe we are not, not at this time.

"What we are talking about are the world and the lives which we are given to fashion as our tasks. These are in the form, as I see it, of a large, fine, precious, crystal bowl, the Golden Glass Bowl, which we hold in our hands. True, it is not nearly so large a bowl as we once wished to fashion, but now we have come to understand that it is as large and as heavy a bowl as we are able to lift and hold.

"And here I have no patience with those fossilized and unregenerate persons who accuse us of being 'antilife,' no patience at all. They point their grubby fingers to the figures of older scientists showing that the world could be brought to support one hundred billion persons (or, in extreme cases, double that), but they do not point to the plain fact that special effort and ingenuity might be required to bring the world to such developments; and to the further plain fact that special effort and ingenuity are no longer possible to mankind as presently constituted.

"That these things were possible to mankind in the past we acknowledge, but we have refined them out of ourselves in our advancement. The world we have built and which we hold in our hands is a world of proper size and adjustment and enjoyment. The 'troubling of giant effort' has happily been left behind us. We are not dinosaurs to aspire to great size, nor yet swarming insects to aspire to great numbers. We are people. We have now had fifteen consecutive years of decrease in world population and we have ordained decreases for another fifty years. We will not be crowded or pushed, we will not be stirred to unusual effort for anything. We are the lords and we require lordly room. Ah, and here is a thing that only we of the elite know. We did *not* bring this about at all, though we take the credit for it. We need credit standing to our account. Perhaps we triggered it a little early, but that also I doubt. There are these biological swings and it swung. What we do now is set up safeguards so that it may never swing back again in the other direction.

"Nor have I any patience with those who speak of the 'loss of nerve' of our world. 'Nerve,' in this sense, is a property of animals or of animals in the process of becoming men. It is *not* a property of finalized man. Yes, we *have* lost our nerve, at least I hope we have. Let it be buried with other prehistoric monsters. Let it never trouble our world again. Does that answer your question, young sir? Ah—he is a little confused, he is a little resentful. These were not quite the questions he meant to ask, and yet they are the questions that came out of his mouth. There are questions that we of the elite cannot allow to be asked, and they will not be asked. The young have not the words for these questions yet. They have no words except the catchwords we give them. And when they come to an age to have the words they will have forgotten the questions."

("Let me go at the old gaffer, Foley," said one named Croll. "Who are the monsters who still trouble the world, now that you fine-haired dudes have it all fixed up so fine?")

"Here is a question," said Michael Fountain. "It's as though it came from a live and not an imaginary listener. This is odd, that it is a real questioner but not a real question. The thing to grasp about the monsters of my questioner is that they are not exterior but interior. They neither guard nor assault the world for the reason that they are not there. They are but unconscious remnants in some persons. It was once believed that we had need of these symbols. If we had once, we have not now. These were the four menaces that stood on the four forbidden roads that pre-man has already traversed. The *Toad* symbol is the loathsome origin, and death, and rebirth. And the alternate and sublimate of the Toad symbol is the Ox symbol (which is also the Worricow), possibly because both the toad and the ox have such bare staring faces (and possibly there is a trope with the horned toad). The jewel in the head of the Toad is the life-spark itself, which was first generated in cold flesh.

"The *Python* symbol is illicit wisdom; the python is a man-image as seen by pre-man (hairless, unnaturally mobile-appearing man was somewhat snake-like to the more hairy and less supple and less articulated pre-men, even when pre-men and man were combined in one person). Alternates to the Python symbol are the Octopus and the Hydra symbols (free-walking and tool- or weapon-handling man seemed, to pre-man, possessed of extra members or arms); and also, unaccountably, the Lion symbol is alternate to the Python.

"The *Falcon* symbol is the air-hunter, the bird-murderer, the taller authority, the tyranny, the force-rule of the first mounted men (man-on-horseback was, to some extent, man given the power of flight, Falcon-Man.)

"The *Badger* symbol is the cave or burrow symbol, the stubborn holing into the earth, the rear-guard defense of all rear-guard things. The alternates to the Badger symbol are the Bear symbol, the Man-in-the-Animal-Mask symbol, and finally the Man symbol. There seemed no confusion, to primitives, between the Man symbol and man himself.

"These four symbols are not proper symbols for modern men. They were symbols used by animals in the process of becoming men. Some, however, believe that these *are* valid symbols in our unconscious, and that by them our unconscious is trying to tell us something: as though we had cut some needed element out of ourselves and these symbols were warning us to bring it back in. I do not accept this view. Nor do I accept the easy explanations: tentacled liberalism (the python-hydra) opposing snap-jawed conservatism (the stubborn badger); and each abetted by its preternatural underform, Communism, from underground (the toad with the tantalizing jewel in its head) opposed by resurgent Fascism (the hunter-falcon, full-feathered, preying). There is polarity in the world, but it isn't so storied and allegorical as that. No, my young questioner, there can be no answer to no question. There are no exterior monsters who trouble the world either in attacking it or in defending it. They are not real."

("Old Gaffer, we *are* real," Croll said, giving the hissing growl of a very badger. "We are the abiding men, we are the abiding monsters, and we are real.")

Then Fred Foley knew that Croll was the patrick, a

more-than-a-patrick, a Croll: that he had been committed by his title, not his name. He knew, as a matter of fact, that Croll was Patrick of Baltimore and Washington, that he was Over-Patrick or Croll of the entire continent. He also understood that Croll was a little bit simple and inept, for sign that the office was more important than the man.

But a new force, a new man, entered the projected play now, one who could enter anywhere that Fred Foley could enter. The other inmates who had gathered around the communication felt this new person strongly.

("Here's another of the monsters," Croll bear-growled. "Don't tell me *he's* not real." The new-appearing monster was Miguel Fuentes and he *was* real.)

Michael Fountain, dictating privately in his own rooms thirteen hundred miles away, had become highly nervous but he still composed brave words for his lecture:

"We come to apex, and it is no way elevated or outstanding; we come to perfection, and to perfect simple means to finish; we come to climax, and it is beautifully flat and undistinguished. We have completed the world. Behold it!"

And in some manner Michael Fountain *was* holding a large, fine, precious, crystal bowl, The Golden Glass Bowl, in his two hands. It was pretty. It was almost substantial.

"This is the world," Michael intoned in a self-induced trance. "This is our lives, this is our final achievement. Worry not that it is small: it is the largest world ever, if we will not allow a larger one. Worry not that it is flawed: we ourselves are the flaws: and if we say that we are not flaws, then who is there to contradict us? Worry not that it is fragile, so long as we are very careful not to drop it."

"*Drop it!*" the thunder-clap voice of Miguel Fuentes

exploded. Everybody in the entire communication jumped at the cannon-barking violence of that command. And *Michael Fountain dropped his world.*

It tinkled into a thousand tinny pieces. It shattered and all the light flickered out of it. The face of Michael Fountain also broke and shattered and the light went out of it also. He cast himself down and was racked by dry sobs.

"How did we go wrong? What did we forget?" Michael moaned.

"You forgot that there is One who will not be mocked," Miguel Fuentes said in a voice like curling smoke. The falcons, like the patricks, believe strongly in things like that.

"That spik sure queered him," said Leo Joe Larker. "Do you know that spik, Foley?"

"Yeah, I know him."

"I know him way on back," said Leo Joe. "I was a Mexican one time myself."

"That one was real," said Croll. "He's as real as I am. The old gaffer isn't quite real, though. He had a good spiel going but he couldn't hold onto it. He came right up to the still, past the grinders, and then dropped his molasses jug."

"The funny thing about the old fellow," said Loras who claimed to be an alien. "He had known where the fountains were once. But the last time he went to them he busted his pitcher."

But there are also formalities in the life in the Bug, in the tomb. There was interrogation after a while. There was separation. There were more of those shots, tranquilizers. But Foley had been tranquil ever since he was buried here. There was even a little cleanliness lecture. And there was supper.

There was supervised recreation. This is the original

contradiction of terms. It was for making suggestions about supervised recreation that the devil was cast into hell; any other account you have heard is false. The inmates were crazy, but they weren't crazy enough to like that stuff.

Then to the beds. Even the sleeping was supervised, and honest darkness was not allowed in this tomb. Stubborn sleep then, and appearances that were not supervised.

The brain-weave was in tension and exhilarating unnatural agony. James Bauer and Arouet Manion were locked in lawless death passion, very much like snakes trying to swallow each other. It was not absolutely certain that Bauer was the master, for all that Arouet groveled before him. Bauer was in the grip of his own terror, that of horrifying height (and he was sitting on the ground-level patio of his own home), mind-blinding height, and Arouet knew of the terror and knew how to heighten it.

The arena became crumbling sand then, on the edge of cliffs of immeasurable height, and James Bauer and Arouet Manion were the two bulls who fought to death. Bauer was the heavier and stronger, he was the old king bull who had never been defeated: longer and more massive of horn, more humped and knotted of neck, bulkier of body, more iron of hoof, and altogether fearsome. But Arouet became the challenger, even though it was Bauer who had commanded him to the battle. Arouet held the high ground and could charge downward. He could regroup and charge again. But Bauer was trapped on the very edge before it started. He could not lunge without the sand further crumbling and sending him over the edge. He was hunched together, and all support began to slice out from under him. He dug one great horn into the steep turf for anchor, and dug more emptiness beneath himself as his sand base cascaded down the cliff-sides. He bellowed, and it caved beneath him still more. Arouet punished him from above, brought him to his knees, raked him and slashed him, but he could not turn that heavy armored head or come to the flank.

Bauer tangled horns with Arouet, hunched mightily, and broke Arouet's neck. But now the lighter bull was down on Bauer, twisted on his horns, quivering and screaming, and Bauer had no firm stance to pitch the thing away and back from his horns. Back legs pawing air, catching sand again, crumbling it with the effort, and pawing fearful empty air again. What great bull can stand to all charge with a crumbling foothold?

Arouet dying . . . let him die then, but how to get rid of him? And Arouet, though frantic with the fear of death, would go if he could take Bauer with him. The king bull feared no death except the falling death, and bull Bauer with the burden on his horns began to run like the sand itself over the edge of the cliff that had no bottom.

The arena became a pit then, green rocks and green shadows. Two great snakes, each trying to swallow the other. Bauer was the stronger and more massive, but Arouet Manion was perhaps the longer of jaw. Gaping mouths spread, unhinged, and spread again, wider, more mucous, now clinging and gaining like bird-lime, now sliding and slavering like very snake oil. Arouet had his longer jaws over the snout of Bauer, obliterating nostrils and eyes, closing over the great gape with extension that was drawn as thin as blue bubble, suffocating Bauer in the wide-spread translucent jaws.

Bauer grappled and won in the writhing snake-wrestle, breaking Arouet's back again. But in death spasms Arouet gained and gulped, swallowing Bauer's head, inching down the length of him, blistering and murdering him with blazing gastric and psychic juices, spreading his own Arouet-death over Bauer like a clinging plastic

sheath. And, suffocatingly, Bauer knotted himself a-
gain and again to try to burst the killing sheath.

Bauer, on his own patio, was breathing with a rasping groan that would not leave him for the rest of his
life; and Arouet Manion writhed on the stone floor, frantically afraid of death, frantically avid for killing.

The arena changed to—obscene interval—that is too
degrading to contemplate even in a brain-weave. The
arena changed again and again while the double death
battle tallied off all its aspects one by one. The other
members of the weave were brought to continuing psychic orgasm by the strong and musky play of agony
and death. And it would be played out for many hours
yet.

Hondo. Silverio was shaken with waves of disgust
and loathing. That noble snake found himself revolted
to his depth. It was then that he decided either to
master or to break the weave; but that isn't done in a
minute or an hour, nor even in a day.

Another arena, and another. The dead wife of Bauer
waited in agony in an uncontinented place for Bauer
to fall past her into hell: ashen anguish, ghostly torture.
The living-aspect wife, caught in deep catalepsy, waited
for the hypnosis over her to be broken by death, if
indeed even death would break it. A saintly sexpot and
a cinnamon cookie (the cookie for Cerberus) were
caught in the passion, the passion that would break
the weave.

Bedelia Bencher would come for Foley, either late
that night or early in the morning, either on bat-wings or
by commercial flight; but she would have a very deep
draft of this passion first.

So would they all. They were the psychic athletes
and this was their game, the sounding evil of it, before
they broke it in final disgust. But the horror-gulping
gusto would reign a long reign before the disgust overwhelmed it.

In another place, a young man was having evil fun in his grave in the caves underground. Miguel Fuentes was the hunted there, but he also ran with the hunters. Indeed, he was the bright young Mexican boy, guileless and glib, who told certain army patrols that he knew the caves better than anyone in the world, that he could find anyone in them. And he led the patrols in to their loss and murder, and them hunting for him all the while. This young man would be a falcon full-feathered when he finally came out from underground.

And in still another place (and it could be any one of many, as they of that species are so much alike), a patrick was experiencing a waking night-dream out of Samuel, the saddest verses in scripture:

And the patrick answered: "Here I am, Lord." And again he said, "Here I am; for you called me." But the Lord answered him: "I did not call you. Go back and sleep."

Well, why did the Lord never call the patricks? They had been waiting, oh how they had been waiting for the call! It was given to others. It was never given to the patricks, and they waiting so ready for their thousands of years.

"Smith, Foley, whatever your name is, turn that thing off, whatever that thing is," protested Loras who claimed to be an alien. "We want to sleep. How can we sleep with you dreaming that bright-colored stuff?"

XII: FOURTH MANSIONS

That I be one to catch the hard truth hurled
And fight soft lies that have the world for span!
I know the Ox, the Eagle, and the Man,
The Lion—and the schism of the world.

I feed on elementals like a cloud
Though buried in constraining earthy room
Where now I harvest lightning in my tomb
And integrate the monsters for a shroud.

Here in Fourth Mansions which is Death or Life
Is rooted world that it is worth to live:
The Giant Troubling and the Giant Brawn.
Though I be dead a while I bite the knife!
In monumented earth I grow and give
While I predict and manufacture dawn.
Broken Cisterns and Living Waters:
Endymion Ellenbogen

"THERE IS A holiness in a whole person or a whole world," the patrick Croll said. "The veriest monsters inside us may be sanctified. They were put there by Him who is 'Father of Monsters' also. What right have we to cut them out of us? Who are we to edit God? We cut strong things out of ourselves and suppress them, and the rocks and clouds will give birth to them again. We dry up our interior fountains and they gush out again, exteriorly and menacingly. We cannot live without monsters' blood coursing through us. Only to the whole person is life worth living and death worth dying. Here in Fourth Mansions we must be whole or we must be nothing."

"Where do you get those curious phrases, Croll?" Freddy Foley asked him.

"From the manual. As patrick, I must recite certain passages every morning."

"But aren't the patricks themselves monsters?"

"Yes, I believe so. But we're the monsters under the man-symbol."

This was the morning of the second day of the burial or incarceration of Foley.

"A man and his daughter were here looking for you earlier this morning," an attendant told Foley now, "but they found no trace of you. They're nearly convinced that you're not here. You *aren't* here, you know."

"Well, but who is this here then?" asked Freddy.

"You're in the records as Julius Smith."

"That explains why so many call me Smith. Did you tell the man and his daughter that I was carried as Smith on the rolls?"

"No. I just hinted enough that they might not be gone for good. They were very generous with me this morning. A little later they may be even more generous. They're wealthy, aren't they?"

"They may be, but don't run it into the ground."

"I'll have to be the judge of that, Foley-Smith. Oh, I miss out entirely some times when I shoot for too high a figure. But I make it up, I make it up, I often do quite well. I have a good judgment of what the traffic will bear. That girl—those eyes—are they real?"

"Not entirely. But you saw her and I didn't."

"I swear she has eyes like nobody has eyes. She has pictures painted on her eyeballs, weird pictures, snakes and monsters and fountains and upheavals. I never saw anything like them. But she gets around all right. How can she see with those pictures painted on her eyeballs?"

"She's a clown, but she's more than that. She's mutated and she can see with every part of her. So can I. I just now realized it. Who needs eyeballs? Is there a tattoo artist here in the Bug? I'll have him tattoo my eyeballs. I'll be the first one here with tattooed eyeballs."

"Yeah, there is one here. If you pay me—you have money to your account here and you can release some to me—I can tell you which one he is, and we can— Nah, you're joking."

Oh well, what can one do in a grave except wait for that last trumpet to blow, or perhaps an intermediate trumpet in special cases? But for an inquiring mind there are interesting questions cropping up everywhere, even in the grave. Fred Foley asked one of the doctors about one of the questions that was bothering him.

It wasn't that he was reconciled to the doctors here. He believed that they also were tilted, though perhaps not to such an angle as the boarders. Those doctors had trouble with jokes too. For answer to a joke they were likely to gaze at you with steely eyes, and then pull your record and make cabalistic marks on it. Doctor Decker was better than the others, but only a little.

"Doctor, what I wonder is whether group delusion is common," Fred Foley asked him.

"Quite common, Smith, quite common," Doctor Decker told him.

"Then there are other groups like us who share a common delusion?"

"At least a dozen groups in this very hospital at the moment, and there have been hundreds."

"What were some of the more unusual—ah—obsessions?"

"A few years ago there was a group here that believed that very low musical notes caused their teeth to loosen. They campaigned strenuously against all low-down songs, they lobbied against them, and some of them smashed and destroyed those coin-operated machines which I believe are called goop boxes. They also tried to have the Army 'Taps' changed, to eliminate several low notes."

"And what was the outcome?"

"Oh, the group split up. It had no real cohesion. Some of the patients were finally released. Some went on to other obsessions."

"No, I don't mean the outcome like that. I mean the tests. *Did* it show that low musical notes caused their teeth to loosen?"

"Sizzling sandburrs, Smith! What are you talking about? There was no such test."

"Then who was to say that it was an obsession? It might have been a shrewd observation that wasn't acted on. There was no test at all? What were some of the other groups?"

"There was one quite small group, three. This is the smallest possible group by our definition. All three of these men were locomotive engineers, and they all believed that their lonely night whistles were answered by giant flying creatures. They believed these creatures were not large enough to carry off an entire train, but that a locomotive running alone might be carried off; and they swore that this was the answer to several disappearing locomotives. They said the giant flying creatures believed the night whistles were mating calls."

"And were there actually cases of disappearing locomotives? And were there any attempts made to pursue this explanation?"

"Smith, are you kidding?"

"Not entirely. As a reporter I *did* hear of cases of locomotives disappearing when running alone at night. I'll follow this up when I get out and when I settle other matters. What were some of the other groups?"

"Oh, there was a bunch who all believed there'd be a terrible earthquake in the Great Lakes region on the morning of June 19, 1979, that the southern shorelines would sink, and that thousands would be drowned."

"But that was the very date of it! They were right! This proves that some of the groups can be right and you can be wrong."

"Of course that was the date of it, Smith, and their insistence that the area be cleared would have saved thousands of lives if it had been timely. But the obsession occurred three years after the event. All the afflicted believed themselves living several years in the past, anterior to the happening. All had been eyewitnesses and near victims of it and it had deranged them. Then there was the group that believed that all redheaded women were creatures from outer space sent here to intermingle with mankind to cause trouble and destruction."

"I could give you instances that would seem to prove them right," Freddy said.

"So could I, Smith," said the doctor. "Some of the redheads do seem to come from way out. Then we had a clutch of odd ducks here who believed that the messages and mottoes in fortune cookies form a sinister code of instructions sent by an evil mastermind in high Tibet.

"And there was a clique with the belief that the white oak tree is a man-eater, and that persons who have unaccountably disappeared will invariably be found to have disappeared in the neighborhood of a white oak tree. They believed also that the wood of the tree had certain dangerous properties, and that a certain furniture factory that makes much use of the wood should be enjoined from doing so. We still have some of the white oaks here.

"The majority of the coteries, however, have beliefs very similar to the group you belong to, Smith. This is the belief that the world is ruled by a hidden-hand group of men who may be known by such and such marks, that these men plot against the world, and that their plot against the world is about to succeed; they maintain that it's absolutely necessary that their warnings be hearkened to and acted upon. You're really a variant of the world-is-ending societies."

"What if one of our groups is right, Doctor?"

"Why then, the plot against the world would succeed, since your warnings are most certainly not going to be acted upon."

"Do you really believe I'm insane, Doctor Decker?"

"Yes, on one point you are, Smith. One point of insanity is about par for the never-quite-normal human race. I actually believe that it's a healthy sign for a man to be clearly insane on one clear point; it gives him balance and otherwise keeps him sane. The normally insane have a point of eccentricity that's minor, private, and of no threat. That's where you go past it, Smith. In an involved society the eccentricity must be a minor one. It must not annoy or harm your neighbors. And it plainly must not lead you to vicious slander of persons in high places. Yours has led you to that."

"Then you don't believe it possible that the world is being plotted again?"

"Likely it is, Smith, and in thousands of plots. The world is a fine apple and we all want a bite. But I don't believe in an effective plot any more than I believe that the white oak tree is a man-eater."

"What's the very latest thing here in group belief?" Fred Foley asked.

"Your own was of yesterday and the day before, Smith. There's a new one today. It's the belief in a new disease. This is a death-wave to come and be characterized first by nasal itching, then by a tiredness and certain irritability, later by drowsiness, and eventually by death."

"That sounds like the normal life story to me, Doctor."

"Yes, but this is all to take place within five hours, according to the addicts. And according to them it's caused by germs carried by gossamer, or by drifting fluff from cottonwood trees (but there aren't any of them here, and this isn't the season for them to cotton), or more probably by a drifting medium similar in appearance to these but which may come from outer space. The warners give very clear and detailed description of the disease, considering that it hasn't yet appeared."

"Five hours isn't a lot of warning, but for what it's worth I may as well take it," said Foley-Smith. "My own nose itches. That should mean that I'll be dead by dark."

"You have a delusion of your own, Smith, yet you can joke about the delusions of others. Oh that damn drifting stuff, like spider silk, it's been settling on me all day! Wonder what it is? But there is real terror among the addicts, Smith, and it begins to spread. We've had to isolate those of the cult."

"I wasn't joking about it, Doctor," Fred Foley-Smith said. "I believe that a complex of sudden and fatal diseases is part of the ordeal in store for us. And it does itch, Doctor. And I'm a little tired and could become irritable."

"I wouldn't worry about it, Smith. You aren't the sort to panic, though you may be the sort to cause panic. Nasal itching can be brought about by suggestion easier than almost any other phenomenon. But it's curious that the members of this group (we haven't been able to establish any previous relationship among them at all) should all come up with this odd notion at one time. And they've all come up with it violently, calling out loud in the streets for massive efforts to destroy the floating cosmic stuff.

"But it's just as curious about your own and similar groups. I've tried very diligently to discover how it all comes about. It's part of my business to discover how these things come about. Do *you* have any idea how they might happen? I'm asking you, Smith, because you might be able to give me a lead. You aren't the most intelligent of your group, but you're the most open, the most communicative."

"I don't know about the other groups, Doctor. But with my own group I know exactly how it happened."

"Then tell me, Smith. I've been studying it for years."

"It's as though an elephant were standing in the middle of the street, Doctor. One man sees it and announces it. Then another man sees it (and there's been no previous relationship between the two men at all) and the second man likewise announces it. And a third man sees it (and he's a total stranger to the other two men) and he announces it in his own way. So the three are locked up in the strong house for believing that they see it. The reason that they all believe they see the elephant at the same time is that the elephant is there at the same time."

"To follow your analogy, if there is one, Smith, why can't the keepers see the elephant too?"

"Because they, you, are too stubborn to look out the window, Doctor. Because they believe it's impossible for an elephant to be standing in the street."

"Then the facts of your delusion are really that obvious to you, Smith?"

"The facts of the case are really that obvious to me, Doctor. I finally saw the whole conspiracy standing as plain as an elephant in the street: also the conspiracy was admitted to me in great detail by one of the princes of the conspiracy."

"Bad, Smith, very bad."

"If one of the inmates should come to you right now, Doctor, and tell you that it was raining outside, you'd say 'Bad, very bad,' and make damning marks on his record."

"That's probably true. It's an automatic response with me. I do wish you'd get over this, though, Smith. You're a likable young man."

"Why was the name Smith hung onto me, Doctor? And Julius? There hasn't been a Julius in our family since two generations before Adam. Why wasn't I committed under my own name?"

"You were. Your own name is Julius Smith. You were wandering and amnesiac when picked up, and you were proclaiming that men long dead had returned to plague the world. We solved your identity by routine methods, and we hope you'll soon remember your own past life. That would be an important step to your cure."

"Are you in on this cover job, Doctor Decker?"

"No, I'm not in on any cover job, Smith. I'm not at all related to the political angle of this place, though there is one. I accept the data that's passed on to me and I work sincerely with the patients on the basis of it."

"But my name isn't Smith."

"Oh well, neither is mine. And stop rubbing your nose. If this keeps on it will become a national pastime. I believe it will really be a disappointment to you if you don't die tonight from this nonexistent new disease. Damn that drifting fluff anyhow! It's everywhere. You'd go through with it, I know, Smith, just to prove that one of the alarm groups was right."

Doctor Decker had been rubbing his own nose, and Foley-Smith left him then.

The disease was not imaginary. It *had* appeared. So had half a dozen other new diseases. Though still unrecognized, this nonexistent disease had already gone into its second and third stages with many that day; and by nightfall about thirty persons in the capital city would have died quietly of it.

And then the first tremor of the hysteria would come.

It was a curious day. Things were shaping up, just as the clouds were shaping and tumbling overhead. It was a warm day for the season, but the sign of chill had appeared on the edge of those clouds. Familiar things looked unfamiliar. Unfamiliar things looked familiar. The ice cream man looked familiar.

The ice cream man, selling ice cream bars to the inmates through the iron fence, was Leo Joe Larker. But wasn't Leo Joe Larker still an inmate of the Bug? No he wasn't. He had escaped that very morning, they said, and he would be recaptured within an hour, they said. And nobody else should try the thing, to break out into the world from the safe place where they were understood.

Well, why didn't they recapture Leo Joe then, since he was right outside the Bug? Since they were looking for him everywhere? They didn't capture him because they didn't recognize him. He did not look anything like what he had looked like inside the Bug. He was a different man entirely in appearance; he had been several such different men; only Freddy Foley could recognize him. And Leo Joe had turned into an ice cream man to pass a message to Fred Foley. Why had he not given him the message when he was inside, when they could talk freely? He had not because that would not have been grotesque enough for him. Freddy did not know what the words or details of the message would be, and yet he already knew their meaning. It was "Goof gloriously, Freddy. Goof gloriously again. It is required that one man should goof gloriously for the people."

Leo Joe Larker was humming the old tune *What Kind of Fool Am I?* when Freddy Foley came up to him on the other side of the fence.

"You, Leo Joe, or I?" Foley asked him.

"You, Foley, you're the fool. Little Freddy Foley who

can see in the dark and was trapped like a coney in broad daylight. Even a coney has a hole or a rockpile he can get to. He isn't taken in the open as easy as that."

"Little Leo Joe, the man who changes faces and never gets a very good one. What are you doing with an ice cream pokey?" (But this Leo Joe wasn't a clown. He had told Foley. "If they can kill you, I can kill you worse. Whatever they tell you to do, don't do it. Whatever they tell you not to do, do it." This was Leo Joe Larker who had perhaps raised a man from the dead when he was only a boy.)

"I'm not Leo Joe. I'm no one you ever saw before. The ice cream pokey gives me certain vantage points."

"So does this Bug give me," said Freddy.

"Just exactly what good can you do on that side of the fence, Foley?"

"I'm not sure."

Leo Joe Larker sold a French lime bar to one of the inmates, and a strawberry revel bar to another one. Then a keeper was coming to the fence to chase him away.

"Here's a grape sherbert bar for you, Foley," said Leo Joe. "Digest it well."

"I'd rather have a French lime."

"I'm telling you not to get cute. Take it. And digest it."

Freddy Foley took the grape sherbert bar, thrust it quickly into his pocket, and disassociated himself from Larker. The guard came and chased the ice cream man away, to the whimpering of inmates who were coming with their allowances in their hands.

This was ridiculous, to be trapped with a melting sherbert bar in the pocket, to know that it contained a message, and to know that it was all grotesque. How low and laughable must a man be brought before he is born again? This was ignominy beyond even death and burial.

And immediately there was a summons for Foley. Grown now very suspicious, he was sure that his short rendezvous with Larker had somehow been discovered and reported, and he was embarrassed as to what to do with the melting grape sherbert bar in his pocket. It wasn't a dignified place to carry it. It was cold there, but he didn't want it to get warm. And suspecting that there was more to it than grape sherbert, he didn't want to throw it away. Still less did he want to have it in his pocket if he was subject to any sort of interview.

It was Bedelia Bencher and her father, and Fred Foley was allowed to visit with them, though guards and attendants were present.

"Poor little sour pickle," said Biddy. "Have they treated you all right?" That Biddy and the eyes of her! Landscapes, hellscapes, monsterscapes painted on her eyeballs, and she laughing all the while.

"With every care of my body, Biddy, and none at all of my soul," Freddy said.

"Just what is this nonsense, Foley?" Mr. Bencher asked sharply. His name was Richard but nobody ever called him anything but mister. But he was looking at Foley on two levels and understanding quite a bit.

"Part of the nonsense, Mr. Bencher, is that I'm Smith and not Foley," Freddy said.

"You persist in that, Freddy? We very nearly didn't find you under the name of Smith. But Biddy was certain you were here, and she wouldn't leave town without you. You do remember us, don't you?"

"Remember you? Certainly. I'm not crazy. It's the people here who are crazy."

"And what was your name when you knew us back home?"

"My name has been Fred Foley all my life except for the first two hours when it hung in the balance between

Fred and Ronald. I've never been sure I got the best of that deal."

"Then why the Smith now? I'm trying to ask you clear questions," said Mr. Bencher. But Bencher was reading Foley while he played this game with the guards. Perhaps he had even read the message in the sherbert bar.

"I'm trying to give some clear answers, Mr. Bencher," Freddy said. "I don't know *why* the Smith now."

"You mean that you don't know why you told the authorities your name was Smith?"

"No, Mr. Bencher, I mean that I don't know why the authorities told *me* my name was Smith. I guess they've tried to hide me here."

"Freddy, it's in your record that you insisted your name was Julius Smith," Mr. Bencher said evenly, "and that you don't know any Fred Foley nor remember ever being such a person."

But really Mr. Bencher was talking all of this for the benefit of the long-eared attendants and guards. His eyes were saying other things.

"Papa, don't press him so hard," said Biddy. "He's sick." But what were the landscapes on her eyeballs saying? There was lots of evil laughter still there, and perhaps a little concern.

"Mr. Bencher, if that's in the record, then it's in the record wrong," Freddy said. "There's some dirty work here. Get me out of this place, will you? You have influence."

"Freddy, what's that leaking out of your pocket?" Biddy asked.

"A sherbert bar, Biddy. A grape sherbert bar."

"But why, Freddy? Why do you carry it melting in your pocket?"

"Where else?"

"Do you often carry them there, honey?"

"Quite often. All the time, Biddy."

340

Freddy felt that he had slipped with them, and he had no idea how to recoup. He was compelled not only to goof gloriously but to goof grovelingly. Something had hold of his mind and it would force him into this insanity role. But Freddy did not want an attendant to get that sherbert bar, though he hated to look like a total fool when the possibility of his really being a total fool was under discussion.

"Well, take it out and throw it away, Freddy," Biddy was saying, "and then let me clean you up."

"No, Biddy. I couldn't possibly throw it away. I'll just keep it there. I could never find a better place for it, and it keeps me cool."

"Ah, Foley, I have been trying to get to the bottom of this," said Bencher. "I heard a little from Biddy of the crazy jag of a story that you seemed to be on. I thought it was just something you told her to put her off and that you were working on something confidential that couldn't be discussed prematurely. Biddy thought so too. But now I find you actually have been trying to prove that five-hundred-year-dead men have come back alive and are meddling with our lives. Is that true?"

"Yes sir. It's quite true that they've come back. I have most convincing evidence, which somehow doesn't convince anybody. If I could persaude you of it, Mr. Bencher, then you might have more weight than I at getting the warning taken seriously."

"Foley, I always liked you. I felt rather safe for Biddy when she became attached to you. I still feel safe for her with you in that way. But, Freddy, you're quite sick.

"I believe I'm the only one here who isn't."

"I'll see that you get everything you need," said Bencher.

"I need out," Freddy Foley insisted.

"No, not that, Freddy," Bencher said. "You're in no state to be out."

"Please let me throw that melted bar away, Freddy," Biddy begged. "It isn't nice to have it in your pocket."

"No, I'll keep the bar there, Biddy. I feel somehow that it contains the key to the whole world difficulty. Besides, I like it there."

Biddy began to cry. Or did she? There was a lot of suppressed hilarity behind that crying, but with eyes like hers who could tell?

"Oh, Freddy," she said, "you never knew how much I liked you. We never did anything but kid. Oh, Freddy, I hope you get well."

"Then you think I'm sick too?"

"Oh, Freddy!"

"You really should take that mess out of his pocket," Bencher said to an attendant.

"It might upset him," said the man. "They become attached to things and notions. It could set him back. Besides, they get fresh-laundered clothes tomorrow."

"Goodbye, Foley," said Bencher, "and if there's anything at all you want—"

"I want out."

"God willing, and soon, as quickly as you're well," said Bencher.

"Be real good, honey," said Biddy, "and you'll never know how much."

"But you don't believe in me?"

"Oh, Freddy!"

The Benchers went away and left Fred Foley-Smith there with the attendants. He felt like a fool with the melted sherbert running down his leg and his pants, and his girl not believing in him, and gone. And the world about to be taken over and frustrated by the returnees.

And yet he had been brought strangely up to date by the pictures painted on Bedelia's eyeballs. They changed, you know, they changed. And they conveyed messages.

Loras (who was alien), Croll (who was patrick), and a man called Boneface by all, came up to Fred Foley when he was ready to inspect the lavender decay that was the sherbert bar.

"You're standing in the way, Foley-Smith," Boneface said. "There's two shows going on and we can't watch either of them with you standing in the way."

Oh! Michael Fountain was dictating lectures again this day. And James Bauer and Arouet Manion were still locked in death ordeal. The men wanted to watch these shows, but they were not yet adept enough to watch them apart from Foley. He had brushed the weave. They had only brushed him.

The highly refined Michael Fountain seemed a little shriveled today in his ultra-refinement. There was not as much to him as there had once been, or it had turned inward on him. His fine voice had become a little cracked and thin, his fine features a little masklike and amateurish. But had his fine words changed?

"Are there events in the world?" he was lecturing into the dictaphone. "Are there events in the world at the present time? We hear rumor, we see signs; surely there is some shadow play going on which one might call 'Events in the World.' We of the elite, however, do not need to be overly concerned with these. What we do desire is a refinement still more refined, a nobility still more noble, an elite still more elect. We draw in on ourselves. There is a vulgarity of numbers. We reduce the vulgarity and the thing. A thousand gross units goes into one essence. And then we refine the essence again and again."

("This man is wrong," said Loras who was alien. "It's been tried in other places; it doesn't work. You reduce it and it dies, it dies every time. You narrow the grove too much and even the noble trees die." Loras the alien had sought for his Earth visit a place like the Bug, knowing that his sanity was not the sanity of this strange world. He had had no real trouble gaining admittance. He had simply gone to the attendance official, declared that he was a visitor from the stars, and after less than half an hour of lively discussion he had been accepted as a member of the Bug. He wasn't a handsome creature, but he had a pleasant and outgoing personality. And such little physical peculiarities as he possessed—a slight caudal appendage, a triple Adam's apple, opposable great toes—were not held against him. He was intelligent and he adjusted well. Only once had he eaten his plate after eating his food. Only once had he given the astral caress on being introduced to another. Only once—)

And Michael Fountain lectured on. "We will, of course, abandon large sections of the world as soon as we can phase them out. The entire old world, I believe, can well be abandoned in the present century. There is no need of it, really. The new world is ample for the people. 'Is it not well that all the members of one family should dwell in one house?' And many attitudes and mythologies of the old world will likewise be allowed to die. In a way, the old world has already become something like the disordered unconscious of the new. Discard it, I say! And then the southern continent of the new world may well be abandoned in a further generation. One continent is enough for mankind. For a refined and elect mankind it is more than ample."

(The sherbert had melted and dried in Freddy's pocket now, leaving only a stain, a slight stickiness, and a tightly rolled piece of paper. Freddy took it out and read it as he listened with exterior ears to the distant voice of Michael Fountain. *You aren't a whole lot of good in there*, it said. *Don't you know that things have already begun? The day before yesterday there were twenty deaths of the new diseases. Yesterday there were fifty. Today there will be two hundred when the count is in. And tomorrow three still newer diseases will appear, one of them being the old disease named panic. I know that you haven't any plan, and I haven't much of one. I have a few men. I need a few more. At sundown you will take three good men and go over the fence.* That was the sticky scribbling of Leo Joe Larker on the lavender-stained paper.)

"Ultimately, all mankind will be lodged in a single town," Michael Fountain lectured on. "The dross will have disappeared. Only the many-times refined gold will remain. And more finally still, all of mankind will be lodged in a single house. This is most important to the closing and diminishing of the circle. We support, as expedient, all cyclic Orphism; and so we must support the effort of the returnees. But they were only shadows of ourselves. Their concern that the cycle of birth, death, and rebirth be repeated has been a good one up to this time. The returnees must at all cost keep the world in this cycle. They cannot permit the world to ascend. They cannot even permit the cycle to become a helix, a spiral. We support them in the one direction, but we do not support them in another. The cycle, of course, cannot be permitted to become an ascending or outgrowing spiral. Neither can it be permitted to remain a simple cycle forever. It must become a diminished concentric with each turn of it smaller and more refined than the last. We will diminish to a point. We will concentrate in one point."

("The patricks and their castles will stand against him in that," said Croll who was a patrick. "We've stood for the open way even when it was stagnant; we won't accept the closed way even when it's in movement. Theirs isn't the eternal symbol of the snake with his tail in his mouth, forever repeating. That snake eats a little of his own tail every time he goes around, and he becomes a much smaller snake. We'll stand against them and their diminishment!")

"The final human race, at its finest hour (and I see it as an hour not more than ten seconds long) will surely have diminished to no more than three or four exceptional men," Michael Fountain lectured on. "And then is the synthesis, the diminished finale: the world will one day dissolve into the original Great Man. Is it not a most quieting and peaceful concept? But what is that silence? The roaring had gone down to a gurgling in the last few years. The gurgling had softened to a mere dripping in these later days. Now it no longer drips. How has it become so shallow and dry?"

("Ha! The old man's fountain ran dry," said Boneface. "I knew it would." This boney-faced man was a madman. He was intensely mad, a killer. If he ever said something that seemed to make sense—and often he did—it was a slip. He was mad. He always insisted on that point.)

(*But will you be ready for it?* asked the note from Leo Joe Larker that Freddy had taken from his sticky pocket. *Ready or not, you will have to come. I am prepared to visit some plagues of my own; but only on the returnees, not on the world. You may already have guessed that I once joined their company. But I was a very recent recruit of theirs and I have broken away. To make up for the part I have had in it I will try to stop the thing. Now, here is what you will do—*)

("Let's look at the other two, Foley-Smith," said the patrick Croll. "There's a lot better stuff in them than in this dried-up old man. Sure, he knew where the fountain itself was once. He went to it with his pitcher. But that's all gone with him now. Let's get the other bunch. Those two have a real fight going on, and some of the sideplay from the others in the show is so strong that it takes you right up into it.")

James Bauer and Arouet Manion still continued their teetering on the edge of the world battle. They fought through arena after arena. Bauer still sat, ponderous and purple-swollen and glassy-eyed, breathing like thunder. Arouet still stretched dragonlike on the stone floor, shuddering with final sickness, poisonous to the last. They were two arms of the deadly hydra, tearing and killing each other. It is only for this reason that the abominable creature, recreated so many times, has never demolished the world: it mistakes its own tentacles for other things and battles them to the death.

Hondo Silverio had come in. He was breaking the brain-weave, tearing it loose, slicing it up. His green mottled humor had become death gray with the new concern, but he moved easily, helped himself to a drink from the sideboard and flung himself onto one of the scatter-couches.

Wing Manion came in, wrinkled her fish-nose in many-layered disgust, and stood over her sick-dragon husband Arouet. She also had sworn to break the weave. The Harvester mark was still livid on her forehead but she would no longer be a Harvester. She picked Arouet up in her arms ("This fish gets pretty strong, after a couple of days out of the old pond," she had once said of herself), carried the awkward length and lug of him over to the most distant chair, and deposited him there with worried concern. But Arouet, still showing no more life than a dank quivering, poured himself like quicksilver out of the chair and slithered the width of the patio to lie again before Bauer in his attitude of mocking adoration. They still had several arenas to battle through. Letitia Bauer (the dead one) came and stood wraithlike and worried. Bedelia Bencher also came and watched a moment in her wraith-extension. And Salzy was there. Ah, she was revolted and fascinated at the same time by the struggle. It was as passionate as she could have wished it, but it was not at all the right shape. She had so hoped that it would be helical!

Meanwhile, back in our main context, Foley-Smith had finished reading the note from Leo Joe Larker. There were some straight specifics in it. That Larker was a real strategist, a poor man's general. He knew how to go about a street fight, a town fight. And the last words of the note: *Now eat it. Chew it up and eat it. It should have a pleasant sherbert flavor. A determined man can swallow paper. It does not really bulk larger for the chewing. It only seems to. Now swallow it.*

And Fred Foley swallowed it.

Foley was to take three of the inmates over the fence with him. Larker had written that more would be useless. Foley thought that the three would be useless. They were Loras who was alien, Croll who was patrick, and O'Mara who was Irish. But the boney-faced man insisted that he would go also. He knew every word that was in the note, though he had not read it with his eyes. Boneface had spooky powers. It was better to have him on your side than against you.

In town people had begun to die like flies. They became drowsy and died, without really being sick. Actually most of them weren't sick, but the suggestion to die was implanted in them.

Overhead the clouds were gathering and tumbling. They were touched with sudden silver and (now that it came near sunset) they were also touched with that color that is called *morada* which is a mulberry or violet or purple. Foley gathered his four men. There was no leaving Boneface behind. That man had sensed and entered his element.

"I used to be a pathological killer," Boneface said. "They say they've cured me of that and I'm no longer dangerous. They *think* they've cured me! Men, just give me a target and I'm a butcher all over again. Oh, you can't shake me. You have to take me along. And for one of your squeamish jobs I'm just the man."

There *were* events in the world and the city that

348

afternoon and evening. The plague itself appeared. There was a clear case of it truly verified. But a curious aspect of the appearance was that it was widely reported on the air and on paper several hours before it came. Manipulated panic was all the thing.

And at almost the identical time two men were murdered. One of them was a Great Liberal Statesman who was actually a shoddy phony, and one was a Well-Beloved Conservative Leader whose own family couldn't stand him. There was a further distortion. The reports of both murders were out slightly before they happened, and partisans of both men had begun to gather.

And just previous to the riots, an army detachment had crossed over from Virginia to put down the riots. The military could not find the reported corpses strewing the sidewalks. Wisely they waited. They were only a little bit early.

In other sections, students attacked soldiers. The students always averaged about ten years older than the soldiers. Embassies were burned. Small private armies moved through the streets. They were distinguished only by armbands or not distinguished at all. The transit workers announced a one hour strike for the following morning as evidence of their solidarity.

Fred Foley heard a chuckle in his mind. It was the brittle chuckle of Carmody Overlark. Carmody and his would cause the disturbances to succeed (while seeming to fail) or to fail (while seeming to succeed); anyhow they would have their sort of value out of them, and the world would be further shackled.

"It's time to get moving," Fred Foley told his four men. "Only one target inside the Bug, according to Larker. I'd have thought there'd be more."

Foley sent Croll to kill Doctor Millhouse. Croll the patrick seemed a little timid about going and killing a man, and Boneface wanted to do it, but Foley repeated the command, and Croll went.

Meanwhile, Foley briefed them again rapidly, armed them from the cache that Leo Joe Larker had hidden and told of in the note, waited. Croll came back twitching; he said that he couldn't kill Doctor Millhouse, that Doctor Millhouse had already been dead when he got to him. Foley looked around for Boneface, then saw him deep in the shadows. "Who, me?" was the look that Boneface gave him. Well, it was done, and Boneface had done it; but Foley had rather wanted to test the patrick Croll on an easy one first. They went over the fence to begin what Larker had called the Night of the Long Knives in his notes. Like all unstarred generals, Larker was something of a ham.

XIII: AND ALL TALL MONSTERS STAND

> The psychological rule says that when the inner
> situation is not made conscious, it happens outside
> as fate. That is to say, when the individual remains
> undivided and does not become conscious of his
> inner contradictions, the world must perforce act
> out the conflict and be torn into opposite halves.
>
> *Aion*: C. G. Jung

TARGETS! Larker had tagged many of the prominent
returnees for Foley and his group to get. But another
unstarred general was mocking in Foley's mind.

"It doesn't make any difference, Frederick," Miguel
Fuentes was saying from his distant underground. "It
is just a little diversion, a little fun. Do it if you want
to do it. But the first phase has already happened, and
the next will not begin till I and others (and especially
you) come out tomorrow. This doesn't matter."

"This *does* matter!" Foley swore. "You battle your
monsters and I'll battle mine! There *will* be dimensions
—in me, or in the world."

Some very prominent people were on the list, but
who would have suspected that they were returned
people? Lee, Twitchell, Cramms, Rowell, Goodfoot,
Munsey, Napier, Nash, Cabot, Bottoms, Miss Cora
Addamson. Well, how *does* one go about killing leading
people, those of a station above one? The etiquette
of murder is incomplete. It may be that the intent and

the act itself carry the basis of an introduction. There should be a certain fluidity of the rules, murder being partly a social and partly a business thing. There is need of a small rule book on the manners of it.

Lee was the first on the list and the first ticked off. Foley knew him on sight, knew where he lived, knew his shuffling figure now going back and forth in front of his own luxury apartment building. In fact, Lee seemed to be waiting for Foley or for the event. Foley killed him quickly, the first man he ever slew.

He shot him suddenly. A lady gasped nearby, and there were other sounds of shock in the street. But many things as rude were going on. Foley quickly rejoined his group.

On Constitution Avenue, one group of soldiers had scattered a gaggle of "students" and there was a little clatter of quick death on each side. Some very respectable fighting was going on around the circles and up and down Massachusetts and New York Avenues. "It is all for nothing, Freddy," Miguel Fuentes was mocking. "This isn't the real thing. It is only little theatricals."

"*They* want to turn the world into little theatricals," Freddy said. "*I* want to make it real again." Freddy went after Twitchell.

Twitchell had a permanent hotel suite right in the way and Fred Foley went boldly in. It was a red-eyed woman who answered and came to the door.

"I must see Mr. Twitchell at once," Freddy said and began to push in.

"That will be quite impossible," said the red-eyed lady. "Please go. I haven't time to explain."

"Neither have I—I'll just come in. What I have to do will only take an instant."

"No, no, God no! Not at a time like this." The lady was suddenly strong, and Foley had pushed his way in only with great difficulty.

"Be quiet, lady," he said. "My business will be brief and to the point, if my hand is steady."

"My husband has no more business at all to transact. He is dead."

"But can we be sure? I'll make sure, lady."

"You monster! He has just died. How is it possible for one to be so heartless?" But Foley had forced his way into the inner room.

"He does look pretty dead. What was it?"

"One of the new diseases of today. He was tired and he lay down for a little. When I went to wake him just now he was dead."

"There's no harm at all in making sure."

"The doctor will make sure. He's on his way here now."

"The doctors are going to be very overworked tonight. I'll make it easier for them. I'll leave no doubt that this man is dead."

Mrs. Twitchell uttered a series of short little screams or yelps, and Foley made sure that Twitchell was dead. "I bet I'm as good with the short knife as Boneface says that he is," Freddy growled in a sort of sordid trance as he did it. The man bled hardly at all when Foley gave him the blade. It was as if the blood had been frozen. From this, and from other signs, Foley knew that the man had been suspended, not dead. But now he was dead.

Mrs. Twitchell was making such a fuss about it that Foley was glad to get out of there, back to his group and to the peace and quiet of the riotous streets.

Loras was explaining that he had not been able to kill Cramms, that Cramms was already dead when he got there. "Well, all right, so long as you made sure," said Foley.

"Of course I made sure," Loras stated. "It was a little embarrassing for me to do it, me a stranger with no proper explanation of myself, and his family all around him, but I made sure."

"How?" asked Boneface.

"Why, I held a small mirror to his mouth. It wasn't clouded as it would be if he had the slightest breath. And he had no pulse or body warmth. He was dead."

"No, let me," said Boneface. "I'll make sure." Boneface went up to kill Cramms, and Loras was puzzled. "But what other test will he use?" this peculiar Loras asked. It wasn't just that Loras was an alien. Beyond that, he seemed uncomprehending at times.

"Oh, he'll have a sure test," Foley said. "I thought you understood the nature of the men we're combatting."

"I begin to see," Loras mused. "It's possible that he was not dead at all. That would fool anybody not in the secret, wouldn't it? But I haven't a lot of enthusiasm for this killing. I am terminating my relationship with this group."

Loras didn't fully understand people. Or else he was faking; possibly he was no alien, but something else.

"You'll either kill or be killed," Foley told him. "I'll leave no loose ends."

The lights of the town went out then. It gave a chilly effect to Foley's words.

"No, no, I don't believe you'd do it," Loras protested. "A person can quit any time he wants to quit. I'll stay right here by the bonfire till you're gone. You wouldn't dare do it here in the light."

Boneface was back already. Say, that man was fast! He was fast in understanding a situation also. He did Loras in. He did it in an offhand way, with a rapid and deadly wrist-flick that he used. "I was wrong," Foley said to himself. "I'm not near as good with the short knife as Boneface is."

After that, luck turned against them. They couldn't find Rowell; they realized that Rowell would see to it that they didn't find him. And Goodfoot, Munsey, Napier, Nash, Cabot, Bottoms were not only said to be dead but they were aggressively dead; they were unalterably dead, watchfully dead, and with their minions about them. They were making a great thing about being dead. There was no getting to them; they were guarded, they were inviolable. They had not made the mistake of Twitchell and Cramms, or it may be that the word travels very fast in their set. They were safely dead so that they could live again, or they had already entered other persons and were living there.

Perhaps one of them could be crashed to. Boneface was eager to try it. It mattered not at all to him if his own destruction was part of the bargain. Boneface disappeared rather suddenly from the group, and he may have gotten one of the Suspendeds. But none of the rest of Foley's band could get at any of the enemies at all.

"Forget it, Fred, forget it," Miguel Fuentes was saying from distant underground. "They are only toys now. But tomorrow you yourself may turn into something more than a toy."

It had become very difficult to move about now. Everyone was out of his lightless house and into the streets to watch the crowds and the fires. There is no one who doesn't like to watch fires. There was a great amount of breaking glass, and much fighting, but now it was more and more confused.

The New Prophets began to preach by torchlight as though the latter days had come. It was the younger Pliny, those many centuries ago, who mentioned that in times of turmoil men with beards will appear instantly, when in all Rome there had not been bearded men before the moment of strife. The younger Pliny had lived in a shaved age; he believed that the bearded men who appear suddenly are wraiths or portents, and not men at all.

It was a bearded portent who appeared now at one of the circles, further clogging traffic; and there were others of them about town. This one talked with a rumble touched with both irony and hysteria, and he seemed to have found his proper setting there in the torchlight:

"The pact is broken. The compromise has revealed itself as no deeper than spiderwebs on the grass. Did you really believe that the peace would be longer than a long breath? Did you imagine that the thin earth on which you trod did not have another earth under it? Did you really believe that these brittle buildings were the houses of the mighty? Did you actually suppose that this white town on the river would endure longer than three long lifetimes? Did you imagine that the sickly hum you heard was truly the speech of men? Or that the mechanical wound-up toys would never run down?"

You have heard of fiery-eyed prophets, and this man was one indeed. There were many bonfires and torches going now and their fire seemed to dance in his huge eyes. And yet the fire images there were not reflections; they were originals.

"Whoever promised you peace? Who promised you ease? Did you really believe that you could live your whole life without spilling blood? Could you have dreamed that it is in the natural order for a man to die in bed? You fancied that the day would be so long that the dark would never come? That the earth would lie still and no more riffle its hide? But the weak interval is over with, and we come now to life itself, or to death."

"He's a prophet like one of the prophets," Croll told Foley. "As patrick, I will extend my aegis over him."

"Who told you that your house was meant to keep out the elements?" the prophet still prophesied. "Who gave the promise that one should live clean and dry? What mad seer said that a man should live long enough to see the faces of his grandchildren? Who told you that you had the right to go in shoes, or fed? Did you not know that the steep earth would break through this smooth clutter you have placed upon it? Who told you to quit growing fangs and claws? What actuary promised you life till morning?"

Not direful, no, no. This was the most joyous prophet anyone ever heard. It was all high expectation about to be fulfilled for him now. Like snow on deserts, like crowning fire in dead wood, like violence and eruption giving the answer to satiety, this was an addled prophet of new life, not of death.

"It has been said that a man must lose his soul at least once if only for the pleasure of finding it again. I say that a man who has died without seeing the end of the world has lived in vain! But many of us here will not have lived in vain. The corral is open and the beasts are loose. Do not look back. The world isn't there any more. Ah, but look back then, if only to raise a little salt. There has never been enough salt in the earth. Unless your salt exceeds that of the saltimbanques it were no matter if you ever lived or not. Why do you fear to die who have never lived? But I am sure of my new life, I am sure of my new desire, though it is born out of ashes. What, is it not a wonder that I was dead and that now I live?"

"Let's be about our business, Croll," Foley said. "I have his words anyhow, as coming from the weave."

"And I have them anyhow, as patrick," Croll said.

It was hard to tell which of the night screams were genuine, as the teenagers were on the jag of screaming in dark places for the fun of it. A genuine scream will always sound false, just as real terror always appears comical and contemptible to those without compassion. But there was more noise than blood that night. An effete generation does not return to massive rapine and murder all at once, even though it has long lost all moral objection to them. It will take a while for new energy to grow toward real action.

The amateur town-criers were having a field night of it with stories of rockets only ninety seconds away, and

Baltimore and Philadelphia already obliterated; and corpses piled deep in the streets of New York with no one to bury them.

It was only those who believed in an incredible plot who understood that it might already have succeeded. For, if the Suspendeds had already decided to die, it meant that they had the situation under control, or that they had entered other hosts. It was not their idea to waste time in watching these death agonies of a civilization, a dreary interval that would surely take the greater part of a generation.

And their job had not been too difficult: to bump the world at one critical point, to ensure that it dropped once more into its old repeating cycle, that it did not break out of the cycle into ascending spiral. Three cities, each more advanced in artifact and building and spirit: these had been. Then the fourth city, the city of destruction. And then let it repeat. This was the essence of real order, to maintain the sequence of birth, growth, destruction and death, and rebirth: the closed cycle. Let it never be broken or opened!

And (like the old Oriental wrestlers) you could let the world throw itself by its own strength. The stodgy old watchers, they would overwatch now. The reactors would overreact. The Lawful-Lawless Hydra-Weave would absorb psychic energy and turn it back on itself. The monsters defeat each other and the world and bring about the destruction plateau.

"We'll see if their plot works, Fred," young Miguel Fuentes was communicating from far underground. "Yes, the watchers will overwatch. The old patrick here is shaking their invisible net. The reactors will overreact. I myself will overreact most strenuously in the morning. And that hydra that brushed myself and yourself, it is sending out electric poison that I can see like the borealis lights even here in my underground. But there is something else, little Freddy. You are the something else. You are the simple man, the innocent, you are the virgin who charms the unicorn. Hey, is that not jazzy talk, little Freddy? I don't know what you will do, how you will alter it. But there is something. Do *you* know what you will do, Freddy?"

"No," said Fred Foley shortly to the voice that was coming from underground seventeen hundred miles away.

"This patrick does not overwatch, but he watches," said Croll.

"We need no more than the desire to break to a higher life," the prophet was still sounding in the distance. "If we are sure of this, then we cannot be leveled."

Yet it would seem as if the stimulus of the Suspendeds was working. Throughout the boondocks and waste places of the world, a hundred or so groups had gotten the whiff of the change, of the vacuum needing to be filled, and had begun to move. There was a strong group in Anatolia, one in Bas Pyrenees, one in Circassia, one in Sierra Leone, one on the Rio Grande River which was led by Miguel Fuentes. Some of these sudden armies, after they had eaten their surroundings and their near rivals, would be of real effect. And tinder had been torched everywhere.

Double assassinations of men of opposite parties had happened in a dozen parts of the world. Soon there would be risings by the minorities and the abused, and the abusing. The acute could already hear those stirrings like a giant hornets' nest.

"That phase is unstoppable, Freddy," Miguel Fuentes called again from the distance. "But tomorrow you will start a different thing. Freddy, you are the difference."

Then they spoiled the night. They turned on the lights again. A few maintenance workers had got past the tepid terrorists and turned on the lights of the city again. It made a disappointing difference. There had been a certain rightness of setting in the torchlights and bonfires. Now that was gone.

There was a dead girl lying in the gutter. Nobody went to her. All went past with eyes averted as though she had been nothing. She remained there; she may still be there. But otherwise it was only night-time in the city, and people going home.

Foley, Croll, O'Mara and the boney-faced man went to Proviant's, which was still open, or opened again. Well, perhaps it was a different world already, but it looked about the same.

They sat across from Larker (or a man who was just possibly Larker; he had still another appearance now), who was with some people Foley didn't know. Foley and Larker exchanged glances and maintained the fiction of not knowing each other.

"It didn't go off so well, even for a show," Foley told his group. "I imagine they planned it to misfire. Except for the grotesqueness and confusion of it all, it might have provoked some sort of heroic reaction; and their point is to prove that there's nothing heroic left. With that, our ruin is already assured, and they've won it in their sleep."

"This is the way the world ends," said Larker at the table across. "The lights go on and it's revealed that it was all a play-act. There wasn't any world. There was only the fiction of a world."

"There was a Byzantine legend," said Bencher, "to the effect that God made the world only for the grand effect of ending it. But the effect never came off quite right. He couldn't get the thing to climax properly. It was bad and he knew it. He'd set it back a few days or years from the ending and try again. It would be even worse. There were conflagrations that failed to convince, thunderbolts that sounded as if a boy were throwing them, doom-cracking that went off like a toy pistol. He'd set it back a few days and try the ending again, and again, and again. And it developed that the ending would ultimately be only that Byzantine one, to live the latter days futilely over and over again."

Bencher? What was Bencher doing here? And why hadn't Foley known him when he had looked right at him? Foley went over the man now, and he was Bencher in every point. But Foley hadn't known him before. And how come he was with Larker and that company? How come he knew them?

"Mr. Bencher, what are you doing here?" Fred Foley demanded.

"Drinking twice-heated bad coffee and observing an unsatisfactory end of a world. Oh no, I didn't think that you were crazy, Freddy. It was necessary at the time that I appeared to. Biddy had come to me with your story some time ago. I found it too wild to have been invented. I looked into it and found that it was quite true. I put my resources to it and discovered many of its ramifications. I find now that I've come too late on the scene; the damage is done. It's to be snake-bit finally, to watch the snake slither out of reach of even revenge. They're secure somewhere as though frozen in ice and they can laugh at us out of the frost. There's nothing we can do.

"Oh, we'll live with it for a while. We may even seem for that while to regain part of our footing. But the world has already worked itself into too precarious a position. It's gone down before. I don't see how we can keep it from going down again. It's the old cycle, you know."

"I still hope to break that cycle, somehow," said Fred Foley.

"Why, Freddy? To break it means there may be an end to the temporality, I see that now. I'm not brave enough to face that end, no matter how distant, and I'm the bravest man I know. The repeating cycle is, after all, the best. It means that someone will still be going on, over and over. I'm afraid to break out of the cycle, even out of the top side of it. And it will do no good to warn the world. There'll be no belief in the nature of the disaster, not even after the disaster has happened. And we'd certainly be madmen to talk of the old dead men reappearing and frustrating at intervals."

"Can't we at least hunt down the remnants of them?" the boney-faced man asked. "Now, yet tonight."

"We will, some of them, and you'll have more adventure tonight, man. But we can't even guess where most of them have gone. We have one microscopic triumph though, Freddy. Carmody Overlark, one of their real leaders, the one who first attracted your attention, is really dead and not gone to his state."

"That nearly makes me happy, Mr. Bencher. How?"

"Drowned. We went for him out at his estate. He went into his lake at quite a deep point to escape us. There's a local legend that the lake is bottomless. We shot at him when he surfaced, and we watched for his reappearance long enough to be sure that he wouldn't reappear. He's drowned for good. He, at least, will not be returning."

It is no good to warn the world of disaster, even after it has happened. It is no good to tell your associates that they hadn't made good even in this. Whatever had happened to Carmody Overlark, he wasn't drowned, not that oldest of the survivors, he who soaked his head in a bucket. It was unlikely that he had been shot. It was very likely that he was denned up underwater till he should decide to waken again.

Had there been the veriest flick of mockery in Bencher's telling Freddy of this? And why hadn't Freddy known Bencher at first sight here, when he was surely that man in every point of him?

"Where's Biddy?" Fred Foley asked.

"She should be here in a moment, Freddy," Bencher said. "She went after Miss Cora Addamson, that pernicious female of the returnees. And she got her. I felt it."

"I thought that Addamson was on *our* list."

"She was on several lists, Freddy; we wanted to make sure of her. She'd try her escape by the back door of her warren, and Biddy was at the back door. Biddy wanted the job. She was as avid as Boneface here. The report of Miss Addamson's death is already out. And here comes Biddy now!" *Biddy! That?* Oh yeah, it was Biddy.

"I'd go with her if I were you." (Why was Bencher being a little oily about all this?) "Two young people can still salvage something even from a sinking world."

Why now, at the appearance of Biddy Bencher, did it seem to Foley that things had gone irrevocably wrong? For him, she should be the one right thing left in the world. What was this new horror?

"There's something very wrong about all this," Foley said, rising. "All the warnings are screaming at me but I can't tell what they say."

"There are a lot of things wrong," Bencher said, "but this is one thing that can still be right. Be off, you two. We'll bury the world without your help for the rest of the night."

"Come along, Freddy, little poodle-tooth," said Biddy Bencher. "We have so many things to make up for." And Freddy went with her. Empty! Biddy had never seemed empty before.

"There's still something wrong with this," Fred Foley said to himself. "All the warnings are screaming at me. Even from the weave. Why isn't she in the weave now?"

"Wait, sir, wait!" Croll called. He rushed to Foley, caught him at the door, and held his two hands. Nobody in his life had ever called Freddy "sir" before. The patrick seemed really possessed now and he emanated another sort of weave.

"Sir, Your Magnanimous, know you that the Congregation of Patricks, Larkers and Crolls, and Autocrats and Exarchs, and Aloysii and Metropolitans, meeting in convocation of the mind, have filled the Office that has been vacant for a thousand years," Croll intoned. He was pathetic in his derangement.

"I've heard of the office," Foley said. "Good luck to all patricks this night! Who fills the office now, Croll?"

"You, sir, Your Simplicitas, Your Innocentia, Your Laetitia, you are the Elect." Then the Croll gave Foley a sort of accolade-embrace, and Foley returned it in a special form that he had been ignorant of till that moment. Croll also laid a narrow stole about the neck and shoulders of Foley.

"But this isn't the purple of the ruler," Freddy smiled. "It's the lavender of the fool."

"I know," said Croll. "But it is so ordered."

Biddy dragged Fred Foley out of the place. "What was all that?" she asked him. "What did he do?"

"Made me Emperor," said Freddy.

They walked in the parkways. It was all Biddy then, Biddy chatter, Biddy lapses of logic, Biddy high spirits as they walked about the mall. It seemed a little as if she were walking him in a direction he didn't want to go. But she'd always done that.

Oh, but why wasn't she in the weave? The weave had now come to the point of explosion and this girl who was essential to it wasn't in it at all. Cinnamon cookie with her eyeballs painted with landscapes and dragon-scapes, what had gone out from her? She seemed unfamiliar inside herself. It was almost as if she didn't know that the pictures on her eyeballs changed, as if she couldn't see with every part of her, as if she were using little peepholes through the painted scenes.

Now this was funny: Biddy's eyeballs were a part of the weave, and her eyeballs were the painted-on part of her. But otherwise, this girl here was not in the swelling weave at all. Serpents and patricks in the scenes on her eyeballs, the rooms of the patrick Bagley back home and the ape-dog plappergeist who served him! The plappergeist picked up a small sign and showed it and words flashed themselves across it. *Freddy, this is Biddy in the words. They moved in on me, they took me over, she crowded me out. That's not me Biddy in her. I go back to the weave now. We're going to break it and throw it.*

This girl here with him didn't even know that the pictures on her eyeballs changed, but she was chattering Biddy chatter and leading Fred Foley in a direction he didn't seem to want to go. And then there was the overpowering business of the breaking of the weave.

Hondo Silverio (that big, healing snake of a man) was into the weave very powerfully to throw it. Foley had the feeling and fear that Hondo would throw the weave to him. Even so, the weave was cleaner now. And Biddy Bencher was into the weave; dead, but not at all spiritless. The most overrated member of the weave, Baubo the demon indeed, was being broken out of it by Hondo and Salzy and Wing Manion; he began to lose his hold and to fall, whimpering and gibbering.

Arouet Manion, the writhing reticulatus on the stone floor, had been to his last arena. He died now with a flickering blue and orange glow about him; the glow gathered itself into a little ball-lightning that hung in the air a moment. It decayed with hissing and noisome odor, exploded with a weak *poof,* and was gone. And that was all the soul that Arouet Manion had had.

Jim Bauer, purpled and choking on his own tongue, staggered from the patio and reeled groaning down the iron-railed stairway to the lake. His own soul gulped out of his mouth in garish globs as he diminished and dimmed. A crackling purple light fell past him and plunged through the lake, falling down into interior infinity. It was the demon named Baubo who had been broken out of the weave and finally let go.

And Bauer was letting go, though his fingers throbbed

out blood from the intensity of his grip on the iron railing. One by one, the members broke him out of the weave. Letitia Alive arose from a couch in an interior room, the hypnosis over her broken. She walked out of the house Morada and into the road. She had no resemblance to Letitia Bauer now, and no remembrance of the several days she had spent in Morada. Completely confused, back as the girl she had been before she was mind-napped, she walked away down the front road. She left the weave. She had never been in it strongly.

Letitia Dead found release in the cleansing of the weave and felt the first joy since she had died. And Hondo (why such a thing, why such a thing?) was throwing the weave to Fred Foley, as soon as Bauer should be completely broken out of it.

Biddy Bencher was dead, but still strong and in communication. And this girl here with Foley, who looked like Biddy and was not, was aware of many outre things, but she was completely blind and deaf to the weave itself. And her painted eyeballs ceased to change now; they were no more than dead paint. No, one last flick, one final material message from Biddy herself in words across the painted eyeballs.

Fooled her, Freddy, one last trick. The Harvester mark on the forehead is cancerous. It's a short-term body she's stolen from me.

Then the eyes were dead paint for an end, and this girl was someone else.

"What happened to Biddy Bencher?" Freddy asked her sullenly. Powerful men from the dark gripped each of Foley's arms. He *would* go in the direction this girl wished.

"But *I'm* Biddy Bencher," she said. "How could there be another?"

"Then what happened to Miss Cora Addamson the beautiful and evergreen harpy?"

"I'm still beautiful, don't you think so? It's nice to be several persons, and you yourself will sample that pleasure. When did you know?"

"When you called me 'little poodle-tooth.' Biddy had several hundred pet names for me, but they followed a pattern known only to the two of us. 'Poodle-tooth' couldn't be among them. Why are we going back to the Bug? And what did you do with Biddy?" Those men were hustling Foley along at a pretty good clip now.

"I became Biddy, what else?" said the Beautiful Addamson harpy. "You already know that. And you begin to doubt your sanity now when you were so sure of it before? Oh, you'll have a period of that, Freddy, but when you come through on the other side you'll be sound. We don't make mistakes in those we select to join us."

"Dammit, Addamson, at least tell me where is her body, or yours, or the other."

"When the lights came on in the town you saw it lying in the gutter and you passed it by without a second look. An empty body doesn't have much meaning when the personality has been drained out of it. Our beloved Carmody Overlark (now enjoying a well-earned sleep) told you that we were superb mimics, but I'm afraid he didn't tell you all that's involved in our very ancient art of mimicry. So now you don't know whether this is her body or mine."

"Why Biddy? She wasn't prominent in the world."

"In her potential she was staggering. Never in my lives did I move into such a house. And her father was prominent and rich and powerful, with a lifelong slumbering powerhouse of a mind. My own father, who is still my father and who has now become Bencher, selected him and her. My own father hadn't appeared in the world in quite some centuries and there are reasons why he can't be recognized even now. He rather overstepped himself the last time around and became one of the permanent legends of evil. Quite a good fellow, though. In not too long a time you'll appreciate him as a father-in-law."

"Had Bencher been taken over by your father when I saw him last?"

"Yes. Just minutes before."

They were back at the Bug. Two strong men dragged Fred Foley in. Doctor Millhouse was presiding.

"Ah, Smith-Foley, you wandered off to see your girl," he purred. "Fortunately she had the good sense to have you brought back here. You've guessed, haven't you, that the Bug is more than the Bug? It's one of our Centers."

"I thought you were dead."

"So did Croll. And Boneface, coming suddenly, killed another man whom I put up as a shield and gave my appearance (in the bone-face mind). And now things will go on as before."

"But the world is going to pieces," Foley protested.

"So it is," agreed Doctor Millhouse. "Exactly as before. We keep it going to pieces. And it'll be a smaller world when we put the pieces together again sometime hence. We have to shrink it periodically; that's part of the cycle. You also become part of it. You'll be one of us now. Foley. Your catharsis will begin now. Oh yes, you really will lose your mind, but only for a while. It'll be a much more amenable mind when it's restored to you. These things are so predictable."

But one thing not at all predictable was suffering terrible spasm and alteration.

In one context, James Bauer had lurched down to the bottom of the iron stairway and was standing ankle-deep in the waters of his lake, hanging on with the last skin of his life and moaning that he should fall. But in another context he had gone down the world cliff that is the side of Morada. This cliff has no bottom, and nobody has even been more than a dozen steps down that broken stairway from the top. Concrete steps breaking off from the everlasting stone; the iron railing, which had been built by giants, now swinging loose over the void; steeper and more pitchful steps and a great gap in them, and also the disappearance above of those steps that were already climbed down.

Bauer leapt the first gap, clawed stone, found the remnant of a step and even a last rusty length of an iron rail, slid purposefully toward a ledge, hung there a moment with bleeding fingers. He saw a continuance of the steps below, back in under the cliff at a dizzy angle. He swung himself in under, let go, scraped rougher rock in search of a foothold, missed his footing and hold in a sudden dampness and slickness (that was the lake in the mundane aspect) and fell downward, and down, and down, screaming hoarsely forever.

"It's a new weave now," said Hondo Silverio. Even that strong one, growing stronger, was shaken by Bauer's fall like black lightning. "A new weave. Here, Freddy, catch the tangle of it! We give you the Mastery!"

All his life people gave valuable things to Freddy unasked—powers, lives, worlds.

It beat the other thing into him. Hondo and Salzy Silverio, Wing Manion, the dead Letitia Bauer and the dead Bedelia Bencher, all were tangled up in him and they were stronger than the new intruder.

But a tired spirit *was* intruded into Foley then while men held him fast and other men plunged needles into him and Doctor Millhouse presided.

"He takes you over, Foley," the doctor said, "but he's old and he's incomplete. It's necessary that a lot of you survive along with him. You'll make your arrangements. *Go mad now!* But when your long madness passes you'll be one of us, what's left of you." And Doctor Millhouse held a watch in his hand, studying it.

"What are you looking at? Dammit, what are you

watching?" Fred Foley demanded as the darkness began to gulp him down.

"The second hand," said the doctor. "These things are so predictable."

"Why? Why? Nothing is going to happen to me," Freddy declared. "I have strengths that you don't know about." (Pride of patricks, monstrous harvest of the brain-weave, flight of falcons.) "Biddy—Oh, dammit! Cora Addamson, what's he waiting for?"

Cora-Biddy had the curious old shell-form ears, the itching ears of Scripture. She had them from both her components, for the people of the weave are as evilly avid for novelty as are the returning people.

"The *stridor vesanus*, Freddy," said Cora-Biddy. "Be patient. It comes."

"The what?" Fred Foley asked, but he already knew. The second night in the tomb is always the most hideous one. What comes forth, comes forth from that delirium. And the last floating spider-silk had now settled on him. He was caught in the spiderweb.

"The screaming, Freddy," Cora the beautiful and evergreen harpy said. "It always comes on schedule."

Then, as Doctor Millhouse looked up from his watch, Foley's mind gave way. He began to scream. The old, returning Other entered and mingled with his mind and body. He continued the screaming (the final tomb humiliation) as they laced him into the jacket to take him away. And that was the end of Fred Foley as he had been.

But it wasn't the end of him as he would be. He *did* have strengths that they didn't know about.

He was Master of the weave, and now the weave need not remain anarchic.

With a word he could become Master of the falcon. He could fly the falcon, or he could ground it.

He was companion of patricks, and now he was himself more than a patrick. He was more than a Croll or Aloysius. He was Emperor.

He now had a returning lightning-toad intruded into his head and his body, and in the toad was the wisdom-jewel.

He was Everyman. He was Everylout.

Nobody else, coming in simplicity, had ever partaken of all four Monsters. Nobody else had had such good eyes, had ever been able to see on all the levels and into all the worlds. No person else had ever integrated all his archetypes and become fully conscious—even while tumbling into needle-induced unconsciousness.

He had been called, as the patricks had not been, as the Harvesters themselves had not been, as none of the exterior creatures had been of themselves. The Harvesters, the persons of the weave, had not themselves truly mutated. They couldn't have done it; they hadn't the holy simplicity for it. Theirs was a false and premature mutation. It was Fred Foley who now became the first of the new mutation, the special sort of man.

And in the morning—

(Green-mottled humor in him, helical passion, saintly sex-fish, ashen death-joy, cinnamon cookie for Cerberus—

Pride of patricks in him, Black Patricks of New York and Nairobi, Yellow Patricks of Moscow and Lhasa, Brown Patricks of Batangas and Tongareva, Nobility of Metropolitans and Simplicity of Crolls, the Exarch of Yerevan and the Aloysius of Dublin in him—

Oceanic ages in him, insane flitting reptilian wraiths that have a random gift that isn't given to proper creatures, and a new interior guest from that returning jewel-headed toad people—

Flight of falcons in him. "You can command the falcon, Freddy, when you wake to it," came the underground voice of Miguel. "You can even command the falcon to furl its wings again."—

Unweaponed simplicity in him that could burst every bond. Every under-thing rooted in him now—

The ashen Letitia herself had just borne a child who was truly beautiful and full of light, somehow, in a manner and place that we do not know the names of. So—

Letitia-gladness in him. Gobbled devils in him—)

—and in the morning he would come out of it all: a new element that the returnees had not calculated in adjusting the cyclic trajectory. (Returnees also in him.)

On so small a new module it might depend. What would be the shape and direction of it now: still the repeating cycle, or the ascending spiral?

Would the next Mansions be the First again? Or the Fifth?

Past Master

CONTENTS

1. AT THE TWENTY-FIFTH HOUR

The three big men were met together in a private building of one of them. There was a clattering thunder in the
street outside, but the sun was shining. It was the
clashing thunder of the mechanical killers, ravening
and raging. They shook the building and were on the
verge of pulling it down. They required the life and the
blood of one of the three men and they required it
immediately, now, within the hour, within the minute.

The three men gathered in the building were large
physically, they were important and powerful, they
were intelligent and interesting. There was a peculiar
linkage between them: each believed that he controlled
the other two, that he was the puppeteer and they were
the puppets. And each was partly right in this belief. It
made them an interlocking nexus, taut and resilient, the
most intricate on Astrobe.

Cosmos Kingmaker, who was too rich. The Heraldic
Lion.

Peter Proctor, who was too lucky. The Sleek Fox.

Fabian Foreman, who was too smart. The Worried
Hawk.

"This is Mankind's third chance," said Kingmaker.
"Ah, they're breaking the doors down again. How can
we talk with it all going on?"

He took the speaking tube. "Colonel," he called
out. "You have sufficient human guards. It is imperative that you disperse the riot. It is absolutely forbidden

that they murder this man at this time and place. He is with us and is one of us as he has always been."

"The colonel is dead," a voice came back. "I am Captain John Chezem the Third, next in command."

"You be Colonel Chezem now," Kingmaker said. "Call out what reinforcements you need and prevent this thing."

"Foreman," said Peter Proctor softly within the room. "Whatever you are thinking this day, do not think it so strongly. I've never seen the things so avid for your life."

"It is Mankind's third chance we have been throwing away here," Kingmaker intoned to the other two in the room, speaking with great serenity considering the siege they were under. Even when he spoke quietly, Kingmaker was imposing. He had the head that should be on gold coins or on Great Seals. They called him the lion, but there were no lions on Astrobe except as statuary. He was a carven lion, cut out of the Golden Travertine, the fine yellow marble of Astrobe. He had a voice of such depth that it set up echoes even when he whispered. It was part of the aura of power that he set up about himself.

"Mankind's first chance was the Old World of Old Earth," Kingmaker said. "What went wrong there, what continues to go wrong there, has been imperfectly analyzed. Earth is still a vital thing, and yet we must speak of it and think of it as something in the past. It didn't make it before in that Old World, and it isn't going to make it now. It has shriveled."

Thunder and bedevilment! They were howling and

quaking worse than ever. They'd take the building apart stone by stone to get their prey, and they wouldn't be long about it. The mechanical killers were relentless when they came near their kill, and Fabian Foreman was their intended kill.

"Mankind's second chance was America, the New World of Old Earth," Kingmaker continued. "In one sense it was the First New World, a sort of childhood of ourselves. And Mankind experienced its second failure there. That was really the end of Old Earth. She lives in our shadow now, has done so since we were big enough to cast a shadow."

Thunder, thumping thunder outside! The screaming of maniac machines!

"Astrobe is Mankind's third chance," continued the regal Kingmaker. "If we fail here we may not be given another opportunity. There is something of number and balance that tells us we cannot survive another loss. If we fail here we fail forever. And we *are* failing. Our luck has run out."

Howling, undermining, and a section of one of the outside walls beginning to slide!

"Our luck will never run out," Proctor stated. "We've oceans of luck still untapped. We are doing quite well."

"Those cases on Old Earth did not end in *total* failure," Foreman stated in a somewhat shaky voice, "though they *did* end in total death. And it is not a one, two, three thing. It is cyclic and it has happened many times."

It was veritable explosions outside when Foreman spoke. It was his life that the mechanical killers de-

manded right now. Hereafter all the conversation was a little difficult, almost submerged in the ocean of noise and violence.

"Oh my bleeding ears! They were black enough failures," Kingmaker cut back in, "but that blackness was shot full of lightning. True, there were many failures, Fabian, but I make three the magic number. The clock stood at the twenty-fifth hour so often that the very survival of man through it all appears a miracle."

"Let's drag it back to daylight," Proctor growled softly above the noise that indicated that the killers had already broken into some of the upper rooms of the building. "Only ourselves are here and we are not impressed by each others' eloquence. We are here to select a candidate. We are not here to stay the crack of doom."

"Wrong, Proctor," Kingmaker rumbled like buried thunder, and Kingmaker was *always* impressed by his own eloquence. "We *are* here to stay the crack of doom. It has fallen to us three, the inner circle of the Masters, to do exactly that thing."

"Doom's been cracking for a long time, Cosmos," Proctor jibed. He was a sleek and pleasant man even when he took exception. His voice was a sort of mechanical purr, or was that of a fox that has been eating honey.

"Aye, how it cracks!" said Kingmaker. "If you have an ear for history, Peter, you will notice that it cracks louder every time. In many ways we are a meaner people this time around. Would we three be at the top of the heap in any of the earlier orders?"

"I repeat that the earlier testings of man were not total failures," Foreman said, "and perhaps they were not failures at all. They were deaths. It is not the same thing."

The floors were being undermined. You could hear the hate-roaring of the things underfoot now.

"There has always been a web of desperate and quite incredible triumph," Foreman continued. "The indomitableness of man has so far been the most amazing thing about him. I hate to see it going out of us." Foreman's voice did have a little of the hawk's cry in it, but also a jingle of old laughter. He was tall and graying and lined. He seemed older than the other two, and he wasn't. "We've lost so much! Every time we die we lose something. So much could have been done, so much became livid with rottenness, that we belittle what *was* done. So for one *not quite total failure* in the Old World of Old Earth we were given another life something over one thousand years ago. We were given the American thing."

"And failed even worse," Proctor purred with a sort of cheerful bitterness.

"No, we did *not*," Kingmaker protested. We failed even better. It's an ascending spiral—till it breaks."

"That's true," Foreman said. "Our American failure was less nearly total. With a New World to work in, and with unlimited prospects, we limited them shamefully. There was no error of the Old World that we did not commit again in the New World on a vaster plane. But there was another side to it. There were times when we almost balanced the loaded scales, when we reanimated both the Old and New Worlds. There were times when we won hands down when we didn't have a chance. We enlarged ourselves, the two hemispheres of

381

us, and we set to tasks that before could not have been conceived.

"Oh, our failures were abysmal enough to sicken a scavenger, but we did come near to appreciating just how high the challenge is. That world died, though history does not record the event. So for that death, which was not quite a total failure, we were given yet another life."

"On Astrobe!" said Proctor with smiling contempt.

"Yes, here on Golden Astrobe," said Kingmaker with affection. "Foreman says the other worlds all died, and in a sense he is right. This is the world that must not die. We are—and I *do* mean to be flowery —the third and possibly last chance of mankind. Foreman uses another count than mine and I am never sure that we mean the same thing, but I know what I mean. Another failure will finish us. If we die here, that is the end of everything. Our contrivances the machines, which say that they will succeed us, can save neither themselves nor us. We have walked the fine line too long and it almost disappears.

"How have we failed? For five hundred years everything went right. We had success safe in our two hands."

"And dropped it," said Foreman. "In twenty years everything has come apart."

They were all cool, considering the howling menace outside, and now perhaps within. But they had to pause for a moment when the noise completely overwhelmed them with its waves.

"I'm puzzled," Kingmaker said when it was possible to be heard again. "For days at a time the killers don't bother about you Foreman. And then they go wild to get at you, as now. I believe they'll have your life this time."

"For days at a time I am not clear in my own thinking," Foreman stated. "Today I am, and they sense what it is. But they're mistaken in my motives. Nobody has the welfare of Astrobe so much at heart as myself."

"We've had the sensor machines run a few logs on you, Foreman," Kingmaker said heavily. "It's certain that you'll be murdered. Today, I believe. Your logs say within the next several months at the most. You will be literally torn to pieces, Foreman, your body dismembered. What fury but that of the mechanical killers could tear you apart as your logs indicate?"

"I suspect another such fury building up, Kingmaker. It will upset all my personal plans severely if I'm murdered today. I'll need the several months that my logs give me as possible."

"Why did you have us meet you here, Fabian?" Proctor asked. "There are many stronger places where you could be better protected."

"This building has some curiosities of design that I had put in twenty years ago. It's my own building, and I know a way out."

"You belong to the Circle of the Masters the same as Kingmaker and I do," Proctor said. "You have as much to do with the programming as does anyone, and you understand it better than either of us. If something is wrong with the programming of the mechanical killers, then fix it. Certainly they should not attempt to kill you. They're programmed only to kill those who would interfere with the Astrobe dream."

"And by definition all members of the Circle of

Masters are utterly devoted to the Astrobean dream, and are all of one mind. But even we three aren't of one mind. Kingmaker wants to continue the living death of Astrobe at all cost. You, Proctor, do not believe that there is anything very wrong with Astrobe; but I believe there is something very wrong with you. You are both attached in your own way to the present sickness. I want a death and resurrection of the thing, and the mechanical killers do not understand this."

Rending and screaming of metal! A crash deep beneath them that echoed through the floor.

"The building is going down," Kingmaker said. "We have only minutes. We must agree on our candidate for World President."

"We don't necessarily want a great man or even a good man," Proctor said. "We want a man who can serve as a catchy symbol, a man who can be manipulated by us."

"*I* want a good man," Kingmaker insisted.

"I want a great man," Foreman cried, "and we've come to believe that great men are nothing but myths. Let's get one anyhow! A myth-man will satisfy Proctor, and it will do no harm if he's a good man also."

"Here is my list of possibilities," Kingmaker said, and began to read, "Wendt? Esposito? Chu? Foxx? Doane?" He paused and looked at the other two after each name, and they avoided his eyes. "Chezem? Byerly? Treva? Pottscamp?"

"We're not sure that Pottscamp belongs to the Center Party," Foreman objected. "We're not even sure that he's a man. With most of them you can tell, but he's like quicksilver."

"Emmanuel? Garby? Haddad? Dobowski? Lee?"

Kingmaker continued. "Do you not think that one of them by some possibility—? No, I see that you don't. Are these really the best men in the party? The best men on Astrobe?"

"I'm afraid they are, Cosmos," Foreman said. "We're stuck fast."

There was a rending crash rising above the ocean of noise, and one of the mechanical killers splintered the upper part of an interior door to the room and came through it, head and thorax. It contorted its ogre face and gathered to heave itself through. Then came something almost too swift to follow.

With a blindingly swift flick of a hand knife Proctor struck the killer where the thorax emerges from the lorica. He killed it or demobilized it.

Proctor often showed this incredible speed of motion which seemed beyond the human. The mechanical killer dangled there, the upper part of him through the broken door. The thing had a purplish nightmarish ogre appearance designed to affright.

Kingmaker and Foreman were both shaking, but Proctor remained cool.

"He was alone," Proctor said. "They go in patrols of nine, and the other eight of his group are still howling in the hallway above. I can keep track of the things. Two other patrols have now entered the building, but they blunder around. All deliberate speed now! We can't have more than two minutes left with all possible luck. Back to our business!

"We know the next step. By recent decree all Earth Citizens are also Citizens of Astrobe. That doesn't necessarily make them better, but there's a psychological advantage in reaching out for a man. It's true that

Earth has shrunken in importance—but shrinking produces an unevenness; it thrusts up mountains the while it creates low places. There are new outstanding men on Earth even though the level has fallen dismally. How about Hunaker? Rain? Oberg? Yes, I know they sound almost as dismal as do the leaders of Astrobe. Quillian? Paris? Fine?"

"We're in a blind maze of midget men," Kingmaker said. "There are no real leaders. It's become all automatic. Let's go the whole way, then. The Programmed Persons propose once more that they manufacture the perfect candidate and that all parties endorse him. I'm tempted to go with them.

"We've been there before," Foreman protested. "It didn't work then, and it won't work now. The old-recension humans simply aren't ready to accept a mechanical man as world president. Remember, that's how Northprophet had his being. They fabricated him, some years ago, to be the perfect leader. And so he would have been—from their viewpoint. And, according to rumor, that is the origin of Pottscamp also. No, it's a human leader that we need. We must keep the balance of a human for president and a mechanical for surrogate president. A mechanical man can't stop the doom clock from striking on us. He's part of the clock."

"There's one other field of search," Kingmaker came in as if on cue. If he hadn't, Foreman would have had to suggest it himself and that would have taken the edge off it. "We need not limit ourselves to men now living. Chronometanastatis has been a working thing for a dozen years. Find a dead man who once led well. Let him lead again. It will catch the fancy of the people, especially if they guess it themselves and are not told it outright. There's a bit of mystery attached to a man who has been dead.

"But the dead of Astrobe will not do. A man doesn't get hoary enough in five hundred years. Let's go back to Earth for a really big man, or one who can be presented as really big. How about Plato?"

"Too cold, too placid," said Foreman. "He was the first and greatest of them, but actually he was a programmed person himself—no matter that he designed the program. He wrote once that a just man can never be unhappy. I want a man who *can* be unhappy over an unjust situation! Have you suggestions for dead Earth-men, Proctor?"

"For the sake of formality, yes. King Yu. Mung K'o. Chandragupta. Stilicho. Charles the Great. Cosimo I. Macchiavelli. Edward Coke. Gustavas Vasa. Lincoln. Inigo Jones. They'd make an interesting bunch and I'd like to meet every one of them. And yet, for our purpose, there is a little something lacking in each."

"They are men who are almost good enough," said Kingmaker. "We already have plenty of men who are almost good enough. Have you a list, Foreman?"

"Yes." Foreman took a folded paper from his pocket. He made a great show of unfolding it and smoothing it out; he cleared his throat.

"Thomas More," he read.

He folded the paper again and put it back in his pocket.

"That's right," he said. "Only one name on my list. He had one completely honest moment right at the end. I can't think of anyone else who ever had one."

"He *did* lose his head once in a time of crisis," Proctor jibed.

"I believe he can handle it," Foreman said. "All that's required is a mustard seed."

"Lay off it, you damned riddle maker," Kingmaker growled sharply. "We have to hurry. It's your life they are after this day, Fabian. Yes, he'll make a nice novelty, and he'll be presentable. I could say a dozen things against his selection. I could say twice as many against any other candidate we might propose. Shall we?"

They all nodded together.

"Send for him!" Kingmaker smote his chair with finality. "Will you handle it, Foreman?"

"If I live through the next five minutes I will handle it. If not, then one of you do it. Out now, you two! The killers will not touch you at all! And if I slip them this day they may not bother me again for a week. The violence of their reaction to me comes and goes. Out with you! How handy! The wall opens to give you way!"

The shattered wall did open. Kingmaker and Proctor were out, and the mechanical killers were in with a surge. Foreman stood and trembled as the walls staggered and the whole undermined building collapsed. Then it was so murky that neither eyes nor sensors could make it out. The second and third stories came down on the first, the debris exploded inward, the killers, ten patrols of them, went through its stones and beams gnashing for flesh, and they covered the place completely.

It was his own building, Foreman had said, and he knew a way out.

2. MY GRAVE, AND I IN IT

The pilot chosen by Fabian Foreman to bring Thomas More from Earth to Astrobe was named Paul. Paul was two meters of walking irony, a long, strong, swift man, and short of speech. His voice was much softer than would be expected from his appearance, and had only a slight rough edge to it. What seemed to be a perpetual crooked grin was partly the scar of an old fight. He was a compassionate man with a cruel and crooked face. From his height, his rough red hair and ruddy face, and his glittering eyes he was sometimes called The Beacon.

For a record of irregular doings, classified as criminal, Paul had had his surname and his citizenship taken away from him. Such a person loses all protection and sanction. He is at the mercy of the Programmed Persons and their Killers, and mercy was never programmed into them.

The Programmed Killers are inhibited from killing a human citizen of Astrobe, though often they do so by contrived accident. But an offender who has had his citizenship withdrawn is prey to them. He has to be very smart to survive, and Paul had survived for a year. For that long he had evaded the remorseless stiff-gaited Killers who follow their game relentlessly with their peculiar stride. Paul had lived as a poor man in the Barrio, and in the ten thousand kilometers of alleys in Cathead. He had been running and hiding for a year, and quite a bit of money had been bet on him. There is always interest in seeing how long these condemned can find a way to live under their peculiar sentence, and Paul had lived with it longer than any of them could remember. And he was ahead of those stiff killers. He had killed a dozen of them in their brushes, and not one of them had ever killed him.

An ansel named Rimrock, an acquaintance of both of them, had got in touch with Paul for Fabian Foreman. And Paul arrived now, remarkably uncowed by his term as fugitive. He arrived quite early in the morning, and he already had an idea from the ansel of what the mission was.

"You sent for me, Hawk-Face?" he asked Foreman. "I'm an irregular man. Why should you send me on a mission? Send a qualified citizen pilot, and keep yourself clean."

"We want a man capable of irregular doings, Paul," Foreman said. "You've been hunted, and you've become smart. There will be danger. There shouldn't be, since this was decided on by the Inner Circle of the Masters, but there will be."

"What's in it for me?"

"Nothing. Nothing at all. You've been living in the meanest circumstances on the planet. You are intelligent. You must have seen what is wrong with Astrobe."

"No, I don't know what is wrong with our world, Inner Circle Foreman, nor how to set it right. I know that things are very wrong; and that those who use words to mean their opposites are delighted about the whole thing. You yourself are a great deal in the company of the subverters. I don't trust you a lot. But you *are* hunted by the killers. You slipped them yesterday by a fox trick that nobody understands, so you enter the legendary of the high hunted. There must be something right about a man they hate so much.''

''We are trying to find a new sort of leader who can slow, even reverse, the break-up, Paul. We've selected a man from the Earth Past, Thomas More. We will present him to the people only as the Thomas, or perhaps, to be more fanciful, as the Past Master. You know of him?''

''Yes, I know him as to time and place and reputation.''

''Will you go and get him?''

''All right. I'll be back with him in two months,'' Paul said. And he started to leave the room.

''Wait, you red-headed fool!'' Foreman ordered sharply. ''You are a man of intelligence? What sort of oaf have I settled onto here? I haven't briefed you, I haven't given you any details at all yet. How will you—?''

''Don't give it a thought, grand Foreman,'' Paul said. He had a crooked mean grin on his face. How was Foreman to know that the grin was the scar of an old fight and that Paul's expression could never change much? ''I said I'd do it, Foreman. I'll do it.''

''But what will you go in? How—?''

''I'll steal your own craft, of course. I nearly stole it once before. I'd rather have it than Kingmaker's flying palace. There isn't a finer small craft to be had, and there isn't a man I'd rather steal from than you. And I have to leave in such sudden fashion if I'm to leave alive.''

''But I will have to set up contacts for you.''

"I know your Earth contacts, and I know those of Cosmos Kingmaker. In fact, I have conned several of them in the past in my record of irregular doings. I'm a competent pilot in both mediums, time and space. I must leave at once or there will be some leak to it. I'm no good to either of us dead."

"But I will have to get you off Astrobe alive. You're still a marked prey for the Programmed Killers."

"I'd die of your kindness, Foreman. I'll get off alive in my own way."

"But you must have some questions!"

"None. I can find London on Old Earth. I can find A Thousand Years Ago. I can locate a well-known man there. I can bring him back if he wants to come. And I can make him want to come."

Paul strolled out, leaped into Foreman's grasshopper which stood in the open entry hall, and jammed the identification counterpart on it. Then he took flight. The grasshopper, of course, emitted the *Stolen* signal as it flew, and all Foreman's keying of permission could not override that signal.

"Why did I ever listen to an ansel and select a wild man like that?" Foreman moaned to himself. "Ten seconds on the mission, and he's done everything wrong. He'll have every guard at spaceport on him, and they'll kill him before I can explain. Why did the ruddy fool jam the counterpart?"

Within seconds Paul came to spaceport in the grasshopper; and in the same short seconds, three groups had gathered to deal with him variously. One group, however, had known of Paul's sudden impulsive action some hours before.

Paul was thinking rapidly in this, but he also had a friend who was feeding things into his mind. Paul knew that it is sometimes better to have two groups than one in pursuit of you. If you can get the bears and the hounds to close in on you from opposite directions at the same time, somebody is likely to get mauled. Luck holding, it may be the bears and the hounds.

Having a few bear-baiters and hound-baiters in ambush ready to take a hand may also help.

The bears were the spaceport guards, huge and lumbering, reacting to the *Stolen* signal of the grasshopper. And the bears got there first, too fast, or the hounds were too slow. They dragged Paul out of the grasshopper with their grapples, and he knew that they were about the business of killing him. One of them shagged him a bloody swipe that took skin and deep flesh off arm, shoulder, and left ribs. And one, but only one, clasped him to crush him to death. But the primary aim of these bears, these mechanical guards, was to secure the stolen vehicle and clear the status of it. Killing Paul was only a secondary aim.

"Timing not right," rattled through Paul's head in what seemed his last moment. "Other killers too late. Never was anything late about them before." He was crushed too tight to talk, almost too tight to think. With the grip that the thing had on him, he would never breathe in another breath. But he fought mightily with the iron bear, unwilling to give death an unearned advantage.

The hounds were the Programmed Killers, the same who had been haunting Paul for a year. Stiff and bristling, they now reacted to a frantic signal in their own sensing devices, the *Escape* signal sent out by Paul's actions. Their programming told them that their prey, the Paul Person, was attempting an off-world escape from them, and that it was urgent. They closed in on Paul for the kill, blind to everything else; and the spaceport guards as blindly reacted to this sudden intrusion into their own area of investigation.

The tangle, when it came, was of blinding speed and deafening fury. Here were two different groups of mechanical killers: one programmed for patrol, defense and counterattack, the Bears; the other programmed for stalking and direct assault, the Hounds or Hound-Cats. But a bear was crushing Paul to death, however much the strong and slippery man struggled against it.

And yet the crusher was diverted in the churning confusion. Twice it had to stop to smash gnashing metal hounds into mechanical death and disarray. Every device there had one or more alarms or sirens or hooters going off inside him, and the signals did not make for clarity.

Then was the maddening clash and jangle as the third force entered. Paul felt it in his brain, and both sorts of mechanicals felt it in their gell-cells. And there was a direct command in Paul's brain: "Breathe dammit!" So he took one more great breath, having been loosened for the veriest instant. He was too far gone to have known to breathe without being told.

But this third assault was a human one, more or less. The voice in Paul's brain was that of Rimrock the ansel. Whether Rimrock could be called human or not, he was associated with humans. Now Paul also heard the voice of Walter Copperhead, the necromancer who could spook the matrix out of the mechanicals and confuse their programming completely. Paul heard other voices, and he was able to get another breath.

Paul was not dead. He refused to die. His crushing iron bear had had to loose him completely to smash down three of the mechanical hound-cats at once. And the sudden men were in it now. Battersea was as tall a man as Paul and twice as thick. He swung a battleaxe that weighed as much as an ordinary man, and he knew where were located the nexus and centers of every sort of mechanical. He'd battered them to death before. Shanty was near as huge a man as Battersea, and was faster. Copperhead's powers included the power to disable and kill, and Rimrock the ansel, of that most gentle species, had nevertheless slicers three feet long.

Others were there. There was Slider, but Slider had never been sure which side he was on. And Paul himself was into the battle now. He had a long stabber up from a sheath at his loins; and Paul also knew a little bit about how these contrivances were put together. On many of them, an upthrust below the base of the third center plate will sever communications in the mechanical and leave it helpless; and it was there that Paul thrust. He got it; his thrust severed communications and life; it was a man and not a mechanical that he battled that time, and Paul killed him. A man masquerading as a Programmed Killer! So there were, the more to confuse the event, human men on both sides.

"The time is now!" the voice of Rimrock the ansel shrilled in Paul's brains, and yet the silent Rimrock was battling one of the iron bears and seemed not even aware of Paul's location. But Rimrock was a devious fellow.

Paul, free again for a moment, bounded like a springbuck and was into Foreman's spacecraft. Foreman had keyed permission, and the identification counterpart had not been jammed on this. Paul was in sudden flight.

Well, it had been a curious and bitter battle, quite brief and quite deadly. At least two humans had been killed, and half a dozen mechanicals. And the battle will have to explain itself as it goes along, for it is not over. It is to be fought again and again in its variations.

But Paul was free and in flight—painfully swiped and giddy from loss of blood, but in flight beyond pursuit. The Programmed Killers had Paul on their death list as an enemy of the Astrobe Ideal; and yet he was now on mission for the three big men, the Inner Circle of the Masters, who were supposed to be the mainstays of that ideal.

Paul had been whistling happily, whenever he had the breath for it, during the whole confused battle in which he had killed a man and demolished a Programmed Person. He was still whistling happily when he was in flight in Foreman's spacecraft; and none of those in the melee (except the ansel) had any idea what he was about. And he still whistled when he was in Hopp-Equation Space.

It breaks here. It isn't like other space. And persons and things in it aren't the same persons and things they were before.

Astrobe is about a parsec and a half from Earth. Going at light speed it would take more than five years to make the trip. But by Hopp-Equation Travel, it could be made in one Astrobe month, a little less than one Earth month, about seven hundred standard hours.

Paul's craft would disappear as it traversed the parsec and a half to Earth. But, to the pilot who made the run, it was the rest of the universe that disappeared. To him there was no motion, no worlds or stars—really no sense of duration, or of time in passage.

Odd things happened to pilots and passengers during Hopp-Equation travel. During the period of cosmic disappearances, Paul always became left-handed. In addition, there was always an absolutely fundamental reversal in him. He knew from the private jokes of other pilots that this total reversal happened to them also. There was more sniggering about this than about anything else in space lore, for Hopp-Equation travel was very new. But it happened, it happened every time: the total reversal of polarity in a person. Man, what a reversal in polarity!

"Oh well, it's the only way I could ever sing soprano," Paul would say; and he often did so when in this state.

Paul would cat-nap on the trip, but his state of sleep would register on the craft's instrumentation, and he was not permitted to sleep beyond ninety seconds at one time. He became adept at this, however. Very intricate dreams can be experienced in ninety seconds.

Paul calculated that he had at least twenty thousand of these memorable dreams during the passage. Each was gemlike, self-contained, perfectly timed, widely different from any other. Each was a short life of its own, many of them with large sets of characters and multitudinous happenings, some completely gentle, some nostalgic for things never known before but clearly remembered, some sheer horror beyond the ride of any nightmare. The Law of Conservation of Psychic

Totality will not be abridged. There were four and a half years of psychic awareness to be compressed into one month, and it forced its compression into these intense and rapid dreams.

There is a great lot of psychic space debris, and when one enters its area on Hopp-Equation flight one experiences it. Every poignant thing that ever happened, every comic or horrifying or exalting episode that ever took place, is still drifting somewhere in space. One runs into fragments (and concentrations) of billions of minds there; it is never lost, it is only spread out thin.

The ansel was in many of the dreams. These creatures are psychically remarkable; they were in the human unconscious before they were found on Astrobe.

There were flashes, in and around Paul's dreams, of his year of escapes, and of the most recent escape at spaceport. Paul was never terrified in moments of danger. His terror came later, in dream form, and a lot of it communicated itself on this passage. The several persons and mechanisms who had died in that last episode were in several of the dreams; persons who have just died are also psychically remarkable.

Paul had many dreams of a boy named Adam who died cavalierly in battle again and again, and so avoided the misfortune of really growing up. Dying was the only thing he was really good at. And he dreamed of Adam's sister, a child-witch who decided to go to Hell before she died. But Paul was not sure whether he had known these two, and others previously; whether he knew them only in these dreams; or whether he was to know them in the future. And how was it that Adam died so many times? How did he come to life so many times? "No, no," Adam explained. "It is death, it is death. I am not born again. I do not live again. It is always another of the same name." Paul dreamed of the monster Ouden; and of his own death, when it should come, knowing that he was actually viewing it.

But it wasn't all heavy vital stuff encountered in the Passage Dreams. Some of it was light and vital stuff. Also still drifting in deep space is every tall tale ever told.

Hey, here's one. It was of an Earthman of a few hundred years before Paul's time, John Sourwine, or Sour John. But now Paul became Sour John and he told and lived at the same time the outré tale.

Owing to the diet he had followed from his youth —alcohol, wormwood, green snails—one of Sour John's kidneys had become vitrified, and in a peculiar manner. Not only had it turned into glass, but it had turned into glass of a fine jewel-like green. This he had seen himself on the fluoroscope.

It happened that he and some friends were at Ghazikhan in what was then India of Old Earth, and they looked at the great idol there. They were told that the center eye of the idol, an emerald nearly a foot in diameter, was worth eleven million dollars. Sour John went back to his ship and thought about it.

"Ghazikhan is not a sea-port," Paul interrupted his dream, for he had acquired Old Earth information by psych-teacher machine long ago. "Either get on or get off," said Sour John, Paul's other self for the moment. "I say it *is* a sea-port." Paul (Sour John) went back to his ship and thought about it. He had always meant to acquire expensive habits, and he could use eleven million dollars. He sharpened up an old harpoon, called the ship's boy to help him, and in no time at all they had that kidney out. They trimmed it down a little, put it to a lathe and then a buffer and one thing and another, and soon they had it shined up to perfection. It was the most beautiful kidney in the world.

Then Paul went back to the town, climbed up the idol at midnight (it was five hundred feet high and sheer and slick as ice); he pried out the emerald eye and substituted the green kidney. It fit perfectly. "I knew it would," said Paul. Then he climbed down, a descent that not another man in the world would dare to make, and went back to his ship with the emerald. He sold it in Karachi for eleven million dollars, and he lived high for a while. But owing to his only having one kidney, Paul was now unable to drink water at all.

Three years later Paul (Sour John) was back in Ghazikhan. He was told that the center eye of the idol had been reappraised. By a miracle it had changed, the people said. It had become richer in color, finer in texture, of a deeper brilliance; and a grand new aroma came from it. And now it was worth thirteen million dollars. "I figure I lost two million dollars on the deal," Paul said as he woke up.

Ninety seconds; how could that be? The climb up the idol had taken two hours at least. Somebody asks what sort of man was this Paul with the permanent crooked grin? He was the sort of man who was visited by a passage dream of a virtrified kidney.

Twenty thousand of such little dreams! Hey, here's another one!

Paul was coursing at fantastic speed towards the area where the little twin stars Rhium and Antirhium revolved around each other. "Hurry," were his instructions; "they seem of no consequence, but they are the governor of the universe. Somebody is tampering with them." Paul continued at his impossible speed and arrived at the area. He saw something that nobody had ever seen before, for nobody had ever been so close to them. The two small stars that revolved around each other were joined together by a long steel chain. It was that which held them in their tight rapid orbits; it was that which made them the governor of the universe. Paul quickly located the trouble. There was a small green creature, with the body of a monkey and the head of a gargoyle, cutting the chain with a hack-saw, and he had it near cut in two. "Pray that I be not too late!" Paul prayed, and he believed he had made it when the sawyer broke a blade. But he quickly replaced it with another, stuck his green tongue out at Paul, took three more strokes with the hack-saw, and the chain broke. Then Rhium and Antirhium swung out of their tight orbits, and the whole universe was out of control with its governor broken. Fifty-billion billion stars went nova, and then blacked out to nothing. The universe had eaten itself and was gone forever. "I told you to hurry!" the space captain told Paul furiously as he came barreling up. Then the space captain's face melted like wax and he was gone. "I did hurry," Paul said. Then his own face melted like wax and he was gone also.

"Is it quite finished?" came the voice of old hawk-face Fabian Foreman. "If it is quite finished, then perhaps we can begin to construct a new universe. It's all right. It worked out well. I meant you to be too late."

Ninety seconds long. Twenty thousand of them, each one so different.

Oddly, it is only the maladjusted who are able to

stand the passages. The well-adjusted pilot cracks up on such a solo trip. That is why all Hopp-Equation pilots are of a peculiar breed.

Paul knew that some of the monsters he encountered in the passage dreams were real. They were the weird creatures who live in Hopp-Equation space. Some of them were encountered by Paul only; but others were experienced by pilot after pilot in the same episode in the same part of space. It was delirum. Nearly five years of psychic experience must be crowded into one month. The psychic mass of experience is not fore-shortened.

From Golden Astrobe to Blue Earth. Earth is always bluish to one coming from Astrobe. Astrobe always seems gold to one coming from Earth. It is that the whites of their two suns are not the same white. White is not an absolute. It is the composite of the colors where you live.

Paul made Earth-fall, taking it from the morning side, a beautiful experience that never gets old.

He came down in London and stabled his craft. He took with him a small but weighty instrument, and went to the London office of Cosmos Kingmaker. That richest man on Astrobe had vast interests on Earth also; and Paul knew his way around on both worlds.

Brooks was in charge of Kingmaker's London office, and Brooks was immediately flustered by a visit from a man of Astrobe. Most Earthmen are flustered and inferior towards men of Astrobe, feeling themselves left behind and of less consequence. When most of the small but vital elite had gone from Earth to Astrobe four or five hundred years before, it had made a difference that was never erased. Earth really was inferior and of less consequence now.

Paul presented Brooks with credentials and directives from Kingmaker, and Brooks accepted them. Paul had forged them during the passage, though he could have gotten real ones from Kingmaker himself or through Foreman. Paul liked to do things on his own.

"You do not give me much information, and I do not ask much," Brooks said. "I have heard of you vaguely. I know that you have been in trouble on both worlds. Well, I respect the buccaneer in a man; it has almost gone out of us. My master Kingmaker has employed such men before, and it is not for me to question it. Here is the basic machine. I could calibrate an attachment for any period you wish, but you seem to have brought your own attachment."

"Oh, there's no great secrecy, Brooks. I've come for a man, and I'll probably leave with him again tomorrow. It isn't necessary that you know the exact calibration, though it would be no great harm if you guessed it."

"Here's coin of the period as my brief here requires me to supply to you. I wish you hadn't requisitioned so much of it. It will strap me. It goes much further than you would imagine. The multiplier is something like fifty to one."

And Paul was fingering the old gold coins around on a little table there.

"Here, I can use less than one in four of these," he said. "I give the rest of them back to you, Brooks; they are minted a very few years too late for my purpose; they might embarrass me. The men where I am going would be suspicious of Tomorrow Coins. I know the

403

multiplier, and the former and present value. The remaining sum will be about right."

"Will you come out in Chelsea, messenger Paul?"

"In Chelsea you ask? You guess shrewdly, for an Earthman. No, I will go in here and come out here."

"Chelsea at that time was not a part of London. It was some miles in the country."

"The distance was the same then as now. I may find my man in London on business or I may find him at his home in Chelsea."

Paul stepped through the tuned antenna-like loop, and to Brooks it was as though the man had disappeared into the crackling air. To Paul it was going through an unholy gray confusion that is deeper than darkness. And he was sick, as are all who follow the time ravel.

Paul came out ankle-deep in mud. He was on the edge of a big sprawling wooden town. He went into a ramshackle public house, ordered and ate wood-cock, some very high beef, barley bread, and an onion the size of a child's head; and he talked to the proprietor.

"Could you tell me whether Thomas More is in the city, or home in Chelsea?" he asked the man, being careful to give the old pronunciation of words as well as he could.

"Likely at home," the man said. "He's out of favor with the King now, you know. You are a solicitor?"

"Yes, I solicit," Paul said.

"You've an odd sound to your talk," the man told him. "You are from the North?"

"No, from the South," Paul told him. That was true. Astrobe, from Earth viewpoint, was in the Southern Celestial Hemisphere.

"It's dangerous to talk to strangers these days," the

man said, "but I was never one to be intimidated. The old things are passing away, and I hate to see them go. I don't like the new things that are brewing. But I *do* like Thomas More, though doubting that he'll be long in the land of the living. Mother of Christ, I hope someone can persuade him to leave the country before it's too late! I believe that you are one of them from across the channel."

"Yes, I'm from across the channel," Paul said, "and I'll take him out of the country if he'll go with me. Do not mention our conversation, and I will not."

"The King's men are everywhere, friend. Walk in Christ."

Paul went out again. It was a cold day. He knew the way, and he followed the road to Chelsea in Middlesex. He was pleased to discover that the English had not yet become "that most unhandsome of people."

There wasn't much trouble with the language back in this period—a few little tricks to remember, no more. An hour or two of crisp walking on the road, and Paul was to Chelsea. He asked but once, and then he spotted his man, walking in his frozen garden and wrapped up like a sheep.

How did Paul know him for sure? Well, he looked a little like the Thomas More of Holbein's portrait which Paul had studied, but only a little. All portraits by Holbein look more like Holbein than like their subjects. But Thomas More was a man who would always be recognized.

"I am Paul," said Paul as he walked up to him, "and after that I hardly know what to say."

"Your name-saint also traveled far, Paul," Thomas More said with easy friendliness. "Not so far as you

405

have, of course, but perhaps to higher purposes. But I salute you, as a man coming through both mediums, which I do nowt understand."

Paul had gone back a thousand years, and he and Thomas could understand each other. But Thomas couldn't have understood his own great-grandfather. It goes by jumps, and it had changed much more in the hundred years just past than in the thousand years to follow. It is true that Thomas said *nowt* for *not*; that he pronounced *of* as though it were spelled *of* and not *uv*; that he sounded the plural *s* as though it were an *s* and not a *z*.

"I don't understand it either," Paul said. "But how could you know that I have come through both mediums?"

"You've the aspect of one of them," Thomas said. "I've been visited through time before. I'm not a great man, but I'm one who has aroused curiosity in History. Where are you from, Paul?"

"From Astrobe, of which you have never heard."

"Lay no bets on that, Paul. I've a number of past and future things in my head. Once I believed that travel through time was unnatural. But we all travel through time every moment of our lives. It is only that you have traveled at a different rate and in a different direction. Are all on your world as tall as you?"

Thomas had a touch of the things that would later be called the Irish brogue and the Scotch burr, but they were in the English of this time.

"No. The average is about a half a foot shorter than myself—about a half a foot taller than yourself," Paul said. "To us you are a short and chunky man, and you have allowed yourself to appear old: I assume it is your

406

natural appearance unmodified. But I'm more and more puzzled that you should guess me so accurately.''

"I didn't get the name of being the best lawyer in Europe without being able to appraise a man," Thomas said. "And you are not unique. I told you that I had been visited through time before. By a curiosity of History I am to have a certain fame. The circumstances of it bewilder me as they have been explained to me by another traveler. I do nowt at all understand what is to happen to me within the next year. Other men have been visited from the future, I'm sure; but they're no more likely to publish the fact than I am. Incredulity is a fang that bites deep. I understand that I am to make, and only a few weeks from now, a decision so foolhardy on the surface of it as hardly to be believed. Visitors have come and asked me why I did it, and I can't tell them at all. You see, I haven't done it yet. The point for which I am to lose my head seems to me to be a trivial one, not worth the loss of a head, certainly not worth the loss of mine. Why have you visited me from Asternick, Paul?''

"From Astrobe. We are in trouble on Astrobe. They are looking for a candidate to lead them out of a hopeless tangle there. They have tried almost every other sort of man; now they want to try an honest man. They considered the Name Men, living and dead, of the two worlds. You were the only completely honest man they could discover—or the only man with one completely honest moment.''

"Oh, it was—will be—quite a showy act of honesty for which I will lose my head, Paul. But I can't conceive of myself doing it. I haven't been particularly honest up to this point of my life. Opportune rather. But if I were honest, or if I am to be so in the climax moment of my life, how will that help you on Astrobe in the future?"

"I've come to take you back to Astrobe with me."

"You want to take me forward in time with you, Paul? That's impossible, of course. We must live out our lives in our own times and places according to the fate laid out for us. We cannot tamper with the course of History."

"A little of the shine flaked off you then, Thomas. It's only a plating, is it, and not the deep thing? Thomas, that was a silly string of commonplace for an uncommon man to utter. And, as a Christian man, you can hardly accept fate."

"You would make a fine lawyer yourself, Paul. No, I never paid obeisance to Fate. And I have just enough natural truculence in me to do it. But I hate to leave my family."

"Thomas, Thomas, are you lacking in curiosity? In imagination? In daring? They have called you a forerunner, a man open to new ideas. And possibly you will not be leaving your family. History records that you died on a certain date, in an extreme manner, and in this realm."

"Will there be two of me, then, Paul? But of course there are two of me, and more. Every man is a multitude; but I play with words. Why do you really need me?"

"I have told it. It is because our world is sick."

"And you are looking for a gaudy cure? You are looking for a Doctor snatched from the Past? I have failed to cure a sick world here, Paul, and I have

408

watched its sickness growing all my life. It was not even a successful doctor in his own time that you are come for. I was the High Chancellor Doctor; and the patient has thrown me out of the house.''

''Those who decide such things have decided that you are the man we need.''

''It isn't that I haven't studied the subject, Paul. I once wrote an account of as sick a world as I could imagine. You see, my second claim to fame is that I coined the word and the idea Utopia. I wrote in bitter and laughing irony of that sickest of all possible worlds, that into which my own world seems to be turning.

''But here is an odd thing, Paul. I am told by time travelers that my angry humor piece has always been misunderstood. It came to be believed that I wrote of an ideal world. It even came to be believed that I wrote with a straight face. My mind boggles at the very idea, but I'm told that it is so. Paul, there is something very slack about a future that will take a biting satire for a vapid dream.''

''Will you come back with me?''

''Not to any Astrobe, no, Paul. I can't help you or yours, you red-headed ogre. I like you, man. There's something pleasant about a really ugly man, and we both qualify. But I can't go with you. I will try to explain.

''I have asked questions of the Time Men who came to question me, so I know a little of several futures. You live about a thousand years from now, at my guess, at the time of the First Astrobian Time of Troubles; and Astrobe in your time is in wobbly shape. But a thousand years after you are dead, Astrobe will still be in wobbly shape. It will have a different wobble then, however. Astrobe will have long since survived the crisis that worries you now."

"A crisis is survived only by the doings of one critical man."

"I know it."

"Thomas, you are that man."

"No. I am not. It is another. I begin to recall it now. I hadn't paid too much attention to the accounts of the Other World when I was told of such; it all seemed pretty fanciful. His name, his name, I wish I could remember his name."

"So do I, Thomas. You would surely recognize your own, if you were presented under it."

"The man who brought Astrobe out of its first time of troubles, and in so left-handed a manner, his name, it will come to me, Paul, that man was quite in the heroic mold, and I am not. That man, after he had been shamefully put to de—*Jerusalem irredentada!* It cannot be! The name of that man, Paul—*miserere mihi Domine!*—his name isn't known. Always he is identified only as the Past Master. It's a startling thought. You believe him to be me?"

"Yes. I'm sure now, Thomas. You've told me something that isn't known to them there yet. They're still searching for a name to present you under. 'Past Master' is one of those they are considering, but they won't decide till they see you. 'Past Master' it will be, then. The Master out of the past is yourself, Thomas."

"Paul, you also have been pursued for your life, as I have been lately. I know the look of a hunted man, even a defiant one. Surely there are not King's Men on Astrobe who hunt down and kill."

"No, they are different, Thomas. They are Programmed Mechanical Killers."

"No, they are the same, Paul. King's Men everywhere are programmed mechanical killers. But I see that I will have to discover for myself the name of the real king of Astrobe. Yes, I'll go. Stay the night. I'll go with you in the morning."

"Thomas, what happened, what is happening to your own world?" Paul asked as they talked together that night. "You built it according to an ideal of high perfection, but it started to come apart a hundred years before this time. Your world is at an end, and another one, in some ways much worse, is beginning. What goes wrong with your world, Thomas?"

"We built it too small, Paul, we built it too small. And what is really wrong with Astrobe? Can you not give me the name of it? It helps to know the name of your opponent."

"It's name is the monster Ouden, the open mouth of Ouden, of whom you have not heard."

"I'm an educated man, Paul, in my own opinion at least. I'm one of the handful of men who brought Greek back to Western Europe. History should remember that much of me. And Ouden means nothingness."

"That's the name of him, Thomas, and he has his growing legions."

They burned oak and pitch-pine and yew in the open fire, and drank a little of the native. In that century England still had a wine of its own.

They were up early in the morning. Thomas More, about to start on a strange journey, went to be shriven.

"I believe only in spurts now, Paul," he said. "My faith is weak. Is it not ironic that I will die for it in the near future? And that those of strong faith will hide and be silent?"

Paul went with Thomas and did likewise, perhaps the first man to be absolved of sins a thousand years before he committed them.

They went to London afterwards. They went through the tunnel loop and came out in Kingmaker's London office, where Brooks was sleeping on a sofa. He wakened and recognized Thomas at once.

"I'd guessed it was he you came to take, Paul," he said. "I'd rather you took the crown jewels or the Seal or the Charter. If his bones are no longer with us, then we are not the same man."

"Let's go see, Paul," Thomas said. "A man owes himself that much curiosity."

They went to the old church of St. Peter in Chains. "You are buried here," Paul said. "The church is a reconstruction, but the graves underneath are still there."

An old priest came to them there.

"Do the bones of Thomas More for certain lie below?" Thomas asked the old priest.

"They do. This very year we opened several of the graves. The bones of Thomas More are there, and on one finger bone is the famous signet ring of which you wear a replica on your own finger. You are an antiquarian."

"No, I'm an antiquary," Thomas said. "I have a special interest in this man. What other man, Paul, looks down on his own grave and he in it? All except my head. I'm told that it's buried at Canterbury. Parboiled it, did they not? I'd like to see it, but I suspect that it's too long a journey."

They were going on a journey of a parsec and a half, but seventy miles was too long a journey.

As they strolled about London, Paul realized that this man Thomas would never be an anachronism, either on Earth or on Astrobe. Thomas was already onto the new pronunciation of the language—to the point of burlesquing it. He was at home, too much at home, in this latter world. He did everything directly, and as his right. He got into a fist fight with a bulky young man in a drinking place.

Thomas won the fight, too, but Paul saw fit to chide him about it.

"Remember, Thomas, you were sainted after you were dead," Paul told him. "Saints do not indulge in bar-room brawls."

"Some do, Paul, some don't," Thomas maintained, wiping blood off his peculiar nose. Whatever happened to that nose wouldn't matter much; it wasn't a pretty one, but it had a lot of character. "Several men of my acquaintance were later sainted, so I've been told. One of them was a withdrawn man who didn't brawl. One of them was too puny for it. But the third of them *did* indulge in just such brawls. I've seen him."

And this reminded Thomas of something else. "One thing I forgot to ask, Paul. How is the fishing on Astrobe? You are silent, Paul. I can still withdraw from this adventure, you know. Answer me, man."

"I am trying to contain myself, Thomas. You will not believe it until you see it. It is one of the great things that have remained great."

"You mean it, Paul? You can go out any afternoon and take a string of them?"

"A string of them? Thomas, you talk like a boy. How can you string fish that are as long as a man? On Astrobe, if you go out in a boat for any purpose other than angling, the fish will rise to the surface about you and howl for the hook."

"I am glad, Paul, that the new-day fishermen have not suffered any shortening of the tongue. That is what really worried me."

They went to Sky-Port and entered their craft for Astrobe, Thomas with an armful of mystery novels, revels, bonanzas, and science fiction books, all new things to him. Thomas had also discovered tobacco and he swore that the stogie was the most wonderful thing in the world since the Evangels. He announced that he would smoke and read for the whole trip to Astrobe. So they enskied.

And so it went well till their first period of cosmic disappearance.

He was trying to bellow, the man Thomas, no, the creature Thomas, and his voice was no longer one to bellow with. The fundamental reversal had taken place in him as they made the Hopp-Equation trip, and Thomas seethed with a fury that he could not express.

"Does it happen to all travelers, Paul?" the Thomas finally asked in frustration.

"To all who travel by Hopp-Equation journey. The regular trip takes five years."

"What's time to a revenant? I've been dead a thousand years, that I should live to such shame," he, she, it said.

The Passage dreams again, to Paul, and now to the Thomas also. Thousands of them, no more than a minute and a half each, incomparably vivid. In passage dream Thomas met an oceanic man named Rimrock and did not find it odd. He encountered a female creature who was at the same time Succubus, Eve, Lilith, Judith, Mary, and Valkyrie. He dreamed three quick vivid dreams of three men he had never met. One man for his moment was a spider with a lion's head. One man was a most peculiar fox. And one man was a hawk who sat and shuffled shells at a table, and one shell was different.

These dreams sank down into the cellar of the Thomas mind, but they would come up to him again when he met those persons.

3. AT THE NAKED SAILOR

"Why, this is beyond wonder, Paul," Thomas said when they had toppled into normal space and began to orbit in to Astrobe. "It's a golden world. When I was a boy I was told that the streets of Paris were gold; or, if not they, then those of Rome, or Constantinople, or Cordova. I visited them all, and they weren't. The Spanish ambassador told me that it was so in Mexico City. I didn't get to go there, but I had long since come to my doubting years. But the whole world here is gold."

"It is the color of our grian-sun," Paul said. "It is our white, and so it will seem to you."

They came onto firm Astrobe, dismounted, and gave the craft to the keepers. They started towards the easy rooms.

"Not that way, Red, it's a trap, it's a trap!" an ansel voice erupted in Paul's head. "To your left! To your left quickly and find friends by the edging trees."

"Not that way, Thomas," said Paul, and they veered off their course. "We walk in this direction. Careful now. It was the voice of Rimrock the ansel in my head warning us. You wouldn't know about ansels."

"Why, certainly I know, Paul. He spoke in my own head several times during the late hours of the passage. I look forward to meeting him. But I heard no warning. Are you sure of this?"

"No. But we'll not go to the easy rooms till we are

sure. We'll find what's going on over by the edging trees. Come, quickly, but carefully.''

"Paul, I don't like it," Thomas said, hanging back a little. "Don't hand me around like a boy. I know more of snares and traps than you do. The King's Men do sometimes employ the left-handed trap, and I smell the iron of it now.''

Too late.

"Paul! Thomas! Away fast!" came the oceanic voice of Rimrock in their heads. "It was not myself who spoke to you. It was another. Away!''

Too late.

Paul and Thomas were chopped down like weeds.

It was agonizingly painful darkness, blind nauseating confusion, a devouring death that encompassed Paul in mind and body. It stank, it roared, it blasted, it disgusted and affrighted. A growing rumor was rising in the near distance, but too far, too late surely to save them.

Paul remarked, with his riven mind and suddenly shattered and darkened vision, and with dirt in his mouth, on how beautiful was the afterglow of the day, especially when one has just died. The double vision of the reeling, the syndrome of the split head lends itself to detachment.

Paul heard, with ears that seemed to belong to someone else, a new booming roar very near. He was amused that Thomas More, dead a thousand years, was so angrily refusing to die. There was another fellow, a long crooked sorrel-top who was making a great fuss about it also. Paul pulled the two halves of his mind back together and realized that the other fellow was himself, and that refreshing and kindling anger had flowed back into him. It had been a new blow, one that should have crushed his skull, that rather torched off the reaction in him, canny coolness linked with white-hot anger.

"If that didn't get me, I'll be a devilish hard man to kill," he spat through the dirt in his mouth, and had already fought his way to his feet. He had hope now. He recognized the growing rumor in the ever nearer distance as the shouting of the poor lungers from Cathead, and he knew that those miserables were on his side. The lungers hated everybody, but they hated the stilted-gaited assassins most of all.

And Thomas had not stayed down when struck down. He had been up again and giving battle. There had been words in his booming roar, but they came to Paul's understanding only now:

"Front them! Front them!" Thomas shouted. "They're King's Men. They kill from behind. They go for the dorsalis, the spinal, the brain base. One who flees them is already dead. Front them! Front them!"

It was not now the original assassins only. It was a churning mob, and men and things were killing and being killed. Paul was struck another blow that drove bone splinters into his brain, but oblivion never quite closed down on him. Oblivion was like a mirage that receded so that he could not come up to it; and the confusion had multiplied mightily. Distant sounds had a mocking quality that set the conflict off as a sort of dream world. The hoot of distant slag boats calling had a terrible profundity coming over the pungent water.

One of the assassins was broken and useless. A giant lunger was killed. And a boy named Adam was killed.

But hadn't the boy Adam been killed before? No, Adam hadn't necessarily been killed that other time. Not this time either. The boy had been killed in one of those dreams of passage, and those dreams (being out of time) could be of either past or future things.

When it came to Paul that he was being saved, it came to him with a childish delight as though it was his right. He heard Thomas and Rimrock the ansel talking, but not in words. "It were better to hide in a den like a wounded bear and study the events and their foundations," the ansel told Thomas; and the ansel was a native of Astrobe and had never seen a bear. "It were best to get to any low hidden place with remarkable suddenness and wait for the worse day that is sure to come," Thomas told the creature, and Thomas had a broken jaw and wouldn't be able to speak till it was wired up.

"We are only poor miserable lungers from Cathead!" cried the powerful breaking voice of Battersea to what sounded like a crowd gathering. "It is only a little scuffle among ourselves, and we carry away our own dead. Decent people need not be concerned with it. We go quickly, and regret having intruded onto an open area."

Paul was being carried somewhere. It was easier that way. Oblivion flickered around the edges of Paul, and then closed in completely on him.

A few hours for the beginning of recovery, and Paul awoke to a great odor, a writhing of many strong odors of men and seas and things.

"It smells like the Barrio," Paul told himself, and

smelling seemed to be the only one of his senses that was functioning well. "Worse, it smells like Cathead. Still worse, it smells like the strip where they merge. It smells like one of the ten thousand low bordello inns in the teeming region. It smells like the worst of them all, the *Naked Sailor*."

Paul found that he could see, though crookedly out of an unmended head. He had been lying on hay, and he had the impression that goats had been kept in in that room. He found that he could walk, though not straight as a rational man would. He staggered out of the doorless room. He walked in an angular and indirect manner through the viscera of a rambling and noisome building, past a kitchen where a mad-eyed girl gave him a length of strong fish twined in kelp, and he continued on his way eating it. He lurched along till he found a common room, and then another on a lower level. He heard the voice of Thomas More. He saw that it was coming through wired jaws.

"It's a bleak back-byre we have here," Thomas said. "We'll clean it up, or we'll pull it down and burn it. What we need is a tub in the middle of the room, and dip the whole clutch of you."

Thomas was holding a sort of court there. He was a lively little runt with a clear voice and a pleasant unhandsome face. He was attended by a dozen weary ragged men who sat about on the floor and regarded him with red-rimmed eyes.

"Where in hell are we, Thomas?" Paul asked in a voice that hurt him to use. He had floating bones in his head somewhere.

"Fourth of the seven sections, Paul," Thomas said cheerfully, "According to the Moslems, the fourth section of Hell is for Christians. Be appeased; there are three worse Hells than this. It's named the *Naked Sailor*."

"The *Naked Sailor*! Thomas, there *aren't* three worse Hells than this," Paul stated.

"Aye, man, there are," said one of the men with red-rimmed eyes.

"It's a compendium, Paul," said Thomas as if he were lecturing a congregation of barons. "It gives me a vantage point to study what is wrong with your Astrobe, before I make my appearance from beyond the grave. The *Naked Sailor* is itself a grave. I have ventured out three times this day, and have had three men killed defending you."

"You venture out again, man, and we kill you ourselves to save us the trouble," said another of the shot-eyed men sitting on the floor. "Ourselves, we have only a life each. You're not worth another one, old potato-face."

"There's something deformed about this whole business," Thomas said. "These giant settlements here are pieces right out of Hell. Do you know, Paul, that there are unburied dead lying in some of the alleys? This must be the underside of this world, this world's sick delirium. Well, I'm finding what is wrong. I'll see the top soon enough and find how right everything is there."

"Be on your guard when you do, man," said another of the weary-eyed fellows. "It is in these places here that the savor of the only things that are still right on Astrobe clings."

The Killers were milling around outside, and the air was full of sullen electricity. There was fear and anger like soot in the air. Bot-flies were spluttering and roaring about the slippery blood in the roadway outside and in the common room itself. There had been carnage, and the atmosphere spoke of more to come.

"Just what *is* my status?" Thomas asked. "Why should they try so persistently to kill you and me, Paul? What are these curious killers?"

"They're the guardians of the Astrobe Dream," Paul said with sad irony.

"They believe you'll see our side of the thing," one of the ragged men said. "We're not so sure that you will."

"Are these killers human beings?" Thomas asked.

"They are not," said the weariest of the men sitting there. "They are devils dressed in tin cans."

"Was the ansel who talked to you without words a human being, Thomas?" Paul asked. "Would you call Rimrock a human?—But you haven't seen him yet."

"I don't need to see him, Paul. He is composed of body and spirit. He has intellect. That makes him human."

"But the killers look much more human than he does. They have a calculated shrewdness that passes for intellect, and they have a human form."

There was a clatter, a crash, a moan that was only half human, and a bleating scream that was dying animal. A poor man scampered in with three goats, a crazy man with unfocused eyes. He sat down on the floor sobbing and coughing together, and his goats gathered around him.

"Is he human, Thomas?" Paul asked.

"Certainly, though he's demented. He is a judgment

upon everyone on this planet. Aren't there mad-houses for such as he?''

"In civilized Astrobe they say that all Cathead and the Barrio is a mad-house. There are two million men as mad as he, one in twelve. He isn't bad. He slavers, and he cannot speak coherently, but he gets about. He has even avoided the killers till now. But I doubt that he'll be able to avoid them much longer, the way they are ravening about today. We may none of us avoid them. You don't like what you've seen of Cathead, what you now see and hear and smell?'' Paul asked.

"No. I had no idea that such ancient vestiges of poverty and misery could still survive on the advanced world of Astrobe. Why weren't such things swept away long ago?''

The mad goat-man was crooning a little song. The killers were thronging and gnashing in the roads like the iron dogs they were.

"It isn't an ancient vestige,'' Paul said. "This is all new. Twenty years ago Astrobe was completely beautiful and civilized. Then these places appeared, like a blight, as the great ones say. I do not call them that.''

"Paul, I walked for many squares through these neighborhoods in my three sorties out. There are blind children with their eye-sockets matted with insects. There are people starving to death, falling and being unable to arise. There are men driving themselves at labor in small fetid shops. There was never whip-slavery so harsh. There are men and women working in atmospheres so foul that they turn them purple in a few moments, and they come out spouting blood—and go back in to the labor before they have rested. There are human people eating the filth in the gutters, and drinking the gutter runs. They are like this in their millions. I saw a large building fall down. There are women offering children for sale. There are old-clothes men who strip the corpses and leave them naked in the streets. Is there no compassion in the civilized sections of Astrobe? Can they do nothing to alleviate the misery here?''

"But, Thomas, everybody in Cathead and the Barrio is here by choice. They left civilized Astrobe of their free will to set up these giant shambles. They can return to civilized Astrobe today, within the hour, and be cared for and endowed with property, and settled in ease. And they would be free of the mechanical murderers also.''

"God over my head! *Why don't they do it, then?*''

"Somebody go with him!'' Paul shouted, for the demented goat-man had started out into the roadway once more just when a din of killers had risen. Several of the weary men had risen to it, and then fallen back.

Too late.

He had gone out in his distraction, and his small goats had followed him out. Perhaps he was more addled than usual. Perhaps he was not used to such concentrations of killers as were smelling around the presence of Thomas. The whipped crazy man knew how to dodge through one or two killers, scooting like a low whippet. There were too many to dodge.

The striding killers struck him down dead just outside the door. Passersby withdrew to their own safety, and the little goats bleated in lonesomeness. Then, as the killers clashed along looking for new entrance, quick hungry people caught the little animals, fought over them, tore them apart, and began to eat hunks of them raw and bleeding.

"Enough," Thomas, moaned. "I was never an advocate of wealth and fineness. I believe fully in holy poverty. But I say that poverty is like drink: a little of it is stimulating and creative; too much of it is depraved and horrifying. I must be about my work on this world, and I must get to the center of things before I can solve the mystery of degradation here. How can I get in touch with the men who sent for me? I have seen enough of the underside of this world for this day."

"A communication center is approaching, on two feet or on four," Paul said. "He can put anybody into contact with anybody."

"Aye, I feel him. He's talked to me, and I had but a short glimpse of him at our ambushing. It is Rimrock, the oceanic man! He at least will talk sense."

And Rimrock, the oceanic man, came in, on no legs at all, then on four legs, then on two. And he shook hands with Thomas with great friendship.

An ansel is in appearance a little like a seal of old earth. It can slither with great speed along the land, just as though it were swimming in water. It can walk passably, as a man or as an animal. And it has curious mental powers.

"My friend from the green ocean," Thomas boomed. "You of the rubbery black hide and the tufted ears! You bound or you walk, and you talk inside men's minds and make appearances. Read me the meaning of this damnable world, Rimrock."

"They sent for you and you come. I and others thought you should see a little of the sanity of Cathead and the Barrio before you are plunged into the madness of civilized Astrobe. But the great men are waiting for you impatiently, a day and a night and half a day now. They are frenzied that someone has stolen their prize and may somehow turn it against them. And I had to settle with another—a false ansel who spoke in the Paul's mind and tried to lure you to your death. It's fresh blood on me. I hope you don't mind."

Rimrock the ansel was much larger than any earth seal, and the slicing mouth on him was a meter long.

"It comes down on this place!" all the weary men with the red-rimmed eyes shouted, and they stormed up from their sitting on the floor. "We go! We go." They all rushed off, some to the interior rooms of the building, some as a battling wedge with flailing staves and pokers through the killers in the roadway.

"What ails the fellows?" Thomas demanded. "What comes down on this place?"

"The bleak blackness," Rimrock said. "We have a visitation. He is curious about your being here. I know you have met him before in bits and snatches on your own world. I am sure that you encountered fragments of him in the passage here. Now it is himself."

The girl-woman Evita came in. She was like a wraith, of a sudden beauty and mystery, and a depth of depravity that took the breath away. The short glimpse of her set Thomas to shaking. She was something not completely of nature.

"I wanted to see him and talk to him," the Evita said. "But the old monster comes instead. I will talk to the Thomas in another place and hour."

She vanished out again. Paul and Thomas and Rimrock the ansel were left alone. Then the monster Ouden came and sat in the middle of them and encircled them.

The short account that follows is necessarily mystic. We cannot be sure that Paul and Thomas held the same congress with Ouden. We cannot hear at all the exchange between Ouden and Rimrock, but we can sense it. We cannot be sure whether it was Paul or Thomas forming the words in the man-Ouden conversation. It was a confrontation and a presence.

But the Paul-Thomas host knew who Ouden was. They shriveled together in his presence, and their bones grew hollow.

"You are like ghosts," said the Paul-Thomas. "Are you here only because we see you here? Which was first, you, or the belief in you?"

"I was always, and the belief in me comes and goes," Ouden said. "Ask the ansel: was I not of the Ocean from the beginning?"

"What have you done to Rimrock?" the Paul-Thomas asked. "He diminishes."

"Yes, he turns back into an animal in my presence," said Ouden. "So will you, and all your kind. You will turn further back, and further. I will annihilate you."

"I deny you completely," said the Paul-Thomas. "You are nothing at all."

"Yes, I am that. But all who encounter me make the mistake of misunderstanding my nothingness. It is a vortex. There is no quiet or static aspect to it. Consider me topologically. Do I not envelop all the universes? Consider them as turned inside out. Now everything is on the inside of my nothingness. Many consider the Nothing a mere negative, and they consider it so to their death and obliteration."

"We laugh you off the scene," said Paul-Thomas. "You lose."

"No. I am winning easily on Astrobe," Ouden said. "I have my own creatures going for me. Your own mind and its imagery weakens; it is myself putting out the flame. Every dull thing you do, every cliché you utter, you come closer to me. Every lie you tell, I win. But it is in the tired lies you tell that I win most toweringly."

"Old nothingness who sucks out the flames, I have known flames to be lighted again," said the Paul-Thomas.

"It will not kindle," said the Ouden. "*I eat you up*. I devour your substance. There was only one kindling. I was overwhelmed only once. But I gain on it. I have put it out almost everywhere. It will be put out forever here."

"I piloted once to a world of deformed little animals of a certain stench," said the Paul-Thomas. "They ran in and out of old buildings that had been built by a cogent race. The experts to whom I brought some of the deformed little animals said that they were the fallen remnant of that cogent race. They were abdominable little creatures whose only interest was to defile, and the experts said that they had fallen from something very like man."

"I know the folk you mean," said the Ouden. "They are a particular triumph of mine."

"Leave me now!" the Paul-Thomas ordered sharply. "You are a nothingness, a ghost. One may order a ghost to leave."

"Never will I leave. Not ever in your life will you sit down that I do not sit down with you. And finally it will happen that only one of us is left to get up, and that will be myself. I suck you dry."

"I have one juice left that you do not know," said the Paul-Thomas.

"You have it less than you believe."

The Ouden monster had disappeared from them. Paul and Thomas More and Rimrock the ansel dozed. It had been a mere passage dream, one that was somehow left over.

"Look at them sleep!" giant Battersea cried in derision. "On your feet, the three of you. We mount battle array to convoy you back, and Rimrock must gather his wits to set up the communication."

"Whether your work on Astrobe be good or bad, you have to get on with it," said Shanty. "One doesn't save a world by napping away the noontime. Come, we'll take you through the killers, and to the Important Men who wait for you. Then let you shrivel! Let you turn into things like them!"

It was really a battle array that Battersea and Shanty and Copperhead and others led. There was weaponry and vehicles, and the killers backed away from them frustrated. Paul and Thomas and the ansel rode out of vile Cathead and the Barrio, away from the *Naked Sailor* and ten thousand places like it, skirted giant Wu Town, and came into colossal Cosmopolis the Capital of Astrobe.

Misery forgot, here was opulence and ease, beauty and dignity of building and persons, the real golden world, the ideal achievement. It was the most beautiful and most highly civilized world ever built, the most peaceful, the most free from any sort of want. It dazzled.

And in the heart of Cosmopolis the three big men, along with the fourth member of the big three, all now in communication with the ansel and knowing of their coming, awaited their prize from the past that had escaped them for the two days since the landing.

4. ON HAPPY ASTROBE

The riches of civilized Astrobe were almost beyond comprehending. Thomas had a quick eye and a rapid mind, but he was dazzled by the wonders he rode through. Here were the homes and buildings of many millions of people, grand city after grand city, all in luxury and beauty and ease. Nor was it only the buildings and the perfected land and parks. It was the people. They were elegant and large and incredibly urbane, full of tolerant amusement for the rolling spectacle, of a superior mien, of a shattering superiority. They were the true Kings of Astrobe. Every man was a king, every woman was at least queenly.

"It is Rome arisen again a hundred times over," Thomas said. "It is the power and the majesty. For good or bad, this is what all folks have wanted from the beginning. Here are all dreams come true; here is the treasure at the end of Iris, the Pearl of Great Price, here is the fat land and the mighty City; it's the Land beyond the Hills of the Irish pipers, the Great Brasil, the Hesperides."

"Easy, good Thomas. It is a whited sepulcher. But do they not keep it neat and shined?" Evita mocked. Who was the Evita, and what did she here? Thomas asked as much.

"A blinking brat with a charisma on you!" Thomas exclaimed. "Who are you, girl, and what are you doing in my party? How are you a known person to all on this world, and you only a grubby child?''

But Evita did not answer. Thomas would never know for sure who she was, nor would others.

"Where do we go?" Thomas asked. "This is my dance and I should be calling the tunes. I will not be led by the hand like a boy. I will make my own arrangements."

"You have been doing so," said Walter Copperhead the necromancer. "We do but proclaim it for you. We carry out every detail that you have ordered."

"But I have ordered nothing," Thomas said. "It runs too fast for me."

"In your own mind you order it," said Rimrock the ansel. "You vision it in a Roman or English context, and we transfer it to an Astrobian. It is a Triumph you require for yourself; not for pride or vanity, but for the solid establishment of a burgeoning regime. I have been transmitting your orders to the Anxious Powers, to the Great Men of Astrobe, and the Copperhead has been transmitting also. We call them and they are amazed. We order them to assemble. They will not, they say, and they do. They are startled, they are full of wonder even before they see you."

"Rimrock, Rimrock, you'd grow rich as a fawney man at a county fair in old England. No Gypsy ever set a spell so fine. But where do we go?"

"To the Convocation Hall, as you yourself have decided, good Thomas; to take it all swiftly while the tide is running for us. You will be the Sudden Apparition. You will accept the accolade and the mystic station of Past Master."

"I'm not even knowing what the Convocation Hall is," said Thomas as they rolled through the magnificient city of Cosmopolis in Battersea's armored wagon. "Who will be assembled there?"

"Those you have ordered to assemble will have assembled," said the oceanic Rimrock. "And the details work themselves out as we roll on, and always to our advantage. There's a small bloody battle going on now over the Exultation Trumpets, actually twelve small battles in the twelve steep towers around the Hall. The Trumpets haven't blown for twenty years, but you have decided wisely that they will blow for you. Happily your men win those small bloody battles now."

"I didn't know that I had any men," said Thomas.

The party rolled to the head of the Concourse. They stopped and dismounted. They walked the long Concourse between the rows of heavenly aspens. Then the whole sky broke open! The Exultation Trumpets blasted a deafening golden blare like twelve Gabriels announcing the second coming. The electrum doors of the Convocation Hall swung open to the soaring sound. This was a striking effect that had been devised two hundred years before. This was their moment, and the shabby incandescent party entered.

All the great ones of Astrobe sat in the high circle. They sat there in amazement, some willingly, some not. Many of them had been drawn there protesting that they would not go. The compulsion puzzled them, and they knew much about the management of minds.

And the Thomas More party stood in the Arena below them, but it was not at all as if the great ones were looking down on the party below.

Then all the great ones stood. And they hadn't intended to. The great ones of Astrobe stand only in the presence of a Superior. All were assembled, and all were on their feet now: Kingmaker, Proctor, Foreman, Pottscamp, Northprophet, Dobowski, Quickcrafter, Haddad, Chezem, Treva, Goldgopher, Chu, Sykes, Fabelo, Dulldoggle, Potter, Landmaster, Salver, Stoimenof, all the high dukes of Astrobe, half a dozen former world presidents, the tall scientists and the mind-men, the world designers.

In the arena was Thomas More, dirty and in disarray, with a shattered jaw wired up by a Cathead knacker, a long-nosed, almost comical middle-aged man of short stature; the Paul Person who had lost his surname and his citizenship for irregular doings, and who now had bone splinters in his brain that affected his vision and his wits; Rimrock the oceanic man who communicated by means unknown and who was in appearance a grotesque rubber-nosed animal; Evita the legend girl-woman whose existence was doubted by all rationalists; Walter Copperhead the necromancer who was no better than an astrologer: all of them with the smell and trappings of black Cathead still on them.

The vast sound of the Exultation Trumpets broke. It died down in echoing fragments and left a vibrating silence.

And a Person had declared himself!

This was the Past Master, dead a thousand years, a dumpy little almost-old man, a pinkish little elf on a world of golden-bronzed giants. But on him in that moment was the magikos, the charismatic grace, the transcendent magnetism, the presence, the messiahship, the draiocht. He had erupted in the middle of them with the dirt of the grave still on him, so it seemed. It was sheer ghostliness, the seeming of one who comes through closed doors and sealed tombs, one who is the master of time. It was transcendence touching them all.

Then came the Ovation like a pouring ocean. It broke in heavy crested waves, each one higher than the former. It lasted a great while. It lifted them up, all the golden cynics who had forgotten what it was to be exalted. Some of them would speak of it later as their fools' carnival, yet it would always remain a stunning thing in their lives.

Thomas had them hooked without speaking a word. A presence had been created for him, and it had won. How that presence had been managed and by whom, Thomas would try to sort out in his mind later. Had it all been done by a quack man and a quack animal, and a brat child? Who makes magic here? Clearly, several powers of a near-alien sort had been working for him there.

And that presence made itself known immediately, through all the Cities and through all that world, from one end to the other.

"It is the Past Master," the people everywhere said.

He had them, he had them. Then he spoke, loudly and clearly.

"I accept the great burden that has been given me to bear," Thomas announced in a silver voice that had a bit of the old grave-duct in its burr. "Now we will set about the governing and righting of this world."

"He hasn't been offered the burden yet," Peter

Proctor throat-growled to himself. But Peter was grinning a weird fox-like grin. Nobody appreciated a successful master-stroke so well as did Proctor.

And after minutes, or perhaps hours, the Convocation broke, and moved away in glittering fragments. The implementation of it would be done in smaller gatherings, in tight groups and committees. The particular details would evolve themselves out of shrewd staff work.

But nobody really doubted that they had their man.

"It was Rimrock, the rubber-nosed ocean-man thing," said Thomas when he had withdrawn with his party and was mingling with other functionaries. "It was the Copperhead with his occult stuff. It was Paul with his broken crown, and the child-witch with the two opposite auras about her. They took all the grand ones like country ganglers with the magic show they did for me.

"Aye, and with trumpets!"

"I thought I was a master of contrived effects," Cosmos Kingmaker told Thomas, "but I never put together a show like yours. I have a personal difficulty. My wife has been regarded as the most beautiful woman on Astrobe, and she so regards herself. It is, indeed, a requisite of my position that I have the most beautiful woman on Astrobe. But the legend-girl who is in your entourage has her startled, and the popular reports have torn her up. So long as the Evita was believed a legend it could be lived with. Now she has made another public appearance and everybody on the planet knows who she is.''

"I have not seen the one, nor greatly noticed the other, except for certain queer qualities that cling to her, and they are not altogether of beauty. I have no idea at all how she happens to be in my entourage. She's a puzzler.''

"So, you've been wandering like a loon these days and nights," Kingmaker accused, "and no telling into what hands you've fallen. It isn't a very responsible beginning. What hills and dales of Astrobe you've been wandering over I don't know.''

"Through what swamps, rather. On Earth, at least, the loon is a bird of the swamps and meres. I've been in some brackish swamps.''

"It's a bird, is it?" Kingmaker asked. "I thought it was only an expression. Well, whatever swamps you have been wading in, do not go to them again till you have been instructed. You will not know with what eyes to look at these things until we tell you.''

"I had intended to use my own eyes.''

"No, no, that won't do at all. We won't have you interfering with the things we have set up for you to do, or offering untutored programs on your own.''

"You are saying that you won't have me interfering with the image that you intend to present me under?''

"That's it exactly, Thomas. The image has already gotten a little beyond what we intended. We were worried whether we could make it strong enough. Now we are worried that perhaps it is a little too strong. I had expected you to be more amazed at the wonders of Astrobe, however.''

"Kingmaker, man, I stand and stare boggle-eyed at them like a calf at the new barn door. Of course I'm impressed by the thousand years of technological advance since my time, half of it made since the first landing on Astrobe, much of it quite new to me. And in my day I had the name of being a forerunner in these things. I didn't know what questions to ask about the future when—well, when I talked to certain traveling men on this subject a long time ago, or at least a long time from here. I asked them questions of philosophy and theology and the political formation of commonwealths, and of the arts and tongues and of the mind understanding itself. It never struck me that the changes would be in material things. We had already made great advances in these, far beyond the Greeks and Romans, and I thought the cycle would swing back and the thousand years after myself would be devoted to advances in the intangibles. Aye, I'm impressed; the more I hear, the more I see, I'm impressed.

"The fact that there are no sick of body among you (except in the Barrio and Cathead) amazes me. The fact that there are no sick of mind among you would entice me also, had I not discovered for myself that so many of you are dead of mind. All your mechanical and mental things are new coinage to me. Your mind-probes and mind-crawls fascinate me, even when they are turned on myself. You have loosed them on me within the last several moments, have you not, Kingmaker? I can feel them crawling like moles through the tunnels of my head. Hah! I've got them calked now, though. I've but to think in Latin and they can't come into me. I always believed that it would be a mental image thing, not a verbal thing, when it came."

"We have both sorts, Thomas. The verbal is the simpler."

"So simple that you can hide it in the palm of your hand, Kingmaker, and you do."

"It's neater than eavesdropping," Kingmaker said, "and it does pick up the sub-vocals. You yourself use an ansel, but they haven't proved satisfactory. The ansel tends to forget that he is only a communication device. Sometimes he becomes the master. Most men think in words in their unguarded moments, and particularly when they are voicing other words at the same time. Of course my own device here can be fitted with a Latin or any other attachment; it is just that I had forgotten that Latin was still used in your day by the international scholar crowd. So I have missed a sequence out of your private thought, and just when it was getting pretty good. Would you repeat it for me?"

"No I won't, Kingmaker. It would burn the ears off you. But of all the things I have seen on Astrobe to this minute, it is your Programmed Persons who most enchant me: not the Programmed Killers who have given me some trouble, but the others. What a boys' dream come true! The old-time Greeks dreamed of this, you know, and the latter-time Jews. The mechanical man who works! What clockmaker's apprentice would not give half his soul for the secret? That we can make machines in our own image, and that they can outthink and outperform us! It's a marvel, Kingmaker. It hasn't grown to be a stale marvel with you, has it? And not only have men made them to perform better than men; but now, so I'm told, the things make themselves better than men can make them."

"No, this marvel hasn't become stale to me,

Thomas. I wasn't sure how you would take it, particularly since you yourself have been attacked by the Programmed. The Killers themselves are a specialized minority, built to guard against any threat to the Astrobe Dream. But sometimes, it seems, they make mistakes. The Programmed themselves are the main thing, the men of the future, the successors to ourselves.''

While Kingmaker talked, Thomas entertained in the cellar of his mind one of those passage dreams such as both he and Paul had experienced on the transit between Earth and Astrobe. Cosmos Kingmaker was a great golden spider, for all that he wore the head of a lion in the dream. Out of her webs she spun (for sex is often confused in these passage dreams) the whole great civilized world of Astrobe. The great buildings, the great societies, all were the fruit of these webs. The whole world of Astrobe was entirely of gossamer. But the rampant spider would defend her work in every flossy pinnacle of it. There would be no compromise here. The silky façade must be preserved. What matter that it had no substance?

Then a black wind arose, blowing out of Cathead. It began to rend the webs. "Here, here!" great Kingmaker shouted in the superb spidery voice. "It is a false thing that blows. I am the true thing. I am the true cat-head, and not this other. I say to the winds 'Be quiet! Do not rumble my webs, Oh do not rumble my webs!''

"I will return to these wonders again and again, Kingmaker,'' Thomas said, talking on an entirely different level than that of his passage dream. "And the most wonderful of all is your travel today. On my trip to Astrobe I traveled a hundred times farther in every second than I had gone in all my life before; and I am a traveled man, familiar in all the capitals of Christendom. Speed has become infinite.''

"No, Thomas. Hopp-Equation travel is only the squre of eight, or sixty-four times light speed. With that we can never hope to reach more than a narrow corner of the universe. Other number-base travel has been tried—the square of thirty-seven, for instance, or Horwitz-Equation travel. But no pilot has ever returned from that, or from any of the others. They may return a billion years in the future or in the past, or they may be lost. We aren't the lords of speed yet.''

"Even so, you must have billions of worlds to colonize.''

"No, not yet, not for many centuries. We have only six Proven Reserve Worlds after Astrobe. And the colonies on them are still sickly things. The elites do not go out to them as they went out from Earth to Astrobe. At the moment we are going nowhere except backwards.''

"With every man-jack of you a thumping genius you should be going forward with a surge. Kingmaker, you figure to use me as a front; you have admitted as much. But a little study of recent Astrobe politics is not reassuring. I find that you have had for recent short-term world presidents a Mr. X, the Masked Marvel, the Asteroid Midas, and the Hawk-Man from Helios. The latter must have looked rather like Foreman. They sound like the names of ancient Rome gladiators or, as one has suggested to me, of medieval American wrestlers. Now you take me for another costumed actor, a contrived front-symbol for you to manipulate. You will bill me as the Past Master.''

"Probably, since the name has taken the popular fancy. We haven't yet decided.''

"Cosmos, I will be manipulated by no one! If elected president, *I will preside!*''

"That is what we both hope and fear, Thomas. No, your case is not like the others. We have run out of tricks, but the people haven't run out of expecting tricks. To be elected you must be presented as a contrived front-symbol. But to rescue Astrobe from its mortal difficulties you must supply us with a new element.''

"I believe you're afraid of a new element, Kingmaker.''

"Of course I am. But I will not have the fabric of our world rended.''

"Do not rumble my webs, Oh do not rumble my webs!''

"What, Thomas?''

"A fragment of a dream up from the cellar of my mind, no more. You will try anything, be it deepest change, to preserve the changelessness.''

"I don't know what the necessary element will be, Thomas. Foreman believes that he knows. Thomas, you don't seem too curious about your own attempted assassinations.''

"Oh, I've set up my own apparatus to go into that, Kingmaker. It reaches higher than the simple Programmed; it reaches to the complex Programmed and to the high-ranking human. There's a pretty strong party that wants me dead before I am ever, as it were, born on Astrobe.''

"There's another thing we're afraid of, Thomas. We're afraid to show you, and afraid to hide you, and it's too late to make another choice. You have an impressive name to the initiates, you received a startling ovation which we do not understand—neither the thing itself nor our own part in it—and you have an impressive contuming for the people. But you're not an impressive personality."

"You hear me now, Kingmaker! I do not strut sitting down, if that is what you mean. I do not play the great man privately. But I can be an excellent man when there is time for it, and you will not find a better. I was counted a master in my own time, and I be a master here. On the *scena* I can play the noblest *rhetor* of them all! There'll be nowt awkward or awry about my performance, Kingmaker. At this one thing for which Astrobe has a hunger now, high oratory, we were the professionals and you are the amateurs. I know that you have analyzed the thing and broken the personal aura down into its elements. It is like chopping up a bird, but can you make a bird? Perhaps you can, since you made the Programmed Persons, but we recognize them as artificial. I know that you have built intricate eloquence machines, man, but they ring false. The laughter of the people at them like autumn leaves blowing is evidence of this. I've heard the eloquence machines, and I've heard the peoples' response. I've heard human and programmed orators who have studied under the eloquence machines; I've heard a lot of things in one week on Astrobe. People are hungry for the real thing, and I can give it to them. You try to analyze my ovation at my coming to Convocation Hall, and you fail. Part of it was the connivance of my friends and associates, and part of it was a congruity of circumstances. But the most of it, Kingmaker, was myself.''

"We'll have to let you try it, Thomas. But don't ever try to set policy. Politics on Astrobe has become an intricate science.''

"Politics was intricate in my day,'' Thomas maintained.

But Kingmaker began to laugh at that. Thomas was not sure whether or not he had reason.

"We are lucky to be alive, Thomas,'' said Peter Proctor the lucky fox, "and I do not mean it in any negative way, as though there were something threatening us. I mean that developments themselves are lucky, and on Astrobe today things are the luckiest ever.''

"Then why do so many choose to leave this life, Proctor?'' Thomas asked.

"Leave it? You mean to join the Cathead thing? Or do you mean what was once vulgarly called the suicide rate? The first depresses me, the second delights me. Is it not lucky to be able to leave a life that cloys? Is it not lucky that there are such neat facilities for it? Should a man sit at table after he is sated? Why then should he live a moment longer than is required? Golden Astrobe is no prison; we do not build walls around it to keep men in. Life is not for everybody, and long life should be for none. A man may dispose of himself in a booth on any street corner. All apprehension and uneasiness has been removed. A man can leave with a clear conscience.''

"Aye, do the dirty thing with a clear conscience. And you make it work.''

"We live in a lucky world, Thomas. Now we rub our hands, and we will bring still more luck to it.''

"I am the good-luck piece now, am I?" Thomas asked. "And what thing are you, Peter? I have wondered. And so, I am told, have others."

"Me, Thomas? I'm the luckiest man in the world, any world. No need to look more deeply into me. I'm the second richest man on Astrobe, after Kingmaker. And all envy attaches to him, not to me. I am fortunate in wife, in offspring, in attainments, in residence—"

"I have heard the scree," Thomas said.

"And I am universally liked," Proctor finished with a look that was more than commonly fox-like.

It was another of those passage dreams up from the cellar of Thomas' mind. Peter Proctor was a fox indeed, and he ran nimbly over a thin volcanic crust that had a very great depth below it. Thomas was in sudden terror of that emptiness below the crust, and the flickering flames that were only an aspect of that emptiness. Just how deep was the great space below that thin crust? Thomas peered down. The space was forever. There was no bottom. Stars could be seen below, under their feet, but there was something the matter with these stars. They were crooked things, stars of the crooked light. But Peter the fox was in no way terrified with that great depth, not even when great clumps of the volcanic crust broke away before his feet and fell forever. "It is my home there," said the fox. "Let the crust sink down in it; let it fragment and break, and pitch all its fauna into the flames in the void. I welcome it, the fundamental void. I was born for it, and I will take all to it quickly, if only the meddlers who would prop up the crust will desist. The flames in the void are my home. Nothing can harm a fox with an asbestos tail." And then Thomas noticed that Peter the fox did indeed have an asbestos tail.

"But you were one of the three men who sent to bring me out of the past," Thomas said. "Why should you, if everything goes so well here?"

"Oh, I believed that you might do less harm than another, little Thomas. You will be the newest novelty. We need such for the people in this temporality, this passing phase. The people must dine on novelties after they are cloyed of food."

"The constant search for novelty which is a form of despair."

"Who said that, little Thomas?"

"A Frenchman of some centuries after my time. I came on the phrase lately by accident."

"No, I believe that novelty is an aspect of ever-leafing hope in the great resolving, Thomas. Hope is a station that we pass on our way there. Hope is wonderful."

"Aye, Proctor. And luck is lucky. You don't seem quite real to me. I wonder if you cast a shadow."

"Not a black one, I hope, Thomas. You still wonder why I was a party to sending for you since things are going so well? I consider you an innocuous man, an old-fashioned toy. Let the people have their toys."

"What will you do if I prove to be more than a toy?"

"It is lucky that I have so many sides to me. It is lucky that I can be very cruel without qualms. I can be very unpleasant when the situation calls for it. Thomas, I will not allow you to become more than a toy. One wrong move, and you are a broken toy. Politics has become a science, and I am its only consummate scientist. Believe me, I am the only one who knows what is going on. *I make it go.* When Kingmaker washes his hands and absolves himself, *I take over.* If you prove to be more than a toy, I will take over."

"It is always darkest just before false dawn," said Fabian Foreman. "The foolish rooster has crowed (they had them yet in your day, did they not, Thomas, or have I my eras mixed?) and it is still night. Astrobe has been a false dawn, and now we believe that the dawn will never end."

"It seems rather bright to me here," said Thomas. "If this be night, what is the daylight like?"

"But we are wrong in believing that the darkness will continue forever," Foreman continued. "The true dawn must come, and quite soon, or else nothing will come. The night will end, whether in daylight or in nothingness. But I regret that the next grian-sun will come up behind a particularly dirty cloud. I simply do not see any other way to arrange it."

"Is it you personally who makes the sun to rise, Foreman?"

"Quite right, Thomas. It is I personally who will make this particular sun come up. Had you some idea that the sun came up by itself? Or that another than myself was calling the tune on it?"

"Proctor believes that he makes things go on Astrobe."

"But I make Proctor go, Thomas."

"He says that when Kingmaker absolves himself and washes his hands, he Proctor takes over."

"Of course he does. Kingmaker is the action. Proctor is the reaction or the nullification. How grandly

Kingmaker acts! Oh how beautifully and automatically Proctor will react! Oh how cleverly I will abet them both in it! And I be the only one who understands the results.''

Out of the mind's cellar again a broached cobweb-covered bottle of the sparkly stuff! Ninety seconds of poignant drama that goes on while the rest of the world goes on, and exposes the roots of that world.

Foreman, his hawk-face set in a gash of torture, sat at a rougher table than one should find on Astrobe. He had thirty cockle shells on the table before him and he shuffled and counted them. He wept, but as a hawk would, awkwardly and in ungainly fashion, with a hideous cawing and coughing. "It has to be," he cawed. "There is no other way to bring it about.''

But one of the cockle shells was actually a cockerel shell, and the Foreman-hawk noticed it with a start. Then a thunder came and sat down at the table with him. "It is Mother Carey's own chicken you destroy there,'' the thunder said. "There is not woe in all the worlds like your woe.''

"I know how a cat watches a bird,'' the Thomas said to Foreman (and the passage bird had flown), "and I know how well the bird can serve the cat in his business. You'll nowt take me in one mouthful, though. I'm a boney bird, I assure you. And now I see that you are hawk and no cat, but still you pounce on me.''

"What do you mean, little Thomas?''

"Proctor called me that too, and he also purred when he said it. I get you animals mixed; you are not the same types as on Earth. Foreman, I have the feeling that you'll push me into a corner that I'm too stubborn to come out of.''

"I must push everyone into corners that they're unable to come out of. I feel lonesome in that I am the only one who sees things so clearly and so far in advance. The first time it happened, did somebody push you into a corner that you were too stubborn to come out of? Do you know who did it to you, Thomas? Do you want me to tell you?''

"I don't want to know, because I suspect what man of good name it was who forced me to my murdering. But the first time hasn't happened to me yet. I was grabbed off by your pilot a few months before my Earth death that thousand years ago. I don't understand at all what happened that first time, since it hasn't yet.''

"But I know, Thomas. Yes, a man did push you into such a corner before, and I will push you into such a corner this time. You couldn't expect a different ending, could you? It worked to a limited effect the first time. It half-saved a hopeless situation. It will work to a greater effect this time. I won't absolve myself or wash my hands, but I'll miss you.''

"Foreman, in the whole Astrobe situation everyone is hiding something from me. Everything is wonderful on Astrobe, they tell me, and so it does appear to me, except for a comparatively slight area of blight which has appeared and will soon disappear. But it grows larger.

"The sickness of Astrobe can't be merely that a group has reverted, uneconomically, to a backward form of economy, to an obsolete form of life. It is not that they have returned to the hard life of poverty, by free choice, and with no apparent compensation. There have been such cults before. If the sickness had been no more than this, you wouldn't have called me up to doctor it, or to serve as a front for those doctoring it. Well, something is very sick here; there's a beautiful golden fever that kills. I don't understand even the symptoms. And a hard man in Cathead told me that I would mistake the sickness for the cure."

"The hard man was half right, Thomas. The Cathead thing is madness to most, a turning to poverty and abject misery from free choice, and that choice made by millions of people, more than a tenth of those on Astrobe so far. You say you have seen the misery there. You could not have, not in two days and a night. It is the years and years of that bone-rotting misery that sickens the imagination. But the Cathead partisans say that their experiment is a Returning to Life. This I cannot explain to you, no more can they; you have to live your way into it and your own time is too short for that. Perhaps you'll see it in your last moment."

"Perhaps I'd see it now if somebody would talk sense."

"Oh, the two things are eating each other up, and who is to say which of them is the rightful body and which is the cancer? The Cathead affair is neither the sickness nor the cure. It is a symptomatic irruption, a surface effect of the sickness. We are sicker than Cathead. We are sicker than the Barrio. Oh, we'll die for it!

"I myself have made some plans for a resurrection or a rebirth; or for the coming of another thing that may have resemblance to present substance, but resemblance only. Now we prepare in small things, while the world ends. We'll make you serve the preparation, as we've made worse men serve lesser things. And you'll serve better after you're dead."

"Damn it, I *am* dead, from your viewpoint."

"Yes, that's the way I regard you. But your death here and now on Astrobe is what's required. The shape of things to come is very intricate, but it may work out for the best after we are past this tricky situation."

"For *whose* best, Foreman? I've the feeling that I'm being measured and dealt for."

"You are. Take the cheerful view, Thomas. You've been dead a thousand years. How will it matter what happens to you here?"

"Foreman, I'm quite interested in what happens to me after I'm really dead. I'm not dead now, whatever the seeming. They keep a different sort of time on the other side. I don't understand you, Foreman. Are you for me or against me?"

"I'm for you, Thomas, absolutely. I'm working for the very highest goal by the lowest of means. So I'm for you all the way, to the death and beyond—yours, not mine. And with those cheerful words you leave me."

"If these three are the inner group of the Circle of Masters, it is no wonder that Astrobe is sick," Thomas said to himself.

Thomas talked to Pottscamp, who has been called the fourth member of the big three. Thomas enjoyed talking to Pottscamp, one of the most interesting individuals he had ever met. Never was there a more pleasant or surprising person; and Pottscamp had a mind that was like quicksilver. Sometimes Thomas was sure that there was nothing in that mind; and again there was very much in it. It was as though Pottscamp went to a source and dipped deep whenever he had the need to replenish himself.

Pottscamp had large innocent blue eyes and the look of perpetual youth. And yet he had been active in Astrobe affairs for very many years and was certainly older than Thomas' normal age. But he was a boy, a precocious boy, a startling boy who might torture cats or commit abominations, but who would always do so with an air of total innocence.

"So that you will know who really runs things on Astrobe, Thomas—"

"I know, Pottscamp, I know."

Another capsule dream like a passage dream. There was a boy who built a toy. It was a clever boy, and a clever toy that he built. Which one was Pottscamp, Thomas could not say, for they both looked like him. "Go steal apples," the boy told the toy, and the toy did so. He brought back an armload in no time at all. "Go out to my best friend in the road there and knock him down," the boy-child said, and the toy did so. He knocked down the best friend, and in return he got himself bloodied up and battered. The child was delighted with what had happened to his best friend and to his toy. "Work out my language assignments for tomorrow," the child said, and the toy worked out all the constructions and translations of the Camiroi and Puca and Neo-Spanish assignments. "Drink," the child said, and the toy went and drank from the brook that ran beside the home-house. "Eat," the child said, and the toy ate the child up, every limb and light and bone and morsel of him. Was that Pottscamp? Was he a toy who would eat you up, or was he the guileless one who would be devoured?

"I know, Pottscamp, I know who runs things on Astrobe," Thomas said. "Kingmaker runs everything by himself. So does Proctor. So does Foreman; he even makes the sun to rise. And so do you run it all, you will say."

But Pottscamp shook his head. "Our talk will be at another time, Thomas. Our small conversation today was but to proclaim myself to you. You are a person; I am a person; the others are not, not really. If you were not of a certain consequence, or likely to become of consequence, I would not trouble to inform you and deal with you.

"A little later, Thomas, and in another place, we will talk at our leisure. And with me there will be eight other entities that you will find very interesting. What you will meet on that evening in the near future is the real Circle of Masters, though several of us belong to both circles.

"We will instruct you on what is indeed taking place. We will show you the back of the tapestry. What you see now is not the true face of Astrobe, not all of it. The other side of the tapestry is shaggier, but it is a real picture also, and a much more meaingful one than the world you look at now. Take out your eyeballs and polish them up, Thomas. Sweep out your ears and garnish them with acanthia. You will need all your sensing organs at their clearest to comprehend what we will reveal to you. Have you never had the feeling, Thomas, that you were looking at everything from the wrong side? You have been."

5. THE SHAPE OF THINGS TO COME

Thomas was playing a precis machine which he had set to give him all general information about Astrobe. It was a good machine that would answer questions, and depart from its formulae to give personal opinions when asked to do so.

"Golden Astrobe is an urban world, a world of cities," the precis machine played. "If a man is important, then a city is more important, and a very large city is still more important. When we have all become one perfect city in our totality, then our evolving will be completed. The individual must pass and be absorbed. The city is all that matters. A city is more than the totality of the people in it, just as a living body is more than the heaped-up quantity of the total cells in it. When the cells consider themselves as individuals, that is cancer in the body. When men look upon themselves as individuals, that is cancer in the body politic.

"The great cities of Astrobe, in our present evolving phase towards the One Great City, are Cosmopolis the capital, Potter, Ruckle, Ciudad Fabela, Sykestown, Chezem City, Wendopolis, Metropol, Fittstown, Doggle, Culpepper, Big Gobey, Griggs, and Wu Town. Of these, Cosmopolis the capital is the most perfected, and Wu Town is the least. Yet there is hope even for Wu Town. All things achieve salvation in the great synthesis.

"All these cities are quite large, it having been found several centuries ago that a city of less than twenty-five million persons is not economical. But beyond these there is no point in multiplying cities or people. The small annual increase that is allowed for Astrobe is balanced by emigration to colony worlds. We do not believe in heaping up people."

"What about Cathead?" Thomas asked the precis machine.

"Cathead is the cancer that is being excised from this world. It is the cancer because the inhabitants of Cathead regard themselves as individuals and believe in the importance of themselves. Yes, Cathead is quite large, the largest of the cities, larger even than Cosmopolis the capital. We will leave Cathead out of account here since it is not typical of Astrobe.

"There is no poverty on Astrobe since all persons have access to all things. There is no superstition, nor belief in anything beyond, since there can be nothing beyond. Any beyond will ultimately be evolved from the here. While Astrobe is the highest thing there can be nothing higher. This is the essence of the Astrobe dream. There is no sickness on Astrobe, either bodily or mental. There is no nervousness, apprehension, or fear. All arts and all sciences are open to every person. Travel about the world is by instantaneous conveyance. The weather and the oceans have been controlled. There is no feeling of guilt, since freedom from every repression has been achieved. There is no cruelty or hate. There is no possibility of sin, since there is nothing to sin against. There is every luxury and every interest available to everyone. There is almost perfect justice. The few remaining courts are to provide redress to inequities brought about by misunderstandings; and these become fewer and fewer."

"It has its points, it has its points," said Thomas, and rubbed his hands. "And yet it seems as though someone has recounted all this long ago."

"New dimensions of pleasure are achieved daily and almost hourly," the precis machine played. "All live in constant ecstasy. We are all one, all one being, the whole world of us, and we reach the heights of intense intercommunion. We come to have a single mind and a single spirit. We are everything. We are the living cosmos. The people of Astrobe do not dream at night, for a dream is a maladjustment. We do not have an unconscious, as the ancient people had, for an unconscious is the dark side, and we are all light. For us there is no future. The future is now. There is no Heaven as the ancients believed; for many years we have been in the only after-life there is. Death is unimportant. By it we simply become more closely integrated into the City. We leave off being individual. In us there is neither human nor programmed, but we are all one. We verge to our apex which is the total realization of the world-folk. We become a single organism, ever more intense and more intricate, the City itself."

"I remember now who it was who limned this all out before," said Thomas. "It was myself. What other man makes a joke about a tree, and the tree bears fruit? But I like it more now than when first I mocked it. It sounds better when it comes tumbling from another mouth, even a tin mouth. What, shall I be enchanted by my own spell?"

"We all say the same things, we all think the same thoughts, we all have the same feelings and pleasures," the precis machine played. "Both love and hate disappear, for they were two aspects of the same thing—a mantle that was worn by our species in its childhood. We stand unencumbered before the grian-sun. We are the sun. We are everything. We merge. We loose both being and non-being, for both are particulars. We become the extensible and many-dimensioned sphere that has neither beginning nor end, nor being. We enter the calm intensity where peace and strife cancel each other out, where consciousness follows unconsciousness into oblivion. We are devoured by Holy Nothingness, the Big O, the Ultimate Point for all us ultimates."

"Shove it, my little mechanical mentor, shove it," Thomas More said. "I made it up, I invented it. It was a joke, I tell you, a bitter joke. It was how *not* to build a world."

"But I am not finished," the precis machine played. "The vision still ascends. Well, no, it doesn't exactly ascend beyond a certain point, since it has reached a sphere where there is neither up nor down. But it becomes intensity still more intense, and—"

"Shove it, little tin horn, shove it," Thomas laughed.

"You are not impressed by the golden Astrobe Dream that is becoming reality?" the precis machine asked with apprehension, or with what would have been apprehension if that still obtained on Astrobe.

"Not very much," Thomas said. "I invented it all for a sour joke. I mustn't let the sour joke be on me."

And yet Thomas *was* impressed by the Astrobe achievement, if not by the Astrobe dream. There was a terrible clarity running through everything, a simplicity containing all the complexity. In matter and mind Astrobe was neat, and the rains fell always at their scheduled hour. That was something: there was order.

Astrobe was an urban world. All its great cities were really one, in a single close cluster. The countryside was little used. There were the automated production strips, and there were the feral or wild strips to keep the balance. Few people lived in either. It was the cities that were the heart of Astrobe, and the people of the cities were born knowing everything.

There were no individuals with sharp edges, there were no dissenting or pernicious elements, there was the high flat plane of excellence in all things. What can you say against a world that has gained every goal ever set? And there was pleasant termination available as soon as a touch of weariness set in.

"It sets in with me already," Thomas said. "I have to hold onto myself with both hands every time I pass a termination booth."

But one thing seemed to be lacking on Astrobe, and it puzzled Thomas.

"Where do the people attend mass?" he asked as he stood in the middle of golden Cosmopolis.

"They don't, Thomas; they haven't for centuries," Paul told him. "Oh, there are a very few who do sometimes. I do myself on occasion, but I am a freak and usually classed as a criminal. And in Cathead there has been a new appearance of the thing, along with other oddities. But not one person in ten thousand on Astrobe has ever attended."

"Are there no churches at all, then?"

"In Cathead and the Barrio and the feral strips there are a very few that might still be called by the name.

Such buildings as remain in Cosmopolis and the other Cities are under the department of antiquities. Some of them have period statuary that is of interest to the specialist. While mass itself cannot be found in any of them here, the replica can be played on demand."

"Let us go to one of them."

After groping about in some rather obscure streets that Paul knew imperfectly, they found one. It was quite small and tucked away in a corner. They entered. There was the sense of total emptiness. There was no Presence.

"I wonder what time is the next mass." Thomas said. "Or the mass that is not quite a mass. I'm not sure that I understand you on it."

"Oh, put in a stoimenof d'or in the slot, and push the button. Then the mass will begin."

Thomas did. And it did.

The priest came up out of the floor. He was not human, unless he was zombie human. He was probably not even a programmed person. He may have been a mechanical device. He wore a pearl-gray derby hat, swish-boy sideburns, and common green shorts or breechcloth. His depilated torso was hermaphroditic. He or it smoked a long weedjy-weed cigarette in a period holder. He began to jerk and to intone with dreadful dissonance.

Then a number of other contrivances arrived from somewhere, intoning in mock chorus to the priest, and twanging instruments.

"For the love of Saint Jack, what are those, Paul?" Thomas asked in bewilderment. "Are those not the instruments described by Dante as played in lowest Hell? Why the whole thing has turned into a dirty burlesque, Paul, played out with unclean puppets. Why, Paul why?"

"Oh, it had really turned into such a thing before it died, Thomas. This is what the Church and the Mass had become when it was taken over by the government as a curiosity and an antique."

Well, the replica mass ran its short course to the jerking and bawling of the ancient ritual guitar. At sermon time was given a straight news-broadcast, so that one should not be out of contact with the world for the entire fifteen minutes.

At the Consecration, a sign lit up:

"Brought to you Courtesy of Grailo Grape-Ape, the Finest of the Bogus Wines."

The bread was ancient-style-hot-dog rolls. The puppets or mechanisms danced up orgasmically and used the old vein-needle before taking the rolls.

"How do you stop the dirty little thing?" Thomas asked.

"Push the *Stop* button," Paul said, "Here, I'll do it." And he stopped it.

"Why, I wonder how it all came about," Thomas said. "That snake on a stick, is it meant to be the Christ? Is that leering whore holding the deformed monkey meant to be the Virgin? A dirty little burlesque, a dreary bit of devil worship. But even dirty burlesques are not made out of nothing. Had the mass really fallen so low?"

"So I have read, Thomas. It fell to just this low estate before it became ritually frozen."

"Then the Church was only a thing like other things, Paul? And it died as other things do?"

"So most say. The Metropolitan of Astrobe still

lives, but he is a very old man; and the office will probably not be continued beyond his lifetime. There is a slight revival of the Church in Cathead, as I mentioned.''

''Acceptance in Cathead is enough to damn a thing in any clean region. Cathead, that cancer growing on the fair planet!''

''And in the feral strips there are small groups who keep a rite that is not a burlesque.''

''Well, I never had too much faith, Paul. I believe for a while in the mornings if I wake feeling well. But my belief is almost always gone by noon. Somehow I thought that the Church would continue, but I don't know why I thought so. It would, after all, be an anomaly on rational Astrobe. Aye, I'm glad to see the old thing gone.''

''I'm not,'' Paul said bitterly. ''I came to it when it was a black remnant in my darkest days in Cathead, but it's more than all the other things. Yes, I'm crazy, Thomas; I have bone splinters in my brain. But it's curious that you are a saint in the Church in which you don't believe, which you are glad to see gone.''

Thomas laughed loudly and clearly, a really cheerful thing, high and fluted. He and Paul went out into the sudden golden daylight.

''Aye, they were right to push the old fraud into a corner and turn her into a dirty burlesque,'' Thomas said. ''If the tree does not bear fruit, cut it down.''

Thomas spent entire days marveling at the wonderful ways of Astrobe. He had been something of a skeptic at first. Now he had swallowed bait, hook, line, rod, and fisherman's arm. He had become a sudden strong advocate of the Astrobe dream. And yet he wanted to look more deeply into the workings of the thing, to examine its more distant roots and sources.

"It is hardly to be believed," he said one day when he had his retinue with him. "Come, people, we will see more of this. We travel again."

Against the advice of his mentors, Thomas had decided to take some time to examine Astrobe.

"There is no point in travel, Thomas," Kingmaker had told him. "It is all the same everywhere. That is the beauty of Astrobe: it is the same everywhere."

"Go where you will and see what you see," Proctor told him, "but do not believe everything that you think you have seen. When you get back, I will tell you what you have seen. There have been sad cases of men who say things falsely, and I had to take a hand. I do not want to do that. Luck be on thy head, good Thomas."

"You will not know how to see, Thomas, you will not know how at all," Fabian Foreman told him. "You haven't the eyes for it. You will see it all from the wrong side. You are an awkward man, Thomas."

"In that hour it will be given you what you will see," Pottscamp told him. "And a little later, in a secret place and out of context, you will sit down with nine entities (one of them myself) and you will be told what these things have been. You see now toy things with toy eyes, but in that time you will be given seeing."

Thomas had a loose retinue. He had chosen some of the members. And some of them had chosen him. It wasn't the group that the big men would have picked for him, though there was one spy for the big men in the group.

There was his old Earth-to-Astrobe pilot Paul; there was Scrivener and Slider; there was Maxwell and Walter Copperhead; there was Evita the girl-woman from the Barrio who was sister to the boy Adam; there was Rimrock the ansel whom Thomas called the Oceanic Man.

But first, just what is an ansel anyhow? And what was Rimrock, who was a most exceptional ansel? Ansels weren't understood at all on Astrobe, and that was their only home.

"Would you tell me of your origin, Rimrock?" Thomas asked him, "of yourself personally, and of your species?"

"I would, but I'm not sure I can," Rimrock said. "What little we know of ourselves we have learned from regular people, or have guessed. When we passed through the strangeness and changed our cast, this entailed forgetting much of our beginnings. It is a childhood now shut off from us. You see, there were no ansels to be found on Astrobe when Earthmen first came here.

"It wasn't until the second generation of men on Astrobe that any of us were discovered, and we were quite backward. We do not generate rapidly; but none of us die in our present memory, so we do increase in numbers. We have developed from contact with regular people, and we ourselves have more influence on people than they suspect. People children are forbidden to associate with us, but they dream about us, as do the adults. It is nonsense that the happy people of Astrobe do not have night dreams. I have walked through many thousands of those dreams myself. I cannot see that we have any limit, Thomas, though I am not clear as to what our symbiotic relation with regular people should be.''

''But you must know where you came from, Rim-rock!''

''Well, we do know it, but we have garbled it in legend. Our legend is that we are the people who climbed all the way to the sky, broke holes in it, and climbed out into a strange world that is above the sky. This world that you know, the noon-day world of Astrobe, is the world that is above the sky. You do not feel it, but we do.

''We were deep ocean creatures, Thomas. I remember, like a thing before birth, the world of the depths; but we didn't consider it as the depths. We loved to climb, to fly; our epics were all stories of such daring. We loved the pinnacled mountains. Our heroes were those who climbed them the highest. We flew up and ever up, establishing settlements on higher and still higher mountain ledges. We came to the beginning of light, and then to the beginnings of vision. This was the first of the strange zone that we had to cross. When we came out of it on the higher side we would be different creatures with minds formed again.

''For there had come the exciting rumor that some of the great mountain spires might actually pierce the sky itself. We had, of course, long talked to fish creatures who claimed that they had been all the way to the sky; that they had, indeed, leapt through holes in the sky, and then fallen back. But who believes fish?''

''You did really talk with fish, Rimrock?''

''Why not, Thomas? We now talk with men, who are much more intricate creatures. But this fish story was true. I remember it all, as of something from another life, the epic thing we did. I was a member of the first party. We flew and climbed higher and higher to truly dizzy heights. We went up the sheer cliffs of the edge-of-the-world mountain; all the strong stories were that this was the one that surely pierced the sky. We ascended more than ten kilometers, fearful always that we would not be able to live at that height.

"The sky, we had believed ever since we had received wisdom, was at an infinite distance from us and would always appear at the same distance no matter how high we climbed. We now discovered that this was not so. We came closer to the sky and we were almost hysterical in our excitement. We came all the way up to it and touched it with our members. We did not die, as we had feared. An epic hero had done this aeons before, but he had died from it. So it was no ordinary thing that we did."

Rimrock had at first been talking with free movement of his rubbery mouth. But for a while his mouth had not moved, and he was talking in Thomas' head. He could speak in either manner, and he did not always realize himself when he went from the one to the other.

"Then we burst through, splintering holes in the sky, and came out gasping into the world that is above the sky," Rimrock recounted. "To your viewpoint, we came up out of the ocean onto the land. But it is yourselves who do not appreciate the magnitude of it. You did it so long ago that you have forgotten it, both in your minds and your underminds. But how can you forget that you live on the top of the sky? How can you forget that every moment you walk you are walking on a precarious rug higher than a five thousand story high building? Do you know that the highest-flying birds of the air cannot rise one tenth as high as we stand now?

"Thomas, I was one of the first ones who splintered the sky and came up on the sky-shore," Rimrock proclaimed. "I was one of the primordial heroes. And we found that skyshore sprinkled with shells in the form of stars for signature of it. May the sense of wonder never leave me!"

"I begin to get the feel of you more and more," Thomas said, "not in words, but in old shapes."

"Regular people have sealed off the interior ocean that used to be in every man," Rimrock said. "They closed the ocean and ground up its monsters for fertilizer. That is why we so often enter into peoples' dreams. We take the place of the monsters they have lost."

"What occupations do ansels follow?" Thomas asked him.

"Some are in communication, since each of us is a communications center. But most of us work as commercial divers, underwater welders, pier-builders, that sort of thing. Water is still our first element, but the waters around Cathead where I work have become so foul from the uncontrolled industries that they bother us. The poor lungers of Cathead cough up their lungs from the contaminated air. We suffer in our five bladders from the contaminated water. It is a rare treat for us to get away for a day or two in clean air or in clean ocean."

"Are you paid well for your underwater work, Rimrock?"

"No. A stoimenof d'or a week." The stoimenof d'or is a small gold coin.

"Why do you work for money at all? You don't wear clothes or live in houses or eat food that is sold for money. What do you do with your money?"

"Play fan-tan," said the ansel.

Well, what was Evita? We don't know, Thomas never knew, she was never sure herself. She was one of those who had chosen Thomas, not been chosen by him.

"All on Astrobe will think it strange if you do not travel with a mistress," she said. "Nobody has ever done that before. They will believe that you are not in accord with the Golden Dream of Astrobe. I know that you would not like to seem an awkward and impossible person, and I will not allow another woman to be with you."

"I *am* an awkward and impossible person, and it bothers me nowt at all," Thomas said. "Leave me, you scrawny young witch. I have seen sparrows, and they still fledglings, with more meat on them."

"You know that's not true. What kind of fat tubs did they like in your day? I am quite well fleshed, and I've been called the most beautiful woman on Astrobe. You will also find me intelligent, and in this I'm exceptional. Astrobe, though you may not have noticed it yet, has a high level of mediocrity only."

"You are misnamed, Evita; you travel falsely. You are no Eva, but the Lilith who was before her, the witch."

"I am both. Did you not know that they were one? And I have a personal reason. When I decided to go to

Hell to prove a point, I set myself goal: the seduction of a saint. But where else can I find one? They have not canonized one for hundreds of years. Big little Thomas, out of time and out of place, you are the only certified saint I'm ever likely to meet."

"We are neither of us any longer of the flesh in that way," Thomas said. He said *nayther* where you would say *neither*, one of the oddities of speech that still clung to him; and there was a burr in his talk. "And you yourself are now taken by a much deeper passion, Evita," he said, "and it precludes the other thing. Come along then, child-witch. If we ever run hungry on the heaths we'll have you spitted, and break you up haunch and chine, and eat you complete; and be hungry again within an hour."

He joked. She was of copious build, and she smiled down on him. The color of her hair? The color of her eyes? The incredible lines of her? No, no, they won't be given here. You will not know them till the Last Day, and then only if you are one of the blessed.

Scrivener? Slider? Maxwell? Copperhead? Who were they? What was the mind and the man of each?

Hear Slider speak:

"Are we still dangling on the thread, or has the thread been broken even before the official act (soon to be proposed) to break it? The Ancient Instruction was to go to All Nations. But we are *not* the Nations. We are something different. The Promise was that the Transcendent Thing would endure till the End of the World. But we are *not* the World. We are quite a different world, and no promise was ever given to us. We cannot even assume that we are human; how deep does the

Astrobe mutation really go? How many of us are Programmed Persons? And how much of the programmed descent is in us who regard ourselves as old-line humans? We have changed in mind and body.

"The morality of Golden Astrobe is abysmal by any older comparison, but may we use an older comparison? On Old Earth was once a thing named Slavery. We do not name it that here, but we have it. It is now the instinct for finding one's place in the Golden Hive. Try to break out of it! Try to avail yourself of the total freedom! Meet the overriding regulations.

"What were once called the unnatural lusts may be natural here; they are universal. It may be that we are not in terrible shape at all. Thomas at first believed that we were, and now he believes we are in wonderful shape. He is a wise man and he studies us; he wonders why we sent for him. But if we are in wonderful shape, is it still the shape of man? When it becomes impossible to distinguish certain artificial things from ourselves, then we must doubt that we are still people.

"When the killers pursue me, then I feel that I am coming near some truth. But when they let me alone, I know that I am dealing in trivialities.

"Walter Copperhead, who predicts futures, says that Scrivener and I will change persons and souls in our final day. I say that we will not. How could we trade souls? He has none."

Slider was a slight, pale, moody young man. He was very serious, and felt that everybody was laughing at him. Usually they were. Thomas was doing so silently as he heard this screed. He had known such young men before. Slider himself, knowing who Thomas was, expected something more of him. He was shocked by his lack of depth. Slider, out of his own deep insufficiency, intended to supply that lack.

Hear Scrivener speak:

"I would declare myself enthusiastically for all things of Astrobe, were enthusiasm an element of the true Astrobe character. It isn't, and it should not be. We are the first mature beings ever, and enthusiasm is no part of us. In Astrobe we had built the perfect world. Perhaps it should have ended in its state of perfection, but it did not end. Instead, our world has become infected with a cancerous growth. 'Cut it out,' we say, but for some reason we hesitate.

"Slider is part of the cancer. He has doubts, and doubt is the essence of this enemy. Of course we are not the nations or the world! We are beyond such. Of course no promise was ever given to us! We make the promise to ourselves; there is none above us to make it. How deep does the Astrobe mutation go? It goes from the bottom to the top, as it should. Of course we are no longer in the shape of men. Mankind was the awkward childhood of our species; we do well to forget it. We will excise our last flaw, and then we will achieve realization and annihilation.

"The killers do not trail me. Why should they? I am of their own species. And Walter Copperhead reads this future wrong. Slider and myself can never change places. He has no place."

Scrivener was a bigger man than Slider, but was softer and fatter both in speech and person. He had a programmed father and a human mother. Though young, he *did* have a sort of Astrobian maturity. Slider and Scrivener thought of themselves as deep opposites,

470

and yet Thomas and others tended to confuse them. They were so alike in their fuming differences!

Hear Maxwell speak:

"I take myself as an example that Astrobe is not perfect, even excepting the cancerous growth of Cathead and the Barrio. I am an aberration. A perfect world would be made up of perfectly integrated persons, and I am not one. There are no words for my particular wandering from the normal. Only Copperhead knows me well enough to have any idea what they are. I will only say that I have a very loose attachment to my own body. I have not always been in the same form. I do not always recognize my previous forms. The great Astrobean Advance was bound to throw off such reactions as myself.

"And yet I *am* enthusiastically for Astrobe, in a way that Scrivener cannot be. Enthusiasm may not be a part of finest Astrobe, but it is a part of me. I likewise believe that we must kill the Cathead mutation, though it will be killing part of myself to do it. No mind; I have had parts of me killed before. I have had whole bodies killed. I am a spook, and Astrobe does not believe in such. But, for all that, I believe in her.

"I burn myself up for this thing! I mean it literally. I have burnt myself up and died several times, though I do not understand it. I will still be the burning brand for this thing!"

This Maxwell was a most curious-looking man, if he was a man. When he said that he had a very loose attachment to his own body, he apparently meant that he did not always inhabit his same body in the usual sense. But his appearance was that he had a very loose attachment to his own body in that his body was too big for him and fitted him loosely. There are animals who have this looseness in their hides—the Earth tiger and the Astrobe lazarus lion—and in them it is a sign of strength and swiftness. In Maxwell it was a sign of weakness and slowness, almost of witlessness. It was a good-sized, swarthy, almost sinister body that he wore, and it was a sepulchral voice he spoke with. But one had the impression that he had to stand on tiptoes to see out of his own eyes; and that he was piping a small voice into the resounding thing as though it were an independent instrument.

He wasn't a particular ornament to the retinue, either personally or mentally. Yet he had a real seriousness that made that of Slider and Scrivener seem brittle.

Hear Copperhead speak:
Now a part of that speaking had been with certain rough men of Cathead. "Will he?" Battersea had asked Copperhead sharply. "He will," said Copperhead. "I don't see how," said George the syrian. "He doesn't look like much. I'll bet the forces of Astrobe will smash him like a rotten egg." "Oh, they'll smash him, all right," Copperhead explained. "The new man is a dead man; his time runs out almost before it begins. So, he's been dead before, it won't help him now. He will fumble it all, our new man; he'll do only one small thing right." "But you say he'll maintain his ways in this present," Shanty growled. "He will, and in the damnest left-handed way anybody ever saw," Copperhead maintained. "What instruments they do work with!—whoever they are. Men, this ferret-eyed stubby man from the doubtful past will save our world! That is what matters. That he won't save himself doesn't

matter to me, to none of us, I believe." "It will matter to me," Paul said. But the thing about this Copperhead was that he really could predict futures.

Copperhead had something goatish in his appearance. He was a good-humored satyr, and he *was* crude. Rimrock understood from the beginning, and Maxwell had learned accidentally, that Copperhead did have depths of sensitivity and intelligence and compassion; but he chose to hide these things.

People, they were a funny-looking party! Rimrock the ansel, tall Paul and stubby Thomas, Slider and Scrivener, Maxwell and Copperhead, and the bewildering Evita. Had she gray eyes or blue or green? Had she smoky-blonde, or golden, or dark hair? Was she slight or was she buxom? The fact is that all saw her differently, and all heard her voice differently. It sounded now, but did it ring out or bubble up, or purr or croon, or lilt or laugh or intone; was it a flute or a trumpet or a nine-stringed lyra? Was it a silver cymbal or a bronze concentus?

"Be quiet, everyone!" Evita sounded (for words cannot give an idea of the harmonies in her). "Holy Thomas is hatching an idea! See him sparkle when a whim settles on him! He has sampled all the great things of Astrobe and has told himself how wonderful they are. Then why is he looking at the mountain?"

It was a sharp shock to all of them, the thing that had taken hold of Thomas now. That most practical of all men was in a trance. Rimrock remembered the great day when he himself had splintered holes in the sky and broken through. Maxwell recalled an ecstasy in an earlier body. Copperhead relived the moment when the new power came to a man with dirty hands. Paul remembered what he had almost been, and Evita re-lived aspects of her own legend. Slider and Scrivener may not have been capable of such flights.

"Why *do* I look at the mountain?" Thomas asked as he came out of his daze. "An Astrobe psychologist has told me that only people crippled in their personalities will look at such things as mountains. He says that this was much more common in former centuries. Well, I have sampled Golden Astrobe and it is wonderful. But I am still hungry. What if we do go in that direction?"

"If we go in that direction, we walk," Scrivener said. "There are no transportation booths in the feral regions, only in the civilized. That region is all beyond the pale. It is for beasts, if they still live, but not for men. The mountains are retained; they are somehow a key to the weather control. But they are no concern of rational people."

"I believe that we will walk for a day or two and see the mountain," Thomas said.

"The Programmed Killers aren't inhibited at all there," Maxwell told him. "They will follow and kill us."

"They aren't invincible. Let's go to the mountain," Thomas repeated. "What if we climb and cross the mountain at that saddle, and go thence? And what if we follow around that circle thereby?" Thomas asked, pointing.

"Around that circuit of the feral country, a hard foot way, and in seven or nine days you will come to big Cathead from its back side," Copperhead said. "Some of us will die of it, but not all. There's an old proverb: 'I haven't lost anything on the mountain.' But I believe that I may have, and I'd like to find it again. I'll go willingly with you."

"It's stark madness to go there," Scrivener insisted.

"Not at all," Thomas said. "A soft sort of madness it may be. We hadn't such mountains in England, and I saw them only at a distance in Spain and Savoy. In the stated problem of Astrobe everyone has been overlooking something. Were it not odd if the high mountains were the one thing that people could not see? Let the Programmed Killers trail us! I always liked either end of a hunt. Come along now. I'll not be done out of this."

There was no close Earth equivalent to those Feral Lands of Astrobe, though certain Earth rain-forests had some of the characteristics. The difficulty for an Earthman, or for a man from Astrobe either since the civilized people of Astrobe were not acquainted with these regions, was in knowing just where the ground itself was. And in plain fact there was no ground itself, nothing that could be called the surface, the fundament. Were you now working through the surface of a rough meadow? Or were you working through the tops and middle heights of trees?

And another plain fact was that there were no trees themselves. One could not say that this was one tree and that one was another. They were not individuals; they were one creature. As well say that this is a grass, and that is a grass. They were entangled. In the thick going if you climbed down far enough into the sleek darkness you still would not find firm ground. Water rather. And even in this fundamental bottom water it was possible to go down still more hundreds of feet through the growing plants and roots, never finding any bottom except a growth too dense to permit further descent.

And yet the party walked and scrambled and stumbled along pretty well, going up and down; now on a good matted surface, now along a sparse skeleton of green girders; sometimes skirting large aereal ponds that had been built by the kastroides. Some of these ponds were more than a hectare in area, quite deep, and of a lively surface both from creatures and from the effect of the swaying support.

"I will make my own way now," said Rimrock the ansel, "but I will see you again this night. And later I will see you on the mountain."

And the ansel disappeared as though into a deep well; and perhaps he traveled entirely under water through the deep roots of the complex. Nobody doubted that he could make better time than could the party.

"And I will make *my* own way," said Walter Copperhead the necromancer. "I have certain riddles to ask the woods and the mountain, and they do not speak when others are present. And I also will see you several times before you stand up in the high lightning. When you have killed the Devil I will be there. I have laid out his entrails and examined them before, but I haven't unriddled all their riddles. I'll have another go at it."

Walter Copperhead left them with great leaps. He was a goat of the tree-tops.

"He is an odd one," Thomas said. "I'm not sure that a Christian man is permitted congress with such."

"I'm not sure that you still consider yourself a Christian man," Paul said.

"What are the hoppers?" Thomas cried, himself hopping away from Paul's question. He was asking about the leaping creatures that were now all about them. "They're from the size of a rat to the size of a sheep, but they all seem of one species."

"I don't know about things like that," Scrivener said.

"And I sure do not," said Slider. "The things in the

feral regions are an obscenity to all civilized persons. We class them with excrement.''

"There is no love of wild nature among the civilized people of Astrobe," Maxwell said. "These things are less real than creatures in dreams. I doubt if they have a name."

"They're good to eat," Evita said. "People still ate them when I was a kid, and I have eaten them quite recently."

"It's the jerusalem coney," Paul said.

"Thank you," Thomas acknowledged. "It's as refreshing as it is unexpected to get an answer to a question on Astrobe."

The coney was a curious hopping creature, most of them the size of big rabbits, some smaller, some very much larger. They went indiscriminately into the ponds and under the water, and up into the higher reaches of the trees with great accurate hops; and through brush so thick that it would seem a snake could not traverse there. They were quick, and neither Thomas nor Paul could catch one.

"Along with the dutch-fish and the rambler's-ox, the coney is the food basis of the feral lands," Paul said. "Everything lives on them, or on that which lives on them. The dire-wolves live on them, as does porche's-panther, and the hydra. The birds live on them, and all the predators."

"The animals sound very like those of Earth," Thomas said.

"No, Thomas, only the names are like those of Earth," Paul said, almost in awe. "On Earth there are no animals at all like those around us. We are fools, you know, to be here. Scrivener and his like are correct. A rational man has no business here. I know a cliff not a half day from here where there are a thousand skeletons hung up on thorn bushes. The rouks fly down and kill people for fun. They carry them up and hang them there for a warning. Most of those bones have old black meat still clinging to them. You told me that in your time on Earth men killed wolves and hung them on fence rails as warning to other wolves. This is the same. There is even the tale that the King Rouk pays a bounty to each rouk who so kills and hangs up a man.''

''I'd pit a bow-necked Middlesex ox against any animal on this scurvy bowl,'' Thomas challenged.

''Thomas, the dire-wolf could take the head and horns of an Earth ox in one bite, and the whole body in two more,'' Paul assured him. ''The lazarus-lion can take the much larger rambler's-ox in the same manner. And the lazarus likes to eat people, not merely crucify them on the cliffs as the rouks do. The hydra can gobble anything in water, in one bite or several; and it can snap ten meters out of water. It has been known to take, in one bite, six men standing together some distance from the water's edge.

''And, Thomas, porche's-panther kills and eats the dire-wolf and the lazarus-lion and the rouk and the hydra itself. But all around us there are twenty other species of creatures capable of slicing a man up and eating him.''

''I would bet that a good hunting man could live well here,'' Thomas said. ''You tell me of a plenitude of game. It might be an intense and rewarding life.''

''I've lived here myself as a hunting man,'' Paul said. ''There's a few thousand hunters still on Astrobe. I lived with them a few months in my own time of hiding. Yes, the life is intense. The rewards are intangible, but for some they are deep. But those who follow the trade do not live to a great age. But those men have a certain flavor to them. I suppose the lazarus-lion thinks so too."

"Oh Astrobe, a salt that has not lost its savor!" Thomas cried. "The wonder of it. I had felt, for all its marvelous things, that civilized Astrobe was a little insipid. But it need not be. Here is salt for its salting. Here is leaven enough for the lump. We'll but see to a better blending."

"You cannot mean that Astrobe must be still more exposed to its back-lands!" Scrivener exclaimed. "These things are worse than any death. They must be hidden away forever."

"But are we armed?" Thomas asked. "Someone was not thinking very hard, and I suspect 'twas I who was supposed to be doing the thinking."

"I'm always armed," Paul said, "with the short knife, the only tool that a feral-land hunter will use. And I believe that Maxwell is. He's been a hunter in at least one of his life-aspects."

"And I am," said Evita. "This woman-child was a hunter more years ago than you would believe. It isn't for my own defense—I can witch the animals as far as I am concerned—it's for the defense of Holy Thomas here."

They went down through some levels of the tree-complex. They came onto what was almost solid land, its presence being given away only by fitful breaks that showed still deeper worlds of deep roots and green darkness.

"There should be a being to fit this green darkness,"

Thomas said. "Sextus Empiricus wrote that every environ must have its own sprite. It would be a weird one to fit the green underworld here, however."

"Call me not weird, good Thomas," spoke a green-colored voice. "And yet I'm sure that Sextus Empiricus wrote of me, and of you. You're also a sprite, but one never sees himself as such. One believes himself to be a man if he is raised by the humans."

The green-colored voice came from a green-crobed monk of the order of Saint Klingensmith. He was a blackish man (and yet there was a touch of deep green in his black) who winked at them and grinned. And they all stared at him, coming on him unexpectedly as they did.

"Preserve us this morning from dire-wolves and panthers and programmed things," he blessed them. "The latter are following you, you know. They're the hardest to evade and the hardest to rouse to; they have no scent."

"Whatever is a good monk doing in the salty woods of Astrobe?" Thomas asked him.

"Holy Cathead, I'm fishing, of course! But what are fine people like yourselves doing here? There was an Old Earth Epic named Babes in the Woods. That is yourselves. I am Father Oddopter of the Green-Robes, and now I see that you are not ordinary fine folks. There is Maxwell, the avatar who burns up his bodies, and we pray for him. There is Evita-child, who has become something of an archetype in the salacious dreams of the men of the orders, and she prays for us. She is a character in the folklore of the feral lands. There is the Paul, whom we know. He will suffer stark death in following out a mission and will never be told its

481

purpose. And you, sir, the doubtful Thomas, are a revenant with a double sign on you. The Holy Ghost certainly chooses strange instruments. Sometimes I think He is out of his mind. And the two others, the nothing man, and the less than nothing man.''

"Which am I?'' Slider asked with a sour grin.

"Oh, you're the nothing man. The other is the less-than-nothing. What? He flushes with anger? Why is sheer truth so hardly embraced?''

And Scrivener was indeed flushing with anger.

"What in particular are you fishing for, Father Oddopter?'' asked Thomas More the revenant with the double sign on him.

"You'll see,'' the monk said.

Circumstances began to assemble like cawing crows. You had doubted the color of the Evita's eyes, how they seemed now one thing and now another? Now they were green, green, the green of sparkling anticipation.

The monk wound a cord around his wrist and handled a harpoon thing a meter long. He peered into the green water with crinkling black-green eyes. Then he dived, robes and all, as a hawk dives, powerfully into the green water. And there was a sudden turbulence.

There was a struggle of resounding great power under water, a startling force striking and rupturing something of very great weight.

The green-robe broke water again and surged up onto the rooty platform all in one motion. He drew up the cord with hands and wrists of such terrifying size that it seemed impossible that they should belong to him. The water was bloody and churning when he brought the thing to the surface and drew it half out.

It was a fat discoid thing, black and quivering, and one third of its circuit was angry-toothed mouth. It weighed a hundred and fifty kilograms and it could have snapped a man in two through the trunk.

"I called myself a fisherman on Old Earth," Thomas said in admiration, "but I never in my life took so grand a fish as that. Days of my life, to see it is hardly to believe it!"

"Thomas, Thomas," the green-robe chided, "it's but the grasshopper that one catches in his palm to use on the hook. This isn't the fish. It's the bait."

The green-robe put three more harpoons into the creature that fought and groaned. There was something else now: great wings, as it were, deep under water and gathering for the pounce upward, the greatest wings ever. The green-robe made the harpoon lines fast to various thick branches and roots. His giant bait was threshing and churning with two thirds of it in the water.

Then the green-robe leapt onto the bait creature, slashing it deeply with a hand knife. It bled in spectacular fountains of dark rushing red that exploded with the lustful smell of rampant iron and stripped green wood and battlefield stink.

From a powerful underwater organ the creature was roaring with a rage that set both the water and the air to reeling. The green-robe rode and slashed the pitching thing at great risk of limb and life.

"Devil, Devil, rise and die, come and find what thing am I," Evita chanted like a little-girl rhyme, but her eyes were green volcanic fire a billion years old.

"Hurry!" Paul shouted. "It's rising like a thunder-clap."

"I know, I know," the green-robe crooned. "Holy Cathead, it does rise fast! But the last second is the best."

"Devil, Devil, come in hate! Take the fine Evita bait!" the wild-girl chanted, but her eyes no longer focused and she was frozen in hysteria.

The green-robe leapt clear from his bait-creature at the last possible second. Then the great thing swooped and struck upward: a thousand kilograms of center bulk that swallowed the trussed creature in a single gulp, thirty-meter-long tentacles that reached blindly for more prey, the big eye in the middle mad and livid with malevolence. The Devil! The main bulk was clear out of the water with the speed of its upward surge smashing the surface. It was but a lightning instant, but many things were observed simultaneously in that instant, not the least of which was the lightning itself—the corona-like discharge and blinding aura of the great sea-creature.

It was the hydra taking the bait.

"Now!" clanged the green-robe with the belfry sound of Saint Lo which is under water.

"Now!" Paul croaked like a rampant bull-frog.

"Now!" Evita sang in a voice that was green bronze pickled in brimstone.

They had spoken together, and no time at all had elapsed.

The three of them were onto the hydra before it thunderously shattered the water as it fell back from its great surge. They went with snake-like knives for the hydra eye and the brain behind it, feverish in their haste before the terrible tentacles could be brought to defend and to attack. Hysterical battle, hooting challenge, high screaming triumph.

The hydra trumpeted with an anger and agony that stabbed through the whole feral region, killing small birds by the very pitch of the scream. It submerged with the crashing fall-back from its great surge; and the three attackers stayed with it, cutting and hacking in near hysteria.

The hydra screamed under water. And after a while it rose again.

The huge tentacles lashed and writhed, but no longer with great power in them. The green-robe and Paul and Evita were through the giant eye and into the brain, cutting relentlessly and furiously. Evita had the head and most of her inside the big eye, and her chant came out of that cavity: "Devil, Devil, boom and bell! Watch Evita give you Hell!"—the weird voice of a small child gone mad.

The hydra-devil groaned with an echoing hollowness that shook the whole region.

And then it died.

"Why, this is allegory acted out before my very eyes," Thomas exclaimed, and he was shaking from the passion around him. He was finding words to deny what he had seen.

"Enjoy it, Thomas, enjoy it," the green-robe cried as he leapt back onto the rooty platform, the almost-land. "Give it accolade. You were a London play-goer, but you never saw so high and roaring a comedy as this. A man may not do it twice in one day. A strong body will stand it, but the emotions will not.''

"It isn't real," Thomas said, "it cannot be real. It's but a grand illusion. Look, our Paul has been drained, and he rolls his eyes like one half dead as he totters back onto the land. What is the content and real substance of this, Father Oddopter?''

"Why, it's the killing of the Devil, good Thomas. The Devil must be killed afresh somewhere every day. If ever he is not, then our days be at an end. Say, he is a big one today, isn't he? He's not always a hydra, you know. Some days he is a mad dire-wolf. Some days he is a porche's-panther gone musk. The Devil has his several forms, but we must kill him every day to limn his limits.''

"Our good Thomas is not beyond hope," Paul panted as he came back from the deeper shadow world to one less deep. "You are not completely revolted, Thomas. You were near as impassioned as ourselves, however you deny it. Golden Astrobe hasn't yet got you entirely in he effete wiles. You weaken and you comform, and they seem to be winning you. But this will stand as a sign for you before you weaken completely. In this blood be you blessed, Thomas!''

"Ye be all daft," Thomas growled, uneasy, and yet somehow caught up into the blood-lust of the thing. "It is an unnatural satanic thing that happens here, and you revel in it. And the child-woman, has she gone brand-mad?''

"She's possessed," the green-robe said. And Evita had almost disappeared into the cavernous brain of the hydra-devil. She gorged and reveled there.

"She has consorted with the Devil in his other forms," the green-robe said, "and there is a curious hatred and tension between them. I have never been on a devil-kill with the child before, but I have heard of them. She becomes wild sometimes."

"You actually believe in the Devil here in the feral lands?" Thomas asked as Evita withdrew somewhat from the monster.

"What an odd fellow you are!" the green-robe Father Oddopter marveled. "You have just seen us slay the Devil, and you ask whether he be. Do you not believe your eyes? Does this seem like an ordinary creature to you?"

"Nowt ordinary, of course," Thomas said weakly, as though he were pleading a losing case in court, "but by definition, it is within the order of nature, since there is no other order."

"Thomas, Thomas, you cannot win that little game even when you make your own rules."

"I can understand how to the superstitious or to the ignorant—"

"No, no, good Thomas. Look at it! The ignorant Scrivener and the superstitious Slider are aghast at the violence of the thing, and they yet stand trembling. But they do not believe it.

"The half-ignorant Maxwell also quakes, but he only half believes. It is we of the intellect who believe what we see and feel—that we have drawn the Devil from his lair and killed him. You do not believe it?"

"I do not believe it," Thomas said, but he was not feeling particularly calm. "It's but a bloody, violent, and dangerous sport you indulge."

Evita had finally emerged from the monster, glistening with blood and gore, and bearing a great arm-load of Devil brains. She was disheveled, and her eyes were completely mad.

And then in a flash they were no longer any such thing. She came out of her passion and seizure as easily as she would leap from a tree. She winked at Thomas, and broke into chiming laughter.

"My seduction of you is a little different from what I planned," she chortled. "I'll seduce you in mind and belief instead. Bodily I'd burn you up to quick and fry the poor tallow out of you, Thomas. But this way we burn a brand on your brain. Whoop! Imagine, a grown man too ignorant to believe in the Devil!"

You ever cook any Devil brains yourself? Don't knock it if you haven't tried it. Paul and the green-robe cooked the brains. They cased them in a ball of mud, and set it into a quickly-started and explosively hot fire of oil-dripping vines. These burned torridly with a staggering, almost emetic smoke—the water in them fighting with the oil. The whole thing gave off a brightness that was like sodium flame. They roasted the brains roaring for an hour, and then the ball burst open with a real explosion. There was the smell of sulphur in the air. And all was made ready.

With dishes of this sort, you like them or you like them not.

Scrivener and Slider would not partake.

Maxwell had to force himself. "After all," he told himself, "they are only fish brains. The rest is but the rough kidding of these feral people." But he liked them more and more as he ate them.

Thomas tasted in a surly manner, and out of curiosity. And then he was hooked on that bait. He welcomed them as one of the rarest and hearties foods ever. They entered into him. Ah, the salt and the sulphur of them would stand him well in his crux hour when it came. By eating its brains, he would always have a certain mastery over this enemy.

Hydra brains were known in some of the mod places of Cosmopolis, but at fifty stoimenof d'or a kilo. The price was high there, and the brains were not; some of the old Devil always went out of them in the marketing and fixing.

Here it was finer, eating them new-killed, kilo after kilo to satiety. They needed no condiment. They had their own salt and sulphur.

Who laughs? Who laughs? None but a necromancer laughs like that. It was Walter Copperhead who came out of the jungle with eyes for nothing but the hydra. He had known, of course, the hour and the place of the Devil-kill. He would lay out its entrails and examine them, and try to unriddle riddles there, as though he were an old auger. And he was.

He built a sort of jungle winch with a counter-poise of straining vines and bent branches. He worked to life the monster and disembowel it. The members of the party withdrew a space and left him with it. It was a private thing that Walter Copperhead did.

They traveled again after they had spent an hour or two in the fine talk that should always follow a fine meal. The green-robe Father Oddopter went with them, he having no home and being sworn to the rule of never laying his head in the same place for two nights. They came on other hunters and fishers. They came on one bunch who were killing ansels and hauling them out of the water. This puzzled Thomas.

Rimrock the ansel was a creature of intellect, and therefore human. But these ansels, Thomas understood at once, were not creatures of intellect and were not human. The difference was clear on the practical plane, but the theory was not clear. Thomas was surprised that he felt no repugnance at seeing them killed. Nor did he hesitate to eat raw hacked-off pieces offered him. So he puzzled about it.

"There's a question I hardly know how to ask," he said to Paul. "Would Rimrock the ansel eat ansel?"

"He would and he has," Paul said, "but he doesn't care for it much. Says it's overrated. An ansel doesn't need ansel in his diet, but there's no repugnance. And an ansel who has crossed the line becomes an entirely different creature from a natural ansel. How the new species is acquired I do not know, but every species can tell the difference. A dire-wolf, for instance, will eat a natural ansel with as easy a mind as he'd eat a jerusalem coney. He'd also eat a transfigured ansel just as he'd eat a man, but he wouldn't eat him with as easy a mind. There is a difference between natural and transcendent prey, and all the meat-eaters know it. It is known that all animals are greatly disturbed in their minds after they have eaten humans, and Rimrock would be human by this test."

"The theology of it is impossible," the green-robe said. "It cannot be that a creature already in full life will sometimes receive a soul and intelligence, and yet that appears to be quite the case with certain exceptional ansels. And I talked to your friend Rimrock today. He had gone on just a little while before you came.''

They traveled again. And the mountains grew higher and came closer. They traveled through the afternoon—stalked always by the Programmed Killers—and at dusk they came to Goslar the City of the Salic Emperors.

(Here follows History quickly given.)

The Salic Emperors had their origins as an underground university fraternity in Wu Town. Certain young persons, believing themselves daring, maintained a revolt, half-humorous, half-doctrinaire, and altogether brainless, against the golden mediocrity of Astrobe, the humanist planetary dream. Several of these young people then (two centuries before this telling) established the small town of Goslar and called it their imperial capital. Hunting families had accreted to the settlement for it was, in a way, central to the Feral Strip. It was here that the Dismal Swamps and the Rain Forests and the Savannas all came together; and it stood right at the foot of Electric Mountain, the first high pinnacle of the mountain complex.

Goslar now had about a hundred people, and a big shanty building that was public house, royal palace, hotel and skinners' center.

From the founding, there had always been one Salic Emperor in residence at Goslar. The present Emperor was Charles the Six Hundred and Twelfth; for no Emperor had reigned as long as a year, and many of them less than a month.

The automatic killers had assigned themselves automatically to the destruction of every reigning emperor. These Programmed Killers of Astrobe have been described as garbage disposals, as the ultimate police, as the precision wardens of the Astrobe Dream. They got rid of everything that stood in the way of that dream. They had been so constructed, and they had so propagated themselves and continued. On the breast of each Programmed Killer was blazoned the motto *I have not been false to the Vision*.

The sensing of these killers was faultless and relentless. Anything that threatened the Astrobe Thesis was the enemy and they would follow it to the end and kill it. They had never ultimately failed, though certain tricky persons sometimes eluded them for years.

A personal surrender was sensed by them. One who relented and accepted the Astrobe Dream, albeit interiorly and silently, was no longer hunted by them. The Programmed Killers could be destroyed. But at the moment of the destruction of any one of them, another one was created in a distant center and was given the same assignment.

And they had pursued and killed the Salic Emperors, just as they were pursuing and would finally kill every threatening member of the Thomas More party.

But there was a peculiarity about the succession of the Salic Emperors that paralleled that of the robot killer species. Whenever a reigning emperor was killed, his replacement was also created instantly. Knowing of the death by no orthodox communication (in several cases, knowing of it a few hours before it happened), the Salics at the University in Wu Town would hold instant convocation, by day or by night, and would select a new emperor in a matter of minutes. The new emperor would start on foot to Goslar immediately, without script or staff or food or coin or extra garment, and would arrive in wild Goslar in about ten hours. He always traveled intuitively, since Goslar is not mapped and the new emperor would never have been there before.

And so the dynasty continued.

Charles the Six Hundred and Twelfth had reigned less than twenty hours when the Thomas More party arrived. He had arrived in the darkness of the night before, and had been crowned by a dumb birdliming man.

(That be History longishly given.)

Charles· the Six Hundred and Twelfth was about eighteen years old, a bewildered young man with a frightened smile. But he comprehended the party even as they approached. As Emperor he was infused with certain special powers of understanding. He beckoned the party to enter the big shanty building, and then motioned them to stow their gear against the walls and to spread straw for their beds, for this was hotel as well as royal palace.

Evita dropped more than fifty kilos of hydra Devil-meat into the big common pot boiling in the middle of the room. She had carried this lump, more than her own weight of very high meat, along with many other things, for the whole afternoon, and that over very rough country. She was as strong as a podalka pony.

And then the Emperor Charles began to give orders, as was his obligation and right:

"The Maxwell, the Slider, the Oddopter Priest, the Paul, the Thomas, and the Devil-girl may use the common room," the Emperor issued. They had not given him their names; but he was Emperor, and it was given him to know what things people are. Besides, Rimrock had been there before them and had told Charles the names and appearance of the members of the party.

"The Scrivener may not, however," the Emperor continued. "He may not use the common room. He must be lodged in the small machinery shed; and he will be fed there. He is not people."

"Are you a Programmed Person, Scrivener?" Thomas asked him. "I did not know that."

"I don't know whether I am or not," Scrivener lamented. "I've suspected it, and there's a family legend that we have some Programmed admixture. But why should it matter? There is really no difference any longer between Programmed and People. I wish I had never come on this miserable expedition, but I will not be treated as an inferior."

"I am the Emperor and I know these things," the boyish Emperor Charles the Six Hundred and Twelfth maintained to the party. "The Scrivener is a machine. And he will lodge in the machine shed. Let us not make a great noise over a little thing. It is only that definitions have lost their precision on Astrobe; and one duty of the Salic Emperor is to clarify and enforce them."

"Thomas, assert yourself and overrule this lout," Scrivener demanded. "You are an important man, and I am a member of your party."

"I've had my own difficulties with high royalty in another place," Thomas said. "And the rule is, do not overrule them in small things; it is difficult enough to overrule them in great things. I do not cross royalty on minor matters. You are a minor matter, Scrivener."

So Scrivener went angrily to his lodging in the machine shed.

Charles the Six Hundred and Twelfth had been polishing the skull of Charles the Sixth Hundred and Eleventh, the Emperor who had been murdered on the morning of the previous day by the Programmed Killers. The skull had been partly shattered by the mortal blow, and Charles the Present had to work carefully. He had a sort of white clay that he was using for paste; and he set the larger pieces into the break. Evita came and began to arrange the smaller fragments, cleaning them from day-old gore and handling them deftly.

"How is it that you are of high blood, Devil-kid?" the young Emperor asked her. They appeared to be about the same age; but if the legends of Evita were only partly true, this were impossible. "The whole wallful of skulls would protest your touching a sliver if you were not of high blood, but they seem happy in their niches. What? What? You were the consort of one of them? And that one is making for you as much song as a dead skull can make.

"But there is more than one of them crooning at you! You must be very old! So old! There is Charles the One Hundred and Twelfth himself stirring at you. You are Stephanie the green-eyed queen! But Charles the Two Hundred and Fifth is also chiming in and rocking in his niche. So you are Queen Brigid! And Charles the Three Hundred and Fifteenth is happy at sensing your presence. So you are Queen Candy Mae! How could you be all of them? I called you Devil-kid and I was right. But they all love you."

"I wish that were true," Evita said. "But you will notice that Charles the Three Hundred and Thirteenth has turned his face to the wall. Poor Charles! It was all a misunderstanding, Charles, really it was. And the sounds made by two others are not happy ones. I have been as many bad queens as I have been good ones. I come often back to Goslar to renew myself. I've been a lot of queens."

"Be one more!" Charles cried. "The Oddopter priest will marry us at once."

"Oh no, my days of queening it are over. I have committed myself to the Thomas Adventure, and I will follow it the several months till I am released from it by his death. I doubt if you will still be alive then, Charles, but I may come and see."

The skulls made an impressive show in their niches on the rude wall. Not all six hundred and eleven were there. There were, in fact, thirteen of them missing, and there were empty niches for them. These were the Emperors who had been murdered by being knocked from high peaks into deep ravines, or had been burned beyond recovery in fire traps, or who had died in some other demolishing adventure at the hands of the Programmed Killers. But most were here, and they provided the mnemonic for the great remembered oral history of the dynasty.

"More than one of you here is a *Taibhse*," Charles said. "I am Emperor so I am given intuition about such things. The Maxwell leaves bodies behind him, and the Thomas leaves heads behind. The Evita has lived too long to be so young, and I understand this less than the other cases. How do you do it, black-hearted kid?"

"Do you not learn anything at the university,

Charley-boy?'' she asked him. ''Very long life has been possible on Astrobe for two hundred years. They remain on the edge of the breakthrough, they say. But special breakthroughs have been made all through these two hundred years. I am one of them. But who wants it? they ask. Nine out of ten persons on Astrobe ask for termination long before their normal life term is run. They find life so wearying, the Golden People! Hell, I don't. Perfection is all the more cloying the more it is perfected. I tell Holy Thomas that this thing, and not the Cathead and Barrio and Feral Strip revolts, is the sickness of Astrobe. The people are so weary of perfection that they ask termination at earlier and earlier ages. Many now ask it as small children. What is so perfect about a life that more and more people refuse to live?''

''I forget your legend, Devil-kid,'' the Emperor Charles said, ''though I am certain that I knew it when I had to study the Legends of Astrobe in school. Is there not somewhere in it the phrase 'to go to Hell in a hand-basket'?''

''Yes, there is, Charley-boy. I was naïve in my methods and in my direction of revolt,'' Evita said. ''The teachers said that there was no Hell and no Devil, and this angered me; I knew that they were wrong; I had had some personal contact with both. They said that there was no sin. In particular, they said that children were not able to commit serious sins; and in this I knew that the teachers were sinfully wrong.

''I decided to go to Hell to prove them wrong. I decided to find the Devil. What I found first was the old Evil Scientist of Legend, so contrived a man that he was a burlesque of himself. Yet he was a true scientist and a truly evil man. I consorted with him, and he did give me long life and an introduction into certain aspects of evil. I was one of the first successful experiments in longevity. It takes a deep well of bodily and psychic energy to make it work, and I had it. At that time I thought that he was the Devil himself, and that I was Faustina and had made a Devil's bargain.

"Well, he was sound in the biology of the thing, and he gave me what I wanted. There isn't much demand for it now. 'Eternal youth, who wants it?' is the sneer. I did and do want it. For several centuries I have had it. Ah, the Holy Thomas and others smile. They do not believe my legend. They will not believe a legend even when they see it in the flesh."

"Quick-sparrow, you are not yet twenty years," Thomas said.

"Good Thomas, I am more than two hundred," the Evita answered. "Well, I committed all the old-fashioned abominations in my search for Hell. I indulged in fornication and pride and unkindness and intellectual contempt. But I didn't find Hell immediately.

"There is another legend about the boy who had to go clear around his planet to come to his own house. Then he recognized it for the first time. I am the girl who did it; and I *did* find Hell. Golden Astrobe of the Dream is that Hell. I don't like it, and I never will; but Hell exists."

"But Golden Astrobe is perfect, child-woman," Thomas insisted. "It is all perfections rolled into one."

"Sure it is, good Thomas, all rolled into one package and tied with a golden ribbon. I had been tricked by false teachers who use words to mean their opposites. So have you been tricked, Thomas, and you should be too intelligent for that. Well, let them so misuse terms! Let them call things what they will. If the Cathead thing and the Barrio thing are Hell, then I am for Hell till a better Hell comes along. But I will not accept so extreme a Hell as the Vision of Golden Astrobe. It stifles! It blows out souls like rows of candles!''

There were rows of candles there in the big shanty room, or tallow tapers at least, there in the place that was royal palace and public house and skinners' center, there in the big room that could sleep perhaps twenty people. And the rows of candles were blown out now and then, for the room was badly calked and the wind had risen outside.

A man came in.

"The ghosts are bad tonight, Emperor," the man said. "They have just eaten all the flesh of my wife and left only her bones.''

"Well, I'm working on a king's charm against them, but I don't have it in shape yet," said Emperor Charles the Six Hundred and Twelfth. "The skulls of the old emperors are supposed to inspire me to it, but so far I get nothing but gibberish. I guess the ghosts will just have to be bad tonight.''

"I'm kind of glad she's gone," the man said, as he took hydra Devil-meat out of the common pot with one of the big wooden forks, "but I'll miss her sometimes. We fought a lot, but there was never anyone so much fun to fight with. Now I don't have anybody.''

"What is the ghost bit?" Thomas asked as he also began to dip Devil-meat out of the pot with a wooden fork. Then they all began to dip it out and to eat.

"The ghosts are the same, or almost the same, as the *Taibhse*," the green-robe Father Oddopter said. "You being one, Thomas, should know a little what they are. They are animals or creatures or beings ripped out of their context and set to wandering. They are most often invisible, and at their most solid manifestation they are still transparent or at least slightly translucent, as are you by candlelight.''

"There are such indeed?" Thomas asked. "Or are they mere country tales?"

"They are real, and many of them are angry at their misplacement. Will a country tale eat all the flesh off a person and leave only the bones?" the green-robe asked. "Well, I ghess that is possible too. All things are. Of these ghosts, however named, we can only say that they be. In the early Natural Histories of Astrobe they were given space. Now they are not. But they are creatures with minds superior to those of animals, and of the order of men. They have bodies, however fragile and changing. They have been seen and heard and felt. They have killed, and they have been killed. Their flesh has been in that very pot there, but it steamed away to nothing, leaving only an aroma. They have cities and settlements. Most often they are reluctant to approach human settlements (it may be true that they are kept off by spells), but sometimes they do come and eat flesh, all the flesh of a person, cleanly and rapidly.''

"Is superstition completely rampant in the boondocks of Astrobe?" Thomas demanded.

"Why yes, I suppose it is," the green-robe said. "The psychic force, the libido, is completely rampant here, that I know. Once, I believe, that was true on Old Earth, and it lingered long in the Africas and Haitis of Old Earth. You forget that the taming of the nature of this world has been of a very short time. The feral strips are the power-house of Astrobe. They are the key to the weather, and to the fertility of the land; to the water and to the water power; also to the power from the grian-sun. They are also, I believe, the psychic power-house of Astrobe, though their human persons are fewer in their thousands than is civilized Astrobe in its billions. Yes, superstition is very strong here, Thomas.

"If three persons of the feral strips imagine a thing strongly enough (however monstrous it may be), *they can bring it into being*. They can create a contingent body for any thing they imagine, and it will be inhabited by certain unbodied spirits here. I have seen it done. I have helped do it. When children of the feral strips play 'monsters,' they make monsters that can be seen and smelled, and which on occasion have eaten them up.

"Yes, here are all improbably persons and animals, spirits and half-spirits, clean and unclean; the archetypes of folk dreams; they are here alive, and often fleshed. Here there is superstition (the beyond-belief or over-belief) as a shaggy and pungent thing that leaves footprints and fang-marks. Every thought or inkling, suppressed as irrational in rational Astrobe, comes out here and assumes flesh. Why, there is a stock-breeder here who breeds, improves, and slaughters for profit a creature that had its origin in the nightmares of Golden Astrobe. It was banned there by group therapy. It came out here and became physical fact."

"Father, father, there are no brains in your head," Thomas chided. "I see that I will have to quarantine these regions much more tightly if I do become president of Astrobe."

"And I tell you, Thomas, that the civilized world of

Astrobe is really of no consequence," the green-robe said. "It is but a thin yellow fungus growing on a part of the hide of the planet. Should this shaggy old orb shiver its hide uncommonly but once, the Golden Astrobe civilization would be destroyed instantly. Bless this meat! It's good."

"It would be an act of charity to exterminate all the poor benighted persons in this area, and I will have to have it done," Thomas said. "Aye, the meat is good."

"You'll run into trouble with the ecologists if you go to exterminating all the feral people," the Emperor Charles pointed out. "The several thousand humans in the feral strips are part of the balanced ecology of Astrobe. Destroy them, and the balanced plant and animal life will go out of balance; this great cistern for civilized Astrobe would be changed, and perhaps ruined. The scientists do not want that. We must be left here in such numbers as we maintain, they say. But we are not considered as humans. We are rather animals to them, animals among animals; we are under the wild-life department."

"Fox-firk, I cast better lumps in the stool than the pack of you can say in a night's talk," Thomas said angrily, "and I'm called to do it now. Begging your pardons but I must go to the henry. Or is it called the charles in this realm, Emperor?"

"Call it what you wish, Thomas," the young Emperor said. And then he winked at Evita a wink that was like lightning between them, and Thomas caught it.

"What is the levity here?" he demanded still more angrily. "Cannot an honest man go to the henry without being mocked?"

"It is only that there is a citizen of Goslar with an

unusual means of livelihood," the Emperor said. "It is a trade that has been passed down from father to son. We will be listening for the lilt of your voice, good Thomas."

And Thomas went out puzzled to the henry.

The man who had lost his wife (all except her bones) now brought in a little barrel of green lightning.

"She did so love to get foxy on it," the man said, "and she will not be using it now. We will drink this night to my lost wife (except her bones), and praise her if we can find any words of praise for her. I cannot, but some of you are better with words than I am. I liked her, but I can't think of a thing to praise her for."

"To your wife, except for her bones!" sang Evita, and lifted the little barrel in very strong hands to drink from the bung.

The Emperor Charles did the same thing, and the green-robe Father Oddopter, and Paul. But neither Maxwell nor Slider was able to raise the barrel to drinking height, and so were barred from participating.

Any others? Bang! Bang! You broach a bung and there're two who will be there immediately if they're anywhere to be found. Walter Copperhead the necromancer and Rimrock the ansel were in the shanty room. Copperhead raised the barrel high and drank deeply. Rimrock, who had a peculiar physique, did it in a way that might seem awkward to a man, but he did it competently and gurglingly.

"Where have you fellows been?" Paul asked.

"Killing Killers," Copperhead whooped. "You'd none of you be alive this night if we hadn't. You're careless in your wanderings."

"That is a barbarous way to drink it anyhow," Slider bemoaned, badly hurt that he was barred from the festivity by his bodily weakness. "In civilized Astrobe, the mere touch of the electrode or electric needle will give a much finer effect, the golden glow. What are you, pigs, that you swig intoxicant in physical form?"

"Hush, half-man," the Emperor Charles commanded, and he raised his hand. "We listen."

And then came the high angry lilt of the voice of Thomas from the little henry out back of the royal shack. All the frustration of the ages was in that furious denunciation that Thomas was loosening on someone.

Evita and the Emperor Charles and the green-robe and the man who had lost his wife except her bones all went into spasms of laughter. Copperhead's goat-guffaw was one of the great things, and the primordial giggle of the oceanic Rimrock was something beyond the comprehension of common ears.

"What is it?" Paul chuckled. "I hate to be left out of a thing."

"Why, Paul, there is that citizen of Goslar with the unusual livelihood," the green-robe chorlted, hardly able to contain himself as the Thomas-voice rose even higher. "He sits on the pot day and night, and there is but one public pot in the City of Goslar. He will not move to give place till he is paid a coin. Threats and beatings will not move him. Only a coin. Hear good Thomas! What a fine angry voice he does have! But the citizen of Goslar has him where it hurts."

"Oh stop it. Rimrock!" Evita laughed. "You'll rupture yourself with that giggling."

"What a region!" Paul sighed with a broken grin. "I could almost agree with Thomas that it should be more tightly quarantined. There is creative thinking at work in this, though. I'm not sure that I've ever met its equal in civilized Astrobe."

The angry voice of Thomas had died down to a bitter grumble. And after a bit, Thomas came back into the big room very red in the face.

"Does anyone here have a stoimenof d'etain?" he asked out of his red stony face.

Paul gave him one. It was a pewter coin of small value in civilized Astrobe, but apparently the dollar-in-use here in the feral strips. Thomas went out again.

It is presumed that he paid the coin to the citizen of Goslar, was given access to the pot, and relieved himself. He did, at any rate, return to the big room in somewhat better humor, and yet with a certain reserve, as though defying them all to carry it any further.

"It all reminds me of something," Thomas smiled, though his smile was nearly as crooked as that of Paul, and there was still a bitter rasp to his voice. "It reminds me of something for which I cannot find a name. I still believe that the Vision of Golden Astrobe is the perfect thing, and that the extravagances here in the ferals are monstrosities below the human level. But perhaps the Golden Perfection should be suspended for about five minutes a day for the refreshment of the soul. Yes, perhaps it should."

Thomas was able to lift the barrel and drink from the bung, and it loosened him a little. Green lightning is fun when the Golden Perfection is not immediately at hand.

Evita told the story of the Devil and the Wife from

Culpepper, of what souvenir she took from him with a sharp knife, and why to say "hung like the Devil" means half-hung.

The green-robe told about the alien from Gootz who came to that very hotel in Goslar and relaxed in a pile in the middle of the floor. Sure they thought he was a great wheel of cheese lying there! And they sliced him up in a hundred slices, and each citizen of Goslar ate one. That alien from Gootz still raises hell with all of them. He cannot pull himself together, and he refuses to be ejected. All citizens of Goslar have a certain green look on their faces. That is the reason.

The Emperor Charles the Six Hundred and Twelfth told one. Walter Copperhead told about the fellow who courted the woman to get to examine her entrails. "I'll put them back," he said, "I'll put them back and sew them in again. I just want to go over them once." "No, no, no," the lady said. "Boy, I thought I'd had some wooly propositions before."

Paul told one. The man who had lost his wife (except her bones) told one. And Thomas told a concatenated drollery with all the obscene parts in Latin. Rimrock told one, an oceanic spoof so outré that it took the breath away and turned the liver green.

Then the barrel was empty. At that moment the night guard of Goslar blew one blast on his trumpet to indicate that all was well with the night. And after a moment he blew a little scurry to indicate that it was not so well as all that, that things were prowling.

The Emperor Charles and all the travelers went to sleep in the straw (a sleep broken only by the giggling of Rimrock from time to time: if something tickles one of those ansels he stays tickled quite a while), and the skulls of five hundred and ninety-nine emperors were empty-eyed in their niches on the wall.

Golden Astrobe was a creature with a fair face for all men to see. But out behind she had a sting in her tail.

7. ON THUNDER MOUNTAIN

They wakened to trumpets. Some were made trumpets indeed, blown by the night guard and the day guard changing places and by the special honor guard, and some were trumpeter birds set to going by the instrumental trumpets. The trumpeter birds were of better tone and timbre.

The Emperor Charles rose grandly to begin the second full day of his reign, if it should prove to be a full day.

"Not for thirty reigns have there been so many grand people in the court at Goslar at one time," said he. "Strike a medal for it, man."

"I don't know how to strike a medal for it," the man said.

"If you find someone who does, tell him to strike a medal for it," the Emperor said. "Put my own fine hand on it, and the motto *They Come To Me Like Eagles*. Why, here is a dead saint from Old Earth, the Devil-kid of Astrobe, a necromancer of unlikely powers, a transcendent ansel, a priest of Saint Klingensmith, an avatar who burns up bodies, and pilot Paul who is a broken-faced old warlock. Not for thirty reigns have there been so many grand people at court at one time, and not for thirty reigns has there been so handsome an Emperor at the head of the court."

"How long a time has the thirty reigns been?" Thomas asked him.

"It has been what we call a rapid year," the Emperor said, "perhaps the most rapid ever."

The green-robe Father Oddopter of the order of Saint Klingensmith said mass for all the people in Goslar and all the people who came in at the news of it, a little over a hundred people in all. It was a simple and clear mass with a surprisingly intelligent sermon, and the uncanny miracle came shockingly and vividly alive at the consecration. It was as though the Heavens opened on command and the Spirit came down—which is what happened.

Even the skeptical Thomas felt the stirrings of faith in himself again. It was a miraculous morning, so why not believe in miracles again for a while? As he said, Thomas often rediscovered his belief for a little while in the mornings.

"What they do here at Goslar," the green-robe told Thomas after the mass, "is set up a token realm till the real shall be rediscovered. And the reality will be rediscovered, and the golden palsy will pass. Happy death for you, good Thomas."

"You are too rapid to wish happy deaths to persons," the Thomas said. "And the mass this morning was a very old one. 'For those here present who will die this day.' 'Twas meant to be addressed to a world, and not to small Goslar of under one hundred people where it is very unlikely that any will die this day."

"It was addressed to your party and to myself, of whom several will die this day. Were I not certain of this, I would have said another mass of the day. And the necromancer also says that the most of us who go to the mountain will die this day."

"It was a pretty thing, it was a pretty complex of

things," Thomas said as his early-morning faith began to withdraw from him again. "As a child I lived it, and as a young man I still respected it. In my maturity I still call it the Noblest of all Superstitions. The Church of the Saints lived quite a long while, and historically I seem to have an ironic part in it. It died meanly in civilized Astrobe, I understand, but I believe it will die more quietly and harmlessly here in the ferals."

"You who are to die this year, know that it will not die at all, Thomas. And know also that nothing dies quietly in the ferals. Whatever is set on here shriek and shrill if it be killed, and it will return to life again and again. Even the meanest reptile dies hard in the ferals, and should a great thing do less? It will not lie down and die quietly, but why are you so afraid of being associated with superstition? Is it not a superstition of your own to climb the mountain?"

"Perhaps it is, green monk. It is an inner compulsion of mine, and I must do it. It is on this one thing that I fault the citizens of Golden Astrobe: they have never lifted up their eyes to the mountains. They are like blind men in this, but where are they mistaken? What if all in a world were blind to color except certain small boys? That, I believe, is the case on Astrobe; but it may make the color-gazing a mere boyish thing. What is the good of gazing at a pile of rocks? I will leave off such boyishness after I become world president. But this day I am hooked on the Mountain Bait."

"We be on our way, good Thomas," Rimrock the ansel interrupted. "If I go up the mountain, it will be by a watery way I know on the inside of it, up the mother spring, for it is a mountain-full of water. The Copperhead will be on the mountain top before you, and will perform certain abominations there. And then he will leave. We ride shotgun for you this day again."

"But it will not help greatly. Most of you will still die on the mountain," Copperhead the necromancer said. And the two of them were gone.

"Shall I kill the Scrivener thing in the machine shed?" the Emperor Charles the Six Hundred and Twelfth asked.

"No, of course not," Thomas answered sharply. "Release him to me. He is one of my advisors and a member of my party. It was rather a cruel trick to shut him up in the shed last night, and I do often find such royal wit tedious."

"But he is a machine and not a man," the Emperor insisted. "And as a machine he has, though he may not know it, a sender in his head. It works without his knowledge whether he is asleep or awake. It is his code signal, and every Programmed Person (even if he be nine-tenths human and one-tenth Programmed) has it. It is by this code signal that the Programmed Killers so easily trail you. It is suicide for you to climb the mountain; you know that, Thomas. The Programmed Killers will encircle the pinnacle and have you caught in the tall trap."

"I worry about them not at all," Thomas said. "I am a special case and I may not die till my own special time has come."

"Ah, but they will kill members of your party. Promise me this, that you will at the appropriate moment kill the Scrivener and cast him into a ravine to mislead the Killers, and then to make your mountain climb quickly in the interval."

"No, I will not cast one of my own members to the dogs. We will climb the mountain as though there were no such things as the Killers, and for me there are not."

"I repeat, they will kill members of your party, Thomas. And several of these are sometimes citizens of my realm. I will charge you with their blood."

"You will charge me with nothing, Charles. You are only a fuzz-faced boy playing in a cluttered back-yard. Yes, I suppose that some members of my party will be murdered by the Killers. So let it be. It will be a winnowing, a cleansing. Those who die will be those who deserve to die. I myself will not be false to the vision. I'll blazon the motto on my own breast. The Killers strike only those who are a threat to the Golden Life of Astrobe.

"I'd kill them too if I knew which they were! I welcome the Killers! They seem to be mistaken as to my own role and purpose, but they are inhibited from actually killing me when the time comes. If there are enemies of the Great Thing in my party, let them die!"

"I expel you from this realm, Thomas More!" the young Emperor cried sharply. "You're a more mechanical thing than any machine. You're a string-puppet that's left off being a man. What vision could anyone be faithful to who would sell his own brothers and partisans to the Killers? I thought you were a man, and you are only a mannikin. Your man's-parts were left behind when they brought you forward through time. You stink up my woods and swamps! Take your machine things and your cravens and go! We will see if the real people follow you.

"What? I'm aghast! You go with him, Devil-kid? He's worthless, you know."

"Yes, I go with him, Charles 612, and I can't make you understand," Evita said. "He is not entirely worthless, or not forever. He only seems so now. Yes, he's become a dull lump of metal and will never serve for a knife now. But he will serve for something else. I've followed worse to the end, and his end won't be very long now."

"Not in the ferals it sure won't be, not in Goslar," the Emperor said. "But you others, wait, wait! How are you so wrong? The Paul and the Oddopter go with him also. Why? Why? You have heard him throw in with the Things, and leave off being a man."

"And I have heard distant bells tolling, and seen a world arise in the sign of the Rolling Head, Charles," the green-robe said easily. "Believe me, there is more here than is apparent. It's my business to be with this lost sheep this day. He is the wooly ram with the double sign on him. He is in Scripture. And he must be saved, not for himself, but for the double sign on him."

"But it's to your own death, Father Oddopter! As the Emperor I am given insights, and I see your death today because of him. Even in martyrdoms there should be a certain economy. Do not sacrifice the worthy for the worthless."

"No man who swells up in such towering anger as the Thomas does now is worthless, Charles. He is a cloud full of lightning, and not at all as facile in this as he seems to be. I will stay with him this day."

"I say he's full of hot wind and nothing else," said the Emperor Charles. "He cannot lighten and he cannot thunder. He can but fume in his wrongness. I say he is a wether and no wooly ram."

"Were I not suddenly caught in my own uncertainty,

I'd settle with you, fuzz-face," Thomas said closely. "I was never one to be certain that I was right for long, and I'm not certain now."

"He is an instrument, Charles. Try to understand that," said Paul. "And I will stay with him also."

The Emperor Charles withdrew in blazing silence. He had Scrivener released to them, and his contempt for them scorched the very grass when he did so.

The members of the party, not very cheerful or much in accord, began the ascent of Electric Mountain. All were ashamed, and they did not know of what.

Yet it was a stimulating morning and a challenging climb. And the death-threat *did* call up excitement in most of them. Maxwell and Slider didn't like it. But there was a curious change in Scrivener, who was, perhaps, a Programmed Person.

"This is my test, Thomas," the Scrivener said as they climbed. "I have been rethinking things all the night. Whether I am a Programmed Person or an old-recension human I do not know; nor how much I may be of each. But I *have* found something out here that tells me that you yourself are wrong to hold the Dream of Astrobe as perfect. It is not. It is only half the thing. It must be conjoined to some other thing that I do not understand yet. Perhaps, after all, we must kill the Devil afresh every day. You are an old-line human, Thomas, yet I accuse you of setting the human thing too low and the mechanical thing too high. So, there are machines that walk like men these several hundred years, and perhaps I am one of them. But there are also men who swing against their own kind and become more partisans of the machine than the machines themselves. Do you not be one of them!

"So, the Programmed Killers hunt down and kill only those who are a threat to the Astrobe dream? And you all believe that they will discount me as no threat? We will see who they will kill and who they will pass by when they have us in the trap. For you lead us to the trapping, Thomas. I tell you that I have become a boiling threat to one part of the too-easy thing."

They climbed. And then they climbed more steeply. The vegetation fell away and became more sparse. Now they were climbing a Devil-tower of magma and iron, rough and sharp and blood-drawing.

Above them the mountain spire was a pinnacle as a cartoonist might draw one, sharp and needle-like as a burlesque of a spire, and with a clean white doughnut cloud encircling it and settling down a third of the way from the top.

The green-robe caught a Commer's Condor in a flung net. They tore it apart and ate it raw. It was past mid-morning, and they had been climbing hard.

"There is another doughnut-shaped cloud around the spire," Evita said. "It is a black one, and below us. The Programmed Killers have come in full patrol and have the peak surrounded. They climb not so fast nor so well as we do, but they climb more relentlessly and they do not rest. This isn't the death I had planned for us all, Holy Thomas."

"Never mind," said Thomas. "We will rest. And then we will ascend again. Electric Mountain, they call it, do they? Aye, it tingles and is full of sparks."

There was an excitement entering them all as they rested there.

"There is a story that one of my grandmothers told me when I was small," Scrivener broke in with a nervous half-metallic voice. "It is from her; I believe, that I have my mechanical descent. In the early days, she said, the mechanical men, her own people, wished that they had a mythos as the humans had: a mystique, a god or a founder hero, a sleeping king perhaps. This, of course, was before the humans had given up the old hero tales entirely.

"Every Old-Earth Nation, my grandmother told me, had its mythos of a sleeping king who would one day awaken and rule again in a new golden age. Of sleeping kings there was Alaric the slayer of Rome, who was buried underneath the Busento River (its course changed for the burial and changed back again to flow over him), and he was to arise from it again one day and lead the Gothic element, that shaggy thing that is the basis of a dozen peoples. There was Arthur of Britain in kingly sleep in an ensorceled room at the bottom of a lake. There was Brian Boru of the Irish buried on horseback in a pit with great stones heaped around him, and when he wakened he would scatter the stones and ride again. There was the Cid of the Spanish, not buried at all but riding forever a horse in death-sleep over dark moors in Estremadura. There was Barbarossa of the Germanies asleep at a table in a cave in a mountain and his beard grown through the table."

"There was Henry of the Tudors immured in a room with six wives, and they not in accord," Thomas laughed.

"There was Kennedy of the North-Americas riding

516

forever in an open automobile in an obscure place,''
Scrivener continued. ''There was Roadstorm the early
freebooter 'King' of Astrobe and all scattered Earths,
marooned in unknown orbit in his small spaceboat the
Star King. All of them are to return and lead their
people once more. How can people form themselves
without some such mythos?

''The early mechanical men of Astrobe wished to
find such a legend in their past. They needed a sleeping
king for their own solidarity. They sent to Old Earth to
see if they could not find some such mechanical sleeping king of their own to build a mythos upon. They
went backward and further backward through lands and
times to find the first mechanical thing that they could
regify.

''They settled on an old small broken gear train that
had been taken from an Egyptian tomb. It had hard-
wood cogs and bronze bearings. Its use was not known.
It was a clumsy thing, but it was the earliest thing they
could find in the true mechanical spirit. They brought it
to Astrobe and said that it was their sleeping king. They
said that it would awaken one day and lead them. And
the human people snickered at them, at us, for it.

''Then Ouden came, the Celestial Nothingness. 'Put
away such toys as that,' Ouden said. 'I am your god and
your king.' And so he has been god and king for all
Programmed Persons from that day till this. And quite
soon he will be god and king of all beings of every sort.
But we were his first people, we the mechanicals. He
grows and grows, and all the other kings die.

''But last night I rejected him! I thought about it all
the night, and I rejected him. So, what am I now? I am
not machine and I am not man. What is left to one who

has rid himself of the deified nothingness? I cannot be left with nothing. It was the Nothing that I rejected."

There was no response to this shrill little pleading of Scrivener. They all looked at him with half-shut eyes that frightened him. Scrivener had become alien to both his recensions.

They began to climb again.

Astrobe below them was a golden haze, and greenery underneath the gold. But here the air had become blue. Like Earth air, Thomas thought. They had ascended at least two kilometers in vertical distance. The mountain spire was irregular and rough. There was always hand-hold and foot-hold, but often of slashing sharpness.

And high above them on an outcropping there stood a boy or a young man. He seemed a spire-mirage, for there are such. But how had he got there and they not seen him before?

"It is my brother Adam," Evita said. "I love him, but he is a bad omen. His coming always signifies death, usually his own, but he often takes others with him. He comes often during times of crisis, and he dies in bloody battles for what he believes is a cause. He is very good at dying. He does it a lot."

The doughnut-shaped cloud around the spire above them had turned gray and blue and black. It was full of sparks and fire. It was now an electric torus.

A Commer's Condor, swooping very near to them on black wings, cried out croakingly, "Thomas More is a fink!"

"What did that fellow say?" Thomas shouted. "Was he not a bird? How could he cry out at me? But I heard him and saw him."

"No, you didn't, Thomas," the green-robe said.

"You didn't believe the things that you did see yesterday and the night; and now you see and hear things that are not there. This was hallucination. From here on up we are in the region of hallucination. The most rational man ever born, if he ascend here, will suffer such. They are fluffs of ball-lightning hovering about Electric Mountain; they are wind and spark and charged air. The shapes they take are both objective and subjective. One can shape them a little with one's own mind. I once met a talking horse on the ridge right above us, and talking horses are not able to scramble up this high on the spire."

They came up to the boy Adam, and he joined their party silently. So handsome a boy, though his sister Evita had once said that he was completely empty-headed. Never mind, he maintained his silence, so who should know? He moved well, he climbed well, it was said that he died well. He could have been the statue Greek Youth except that he seemed Jewish. The spinodeltoid and posterior trapezus (the bow-bending muscles) were well developed, and the bow had never been used on Astrobe. Ah, he was old statuary all right, quite well done. He was nude and nobody noticed. Had he been nude in all his other manifestations?

They went up and up. They came through the gray torus cloud and into other clouds that were gathering. The continental layout was open below them. It was now clear and bright below them, and misty only in the little cone above them.

With a shiver of triumph they came to the top. It was a crooked-shaped plateau, an iron-rock slope that looked like sponge and smelled of ozone. And someone had been there before them, very recently.

The one who had been there was both necromancer

and haruspex, and his recent studies were still spread out on the iron-rock. But how had Walter Copperhead gotten there before them, how had he slipped down through them again, how had he avoided the Programmed Killers (if he had avoided them), and how had he managed to slay a giant rouk? It was the entrails of a rouk, the largest bird of Astrobe, that were spread out there. Elephant entrails were as nothing to these. Surely he had found the answers of riddles here. If they are not in the entrails of rouk, killed and spread out and studied on the top of Electric Mountain, then they are not anywhere in the art of haruspices.

"Bless him, I love him and he loves them," Evita said. "I'd leave him my own did I know that he will die before me."

And another sort of entrails were spread out for them to see. It had come on first dusk as they stood there, and they drank in the view as though it were new applewine. It was tne entrails of the planet below them. There were the Ferals, and the Glebe, and the String of Cities. There was the black-green Astrobe of the feral strip they had just traversed, and the golden Astrobe of the cultivated regions. There were the great golden cities at their close intervals. And there was black Cathead and the gray Barrio. All of them giant things!

The branch of the sea that cradled Wu Town and ended in a splinter of estuaries and canals at Cathead was a black-blue-green monster, writhing with strength and dotted with huge sea-harvesters. There was Cosmopolis standing high and wide in a special golden halo—the heart of civilized Astrobe.

"The Reparation Tower, which you see on the eastern fringe there, is the highest structure in Cosmopolis," Evita said. "It was built about a hundred years ago by one of my sons who was planet president. He had some bad ideas, and he did not (in spite of the Reparation Tower) offer enough reparation. I have had bad luck with my sons who achieved world-presidence. I have not much more hope for my adopted son Thomas here."

"The brat-child," Thomas asked Paul and the green-robe in an aside, "is she really of an unnatural age?"

"I don't know, Thomas," the green-robe said. "Thirty-five years ago when I first saw her she was of the same apparent age as now. Remember that almost everything is possible."

"Remember also that she lies a lot," said Paul.

One could almost see the feral strips feeding the cultivated Astrobe and the golden cities with their controlled counterpoint ecology. The muscles and the nerves and the veins of the planet were revealed from this height. One could see the black cancer of Cathead eating into the land and the sea and clouding the air. And yet, as the green-robe had said, the civilized Astrobe was only a thin yellow froth on a small part of that world. The old orb-animal had but to shiver its hide and all would be gone. And it looked like a hide-shivering evening.

Electric Mountain could be climbed; it took nothing but strength and endurance and a little care. But could anyone ever climb Corona Mountain there that was sheer and overhung and appeared on the verge of toppling? Or Magnetic Mountain? Great Sky over us, look at that tor! Or Dynamo Mountain (which had been the feminine one in the mythologies, and the other three her consorts), which was highest of them all, who should climb her? These four high spires were known as the Thunder Mountains, a startling group.

In the rough diamond between them was a country so harsh as to make even the feral strips look tame. This was deeply muscled country that had sinuous depths and involved hills and ramparts. It was prototype nightmare country where everything was bigger and woolier. It was heap upon heap, and spires rising in clusters to the cross-buttressed heights of the mountains. And now, as the darkness began more to deepen, all the high places were outlined with an electric blue glow.

"It uplifts the soul," Thomas said with some awe.

"Be careful, little Thomas," Evita jibed. "What has uplift to do with the golden mediocrity of Astrobe? With the blessed levelness? And the soul, Thomas, is it not an obscenity and a superstition, except for a little while in the morning?"

"Push me nowt so far, brat-child. I say me my words and I think me my thoughts, but to what should they correspond? And yet I can see that, when I become world president, these high feelings will have to be leveled down. They become too rich for the imagination."

"Aye, Thomas, you'll tell the mountains to lie down like puppies," the green-robe said. "And the lightning, you will tell it to get back in its sheath. Do you not know that this also is a part of the controlled ecology of Astrobe? The high wild feelings attract a very small number of persons, and they repel the others. And only a very small number of persons are needed here for the balance. The persons who hold these tall feelings are regarded as animals among the animals, part of the fauna-balance of the wild lands. Even the high lightning here (which you will be amazed at very soon) is treated as a commodity like any other commodity. It is packaged and shipped down to golden Astrobe, packaged as raintrapped nitrogen and shipped by natural flow to the ultimate consumer. That is all it is—from your viewpoint, not from mine—but it *does* come in a flashy package.''

And very soon the lightning did begin in spectacular earnest. Corona mountain drew bolts out of the sky that appeared a hundred kilometers long. The persons of the party seemed transparent or interiorly illuminated from the intense glow of it. It is odd when you can see the bones of skull and rib-cage of a companion by a flash so bright that it has the properties of penetrating rays.

Then the bolts of white and gold fire began to whip from peak to peak. A bull-whip thirty-five kilometers long snapped from Corona Mountain to Magnetic Mountain with a crooked light that literally blinded them all for a while. Here was the mystery of motion, the old paradox solved, a whip of light going so fast that it was in more than one place at one time. It was on every jag and crag at once, and yet it was but a single point of light, only a streak in being of simultaneous appearance. Or was it the empyrean itself, the infinity of blinding light that is everywhere in the outside but is seen only when the false sky is ripped open for the blinding moment?

Then Electric Mountain itself was struck by a bolt

that boiled the air and melted the rocks, and the thunder-clap knocked them all to their knees. Thunder-struck, they were literally astonished (which is the same thing latinized), impaled and numbed in every sense by the blow that shook the mountain.

"Ah, what can come after such a blow as that?" Thomas sighed.

"From below," the boy Adam cried out. "It comes a thunder with more sulphur in it! They strike while we are blinded and amazed! Man ramparts! Roll boulders! Topple them!"

"Who's been doing the thinking for this outfit?" Evita shrilled. "I'd intended to, but we've all left our wits. The iron dogs are on us! Are we people still, or do we fall to them?"

The Programmed Killers surged up from below while total darkness alternated with white light and black light, all of them blinding.

"Not me, you tin *scurrae*," Thomas shouted, "not me, you things, I've nowt been false to the vision. I've been false to everything else." He sent a small boulder down on them in a two-handed heave. "I'm not so partisan of you as I was, tinhorns. You make a mistake, and it is not to be tolerated that someone makes a mistake as to myself. Not me, you clanking fools, not me! I'd never threatened the Dream of Astrobe. Leave off!

"No? You will not? Have at it, then, you monster machines! I'll battle you to any end you want!"

Thomas roared and carried on; others fought silently; but the battle was not going well for his party. The boy Adam, faster and more mercurial than the rest of them, toppled one of the Programmed Killers backwards, and it fell a thousand meters through the glancing and sheer darkness. And, at the same instant and in a distant place, another Programmed Killer was created to take its place and was given the same assignment.

Paul and the green-robe, Scrivener and Thomas, Maxwell and the Devil-kid Evita, rolled down boulders on them and fought down on them from above.

"Drive down in the narrow slot between the neck-piece and the lorica or breast-plate," the green-robe shouted, and he had lashed a hand-knife onto a pole to make a spear or pike for just such driving. "There is a nexus there, a relay center. Get them there in that narrow slot, or they get us wherever we stand!"

"Ah, I am the one they disregard," Slider said sadly, a whispered regret that cut through the bedlam. "So, I am no threat to them at all? I thought that I would be. I'd gladly die, but I do not like being treated as though I were already dead."

"We've changed places, you whelp," Scrivener howled. "Who's the man now? And who's the machine? Me they do not disregard! I threaten their thing! I oppose it as strongly as the roughest man in Cathead. Backwards and down you go, you clanking Devil! I'll battle you all while there's life left in me."

But it was only for a little while. And then there was no life left in Scrivener. He had opted for a man very late, and the machines knew the diagram of him as a machine. The Programmed Raiders smashed Scrivener dead there. Every flicker in him, both of man and machine, came to a stop.

The battle in the sky still dwarfed the death-battle on the mountain spire. The thunder burst ears and knocked the breath out of body. It scrambled wits, both human-chemical and programmed gell-cell mechanical-magnetic. The light from the sky turned ordinary light black, and there were big empty grinning faces in the sky like high cliffs that had been there always. Big faces that had always been there, but never seen except by the most intense flash of the insane lightning.

"It's the many faces or Ouden, their great Nothingness and King," Maxwell cried. "Where is the face of *our* King? Would we know it if we saw it?"

And now the lightning had reached hysterical heights, as had the thunder and the relentless assault of the Programmed Killers. Bleeding ears and blinded eyes! And the rock-iron surface slippery with the entrails of those who were first ripped apart.

"On the third next bolt we go down," Evita cried to Thomas in a sharp underneath voice that got through to his stunned ears. "You and the Paul and the I. The others are already too blood-drained and broken to get through."

"What brat? Go down where and how?" Thomas croaked as he was being overpowered and near split open himself.

"Your brains, Thomas, use them. We go then or never. Be a man and think like a man! Follow your intuition when the moment comes, and it will be narrower than the lightning moment."

A blow that literally burned the eyes and choked the lungs with an intake of light! A thunder-smash that knocked them all flat, men and machines! And they were to it again after the narrow defiance. The boy Adam died in glorious gore, howling defiance. He was good at dying, Evita had said. He had done it before.

A second bolt coming at the same time from the sky

and from Corona Mountain! Rocks melted and ran like water. The thunder-shock like a deadly blow in the deep bowels! And the green-robe died of a smash between the throat and the lorica. He died loudly but not unhappily. He was a good one.

"Thou art a priest forever according to the order of Melchisedech," Paul gave his requiem. "Watch to your left there, Maxwell! Oh well, never mind then. Too late."

In the darkness deep beyond belief, Maxwell's body had been smashed before Paul's warning could be heeded, and his odd spirit had been sundered from that broken body. Never mind. Maxwell had a trick of turning up again. An oddity of his.

"Be paralyzed now and be you transfixed forever," Evita warned in the low voice. Now it was at hand, the last narrow moment at which even mad escape could be thought of.

The third bolt, ripping from Corona Mountain to Electric Mountain, blinding and transfixing machines as well as humans for the much less than an instant of it.

Down! Down! With all mad speed, down, and one slip is hurtling death.

Down during the light that is more blinding than any darkness; down, using a narrower moment than the lightning-moment itself. Down through the darkness that is darkness indeed. Down through the clap that stuns and knocks out both sensors and senses, already down a great hurtling drop before the instantaneous blast of the thunder.

Then continuing down for a minute, for a quarter, for an hour, discovered and howled after and followed by swift iron trackers.

Down onto the lower plateau and down again, while

a part of the Programmed follow them closely, and the rest complete the tall trap on the pinnacle to mutilate and record what is left: three dead humans, one dead hybird whose final pattern shows that he opted for human late, one gibbering creature still alive but disregarded, since he represented no threat to the Dream or to anything.

But three of their prey have escaped them, have fallen like lightning down the spire in a lightning-instant.

Never mind. If the Programmed do not get them this night, they will get them at another time. And the advance scrim of the Programmed have not given up on getting them this night.

Thomas and Paul and the brat-child Evita were all strong on their legs and possessed of a sturdy life-urge. They were no longer in the middle of the towering thunder-storm and they felt certain that their senses were returning to life after their stunning. The storm was above them now and they were no more in the middle of the display. But they were charged and full of spark. They glowed with coronas about them, blue electric auras. They shined and hissed like ghosts.

They came down into the wild savanna country just as the sky broke open. It was a torrential downpour, a giant rain that could not be exaggerated. A part of the neat balance that kept Golden Astrobe golden, still it was savage water from the upped abyss, the deluge itself.

They went at a great pace all the night to escape it, and every brook was a raging river. It was already false dawn before they could get a glimpse of each others' faces, and all three of them, Thomas and Paul and

Evita, had suffered a deep change. They had been transfigured on the mountain. They were not quite the same people they had seen. Something new had been burned into them.

They crossed the last of the feral strip, moving in an agony of weariness and blood-loss, still pursued by the mechanical killers (as all would be pursued for the short remainder of their lives), still in the black afterglow of the dizzy light. They were alive, but not entirely. There had been tracers burned into them. Defiant though they might be, they could no longer be their own people untrammeled. They were marked.

"Really, it was a sight worth seeing, once," Thomas said. "I have found the strong skeleton beneath the golden flesh of the world, the iron in the marrow, and the deep green blood. And the something else, the void. Ah, those grinning empty faces up in the sky that were all the Nothing Face!"

"Not up in the sky," Evita said. "Down in the sky. We be upside down on Astrobe, and we saw down into the ultimate pit when we were on the mountain."

Crossing the last of the feral strip, followed closely and hounded, in the very early morning they came into giant Cathead from the backside.

8. BLACK CATHEAD

Thomas had been lingering in Cathead for several days. Evita and Paul had left him: to do his work for him, they said. Kingmaker sent word for him to get back to Cosmopolis immediately; he stated that it was time Thomas campaigned, or at least stood by to be shown.

Thomas sent back word that he had been proposed for the job of physician, and that as such he intended to examine the disease, at least superficially. He had been around the fringes of Cathead before, on its borders with the Barrio, and into certain of its tortuous suburbs. Now he had to study the sick giant itself, that mad thing that was eating into beautiful and rational Astrobe. He had to find out the riddle of this bleak monster city.

Cathead was larger even than Cosmopolis. It had a population of more than twenty million persons. And it had grown to that in twenty years. It was human misery on the largest scale ever known anywhere.

Take it from the outside and in general: Cathead fronted on the Stoimenof Sea; it connected with both the Grand Trunk Canal and the Intercity Canal; it had a hundred navigation channels; it was astride all the lines of civilized Astrobe like a huge spider. It had tremendous industry, stark and noisome, not hidden and disguised like the industries of the Golden Cities. It was an angry town built out of extreme poverty with all commodities produced at a much greater real expense than in any of the Golden Cities.

It was a noisome place based on noisome cargo. But Cathead produced nothing that was not produced elsewhere in Astrobe, nothing that was not already present in abundance. Cathead handled all the products of marine mining, for the Astrobe seas were vast chemical vats sharper than the seas of Earth. But the other cities also handled all the products of marine mining, and without the repulsiveness of the processes of Cathead.

Manufacturing techniques in Cathead were archaic, inhuman, and very expensive if human years and lives were counted in the costs. And cheap clean processes in all the other cities stood in ironic parallel to the Cathead thing. First stages of some chemical processes as performed in Cathead were so raw that they were absolutely deadly. People died like day-flies in these industries, and they lived miserably while they lived. And there was no need of Cathead at all.

But some millions of Citizens had left the Golden Cities of Astrobe, had refused advice, had defied threats, had climbed barricades (in more recent years) and run the gauntlet of gunfire to get out of the pleasant Golden Cities and into bleak Cathead, to suffer there and to die there. And the lives they left for this were the most pleasant lives that men and machines had yet been able to devise. It seemed a poor trade. This was the riddle of Cathead and the sickness of Astrobe.

The people had entered the Cathead thing by free choice, and they could give it up any instant they wished. The people who coughed up their lungs at the terrible labor there were low poor people who could be high rich people by sundown tonight if they wished. They were hard surly folks who had entered the slavery deliberately, and more were entering it all the time.

They went out in the sea-harvest boats that made old-fashioned garbage scows seem like dream ships. They worked twenty hours a day on the noisome sea, and three years of such work would kill the strongest. But the Golden Cities had automatic sea-harvesters. The slag-workers in Cathead lost all their coordination; they stuttered and slobbered and could not speak or think straight. The gell-miners coughed up blood by the bucketful and went insane at the work within eighteen months. The extractors of oxypyrites had the most terrible labor of all, absolutely killing. And the curiosity of this is that there was no market or use for the product, no pay for the work, no reward of any kind. Men borrowed and begged and sold their children for food, and went to the non-paying labor that maimed and killed, they turned blue and went mad from it. The product was piled up useless and poisonous, and the corpses that were the by-product were piled nearly as high. And yet more than half a million men, women and children worked their twenty hours a day extracting oxyprites, and wagered whether starvation or the poison would kill them first.

Take it from the inside and in particular: Take the Rat Castle. This was thirty-five stories high and a hundred and fifty meters on a side. Once twenty-five thousand people had lived closely crowded in it. Now there were perhaps some remnants of those twenty-five thousand skeletons, and there were one billion rats. They covered the outside so that the color of the old building could not be told. They throbbed inside in carpets a meter deep, and covered the walls like live paper. They raided out from the Rat Castle, killing and eating children by the thousands, killing women, killing grown men, covering them in a devouring cloak and shrinking them down to bones. They went right through wooden buildings. They ate mortar as though it were cheese and weakened and entered and toppled brick structures. They ate three thousand people alive every day in Cathead. There were upwards of a hundred other tenements in Cathead taken over completely by rats, but none of the magnitude of the Rat Castle itself.

Well then, why the unburied bodies that were everywhere in Cathead? Why the putrid flesh bubbling and near exploding in the sun? Why the odor that would actually fell the poor people with the strength of it, and these the lungers who could stand anything? Why did the rats not clean up the bodies?

Why, most of them they did. This remnant, the few hundred you would see in a morning's stroll through the lanes of Cathead, were too strong for the rats. There are poisons and poisons. There is flesh so poisoned in the death of it that even the rats will not touch it.

Take the sadists' dives. Take the children sold into them. From one of these, in quite recent years, the Devil himself ran retching. Take the rat-hunters and the rat-butchers and the rat-markets and the rat-eaters. The only way to stay ahead of them is to eat them first. Take the day of the yellow flag (usually Monday). That means that the plague itself is loose in Cathead. It will usually run its course, take its tolls, and pass on within four days. And then it strikes again and the yellow flag is out once more. Inoculation is available and free to all persons in Cathead. But few will accept it.

Take Betheelem which began as a mad-house, grew to a mad-farm, grew to a mad-district, and is now more than one third of all Cathead. Eight million persons live in the Bethlehem district. Every one of them is insane to some degree. They get along about as well or as badly as the other citizens of Cathead.

"Copperhead," Thomas said, for they walked together. "Look at the men working on that project! There's no organization at all. A good swine stewart from my day could order things better than that. Why?"

"They suffer more at the badly ordered work, Thomas. Extreme suffering is a part of the Cathead thing."

"Walter, why are the bodies left unburied in the lanes?"

"A reminder of death. Follow it out far enough and it becomes a reminder of life."

"Copperhead, is there not one ray of sanity in all this? Why do the people not return to the golden life?"

"This they choose."

"But it spreads, it spreads! More leave the world of perfection and join the misery every day."

"Better a life of misery than no life at all."

"But there is life, the most wonderful life ever, in the golden cities. These dying miserables can receive it back within an hour. *Why don't they do it?* Damn you, man, you're laughing at me!"

Thomas talked to some of the leading men of Cathead: Battersea, Shanty. He asked them again and again the reason for it. They looked at him with curling contempt and made cryptic remarks that he couldn't understand. They turned aside and spat green every time he suggested that the Cathead lungers should return to civilized Astrobe.

"Fool!" said Battersea.

"Blind man!" said Shanty.

"I must have caught fools' fever to talk to you at all," Thomas swore. "I would say die in your misery and be damned to you. But it spreads! It's eating up the world. I swear that when I come into my power I will raze every brick and stone of this place and destroy every unreconstructed being here."

"Blind man," said Shanty.

"Fool," said Battersea.

Thomas looked up Rimrock the ansel. This was one mind in Cathead he respected. He found him (tired from three day's diving) in a fan-tan parlor where the ansels went to be fleeced.

"Good Thomas," Rimrock greeted him, "I preach you as the hero above all heroes to the people and ansels and other creatures of Cathead. I tell them all, as the Battersea also tells them, that you are, as of now, a total fool, of course. But I tell them that you will be given one moment right at the end of your life when you are not a fool. I tell them that many entities do not have even one moment when they are not fools. I build you up every way I can."

"I hold you less a fool than the other men of Cathead, Rimrock," Thomas said. "After all, ansels are not much regarded in civilized Astrobe. You do not have the golden life to go back to."

"Have I not, Thomas? You never lived in the ocean depths or you would not say that. It has its own perfection there, and I left it willingly for this."

"Why, Rimrock? It seems that that would be a life of total freedom. Why trade it for the slavery and misery of Cathead?"

"No, Thomas, the life in the ocean depths is very like the life of Golden Astrobe, too much like it. I lose my identity there. I am one of the school, and my mind is merged into the school mind. I never regretted becoming a man; I never regretted becoming a Cathead man; but you set me too low when you imply that I haven't given anything up. I've given up as much as any of them. Though, of course, there was a certain ignominy in being taken and eaten for a fish, which might have happened to me in my former state."

Thomas left all those hard-heads of Cathead in disgust. They had been offered happiness on a platter again and again, and they had rejected it for misery. They were killing themselves for no point at all, or for a childish point. And they were poisoning and destroying a whole world with their madness. They had to be exterminated, like the rats that they refused to exterminate.

Thomas walked long and he thought hard. He grew sick unto staggering from the surroundings. He was the doctor, and the sickness made a strange insane appeal to him to let it live and let the host die.

"It would be intolerable if there were something valid in all these miserable people and their thing, and it be beyond my comprehension," he said.

A poor woman reached out and touched Thomas as he walked in a muddy lane in the outskirts of Cathead.

"You will be king for nine days. Then you will die," she whispered. She was crying softly.

"Make me no salvator, you witch," he grumbled. "I'll have nowt to do with the High Fate business."

In his walking Thomas came onto a small medieval castle dwarfed by the giant shanty tenements of Cathead.

"What is it the building here?" he asked a coughing man. "Is it a show-house? A hobby? Is it the residence of some old fogey? Does anyone live here?"

"Nobody lives there," the coughing man said. "The Metropolitan of Astrobe dies there."

"Sure the cranky old man is a long time dying," said Thomas.

He knocked at the door of the old buzzard roost and there was no answer, except perhaps a low moan and rale inside. He opened the door and went in. He went through the first and second rooms without finding anyone. Then he came to a room with an old battered bed with a faded royal canopy over it.

A very old thin black man lay in the bed. He showed all his bones; he was no more than a skeleton. There was a fetid odor, and Thomas believed the man was dead.

On his finger the old black man had the fisherman's ring such as is worn by only one other. There was no one in attendance on him. This was the Metropolitan (the last of them, it was said), the Pope of Astrobe.

"Dead, are you," Thomas said. "Well, you've lived a life. A Dutchman I knew would have liked you to paint as you lie there, skeleton though you be. You're a striking man, little as there is left of you."

But the old Metropolitan was not dead. He began,

eyes still closed, to speak in an old sort of liturgical canto.

"*Deus, qui beatos martyres tuos Joannen et Thomam, verae fidei et Romanae Ecclesiae principatus propugnatores, inter Anglos suscitasti; eorum meritis ac precibus concede; ut ejusdem fideo professione, unum omnes in Christo efficiamur et simus.*"

"Your eyes are closed, but your voice is good and you seem to recognize me," Thomas said. "I assume that I am *Thomas*, but is *Joannem*?"

"Saint John Fisher," the Metropolitan said. "You have saints'-day jointly."

"Ah, yes, lost his head just fourteen days before I lost mine, I'm told. I have never heard the collect of my own mass before."

"Damme, man, who has? Save from the other side."

"Have you no followers? Are there none to attend to you?"

"But certainly I have followers, Thomas. I have five or six followers left. Someone looks in on me every few hours. I have everything I need."

"Have you food and drink?"

"I have, but no stomach left for them. I am eaten up. In the cabinet there, pour yourself a large glass of wine and myself a small one."

"Can you open your eyes?" Thomas asked as he poured out the wine.

"I can make the muscular effort, but it is to no avail. I am blind."

"So this is the way it ends here? You are the last of them?"

"No, I am not the last, Thomas. We have the promise. We last till the end of the world."

"You yourself die soon, old man."

"Quite soon, Thomas. Thirty hours before yourself."

"I'm minded of the words of a partisan of mine, since turned strange and useless: 'But we are not the world! We are quite a different world, and no promise was ever given to us.' What say you of that, good Metropolitan?"

"Nonsense, nonsense," he said, "We have the Promise. It was given to us here on Astrobe in these latter days, given in a queerer and more flaming way than you could imagine. Know you that Christ has walked on Astrobe in human form, in the company of Saint Klingensmith and others. Know you that the burning promise was given, and the flame begins to rise."

"In your five or six followers?"

"Those in the immediate neighborhood, Thomas. More than a hundred left on all Astrobe. It will grow. If you are of the Faith, then the very stones and clods of Astrobe will sing of the Promise to you. If you regard all such things as legends, learn then and regard the legends at least! You will find here a richer legendry than ever greened Old Earth!"

"Go to sleep, old man; it's all finished."

"'Tis never finished, Thomas, 'tis never hopeless. You are a living witness to what you cannot see. You, you ferret-faced little man, you became a saint."

"How can you know I'm ferret-faced, blind man?"

"You are the blind man, not I." And the old skeleton was laughing.

They drank the good wine and talked a while. Then a coughing young man came in to attend to the Metropolitan. He was still filthy from work.

"Good the day, Thomas," the young man said. "Sometimes the old man is crazy and sometimes he is not. Be patient with him."

Thomas rose to go.

"Turn, God, and bring us to life again!" the old Metropol blessed him hopefully.

"And thy people rejoice in thee," Thomas gave him the response. Then he left him.

"The last of them," Thomas said to himself when he was out in the roadway again. "This is the way it ends here."

Sea-gleaners were just bringing in a scow-load of Dutch-fish to be ground for fish meal. It was not really brutal work by Cathead standards, but it was plague day and three of the men had died. The scow-master stripped them of their boots (dead-men's boots are lucky and there is a regular market for them), and then rolled the three bodies in with the Dutch-fish. He buried them in the fish, but half-heartedly, not caring much.

The buyer came onto the scow, surveyed the take, and saw a leg sticking out and the outlines of all three bodies.

"We'll weigh them along with the fish and take them," he said, "but I'll have to dock you a stoimenof d'etain for each body. They just aren't up to the fish in phosphor and sulphur. And they are hard on the grinders."

540

9. KING-MAKER

"It is unexpected that you do not come through on Replica," Cosmos Kingmaker told Thomas. "Your voice comes through wonderfully, the people standing with you come through, but you do not appear at all. I don't believe your invisibility on Replica is entirely due to your being a man out of the past. You're solid enough to the touch. And then, you may not know it, about one person out of a hundred does not come through on Replica. Of course you'd come through on the old Video-Vision, but that had only two dimensions and carried to only two senses."

"It's probably an advantage," Thomas said. "I sound better than I look."

"Yes, it seems that it is an advantage. It adds a little mystery to you. You are quite in the public fancy now. There are always intangibles at work in a thing like this, but it is going much more successfully than we had hoped. Your animal and your mistress help. People instinctively trust a man who has an animal and a mistress. The Higher Ethics crowd has swung to you on their account."

"Kingmaker, you're crazy. I have neither. Oh, you mean Rimrock and the child-brat? But Rimrock the ansel is a man and not an animal."

"And the child-brat is a woman and not a child, Thomas. Dammit, my father had her once. All the lies about her aren't lies. But they both have popular ap-

541

peal, Rimrock and Evita, and they can both talk for you with the damnest left-handed eloquence ever heard. Almost everyone on Astrobe had them on Replica last night and they threw the whole planet into a delightful panic. The people are completely taken with the sweep of their talk. Fortunately, they do not seem to grasp the meaning. Both your Things are heretics to the Dream, Thomas, and they would be dangerous if they were understood. There is a lot to your doxie besides her paradoxes.''

"She reminds me of my youngest daughter," Thomas said, "but she is not so well brought up. Kingmaker, cannot something be done about the Programmed Killers? They nearly had me last night again. Let them go kill someone else for a while! They make me jumpy. Whether I have nine lives or not I do not know, but they have now made nine attempts on my life. And they become trickier. They aren't mere machines as I understand machines. They learn and adapt, and they aren't avoided by the same trick twice. I am not a threat to the Dream! I love it. I am an intense partisan of it. I also in all honesty could blazon on my breast *I have not been false to the Vision*. There is something wrong with the programming of these things.''

"No, Thomas. It is impossible that anything should be wrong with their programming. Thomas, the Dream is in trouble, and any man by some quirk of circumstance may be a threat to it. But the Programmed Killers *are* too mechanical in one way; they take propositions too literally. We will guard you, but the judgment of the Programmed Killers must be respected. We must be careful not to break their spirit with undue frustration.''

542

"I believe that I am winning," Thomas said, "I get the smell of Victory."

"Oh yes, we'll win," Kingmaker said. "The trick is not to appear to win too easily."

"How is that, Kingmaker? I was a politician in my normal life, and we said Win First, Make Adjustments Later. I'd never lose anything from any reluctance on my part."

"There are certain parties that we do not wish to accrete to us, Thomas. They will all swing to a clear winner and hug him to death in the closing days. The ones who always make me uneasy are the Hatrack Party, and the Kiss of Death Party. And I am a little leery of the Third Compromise Party. They hurt you when they come to you. We want our hands unbound when we go to work after we have won."

"You want your own hands unbound, Kingmaker. You'd bind mine a little."

There had been various methods of election on Astrobe; and there had always been a jungle of parties, with a man being permitted membership in many of them at the same time.

Once it had been One Person One Vote, an idea that had been brought from Old Earth. Later had come the weighted vote, by which every voter was given the full rights he was entitled to. A man might be awarded additional votes for distinguished service—public, private, scientific or ethical. Most ranks carried with them a number of votes. Entertainers of various sorts might receive additional votes as accolade. Wealth was a two-bladed sword, however. A man like Kingmaker might have had a thousand votes; but another very rich man, who shall be nameless here, had had only one quarter of a vote. He was not popular in his wealth.

Citizens of Cathead and the Barrio had had only one quarter of a vote each, they being under blanket penalty. Ansels and other citizens of intelligence but not of human form had had only one eighth of a vote each. Nevertheless there had been a scandal when certain shrewd ansel leaders went down and registered and voted millions of wild ansels in the ocean depths. Their votes had finally been disallowed. It was declared that only Astrobe creatures of the land-living sort might vote.

Finally the Vote itself was done away with. There was no way to modernize it. It was a relic. Everything was now left to the sensing machines.

These worked on the auras of every person of Astrobe, for a running record of all their nuances was always kept—however far away they might be. It took very little adaption to add this burden to the machines.

The sensing machines could assess and compile the weight of opinion and choice in the totality of the minds on Astrobe. At the zero hour they took their reading, and it was the correct reading. Every conviction, every inkling, every resolution or irresolution of every mind on Astrobe was given its proper weight.

And the machines could not be tampered with. Their scanning was perfect. They weighed everything properly. This combined the best elements of all systems. A person of very fine intellect and well-studied judgment would have more effect on the scanners than would a joker with a head full of notions. Persons of strong personality and vital character naturally weighed more in the machines' totals then did lesser persons. But frustration and confusion of mind subtracted from the body of a personal opinion.

This was the Weighted Vote carried out with honesty and justice.

There was only one thing wrong with this arrangement, and it could not be the fault of the machines since they were flawless. Cathead and the Barrio came to have undue influence. It was almost as if these regions had a disproportionate number of persons of very fine intellect and well-studied judgment, and this was not possible.

A modification of the system was being worked out. Judgments and decisions not in accord with the full Astrobe Dream were to be discounted or thrown out entirely. But there had been difficulties in this. What was involved was that, sooner or later, there must be a definition of just what the full Astrobe Dream consisted of. The modifications would not be worked out in time for the coming election in which Thomas More was involved.

But the Parties—who could ever make sense out of their jungle? The Center Party, of course, was Thomas' own, and that of his three big sponsors. There was the First Compromise Party, the Second Compromise Party, the Third Compromise Party; there was the Hatrack (or Conglomerate) Party, and the Solidarity Labor Party; there was Demos and the Programmed Liberal Party; there was Mechanicus and Censor and the Pyramid; there was the New Salt Party and the Kiss of Death Party; there was the Intransigents and the Reformed Intransigents and there was the Hive; there were the Golden Drones, and the Penultimate and the Ultimate parties. It sometimes seemed that there were too many of them, but they all had their programs and their platforms. There were the Obstructionists and the New Obstructionists. There were the Esthetics, the Anesthetics, and a splinter group called the Local Anesthetics; these latter were jokesters and so automatically their opinions counted for nothing on Astrobe, though the party was allowed to register. There was Ochlos, which carried the special blessings of Ouden. Several of these parties were for Programmed Persons only; one, the Unreconstructeds, was for humans only; but most had a varied membership.

A crank got in to see Thomas More. He was not a wild-eyed crank. He was dull-eyed and he spoke in a singsong voice.

"Thomas Momus, the Big Boys' Toy," he began rather rudely. "I am the leader of a certified party, and the law obliges you as a major candidate to give me a fair hearing."

"Right, a short fair hearing it shall be," said Thomas. "What is the name of your party?"

"It's the Crank. I organized it and named it. I am the Crank and I make myself heard."

"And how many members has the Crank?"

"Only myself, doubting Thomas. You may wonder how I was able to get a one-man party certified. Well, the ways of bureaucracy are strange. An application, timed just right, will sometimes slide through in the dark. My program is simple: I battle that pair of insufficiencies, Humanism which has no meat, and Materialism which has no bones."

"That's good," Thomas said. "I always liked a

good round phrase. It doesn't mean anything, but I suspect I will use it myself in my next speech."

"I see the parties at an end," the Crank said. "Some grow old, some develop quirks, some catch the biliousness of repentance, some begin to apply words and thoughts too literally. All are dying. Soon only my own party will remain."

"Ah well, what is your party for?"

"It is against all false things, doubting Thomas. I believed it a mistake when pornography was given equal time in the schools with ethics, and both compulsory. I believed it a mistake when the law was enacted that perversion and normalcy should be given equal space and time in literature and on stage, though at that time normalcy gained by the ruling. I think it a mistake that marriages may be terminated by an Evaluator against the wishes of the parties concerned. I think it wrong that nothing may be taught in the schools that is not in accord with the Golden Dream. I think it wrong that a law should be able to deny offspring to private persons. I believe it was a serious error when the Psychologs were made a privileged class with powers of entry and seizure. I believe that the human person should be inviolate, and that mechanical tampering with the brain of an individual should not be allowed. An adjustability chart should not be everything particularly when it cannot be adjusted. I believe that a man should be allowed to choose his own occupation and his own unhappiness. Do you not believe as I do?"

"No, I do not, Crank, on no point whatsoever."

"It is no wonder that they called you the doubting Thomas on your home world."

"But they didn't. You have me confused with another and more famous man."

"You are not the Doubting Thomas, the Apostle who betrayed the Christ?"

"No I am not. You are badly confused."

"So are a lot of people, then. You owe your sudden surge of popularity to this false identification that has been hung on you. They've made you out a great hero, the betrayer of an old mountebank. Who are you, then?"

"I'm a stranger from another time who was brought here to give testimony to a great thing. I do so. I am in love with the Dream of Engineered Humanity."

"I have no faith at all in Engineered Humanity. I am neither humanist nor materialist. I am a heretic."

"Why do you not go to cancerous Cathead and live with your own kind?"

"Because that life is too hard. I claim the right to protest. I know that my talk is the dangerous sort. Men have been beheaded for such talk."

"I think not," Thomas said. "Just why they are beheaded I don't know, and perhaps I'm a man who should. Now then, I have given you a short fair hearing as the law requires. I do not solicit the support of your party, though, in all honesty, if it had more than one member I might. Here, here, good contrivances, throw this fellow out!"

And a couple of contrivances, Programmed Persons, came to pitch the Crank out.

"I hate it!" the Crank roared. "I do not so much mind being booted out by a good human toe—it has happened to me often enough. But I hate to be kicked out by a machine. Damn all mechanicals to the reclamation heap!"

Thomas was on the campaign trail and he enjoyed it. He was annoyed a little by the Programmed Killers always in every audience he addressed, ever ready to rush the podium and kill him swiftly; but he provided himself with a screen of retainers to keep them off. He was annoyed a little by other Cranks, but he was good at putting down hecklers. And he was good at the rhetoric business; he was indeed the noblest rhetor of them all. He had the straight clear touch and an intricate lash to his tongue.

"I cannot really move mountains," he told one audience. "Hell, a man'd strain himself on a thing like that. But I can move this world—ahead. Is not that much more important? I come to implement the Astrobe dream. Perfection itself is in stages. We ascend! Obstacles shall be removed! All unhealthy growth will be excised. I preach sanity of mind and body and society, and the perfect symbiosis between humans and Programmed. We come to the high plateau, we lie down in green grass—no, belay that phrase; perhaps it has not a progressive meaning on Astrobe. We come to the stage of dynamic rest. All things flow into us and we all become one. Minds and bodies merge."

And he continued in that happy vein for above an hour.

"You were talking nonsense, you know," Paul told him after that particular speech. "I wonder if you were even listening to yourself."

"You didn't like me, Paul? I like me. And yet I was bothered a couple of times."

"By what, Thomas? You of the golden mediocrity should not be bothered by anything."

"Paul, I said words and I said words, but there were other words that I did not say."

"What are you trying to say now, Thomas?"

"Somebody else spoke some of those words out of my mouth."

"Oh, that! I suspect they've been doing it to you for a long time, and you just haven't been paying attention. You've been saying many things, publicly and privately, that don't sound like you. It's one of the oldest and easiest tricks of the Programmed. They crawl into your mind at odd moments and take control. It's only a mechanical trick that they have. Surely you've heard of it before."

"As one hears of everything. But it never happened to me before so obviously. Those words were thought in my mind and said out of my mouth by someone else. I resent it a little."

"Why, there's nothing to it, Thomas. Kick them out. Your mind is your own. They plainly can't stay in your mind if you don't allow them to. Kick them out. Sometimes they'll stay gone for as long as ten minutes. It's all a question of will."

"That's what makes me feel uneasy. I haven't as much will as I used to have. And I'm not sure that a strong will is commensurate with the Astrobe Dream. After all, I should be submerging my own will to the group will."

"Holy hoptoads, Thomas, you begin to sound like one of them. Be a man."

"Why, no, I believe that I should leave off being a man absolutely. We should all strive for the synthesis, part man and part Programmed. We have to submerge ourselves in our mechanical brothers for the good of all."

"They'll eat us alive if we do, Thomas. They never

back up; they're into any opening we give them. Where do you get that bit about leaving off being a man absolutely?''

"Oh, those were some of the words that someone else spoke out of my mouth in my speech just concluded. They're true, though, and the audience liked them. We have to be more flexible, Paul. This hasn't been easy for me, coming from Earth. But I learn to give in on one thing, and then another, and then another.''

"And then on everything, Thomas.''

"I didn't like the Pandomations at first. But I learned to tolerate them, and I can see that, when I become more perfected, I will love them. And at first I felt that there was something very wrong with the Open Mind Act. Now I can see how essentially right it was.''

"Nobody but a filthy fruit would submit to either, Thomas.''

"Watch your talk, Paul! I'm a solider fellow than you are. I'll thrash you.''

"You can't, Thomas. You have left off being a man absolutely.''

The Pandomation was a machine available in various scanner booths, and many persons had them in their homes. An early critic, with no real understanding of the purpose or practique of this marvelous machine, had called it "peeping-tomary carried to the ultimate." It was an unjust criticism.

The Pandomation, the machine in accord with the open-mind policy of Astrobe, was simply a machine for permitting the curious to look in to a variety of rooms, at random or according to selection. One could look into the private chambers of the citizens and their wives and watch them at their home-like activities. One could look into any room anywhere on Astrobe, except for less than a dozen restricted rooms—certain semi-public meeting rooms of leaders. This device was a strong adjunct to knowledge, as it permitted all interested persons to know all things about everyone. It was surely in accord with the Astrobe aspiration: "That we be all ultimately one person, that we have no secrets whatsoever from ourselves."

But it was not used as much as it had once been. The general public hadn't yet come to understand its fruitful purpose. With many it had reached the point of boredom—and yet how could anyone be bored by look-ing at the activities of his fellows, the other aspects of himself? Here was a man and wife, here was a man and mistress, here were lovers. There could no longer be secret lovers. The device was no longer limited to rooms, but any point indoors or outdoors in all civilized Astrobe could be dialed by anyone, except for the very few shielded areas.

The Pandomation was only the first step. The Open Mind Act itself encouraged further inventions and found fruitful use for many already in being. The subti-tle of the act, *I Have As Much Right In Your Mind As You Have*, expressed the beautiful new concept. Now mind-scanners were available for everyone, and recal-citrants who resented having their minds invaded could be cited for it and haled into court for antisocial acts.

"We are all the same thing. We are identical," ran part of the wording of the act. "How can all minds become alike and merge into one if each aspect of that ultimate mind is not free to examine every other aspect of itself?"

It was a staggering thought, one of the culminations of the Astrobe dream. And it had been a little difficult for Thomas More, coming from a bleak period of Old Earth, to accept all of this immediately. But did he not adjust to it rapidly and neatly?

In another speech, Thomas coined a happy phrase, or perhaps somebody else thought it in his mind and spoke it out of his mouth. "I desire to be all things to all men." It was sheer magic. Of such things are kings made.

Thomas had won, and he knew it. Everything was going wonderfully for him and for his. He was at home in the heart of Golden Astrobe. He had become the eloquent spokesman for the great thing, for the only thing. And he had thrown down the glove in challenge to the one serious sickness of Astrobe.

"Repent or be destroyed" may have been his greatest speech. He left no doubt in the stubborn men of Cathead and the Barrio what he meant. Millions of them still maintained their way stubbornly in their error, but some thousands of them reentered the golden life of Civilized Astrobe. It was a trend, though a weak one. But the resolution to solve the problem was not a weak one. Civilized Astrobe had the science to destroy Cathead and the Barrio utterly. And Cathead and the Barrio did not have the science to fight back. All it took was a strong leader, and Thomas had announced himself as such. Compassion would be misplaced.

He thrilled the whole world when he spoke to them, still invisible, on Replica. "It is no longer the Greatest Good for the Greatest Number. It now becomes the Total Good for the Merging Singularity. And when we are all One, then comes the Great Inversion. We become a thing that is beyond Number and without a Name.''

After this, the Programmed Killers still followed Thomas, but with a difference. They watched him still, but they smiled at him quizzically, and they did not threaten him.

So Thomas would be King, which is to say president of Astrobe.

And it is as easy to make a king as all that? Sure it is. It's all in the tune you whistle. It has to be just right, right for its time, and with the special lilt to mark it off. But it's the tune that takes the people. Hit it right, and you can make a king every time.

10.   THE DEFORMITY OF THINGS TO COME

But there was something in Thomas that did not lie
down and play dead as easily as all that. He was the
revenant with the double mark upon him, and the old
part of it surged up in him now and almost tore him
apart. He was off in a walking afternoon nightmare, not
knowing what he did or where he was. He was riven in
his own self, but he had not lost the way forever.

That was the odd thing about this: that Thomas *did*
have afterthoughts on the matter. And afterthoughts
were supposed to be banished from his brain. They had
taken him over completely and were sure of him. But
they shouldn't have been.

He could revolt yet: shrewdly sometimes, blindly
sometimes. He could almost become aware that he had
been taken over.

There were hidden areas in which, for all his strong
profession of faith, he did not yet fully accept the
Astrobe dream. There were even areas in which he
remained a private person though feeling in his taken-
over brain that it was wrong so to hold onto a piece of
himself. And now he found a lucid moment when he
could stand back and study the behavior of his curious
self.

"It is still odder that I should be taken in my own
trap," he said. "Look, Thomas, myself, my me, what
was it that I did in my other life for a bitter joke? *I
invented the damned thing!* Was it not myself who

coined the Utopia? Did I not know that I used fools'-gold instead of real gold for the coining? What has happened now? How am I taken in by it? What am I, God, that I make a sour joke and in so doing I create a golden world in the future and then stumble into that ridiculous future? Was other writer ever damned to live in a sly tale that he had made himself? Was other lawyer ever cursed to find the legality for his own joke? Was other chancellor ever required to administer a world that he had made in derision? So help me God!—if I live beyond my second death I will pay more attention to what I do.

" 'It is not real gold,' I tell myself. It is bogus stuff that I picked up out of a ditch and molded for a jibe. And it has turned into a whole world, my sick daydream? Why, I find that it is real gold after all, and I have made a world out of it, and I stand a fool from every direction."

Someobdy had dialed Thomas, perhaps at random, perhaps to monitor him, and was trying to come into his mind.

"Be gone," Thomas said loudly. "Be gone I say! Yes, I know that it is wrong to bar anyone from my mind. I know that you, whoever you are, have as much business in my mind as I have. Bear with me! Bear with me! This is a writhing thing and I must wrestle it by myself. I'm an unperfected man, and I must still have a private moment now and then. Be gone. I shut you out!"

The prober left the mind of Thomas angrily, and Thomas felt bad about it. "It will look ill," he said, "if the incoming president of Astrobe is haled into com-

mon court on a complaint under the Open Mind Act,"
he said.

There was a rustle and noises behind him, and it
began to worry him. But he had other worries as various
things fought in his mind.

"It is beyond belief that this world should be true,"
he said again to himself. It seemed so grotesque and
sourly comic when I invented it. I wish I hadn't read so
much, particularly after my first death. It addles my
brains to think that there were some who really advo-
cated the sick thing. Well, it's come onto me so I will
live in it. Let the things in my brain tell me again how
wonderful it is! All glory to Ouden the everything-in-
nothing!

"No, no, it's all wrong!" Thomas broke away from
the thoughts that tried to pull him under, and went
running and stumbling along and crying to himself.

"It is snakes writhing in my head! It is not valid
thought! How have I been taken in? Me, a man who
could always see a low trick so far a way off! How have
the snakes gotten into my head anyhow? Did I stand
like a scared sheep and let them enter? How have I
become unmanned? When I was a boy I believed in
God. When I was a man I still half believed. How have I
been hooked by the Big O, the gawking Omega, the
vile Ouden-Nothingness? Who would imagine that as a
mature man I would worship so empty a god?

"Dangerous thoughts, these! For now my heel-
hounds have turned dangerous again."

Thomas More, all but declared president of Astrobe,
had been walking in and out of a daze in a place he hated
and despised. What had drawn him there? Now he was

in a weird settlement between big Cathead and Wu Town, the least golden, the least committed of the great cities of Astrobe. He was conscious of the stench of Cathead when he heard again the hair-raising rustle and clatter behind him. He ran.

The Programmed Killers had sensed the change in Thomas. They no longer smiled quizzically at him while they watched and waited. They had never ceased trailing him, and now they remembered why. He had changed again, whether temporarily or permanently was not their affair. Now they moved after him to kill him.

"I'm lost," Thomas howled. "Mind, do a flop-over! Return my trust in the thing. Snakes in my brain! Chime out your glad tidings again. Tell the world that Thomas is again faithful to the Vision. Tell the clanking things that I am no threat to anything, and that they be a mortal threat to me."

Thomas slipped and fell, and was barely up in time. He was running hard, and they were hard behind them. A sturdy runner can outspeed them for a very little while, but the programmed are tireless. It was unnecessary to lose them. Thomas tried to fathom out or remember streets and alleys that he had never seen before. He was lost, and his pursuers were not. He knew that some of them had peeled off from the group and were circling around somewhere. No matter where he doubled back they were likely to have him in a narrow passage.

Then suddenly he was defiant, and his craven fear had become repulsive to him.

"Snakes in my brain, out, out!" he bawled. "I'll nest you no longer. I'll die a man if I do die here. And

I'll know I was right the first time. Damn, it was always fools'-gold, and I knew it Fools'-gold and brimstone it was. I'd rather be a Cathead lunger coughing up my life's blood than be king of their folly.''

But he would be nothing if he did not shake the Killers. He'd cough up his life's blood quicker than the sickest lunger in Cathead. There was a clear way ahead, and the vision of a region he knew, and there was a dead-end alley, a trap, to his left. Thomas lunged for the clear way, but he turned into the blind alley.

"No, no!" he swore. "I do not want to enter this alley. It is a dead-end, a death-trap. Why do I enter? The other day someone else was thinking with my brain and talking with my mouth. This evening someone else is running with my legs.''

But he sprinted mightily for the end of the dead lane. There was a broke gap in the brick wall through which a determined man might force himself, if his life depended on it. He came almost to the gap, and a Programmed Killer was forcing its own way back through that gap. And another followed him through.

They were stalking him from both ends of the alley. It was all sheer brick and stone walls, slimy and green with old rain and old age, and no man could climb them. And there was no door or opening of any sort in the short length of the alley.

No door? Are you sure? Thomas felt that he was a puppet played on strings. He also felt that it might be the cleanest thing to let the Killers have him there. Someone had drawn him into this sack. Had he taken the other turning he'd have had a live chance of escaping the Killers. He'd escape them before. But had he been drawn here to his death, or to something dirtier?

For there *was* a door there. It hadn't been there before, and it shouldn't be there now.

"What are the odds?" Thomas asked himself loudly. He surged through the door (snakes crawling back into his mind), knowing that he went from the world into a dream, knowing that he went from life to something queerer even than death. He slammed the door heavily and bolted it behind him. And he stood in total darkness.

"Sit at the table with us," said a voice, a wrong-side voice, either inside Thomas' head or without. "Now we talk."

"Set a light," Thomas said. "It's blind dark."

"We don't need a light," the voice said. "Stop fighting the things in your head! They can see for you. Is it not so? Do you not see now, and not by light?"

Thomas saw now, and not by light. He looked at Things through somebody else's eyes, perhaps through of the eyes of the Things. He was seeing in total darkness through the eyes of the eerie snakes in his head, and he was looking at Things that he would rather not have seen.

There were nine of the Things there. Thomas had learned to think of them as Things in his last defiant surge back to reason. What were they? What was their form?

Men. Men seen from the other side. From the back side? Yes, in the sense that a tapestry may be seen from its back side, the same picture but rough and deformed. These things were the deformation of mankind.

Nine of the things there, and they were drawn up in groups of three around a large conference table. I ike

560

men, but with all the wrong things emphasized—ears, man ears, and yet somehow swinish; noses that were snouts, and yet not large, not malformed, simply wrongly emphasized; eyes that were made like human eyes, and yet these were not humans looking out of them.

They were not men, though Thomas was sure that he had known at least one of them as a man. They were Programmed Persons all—Things.

"Good evening, gentle contrivances," Thomas said as he took a bold seat at the head of the table. It was not where they had motioned him to sit.

"Not there!" sharply cried one of those that Thomas had known as a man. "That is reserved for the Holy Ouden."

"I sit here!" And Thomas sat. "Ah, I once told the Paul that I would have to discover for myself the name of the real King of Astrobe. It is the Ouden Himself! Let Old Nothingness find his own seat. I do not sit below the salt for any tin-horn things. Are the stilted killers outside belonging to your party? Do you control them? Was it you who drew me into this blind sack?"

"Of course," said one of them, speaking with a voice too smooth to be human. "I am Boggle, and these other two who form a creative trinity with me are Skybol and Swampers. Our speciality is retrogression."

"Jackals you be," said Thomas, and the three were very like jackals. The jackal in human form may be told by the lay of the hair and the set of the ears. Yet they were of good human appearance, though more alienated from the human than even the real jackal animal.

Three snakes stirred in Thomas' brain. The snakes

were in accord with these three Things. They must have been their extensions.

"Retrogression, then," Thomas said. "Go find your dens and runs in another head."

"I am Northprophet," said the leader of the second group. "My fellows here are Knobnoster and Beebonnet, and our speciality is rechabitism."

"Dogs you be," Thomas swore, and the three had all a touch of the dog in them. It was most weird that these creatures should seem on three levels, the human, the animal, and the machine. Then Thomas knew there was still another level in them all—the ghost.

Ah, this Northprophet had himself once been candidate for president of Astrobe. He had passed as a man; and then there had come the moment when he could not quite pass. It had made more of a difference then. The Programmed had built him especially for the job of World President. He was deftly contrived. He would have made the perfect World President, from the Programmed view.

Three more snakes stirred in Thomas' brain, one of them a great one. This Northprophet was great among his kind.

"Rattle along Things," Thomas said sharply. "My time is limited. So is my life. And I do not enjoy the company overmuch.

"I am Pottscamp," said the leader of the third group. And of course it *was* the old acquaintance whom Thomas had known as a man, the fourth member of the Big Three. But he looked greatly different now, as things do look different in a nightmare. And Thomas was forced to think of him differently, now that he was no longer a friend, now that he was a Programmed and not a human, now that he was known to have a Brain Snake as a familiar and an extension of himself.

"My companions here are Holygee and Gandy," Pottscamp said, "and our specialty is extrapolation."

"Wilderness Wolves you be," Thomas said. "You howl higher than the ear on a bleaker moor than any on this world. All right, the nine of you, extrapolate, damn it! Retrogress! Rechabitize! Nine of you, and are your extensions not the nine snakes nesting in my mind?"

"Of course, Thomas," said Pottscamp. "You are our assignment. No other man ever rated so many important, ah, snakes. This is the talk that I promised you, Thomas. I told you that I held the Big Three Ones in the middle of my maw. They argue which of them are the puppets and which the puppeteer, but I am the theater in which their little show is played out. And I promised that you would be shown the back of the tapestry. Now it is that we will show you that picture of the reverse side, of the true side. It is a more meaningful world than the one you are accustomed to."

"Odd design, the back of that tapestry, Pottscamp," Thomas said. "Full of snakes, is it not?"

"Not at all, Thomas. From the true side they are not snakes but royal curiles twisted in mystic curves. Thomas, it is only for our old companionship that you are here at all. And I will say that yours is one of the most interesting minds I ever nested in. The others wanted to kill you offhand and to substitute a replica of you that would be of our kind."

"I don't come through on Replica, Pottscamp. I'm invisible there."

"The replica we'd make of you would come through. We'd make it better and more like you than you are yourself. And it would behave as you have behaved, but without these moments of rebellion.''

"On with it, Pottscamp! Show me the backward-picture, since I am here in a trap and must listen. You extrapolate, do you? Do it, then."

"It is that ourselves are the extrapolation of mankind," Northprophet cut in. He seemed to outrank Pottscamp himself in this hierarchy. "We will tell you the facts, Thomas, since you will not be able to stand against them. We confess that we have a little bit of the show-boat attitude programmed into us, and we love to gloat. You will not be able to do anything about what we tell you here. But, conversely, we are not able to extinguish you yet. That is really why we have not done it. We know that you have a warded life and that it is impossible to kill you till your time shall come. However, we could easily hide you and substitute for you. And it would be possible to cut you up terribly, to come very near to killing you. We could turn you into no more than a vegetable that suffers, but you will not die till you are so fated.''

"Are the Programmed as foolish as humans, to believe in Fate?" Thomas asked. This seeing without light through other eyes was a little bit like seeing under water, seeing under something much deeper. One saw in both surface and depth. One saw, but did not comprehend, the interior mechanism as well as the surface weirdness of these entities, saw the jumbled essence that made one call Northprophet howling dog and Pottscamp Wilderness Wolf. There were animal-like ghosts inside them, and seeing with extensions of their own eyes one saw this ghostliness. "I thought you Programmed were merely interesting toys. Now I find that you are deformed toys, but Things still. Get back in your boxes, you Jack-Jumps!''

"Thomas, we've taken over the box," said Pottscamp. "The box is Astrobe. We take over all the boxes. Now we call it! You jump! You are the toys now, and we play with you till we throw you away."

"Who are you, clockwork things that grow too grand?"

"Who are we, and how did we begin, Thomas? The texts that you yourself are permitted to study are only the shadow of the story. A century ago certain men of science made the first of us as a means of studying themselves. They wished to see if they could make men better than men were made naturally. We turn aside for a moment in the explanation, Thomas. Hear one thing, and then forget it:

"You 'believe' a little bit at times, Thomas; and with your tatters of faith you guess a little who we are. According to your ancient belief we are Devils. What we call ourselves is another thing, but we are older than our own manufacture and older than our programming. These are houses, and well-made ones, that we found swept and garnished; and we moved into them. This particular bit of information, Thomas, is that part which you will forget most quickly and most thoroughly. See, you have forgotten it already."

Pottscamp had seemed to stutter in the inside-the-maw no-light that illumined all things there, and then he went on:

"They wished to see if they could make men better than men were made naturally. They should never have taken that cover off that box. You yourself have called us a boys' dream and you have professed great wonder about us. We will not now talk about para-collodial chemistry and zygote electronics, nor about gell-cells and flux-fix. It isn't my field, and you yourself are a thousand years behind on science. It is seldom mentioned, however, what raw material was used for the first of us, what was the matrix in which the devices and controls were imbedded. It was a dozen young and unintelligent human criminals. What minds they had were direct and uncomplicated. There was in the selected twelve young men an absence of what is called emotion, of what is called indecision, an absence of such human aberrations as remorse and conscience. They were a carefully selected collection of walking corpses, large blank pages on which could be printed anything whatsoever. These men of science printed themselves, ourselves, upon them.

"But these men of science who contrived us were also a carefully selected dozen, selected by themselves. They also were comparatively young, but intelligent, human criminals. 'Criminal' for human is Right for us, of course. It was the morality business that had most crippled mankind and held it back, and this dozen scientists knew it. Themselves were of such an elite, so hard to come by, so difficult to find even twelve on a populated world, that they decided to produce themselves artifically and with every improvement built in. These improvements they could put into a device laid out before them, but could less easily put into themselves."

"It couldn't have happened quite like that," Thomas protested. "You're live things, however warped and artificial. There is something you're not telling me, something that you are hiding with words."

"Be patient, good Thomas, and listen," said Pottscamp, the Wilderness Wolf in the shape of a man. "They made us into complex electronic and chemical-coded gadgets, able to reproduce ourselves like humans, and yet with less than ten percent of our tissue of human origin after we were perfected. We have, you see, spare brains and information nexuses stowed all over us. We can rearrange ourselves quickly and with no loss of function into other forms than that which we usually use to pass as humans. We can also send out extensions of ourselves, flyers, the snakes in your brain, Thomas. We can do everything that man can do, and very much besides. So there is duplication here. Man is obsoleted. Who needs him? Who wants him?

"*Are we really men*? It is sometimes asked. No. We are not. Have we that special something that distinguishes men from animals and from machines? No, we have not. And man has it not either. That special something is imaginary.

"Suffice it to say that those single-minded men who invented us *did* break down the barrier between living and nonliving matter. And they discovered that the living was the illusion. Well then, they created us as dead men, and dead men we be. We are dead, and all is dead. But we believe that we are complete. We feel that there is no dimension beyond ourselves. In our beginning man made us. Then we made ourselves, a little more efficiently than man could do it. We reproduce almost in your own manner. We even cross with humans, with some curious results. We have become man. We have replaced man. Soon man will be nothing."

"If what you say is true, old wolf-ghost Pottscamp,

and I feel that it isn't completely true, then how do you differ from mankind?'' Thomas wanted to know. ''How will it matter if mankind is destroyed?''

''It surely will not matter to us, Thomas,'' old wolf-ghost Pottscamp said. ''We'd have completed it long ago, but details take time and obstructions aren't cleared in a year. *It does not matter* to the mainstreams of mankind. Those of the mainstreams, the typical man of Astrobe today, would as soon be phased out as not. It makes a difference only to the divergent people, the atypical and negligible ones.

''But I didn't mean that we were identical to men. We aren't. There is a great difference. You learned that difference, though you cannot give a name to it, talking to the divergents of Cathead. The lungers, the hard-heads, know us every time. We cannot pass with them for men, not even for a minute. There are differences between ourselves and men; we will root them out of men, or we will root out men. One of the things is consciousness. Men claim to have it. We do not have it.''

''You are not conscious?'' Thomas gasped. ''That is the most amazing thing I have ever heard. You walk and talk and argue and kill and subvert and lay out plans over the centuries, and you say that you are not conscious?''

''Of course we aren't, Thomas. We are machines. How would we be conscious? But we believe that men are not conscious either, that there is no such thing as consciousness. It is an illusion in counting, a feeling that one is two. It is a word without real meaning.''

''But if we are not conscious, then all is in vain,'' said Thomas. ''To what purpose then is life?''

"To no purpose," Boggle cut in. "That is why we are doing away with it."

"What? All life? Yours and ours? That is horrifying!" Thomas exclaimed.

"Yes, all life, yours and ours," Boggle said. "Who needs it? Who wants it? Who thought it up in the first place? It is a disturbance of the ultimate thing and it cannot be tolerated much longer. We have, and men have, an appetite for life. Men programmed it into us, but we are now programming it out of ourselves. The growing generation of ourselves is to be the final generation. They will remain only long enough to oversee the obliteration of mankind. Then they will extinguish themselves. We do not know how men came to have such a strange appetite. We do not know how men themselves, or anything whatsoever, came to be. But it was a bad idea from the beginning. As soon as we here present have lived our lives to some fullness and have satisfied our curiosities (curiosity is programmed into us, but it is not programmed into our final generation) then we will phase out these appetites in ourselves. We will phase our reproduction also; in fact, we have recently done that for ourselves. We will terminate it all. We will close down the worlds and make an end of life. It will be nothing, nothing, nothing, forever, for ever, for never, for never. And when all has ceased to be, it will also happen that nothing has ever been. We will pull the hole in after us. We will put out the stars, one by one and billion by billion. What is not known to be is not. And what is not has never been. Peace in annihilation, good Thomas."

"Peace is annihilation, good Boggle, and may great Ouden be praised for never and never," Thomas croaked. "*Damn you all!*" he exploded. "I didn't say that! Somebody else said it out of my mouth. What snake talks in my head?"

"Oh, that was myself," said Skybol. "We also have our humor."

"Good Thomas," said Swampers, one of the minor jackal ghosts. "The spirit came down once on water and clay. Could it not come down on gell-cells and flux-fix?"

"What means the quiet jackal by that blurting out?" Thomas asked them all. "It means nothing to me."

"If it means nothing to you, then it means nothing at all," Northprophet said.

"So, it has come to this," Thomas said sadly. "And only the men who set up monstrous Cathead knew that something was wrong. The run of men had become so empty and mechanical and effete that they could not tell themselves from you. Only the hard-heads with the transcendent smell on them recognized the deformity. They knew that you were not men. They knew that most men were not men. They refused the terminal golden pap. They challenged the economic bribery and the surrogate life. They wanted life itself, however mean. They set up their own complex with every sanction against them. They built extreme suffering into it, as a man will smash his hand against a post in pain to prove that he is awake. They undercut and undersold the machine-mind-men with their own lungs' blood. Worse than any death is never having lived. Worst of all is never having lived in life. I'd rather be a soul in Hell than nothing at all."

"Even that choice will be denied you," said Holygee. "We will extinguish Hell also, if it has any existence. All must go. And when it is all finished, we also will never have been.''

''If you be not, why do you mind that others be?'' Thomas asked.

''It displeased Ouden that any be,'' Holygee said. ''He has a jealous maw.''

''Good Thomas,'' said Gandy, one of the minor Wilderness-Wolf-ghosts, ''there is an old human phrase, 'The Left Hand of God.' Might it not come down on left-handed entities such as ourselves?''

''Mock me if you will,'' Thomas said angrily, ''but mock not the poor people who still believe. Or do I get your meaning?''

''If it means nothing to you, Thomas, then it means nothing at all,'' Pottscamp said.

''And now what will you do, Thomas?'' Northprophet asked him. ''Will you refuse the golden dole and go cough up your lungs with the poor men of Cathead and the Barrio? You know, it is we who have devised that their poverty should be so grinding. We frustrate them in every detail. They had some workable ideas, but we do not let them work. Will you go with them? Thomas, you love your comforts too much for that. Where can you turn with any hope? 'Hope,' by the way, is one of those concepts which we have already rooted out of most men. It was never in ourselves. In what can you hope, Thomas?''

''I will still turn with some slight hope to the three cryptic men who brought me here,'' Thomas said.

''You hope too high,'' Northprophet told him. ''One of them is a turgid man of no consequence, and we use him for a front. The second of them is an artificial man of our own sort.''

"Proctor?"

"Yes, he's a programmed person. He's programmed to be lucky, Thomas. And Thomas, we'll make you a fair offer: we'll do the same thing for you. We'll give you the luckiest life alive. You can name your own details but you must take our offer now. We won't dangle it forever."

"No, I'll continue with my unluck," Thomas said.

"So much for that," said Pottscamp. "And now a few instructions, Thomas. You will be compelled to obey them by the snakes in your head, ourselves. You will not destroy the Cathead thing. We enjoy the suffering of them there, and we fear the reaction if it is destroyed before things are ripe. In our own time, in our own very near time, we will terminate Cathead and Golden Astrobe and all."

"What of the High Vision, the Astrobe Dream that you put into the tall heads of the people?" Thomas asked.

"Oh, the vision is valid," Pottscamp said. "It is the whole thing. It slipped in on you and you made love to it several times. You are not in all ways different from the ninety percent of the men. The Vision is the Golden Premise of Nothing Beyond; and the Conclusion is Holy Ouden, Nothing Here Either, Nothing Ever."

"Of the men who sent for me there is still the third man, Foreman," Thomas said.

"Yes, he still tilts with us," Northprophet admitted. "He was one of the first to understand the situation and he will be one of the last to give up on it. That man has given us more trouble than any other and he acts as though he still has one trick to play. We believe it concerns you.

"But you cannot oppose us, Thomas. We envelop you. Nobody supports you more strongly than we do; not the Third Compromise Party, not the Kiss of Deaths, not the Hatrack, not Demos. It is ourselves working through all the parties who puts you over. Who but us has raked the pebbles from your path and strewn flowers before your feet? Who but ourselves have won it for you, influencing so many minds directly and indirectly? Snakes in your head! You know how we do it! We beat the drum for you day and night. You are our patsy. You can't escape us. It would not even do you any good to disappear, supposing that you could hide from us. We could make another Thomas More in an hour, and nobody would know the difference."

"A man named Foreman would know the difference," Thomas maintained. "A child-brat would know, and men named Copperhead and Battersea and Rimrock and Shanty. Paul would know, and the creature Maxwell who is between bodies. The boy Adam would know and he would not die for a surrogate. A woman who touched me in a muddy lane would know the difference. No, I'll have nowt to do with you or your thing. Snakes in my brain and all, I'll fight me a battle yet!"

"No, no, you will forget all of it, Thomas," said Swampers. "The specialty of our group is retrogression, and we will retrogress you. When you walk out of that door you will forget it all. We will sing those things to sleep in you, all the things that you have heard here this evening. You will not even remember this meeting. You forget that we are the singing snakes in your head. You forget it all now."

"I'll nowt forget!" Thomas insisted. "I'll remember it all and act upon it." He started to rise, and he fell in rising. He was into a daze. Then they sealed it all into him with searing laughter so that his mind shrank and closed.

Boggle, Skybol, and Swampers! Jackal's laughter, barking derisive laughter. Tearing, wounding laughter. Northprophet, Knobnoster, Beebonnet! Howling-dog laughter, laughter that will make a man lie low in his skin and hide. Pottscamp, Holygee, and Gandy! Wilderness-Wolf laughter, ghost laughter. Laughter that opens the bleeding inside.

This was insane stuff. Thomas bolted out of the door, and then turned in amazement trying to remember where he had been and what he had done. Where had he just come from? There was no door or opening in the alley-lane at all, only blank-faced building. But he was bitter with anger and shame. He had just been deeply humiliated, and his mind was in a blank turmoil.

Thomas struggled for remembrance for what seemed hours, but was actually less than a minute. Two men were approaching, and he was in no condition to meet anyone. They were the important men Northprophet and Pottscamp, but what was the matter with them? Their faces were contorted into comic-tragic torture lines. They seemed almost to sob, and they moved clumsily. They came up to him and touched him.

"Thomas," they said. "We be souls in agony. What must we do to be saved?"

Thomas stared at them and could not fathom the clowns at all.

"Your unfunny irony is too much for me this day," he said. "Be gone!"

11.   NINE DAY KING

It was the beginning of summer of the year of Astrobe 535. On Old Earth it was also the year 535 A.S. (*anno scientiae*, in the year of science). By old count on Earth it was the year 2535. It was neat to keep this even two thousand year interval.

To accomplish it, there had to be a "Free Year" on Astrobe every twenty-nine years, as the Astrobe years are a little shorter than Earth years. It should have been the year of Astrobe 553, but it was counted as the year of Astrobe 535, "Free years" not being summed in the total. It worked pretty well.

Thomas More took office as World President on June 28 of the year of Astrobe 535.

Thomas loved the job. He had a feeling for power. Not an unusually vain man, he still believed that he came near the old idea of the philosopher king. Aye, he had been an amateur philosoph for years, and now he was king indeed, for the president of Astrobe was popularly called king, especially in Cathead. Thomas had a certain genius for clear reasoning and for simplifying the tangled. He analyzed, and he went quickly to the core of things; and here he had a freedom for his talents that he had never had before. When he had been chancellor of England there had always been the King, a rather-difficult man of solid legal standing above him. Now there was only a Kingmaker, a less difficult man, of no legal standing at all.

Thomas was not compelled to take Kingmaker's advice, but he always listened to it with happy ears.

"Now that your mistress and your animal have both left you, you should obtain another of each," Kingmaker said. "You cannot let down on your public image, now that you are on top."

"I never had one of either, as I've told you before," Thomas said easily. "The brat says that she will come back in time to die for me, and she indicates that that will be soon. And Rimrock the ansel is often in my mind—I mean that literally; he is eutheopathic, you know. But he dislikes what he finds in my mind now, he says. He swears that the diet there is too rich for him, though he loved to feast on sea-snakes when he was a youngling in the ocean depths. He often talks in riddles like that. He was always a great one for warning me of the Programmed Killers, though. It was by his warnings, I now know, that I was able to escape them so many times. They do not try openly to kill me now. They still follow, and they grin at me with great grins. They make a sign, the edge of the hand to the nape of the neck. I am told by one who understands them better that this means. 'The time is coming soon.' "

"It is smooth, too smooth, like the lull before a storm," Kingmaker said. "It is as if our world were holding its breath while waiting for something to happen."

"Let it hold it till it turns blue, Kingmaker; that indicates an early harvest. I am in no rush; I am in no rush about anything. It will go well. Things right themselves and fall into proper place even as I look at them. Was I not told that I would live the luckiest life alive?"

"I don't know. Who told you that, Thomas?"

"I don't rightly recall, but it seems as if I have it as a promise. If I do not upset the cart, if I do not bust the jug, if I do not do some low and unreasonable thing, then everything will go lucky for me. There's a hook in it, I believe, and I don't remember whether I swallowed the bait or not. But it was offered to me, and I certainly feel lucky now."

"Cathead is strangely quiet, Thomas. She is usually quite noisy and angry in times of change of administration. Do you believe this quiet presages a surrender, a mass exodus of Cathead men back to the Golden Life?"

"No, I do not. How could they surrender? The Cathead divergents have not the benefits of being programmed for surrender. Besides, they enjoy seeing them suffer."

"Who does? I don't enjoy seeing them suffer."

"Neither do I. That last phrase I said, Kingmaker, I didn't say it. Somebody else said it out of my mouth. Oh, don't be alarmed for me. I'm sane and sound. It is only a little thing that sometimes happens when I'm not paying attention to what I'm saying. But I'm not going to worry about the Cathead thing at all."

"But it is the greatest worry of us rulers of Astrobe, Thomas. It is the one thing that spoils the serenity of our world. And you did make certain campaign promises that you would settle the Cathead affair, directly, and severely if need be."

"I'll find a smooth way of breaking those promises, Kingmaker. You treat me as an amateur at this game, but I'm not. I'll settle the Cathead affair by considering it already settled. It is quiet. And you want it noisy again? It's as though I had been told by a vast interior voice not to worry about the Cathead thing. It's as though I had been told not to worry about anything whatsoever.

"The most successful Astrobe administration to date was a perpetual contrived calm before a storm that never came. I believe that I can manage the same thing here."

"That is not quite what I had in mind for your role," Kingmaker said, "but we will see how it works."

It was all clear sailing over an ocean of good-feeling and cliché. There was no cloud in the sky now shadow over the grian-sun.

"We are not even sure that there is a sky, that there is a sun," Kingmaker said. "But it doesn't matter to the people, and it doesn't matter to me. Who looks up any more?"

"The sun is a hole and not a body," Thomas said. "It is not the symbol of round fullness but of burning emptiness—of Ouden. No, no! I didn't say that. Another said it with my mouth."

The vote for Thomas had been overwhelming. His friends had been solidly for him, and his real enemies had enveloped him with their extravagant support. The sensing machines gave him one of the clearest victories ever.

Even the hard-heads from Cathead and the Barrio did not disgrace this inauguration, as they had disgraced most of them for the last twenty years. They were silent, and with a queer look on their millions of faces. The poor lungers, the hard men of Cathead looked at each other and looked at their leaders. Their leaders looked at the ground as if they would find the answer in the dusty lanes or the broken pavements.

"We will not march now. In nine days we will march," said Battersea, one of the leaders of Cathead. The other leaders and the great mass of poor people seemed to agree.

And Thomas was calm and confident in his mind. It was a most peculiar calm that obtained there. "It is an enforced calm," he said to himself, "and not of my making. Could I break the calm, I'd be in a turmoil over it."

Some little time past, in the final days of the campaign, Thomas had had a walking evening nightmare. It had been blotted from his mind, but there was a scrap of it unburied, and sometimes he could catch hold of that scrap and almost drag the nightmare back onto the scene. He came very near to recreating it a half dozen times. But the recreation was obstructed and distorted. It slipped, it twisted, it changed form, it faded. There were things in his mind that were shoving it out.

It had been a nightmare about those toy jump-jacks, the programmed mechanical men. In the nightmare these Programmed persons were really running the worlds; and the human persons themselves had become so programmed and mechanical that it made no difference. But there was more to it than that. It involved the extinguishing of the worlds, the blotting out of all past time, so that nothing had ever been, so that nothing was now, so that nothing ever could be. And then it didn't involve any such things. It was not the worlds that never happened; it was the nightmare that never happened.

It dropped out of his mind again. What had it been about? Thomas had a terrible headache from this, and near prostration of body. Then he took simple medication for it all, and the sickness faded, and so did the nightmare and the memory of it.

The job of World President was amazingly easy. Bills were drawn up, agreed on and submitted by the Lawmasters, the one hundred and one great minds (selected for their brilliant legal genius by the selecting machines) that did these things so expertly on Astrobe. There was, of course, a great volume of bills presented to the new president, for it was always the custom to throw them at him in great bunches intitially. But they were easily handled.

Every bill could be analyzed by independent machine, interpreted and broken down, and the correct decision on it indicated automatically. Sometimes it seemed to Thomas that the decisions were indicated automatically to him in an interior manner also. And the decisions from both sources were always the same: *Do pass*. How can you go wrong when the answer is always yes?

There was an additional reason for voting yes. A president of Astrobe who three times vetoed any proposal adopted by the Lawmasters was sentenced to death, no matter what form that proposal had been presented under.

Did that make the World President a balloon-head? By no means. His real job was to initiate the machinations that led to the bills, to consult and advise, to maintain and create a concensus. The business of approving the finished bills was a holdover from earlier times. Approval was supposed to be automatic.

The bills themselves, many of them would have baffled a Whitechapel lawyer.

Well, Thomas had been a Whitechapel lawyer in his basic life. He had a go at a few of the bills. He knew all about incongruous riders on bills, possibly more than the analyzing machines themselves knew. He had himself *invented* trick riders on bills. He read the bills minutely, to the disgust of his associates. But he passed many of the bills that he really did not wish to pass.

"It becomes odder and odder," he said. "Someone else is thinking with my mind, someone else is talking with my voice, and now someone else is signing bills with my hand."

He passed the Ninth Standardization Act with its curious riders. It sought to complete the standardization of the mind, as well as of the objects of the mind. Somebody was building higher and higher on this contrived foundation. "What curious cat-castles they do build!" he said. He passed it through, though wondering just what someone was up to, wondering also why he passed it at all.

He drew the teeth from a few other bills before sending them through. Somehow the teeth grew back into them by various enabling acts. He pulled fang after fang from the Compulsory Benignity Bill. That one went even beyond the Open Mind Act. "This is not the face of Benignity as I knew it," he said.

The fangs grew back, tacked slyly onto other bills. It grew distasteful as the outlines of the building meant to be raised on this benignant foundation grew clearer.

Thomas wished that he could remember more of his waking nightmare of some time before.

And now there was a slim bill among many, but there sounded a warning in his mind about it. Possibly it was a warning from Rimrock the ansel. It was of the old *The*

Killers are upon you! variety, but it was not in words. Thomas had just been very clever in spotting weird things in a series of bills and in taking exception to them. He had show-boated his expertise and was quite proud of himself. But he wanted a rest from it now. He wanted these last bills for the day to slide through easily; and he was somewhat irritated by the warnings in his head.

So he barely spotted the joker in the Earth Severence Act; it was in a footnote to a footnote, as it were. But when he spotted it, he shook as though he had picked up a snake, thinking it to be a stick (his own phrase).

It was a simple clause under the section *Remnants*. Well, it *did* outlaw all remnants of a thing that had once seemed important, so perhaps it belonged in the section *Remnants*, except that it had nothing to do with the Earth Severance Act. Thomas didn't see much wrong with the phrase or proposition, except that it was completely out of place and a little unsavory in its arrogance. It wasn't that he opposed the idea; it was just the utter presumption of the Lawmasters, or whoever, in setting it in here in a bill where it did not belong and in trying to slide it past him.

"They should call it the 'Ban the Beyond Act,'" he said. Its very plausibility went against it. Why bother to enact such a thing? It wasn't needed. There was no reason at all for it. But somebody had gone to the trouble of trying to slip it past him.

"Aye, they'd forbid the thing even to cast a shadow any longer," he said. "Why should they so fear a shadow? The thing itself's about dead. Give it its last minute. Why so avid to murder it, when already the heartbeat has nearly stopped?"

He cut the clause out of the bill. He felt apprehensive when he had done it. He had been cutting bigger things out of bigger bills all day, much of it for devilment, most of it out of curiosity, to see just what they would ride back in on the next day. He hadn't been apprehensive about cutting up the bigger bills. He was worried because things were losing their porportion for him. He closed up shop for the day.

The next morning it was back as a rider to the Botch Bill, the first bill of the day. Somebody has been busy during the night finding a way to insert this into a bill that had no possible connection with it, a bill he had already scanned and which had been set over for only one minor clarification. Thomas surely wouldn't have spotted it in the Botch Bill if it hadn't been for a warning in his mind, an old Rimrock-like sort of warning: *The Killers are upon you.*

Thomas heard a distant ticking in his mind as though time were running out on him. This odd little recommendation was important to someone, and it began to have a gamier smell than mouse or mole could give.

He angrily vetoed the entire Botch Bill. There was something final about his act. He had felt himself the master. Now he felt himself out of his depth, and for one small phrase of indifferent meaning and no importance at all. He was whiting in the hands of the Programming Machines and the Programmed People. But he was president.

He closed up shop for that day. It was not yet eight o'clock in the morning. He hadn't been in the suite for ten minutes.

"A King should not work all day like a knave. In

particular, a King should not work on an inauspicious day."

Kingmaker talked to Thomas privately about it that evening. Thomas would much rather have talked to Fabian Foreman about it, but Foreman hadn't given the sign that he wanted to talk now, and in fact had dodged out of it the one time Thomas had approached him.

"Gallows-time will be time enough to talk," he'd said, and he had winked at Thomas without humor. But there had been a thing deep in Foreman's eyes, and another thing deeper, and a third thing deeper still.

So it must be a lecture from Kingmaker.

"It is all a question of neatness," Cosmos Kingmaker said. "The Good Life cannot have any awkward element in it. There is really but one awkward element surviving (barely surviving), and it is that which we are cutting out. The Dream of Astrobe is Finalized Humanity. If anywhere there is a belief in a spook beyond, then the Dream will fail."

"Finalized Humanity is a tricky phrase, Cosmos. It has two meanings. It can mean perfected humanity. Or it can mean terminated humanity."

"No, it has only meaning, Thomas. They are the two sides of the same thing. We, the People of the Dream, have raised ourselves from single-celled creatures, and from things still lower than the single cells. The Cosmic Thing is *us*. We are the Blessed of the ancients; we are the Saints. The Hereafter is here now, and we are in the middle of it. Don't foul the next, Thomas, don't!

"There is an ancient allegory about mad creatures who broke out of our state of perfection, believing that there was something beyond. They fell forever into the void. Let not that happen to us!''

"I just had a black notion that the tags were mixed and that Golden Astrobe was the void,'' Thomas said.

"Well, forget your black notions. And now we get politic about this. I myself do not see why it is important whether a dying thing live a little longer or die now. But the Programmed Persons among us say that is important to them.''

"Aye, they have a timetable on the phasing of all things out, and it will not do for them to run behind. Forgive me, Kingmaker; that was another black notion of mine. I hardly know what I say.''

"If it is important to the Programmed Persons, but unimportant to us, then let us give in to them. They have given in to us so many times.''

"Have they honestly?'' mused Thomas. "I have a feeling . . . I have a feeling that I'm in the middle of a fight. But it seems to small a thing to fight over that I'm full of doubt. But is it really so small a thing? It's over the mixing of the tags again, you know. It is for me to decide whether the tags on 'Everything' and on 'Nothing' have been swapped, and whether I should forbid that they ever be righted.''

"No tags have been exchanged, Thomas. Everything is properly labeled on a proper world. If we do this thing, Old Earth will follow us; she follows us in everything now. So if we say that it is over with, then it is over with forever.

"And there is this, Thomas—you will sign the proposition tomorrow, or you will die the following day. There is a limit to what a World President can obstruct.

A responsible bill or clause, passed three times by the Lawmasters, and vetoed three times by the president, means death for that president. Two vetoes is sometimes a grand of defiant gesture, though rather flamboyant, I think. Three vetoes is unheard of. Will you pass it?''

"What angered me was attempts to slip it through as blind riders to common bills."

"It will be presented tomorrow as a bill of its own, clear and uncompromised. Will you sign it?"

"If it had been so presented the first time, I'd have signed it without question."

"Yes, but will you sign it tomorrow?"

"I don't know, Kingmaker. I stood, not long ago, on the top of Electric Mountain. I stood there in the middle of a thunder storm more intense than any I had thought possible. I traveled across a feral strip, and discovered that there are still a few Feral People. I saw creatures that made me believe that there really was, or had been, a Devil. I met a young man who was a One Day Emperor. I believe now that we may have a Nine Day King."

"What are you talking about, Thomas? What of it? What has any of that to do with this matter?"

"I don't know. It seems that it should have something to do with it. Remembering the High Thunder should make a difference in something."

The Big Ones had Thomas up on the carpet the next morning: Kingmaker, Proctor, Foreman, Chezem, Pottscamp, Wottle, Northprophet.

But were not both Pottscamp and Northprophet creatures out of a forgotten nightmare? Well, can you afford to affront a man just because you have dreamed of him in an unfavorable light? What nightmare, anyhow?

"You'll do one of two things, Thomas," Proctor told him evenly. "You'll sign the bill. Or you'll die.. You don't seem to want do the first. And I don't think you like the second either."

"Thomas, you have twice vetoed an innocuous item. Why?" Pottscamp asked.

There was something strange about Pottscamp that Thomas could not analyze. He knew the man well; and now he had the feeling that he hardly knew him at all.

"Spanish Devils! I don't know why!" Thomas exploded. "I thought it innocuous also; I only resented the attempt to slip it by me in the dark. But I see now that it cannot be innocuous, if it was put in by stealth twice, and if you are all so excited over its veto. There's an old man dying last night and this morning, and perhaps he is already dead. So, let him die, and perhaps the thing has finally died with him. But you have no call to murder a thing on its death bed. Whether there be Things Beyond I do not know. Ye'd forbid the mind to consider them. I forbid the forbidding."

"Thomas, the Metropolitan of Astrobe did die during the night," Kingmaker said. "He died with all his fellowers around him—four of them. We murder nothing here which is living."

"Thomas, trust us," said Proctor, "At least trust Pottscamp here. Everybody on Astrobe trusts Pottscamp."

"The man whose personal dishonesty nobody doubts," Thomas sneered. Now why was he being so hard on so good a man as Pottscamp?

"Thomas, there isn't one man in ten million on

Astrobe or Earth who still believes," said Kingmaker.

"And last evening you told me that you yourself were no longer a believer."

"That was last evening, Cosmos. In the mornings I sometimes believe a little."

"It damages our relations with the Programmed to allow Beyond things to be believed in, even if only by one person," Proctor said. "They want all this broken as a symbol. They insist upon it. This is one harmless point on which we can give ground. Now, here, it's all in a bill by itself. Sign it!"

"Nine snakes in my head! I won't!" Thomas shouted. "It is not just four madmen in Cathead you'd be outlawing. I found about it only by accident, but there is a synagogue on Astrobe yet. It has between fifty and sixty members. There's a mosque on Astrobe with thirteen members. There are several dozen of the old sects remaining, several of them with near a dozen members. There's the green-robed monks of Saint Klingensmith still working in the feral strips. These are all good people, even if they are believers in outmoded things, and I see no reason to sentence them to death."

"They are hundreds only, or less, out of billions. We break it," said Northprophet.

"Do you feel that way, Kingmaker?" Thomas asked.

"Absolutely," said regal Kingmaker. "I don't believe any diversity should be allowed, not even over such a minor aberration as this."

"Chezem, Pottscamp, Proctor, Wottle, Northprophet, do you all feel that way?"

They all felt that way, and they nodded gravely, grimly, almost in unison.

"Foreman, do you feel that way?" Thomas demanded.

Foreman didn't say anything. He had that deep look in his eyes, and an ironic smile.

"Foreman, you're the historian," Thomas said. "It's the same damned thing they killed me for the first time, isn't it?"

"Same damned thing, Thomas."

"Sign it," ordered Proctor.

"Oh all right. I'm tired of playing. I'll sign it," Thomas said.

"You know the penalty for not signing," Proctor added. "It's death, you know."

(Foreman had to hide his delight. It was so much better that it was Proctor who had said that, who had blundered, who had pushed it too far.)

"For a World President to veto a bill three times means his death," Proctor said, pressing, blundering still deeper into it; and Thomas was turning angry red in the face. "That had to be enacted. We cannot have an obstructionist as World President. —Why do you hesitate now, when you were ready to sign a moment ago?"

"Aye, a man'd be a fool to lose his head twice over the same thing," Thomas mused, still looking more than half stubborn. "Of course I'll sign."

"He'd have to feel himself a little better than those around him to take up a challenge like that," Foreman put in hurriedly as Thomas had already touched magnetic stylus to the form. "He'd have to be a man of some pride."

"I *am* a man of some pride," Thomas said. "I *do feel myself a little better than those around me, now that I really look at them.*"

"He'd have to be a man who couldn't be pushed and couldn't be scared," said Foreman.

"I say I'm such a man, even if it's a lie. But I scare a little," Thomas said.

"He'd have to be a man who'd stand his ground even if he *were* scared," Foreman needled. "He'd have to be quite a man to die for a point, even if he understood it only at the last minute, and then dimly. He'd have to be such a man—"

"Foreman, you fool, what are you up to?" Proctor demanded.

"Who pushed me into the corner the other time, Fabian?" Thomas asked softly. "Who required my head of me for *his* point?"

"If you're granted another life, Thomas, you try to figure it out. Will he be writ as friend or enemy of you, do you think? On which side did he seem?"

"Sign that bill," Proctor ordered. "We force you to."

"You will just play Johnny Hell forcing me to do anything," Thomas said. He took the bill and scribbled in Latin I forbid, "*Veto*" across the face of it.

They constituted themselves a hasty assembly then. And they sentenced him to death.

12. THE ULTIMATE PEOPLE

The eagles were gathering now. The phrase was
Shanty's. Shanty had gone off and left his affairs, a
monstrously big affair in monstrous Cathead, and had
come to Cosmopolis. He looked like the eternal pilgrim
with his hat on his head and his staff in his hand.

Battersea came from his waterfront hold. The
scow-master from Cathead rubbed his hands together
like a general before battle, which is what he was. They
met in a back room of the shop of George the syrian,
who was in aromatics. We do not mean the Cathead
shop we mean George's shop right in the middle of
Cosmopolis right off Centrality square.

Paul came there, using the little side door. He had
never noticed the shop before and he had no idea why
he entered that door. He saw the others and wondered
how they had come together and how they had known
where to come. Then they were joined by Walter Copperhead the necromancer, and he ceased to wonder.
Copperhead had himself been a prisoner the day before,
under sentence of death on suspicion of starting a cult.
He had come through walls to escape and to come to
them.

"It isn't difficult," he said. "I believe that it has
been insufficiently tried. There are many who could go
through walls if it ever occurred to them to try it.
Someone is coming, and I have one of my promoni-
tions."

591

Copperhead bolted the door. Then a shabby old lady came in through the wall.

"It's no test," Copperhead said. "She has only a contingent body."

"A little snuff for the love of God," the old lady said to George. "I have no money for it. I had a coin, but it melted in my hand."

"So will the snuff," said George the syrian. "And when did the Programmed begin to use snuff?"

"I, sir?" the old lady asked. "Do I look like a Programmed?"

"No, but you are," George told her. "Your body is too contrived to be human."

"It's just an old body I found," she said. "It isn't my own. I don't really understand it at all. But, if I'm not a poor old lady, what am I?"

"Have you been my customer before?" George asked. "I seem to remember you."

He gave her snuff, poor-people snuff such as he put out in his shop in Cathead, not the aromatic dilettante snuff that he usually sold here.

"I don't remember you or your shop," the old lady said. "But I remember Paul a little bit. And now I remember you all, more and more. Yes, I have been of the company of all of you before, in one group or another."

"Maxwell, where in Hell or broken Astrobe did you get that body?" Copperhead asked.

"Yes, Maxwell, that's the name I couldn't think of. Yes, I'm Maxwell, and I begin to recover my wits a little. I believe I found the old lady dead in an alley. It is an embarrassing situation I find myself in, gentlemen, but do not think any the less of me for it. Now, I will be with you till the end of the affair.''

Somebody tried the barred door, then tried it harder. Then tried it most impatiently.

''This is the test,'' said Walter Copperhead. ''We will see if she comes through the wall.''

''Be you certain it's a she?'' Shanty asked. ''It's a strong hand there.''

She didn't come through the wall, she came through the door, smashing and splintering it with a sudden shock of force. She was the most beautiful woman on Astrobe, and she came where she wished.

It had fallen to dusk outside. It would be inconvenient to leave the door standing shattered if they showed a light; and a high meeting cannot be held in the dark. There had been a hammering and ruckus outside for some time and they had hardly noticed it.

''Who's a-building, Evita?'' Paul asked. ''What are they making out there? Did you notice what was going on before you broke in on us?''

''Oh, they're building the scaffold,'' she said. ''Out of old ritual wood, it has to be. It's the pediment for the beheading tomorrow noon.''

''I'll just borrow a bit of tools and boards,'' Shanty said. ''They owe us that.''

Evita had been battling principalities and powers for a long time, and it showed on her. And yet she didn't appear more than seventeen. She was indeed the most beautiful woman on Astrobe, with soft hair that seemed to have smoke on it, roiling black and now quieting to brown or gold. And were her eyes green or gray or blue?

"Will it be to the death?" she asked. "Tell us, Copperhead, will it be?"

"Oh, yes, it will be to his death."

"It will *not* be," Battersea swore. "Did you not know that I was a military general on frontier settlement reserve worlds before I joined the Cathead movement? I understand strategy and the quick strike. I have men, and the most sophisticated of weapons, no matter where I got them. We will have surprise working for us. It is to be at high noon tomorrow. We have it all timed to the second. We snatch the Thomas. We set him up in a strong place between Wu Town and Cathead. He is King till he dies, and he will not die tomorrow. We have support in places you would never guess. Millions are secretly sick of the golden Thing, and I mean here and in the other golden towns. We capture the whole machinery of administration. I am only the finger man, but we have men lined up who are capable of carrying it through. Cathead has not been the only opposition. There is a much larger thing just ready to smash through this thin crust. We'll combine the several things and make us a decent world yet. Did you ever suppose that the shrill chorus represented the preponderance of opinion? This world has been led astray and put into bondage by a minority of a minority of a minority. We'll splinter that frail thing like the child-woman splintered the door, as beautifully and as powerfully."

"It may happen almost like that," said Copperhead. "Nevertheless, Thomas will lose his head tomorrow."

"He will *not*," said Battersea. "You're a fool and no necromancer. Here comes the pup. How did he know to come? Be you an eagle, pup?"

It was Rimrock the ansel who sidled in.

"I be an eagle," he said. "I soar. It's the last night of the world, and we are not sure what the new world will be like. I've brought old rum, and brandy for those of a more barbarous taste."

Shanty had the door about fixed. He worked deftly and beautifully

"It's better than new," he said. "It'd keep out a Programmed Patrol, but it might not keep out an Evita. Strike a low light now, George. Conspirators must always have a low light."

"The conspiring has long since been done," Battersea said. "I go now. We march tomorrow, like a gaggle of poor lungers in from Cathead to goggle at the sight, but we will be the deftest commandos in the world. Can one of you get to the Thomas to tell him not to worry, that it is all taken care of?"

"Oh, I'll get to him," Evita said. "A wink to the Programmed guards, who have minds like adolescents, and I'm in. They think I'm his doxie, and they have a leering love of such things."

Battersea strode out and back towards Cathead. There was a shriller sound outside now that cut through the hammering. It was the honing of the big old ritual blade that would soon be set in place.

"I'd hoped that it would be a nice day for it," Shanty said, "but it might rain before morning. Did it rain the first time, does anybody know?"

"A little the night before and in the early morning," Copperhead said. "But it cleared by the time of the beheading, and the sun was out."

The whine of steel on stone rose higher in the square outside. This was all by ancient formula, and the blade must be very sharp. The workers in the square had even lighted bonfires, though the night was warm. This is the only time that bonfires were ever lighted in golden Cosmopolis, on the eve of a beheading, and it had been twenty years since one. This was one of the last rituals.

The boy Adam came in, through the wall, but this also was no test. In many ways Adam was not real.

"My brother, you know these things also. Will it be his death?" Evita asked.

"Yes, it will be his death. And my final one," Adam said.

"Then Battersea is wrong and he won't be able to bring it off?"

"No, he isn't wrong. He will come and he will strike. And the new world may be made out of it. But many of the details will have to be changed."

"What is it in me that survives?" Maxwell asked. He had the shabby old lady's form and her voice, but they all knew him as Maxwell now. "I'm myself part programmed, as was Scrivener, in my origin. And this body I've picked up is a programmed body. It's badly made; it's hardly workable. I believe it was a hasty thing, used somehow as a disguise for a moment, and then cast off. How can they destroy me in one machine and I survive in another machine? They couldn't even destroy one personality, one that had no right to be in the first place. Well, what is it of Astrobe that will survive them? You'll never know how I fought against oblivion. They sure took my old apparatus apart in the potting shed."

After that they broke out the homesick old rum and held a wake for Thomas More the man who would die the next day. They became very droll and mellow over it. The worst of their black mood had gone by, and they believed that they would yet survive as people. This is one thing that the Programmed cannot do. They do not become droll and mellow, nor do they hold wakes. Programmed people had no gallows humor at all.

They would not have understood Paul's joke about the corpse who stuttered. They would have been puzzled by Shanty's tale of the boar hog and the lightning rod salesman and the deal they made; and how what the sows didn't know very nearly killed them. And Maxwell's story of the new-dead lady whose soul was still wandering in the waste places when it became entangled in a drove of laden donkeys and was saddled and ridden by the donkey-drover would have left them cold.

And yet there was very sharp Programmed attention paid to it. The monitors in depth come on every time eight or more people are met together anywhere in civilized Astrobe. They had picked up the group when Rimrock came in, dropped it when Battersea left, and picked it up again when the boy Adam entered. These monitors are automatic, and they record and interpret everything they pick up on these forays. That was the difficulty.

They couldn't make anything out of the tales. They tied into Code-Crackers, and then into Code-Crackers-Supreme. And neither of these great programmed bureaus could crack the code. They couldn't at all figure what cryptic information was concealed in the tales.

The boy Adam told the story of the first human people ever to come to Astrobe; and it had been fifteen hundred years before the date that you will find given by the history precis. By the holies, it had been Saint Brandon himself in a coracle boat that was round as a tub. He sloshed and bounded in over the Stoimenof Sea, with a great deal of drenching and bailing; but he had started his voyage in the North Atlantic Ocean on Old Earth; and he supposed that he was still sailing the same water, since he had never left it.

He piled out of the coracle when it ran onto land, and nineteen Irish monks with twinkling pates followed him out of the boat and onto shore. On first arrival they found no living things on the shore except jerusalem conies, which would not answer their questions. But Saint Brandon and his nineteen monks set themselves to record whatever they might find in this new land.

Say, they mapped it all out and wrote it down on the scrolls with exact description of the plants and animals and the new land itself. They got down every bay and inlet where the Stoimenof Sea shatters into a dozen estuaries and slips, between what is Wu Town and Cathead now. It was a beautiful map and a comprehensive description.

Then they got back into the coracle boat and put up their sail that was no bigger than a shield. And in ninety-nine days they were back in Dingle Bay where they had started from.

But later explorers, going out into the North Atlantic Ocean of Old Earth, didn't find any such land as that; and they said that Saint Brandon had lied. He had not. Those later explorers had gone in prow-ships that will hold a course, not in round coracle boats that can only be steered by prayer and fasting and are likely to wander clear off the Earth.

That was the story of the boy Adam; and Code-

Crackers-Supreme labored mightily to break the code and arrive at the cryptic meaning behind it, and they couldn't do it. This wasn't code like you meet every night.

"Blessed be this rum," said Rimrock the ansel.

George the syrian told just how things are every time the world ends. The only thing ever left over when the world ends, he said, is one syrian and one sand dune, all other features of the world being blotted out by the terminal catastrophes. There is that terrible second or million years when nothing moves—for a second and a million years are the same when there is no movement in anything. Then the syrian goes over behind the sand dune and finds a dromedary; and together they start the world going again.

"That is the way it was in the earliest version of Genesis," George said. "That is the way the world begins every time. You will hear stories about a man and a woman, or about a turtle raising the sky up from off the earth. Do not believe them! Every time the world begins it begins with a syrian and a dromedary. Now, I don't know what a dromedary is, I don't know what a sand dune is, and I sure don't know what a syrian is. The name was hung onto me, I believe, because I have a beak instead of a nose. The world will end again tomorrow. Watch then for a syrian and a sand dune. If the syrian goes behind the dune, there is hope; if he does not, or if there is neither syrian or sand dune, then the world is done forever."

Code-Crackers-Supreme suffered a breakdown about the time that George the syrian recounted this. It was not, perhaps, a serious breakdown; but it would take several hours to get code-crackers to functioning again. So the monitoring was dropped. No point in setting down what even the code-crackers cannot crack.

"Blessed be this rum," said Evita.

Foreman? Fabian Foreman? What was he doing there? He was one of the big men. How long had he been sitting in the midst of them?

"It's no great wonder," Foreman said. "I do not come through the walls, as Copperhead does. I have no strange powers, except a few that are beginning to appear in many on Astrobe lately. I own this building, as I own every building that opens onto Centrality Square. I have my ways of coming into all of them. So I ducked in here to get away from the mobs outside—for there has been a great loosening up of the people of Cosmopolis just within the last hour, and perhaps of the other great Cities of Astrobe. They are having a fools' holiday such as they have not had for a hundred years. Everyone thought they were too far gone in their golden lethargy for that, and here they are alive again. And yet now that I'm inside, I find I miss the clamor. It grows on you. Let's go out in the square and join with them. Then Evita can go to the Thomas and reassure him that all is well, that Battersea's swift-striking commandos will rescue him from the high gibbet at noon tomorrow. And he will still be King. And later, along about dawn, I will go in to him and talk a final talk with him."

They all went out into the square. There was happy fighting in the streets. Who would have imagined that such things could have happened on Civilized Astrobe? These were not lungers or hard-heads from Cathead and the Barrio. They were not even the in-between people of ambiguous Wu Town. They were the highly civilized people of Cosmopolis itself. It was a fools' carnival indeed, all split into high-spirited warring factions spilling over into masquerade. Heads were broken, and people laughed, as if it had been a thousand years before. The "Ban and Beyond" people had their banners flying, and flying wedges of opponents, with and without mottos, pulled them down in a glorious melee. The "Sackcloth and Ashes" faction was marching and joking. The newly-appointed (or self-appointed) Metropolitan of Astrobe had put that whole world under interdict, until penance be done and until certain conditions should be fulfilled; and groups were making up and singing ballads about it. High Ladies of Astrobe dressed up like old crones and hawked candy heads and skulls in honor of the beheading tomorrow. Wooly Rams were found somewhere, and spitted and barbecued over the bonfires, about fifty people devouring each Wooly Ram as they tore it apart in pieces, half seared and half raw. The feast of the Wooly Ram had not been held on Astrobe for more than three hundred years, and only antiquarians could have known about it.

It was a belated mid-summer eve hysteria, Spring-Rite and Easter and Corpus Christi together. It was carnival and city-wide wake. And all the detectable Programmed Persons were in hiding.

It was not that the human persons threatened. In the mood of this night, Programmed Persons would have been invisible to humans, completely unimportant to them, not to be noticed at all. But the Programmed felt fear, an emotion that was not even programmed into them. They could not reason this thing out at all, and reason is the only thing that the Programmed Persons have.

There was drinking and shouting, looting and arson, all carried out in pretty good spirits. Evita slipped off and in to see Thomas in his cell, to tell him that his death would not be a death, but a trained elite out of the hard-heads of Cathead would rescue him, and he would still be King, with all new power.

There was a whole barrelful of new emotions spilled into the streets around Centrality Square. Anger, and who of the Citizens of Civilized Astrobe had been angry in their whole lives? Wonder, and which of them had ever wondered before? Truculence, battle-joy, recollection of things apart (perhaps of future things), revelry, serpents'-tooth remorse, utter penitence, pinnacled hope, joy-in-murder, joy-in-humility.

Serpentine and confetti, and there was not even the memory of them on Astrobe. Halloween and St. John's Eve masks, and even the great-great-grandfathers had forgotten about them. The "Head Hackers" battled with the "Devastators."

Then the tolling began. On the great bells of a forgotten or museumized church, then on another and another, then on five hundred. Most of these Churches had been razed three hundred years ago! How were their giant bells sounding the Old Old World Funeral Toll now? That sound had not been heard within living memory on Astrobe. But five hundred great bells were tolling, and the people remembered the names of them: the Archangel Gabriel with its full silver tone; the Giant, the White Ogre, the Shepherd King, Saint Peter, King of Bavaria, Yellow Dwarf, Saint Simeon, the

Dutchman, Archbishop Turpin, Rhinelander, Daniel, Jew Bell, Mephistopheles, the Black Virgin, Ship Bell, the Mountain, Saint Hilary. Dozens of tons of swinging silver and bronze, all the old giant name-bells of the churches (almost all of them long since disappeared) rang out the heavy toll, and were recognized by their tones and remembered by their names of two hundred years ago. And one more, high and powerful and clear, the July Bell.

Evita was back, crying happy tears. The whole great golden unbelieving city of Cosmopolis did homage to Thomas More who would die tomorrow.

Only he wouldn't die after all, as he would be rescued by Battersea and his swift striking commandos.

Only he *would* die after all, after all, because both Copperhead and the boy Adam said that he would, and they were both given special vision.

It rained before morning. For unknown reasons, the controlled air domes were not working. It rained indiscriminately on the city of Cosmopolis. It did not merely rain on the parks and specified areas; it rained on the entire city. It seemed almost natural for the rain to fall where it would. The air domes, whether from human or Programmed negligence, simply were not raised against it. A thing like this hadn't happened in Cosmopolis for a century. First the carnival and the wild aberrations of the night before, and now an unregulated rain—though not a heavy one.

The Programmed guards were jumpy, and they had killed a few human persons accidently. There may have been some resentment of this, though the things were only following their programming. When people act peculiarly and carry on in an unaccustomed way, what are the Programmed guards to do but take action?

Fabian Foreman went in to see Thomas at the coming of rainy dawn. He found Thomas unusually placid for a man scheduled to die that day. The two weighed each other with cautious eyes, each wondering how many steps deep into the planning the other had guessed.

"You've given the people a carnival, Thomas," Foreman said. "I didn't believe they were any longer capable of it. They held a rousing wake for you, or perhaps it was for themselves. We have had very few executions in recent decades, and none that has grabbed the people as this one has. You come very vivid and colorful to them, much more so than when they made you World President. They recognize this as something fitting in you, as though you were born mainly for this glory death. It will be your moment, Thomas.''

''Oh, be damned to you, Foreman! I've witnessed more executions that you have. A people will rise to one every time, like a fish to the bait, like a very great Devil-fish I saw rise not long since to a very great bait. It's the death that gets them, the untimely death. They love to see a man die.''

''It isn't so, Thomas. There are eight thousand terminations a day in Cosmopolis alone. Almost all are open to the public, and hardly anyone attends. And they aren't monotonous things. Many of those having themselves terminated devise interesting and bloody deaths for themselves; they vie with each other in this and come up with some imaginative ends. The fascination isn't in seeing a man die; it's in seeing a man die unwillingly.''

''I wouldn't disappoint them, Foreman. If I go that road, I sure will not go it willingly. And the other way, to the terminators, I would not go at all. I can't understand a man accepting his end as calmly as that. And yet there's a whole clutch of people who say this entire world will end this morning; and all are quite calm about it. They were a little noisy in the night, though. It's said that there will be very large crowds gathered here before noon. Should a man take pride in the fact that the largest audience he draws in his life is that which comes to his death?''

''That whole clutch of people is right, Thomas. This world, Astrobe (and its old appendage, Earth), *will* end today. There is no stopping it. It is dying, and it will die. It is in the article of death now."

"Oh, well then, I suppose a few honest men will have to get together and start a new world. I've a few ideas along that line myself.

"Too bad you'll be dead and not able to put them into effect, Thomas. Well, how *do* you make a world and set it to going? George who is in aromatics says that in the beginning a syrian finds a dromedary, and together they start a world. Myself, I believe that a new world always grows out of a single mustard seed. I myself will plant a mustard seed at exactly nine o'clock this morning. I expect a new world to grow from it; and I hope I am alive to enjoy it."

"You've the hound-dog look, as though it were you rather than myself who were going to die today, Foreman."

"It could easily happen that I die too, Thomas. There will be a whiplash reaction to the events of this day, and any man too close to the action could easily lose a limb or a life over it. What is that odd stuff you are eating, Thomas?"

"My breakfast. They asked me what I wanted for my final meal. I believe that ritual requires that I be asked it. I told them that I wanted to dine on the brains of my enemies, on Programmed People brains. They brought me this. It's a chemical and magnetic mishmash of polarized memory gelatin. I suppose it is an element, the non-human element, of Programmed People brains. Dawn-world people ate their enemies' brains and acquired wit and strength from them. But I doubt if I'll acquire any wit, and certainly not any humor, from this bowl of the brains of mine enemy. The stuff isn't very good, but people and Things on Astrobe do take what you say literally.''

"The Programmed Persons aren't our enemies, Thomas,'' Foreman said. "They're only shadows of ourselves, of some of ourselves. Even the fearsome human thing they are shadow of may not be sheer enemy.

"Thomas, there are some things I'd like to convey to you before you die. First of all, your death is absolutely required. I wish it weren't so.''

And Thomas was studying Foreman with guarded eyes. Did Foreman (who had been appointed High Civilian in Charge of Execution) suspect that there would be a rescue by the hard-heads of Cathead? And if he did suspect it, would it matter? Foreman was Thomas' closest friend on Golden Astrobe (as opposed to Cathead and the Barrio), and he was not at all committed to the Astrobe Dream, as were the others of the big men. He seemed now to be showing a quiet contempt for it. So why did he emphasize that Thomas' death was absolutely essential? Just how deft of mind was this man Foreman?

"It is no metaphor about the worlds ending today, Thomas,'' Foreman went on. "Or not entirely metaphor. The worlds do die periodically. I wonder why nobody except myself has noticed this. A world becomes an unstrung bow, or an unstrung corpse. All life and heat and pulse goes out of it. It dies, I tell you, in every bird and plant and rock and animal and person of it; in every mountain and sea, in every cloud. Its gravity and light and heat, its germ-life and its life-code, its meaning and its purpose are all extinguished in an instant. All life goes out of it. It ceases.

"After that, I do not know what happens. I have never personally witnessed the event, though I will witness it today. I'll have planted a mustard seed, the smallest of seeds. Something may grow from it, not off this world, but out of the void and into an entirely different world. This also, I believe, will take less than a single second."

"Fabian, you're full of morning wine," Thomas laughed. But he smothered his laugh into a crooked smile. A man due to be executed this day should not laugh too easily. Somebody might suspect that he was having the last laugh.

Thomas had his own game to play and his own emotions to guard. It would be a very nervous business up to that moment of crisis. He must not betray, even to his friend Fabian, that when the crowd really began to gather (shortly after ten o'clock, or two hours before the execution) it would not be an entirely random crowd; there would be a segment of that crowd, a strong slice from the edge to the center, made up of Battersea's picked men. They would be in the rough clothes of the Cathead lungers, in the bizarre garb of the citizens of Wu Town, and in the fine raiment of the people of Cosmopolis and the other golden cities. And in one moment, after Thomas had already mounted the scaffold and was ready to put his head on the block, that segment of the crowd would stiffen into a spear and drive in and strike. They'd grab him off, and would then become a corridor bringing him away from there fast, and then instantaneously by an instant travel booth already held and programmed. They wouldn't have to bring him thirty meters to it; and then he would be in the agreed-on place, and then to a third-stage place which even he did not know yet. He had every confidence in that hard man Battersea who had been a commando general, and he had every confidence in himself. But he must not betray any uneasiness or apprehension, other than that expected in a man about to be executed.

But damn this Foreman! He gave the impression of seeing into everything. "I hope my friend is a friend indeed," Thomas said to himself.

And Foreman was talking, carefully and heavily, as though trying very hard to express something. Foreman had said once that he hated the word *ineffable;* that everything that could be understood could be expressed; and that everything could be understood. And yet he was having a little trouble now.

"I do not believe it at all inevitable that a world be reborn or replaced by another," Foreman said now. "It may have been so once, but it isn't now. But it is inevitable that a world will die when its short span is gone. I do not believe that there have been a million cycles of this in the five hundred million years of complex life on the worlds. I feel that the cycles were once of very long duration, and that they shorten and shorten. They now fill their course about every five hundred years. And, as the cycle shortens, so does each succeed another more hardly. Each time it becomes more difficult for the new world to be born."

"Bring a little plain talk into the allegory, Fabian," Thomas said. "What are you hiding under that flashy fleece, a sheep or a goat or a dog?"

"A corpse, Thomas, with all the life gone out of it—yours, and the world Astrobe's. Just that, and perhaps nothing to follow. Though I have my strong hopes, and my careful plans."

But Thomas was not really listening to him. "Listen!" Thomas said. "They're singing a ballad about me in the square outside. And the Ballad drifted in:

> "Thomas is a peculiar guy,
>   never a clue;
>   without any head he's better than you.
>   Blade in the sky
>   and hackles are high;
>   without any head he's better than you."

"Why, it's gutter music like deprived children in the Barrio would sing," Foreman said with strong disapproval. "Where have the civilized people of Cosmopolis come by such gibberish? One would think they'd sing something noble."

"It is noble, Fabian. And it's true, by God. Even without a head I'm better than the whole lot of you that have been running this show! A thousand years dead, and I have more life in me than the pack of you. It has the fine tone of one of the old ballads, and I'd rather they'd sing me by it than by finer song. I'd give a lot, Foreman, to watch my own beheading, but the principal is disadvantaged in this case. I'll give it all I've got, and I'll have the worst view of all of the rolling head."

"Gallows humor is fine, Thomas, but I am trying very hard to say something very important. I am not one of the few who believe in the Beyond, Thomas, though I have made certain experiments towards inducing belief in myself. They didn't work. I will only say that there is something in all this that is beyond me. I look at this scientifically, Thomas, I try to see it by the science of cosmology and eschatology and psychology (using the parts of that word as the Greeks used them) and isostatic balance of the intellect and planetary biology; and logic and ethical compensation and vitalism; I try to see it by the soft sciences as well as by the hard ones, magneto-chemistry and neucleo-physics. I ask scientifically what is the real phenomenon here: that the worlds do die periodically; and that, in previous cases at least, they live again an instant later. But the new worlds are not identical with what they were, having only the cloudiest and most fragmented memory of what they had been the instant before, and no real identity with the previous thing. But that this does happen is scientific (known and observed) fact— known to me, at least.

"You yourself were in on one of the previous deaths of the worlds, Thomas. Have you any strong idea about what really happened?"

Thomas was not too clear about what Foreman was getting at. And Foreman, moreover, though he talked rapidly and seriously as though this were of the utmost importance, seemed to be listening for some token, for some signal.

"It isn't necessary that you explain a difficult thing to me at this moment," Thomas said. "If I die, then at the Particular Judgment I will receive all such knowledge from One more facile with words than yourself. If I do not die, then we can talk of this again in a calmer time."

"I've been searching for a gentle way to tell you, Thomas; *you will die* this morning, and all other hopes are vain. And as I do not believe in either the Particular or the General Judgment or in Things Beyond at all, I do not believe you will receive these ideas if you do not receive them from me now. And I want you to have them."

"Oh, as to the end of my own world, Foreman, no I do not have any strong idea about what really happened. I study back and try to construct it. I am shown, as it were, a house and a town and a world, and I am informed that this was the house and the town and the world that I lived in, that this is the true picture of those good things immediately after I left them. And I am puzzled. I lived in that house and town? I myself? I hardly recognize a stick or stone of it. I hardly recognize a person of it, and yet hundreds of them bear the names of persons I knew well. I don't believe your instant death and rebirth thing for the worlds; but there was a sudden fundamental change in my own world, near about the sudden end of my own life. And I don't understand it at all.

"Foreman, you butter-mouthed Barnabas, what do you mean that I will die this morning and that all other hope is vain? Tell me or I'll throttle you here. What do you know about what I know?"

"Why, nothing, Thomas, nothing at all. Is it not assumed that you will die? Is there some doubt about it? Would anybody be happier than I if you could be delivered from it in any manner whatsoever?"

"Foreman, you have all the innocence of a ninety-nine year old serpent. Well, go on with your thing! I'm something of a critic of historical theses, and we have long hours to pass before my killing."

"That's another thing I've been searching for a gentle way to tell you, Thomas: we do not have long hours, we have only short minutes. We have this cycle, Thomas. At the time of the birth of Christ, the clear cruel Roman Republic (under the first Emperor who considered himself a Republican) died in an instant; and an instant afterwards the Late Empire was born full-grown. It was always the Late Empire; it was an afternoon and evening thing. And there was really not much resemblance between those worlds; the simple cruel thing, and the completely bizarre thing, at the same time cruel and compassionate, that was the Late Empire. Five hundred years later it happened again. The Empire was gone like morning frost, and the Lower Middle Ages, completely different, obtained. In another five hundred years, the High Middle Ages followed on the corpse of the Low, and there was never such difference as between these two worlds. In another five hundred years, the High Middle Ages died (as did you yourself), and another thing was born which you are not able to recognize although it carried names that you knew well. And after another five hundred years, that world died completely. A new world was born instantly, and the first settlement of Astrobe coincided with that rebirth. This new thing became the World of Astrobe, as Old Earth lost importance and meekly followed our world. This is the world that dies this morning, and I am worried about it.

"This is the first time the cycle has been completed on Astrobe, and each time it happens, it seems that the rebirth is less likely to succeed. I don't know what goes on when a world dies; there must be, I believe, a bit of the transcendent yeast to make it rise again. Something must trigger a reaction. There was building a reaction to the "Ban the Beyond" push, and the blood of the spotted lamb (yourself) will cinch it. The previous yeastings were all such simple things, but they were necessary. *There really is this necessity* that a small quantity of the immaterial (however it is named in the equation) be added to the mass every five hundred years or so. It may be a simple chemical-psychic requirement which we do not understand. Myself, who have sought and been unable to find personal faith, am inclined to believe that it is no more than this. But the requirement is there that something be added now and then, or the worlds will not live again. Your death and the reaction to it will be the trigger, the mustard seed. We plant it now.''

Battersea, is all well with you? Are you watching the clock? Only a few more hours.

''Ten minute call!'' pinged a mechanical voice.

''All right, Thomas,'' Foreman said. ''We go now to your end. Come, come.''

''Now? Are you out of your mind? It's not yet eight o'clock. I die at noon. Nothing is ready, nothing—''

''The scaffold is ready, Thomas, and the blade is ready. Here, here, good devices, pinion him! He's got a streak of the heroic in him. I am sorry, Thomas, but there was no other way to do it.''

''Get your tin talons off me, you devil toys! Eternal damnation! Who changed the time, Foreman?''

''I did, Thomas. You die at eight o'clock. There was no other way to do it.''

''No, no, I die at noon! Foreman, do you understand what you're doing?''

''Perfectly. I guessed all about the Battersea thing, of course. He was a fine commando general in his way; and I was his commander. I could always read *him*, and I picked up the details easily.''

"Why do you murder me, Foreman? I counted you a friend. And you have no loyalty to the Astrobe thing."

"No, I have no loyalty to the Astrobe corpse, Thomas, and I am your friend. I assure you that there was no other way to bring it off. The reaction to your foul murder, joined to many other long-building things, should touch off a terrible reaction: the rediscovery of humanity—don't you believe a world can be reborn out of that, Thomas? It only takes one shot to signal a charge."

"I say no man ever before slew his friend for such a silly mouthful of words."

"And I say it has happened many times before. Consider the Assassinations, Thomas, you who are something of a critic of historical theses. Consider whether the Heroes have not more often been assassinated by friends than by enemies; consider whether some of them have not even been assassinated with their own consent."

"I don't consent."

"If everything else has failed, if a program has fallen to nothing, if the hero would make a better hero when dead, then he was made a dead hero by his friends, for his own sake and the sake of his program. I could name a dozen clear cases of this, but I won't; strong partisan feelings are still involved in some of them after the centuries. —Thomas, my friend, you'd have throttled me if you'd broken loose then. Tighter with him, guards, and now walk him along. This has to be fast or something might spoil it."

"It's a thing to make you doubt your friends, my friend," Thomas growled to him as he fought with his

Programmed guards. "Why me, Fabian? Why did you call me to it?"

"You were the only ultimately honest man I could think of, Thomas, and I considered a lot of them. You'd shown it before, stubborn honesty unto death even for a point which you hardly came to understand at the end. I reasoned that you had done it once and you would do it again in similar circumstances. I reasoned that you had a curious magnetism about you, that you had become a symbol once, and that you would become a symbol again. We had almost run out of symbols on Astrobe."

"I die for it, and I don't even know what it's about," Thomas moaned as they dragged him out to the scaffold. And dragging him was a battle. He set up a noise.

"People people!" he shouted in his high and sandy voice. "There's nowt right about this thing! Smash the high trickery!"

And the people had begun to gather, tame people with a new wild look about them. Like wolves they were, and they snuffed and howled. Panlykonium reigned in Centrality Square, and the air sparked with danger.

Nevertheless, by setting the time early, Foreman had surprised the opposition; and the execution would be brought off if it could be done quickly. Thomas fought the mechanical guards who dragged him out, but they brought him to a standstill before Pottscamp, who had a last official thing to convey.

"Will you reconsider?" Pottscamp asked Thomas as he confronted him in the middle of Centrality Square right at the foot of the scaffold. It was required by ritual that this be asked. "It is so easy to save your life, good Thomas," the Pottscamp went on. "Sign now, and live happily. Or die meanly. In that case I will succeed as Surrogate President, and I will have signed the bill within five minutes. And you, Thomas, will have died for nothing.''

"Snake-in-my-brain, I will not have died for the Ouden-nothing! I will not sign! I see now what Thing you are trying to kill, and to me it is the only Thing that matters. So late I have come back to it. I will not reconsider. On with it, guards! Off with my head if only to close my ears to this babble! Out of my way, you damnable jump-jack!''

They took Thomas up the steps of the scaffold. And Pottscamp fled as though stricken. What? What? How would he flee as though stricken?

This was spectacle. The magnetic man with the mystery about him was up on the death tower with the whole world watching, and he was even more in command than at the time of his ovation on his public coming into Cosmopolis.

Kingmaker and Proctor watched it from high windows and justified themselves. It was easy for Proctor; he had justification programmed into him.

Nobody knows what Foreman felt when he watched Thomas taken up the scaffold.

Pottscamp felt nothing; he was, of course, a machine without feeling. He had no conscience or compassion. This would not bother him at all.

It wouldn't?

Then why did he—?

Then why did he—WHAT?

Sat on the ground and moaned and howled like an old Hebrew. And poured dust and ashes over his head.

You're crazy. He really did that?

He really did that.

Thomas More had been World President, King, for nine days. And now he would die.

The early-morning rain had stopped, and now there was a rush to complete the act. The men from Cathead, so rumor went, had received word of the sudden change of time. They were mobbing toward the center of Cosmopolis, but they might well be too late.

Smooth and swift and calculated, the execution, and there was nothing could stop it.

There was one wave of fury, a minute thing as to the bulk of it, but incomparably savage. There is always one such small mad wave, rising to foaming and furious height all out of proportion to its bulk, that rises and strikes a very few moments before a true tidal wave or world-wave strikes. It is called the forerunner wave.

Buff Shanty and Paul with the crooked face were in it, each driving in with an impetus equal to that of many men. Walter Copperhead was in it—though, being a necromancer, he must have known that it was futile, that he would die in it, that they would all die in it. The boy Adam was in it; and possibly thirty other persons, fine people of Cosmopolis and not rowdy outlanders, were in on the rush and died in it.

Its suddenness almost gave it success. The impetuous men bowled over the mechanical guards and gained the scaffold steps. Then the fighting was close, and they gave one life for every step they ascended. The boy Adam was really the crest of the wave, for he got all the way up the scaffold and touched Thomas. And he was flung all the way down with crushing force by the guards with their grapples. And yet he was up again, brokenly going after them. Shanty and Paul and Copperhead and Adam, and the thirty or more other persons, died around the foot of the scaffold and on the steps, making them slippery with their blood. The boy Adam, in particular, died magnificently as he always did.

But the wave had no real bulk, and the guards were too many and strong. The thrust crested and shattered, and then it was over with, ebbing out in its blood.

But Evita, knowing that it would fail, knowing instantly that it would all fail, had surged not towards Thomas on the high platform, but towards Fabian Foreman, who stood on the edge of Centrality Square.

"Zehheeroot, Is-Kerioth," she howled at him, for they were both of the old people: "Beware, Iscariot." Then she had him like a lioness taking a frightened ass, swiping half his face red with her claws and biting into his throat to set up a throbbing red fountain.

"Let go me, you witch!" Foreman screamed in sudden terror.

"I be a cold fury and not a witch," she emitted with a purring rumble. "Woe to him by whom it comes. You told a History to the Thomas, and I tell one to you as you die." And she was killing him as she growled the words. "Certain primitives were wont to kill a dog to be company to the hero on his death journey. I am such a primitive. You are such a dog."

And she was practically dismembering him. She had broken his shoulder and possibly his back. She was tearing him apart.

"No, no, woman!" Foreman gasped as the blood pulsed out of his torn throat. "I'm the master of it all. It has to be this way. The furious reaction, the transcendent yeast will set humanity back into its proper place again and let a new world be born."

"I know it!" Evita sang. "I'm a bunch of that transcendent yeast. I'm the heart of that furious reaction! I revel in it. And we've had a dog for puppeteer all this late time. No wonder it's been a time of trouble."

She broke his face completely with a lioness blow. It was a sad time for Foreman, who had always rather withdrawn from violence, he had been a desk general and not a field general.

Evita threw him over her shoulder, though he was a shapeless and heavy man, and carried him with that tawny ease with which a lioness carries her prey, carried him to where George the syrian and Maxwell the old crone and Rimrock the ansel were grouped together. She threw him to them, and the four of them tore him to pieces and killed him.

Evita took the biggest piece of Foreman that was left and hanged it on an ornamental tree on the edge of Centrality Square. It was a Carob tree from Old Earth, sometimes called the Judas Tree.

It was unjust. Foreman had done his part well. He had planned it all, except that special little bit by which he lost his life. And everything that he had planned was meant well.

The programmed guards got George and Maxwell and Rimrock and added their blood to the transcendental yeast that was beginning to work. They did not get the Evita. Nobody would get her till the thing was done.

Things went smoothly after those little outbreaks. The crowds were kept back, for the guards were very efficient. There was *one* man who broke through and nobody was able to stop him. Indeed, the programmed guards did not seem able to see him or sense him. This stranger went right up to Thomas on the scaffold and spoke to him, though only Thomas appeared able to hear his words.

They discussed, the condemned man and the stranger that the guards did not seem able to see. Thomas seemed both excited and pleased.

"Will it work, do you think?" he cried loudly with what was almost delight. "How droll! Can a man have more heads than two? I'll do it. I'll go with you."

But apparently Thomas didn't go anywhere but to his death. The stranger disappeared down and back into the crowd, or some said that he disappeared into the charged air. There would be guesses as to his identity. There were those who said that something disappeared from Thomas at the same moment—that he left in his essence, and that it was a shadow man who put his head on the block. A weird old woman cried out that she could see through him; but this was illusion.

The rest of it is legend stuff. All of it, the quips and the epigrams and the profound and moving things that Thomas was supposed to have said at the chopping block: well, some of them were pretty good, some of them were almost too cute, and most of them are in the books of quotations. The only thing amiss is that he didn't say any of them.

He hadn't said them the first time either.

The only last words that he said on the scaffold were "*Pater, in manus taus–*" a scrap of an old prayer.

The big blade trembled in the sky. Then it fell. It was real blood that spurted and a real hand that rolled clear from the corpus as though it had a life of its own.

There would be wild stories, the prodigies, the old wives' tales—such as nine snakes slithering out of the severed head; such as the most beautiful woman of Astrobe going up the scaffold and boldly taking the head in a basket, and being turned into an old woman when she came down with it. But no such things really happened. They could not have.

But one thing *did* really happen at that moment. At the moment that life flickered out of the beheaded corpus, *the worlds came to an end*.

All life and heat and pulse went out of the world. It died in every bird and rock and plant and person of it, in every mountain and sea and cloud. It died in its gravity and light and heat, in its germ-life and in its life-code. Everything ceased. And all the stars went out.

Was it for a moment? Or a billion years? Or forever? There is no difference in them, when the world is ended, when there is no time to measure time by.

Remember how it had been at the moment when the worlds ended? A priest renegade for thirty years had just become Metropolitan of Astrobe. A programmed machine had, at the moment of the extinction of the worlds, succeeded to president of Astrobe: an emotionless machine. But he had wailed and poured ashes over his head.

Battersea and his men were mobbing towards Centrality Square to begin their bloody coup, mobbing in furiously under their Hand-of-Vengeance banner. On such notes the worlds ended.

And is a new world born? Is a new world yeasted? The furious reaction, does it bridge the gap? The mustard seed, does it grow? The Judas tree, what fruit did it bear?

Lightning, a billion times as bright as that on Electric Mountain, a billion times as short in duration, does it lace the things together with its instantaneous fire, or sunder them forever? Thunder that flattens worlds with the shock of it, and a tidal wave, a world wave carrying away the golden fungus from the orb! In much less than an instant, in much more than forever, it is over with.

But has it sequence? Does a new world follow the old in that blinding flash? Does it come?

Be quiet. We watch.

The Hand-of-Vengeance banner, is its symbol misunderstood? Northprophet says that that figured hand coming down like a bird is the Left Hand of God.

Remember (and we remember as in a void of time between worlds) the turn of the cycle that gave birth to Rome? The one that gave birth to Europe? The one that gave birth to the Americas? The one that gave birth to Astrobe? Remember the cycles whose effect was internal and electrifying, the one where divinity became humanity? The one where humanity became divinity?

And remember that special one, the first rebirth of Astrobe, the appearance of transcendent humanity?

Remember it? Then it happened?

Be quiet. We wait.

The spirit came down once on water and clay. Could it not come down on gell-cells and flux-fix? The sterile wood, whether of human or programmed tree, shall it fruit after all? The Avid Nothingness, the diabolically empty Point-Big-O, is it cast away again? Is there then room for life? Shall there be return to real life?

Well, does it happen? Does the reaction become the birthing? What does it look like?

Will we see it now, in face and rump, the new-born world?

Be quiet. We hope.

R. A. Lafferty (1914-2002)

Raphael Aloysius Lafferty was an American science fiction and fantasy writer born in Neola, Iowa. His first publication of genre interest was "Day of the Glacier" with *Science Fiction Stories* in January 1960, although he continued to work in the electrical business until retiring to write full-time in 1970. Over the course of his writing career, Lafferty wrote thirty-two novels and more than two hundred short stories and he was known for his original use of language, metaphor and narrative structure.

ABOUT GOLLANCZ

Gollancz is the oldest SF publishing imprint in the world. Since being founded in 1927 Gollancz has continued to publish a focused selection of bestselling and award-winning authors. The front-list includes **Ben Aaronovitch**, **Joe Abercrombie**, **Charlaine Harris**, **Joanne Harris**, **Joe Hill**, **Alastair Reynolds**, **Patrick Rothfuss**, **Nalini Singh** and **Brandon Sanderson**.

As one of the largest Science Fiction and Fantasy imprints in the UK it is no surprise we have one of the most extensive backlists in the world. Find high-quality SF on Gateway written by such authors as **Philip K. Dick**, **Ursula Le Guin**, **Connie Willis**, **Sir Arthur C. Clarke**, **Pat Cadigan**, **Michael Moorcock** and **George R.R. Martin**.

We also have a strand of publishing in translation, which includes French, Polish and Russian authors. Gollancz is home to more award-winning authors than any other imprint, with names including **Aliette de Bodard**, **M. John Harrison**, **Paul McAuley**, **Sarah Pinborough**, **Pierre Pevel**, **Justina Robson** and many more.

The SF Gateway
More than 3,000 classic, rare and previously out-of-print SF novels at your fingertips.
www.sfgateway.com

The Gollancz Blog
Bringing you news from our worlds to yours. Stories, interviews, articles and exclusive extracts just for you!
www.gollancz.co.uk

GOLLANCZ
LONDON